D0405864

ASHES OF
VICTORY

Baen Books by David Weber

Honor Harrington novels:
On Basilisk Station
The Honor of the Queen
The Short Victorious War
Field of Dishonor
Flag in Exile
In Enemy Hands
Echoes of Honor
Ashes of Victory

Edited by David Weber:
More Than Honor
Worlds of Honor

Mutineer's Moon
The Armageddon Inheritance
Heirs of Empire

Path of the Fury

Oath of Swords
The War God's Own

The Apocalypse Troll

with Steve White:
Insurrection
Crusade
In Death Ground

ASHES OF VICTORY

DAVID WEBER

Ashes of Victory

This is a work of fiction. All the characters and events portrayed in this book are fictional, and any resemblance to real people or incidents is purely coincidental.

Copyright © 2000 by David Weber

All rights reserved, including the right to reproduce this book or portions thereof in any form.

A Baen Books Original

Baen Publishing Enterprises
P.O. Box 1403
Riverdale, NY 10471

ISBN: 0-671-57854-5

Cover art by David Mattingly
Interior schematics by Russell Isler
Interior map by Hunter Peddicord

First printing, March 2000

Library of Congress Cataloging-in-Publication Data
Weber, David, 1952–
    Ashes of victory / by David Weber.
       p.   cm.
    ISBN 0-671-57854-5 (hc)
    I. Title.
PS3573.E217 A87 2000
813'.54—dc21   99-054523

Distributed by Simon & Schuster
1230 Avenue of the Americas
New York, NY 10020

Typeset by Windhaven Press, Auburn, NH
Printed in the United States of America

10   9   8   7   6   5   4   3

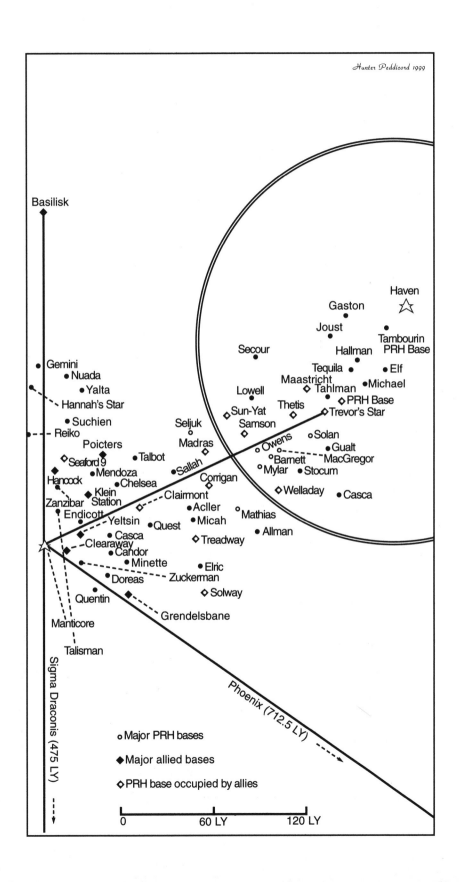

Hunter Peddicord 1999

Basilisk

Haven

Gaston

Joust

Secour

Tambourin
PRH Base

Hallman

Tequila

Elf

Maastricht

Michael

Gemini

Nuada

Lowell

Yalta

Tahlman

Hannah's Star

Sun-Yat

PRH Base

Thetis

Suchien

Samson

Trevor's Star

Seljuk

Reiko

Solan

Madras

Poicters

Owens

Gualt

Talbot

Barnett

MacGregor

Seaford 9

Mendoza

Sallah

Mylar

Stocum

Hancock

Chelsea

Corrigan

Klein
Station

Welladay

Casca

Zanzibar

Clairmont

Endicott

Acller

Mathias

Yeltsin

Micah

Quest

Allman

Casca

Treadway

Clearaway

Candor

Minette

Elric

Doreas

Zuckerman

Quentin

Solway

Grendelsbane

Manticore

Talisman

○ Major PRH bases

◆ Major allied bases

◇ PRH base occupied by allies

Sigma Draconis (475 LY)

Phoenix (712.5 LY)

0   60 LY   120 LY

30.9 METERS

GHOST RIDER MISSILE

CAPITAL MISSILE

CA/BC MISSILE

CL/DD MISSILE

SHRIKE MISSILE

COUNTER MISSILE

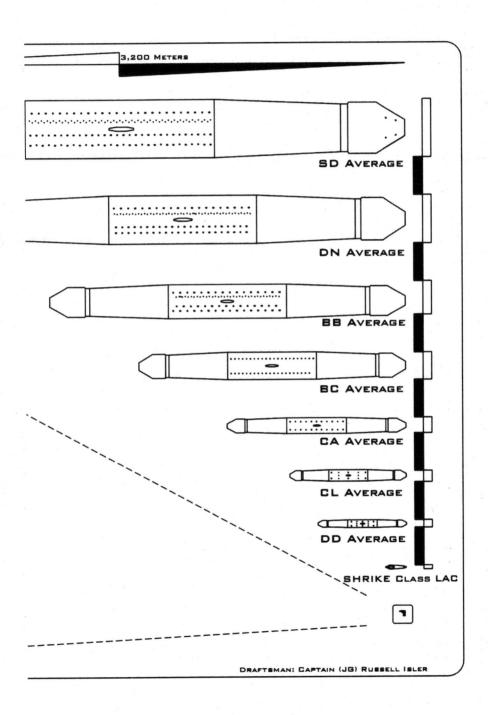

3,200 Meters

SD Average

DN Average

BB Average

BC Average

CA Average

CL Average

DD Average

SHRIKE Class LAC

DRAFTSMAN: CAPTAIN (JG) RUSSELL ISLER

Royal Manticoran Navy
Bureau of Ships
Saganami Island Design Campus

SD HULL/SD(P) HULL CONTRAST TREATMENT

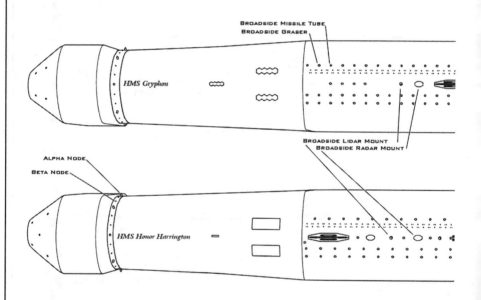

BROADSIDE MISSILE TUBE
BROADSIDE GRASER

HMS Gryphon

BROADSIDE LIDAR MOUNT
BROADSIDE RADAR MOUNT

ALPHA NODE
BETA NODE

HMS Honor Harrington

HARRINGTON CLASS STERN HAMMERHEAD

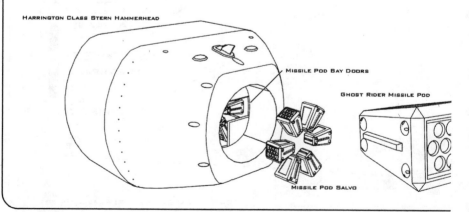

MISSILE POD BAY DOORS

GHOST RIDER MISSILE POD

MISSILE POD SALVO

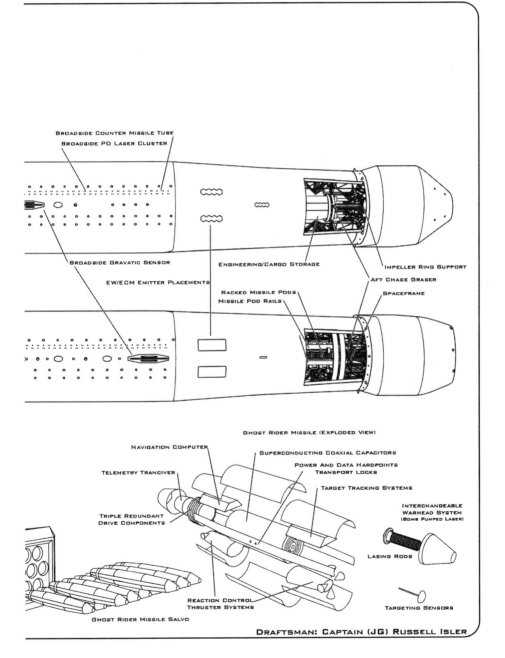

BROADSIDE COUNTER MISSILE TUBE

BROADSIDE PD LASER CLUSTER

BROADSIDE GRAVATIC SENSOR

EW/ECM EMITTER PLACEMENTS

ENGINEERING/CARGO STORAGE

IMPELLER RING SUPPORT

AFT CHASE GRASER

RACKED MISSILE PODS

MISSILE POD RAILS

SPACEFRAME

GHOST RIDER MISSILE (EXPLODED VIEW)

NAVIGATION COMPUTER

SUPERCONDUCTING COAXIAL CAPACITORS

TELEMETRY TRANCIVER

POWER AND DATA HARDPOINTS

TRANSPORT LOCKS

TARGET TRACKING SYSTEMS

INTERCHANGEABLE
WARHEAD SYSTEM
(BOMB PUMPED LASER)

TRIPLE REDUNDANT
DRIVE COMPONENTS

LASING RODS

REACTION CONTROL
THRUSTER SYSTEMS

TARGETING SENSORS

GHOST RIDER MISSILE SALVO

DRAFTSMAN: CAPTAIN (JG) RUSSELL ISLER

(1) Point Defense Laser Cluster
(2) GRASER main armament
(3) Anti-ship Missile Tube
(4) Anti-ship Missile "Revolver" Magazine Cell
(5) Point Defense Missile Tube
(6) Small Craft Hangar
(7) Folding Wing Cutter/Lifeboat
(8) Anti-ship Missile
(9) Sidewall ("Bow Wall") Generator

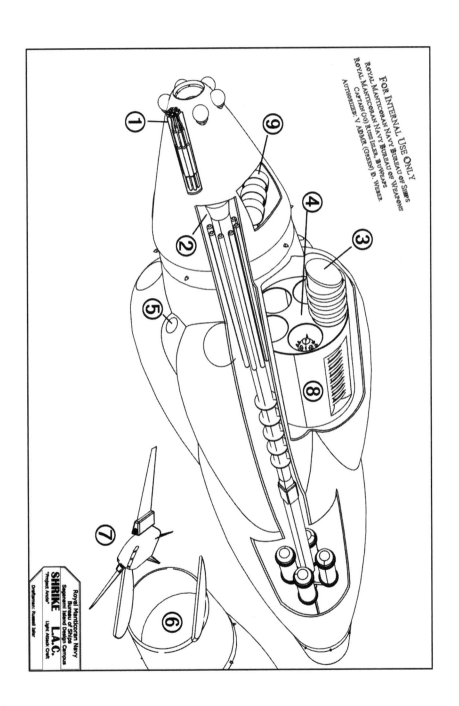

FOR INTERNAL USE ONLY
ROYAL MANTICORAN NAVY BUREAU OF SHIPS
ROYAL MANTICORAN NAVY BUREAU OF WEAPONS
CAPTAIN (JG) RUSS ISLER, BUWEAPS
AUTHORIZED: V ADMR (GREEN) D. WEBER

Royal Manticoran Navy
Bureau of Ships
Saganami Island Design Campus

SHRIKE   **L.A.C.**
"Project Anzio"   Light Attack Craft

Draftsman: Russell Isler

(1) Point Defense Laser Cluster Emitters
(2) Standard Beta Node
(3) New "Beta-Squared" Beta Node
(4) Alpha Node
(5) Graser Broadside Armament

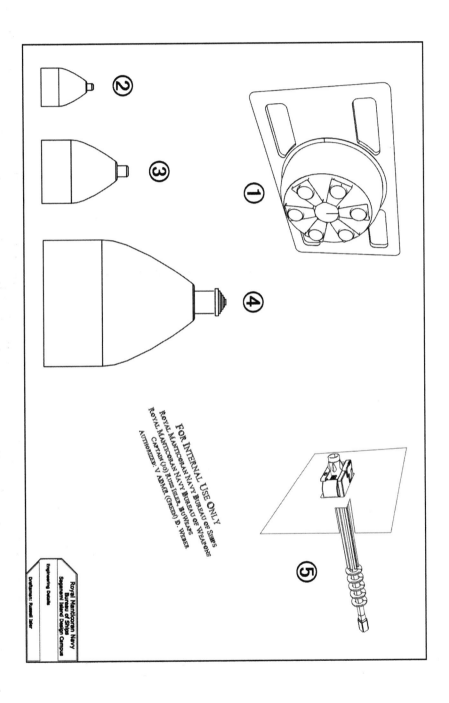

For Internal Use Only

Royal Manticoran Navy Bureau of Ships
Royal Manticoran Navy Bureau of Weapons
Captain (JG) Russieler, BuWeaps
Authorized: V Admr (Green) D. Weber

Royal Manticoran Navy
Bureau of Ships
Saganami Island Design Campus

Engineering Details

Draftsman: Russell Isler

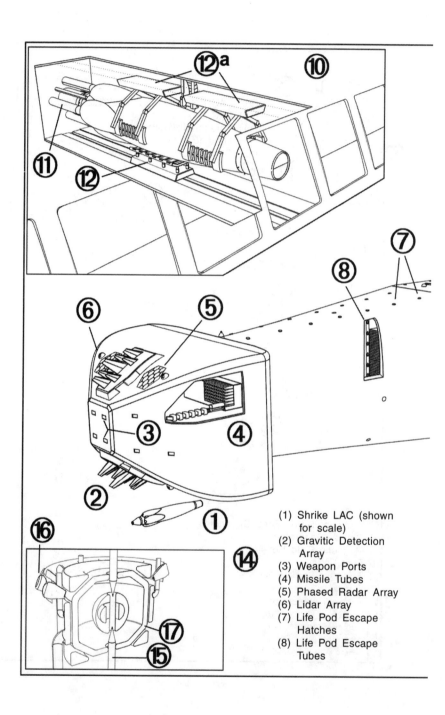

(1) Shrike LAC (shown for scale)
(2) Gravitic Detection Array
(3) Weapon Ports
(4) Missile Tubes
(5) Phased Radar Array
(6) Lidar Array
(7) Life Pod Escape Hatches
(8) Life Pod Escape Tubes

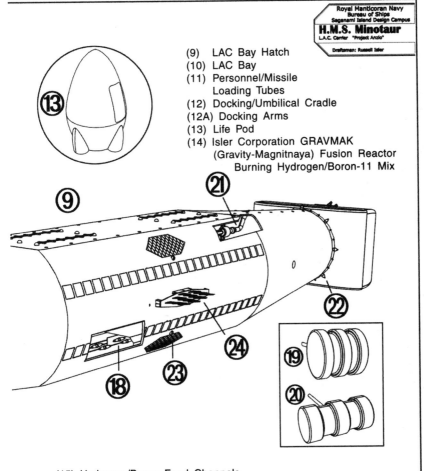

Royal Manticoran Navy
Bureau of Ships
Saganami Island Design Campus

H.M.S. Minotaur
L.A.C. Carrier "Project Anzio"

Draftsman: Russell Isler

(9) LAC Bay Hatch
(10) LAC Bay
(11) Personnel/Missile
     Loading Tubes
(12) Docking/Umbilical Cradle
(12A) Docking Arms
(13) Life Pod
(14) Isler Corporation GRAVMAK
     (Gravity-Magnitnaya) Fusion Reactor
     Burning Hydrogen/Boron-11 Mix

(15) Hydrogen/Boron Feed Channels
(16) Gravity Generators
(17) Magnetic Field Housing
(18) Boat Bay
(19) Radiation/Particle Shield
     Generator
(20) Sidewall Generator
(21) Vectored Thrust Auxiliary
     Fusion Reactor Thruster
(22) After Impeller Ring
(23) Broadside Phased Array Radar
(24) Broadside Gravitic Array

FOR INTERNAL USE ONLY
ROYAL MANTICORAN NAVY BUREAU OF SHIPS
ROYAL MANTICORAN NAVY BUREAU OF WEAPONS
CAPTAIN (JG) RUSS ISLER, BUWEAPS
AUTHORIZED: V ADMR (GREEN) D. WEBER

CHAPTER ONE

Admiral Lady Dame Honor Harrington stood in the gallery of ESN *Farnese*'s boat bay and tried not to reel as the silent emotional hurricane thundered about her.

She gazed through the armorplast of the gallery bulkhead into the brilliantly lit, perfect clarity of the bay itself, and tried to use its sterile serenity as a sort of mental shield against the tempest. It didn't help a great deal, but at least she didn't have to face it alone, and she felt the living side of her mouth quirk in a wry smile as the six-limbed treecat in the carrier on her back shifted uneasily, ears half-flattened as the same vortex battered at him. Like the rest of his empathic species, he remained far more sensitive to others' emotions than she, and he seemed torn between a frantic need to escape the sheer intensity of the moment and a sort of euphoric high driven by an excess of everyone else's endorphins.

At least the two of them had had plenty of practice, she reminded herself. The stunned moment when her people realized their scratch-built, jury-rigged, half-derisively self proclaimed "Elysian Space Navy" had destroyed an entire Peep task force *and* captured the shipping to take every prisoner who wanted to leave the prison planet of Hades to safety lay over three standard weeks behind them. She'd thought, then, that nothing could ever equal the explosion of triumph which had swept her ex-Peep flagship at that instant, but in its own way, the emotional storm seething about her now was even stronger. It had had longer to build on the voyage from the prison the entire People's Republic of Haven had regarded as the most escape-proof facility in human history to freedom, and anticipation had fanned its strength. For some of

1

the escapees, like Captain Harriet Benson, the CO of ENS *Kutuzov*, over sixty T-years had passed since they'd breathed the air of a free planet. Those people could never return to the lives they'd left behind, but their need to begin building new ones blazed within them. Nor were they alone in their impatience. Even those who'd spent the least time in the custody of the Office of State Security longed to see loved ones once more, and unlike the escapees who'd spent decades on the planet inmates called "Hell," they *could* pick up the threads of the lives they'd feared they would never see again.

Yet that hunger to begin anew was tempered by a matching emotion which might almost have been called regret. An awareness that somehow they had become part of a tale which would be told and retold, and, undoubtedly, grow still greater in the tellings . . . and that all tales end.

They knew the impossible odds they had surmounted to reach this moment, in this boat bay gallery, in this star system. And because they did, they also knew that all the embellishments with which the tale would be improved upon over the years—by themselves, as likely as not—would be unnecessary, peripheral and unimportant to the reality.

And that was what they regretted: the fact that when they left *Farnese*, they would also leave behind the companions with whom they had built that tale's reality. The unvoiced awareness that it was not given to human beings to touch such moments, save fleetingly. The memory of who they'd been and what they'd done would be with them always, yet it would be only memory, never again reality. And as the heart-stopping fear and terror faded, the reality would become even more precious and unattainable to them.

That was what truly gave the emotions whirling about her their strength . . . and focused that strength upon her, for she was their leader, and that made her the symbol of their joy and bittersweet regret alike.

It was also horribly embarrassing, and the fact that none of them knew she could sense their emotions only made it worse. It was as if she stood outside their windows, listening to whispered conversations they'd never meant to share with her, and the fact that she had no choice—that she could no longer *not* sense the feelings of those about her—only made her feel perversely guilty when she did.

Yet what bothered her most was that she could never return what they had given her. They thought she was the one who'd achieved so much, but they were wrong. *They* were the ones who'd done it by doing all and more than all she'd asked of them. They'd come from the military forces of dozens of star nations, emerging from what the Peeps had contemptuously believed was the dustbin of history to hand their tormentors what might well prove the worst defeat in the history of the People's Republic. Not in tonnage destroyed, or star systems conquered, but in something far more precious because it was intangible, for they had delivered a potential deathblow to the terror of omnipotence which was so much a part of State Security's repressive arsenal.

And they'd done it for her. She'd tried to express even a fraction of the gratitude she felt, but she knew she'd failed. They lacked the sense she'd developed, the ability to feel the reality behind the clumsy interface of human language, and all her efforts had made not a dent in the storm of devotion pouring back at her.

If only—

A clear, musical chime—not loud, but penetrating—broke into her thoughts and she drew a deep breath as the first pinnace began its final approach. There were other small craft behind it, including dozens of pinnaces from the three squadrons of the wall which had come to meet *Farnese* and more than a dozen heavy-lift personnel shuttles from the planet San Martin. They queued up behind the lead pinnace, waiting their turns, and she tried not to let her relief show as she thought about them. She and Warner Caslet, *Farnese*'s exec, had packed the battlecruiser, like all the other ships of the ESN, to the deckheads to get all of the escapees aboard. The massive redundancy designed into warship life-support systems had let them carry the overload (barely), but it had done nothing about the physical crowding, and the systems themselves were in serious need of maintenance after so long under such heavy demand. The personnel shuttles outside the boat bay were but the first wave of craft which would transport her people from the packed-sardine environment of their battlecruiser to the mountainous surface of San Martin. The planet's heavy gravity scarcely qualified it as a vacation resort, but at least it had plenty of room. And after twenty-four T-days crammed into *Farnese*'s overcrowded berthing spaces, a little thing like weighing twice one's proper weight would be a minor price for the glorious luxury of room in which to stretch without putting a thumb into someone else's eye.

But even as she felt her crew eagerly anticipating the end of its confinement, her own attention was locked upon the lead pinnace, for she knew whose it was. Over two T-years had passed since she'd last faced the officer to whom it belonged, and she'd thought she'd put her treacherously ambiguous feelings about that officer aside. Now she knew she'd been wrong, for her own emotions were even more confused and turbulent than those of the people about her as she waited to greet him once again.

Admiral of the Green Hamish Alexander, Earl of White Haven and Commanding Officer, Eighth Fleet, forced his face to remain immobile as GNS *Benjamin the Great*'s pinnace approached rendezvous with the battlecruiser his flagship had come to meet. ENS *Farnese—and just what the hell is an "ENS?"* he wondered. *That's something else I should have asked her*—was a *Warlord*-class unit. The big ship floated against the needle-sharp stars, well out from San Martin, where no unauthorized eye might see her and note her Peep origin. The time to acknowledge her presence would come, but not yet, he thought, gazing through the view port at the ship logic said could not be there. No, not yet.

Farnese retained the lean, arrogant grace of her battlecruiser breed, despite the fact that she was even larger than the Royal Manticoran Navy's *Reliant*-class. Small compared to his superdreadnought flagship, of course, but still a big, powerful unit. He'd heard about the *Warlords*, read the ONI analyses and appreciations of the class, even seen them destroyed in combat with units under his own command. But this was the first time he'd ever come close enough to see one with the unaided human eye. To be honest, it was closer than he'd ever anticipated he might come, except perhaps in that unimaginable time somewhere in the distant reaches of a future in which peace had come once more to this section of the galaxy.

Which isn't going to happen any time soon, he reminded himself grimly from behind the fortress of his face. *And if I'd ever had any happy illusions in that respect, just looking at* Farnese *would disabuse me of them in a hurry.*

His jaw set as his pilot, obedient to his earlier orders, swept down the big ship's starboard side and he studied her damage. Her heavy, multilayered armor was actually buckled. The boundary layers of antikinetic armor seemed to have slagged and run; the inner, ablative layers sandwiched between them were bubbled and charred looking; and the sensors and antimissile laser clusters which once had guarded *Farnese*'s flank were gutted. White Haven would have been surprised if half her starboard weapons remained functional, and her starboard sidewall generators couldn't possibly have generated any realistic defense against hostile fire.

Just like her, he thought moodily, almost angrily. *Why in Christ's*

name can the woman never *bring a ship back intact? What the* hell
is it that makes her—

He chopped the thought off again, and this time he felt his
mouth twist in sardonic amusement. His was not, he reflected, the
proper mood for an officer of his seniority at a moment like this.
Up until—he glanced at his chrono—seven hours and twenty-three
minutes earlier, he, like all the rest of the Manticoran Alliance, had
known Honor Harrington was dead. Like everyone else, he'd seen
the grisly HD of her execution, and even now he shuddered as
he recalled the ghastly moment when the gallows trapdoor sprang
and her body—

He shied away from that image and closed his eyes, nostrils flaring while he concentrated on another image, this one on his own
com less than eight hours earlier. A strong, gracefully carved, half-
paralyzed face, framed in a short mop of half-tamed curls. A face
he had never imagined he would see again.

He blinked and inhaled deeply once again. A billion questions
teemed in his brain, put there by the raw impossibility of Honor
Harrington's survival, and he knew he was not alone in that. When
word of this broke, every newsie in Alliance space—*and half of those
in Solly space, no doubt,* he thought—would descend upon whatever hiding places Honor or any of the people with her might have
found. They would ask, plead, bully, bribe, probably even threaten
in their efforts to winnow out every detail of their quarry's incredible story. But even though those same questions burned in his
own mind, they were secondary, almost immaterial, compared to
the simple fact of her survival.

And not, he admitted, simply because she was one of the most
outstanding naval officers of her generation and a priceless military asset which had been returned to the Alliance literally from
beyond the grave.

His pinnace arced down under the turn of *Farnese*'s flank to
approach the boat bay, and as he felt the gentle shudder when
the tractors captured the tiny craft, Hamish Alexander took
himself firmly in hand. He'd screwed up somehow once before,
let slip some hint of his sudden awareness that the woman who'd
been his protégée for over a decade had become something far
more to him than a brilliant junior officer and an asset of the
Royal Manticoran Navy. He still had no idea how he'd given
himself away, but he knew he had. He'd felt the awkwardness
between them and known she'd returned to active duty early in
an effort to escape that awkwardness. And for two years, he'd
lived with the knowledge that her early return to duty was what

had sent her into the Peep ambush in which she had been captured . . . and sentenced to death.

It had burned like acid, that knowledge, and he'd watched the Peep broadcast of her execution as an act of self-punishing penance. In an odd way, her death had freed him to face his feelings for her . . . which only made things immeasurably worse now that he knew she wasn't dead, of course. He had no business loving someone little more than half his age, who'd never shown the least romantic interest in him. Especially not while he was married to another woman whom he still loved deeply and passionately, despite the injuries which had confined her to a life-support chair for almost fifty T-years. No honorable man would have let that happen, yet he had, and he'd been too self-honest to deny it once his face had been rubbed sufficiently in it.

Or I like to think I'm too "self-honest" to lie to myself, he thought mordantly as the tractors urged the pinnace from the outer darkness into the illuminated boat bay. *Of course, I had to wait until she was safely dead before I got around to that sudden burst of honesty. But I did get there in the end . . . damn it.*

The pinnace rolled on thrusters and gyros, settling towards the docking buffers, and he made himself a silent promise. Whatever he might feel, Honor Harrington was a woman of honor. He might not be able to help his own emotions, but he could damned well see to it that she never knew about them, and he would. That much he could still do.

The pinnace touched down, the docking arms and umbilical locked, and Hamish Alexander pushed himself up out of his comfortable seat. He looked at his reflection in the view port's armorplast and studied his expression as he smiled. Amazing how natural that smile looked, he thought, and nodded to his reflection, then squared his shoulders and turned towards the hatch.

A green light glowed above the docking tube, indicating a good seal and pressure, and Honor tucked her hand behind her as the gallery-side hatch slid back. It was amazing how awkward it was to decide what to do with a single hand when it had no mate to meet it halfway, but she brushed that thought aside and nodded to Major Chezno. The senior officer of *Farnese*'s Marine detachment nodded back, then turned on his heel to face the honor guard drawn up behind the side party.

"Honor guard, attennnnnn-*hut!*" he barked, and hands slapped the butts of ex-Peep pulse rifles as the ex-prisoners snapped to parade-ground attention. Honor watched them with a proprietary air and wasn't even tempted to smile. No doubt some people would have found it absurd for men and women packed into their ship like emergency rations in a tin to waste time polishing and perfecting their ceremonial drill, especially when they all knew they would be broken up again once they reached their destination. But it hadn't been absurd to *Farnese*'s ship's company . . . or to Honor Harrington.

I suppose it's our way of declaring who and what we are. We're not simply escaped prisoners, huddled together like sheep while we run from the wolves. We are the "wolves" of this piece, and we, by God, want the universe to know it! She snorted in amusement, not at her Marines and their drill, but at herself, and shook her head. *I think I may be just a* wee *bit guilty of hubris where these people are concerned.*

The Navy side party snapped to attention as the first passenger floated down the tube, and Honor drew another deep breath and braced herself. The Royal Manticoran Navy's tradition was that the senior passenger was last to board and first to exit a small craft, and she knew who she would see well before the tall, broad-shouldered man in the impeccable black-and-gold of an RMN admiral caught the grab bar and swung himself from the tube's weightlessness into the gallery's one standard gravity.

Bosun's pipes twittered—the old-fashioned, lung-powered kind, out of deference to the traditionalists among the Elysian Space Navy's personnel—and the admiral came to attention and saluted *Farnese*'s executive officer, standing at the head of the side party. Despite sixty years of naval service, the admiral was unable to conceal his surprise, and Honor could hardly blame him. Indeed, she felt an urchinlike grin threatening the disciplined facade of her own expression at the sight. She'd deliberately failed to mention her exec's identity during the com exchanges which had established her ships' bona fides for the Trevor's Star defensive forces. The Earl of White Haven deserved some surprises, after all, and the last thing he could possibly have expected to see aboard this ship was a side party headed by a man in the dress uniform of the People's Navy.

Hamish Alexander made his expression blank once more as the side party's senior officer returned his salute. A Peep? Here? He knew he'd given away his astonishment, but he doubted anyone could have faulted him for it. Not under the circumstances.

His eyes swept the rainbow confusion of the ranks beyond the Peep as the bosun's pipes continued to squeal, and another surprise flickered through him. That visual cacophony had never been designed for color coordination, and for just an instant, the assault on his optic nerve kept him from understanding what he was seeing. But realization dawned almost instantly, and he felt himself mentally nodding in approval. Whatever else Hades might have lacked, it had obviously possessed fabric extruders, and someone had made good use of them. The people in that bay gallery wore the uniforms of the militaries in which they had served before the Peeps dumped them in the PRH's "inescapable" prison, and if the confusion of colors and braid and headgear was more visually chaotic than the neatly ordered military mind might have preferred, so what? Many of the navies and planetary combat forces those uniforms belonged to hadn't existed in well over half a T-century. They had gone down to bitter defeat—often clawing and defiant to the end, but still defeat—before the juggernaut of the People's Republic, and again, so what? The people wearing them had won the right to resurrect them, and Hamish Alexander rather suspected that it would be . . . unwise for anyone to question their tailoring.

The pipes died at last, and he lowered his hand from the band of his beret.

"Permission to come aboard, Sir?" he asked formally, and the Peep nodded.

"Permission granted, Admiral White Haven," he replied, and stepped back with a courteous welcoming gesture.

"Thank you, Commander." White Haven's tone was equally courteous, and no one could have been blamed for failing to realize it was an absent courtesy. But then, no one else could have guessed at the emotions raging behind his calm, ice-blue eyes as he glanced past the Peep to the tall, one-armed woman waiting just beyond the side party.

They clung to her, those eyes, but again, no one could reasonably have faulted that. No doubt people had stared at Lazarus, too.

She looks like hell . . . and she looks wonderful, he thought, taking in the blue-on-blue Grayson admiral's uniform she wore instead of her Manticoran rank. He was glad to see it for at least one intensely personal reason. In the Grayson Space Navy, her rank actually exceeded his own, for she was the second ranking officer of that explosively growing service, and that was good. It meant that at least he would not have to address her from the towering seniority of a full admiral to a mere commodore. And the uniform looked good on her, too, he thought, giving her unknown tailor high marks.

But good as she looked, he could not pull his eyes away from the missing left arm, or the paralyzed left side of her face. Her artificial eye clearly wasn't tracking as it was supposed to, either, and he felt a fresh, lavalike burn of fury. The Peeps might not actually have executed her, but it seemed they'd come close to killing her.

Again.

She has got to stop doing this kind of thing, he thought, and his mental voice was almost conversational. *There are limits in all things . . . including how many times she can dance on the edge of a razor and survive.*

Not that she would pay him any attention if he said as much. Not any more than he would have paid if their roles had been reversed. Yet even as he admitted that, he knew it wasn't the same. He'd commanded squadrons, task forces, and fleets in action, in an almost unbroken series of victories. He'd seen ships blown apart, felt his own flagship shudder and buck as fire blasted through its defenses. At least twice, he'd come within meters of death. Yet in all that time, he'd never once been wounded in action, and not once had he ever actually faced an enemy. Not hand-to-hand. His battles had been fought across light-seconds, with grasers and lasers and nuclear warheads, and for all that he knew his personnel respected and trusted him, they did not idolize him.

Not the way Honor Harrington's people idolized her. For once, the newsies had gotten something exactly right when they dubbed her "the Salamander" from her habit of always being where the fire was hottest. She'd fought White Haven's sort of battle all too often for someone of her comparative youth, and she had the touch, the personal magic, that made her crews walk unflinchingly into the furnace beside her. But unlike the earl, she had also faced people trying to kill her from so close she could see their eyes, smell their sweat, and God only knew what she'd been doing when she lost her arm. No doubt he'd find out soon enough, and, equally no doubt, it would be one more thing for him to worry that she might be crazy enough to repeat in the future. Which was irrational of him. It wasn't as if she actually went out *looking* for ways to get herself killed, no matter how it sometimes seemed to those watching her. It was just—

He realized he'd been motionless just a moment too long. He could feel the curiosity behind the countless eyes watching him, wondering what he was thinking, and he forced a smile. The one thing he couldn't have any of them do was to actually figure out what had been going through his mind, and he held out his hand to her.

"Welcome home, Lady Harrington," he said, and felt her long, slender fingers tighten about his with the careful strength of a native heavy-worlder.

"Welcome home, Lady Harrington."

She heard the words, but they seemed tiny and far away, at the other end of a shaky com link, as she gripped his extended hand. His deep, resonant voice was just the way she'd remembered it— remembered, in fact, with rather more fidelity than she might have desired—yet it was also completely new, as if she'd never heard it before. And that was because she was hearing him on so many levels. Her sensitivity to others' emotions had increased yet again. She'd suspected that it had; now she knew it. Either that, or there was something special about her sensitivity to *his* emotions, and that was an even more disturbing possibility. But whatever the cause, she heard not simply his words, or even the messages communicated by the smile in the blue eyes. No, she heard all the things he *didn't* say. All the things he fought so hard, and with such formidable self-control, against allowing himself even to hint that he might want to say.

All the things he might as well have shouted at the top of his lungs yet didn't even guess he was giving away.

For a fleeting moment of pure self-indulgence she let the emotions hidden behind his face sweep her up in a dizzying whirl. She couldn't help it as his joyous surprise at her survival swept over her. His soaring welcome came on its heels . . . and his desire to sweep her into his arms. Not a trace of those things showed on his face, or in his manner, but he couldn't possibly hide them from her, and the sheer lightning-strike intensity of the moment burned through her like an explosion.

And on its heels came the knowledge that none of the things he longed to do could ever happen.

It was even worse than she'd feared. The thought rolled through her, more dismal still for the moment of joy she had allowed herself to feel. She'd known he'd stuck in her mind and heart. Now she knew that she had stuck in *his*, as well, and that he would never, ever admit it to her.

Everything in the universe demanded its own price . . . and the greater a gift, the higher the price it carried. Deep inside, in the secret places where logic seldom treads, Honor Harrington had always believed that, and she'd realized over the last two years that this was the price she must pay for her bond with Nimitz. No other 'cat-human bonding had ever been so close, ever spilled across to the actual communication of emotions, and the depth of her fusion with her beloved companion was worth any price.

Even this one, she told herself. Even the knowledge that Hamish Alexander loved her and of what might have been had the universe been a different place. Yet just as he would never tell her, she would never tell him . . . and was she blessed or cursed by the fact that, unlike him, she would always know what he had never said?

"Thank you, My Lord," Lady Dame Honor Harrington said, and her soprano was cool and clear as spring water, shadowed only by the slight slurring imposed by the crippled side of her lips. "It's good to be home."

CHAPTER TWO

White Haven's pinnace, unlike the ones which had followed it into the boat bay, was almost empty when it left. He and Honor, as befitted their seniority, sat in the two seats closest to the hatch, but those seats were a virtual island, surrounded by emptiness as their juniors gave them space. Andrew LaFollet, Honor's personal armsman, sat directly behind them, and Lieutenant Robards, White Haven's flag lieutenant, sat two rows back from there, with Warner Caslet, Carson Clinkscales, Solomon Marchant, Jasper Mayhew, Scotty Tremaine, and Senior Chief Horace Harkness scattered out behind him. Alistair McKeon should have been there, but he had remained behind with Jesus Ramirez, Honor's second-in-command, to help organize the transfer of her Elysians to the planetary surface.

She really ought to have stayed aboard *Farnese* and organized that transfer herself, but White Haven had been politely insistent about the need to get her and her story on their joint way to higher authority. So Alistair had remained behind, along with the other survivors who'd been with her since their capture in Adler, and she glanced over her shoulder one more time at the handful of people who would accompany her on the next stage of her journey, then returned her attention to the man seated beside her.

It was easier than it had been. One thing about moments of tempestuous emotion, she'd discovered: they simply could not be sustained. Indeed, the stronger they were, the faster it seemed people had to step back to gather their inner breath if they intended to cope with their lives. Which, fortunately, both she and White Haven did. The murmuring undercurrent remained, flowing between them even if she was the only one who could sense it, but it was bearable. Something she could deal with, if not ignore.

Sure it is. I'll just keep telling myself that.

"I'm sure it will be months before we get all the details straight, Milady," the earl said, and Honor hid a wry mental grimace at his formality. He clearly had no intention of calling her by her given name . . . which was probably wise of him. "Lord knows we've only scratched the surface so far! Still, there are a few things I simply have to ask you about right now."

"Such as, My Lord?"

"Well, for one thing, just what the devil does 'ENS' stand for?"

"I beg your pardon?" Honor cocked her head at him.

"I can understand why they're not 'HMS,' given that you've been acting in your Grayson persona, not your Manticoran one," White Haven said, gesturing at the blue uniform she wore. "But that being the case, I would have expected your units to be designated as Grayson ships. Obviously they aren't, and I haven't been able to come up with any other organization, except perhaps the Erewhon Navy, to fit your terminology."

"Oh." Honor gave him one of her crooked smiles and shrugged. "That was Commodore Ramirez's idea."

"The big San Martino?" White Haven asked, frowning as he tried to be sure he'd fitted the right name to the right face on a com screen.

"That's him," Honor agreed. "He was the senior officer in Camp Inferno—we never would have been able to pull it off without his support—and he thought that given the fact that we were escaping from a planet officially called Hades, we ought to call ourselves the Elysian Space Navy. So we did."

"I see." White Haven rubbed his chin, then grinned at her. "You do realize you've managed to open yet another can of legal worms, don't you?"

"I beg your pardon?" Honor repeated in a rather different tone, and he laughed at her obvious puzzlement.

"Well, you were acting as a Grayson, My Lady . . . and you're a steadholder. If I remember correctly, the Grayson Constitution has a very interesting provision about armed forces commanded by its steadholders."

"It—" Honor broke off and stared at him, her single natural eye very wide, and she heard the sudden hiss of an indrawn breath from the armsman behind her.

"No doubt you're better informed than I am," White Haven said into her sudden silence, "but it was my understanding that steadholders were specifically limited to no more than fifty personal armed retainers, like the Major here." He nodded courteously over his shoulder at LaFollet.

"That's correct, My Lord," Honor agreed after a moment. She'd been Steadholder Harrington for so long that it no longer seemed unnatural to have somehow become a great feudal magnate, yet she hadn't even thought about the possible constitutional implications of her actions on Hell.

She should have, for this was one point on which the Constitution was totally unforgiving. Every armsman in the service of Harrington Steading answered to Honor in one way or another, but most did so only indirectly, through the administrative machinery of her steading's police forces. Only fifty were her personal liege men, sworn to *her* service, and not the steading's. Any order she gave those fifty men had the force of law, so long as it did not violate the Constitution, and the fact that she'd given it shielded them from any consequences for having obeyed even if it did. *She* could be held responsible for it; they could not, but those fifty were the only personal force Steadholder Harrington was permitted.

Steadholders might command other military forces from within the chain of command of the Grayson Army or Navy, but to satisfy the Constitution, the command of those forces must be lodged in the established Grayson military with the specific approval of the planet's ruler. And Protector Benjamin IX had not said a word about anything called "the Elysian Space Navy."

She looked over her shoulder at LaFollet, and her armsman gazed back. His face was calm enough, but his gray eyes looked a bit anxious, and she raised an eyebrow.

"Just how badly have I stepped on my sword, Andrew?" she asked him, and despite himself, he smiled, for "sword" had a very specific connotation on Grayson. But then he sobered.

"I don't really know, My Lady. I suppose I ought to've said something about it, but it never occurred to me at the time. The Constitution is pretty blunt, though, and I think at least one steadholder was actually executed for violating the ban. That was three hundred years ago or so, but—"

He shrugged, and Honor chuckled.

"Not a good precedent, however long ago it was," she murmured, and turned back to White Haven. "I guess I should have gone ahead and called them units in the Grayson Navy after all, My Lord."

"That or the RMN," he said judiciously. "You hold legal rank in both, so the chain of command would have covered you in either, I imagine. But it might be just a little awkward the way things actually worked out. Nathan and I—" he flicked a small nod at the imperturbable young lieutenant behind them "—discussed this on our way to *Farnese*. He actually went so far as to consult *Benjamin the Great*'s library. I don't believe there's been a precedent since the one Major LaFollet just referred to, but the fact that a steadholder not only held command in but actually created a military force not authorized by the Protector could be a real problem. Not with Benjamin, of course." A casual shooing gesture of his right hand banished that possibility to well-deserved limbo. "But there are still those on Grayson who feel more than a little . . . uncomfortable with his reforms and see you as the emblem of them. I have no doubt that some members of that faction would love to find a way to embarrass you—and him—by seizing on any weapon, even one as specious as that sort of pettifogging legalism. I'm sure Benjamin's advisers will see the problem as soon as I did, but I thought it might be as well to point it out to you now so you could be thinking about it."

"Oh, *thank* you, My Lord," Honor said, and both of them chuckled. It was a brief moment, but it felt good. *At least we can still act naturally around one another. And who knows? If we act that way long enough, maybe it will actually* become *natural again. That would be nice. I think.*

She brushed the thought aside and leaned back, crossing her legs and ignoring Nimitz's mock-indignant protest as her lap shifted under him.

"I trust you haven't had any more interesting thoughts, My Lord?" she said politely to White Haven, and the earl smiled.

"No, I haven't," he assured her, then rather spoiled the reassurance by adding, "On the other hand, you have been gone for over two T-years, Milady, and everyone thought you were dead. There are bound to be quite a few complications waiting for you to straighten out, don't you think?"

"Indeed I do." She sighed, and ran the fingers of her hand through her short-cropped hair. She missed the longer, more luxurious length she'd managed to produce before her capture, but the Peeps had shaved it all away in the brig of PNS *Tepes*, and the loss of her arm had made it impractical to grow it all the way back out.

"I'm sure there are, as well, Milady." White Haven said, and shrugged as she glanced at him again. "I have no real idea what they might be. Well, there are one or two things I can think of, but I feel it would be more advisable to let Protector Benjamin discuss them with you."

His face was admirably calm, but Honor felt a sudden prickle of suspicion. He *did* know something, she thought, but whatever it was, he didn't expect it to have serious or unpleasant repercussions. There wasn't enough worry in his feelings for that. But there was a hefty dose of wicked amusement, a sense of anticipation that fell short (barely) of gloating but was definitely of the naughty little boy "I've got a *seeeeecret!*" sort.

She eyed him with scant favor, and he smiled beatifically. Like their shared laughter of a few moments before, the amusement flickering in his depths was a vast relief compared to the emotions he had no intention of ever expressing to her, and she was glad. That did not, however, make her feel a bit better when it came to worrying over just what sort of land mines could afford him so much anticipatory delight.

"There've been a few problems back home in the Star Kingdom that I do know about, however," he went on after a moment. "For one thing, your title was passed on to your cousin Devon when you were officially declared dead."

"Devon?" Honor rubbed the tip of her nose, then shrugged. "I never really wanted to be a countess anyway," she said. "Her Majesty insisted on it—I certainly didn't!—so I really can't complain if someone else has the title now. And I suppose Devon is my legal heir, though I hadn't thought much about it." She grinned crookedly. "I suppose I should have considered it long ago, but I'm still not really used to thinking in dynastic terms. Of course," she chuckled wickedly, "neither was Devon! Do you happen to know how he took his sudden elevation?"

"Grumpily, I understand." White Haven shook his head. "Said it was all a bunch of tomfoolery that would only get in the way of his research on his current monograph."

"That's Devon," Honor agreed with something very like a giggle. "He's probably the best historian I know, but getting his nose out of the past has always been all but impossible!"

"So I was told. On the other hand, Her Majesty insisted someone had to carry on the Harrington title. She was quite firm about it, according to my brother." White Haven paused, and Honor nodded her understanding. William Alexander was Chancellor of the Exchequer, the second ranking member of the Cromarty Government. If anyone was likely to be privy to Queen Elizabeth's thinking, he was. "She personally discussed it with your cousin . . . at some length, I understand," the earl added.

"Oh, dear!" Honor shook her head, her good eye brimming with delight. She'd had her own experience of Elizabeth III in insistent mode, and the thought of dear, stuffy, bookish Devon in the same position filled her with unholy glee.

"Well, she also got around to actually providing some lands to go with the title, as well," White Haven told her. "So at least the new Earl Harrington found himself with the income to support his new dignities."

"She did?" Honor demanded, and he nodded. "What sort of lands?"

"Quite a nice chunk of the Crown Reserve in the Unicorn Belt, I believe," he said, and Honor blinked.

The term "lands" was used in the Star Kingdom as a generic label for any income-producing holding associated with a patent of nobility. It was a sloppy term, but, then, both the original colonial charter and the Constitution tended to be a bit sloppy in places, as well. The same term had been used from the very earliest days of the Manticore colony to refer to any income source, whether it was actual lands, mineral or development rights, fishery rights, a chunk of the broadcast spectrum for HD, or any other of a whole host of grants, which had been shared out among the original colonists in proportion to their financial contributions to the colonizing expedition. Probably as much as a third of the Star Kingdom's current hereditary peerage held no actual land on any planetary surface as a direct consequence of its ennoblement. Well, no, that wasn't quite true. Virtually all the hereditary members of the Lords had at least acquired properly titled seats somewhere to support their aristocratic dignity, but the real income which had permitted them to do so often came from very different sources.

Still, it was highly unusual these days for the Crown to dip into the Crown Reserve to create those income sources, if for no other reason than that the Reserve had dwindled over the years since the Star Kingdom's founding. The usual procedure was for the Crown to request the Commons to approve the creation of the required "lands" as a charge on the public purse, not to split them off from the bundle of lands which still belonged personally to Elizabeth III, which was what the Crown Reserve really was. And that was especially true for a hereditary title like her own, since unlike the grants for life titles, its holdings would remain permanently associated with it. So if the Queen had irrevocably alienated part of the fabulously wealthy Unicorn asteroid belt from the Crown in Devon's favor, she'd clearly been serious about her desire for the Harrington title to be properly maintained.

A sudden thought struck her, and she stiffened in her chair.

"Excuse me, My Lord, but you said Devon inherited my Manticoran title?" The earl nodded. "Do you happen to know what Grayson did about my steadholdership? Did they pass it on to Devon, as well?"

"I believe there was some discussion of that," White Haven said after a moment, and Honor's eye narrowed as the sense of amusement she'd already tasted peaked momentarily. "In the end, however, they made other arrangements."

"Such as?"

"I really don't think it would be proper for me to go into that, Milady," he told her, with a commendably straight face. "It's a rather complicated situation, and your sudden return from the dead is only going to make it even more complicated. And since it's a purely domestic Grayson problem, I'm not entitled to any say in its resolution. In fact, it would probably be inappropriate even for me to express an opinion about it."

"I see." Honor regarded him very levelly for a moment, then smiled thinly. "I see, indeed, My Lord, and perhaps someday the opportunity will arise for me to repay your admirable self-restraint in kind."

"We can always hope, Milady," he agreed. "On the other hand, I doubt very much that I'll ever make a dramatic return from the dead following my very public execution."

"If I'd guessed that whatever it is you're so darkly hinting at was waiting for me, *I* certainly would have thought twice about the idea," Honor said tartly, and he chuckled. But then his face and his emotions sobered.

"In all honesty, Milady, and all jesting aside, Grayson was thrown into far more disorder by the report of your death than the Star Kingdom was. We have scores of earls and countesses in the Star Kingdom; there are less than ninety steadholders on Grayson. There were all sorts of repercussions there, and that's why I agreed with Admiral Kuzak and Governor Kershaw that you ought to return to Grayson first."

Honor nodded yet again. Although White Haven's Eighth Fleet was based on Trevor's Star while it prepared for operations elsewhere, Theodosia Kuzak was the system's military CO. She was junior to White Haven, but her Third Fleet was still tasked as the system's primary defensive unit.

Governor Winston Kershaw was her civilian counterpart: the Manticoran Alliance's official administrator and head of the commission overseeing the organization of San Martin's post-liberation planetary government. He was also a younger brother of Jonathan Kershaw, Steadholder Denby, and one of Benjamin IX's stronger supporters, and he'd been quite . . . firm about how best to handle the political aspects of Honor's return. In particular, he'd been adamant in insisting that word of her return must remain completely confidential until she'd had a chance to meet personally with Benjamin.

"I still don't know if I completely agree with the Governor," she said after a moment, but White Haven shook his head.

"I think he's absolutely correct," he disagreed. "The political and diplomatic consequences of your escape are going to be enormous, and Grayson deserves to know the full details first. We'll send a courier boat ahead to both Yeltsin and Manticore, but the dispatches will be classified at the highest level available to us. Not even the courier boats' crews will know what they say, and we're clamping a security blackout on the story here. I can't guarantee it, but I doubt very much that Her Majesty will allow a hint of the information to leak into the system data nets until the Protector's government has had an opportunity to debrief you in person and decide how to deal with it."

"Are you certain about that, My Lord?" Honor asked him. "I don't question the basic logic, but why not send *me* in a courier boat rather than a dispatch? And why the long way around instead of by way of Manticore? It's going to take over three weeks for me to get to Grayson without using the Junction. That seems like an awful long time to try to keep the arrival of so many people on San Martin a secret!"

"As far as keeping secrets is concerned, there's no real problem. Oh, I doubt the secret will keep very long in local space. The story's just too good. It's bound to get out, sooner probably rather than later, but we control both termini of the Junction. That means nobody outside this system will hear a thing about it until we let the word out through Manticore or somebody carries the news elsewhere through a regular hyper trip. Which means no one on the outside is going to hear a thing about it for at least several weeks, and probably a lot longer than that, given the traffic control we've clamped down locally. Especially since McQueen sprang her damned offensives."

He frowned.

"One thing that did was make it very plain that we've been lax in our security arrangements. They clearly had hellishly good intelligence for most of their ops, and they had to have gotten it someway. 'Neutral shipping' in the Junction probably explains a good bit of it, at least in the case of Basilisk and Trevor's Star. Plain old visual examination can tell them a lot about what they see, and the Government has decided that we simply can't restrict Junction traffic patterns much further. That's the real reason we're cutting down on military Junction transits as much as we can, especially transits by new construction we don't want the Peeps to know about."

He shrugged, in acceptance of orders from his civilian superiors, if not in actual agreement with them.

"Anyway, I'm confident we can at least keep the news from breaking until after Grayson's had an opportunity to decide how to handle it domestically. As for sending you the long way around, that's a consequence of the ship we're using, since it's part of that new construction we're keeping people from seeing. But that was Governor Kershaw's call, and while I'm sure you would have preferred a shorter voyage, it's certainly appropriate to send you home on the senior Grayson ship present. And even if it weren't, *I'm* not foolish enough to argue with a bunch of Graysons about it!"

He grinned at her expression, then sobered.

"In addition, your transit time will give Her Majesty and the Protector both some time to consider how they want to handle the official announcement before you actually arrive. And they're going to want to give it some very careful thought, I'm sure." He shook his head. "I can't even begin to imagine how it will all play out on the diplomatic front. You do appreciate what a monumental black eye you've just given the Peeps in general and State Security and Public Information in particular, don't you?"

"I have wiled away the occasional hour on the way here thinking about that," Honor admitted, and it was White Haven's turn to smile at the wicked gleam in her eye. "In fact, honesty compels me to admit that I've actually spent a bit of time here and there *gloating* over it," she went on. "Especially the bit about my execution." The amusement in her eye vanished, replaced by a hard, dangerous light which would have made White Haven acutely uneasy if it had been directed at him. "I've seen the imagery myself now, you know. It was in *Farnese*'s memory." She shivered involuntarily at the memory of her own brutal "execution," but the light in her eye never faded. "I think I know exactly how my parents must have reacted to that. And Mac and Miranda." Her jaw tightened for a moment. "Whoever put that particular bit of sick, sadistic footage together has a lot to answer for, and knowing how hard Pierre and Saint-Just will shortly be looking for a scapegoat has afforded me considerable consolation over the past few weeks."

"I'm sure it has," White Haven agreed. "And judging from even the brief report you've had time to give us so far, I imagine the consequences will actually go a lot further than that in the end. You do realize that you've just executed—you should pardon the expression—the largest mass prison break in the history of mankind, don't you? You got out—what? Four hundred thousand people?"

"Something close to that, once Cynthia Gonsalves gets here," Honor said, and he nodded at the correction. Captain Cynthia Gonsalves, late of the Alto Verdan Navy, had left the Cerberus System well before Honor, but her transports were far slower than the warships and assault ships Honor had managed to secure. Which meant it would be weeks yet before the first wave of escapees actually arrived.

"Well, that has to be the largest number of POWs ever to escape in a single operation," White Haven pointed out, "and the sheer scale of the thing is almost unimportant beside where you managed to escape *from*. State Security will never recover from the blow to its reputation, and that doesn't even consider what's going to happen when people like Amos Parnell start talking to the newsies about who actually carried out the Harris Assassination—!"

The earl shrugged, and Honor nodded. No doubt Public Information would do its best to discredit anything the ex-Chief of Naval Operations of the People's Navy might say, but not even Public Information was going to able to shrug this one off, especially in the face of the files Honor's people had lifted from Camp Charon's own security records. She suspected that PubIn was going to have just a bit of a problem convincing people that the commandant of StateSec's most important prison hadn't known what he was talking about when he taunted Legislaturalist prisoners with the truth behind the Harris Assassination's civilian massacre. And once it truly registered that the Committee of Public Safety, organized to prevent the overthrow of the state by the "traitorous" naval officers responsible for the coup attempt, was headed by the man who had in fact masterminded the entire operation, the effect on interstellar diplomacy was likely to be profound.

"As a matter of fact," White Haven went on much more quietly, breaking into her train of thought, "as delighted as I am to see you back on both a personal and a professional basis," she felt his emotions shy away from the word "personal," but the intensity of his train of thought helped pull him past it, "the effect on the Alliance's morale will probably be even more important, in the short term, at least. Frankly, Milady, we need some good news rather badly. Esther McQueen's managed to throw us firmly back onto the defensive for the first time since Third Yeltsin, and that's shaken the Alliance's morale seriously, especially among its civilians. Which means *all* the Allied governments are going to be absolutely delighted to see you."

Honor shuddered. She knew he was right, yet she hated even to think about the media circus the news was bound to spawn. All she wanted to do whenever she contemplated it was to run far, far away and hide, but she couldn't. She had responsibilities she couldn't evade—*even,* she thought smolderingly, *if he won't tell me just what sort of "arrangements" they made on Grayson!* And even if she hadn't had those responsibilities, she could see the propaganda value too clearly. She detested the idea of being turned into some kind of larger-than-life icon. She'd already had more than her fair taste of that, had to put up with more media intrusiveness than any individual should have to tolerate, and this was going to be infinitely worse.

But none of that mattered, except, perhaps, on a personal basis.

"I understand, My Lord," she said. "I hate it, and I'd do anything I could to avoid the media frenzy, but I understand."

"I know you do, Milady," he said. Very few people, perhaps, would have believed she truly loathed the very thought of the adulation soon to be channeled her way, but Hamish Alexander was one of those few, and she smiled gratefully at him.

He began to say something else, then stopped as a soft chime sounded. He leaned forward to look across her and out the view port beside her, and nodded in satisfaction.

"And here's your transport to Grayson, Milady," he announced. Honor glanced at him for a moment, then turned to look out the port herself, and Nimitz pushed up to stand in her lap. He pressed his nose to the armorplast, then twitched his whiskers as he, too, saw the white mountain of battle steel drifting in the void, bejeweled with the green and white lights of an "anchored" starship.

The superdreadnought was one of the largest ships Honor had ever seen. Possibly *the* largest warship, she reflected, her experienced eye estimating its tonnage from the relative size of the huge ship's weapons hatches and impeller nodes, although she supposed she might have seen larger merchant vessels. That was her first thought, but then she noted the odd, distinctive profile of the after hammerhead, and her eye narrowed in sudden recognition.

"That's a *Medusa!*" she said sharply.

"In a manner of speaking," White Haven agreed. "Actually, though, the Graysons built her, not us. It seems they got hold of the plans for the new class about the same time BuShips did back home . . . and they had a bit less deadwood and conservative stick-in-the-mud opposition to deal with."

He added the last phrase in a dust-dry voice, and Honor turned back to the port to hide her expression as her mouth quirked uncontrollably. She remembered that shattering night in her library only too well for personal reasons, but she also recalled that one Hamish Alexander had been one of the conservative sticks-in-the-mud who'd opposed the initial concept of the hollow-cored, pod-armed missile SDs. She, on the other hand, had written the final recommendations which had led to the *Medusa* design's actual formulation as her last duty as a member of the Weapons Development Board.

"And have they been tested in action, My Lord?" she inquired after a moment, as soon as she felt she could keep her voice level.

"On a limited scale," he said very seriously, "and they performed exactly as you predicted they would, Milady. We don't have enough of them yet, but they're absolutely devastating when used properly. And so—" he glanced over his shoulder at the other, lower-ranking officers behind them, none of whom had been cleared for information they had no pressing need to know "—have certain other elements of the new fleet mix you described to me that night."

"Indeed?" Honor turned to look at him, and he nodded.

"Indeed. We haven't used any of them, including the new SDs, en masse yet. We're still ramping up our numbers in the new classes and weapons, because we'd like to commit them in really useful numbers rather than penny-packets that will give the enemy time to adjust and work out countermeasures. At the moment, we hope and believe that the Peep analysts haven't been able to put together a clear picture of their capabilities from the limited use we've been forced to make of them so far. That's one reason we're not sending any of the new types through the Junction except in emergencies; we don't want anyone who might whisper in StateSec's ear getting a good look at them. But within a few more months, Citizen Secretary McQueen and the Committee of Public Safety ought to be getting a very unpleasant surprise."

She nodded in understanding without taking her attention off the ship waiting for her. There were a few differences between the completed ship and the design studies she'd seen, but not very many, and she felt a curious, semiparental surge of pride as she saw the reality of the concept she and her colleagues on the WDB had debated so hotly.

"Just one more thing," White Haven said very quietly, pitching his voice too low even for Robards and LaFollet to have heard, and she glanced at him. "This ship, and the others like her in Grayson service, were all built in the Blackbird Yard you arranged the basic funding for, Milady. So, in a very real sense, you're a keel plate owner of all of them. That's one reason we felt she'd be the perfect ship to take you home again."

Honor met his eyes, then nodded.

"Thank you for telling me, My Lord," she said, equally quietly.

Even as she spoke, the pinnace gave the tiny quiver trained reflexes recognized as the lock-on of docking tractors. The ship was no longer a ship beyond the port; it was simply a vast, endless expanse of alloy and weapons, completely filling the view port and waiting in all its megaton majesty to receive her as the minnow of their pinnace drifted into the brilliantly lit belly of the white whale.

The tractors adjusted the pinnace with finicky precision before settling it into its docking cradle, and Honor felt her breathing quicken and blinked on tears as she gazed in through the armorplast wall of the boat bay gallery. The massed ranks of Grayson blue, leavened here and there with the black-on-gold of RMN personnel on detachment to their ally's navy, woke a sudden, almost unbearable stab of homesickness, and even from here she could feel the fierce, exultant beat of their emotions.

It was odd, she reflected. She truly had become a woman of two worlds. Child of the cold, mountainous majesty of the Star Kingdom's Sphinx, yes, always that. But she was also a woman of Grayson, and something of that sometimes backward and maddening world, with its almost frightening dynamism and fierce, direct loyalties and animosities, had infused itself into her, as well. She understood its people now, as she never had when first she met them, and perhaps that had been inevitable. However different they might have been on the surface, in one respect they had always been alike, she and the people of Grayson.

Responsibility. Neither she nor they had ever been able to run fast enough to escape it. In an odd way, even those who'd hated her most for the changes she'd brought their world had understood her almost perfectly, just as she'd come to understand them. And so, as she felt those exultant waves of emotion rolling over her from the bay gallery, she understood the people behind them, and the understanding welcomed her home.

"After you, Milady," White Haven said, standing and gesturing at the hatch as the green light blinked above it. She glanced at him, and he smiled. "In this navy, you're senior to me, Lady Harrington. And even if you weren't, I would never be stupid enough to come between you and a shipload of Graysons at a moment like this!"

She blushed darkly, but then she had to laugh, and she rose with an answering smile.

He helped her get Nimitz's carrier back into place on her back, then let her precede him down the docking tube, and she felt the beat of the superdreadnought crew's excitement, almost as if waves of over-pressure were pulsing down the tube to meet her. It was as overwhelming, in a very different way, as the emotional storm aboard *Farnese* had been, making it difficult to think. But swimming a tube, even with only one arm, was something she could have done in her sleep, and she fell back on the almost instinctive skills of a forty-plus-year naval career. Yet as she approached the grab bar at the end of the tube, she felt something else, even through the pulse beat of welcome from the waiting Graysons. It was a small thing, yet it glittered with its own brilliant delight and anticipation, and it came from behind her.

She wanted to look over her shoulder at White Haven, just to see if his expression matched the ripple of someone else's laughter echoing in the back of her mind. And, she admitted, for any clue as to what he was so amused over. But there was no time, and she gripped the bar and swung out into the rich, golden notes of the Steadholder's March.

She'd braced herself as best she could, but nothing could really have prepared her. The music, the storm of uniforms, lit by the lightning flashes of gold braid and rank insignia, the presented arms of the Marine honor guard, the whirlwind of emotion and welcome—and, yes, vengefulness as they saw her missing arm and paralyzed face—all of it crashed over her. And with it came something else: a roar of cheering not even Grayson naval discipline could have hoped to stifle. She felt Nimitz quivering in his carrier, shared his almost dazed response to the sensations flooding through him like some polychromatic roll of thunder that went on and on and on, and it was all she could do to carry through the instinct-level protocol for boarding a ship.

She turned to salute the Grayson planetary flag on the boat bay's forward bulkhead, then turned back to salute the ship's captain, and felt her heart leap as she recognized Captain Thomas Greentree. The chunky, brown-haired Grayson's face looked as if his smile were about to split it in two, and beyond him, she recognized another familiar face. Admiral Judah Yanakov's smile was, if possible, even broader than Greentree's, and somehow its welcome went perfectly with the hard, dangerous light in his eyes as he saw the stump of her arm. She knew him too well to doubt what that light portended, and she made a mental note to talk to him—at length—as soon as possible. But now was not the time, and she looked behind him, letting her gaze sweep the gallery as she waited for the cheers to fade.

It was a spacious gallery, even for a superdreadnought, and—

Her thoughts chopped off as she saw the ship's crest on the bulkhead behind the honor guard. The basis of the crest was glaringly obvious. She'd seen the same set of arms every time she looked at her own steadholder's key . . . and if there'd been any question at all of where it had come from, the ship's name blazoned above it would have dispelled it immediately.

She stared at the crest, unable to look away even though she knew her reaction was fully validating the torrent of amusement she felt flooding from the Earl of White Haven. And it was probably as well for the earl's continued existence that she *couldn't* turn away, she realized later, for if she'd been able to, and if he'd been smirking even a tenth as broadly as she suspected he had, and if he'd been in arm's reach . . .

But she had no time to think about such things just then, for the tumult about her was dying, and Thomas Greentree decided to ignore the strict demands of naval protocol just this once. His hand came down from its salute even before hers did, and it reached out, catching hers in a crushing clasp of welcome before she could say a word.

"Welcome home, My Lady!" he said, and if his voice was husky with emotion, it also echoed in the sudden quiet. "Welcome home. And welcome aboard the *Honor Harrington!*"

CHAPTER THREE

High Admiral Wesley Matthews gazed out from the palatial shuttle pad lounge and puffed his cheeks. His hair, dark brown back in the simpler days when he'd been a mere commodore in what had been no more than a system-defense fleet, was now so heavily shot with silver it seemed to gleam as the dawn light of Yeltsin's Star spilled down over Austin City. There were more lines in his intelligent, mobile face than there had been, too, but there was also a solid satisfaction in his hazel eyes. Usually, at least. And with reason, for he had overseen the transformation of the Grayson Space Navy which had been all but destroyed in the Masadan War as it rose phoenixlike from the ashes to become, by almost any standard, the third most powerful fleet in a hundred-light-year radius of his world. To be sure, that fleet was also locked in battle with the *largest* fleet within that same radius, but it had puissant allies, and, by and large, High Admiral Matthews had much of which to be proud.

None of which helped damp the exasperated, affectionate, respectful irritation he felt at this particular moment. He glowered for just a moment, with infinite deference, at the back of the short, wiry man standing with him in the lounge, then returned his attention to the scene beyond the window.

Austin City was the oldest city on Grayson. While many of its public buildings had been placed under protective domes, the city as a whole had not, and it was winter in Grayson's northern hemisphere. Fresh, heavy snow had fallen overnight, and banks of it lay more than man-high where the landing field's plows had

27

deposited it. Matthews had never been particularly fond of snow, but he was prepared to make exceptions at times. Like this year. The four-thousand-year-old Christian calendar which Grayson stubbornly clung to for official dating was in unusual agreement with the actual planetary seasons, and that had given him extra enjoyment as he listened to his favorite carols. It wasn't often that a Grayson had a chance to see for himself what the ancient songs' enthusiasm for "white Christmases" was all about.

But Christmas had been two days before. Matthews' mind was back on military matters once more, and he grimaced as he glanced at the dozen or so armsmen in Mayhew maroon and gold standing about the foot of the lounge lift. Their breath plumed in the icy air, and beyond them, several dozen Marines had been scattered, apparently randomly, around the approaches. That randomness, Matthews knew, was deceptive. Those Marines had been very carefully deployed, with plenty of support a com call away, and they were heavily armed, alert, and watchful.

And unless he missed his guess, every one of them was as irritated as he was with the latest antic of their Protector.

One of these days, Benjamin is simply going to have *to grow up. I know he enjoys slipping the leash whenever he can, and Tester knows I can't blame him for that, but he has no business standing around in a spaceport lounge with no more security than this! And speaking of standing around, it would be nice if he'd bothered to give me some reason to be standing around with* him. *It's always flattering to be invited along, of course, but I* do have *several hundred other things I could be doing. Not to mention the fact that the crack of dawn is* not *my favorite time to get up and haul on a dress uniform just because my Protector's decided to play hooky from the Palace for the day.*

Benjamin Mayhew turned his head and smiled up at the taller high admiral. It was a charming smile, from a charismatic man, and Matthews felt himself smiling back almost against his will, for the Protector had that bad-little-boy-escaped-from-the-tutor look he'd come to know entirely too well in the last decade. It made Benjamin look much younger than his forty T-years (to Grayson eyes, at least; to eyes from a planet where prolong had been available from birth, he would have been taken for a man of at least fifty or sixty), even if it didn't do a great deal to soften his senior naval officer's mood.

"I suppose I really ought to apologize, Wesley," the Protector said after a moment, but then his smile turned into a broad grin. "I'm not going to, though."

"Somehow that doesn't surprise me, Your Grace," Matthews infused his reply with all the disapprobation he was prepared to allow himself with the ruler of his planet.

"Ah, but that's because you know me so well! If you *didn't* know me, if you'd been taken in by all the nice things the PR flacks say about me for public consumption, then I'm sure it would surprise you, wouldn't it?"

Matthews gave him a fulminating look but, aware of the two Marines standing vigilantly just inside the lounge entry, declined to answer in front of military personnel. Although, if the only other ears had belonged to the square-shouldered, weathered-looking armsman standing behind the Protector, watching Benjamin's back with much the same irritated affection as Matthews, it would have been a different matter.

Major Rice had been the Protector's personal armsman for over ten years, since his predecessor's death during the Maccabean coup attempt, and he had not been selected for his position for his social skills. Indeed, his social skills were a bit rudimentary. But back before joining Palace Security, Sergeant-Major Robert Rice, known to his fellows as "Sparky" for some reason Matthews had yet to ferret out, had been the senior noncom of the Orbit Dogs. Officially known as the 5019th Special Battalion, the Orbit Dogs were *the* elite battalion (except that the outsized "special" battalion was bigger than a normal regiment) of the Grayson Space Marines. After the Protector's hairbreadth escape from assassination, Palace Security had decided he needed an especially nasty guard dog, and "Sparky" Rice had been their choice. It was not, Matthews suspected, a post the slightly graying, red-haired veteran had accepted without some severe qualms. On the other hand, his long, distinguished, and risky military career had probably stood him in good stead by helping develop the sort of patience required to ride herd on a charge as . . . incorrigible as Benjamin IX. What mattered at the moment, however, was that the Protector had no secrets from the head of his personal security detachment, and that Rice had seen him in this sort of mood too often to have taken anything Matthews might have said wrongly.

The high admiral realized the Protector was still grinning at him expectantly and shook himself.

"I assure you, Your Grace," he said, taking a mild revenge by resorting to tones of exquisite, courteous respect, "that no service you might request of me could be anything other than an honor and a pleasure to perform."

"That's given me my own back!" Benjamin observed with admiration. "You've really gotten very good at that, Wesley."

"Thank you, Your Grace," Matthews replied, hazel eyes twinkling at last. A soft warning tone sounded and he glanced up at the data display on the lounge wall. A Navy shuttle was ten minutes out, and his eyebrows rose. Obviously, they were here to meet the shuttle, but why? And how did it come about that the Protector clearly knew more than the uniformed commander of the Grayson Navy did about who—or what—was aboard one of its shuttles? And what the *hell* was Benjamin *grinning* about that way?

An almost unbearable curiosity nearly forced the question from him, but he bit his tongue firmly. He would *not* give his maddening ruler the satisfaction of asking, he told himself doggedly, and returned his gaze to the landing apron of the pad.

Benjamin watched him for a moment longer, then smothered a laugh and joined him in gazing out through the crystoplast.

Several more minutes passed in silence, and then a white contrail drew a pencil-thin line across the rich blue morning sky behind the gleaming bead of a shuttle. The bead grew quickly into a swept-winged arrowhead, and Matthews watched with professional approval as the pilot turned onto his final approach and swooped down to a perfect landing. The landing legs deployed, flexed, and settled. Then the hatch opened and the stairs extended themselves, and Matthews forced himself not to bounce on his toes in irritation. He really did have far too many things to do, and as soon as this foolishness—whatever it was—was out of the way, perhaps he could get back to them and—

He froze, hazel eyes flaring wide as they locked on the tall, slim figure in a blue-on-blue uniform identical to his own, and his mental grousing slithered to an incoherent halt. He could not possibly be seeing what he thought he was, a small, still voice told him logically. Only one woman had ever been authorized to wear the uniform of a Grayson admiral. Just as only one woman in the Grayson navy had ever carried a six-legged, cream-and-gray treecat everywhere she went. Which meant his eyes must be lying to him, because that woman was dead. Had been dead for over two T-years. And yet—

"I told you I wouldn't apologize," Benjamin IX told his senior military officer, and this time there was no amusement at all in his soft voice. Matthews looked at him, his eyes stunned, and Benjamin smiled gently. "It may be a little late," he said, "but better late than never. Merry Christmas, Wesley."

Matthews turned back to the lounge windows, still grappling

with the impossibility of it all. One or two of the Marines and armsmen on the pad apron had made the same connection he had. Astonishment and disbelief were enough to yank even them out of their focused professionalism, and he saw them gaping at the tall woman with the short, curly hair. He knew he was doing exactly the same, but he couldn't help it, and he felt disbelief giving way to an exultant inner shout that threatened to rattle the bones of his soul like castanets.

"I know how much she meant to you and the rest of the Navy," Benjamin went on quietly beside him, "and I simply couldn't take this moment away from you."

"B-but how—? I mean, we all knew . . . and the newsies all said—"

"I don't know, Wesley. Not yet. I received the original dispatch from Trevor's Star over two weeks ago, and an encrypted message direct from her shortly after the *Harrington* came out of hyper and headed in-system, but they were both maddeningly brief. They didn't give many details, aside from the most important one: the fact that she was alive. I suppose she and Judah really ought to have gone through your channels instead of directly to me, but she was acting in her capacity as steadholder, not admiral, and she was right about the need to consider the political repercussions of her return before anything else. But do the details really matter?"

The Protector of Grayson's voice was very soft, and his eyes gleamed as he watched the tall, one-armed woman make her way towards the lounge lift, followed now by a major in Harrington green, another half dozen or so officers, and one burly senior chief missile tech in Manticoran uniform.

"Does *anything* really matter . . . besides the fact that she's come home again after all?"

"No, Your Grace," Matthews said equally softly, and drew a deep, shuddering breath—his first, it seemed, in the last standard hour or so—then shook his head. "No," he repeated. "I don't suppose anything else *does* matter, does it?"

Honor Harrington stepped out of the lift and started to come to attention, but Benjamin Mayhew reached her in a single stride. His arms went about her in a bear-hug embrace far too powerful for his wiry frame to have produced, and her working eye went wide. It was unheard of for a Grayson man to so much as touch an unmarried Grayson woman, far less to throw his arms around her and try to crush her rib cage! For that matter, no properly reared Grayson male would embrace even one of his own wives so fiercely in public. But then the surprise flowed out of her eye, and her remaining arm went around the Protector, returning his hug, as his emotions swept through her. She shouldn't have done it, even if Benjamin was the one who'd initiated the contact, but she couldn't help it, for in that moment, he wasn't the Protector from whose hands she had received her steadholdership ten T-years before. He was the friend who'd seen her die and now saw her returned to life, and just at the moment, he didn't give very much of a damn what the ironbound strictures of Grayson protocol had to say about the proper behavior of a Protector.

The moment was as brief as it was intense, and then he drew a deep breath, stood back, and held her at arms' length, hands on her shoulders, while he looked intently up into her face. His eyes weren't completely dry, but that was all right. Hers weren't either, and she tasted the cold anger flickering deep within his joy at seeing her again.

"The eye's gone again, too, isn't it?" he said after a moment, and she nodded, the live side of her mouth twisting in a wry smile. "That, and the nerve repairs've been shot to hell again . . . And the arm," he said flatly. "Anything else?"

She gazed back at him, all too well aware of just how much a lie his apparent calm was. She'd been afraid of how he might react to her injuries, and especially to how she'd received them. She'd had a sufficient foretaste from Judah Yanakov and Thomas Green-tree . . . not to mention every other Grayson officer who'd heard the story.

She'd always known she enjoyed a unique status in her adopted Navy's eyes. That probably would have been enough to wake the bleak, harsh hatred she'd tasted in them as she tried to brush over her imprisonment and starvation and StateSec's degrading efforts to break her. But they were also Grayson men, and despite any changes Benjamin Mayhew might have wrought, Grayson men were programmed on a genetic level to protect women. She suspected that the reports of her death had been enough to push quite a few of them to a point only a step short of berserk rage. Indeed, she *knew* it had, for she'd felt the echoes of fury still reverberating within Judah Yanakov . . . and Greentree had told her about his order to the Grayson forces at the Battle of the Basilisk Terminus. Yet in some illogical way, the discovery of how she'd actually been treated was even more infuriating to them, now that they knew she was alive, than even the HD imagery of her supposed death had been when they'd believed she was dead.

Men, she thought with exasperated affection. *Especially* Grayson *men! Not that Hamish was a bit better. They really aren't that far from the bearskins and mastodon days, any of them, are they?*

But however that might be, she must be very careful about exactly how she related her experiences to *this* man. Benjamin Mayhew was the Planetary Protector of Grayson and the liege lord of Steadholder Harrington, with all the complex, mutually interlocking obligations that implied, including the responsibility to avenge injuries done to his vassal. Worse, he was a Grayson male, however enlightened he might be by his home world's standards. Worse yet, he was her friend . . . and he'd never forgotten that he owed his family's lives to her and to Nimitz. And worst of all, the fact that he *was* the Protector of Grayson meant he was in a position to give terrifying expression to the rage the man within him felt at this moment.

"That's about the entire list for me," she said, after only the briefest pause, and her soprano was calm, almost detached. "Nimitz needs a bit of repair work, too." She reached up to rub the 'cat's ears as he stood in the carrier. "He had a little collision with a pulse rifle butt. Nothing that can't be fixed for either of us, Benjamin."

"*Fixed!*" he half-snarled, and she felt his fresh spike of anger. Well, she'd expected that. He knew she was one of the minority for whom regeneration simply did not work.

"Fixed," she repeated firmly, and violated a thousand years of protocol by giving the Protector of Grayson a gentle, affectionate shake. "Not with all original parts, perhaps, but the Star Kingdom makes excellent replacements. You know that."

He glared at her, almost angry at her for trying to brush her mutilation aside. Both of them were perfectly well aware that not even Manticoran medicine could provide true replacements. Oh, modern prostheses could fool other people into never realizing they were artificial, and many of them, like the cybernetic eye the Peeps had burned out aboard *Tepes*, offered some advantages over the natural parts for which they substituted. But the interface between nerve and machine remained. There was always some loss of function, however good the replacement, and whatever enhancements a replacement might add in partial compensation, it never duplicated the feel, the sensitivity—the *aliveness*—of the original.

But then his face relaxed, and he reached up to pat the hand on his shoulder and managed a nod, as if he recognized what she was trying to do. Perhaps he *did* recognize it. Honor couldn't parse his emotions finely enough to be sure, but he was certainly intelligent enough to understand how dangerous his anger could be and to grasp her efforts to turn that anger before it launched him on a charge to seek vengeance.

Speaking of which . . .

"Actually," she said in a lighter tone, "I'm much luckier than the people who arranged for me to need those replacements in the first place, you know."

"You are?" Mayhew asked suspiciously, and she nodded, then flicked her head at the burly senior chief who'd finally arrived in the lounge, trailing along behind the commissioned officers from the shuttle.

"Senior Chief Harkness here sort of saw to it that everyone who had anything to do with what happened to me, including Cordelia Ransom, came to a very bad end," she told the Protector.

"He did?" Mayhew regarded Harkness approvingly. "Good for you, Senior Chief! How bad an end was it?"

Harkness flushed and started to mumble something, then slid to a halt and stared imploringly at Honor. She gazed back with a demure smile, right cheek dimpling, as she let him stew for a moment, then took mercy on him.

"About as bad as they come, actually," she said. Mayhew looked back at her, and she shrugged. "He arranged for a pinnace to bring up its impeller wedge inside a battlecruiser's boat bay," she told him much more soberly.

"Sweet Tester!" Matthews murmured, and her smile went crooked and cold.

"If there were any pieces left at all, they were very, very small ones, Benjamin," she said softly, and his nostrils flared as he inhaled in intense satisfaction.

"Good for you, Senior Chief," he repeated, and Honor felt a tingle of relief as he stepped back from the precipice of his rage. He could do that, now that he knew those actually responsible for what had happened to her were safely dead. It wouldn't make him one bit less implacable where those people's superiors were concerned, but his need to strike out at someone—anyone—had been muted into something he could control.

He gazed at Harkness for a few more moments, then gave himself a little shake and turned back to Honor.

"As you see," he said in a more normal tone of voice, "I took your advice and restricted the news to a minimum. Even Wesley didn't know who he was waiting for." He smiled a devilish smile far more like his own. "I thought he'd enjoy the surprise."

"No you didn't," Matthews replied, deciding that just this once *lèse-majesté* was fully justifiable, Marine sentries or not. "You decided that you'd enjoy *watching* me be surprised . . . just like any other adolescent with a secret!"

"Careful there, High Admiral!" Benjamin warned. "Officers who tell the truth about—I mean, *insult* their Protectors have been known to come to gory ends."

"No doubt they have," Matthews retorted, eyes twinkling as he held out his hand to Honor, "but at least they perished knowing they'd struck a blow for freedom of thought and expression. Didn't they, Lady Harrington?"

"Don't get me involved in this, Sir! We steadholders have a legal obligation to support the dignity of the Protector. Besides, I'm 'That Foreign Woman,' remember? Having me on your side would only make things worse in the eyes of the unthinking reactionaries who'd undoubtedly carry out his orders to scrag you without turning a hair."

"Perhaps in the past, My Lady," Matthews said. "But not in the future, I think. Or not the immediate future, at any rate. I realize we're talking about *Grayson* reactionaries, but not even they are going to be immune to having you come back from the dead. For a while, at least."

"Hah! I give it three weeks. A month tops," Mayhew snorted. "Fortunately, there are less of them than there used to be, but the ones we still have seem to feel some sort of moral imperative to become even more obstructionist as their numbers dwindle. And they're concentrating on our interstellar relations now, not the domestic side, anyway. Not that they aren't planning on back-dooring their way back to the domestic front as soon as they can! It's too bad these aren't the bad old days right after the Constitution was ratified. There are quite a few of my Keys I'd like to introduce to some of the more . . . *creative* chastisements Benjamin the Great reserved for irritating steadholders. Especially the ones like—"

He broke off with a grimace and waved one hand dismissively.

"Let's not get me started on that. One thing of which we can be unfortunately certain, Honor, is that there'll be plenty of opportunities for me to make you dismally well aware of just how the conservatives have managed to irritate me in your absence."

"I'm sure," she agreed. "But that brings another point to mind. Certain admirals, including a Manticoran one and your own despicable cousin, have flatly refused to tell me just what the lot of you did with my steading! I'm pretty sure Judah ordered no one else to tell me anything, either, and he doesn't fool me for a minute with that 'military personnel shouldn't dabble in matters of state' nonsense! He's *grinning* too much."

"He is?" Mayhew raised both eyebrows, then shook his head. "Shocking," he sighed. "Simply shocking! I see I'll have to speak to him quite firmly." Honor glared at him, and he smiled back. "Still, the ins and outs of two-plus years of history aren't something to try to explain in a spaceport lounge, either. Especially not when we have a few other things to take care of before Katherine and Elaine descend upon you and begin planning the planet-wide gala to welcome you home."

He chuckled at Honor's groan, then nodded to Rice. The major touched his wrist com and murmured something into it, and the Protector took Honor's elbow and began escorting her towards the lounge exit while Rice and Andrew LaFollet trailed quietly along behind them.

"As I said, Honor, I've restricted the information about your arrival to a very small group, for the moment, at least, but there were a few people here on Grayson who I thought really ought to know immediately."

"Oh?" Honor eyed him warily.

"Yes, and— Ah, here they are now!" he observed as the exit doors slid silently open, and Honor stopped dead.

Seven people appeared in the opening: five with four limbs, and two with six, and all of them seemed to shimmer as her vision hazed with sudden tears. Allison Chou Harrington stood beside her husband, small and elegant and beautiful as ever, and tears gleamed in almond eyes that matched Honor's own as she stared at her daughter. Alfred Harrington towered over her, his face working with emotions so deep and so strong they were almost more than Honor could bear to taste. Howard Clinkscales stood to Allison's left, his fierce, craggy face tight with emotion of his own while he leaned on the silver-headed staff that was the badge of office of Harrington Steading's Regent. Miranda LaFollet stood to his left, cradling the treecat named Farragut in her arms, smiling with her heart naked in her eyes as she saw her Steadholder and her brother at last. And to Alfred's right stood a man with thinning sandy hair and gray eyes, staring at her as if he dared not believe his own eyes. She felt James MacGuiness' towering joy— joy that was only now beginning to overcome his dread that somehow the impossible news of her return was all a mistake—and wrapped about that joy was the dizzying spiral of welcome and jubilation welling up from the slim, dappled shape riding on his shoulder as the treecat named Samantha saw her mate.

It was all too much. Honor had no defense against the emotions pouring into her from those people who meant so much to her, and she felt her own face begin to crumple at last. Not with sorrow, but with a joy too intense to endure.

He did it on purpose, she thought, somewhere down deep under the whirlwind of her own emotions. *Benjamin knows about my link with Nimitz, and he deliberately saw to it that I could meet them with no one else present. No one to see me lose it completely.*

And then there was no more room for thought. Not coherent ones, anyway. She was fifty-four T-years old, and that didn't matter at all as she stepped away from Benjamin Mayhew, holding out her arm to her mother through her blinding haze of tears.

"Momma?" she half-whispered, her soprano hoarse, and she tasted salt on her lips as her parents came towards her. "Daddy? I—"

Her voice broke completely, and that didn't matter, either. Nothing in the universe mattered as her father reached her and the arms which had always been there for her went about her. She felt the crushing strength of Sphinx in them, yet they closed around her with infinite gentleness, and her visored cap tumbled to the floor as her father pressed his face into her hair. Then her mother was there, as well, hugging her and burrowing her way into the embrace Alfred had widened to enfold them both, and for just a moment, Honor Harrington could stop being a steadholder and a naval officer. She could be simply their daughter, restored to them by some miracle they did not yet understand, and she clung to them even more tightly than they clung to her.

She never knew how long they stood there. Some things are too intense, too important, to slice up into seconds and minutes, and this was one of them. It was a time that lasted as long as it had to last, but finally she felt her tears ease and she drew a deep, deep breath and pushed back in her father's arms to stare mistily up at his face.

"I'm home," she said simply, and he nodded.

"I know you are, baby." His deep voice was frayed and unsteady, but his eyes glowed. "I know you are."

"We both know," Allison said, and Honor gave a watery giggle as her mother produced a tiny handkerchief and, in the manner of mothers since time immemorial, began briskly wiping her daughter's face. She was barely two-thirds Honor's height, and Honor was fairly sure they must look thoroughly ridiculous, but that was fine with her, and she looked across her mother's head at Clinkscales.

"Howard," she said softly. He bowed deeply, but she saw his tears and tasted his joy, and she held out her hand quickly. He blinked as he took it, his grip still strong and firm despite his age, and then he drew a huge, gusty breath and shook himself.

"Welcome home, My Lady," he said simply. "Your steading and your people have missed you."

"I got back as soon as I could," she replied, making her tone as light as she could. "Unfortunately, our travel plans hit a couple of glitches. Nothing Chief Harkness and Carson couldn't straighten out for us, though."

Ensign Clinkscales stepped up beside her as she spoke his name, and the Regent smiled as he enfolded his towering nephew in a huge hug. Howard Clinkscales had been a powerfully built man in his prime, for a Grayson, but he'd never matched Carson's centimeters, and he was eighty-seven pre-prolong T-years old. The two of them looked as mismatched in height as Honor knew she and Allison had, and she chuckled as she put her arm affectionately back about her mother.

Then she paused. She hadn't noticed in the intensity of their initial embrace, but each of her parents wore a carrier much like the one in which she herself carried Nimitz, and her eyebrow quirked. Now why—?

Then her father half-turned to make room for MacGuiness and Miranda, and Honor's eye went even wider than it had gone when the door opened. The carrier on his back wasn't like hers after all, for it wasn't for a 'cat. It was—

"Don't stare, dear," her mother said firmly, and reached up to grasp her chin, turning her head to wipe the left side of her face. Honor obeyed the grip meekly, so surprised she was unable to do anything else, and her mother shook her head. "Really, Honor," she went on, "you'd think you'd never seen a baby before, and I happen to know you have!"

"But . . . but . . ." Honor turned her head once more, staring into the dark eyes that gazed drowsily back at her, and then gulped and turned back to her mother, using her height to lean forward over her and look into the carrier on *Allison's* back. She was sure the eyes in that small face were equally dark, but they weren't drowsy. They were closed, and the tiny face wore the disapproving, sleepy frown only babies can produce.

"Really, Honor!" her mother said again. "Your father and I *are* prolong recipients, you know."

"Of course I do, but—"

"You seem to have grown entirely too fond of that word, dear," Allison scolded, giving Honor's face one last pat before she stepped back to examine her handiwork. Then she nodded in satisfaction and tucked the damp square of fabric back into whatever hiding place it had emerged from in the first place.

"It's all your fault, actually," she told Honor then. "You hadn't gotten around to producing an heir, so when they tried to make poor Lord Clinkscales Steadholder Harrington, he had to think of *something* in self-defense." She shook her head, and Clinkscales looked at her for a moment, then gave Honor a half-sheepish grin.

"You mean—?" Honor shook herself and drew a deep, deep breath. She also made a mental resolution to personally hunt Hamish Alexander down and murder him with her bare hands. Or *hand*, singular, she thought as she recalled his devilish amusement and vague talk about "other arrangements" on Grayson. Given the nature of the offense, waiting until she could be fitted with a replacement for her missing arm was out of the question. If she left this afternoon aboard a courier boat and went by way of the Junction, she could stop by the *Harrington* to wring Judah Yanakov's neck and still be back at Trevor's Star in just four days, and then . . .

She exhaled very slowly, then looked back down at her mother.

"So I'm not an only child anymore?"

"Goodness, you figured it out after all," Allison murmured with a devilish smile. Then she reached up and slipped the carrier straps from her shoulders. She cradled the sleeping infant, carrier and all, in her arms, and when she looked back up at Honor the deviltry had disappeared into a warm tenderness.

"This is Faith Katherine Honor Stephanie Miranda Harrington," she said gently, and giggled at Honor's expression. "I know the name is longer than she is just now, poor darling, but that's your fault, too, you know. At the moment—which is to say until *you* get busy in the grandchild department—this long-named little bundle is your heir, Lady Harrington. As a matter of fact, right this second *she's* actually the legal 'Steadholder Harrington,' at least until the Keys get around to discovering that you're back. Which means we were lucky to hold her to just five given names, all things considered. I expect the assumption, up until a few hours ago, was that she would become Honor the Second when she chose her reign name. Fortunately—" Her lips quivered for an instant, and she paused to clear her throat. "*Fortunately*," she repeated more firmly, "she won't have to make that decision quite as soon as we'd feared she might after all."

"And *this*," Alfred said, having slipped out of his own carrier's straps, "is her slightly younger twin brother, James Andrew Benjamin Harrington. He got off with two less names, you'll note, thus duly exercising his prerogative as a natural-born male citizen of the last true patriarchy in this neck of the galaxy. Although we did, I hope you will also note, manage to butter up the local potentate by hanging *his* name on the poor kid."

"So I see." Honor laughed, reaching out to stroke the baby boy's satiny cheek. She shot a sideways glance at Benjamin Mayhew and noted his happy, almost possessive smile. Obviously her parents and the Mayhews had grown even closer to one another than she'd dared hope they might, and she returned her attention to her mother.

"They're beautiful, Mother," she said softly. "You and Daddy *do* do good work, even if I say so myself."

"You think so?" Her mother cocked her head judiciously. "For myself, I could wish we'd figured out a way to skip straight from the delivery to the first day of school." She shook her head with a pensive air that fooled no one in the lounge. "I'd forgotten how much sheer *work* a baby is," she sighed.

"Oh, of course, My Lady!" Miranda LaFollet laughed. Honor turned to her maid and found Miranda in the circle of her brother's arm . . . which would have represented a shocking dereliction of duty on the major's part under normal circumstances. Which these weren't. Miranda saw Honor's questioning expression and laughed again. "It's so much 'work' she insisted on carrying them to term the natural way, despite the fact that her prolong added two and a half months to the process, My Lady," she informed Honor. "*And* so much work that she flatly refuses to let us provide full-time nannies for them! In fact, it's all we can do to pry her loose from them—to pry *either* of your parents loose, actually—long enough for them to go to the clinic! I don't think even people from our steading were quite ready for the sight of two of the best doctors on the planet making their rounds with babies on their backs, but—"

She shrugged, and Honor chuckled.

"Well, Mother *is* from Beowulf, Miranda. They're all a little crazy there, or so I've heard. And they go absolutely gooey over babies. Not," she added reflectively, gazing at the tiny shapes of her brother and sister, "that I can fault them, now that I think of it. These two have to be the most beautiful pair of babies in the explored universe, after all."

"Do you really think so?" her mother asked.

"I really think so," Honor assured her softly. "Of course, I may be just a tiny bit prejudiced, but I really think so."

"Good," Allison Harrington said, "because unless my nose is

mistaken, Faith Katherine Honor Stephanie Miranda here has just demonstrated the efficiency with which her well-designed internal systems operate. And just to show you how delighted I am by your opinion of her beauty, I'm going to let *you* change her, dear!"

"I'd love to, Mother. Unfortunately, at the moment I only have one hand, and since that's obviously a job which requires *two* . . ." She shrugged, and her mother shook her head.

"Some people will do anything to avoid a little work," she said, much more lightly than she felt as her eyes flicked to the stump of Honor's left arm, and Honor smiled.

"Oh, I didn't have to do this just to get out of work," she assured Allison, smile broadening as James MacGuiness approached with Samantha. "Mac spoils me shamelessly. I'm sure he'd have been delighted to do my share of the diaper-changing even without this. Wouldn't you, Mac?"

"I'm afraid that's one thing that isn't covered in my job description, Milady," the steward said. His voice was almost normal, but his eyes were misty and his smile seemed to tremble just a bit.

"Really?" Honor's smile softened and warmed, and she reached out to put her arm around him. He let himself lean against her for just a moment as she hugged him hard, then held him back out at arm's length to look deep into his eyes. "Well, in that case, I guess you'll just have to settle for being 'Uncle Mac' . . . because we all know uncles and aunts are responsible for spoiling kids rotten, not doing anything constructive."

"What an interesting notion," Alfred Harrington observed. "And the job of big sisters is—?"

"Depends on how much 'bigger' they are, doesn't it?" Honor replied cheerfully. "In this case, I thin—"

She broke off suddenly, so abruptly her mother looked up from Faith in quick alarm. Honor's smile had vanished as if it had never existed, and her head snapped to her left, her single working eye locking on the 'cat on MacGuiness' shoulder.

Samantha had reared up, her ears flat to her skull, her eyes fixed on her mate. Allison whipped her head around to follow that intense stare, and her own eyes widened as she saw Nimitz recoiling as if he'd been struck. For just an instant, she had the insane thought that he'd somehow infuriated Samantha, but only for an instant. Just long enough for her to recognize something she had never, ever expected to see in Nimitz.

Terror. A fear and a panic that drove the whimper of a frightened kitten from him.

MacGuiness and Andrew LaFollet had looked up when Honor

broke off, and both of them went white as they saw Nimitz. Unlike Allison, they *had* seen him that way before—once—in the admiral's quarters of GNS *Terrible*, when the terrible nightmares lashing his person's sleeping mind with the Furies' own whips had reduced the empathic 'cat to shivering, shuddering helplessness. Now they saw the equal of that terror ripping through him, and as one man, they stepped towards him, reaching out to their friend.

But even before they moved, Honor Harrington had hit the quick release of the carrier straps where they crossed on her chest. She caught the straps as they opened, and, in a single, supple movement which ought to have looked awkward and clumsy for a one-armed woman, stripped the carrier from her back and brought it around in front of her. She went to her knees, hugging Nimitz, carrier and all, to her breasts, pressing her cheek against his head, and her eyes were closed as she threw every scrap of energy she had into the horror raging in her link to him.

I should have felt it sooner, some fragment of calm told her. *I should have realized the instant we saw Sam . . . but* he *didn't realize it. My God, how could we have* missed *it?*

She held the 'cat with the full power of her arm and her heart, and for just an instant, as the terrible storm front of his emotions spun its tornado strength through them both, he struggled madly to escape her. Whether to run and hide in his panic or in a desperate effort to reach Samantha physically Honor could not have said, probably because *he* couldn't have. But then the terrible panic flash eased into something less explosive . . . and far, far bleaker. He went limp with a shudder, pressing his face against her, and a soft, low-pitched keen flowed out of him.

Honor's heart clenched at the desolate sound, and she kissed him between the ears while she held him close.

The pulser butt, she thought. *That* damned *pulser butt on Enki! My God, what did it* do *to him?*

She didn't know the answer to that question, but she knew the blow which had shattered his mid-pelvis had to be the cause of the dark and terrible loneliness of a full half of Nimitz's mind. Nothing else *could* have caused it, and the shock and terror it produced were infinitely worse than they might have been because neither he nor Honor had even realized that silence was there.

She crooned to him, holding him tightly, eyes closed, and she felt Samantha standing high on her true-feet beside her. Nimitz's mate had exploded off of MacGuiness' shoulder, racing to Nimitz, and her true-hands and feet-hands caressed his silken fur. Honor felt her matching panic, felt her reaching out to Nimitz with every sense she had, trying desperately to hear some response from him, pleading for the reassurance her mate could no longer give her.

Honor tasted both 'cats' emotions, and her tears dripped onto Nimitz's pelt. But at least the initial panic was passing, and she drew a deep, shuddering breath of relief as they realized, and Honor with them, that they could still feel one another's emotions . . . and Samantha realized Nimitz could still hear *her* thoughts.

The exact way in which the telempathic treecats communicated with one another had always been a matter of debate among humans. Some had argued that the 'cats were true telepaths; others that they didn't actually "communicate" in the human sense at all, that they were simply units in a free-flow linkage of pure emotions so deep it effectively substituted for communication.

Since her own link to Nimitz had changed and deepened, Honor had realized that, in many ways, both arguments were correct. She'd never been able to tap directly into Nimitz's "conversations" with other 'cats, but she had been able to sense the very fringes of a deep, intricate meld of interflowing thoughts and emotions when he "spoke" to another of his kind. Since he and Samantha had become mates, Honor had been able to "hear" and study their interwoven communication far more closely and discovered Nimitz and Samantha truly were so tightly connected that, in many ways, they were almost one individual, so much a part of one another that they often had no need to exchange deliberately formulated thoughts. But from observing them together and also with others of their kind, she'd also come to the conclusion that 'cats in general definitely did exchange the sort of complex, reasoned concepts which could only be described as "communication." Yet what she'd never been certain of until this dreadful moment was that they did it over more than one channel. They truly were both empaths *and* telepaths. She knew that now, for Samantha could still "hear" and taste Nimitz's emotions . . . but that was *all* she could hear. The rich, full-textured weaving which had bound them together had been battered and mauled, robbed of half its richness and blighted with unnatural silence, and she felt herself weeping for her beloved friends while they grappled with their sudden recognition of loss.

How could we not have noticed it on Hell? All that time, and we never even guessed—

But then she drew a deep breath of understanding. Of course. Her link with Nimitz operated through the 'cat's empathic sense. They'd never used the telepathic "channel" to communicate, and so Nimitz had never even suspected that it had been taken from him. Not until the moment he'd reached out to his mate . . . and she hadn't heard him at all.

"Honor?" It was her mother's soft voice, and she looked up to see Allison kneeling beside her, her face anxious, her eyes dark with worry. "What is it, Honor?"

"It's—" Honor inhaled sharply. "In the Barnett System, when Ransom announced her plans to send me to Hell, she ordered her goons to kill Nimitz, and—" She shook her head and closed her eyes again. "We didn't have anything left to lose, Mother, so—"

"So they attacked the StateSec guards," Andrew LaFollet said softly, and Honor realized her armsman, too, was kneeling beside her. He was to her left, on her blind side, and she turned towards him. "That must have been it, My Lady," he said when his Steadholder looked at him. "When that bastard with the pulse rifle clubbed him."

"Yes." Honor nodded, not really surprised Andrew had realized what must have happened. But she could taste the confusion of the others, even through the emotional tempest still rolling through the two treecats. She loosened her grip on Nimitz, setting the carrier on the floor, and watched as he climbed out of it. He and Samantha sat face-to-face, and he pressed his cheek into the side of her neck while her buzzing purr threatened to vibrate the bones right out of her, and her prehensile tail wrapped itself about him and her true-hands and hand-feet caressed him. Even now he sat awkwardly hunched, twisted by his poorly healed bones, and she looked back up to meet her mother's worried eyes.

"No one's ever known if the 'cats were truly telepaths . . . until now," she told Allison softly. "But they are. And when that SS thug clubbed him, he must have . . . have broken whatever it is that *makes* them telepaths, because Sam can't hear him, Mother. She can't hear him at all."

"She can't?" Honor looked up. Her father stood beside her, cradling one of the babies in either arm, and frowned as she nodded at him. "From the way he's sitting, the pulser must have caught him—what? Almost exactly on the mid-pelvis?"

"A little behind it and from the right we think, My Lord," LaFollet said. "Most of the ribs went on that side, too. Fritz Montoya could probably give you a better answer, but it looked to me like it came down at about a seventy-degree angle. Maybe a little shallower than that, but certainly not by very much."

The armsman's eyes were intent, as if he recognized something behind the question from his Steadholder's father, and Alfred nodded slowly.

"That would make sense," he murmured, staring for a moment at something none of the others could see while he thought hard. Then he gave his head a little shake and looked back down at his elder daughter.

"We've wondered for centuries why the 'cats spinal cords have those clusters of nervous tissue at each pelvis," he told her. "Some have theorized that they might be something like secondary brains. They're certainly large enough, with sufficiently complex structures, and the theory was that they might help explain how something with such a relatively low body mass could have developed sentience in the first place. Others have derided the entire idea, while a third group has argued that even though they may be secondary brains, the physical similarities—and differences—between them indicate that they must do something else, as well. Their structures have been thoroughly analyzed and mapped, but we've never been able to link them to any discernible function. But, then, no one ever had a 'cat expert quite like you available for consultation, Honor. Now I think we know what at least one of those superganglia do."

"You mean you think the mid-limb site was his . . . well, his telepathic transmitter?"

"I'd certainly say that's what it looks like. I noticed that you said Sam can't hear *him*, not that he can't hear *her*. Is that correct?"

"Yes. I think so, anyway," Honor said after a moment. "It's hard to be sure just yet. When he realized she couldn't hear him, he just—"

"Reacted very much the way I would have in his place," her father interrupted. "And not surprisingly. I've always wondered what would happen to a telempath who suddenly, for the first time in his life, found himself isolated and alone, locked up in his own little world. We still don't begin to know all we ought to about the 'cats, but one thing we do know is that they all seem to share that constant awareness, that linkage, with every other 'cat and most humans, at least to some extent, around them. It's *always* there, from the day they're born, and they must take it as much for granted as they do oxygen. But now—"

Alfred shuddered and shook his head, and Honor nodded mutely, astounded by how accurately her father had described an interweaving of minds and hearts he had never been able to taste himself.

"If I'm right about how he was injured, this can't be the first time something like this has happened to a 'cat, either. God knows they get banged up enough in the bush that at least some of them must have sustained similar injuries and lived. So they have to know it can happen to any of them, and it must be one of their most deep-seated fears. When Nimitz realized it had happened to *him* . . ."

He shook his head again and sighed, his eyes dark with sympathy as they rested on the two 'cats and he listened to Samantha's soft, loving croon.

"Is there anything we can do?" Honor asked, and there was an odd edge to her voice, one LaFollet didn't understand for several seconds. But then he remembered. Alfred Harrington was one of the Star Kingdom of Manticore's four or five finest neurosurgeons. This wasn't just a daughter asking her father for reassurance; it was a woman asking the man who'd rebuilt the nerves in her own face, and who'd personally implanted her own cybernetic eye, if he had one more miracle in his doctor's bag for her.

"I don't know, honey. Not yet," he told her honestly. "I've paid more attention to the journal articles on 'cats than most other neurosurgeons, I imagine, because of how much a part of all our lives Nimitz is, but my specialty is humans. Native Sphinxian life forms have always been more of a veterinary specialization, and there are a lot of differences between their neural structures and ours. I'm positive that fixing the bone and joint damage won't be a problem, but I don't have any idea where we might be on the matter of neural repairs." The live side of Honor's face tightened, and he shook his head quickly. "That doesn't mean anything, Honor! I'm not just trying to be a doctor throwing out an anchor to windward; I truly don't know, but I certainly intend to find out. And I'll promise you—and Nimitz and Samantha—this much right now. If it *can* be fixed, then I will damned well find the way to do it!"

Honor stared up at him for two more heartbeats, and then she felt her taut shoulders relax just a bit, and the worry in her face eased ever so slightly. She trusted both her parents' judgments in their medical fields. She'd seen and heard about what they'd accomplished far too often not to have learned to trust them. If her father said he thought there might be a way to correct the crippling damage Nimitz had received, then he truly believed there might be one, for one thing he did not do was tell comforting lies.

And one other thing he did not do, she thought. Never in her entire life had he made her a promise he'd failed to keep . . . and she knew he would keep this one, as well.

"Thank you, Daddy," she whispered, and felt her mother's arms go around her once again.

CHAPTER FOUR

"**I** don't fucking *believe* this!"

More than one of the people seated around the conference table flinched at the venom in Secretary of War Esther McQueen's snarl. Not because they were afraid of her (although some of them were), but because no one who wasn't completely insane spoke to Rob Pierre and Oscar Saint-Just that way.

Despite himself, Pierre felt a grin—more of a grimace, really—twitch the corners of his mouth. There were nine people at the table, including himself and Saint-Just. Among them, they represented the core membership of the most powerful group in the entire People's Republic. After better than eight T-years, the Committee of Public Safety still boasted a total membership of twenty-six, almost thirty percent of its original size. Of course, that was only another way of saying that it had been reduced by *over* seventy percent. And allowing for new appointments to replace those who'd disappeared in various purges, factional power struggles, and other assorted unpleasantnesses (and for the replacement of several of those replacements), the actual loss rate among the Committee's members had been well over two hundred percent. Of the original eighty-seven members, only Pierre himself, Saint-Just, and Angela Downey and Henri DuPres (both of whom were little more than well-cowed place-holders) remained. And of the current crop of twenty-six, only the nine in this room truly mattered.

And six of them are too terrified to breathe *without my permission. Mine and Oscar's, at any rate. Which was what we thought*

47

we wanted. They're certainly not going to be hatching any plans to overthrow me . . . but I hadn't quite counted on how useless their gutlessness would make them when it hit the fan.

Which—fortunately or unfortunately, depending on one's viewpoint—is at least not something anyone would ever consider saying about McQueen.

"I can understand your . . . unhappiness, Esther," he said aloud after a moment. "I'm not too happy myself," he added with gargantuan understatement. "Unfortunately, it seems to have happened, whether either one of us likes it or not."

"But—" McQueen started to snap back, then made herself stop. Her mouth clicked shut, and she reined in her temper with visible, nostril-flaring effort.

"You're right, Citizen Chairman," she said in the tone of a woman coming back on balance. "And I apologize for my reaction. However . . . surprising the news, it doesn't excuse such intemperate language. But I stand by my original sentiments. And while I imagine there will be time for proper recriminations later—" she glanced at one of the only two people at the table who were junior to her, and Leonard Boardman, Secretary of Public Information, wilted in his chair "—the immediate consequences are going to be catastrophic . . . and that's if we're lucky! If we're *unlucky.* . . ."

She let her voice trail off and shook her head, and Pierre wished he could disagree with her assessment.

"I'm afraid I have to concur with you there," he admitted, and it was his turn to shake his head.

Joan Huertes, Interstellar News Service's senior reporter and anchorwoman in the People's Republic of Haven, had commed Boardman directly, seeking his comment on the incredible reports coming out of the Manticoran Alliance. The good news, such as it was, was that Boardman had been smart enough to give her a remarkably composed (sounding, at any rate) "No comment," and then to contact Saint-Just immediately rather than sit around and dither over what the PR disaster might mean for him personally. Judging from his expression, he'd made up for the dithering since, but at least he'd gotten the information into the right hands quickly.

Equally to the good, Saint-Just hadn't even considered covering up or trying to sugarcoat the situation for Pierre. Some people, including some at this table, would have in his place, for it was Oscar's people who'd screwed the pooch. But he'd made no attempt to delay while he sought scapegoats. And, finally, they were at least fortunate that the story hadn't come at them completely without warning.

Citizen General Seth Chernock had opted to send his dispatch, with its preposterous conclusion that something must be very wrong in the Cerberus System, aboard a StateSec-crewed vessel in the name of security rather than using the first available dispatch boat. By his most pessimistic estimate, however, he ought to have arrived in Cerberus over two months ago, yet no report from him had reached Saint-Just. No one had worried about that at first. After all, Chernock *was* the StateSec CO of the sector in which Cerberus lay. That meant any decisions about how to deal with problems there were properly his, and he wasn't the sort to ask prior approval for his actions. Besides, what could possibly have happened to such a powerful force?

Yet as the silence dragged out, Saint-Just had begun to grow anxious at last, and last week he'd finally dispatched his own investigators—*very* quietly—to look into Chernock's ridiculous worries. None had reported back yet, and wouldn't for at least another three weeks, but at least he'd already begun the information-seeking process.

Unfortunately, that was all the good news there was . . . and Pierre was grimly certain they'd scarcely even begun to hear the *bad* news.

"Excuse me, Citizen Chairman," Avram Turner, the thin, intense, dark-haired Secretary of the Treasury (and most junior member of the Committee), said after several seconds of silence, "but I'm still not clear on how any of this could have happened."

"Neither are we—yet," Pierre replied. "Obviously no one saw it coming, or we would have acted to prevent it. And at this particular moment, all the information we have is what's coming to us from the Manties."

"With all due respect, Citizen Chairman, and while that may be true, it would have helped enormously if StateSec had informed the Navy when it first received Citizen General Chernock's initial dispatches," Esther McQueen said. "We couldn't have prevented what had already happened to Hades, and we couldn't have hoped to intercept Harrington en route to Trevor's Star, but you do realize that our frontier fleets and star systems are going to hear about this from the Manties and Sollies well before they hear anything about it from *us*." She twitched her shoulders. "I can't begin to estimate the impact it will have on Fleet morale and the loyalty of our more, um, *fractious* planetary populations, but I don't expect it to be good."

"I know." Pierre sighed, and ran the fingers of one hand through his hair. "Unfortunately, the communications lag really bit us on the ass on this one. I'm not defending my decision to keep

Chernock's original report to myself, but be honest, Esther. Even if I'd shared his dispatch with you, what could we have done about it until we had confirmation of whether or not he was correct? And without sending a courier to Cerberus to see for yourself, would *you* have believed a completely unarmed group of prisoners, denied any technology above the level of windmill water pumps, the closest of them separated from our main on-planet base by over fifteen hundred kilometers of ocean, on a world whose native flora and fauna are totally inedible, could somehow have seized control of an entire star system? Of course Oscar and I thought Chernock had gone insane! And even if he hadn't, the force he took with him should have been capable of dealing easily with anything the prisoners could do to resist it."

He met McQueen's eyes levelly, and the small, slender Secretary of War had to nod. She didn't feel like agreeing, but she really had no choice. None of the fragmentary information so far available explained how the prisoners had seized the planet in the first place, far less how they could possibly have defeated the powerful force Chernock had put together to go and take it back again.

And the bastard had the good sense to ask for a regular Navy CO for his collection of Navy and SS units, she admitted to herself unhappily. *Let's not point that little fact out just now, Esther.*

She pushed herself back in her chair, eyes closed for a moment, and pinched the bridge of her nose. Until their own couriers got back from Cerberus, they had only the fragments Huertes had used to prime the pump in her interview attempt with Boardman, and it was entirely possible Boardman had read too much into those bits and pieces. Unfortunately, it didn't feel that way to McQueen, and she'd learned to trust her instincts. And if Boardman hadn't overreacted—hell, if only a *tenth* of what he thought Huertes had meant was true—the disaster sounded pretty damned close to complete.

She puffed her lips in silent frustration and anger, wondering how in hell it could have happened. She'd never met Citizen Admiral Yearman, but she'd pulled his record within minutes of hearing from Saint-Just—*finally!*—about Chernock's dispatch. From what she could see, Yearman wasn't (or hadn't been; no one was certain at the moment if he or Chernock were still alive) an inspired strategist, but he was a sound tactician. If Chernock had been smart enough to realize he needed a professional to ride herd on his SS thug starship crews, then one had to assume he'd also been smart enough to let that professional run the show once they arrived in Cerberus. And whatever Yearman's weaknesses in the area of strategy, he certainly ought to have been able to deal with the orbital defenses guarding Hades, even if they'd been completely under the escapees' control. Particularly since Chernock had specifically informed Saint-Just that he was giving Yearman the full technical specs on those defenses.

But still . . .

"The fact that Harrington is still alive may actually be even more damaging than the escape itself," Turner pointed out, and, again, McQueen nodded. Privately, she was impressed by the other's nerve. His point was glaringly obvious, but making it in front of the two men who'd decided to have Public Information fake up the imagery of Harrington's execution took guts, especially for the most junior person present. On the other hand, as McQueen herself demonstrated, actual power within the Committee of Public Safety wasn't necessarily linked with how long one had been a member. Rob Pierre had handpicked Turner to take over the Treasury just over a T-year ago, when he decided to ram through a long-overdue package of fiscal reform, and whatever his other failings might be, the thin, aggressively energetic Turner had performed impressively in implementing those reforms. His star was definitely in the ascendant at the moment.

Then again, my *star is "in the ascendant"* . . . *and I know perfectly well that Saint-Just would shoot me in a second if he thought he could dispense with my services. Hell,* McQueen gave a mental snort of amusement, *he'd probably shoot me* anyway, *just on general principles. Pierre's the one who's smart enough to know the Navy needs me running it. Saint-Just's just the one who's smart enough to know I'll shoot both of* them *the instant I think I can get away with it.*

"Again, I'd like to disagree, and I can't." Pierre sighed in response to Turner's observation. It was his turn to pinch the bridge of his nose, and he shook his head wearily, then managed a wan smile. "It seemed so simple at the time. She was already dead—we knew that—and whatever we said, the Manties and Sollies would never believe *we* hadn't killed her. At least this way we could pass it off as the end result of due process instead of leaving the impression that we'd just shot her out of hand and dumped her in a shallow grave. And we were hardly in a position to risk shaking public confidence by announcing Cordelia's death or what had really happened to *Tepes,* so—"

He shrugged, and no one in the conference room needed any maps to figure out what he'd left unsaid. None of them had been part of Cordelia Ransom's faction on the Committee. If they ever had been, they would not have been in this room . . . or any longer on the Committee. They all knew how useful Pierre and Saint-Just had found the delay in the official announcement of Ransom's death when it came time to purge her supporters. But still . . .

"That's the thing I find hardest to understand," Turner murmured with the air of a man thinking out loud. "How could she possibly have survived what happened to *Tepes*? And if she did, how could we not have known?"

"Esther?" Pierre glanced at McQueen. "Would you have any thoughts on those questions?"

Carefully, now, she thought. *Let's speak* very *carefully, Esther.*

"I've had a lot of thoughts about them, Citizen Chairman," she said aloud, and that much at least was true. "I've gone back and pulled the scan records from *Count Tilly's* flag deck and combat information center, and I've had them analyzed to a fare-thee-well over at the Octagon." She reached inside her civilian jacket and extracted a thin chip folio, tossing it on the table so that it slid to a stop directly in front of Pierre. "That's the result of our analyses, and also the actual records of the explosion, and none of my people have been able to find anything to explain how Harrington and her people could have gotten off the ship and down to the planet before she blew. Or, for that matter, how Citizen Brigadier Tresca and his people groundside could possibly have missed something like that. Obviously they must have used some of *Tepes'* small craft, although how they could have taken control of them in the first place is beyond me. There were less than thirty of them aboard, and I can't even begin to imagine how so few people could fight their way through an entire ship's company to the boat bays. But even assuming they could pull that off, the only small craft anyone actually saw was the single assault shuttle that Camp Charon used the orbital defenses to destroy."

She paused, watching Pierre (and Saint-Just) as neutrally as possible. The chips she'd passed to the Citizen Chairman contained exactly what she'd said they did. What they did *not* contain was the footage from *Count Tilly's* flag deck immediately after *Tepes* had blown up. McQueen had been very specific about the time chops she'd assigned when she instructed the Navy experts to analyze the records. She still wasn't certain what Citizen Rear Admiral Tourville had been up to when he bent over his tac officer's console, and she had no intention of allowing anyone *else* to figure that out if there was anything at all she could do to prevent it. Lester Tourville was entirely too good a fighting officer to hand over to StateSec. And the fact that she'd covered for him, once she found a discreet way to let him know she had, ought to prove extremely useful as a loyalty enhancer down the road . . .

"The one thing I can suggest with some degree of confidence," she went on after a moment, "is that Harrington and her people must have used the temporary degradation of the Hades sensor net caused by the destruction of the known shuttle to slip their own small craft through to the surface without anyone groundside seeing them coming."

"Degradation?" Turner repeated, and she cocked an eyebrow at Pierre. The Citizen Chairman nodded almost imperceptibly, and she turned to Turner.

"The ground defense center at Camp Charon used high mega-ton-range orbital mines to destroy the Manties' escape shuttle—or what everyone had *assumed* was their escape shuttle—just before *Tepes* blew up. The blast and EMP from that, coupled with the effect of *Tepes'* own fusion plants when they let go, created a very brief window in which the sensor net was effectively 'blinded' and reduced to a fraction of its normal efficiency. That has to be when Harrington's people slipped through to the planet."

"Are you suggesting that they planned from the beginning to use our own response to open the way for them?"

"I think it's obvious that they must have," McQueen replied. "And we're talking about Honor Harrington here, Avram."

"Harrington is *not* some sort of boogeyman," Saint-Just said in frosty tones. Several people cringed, but McQueen met his cold eyes steadily.

"I didn't say she was," she said. "But it's obvious from her record that she's one of the best, if not *the* best, Manty officers of her generation. With the sole exception of what happened at Adler—where, I might add, she still succeeded in her primary mission of protecting the convoy under her command, despite atrociously bad luck—she's kicked the crap out of every commander we've put up against her, Navy and StateSec alike, apparently. All I'm saying here is that this is exactly the sort of maneuver I would expect from her." She raised a hand as Saint-Just's eyes narrowed and continued before he could speak. "And, no, I'm not saying that *I* would have anticipated something like this before the fact. I wouldn't have, and I have no doubt she would have taken me completely by surprise, as well. I'm simply saying that, looking back after the fact, I'm not in the least surprised that she managed to anticipate Camp Charon's logical response to an 'escaping' shuttle and found a way to use it brilliantly to her advantage. It's exactly the sort of thing she'd been doing to us for the last ten or twelve years now."

"Which is why she *is* a boogeyman." Pierre sighed. "Or why altogether too many of our people regard her as one. Not to mention the reason the Manties and their allies are so ecstatic about having her back." He showed his teeth in an almost-smile. "Bottom line, it doesn't really matter whether or not she's some sort of warrior demigoddess if that's what her people *think* she is."

"I wouldn't go quite that far, Sir," McQueen said judiciously. "What she actually manages to do to us is nothing to sneeze at. Still, you're essentially correct. She's much more dangerous to us, right this moment, as a symbol than as a naval officer."

"Especially given how badly shot up she seems to be," Turner agreed with a nod.

"I wouldn't count too heavily on her injuries to keep her out of action," McQueen cautioned. "None of them appear to have affected her command abilities. Or not," she added dryly, "to judge by the rather neat little operation she apparently just pulled off, at any rate. And it's entirely possible, if the situation turns nasty enough for them, for the Manties to send her back out, arm or no arm."

"On the other hand, that would appear, at the moment, to be one of the brighter spots of the situation," Pierre pointed out. "For right now, at least, your people are still pushing the Manties back, Esther. Are you in a position to keep on doing that?"

"Unless something changes without warning, yes," McQueen said. "But I caution you again, Sir, that my confidence is based on the situation as it now exists and that the situation in question is definitely open to change. In particular, we know from the Operation Icarus after-battle reports that the Manties hit us with something new in both Basilisk and Hancock, and we're still not certain exactly what it was in either case."

"I still believe you're reading too much into those reports." Saint-Just's tone was just a tiny bit too reasonable, and McQueen allowed her green eyes to harden as they met his. "We know they used LACs at Hancock," the StateSec CO went on, "but we've known ever since our commerce raiding operations went sour in Silesia that they had an improved light attack craft design. My understanding is that the analysts have concluded the Hancock LACs were simply more of the same."

"The *civilian* analysts have concluded that," McQueen replied so frostily several people winced.

McQueen and Saint-Just had clashed over this before, and their differences, however cloaked in outward propriety, had become ever more pointed over the last few months. McQueen wanted to resurrect the old Naval Intelligence Bureau as a Navy-run shop, staffed by Navy officers. Her official reason was that the military needed an in-house intelligence capability run by people who understood operational realities. Saint-Just was equally determined to retain the present arrangement, in which NavInt was merely one more section of State Security's sprawling intelligence apparatus. *His* official reason was that centralized control insured that all relevant information was available from a single set of data banks and eliminated redundancy and the inefficiency of turf wars. In fact, his real reason was that he suspected that *her* real reason was a desire to cut his own people out of the loop in order to give herself (and any personal adherents in the upper echelons of the Navy's command structure) a secure channel through which to intrigue against the Committee.

"I could wish for more complete and detailed data from Hancock," she went on after the briefest of pauses and in slightly less chill tones. "Only one of Citizen Admiral Kellet's cruisers got out, and every one of her surviving battleships took severe damage. And, of course, only six of *them* came home again."

She paused once more to let the numbers sink in, and her eyes surveyed her fellow Committee members cooly. *I don't think I'll mention Citizen Admiral Porter again just now,* she decided. *I've made the point plainly enough to both Pierre and Saint-Just in the past, and it would be . . . untactful to make it again in front of the others. But, Christ! If the idiot hadn't panicked when he realized he was in command, if he'd only stayed concentrated for another thirty minutes, we'd've gotten a hell of a lot more battlewagons home. Kellet and Hall had them clear of the Manty SDs, and it's obvious the LACs were about to break off the action, but then the fucking idiot went and ordered his units to* scatter *and "proceed independently" to the hyper limit! He might as well have dropped fresh meat into the water for a bunch of Old Earth piranha! I know it, the rest of the Octagon staff knows it, and Saint-Just and Pierre know it, but the bastard's political credentials were so good Pierre let Saint-Just turn the entire board of inquiry into one gigantic whitewash. So there's still no open channel I can use to let the rest of the officer corps know what really happened, and that's making all of them even more nervous than they ought to be over whatever "secret weapons" the Manties are coming up with* this *time around. Thank God Diamato got back alive . . . but it took over two months for the medics to put him back together well enough for us to get anything coherent even out of* him.

"Because so few units got out, and because those who did had suffered so much damage to their sensor systems," *and because you won't* let *me,* "I've still been unable to reconstruct the events at Hancock with any higher degree of certainty and confidence than the official board managed immediately after the operation," she went on. "I've got a lot of theories and hypotheses, but very little hard data."

"I'm aware of that, Esther," Saint-Just said with ominous affability. "There doesn't seem to be much question but that Kellet allowed herself to be ambushed by LACs, however, does there?"

"It could certainly be described that way," McQueen agreed, showing her teeth in what not even the most charitable would have called a smile.

"Then my point stands." Saint-Just shrugged. "We've known for years that they have better LACs than we do, but they're still just LACs, when all's said and done. If it hadn't been for the circumstances under which they were allowed into range, they surely wouldn't have been any real threat."

"They weren't *allowed* into range, Citizen Secretary," McQueen said very precisely. "They utilized stealth systems far in advance of anything we have—*and* far more capable than any LAC should mount as onboard systems—to intercept before anyone could have detected them. And once in range, they used energy weapons of unprecedented power. Powerful enough to burn through a battleship's sidewall."

"Certainly they used their stealth systems effectively," Saint-Just conceded, his almost-smile as cold as her own had been. "But, as I already said, we've known for years that they were upgrading their LACs. And as you yourself just pointed out, our sensor data is scarcely what anyone could call reliable. My own analysts—civilians, to be sure, but most of them were consultants with the Office of Construction before the Harris Assassination—are uniformly of the opinion that the throughput figures some people are quoting for the grasers mounted by those LACs are almost certainly based on bad data." McQueen's face tightened, but he waved a hand in a tension-defusing gesture. "No one's arguing that the weapons weren't 'of unprecedented power,' because they clearly were. But you're talking about battleship sidewalls, attacked at absolutely minimal range, not ships of the wall, or even battleships or battlecruisers attacked at realistic ranges. The point my analysts are making is that no one could fit a graser of the power some people seem afraid of into something the size of a LAC. It's simply not technically feasible to build that sort of weapon, plus propulsive machinery, a fusion plant, and the sort of missile power they also displayed, into a hull under fifty thousand tons."

"It wouldn't be possible for *us*," McQueen agreed. "The Manties, however, have rather persistently done things we've been unable to duplicate. Even our pods are less sophisticated than theirs. We make up the differential by using larger pods, more missiles, and *bigger* missiles, because we can't match the degree of miniaturization they can. I see no reason to assume that the same doesn't hold true for their LACs."

"I see no reason to assume that it automatically *does* hold true, either," Saint-Just returned in the voice of one striving hard to be reasonable. "And the LACs they've been operating—still *are* operating, for that matter—in Silesia show no indication of the sort of massive, qualitative leap forward my analysts assure me would be necessary to build LACs as formidable as some people believe we're facing. Granted, it's the job of the Navy to err on the side of pessimism, and it's better, usually, to overestimate an enemy than to *under*estimate him. But at this level, we have a responsibility to question their conclusions and to remind ourselves they're only advisors. *We're* the ones who have to make the actual decisions, and we can't allow ourselves to be stampeded into timidity. As you pointed out yourself, quite rightly, when you proposed Icarus in the first place, we have to run some risks if we're to have any hope at all of winning this war."

"I haven't said we don't, and I haven't proposed sitting in place out of fear," McQueen said flatly. "What I *have* said is that the situation is unclear. And the LACs aren't the only thing we have to worry about. Citizen Commander Diamato was quite adamant about the range of the shipboard missiles used against Citizen Admiral Kellet's task force, and nothing we have in inventory can do what *they* did, either. And that doesn't even consider what happened to Citizen Admiral Darlington in Basilisk. Unless the Manties were in position to bring their entire Home Fleet through, or unless our intelligence on the terminus forts was completely wrong, *something* very unusual was used against him, and all any of the survivors can tell us is that there were one hell of a lot of missiles flying around."

"Of course there were. Both of us have pods, Esther, as you yourself just pointed out. Our intelligence on the numbers of forts was accurate, we simply underestimated the numbers of pods which had already been delivered to them. Besides, I just received a report from one of our sources in the Star Kingdom which suggests that the answer was probably White Haven and Eighth Fleet."

"We have?" McQueen cocked her head, and her eyes flashed. "And why haven't *I* heard anything about this report over at the Octagon?"

"Because I just received it this morning. It came in through a purely civilian network, and I directed that it be forwarded to you immediately. I assume you'll find it in your message queue when you get back to your office." Saint-Just sounded completely reasonable, but no one in the room, least of all Esther McQueen, doubted for a moment that he'd saved this little tidbit until he could deliver it in person . . . and in front of Rob Pierre. "According to our source, who's a civilian employed in their Astographic Service, White Haven brought all or most of his fleet through from Trevor's Star in a very tight transit. I'm not conversant with all the technical terms, but I'm sure the report will make a great deal of sense to you and your analysts when you've had a chance to study it. The important point, however, is that what happened to Darlington was simply that he walked into several dozen super-dreadnoughts who weren't supposed to be there *and* into the fire of a store of missile pods we thought hadn't been delivered."

He shrugged, and McQueen bit her tongue hard. She knew Pierre well enough by now to realize he understood exactly what Saint-Just had just done, and why . . . and that it had worked anyway. For herself, she had no doubt the report said exactly what he'd said it did. And it made sense, too. Indeed, she'd considered the possibility, but the Manties had played things awfully tight about exactly how they'd pulled off that little trick. Unfortunately, the rabbit he'd just produced about *one* thing the Manties had done lent added authority to his voice when he argued about *other* things the Manties had done. As he proceeded to demonstrate.

"I think my analysts are probably on the right general track about Hancock, too," he went on, as if his analysts had already suggested that Eighth Fleet had successfully rushed to the defense of Basilisk, as well. "The LACs in Hancock just happened to be there. No doubt they do represent an upgrade on what we've already seen in Silesia, and Hancock would be a reasonable place for them to work up and evaluate a new design. The logical answer is that they were already engaged in maneuvers of some sort when we turned up and they were able, by good luck for them and bad luck for us, to generate an intercept. Unless we want to stipulate that the Manties' R&D types are magicians in league with the devil, though, the worst-case evaluation of their capabilities is much too pessimistic. Probably there were more of them than any of Kellet's survivors believed and they made up the apparent jump in individual firepower with numbers. As for the missiles Diamato talked about, he's the only tac officer who seems even to have seen them, and none of his tactical data survived *Schaumberg's* destruction. We have no way to be sure his initial estimates of their performance weren't completely erroneous. It's far more likely there were additional ships back there, ships he never saw because of their stealth systems, and that the apparent performance of the missiles was so extraordinary because what he thought was terminal performance was actually a much earlier point in their launch envelope." He shrugged. "In either case, no one *else* has seen any signs of super LACs or missiles since, and until we do see some supporting evidence . . ."

He let his voice trail off and shrugged again, and McQueen drew a deep breath.

"That all sounds very reasonable, Oscar," she said in a very even tone. "But the fact that they haven't used whatever they used then since might also suggest—to me, at least—the possibility that they've decided to hold off on using their new toys until they have enough of them, in their estimation, to make a real difference."

"Or until they're pushed so far back they have no choice but to use them," Saint-Just suggested a bit pointedly. "I agree with your basic analysis, Citizen Secretary, but it's been over a year since you launched Icarus, and you've hit them hard a half dozen times since then without seeing any sign of new hardware. Let's say for the sake of argument that they do have a new LAC and a new missile and that the performance of each falls somewhere between what your analysts think we actually saw and what my analysts believe is theoretically possible. In that case, where are those new weapons? Isn't it possible the Manties haven't used more of them because they don't *have* any more? That we ran into prototypes of a design they still haven't been able to debug sufficiently to put into series production? That being the case, they may still be months from any actual deployment. And the need to defeat them before they do get it into full production lends still more point to the importance of continuing to hit them as hard, frequently, and quickly as possible."

"That's certainly possible," McQueen agreed. "On the other hand, it *has* been over a year. My own thought is that even if they were prototypes, a year is more than long enough for the Manties to have put them into at least limited production. And we *have* been pushing the pace since Icarus. They know that at least as well as we do, and I would have expected to see them using their new weapons, even if they only had a relatively low number of them, in an effort to knock us back on our heels . . . *unless* they're deliberately holding off while they build up the numbers to hit us hard at a moment of their own choosing. They've lost nine star systems, but none were really vital, after all. While I hate to admit it, we're still at the stage of hitting them where we *can* hit them, not necessarily of attacking the targets I *wish* we could hit.

She paused for a moment, gazing levelly at Saint-Just, but it was Pierre she watched from the corner of her eye. The Citizen Chairman frowned, but he also nodded almost imperceptibly. McQueen doubted he even realized he had, but the tiny response was encouraging evidence that he, at least, was reading her reports and drawing the proper conclusions from them. More to the point, perhaps, it was an indication that even if Saint-Just had just scored points in his ongoing fight over the control of NavInt and his suspicion that she was deliberately slowing the operational pace to make herself appear even more irreplaceable, the Chairman still recognized what was going on.

"I feel sure the Manties' senior planners realize that as well as we do, Oscar," she went on. "It would take some gutsy decisions by their strategists to hold back at this point even if they do, of course, but if I were in their shoes and thought I could pick my moment, I'd certainly do it. *And* I'd do my best to keep my opponent from getting an early peek at my new systems until I was ready to use them, too. There's never been a weapon that couldn't be countered *somehow*, and I wouldn't want to give the other side a good enough look at my new weapons to begin figuring out a doctrine to offset them."

"You've both raised excellent points," Pierre said, intervening before Saint-Just could reply. He knew the StateSec commander was increasingly unhappy about the degree to which the Navy, and even a few of StateSec's shipboard commissioners, were beginning to venerate McQueen. Saint-Just was too disciplined and loyal to move against her without Pierre's authorization, but he was also more attuned by nature to the implications of internal threats than to those of external ones. In many ways, Pierre shared Saint-Just's evaluation of the domestic threat McQueen represented, but he was afraid the SS commander's legitimate concerns in those areas caused him to underestimate or even dismiss the severity of the danger still posed by the Manticoran Alliance's military forces. Quiescent and apparently defensive minded though they'd been since Icarus, Pierre was far from convinced that they were down for the count.

"For the moment, however," he continued, deliberately pulling the discussion back from the confrontation between his internal watchdog and his military commander, "our immediate emphasis ought to be on how we respond to the consequences of Harrington's escape. Our military operations have already been planned and set in motion, and there's not much we can do about them right this minute, but Huertes is still going to want a response from us, and we can't afford to let the Manties' version of what happened totally dominate the coverage in the Solarian League."

"I'm afraid I don't see how we can prevent that, Citizen Chairman," Leonard Boardman said. His voice was a bit hesitant, but firmer than McQueen would have expected, and he didn't cringe too badly under the daggered look Pierre shot him.

"Explain," the Citizen Chairman said flatly.

"Huertes came to us once the story got *back* to her, Sir," Boardman pointed out. "It didn't originate in the Republic; it originated with the Manties' announcements in Yeltsin and Manticore. There's no possible way it could've gotten back to us here until well after they'd already dumped it through Beowulf to the rest of the Solarian League."

He paused, and Pierre nodded, grudgingly and almost against his will. The Star Kingdom of Manticore's control of the Manticore Worm Hole Junction gave it an enormous advantage in terms of turnaround time on any message to the Solarian League, and on something like this, the Manties would have exploited it to the maximum.

"That means anything we do in the League will be playing catch-up," Boardman went on a bit more confidently. "Here in the Republic, we'll have the opportunity to put our spin on it—" *and just how,* Esther McQueen wondered, *can anyone possibly put a good "spin" on something like this, Citizen Secretary?* "—but in the League, we'll be trying to overcome the *Manties'* spin. And, quite frankly, Sir, I'm afraid Huertes already knows at least something we don't."

"Such as?" Saint-Just demanded, and McQueen hid a grimace. There didn't seem to be a great deal of sense in demanding an opinion about something when Boardman had just said they didn't know what that something was.

"I have no idea—yet," Boardman replied. "But from the tone of her questions, she knows more than she told us about. It's as if she's trying to get us to commit ourselves so she can catch us out."

"I don't much care for the sound of that," Wanda Farley, the Secretary of Technology grunted. The heavy-set woman had been silent throughout, and especially during the debate on the technical feasibility of the new Manticoran LACs, but now she frowned like a dyspeptic buffalo. "Just who the hell does she think she is, playing some kind of game with us?"

Who she thinks she is, McQueen very carefully did not say aloud, *is a real newsie trying to report the biggest human interest story of the entire war. I'm not surprised you're confused, after the way INS and the other services have let PubIn play them like violins for decades, but you idiots had better wake up pretty damned fast. They've caught us red-handed,* with *proof we fed them a special-effects chip and lied at the very highest level about Harrington's execution. Worse, they're not all cretins. Some of them see themselves as* real *reporters, with some sort of moral obligation to tell their viewers the truth. And even the ones who don't know that the folks back home know they let themselves be suckered. So they're pissed off at us for using them, and at the same time, they have to do* something *to win back their audience's confidence. So for the first time in fifty or sixty T-years, we're going to find ourselves with genuine investigative reporters climbing all over us right here at home, unless we decide to evict them all the way we did United Faxes Intergalactic. Which we can't do just this minute without convincing every Solly we've got things to hide. Which, of course, we do.*

Unfortunately, getting someone like Farley to understand how things worked in a society without officially sanctioned censorship was a hopeless cause.

"That doesn't really matter, Wanda." Pierre sighed. "What matters are the consequences."

"I think our best bet is to be as cautious as we can without completely clamming up, Sir," Boardman said. "There's no point in our denying, to the Sollies, at least, that *something* happened at Cerberus and that at least some prisoners apparently managed to escape. At the same time, we can say, honestly, that we haven't yet heard back from the forces we'd already dispatched to Cerberus in response to concerns previously raised by StateSec personnel. That will indicate that we were as well informed as possible, given the communications lag, before Huertes came to us. And it will also buy us a little more time. We'll obviously have to ascertain the facts for ourselves before we can offer any comment, and we can respectfully decline to engage in useless speculation until we *have* ascertained the facts."

"And then?" Saint-Just prodded.

"Sir, it will depend on what the facts are, how bad they are, and how we want to approach them," Boardman said frankly. "If nothing else, however, I feel confident Huertes will have dropped the other shoe by then. Or, for that matter, we'll have direct reports from our own sources in Manticore. We can at least buy enough time for that to happen, and for us to decide on the best angle from which to spin the story."

"And domestically?" Pierre asked.

"Domestically, we can put whatever spin we like on it, Sir, at least in the short term. Whatever they may want to do for their home audiences, I doubt very much that any of the services is going to risk being tossed out of the Republic just to dispute Public Information's reportage locally. And if they try, we've got the mechanisms in place to stop them cold. In the short term. In the *long* term, at least a garbled version of the Manties' version is bound to leak out here at home, but that will take months at the very least. By the time it does get out, it will have lost a lot of its immediacy. I don't expect the greatest impact to be here at home, unless we really drop the ball. It's the consequences in the League that I worry about."

"And me," McQueen said quietly. "It's largely the Solly tech transfers which have let us get within shouting distance of the Manties' naval hardware. If this story is going to jeopardize that technology pipeline, we could have a very serious problem."

"Unless we finish the Manties off before it *becomes* 'serious,'" Saint-Just observed with a wintery smile.

"With all due respect, that isn't going to happen anytime soon," McQueen replied firmly. "Oh, it's always possible we'll get lucky or their morale will suddenly crack, but they've redeployed to cover their core areas in too much depth. We're punching away mainly at systems *they* took away from *us*, Oscar. If they let us hang onto the initiative, we'll wear them down eventually. That's the great weakness of a purely defensive strategy; it lets your opponent choose her time and place and achieve the sort of concentrations that grind you away. But we're still a long way from reaching any of the Alliance's vitals—except, of course, for what happened in Basilisk. Raids on places like Zanzibar and Alizon may have profound morale effects, but they don't really hurt the Manties' physical war-fighting capability very much, and now that they realize we're on the offensive, the systems where we really *could* hurt them, like Manticore, Grayson, Erewhon, and Grendlesbane, are far too heavily protected for us to break into without taking prohibitive losses."

Saint-Just looked stubborn, and Pierre hid a sigh. Then he rubbed his nose again and squared his shoulders.

"All right, Leonard. I don't like it, but I think you're right. Draft a statement for me on the basis you've suggested, then com Huertes and offer her an exclusive interview with me. I'll want to be briefed very carefully, and you'll inform her that certain areas will be off-limits for reasons of military security, but I want to come across as open and forthcoming. Maybe I can coax her into letting that other shoe fall . . . or bait her into trying to mousetrap me with it, at any rate. But what I really want is to remind her and her colleagues how valuable access to my office is. Maybe then they'll think two or three times before they do something that might piss us off enough to *deny* them that access.

"In the meantime, Esther—" he turned to McQueen "—I want you to expedite operations. In particular, I want you to put Operation Scylla on-line as soon as possible. If we're going to take a black eye over Cerberus, then it's going to be up to you to win us some countervailing talking points by kicking some more Manticoran butt in the field."

"Sir, as I told you yesterday, we—"

"I know you're not ready yet," Pierre said just a bit impatiently. "I'm not asking for miracles, Esther. I said 'expedite,' not charge off half-cocked. But you've demonstrated you can beat the Manties, and we need it done again as soon as you possibly can."

He held her eyes, and his message was clear. He was willing to back her military judgment against Saint-Just's—mostly, at least, and for the moment—but he needed a miracle, and the sooner the better. And if he didn't get one, he might just rethink his faith in her . . . and his decision to restrain Saint-Just from purging her.

"Understood, Citizen Chairman," she said, her tone resolute but not cocky. "If you want some Manticoran butt kicked, then we'll just have to kick it for you, won't we?"

CHAPTER FIVE

"**S**o how does it feel to be alive again?"

The question came out in a husky, almost furry-sounding contralto, and Honor's mouth quirked as she looked across from her place in the improbably comfortable, old-fashioned, unpowered armchair that seemed hopelessly out of place aboard a modern warship. HMS *Edward Saganami*'s captain smirked insufferably back at her, white teeth flashing in a face barely a shade lighter than her space-black tunic, and Honor shook her head with a wryness that was no more than half amused.

"Actually, it's a monumental pain in an awful lot of ways," she told her oldest friend, and Captain the Honorable Michelle Henke laughed. "Go ahead, laugh!" Honor told her. "*You* haven't had to deal with people who name superdreadnoughts after you—and refuse to change the name when it turns out you weren't quite dead yet after all!" She shuddered. "And that's not the worst of it, you know."

"Oh?" Henke cocked her head. "I knew they'd named the *Harrington* after you, but I hadn't heard anything about their refusing to change the name."

"Well, they have," Honor said grumpily, and rose to stalk around the spacious quarters the RMN's designers had provided for the brand-new heavy cruiser's lady and mistress after God. All of *Saganami*'s personnel spaces were bigger on a per-crewman basis than those of older ships, but Henke's day cabin was as big as the captain's cabins of some battlecruisers. Which at least gave her plenty of room in which to pace.

She set Nimitz on the back of the chair, and Samantha flowed up from where she'd perched on its arm to wrap her tail about him once more. Honor watched the two 'cats for a moment, grateful that the harsh, metallic-tasting bitterness of Nimitz's fear and sense of loss had retreated into something all three of them could handle, then looked back at Henke and began to pace with proper vigor.

"I argued myself blue in the face, you know, but Benjamin says he can't overrule the military, the Office of Shipbuilding says it would confuse their records, Reverend Sullivan insists that the Chaplain's Corps blessed the ship under her original name and that it would offend the religious sensibilities of the Navy to change it now, and Matthews says it would offend the crews' belief that renaming a ship is bad luck. Every one of them is in on it, and they keep playing musical offices. Whenever I try to pin one of them down, he simply refers me—with *exquisite* courtesy, you understand—to one of the others. And I *know* they're all laughing in their beers over it!"

Henke's grin seemed to split her face, and her throaty chuckle rippled with delight. She was one of the people who'd figured out the truth about Honor's link to Nimitz long ago, which lent a certain added entertainment to Honor's certainty about how much the highest Grayson leaders were enjoying themselves.

"Well, at least the Admiralty agreed to back off from calling them the *Harrington*-class," she pointed out after a moment, and Honor nodded.

"That's because the Star Kingdom has a slightly less low so-called sense of humor," she growled. "And," she added, "Caparelli and Cortez know I'd've resigned my commission if they hadn't gone back to designating them the *Medusa*-class. I only wish I thought I could get away with making the same threat stick against Matthews."

She glowered, and Nimitz and Samantha bleeked in shared amusement as they tasted her emotions. She raised her head to shake a fist at them, but the living corner of her mouth twitched again, this time with true humor at the absurdity of her situation.

"I think it's a sign of how much they care about you that a reactionary old batch of sticks is willing to give you such a hard time, actually," Henke observed. Honor shot her a sharp glance, and the other woman shook her head. "Oh, I know Benjamin is the cutting edge of what passes for liberalism on Grayson, Honor, and I respect him enormously, but let's face it. By Manticoran standards, the most liberal soul on the entire planet is a hopeless reactionary! And with all due respect, I don't think I could legitimately call either Reverend Sullivan or High Admiral Matthews liberals, even for Grayson. Mind you, I like them a bunch, and I admire them, and I don't feel particularly uncomfortable around them. In fact, I'll even admit they're both doing their level best to support Benjamin's reforms, but they grew up on pre-Alliance Grayson. Matthews has done an excellent job of adjusting to the notion of allowing foreign women into Grayson service, and an even better one of treating them with equality once they're there. But deep down inside, he and Sullivan—and even Benjamin, I suspect—are never really going to get over the notion that women need to be coddled and protected, and you know it. So if *they're* willing to give you a hard time, they must really, *really* like you a lot."

She shrugged, and Honor blinked at her.

"Do you even begin to realize how ridiculous that sounds? They respect women, and want to protect them, so the fact that they're all willing to drive me totally insane means they *like* me?"

"Of course it does," Henke replied comfortably, "and you know it as well as I do."

Honor gave her a very direct look, and she gazed back with an expression the perfect picture of innocence until Honor finally grinned in ironic acknowledgment.

"I suppose I do," she admitted, but then her smile faded just a bit. "But that doesn't reduce the embarrassment quotient one bit. You *know* some Manticorans are going to think I signed off on keeping the name. And even if they weren't going to, *I* think it's about as pretentious as anything could possibly get. Oh—" she waved her hand as if brushing away gnats "—I suppose it made sense, in an embarrassing sort of way, to name a ship after a naval officer who was safely dead, but I'm *not* dead, darn it!"

"Thank God," Henke said quietly, and all the laughter had gone out of her face. Honor turned quickly to face her as she felt the sudden darkness of her emotions, but then Henke shook herself and leaned back in her chair.

"By the way," she said in a conversational tone, "there's something I've been meaning to say to you. Have you seen the HD of your funeral on Manticore?"

"I've skimmed it," Honor said uncomfortably. "I can't stand to watch too much of that kind of thing, though. It's like seeing a really bad historical holodrama. You know, one of the 'cast of thousands' things. And that doesn't even consider the crypt at King Michael's! I mean, I realize it was a *state* funeral, that the Alliance thought the Peeps had murdered me and that that had turned me into some sort of symbol, but still—"

She shook her head, and Henke snorted.

"There was some of that kind of calculation involved, I suppose," she allowed, "if not nearly as much as *you* probably think. But what I had in mind was my own humble participation in your cortege. You knew about that?"

"Yes," Honor said softly, remembering the images of an iron-faced Michelle Henke, following the anachronistic caisson down King Roger I Boulevard at a slow march through the measured tap-tap-tap of a single drum with the naked blade of the Harrington Sword upright in her gloved hands and unshed tears shining in her eyes. "Yes, I knew about it," she said.

"Well I just wanted to say this, Honor," Henke said quietly. "And I'll only say it once. *But don't you* ever *do that to me again*! Do you read me on that, Lady Harrington? I *never* want to go to your funeral again!"

"I'll try to make a note of it," Honor said, striving almost successfully for levity. Henke held her gaze for a long, still moment, then nodded.

"I suppose that will have to do, then," she said much more briskly, and leaned back in her own armchair. "But you were saying your friends back on Grayson have done something else to offend your fine, humble sensibilities?"

"Darn right they have!" Honor took another turn about Henke's day cabin, the hem of her Grayson-style gown swirling about her ankles with the energy of her stride.

"Stop stomping around my quarters, sit down, and tell me what it is, then," Henke commanded, pointing to the chair Honor had previously occupied.

"Yes, Ma'am," Honor said meekly. She sat very precisely in the chair, chin high, feet planted close together, hand resting primly in her lap, leaned forward ever so slightly, and looked at her friend soulfully. "Is this better, Ma'am?" she asked earnestly.

"Only if you want to be thumped," Henke growled. "And in your present condition, I might even be able to take you."

"Ha!" Honor snorted with lordly disdain, then leaned back and crossed her legs.

"Better. Now tell!"

"Oh, all right," Honor sighed. "It's the statue."

"The statue?" Henke repeated blankly.

"Yes, the statue. Or maybe I should call it 'The Statue'—you know, capital letters. Maybe with a little italics and an exclamation point or two."

"You do realize I don't have even a clue what you're babbling about, don't you?"

"Oh? Then I take it you haven't been down to Austin City since my recent untimely demise was reported?"

"Except to ride the pinnace down to pick you up from the Palace, no," Henke replied in a mystified tone.

"Ah, then you haven't been to Steadholders' Hall! That explains it."

"Explains *what*, damn it?!"

"Explains how you could have missed the modest little four-meter bronze statue of me, standing on top of an *eight*-meter—polished!—obsidian column, in the square at the very foot of the main stairs to the North Portico so that every single soul who ever walks through any of the Hall's public entrances will *have* to walk right past it at eye level."

Even the ebullient Henke stared at her, stunned into silence, and Honor returned her goggle-eyed gaze calmly. Not that she'd felt the least bit calm when she first saw the thing. It had been another of Benjamin's little "surprises," although she believed him when he insisted the idea had been the Conclave of Steadholders', not his. He was simply the one who hadn't bothered to mention its existence to her before she found herself face-to-face—well, face-to-column, anyway—with the looming monstrosity.

No, she made herself admit judiciously, calling it a "monstrosity" wasn't really fair. Her own taste had never run to heroic-scale bronzes, but she had to agree, in the intervals when she could stop gnashing her teeth, that the sculptor had actually done an excellent job. The moment he'd chosen to immortalize was the one in which she'd stood on the Conclave Chamber's floor, leaning on the Sword of State while she awaited the return of the servant Steadholder Burdette had sent to fetch the Burdette Sword, and it was obvious he'd studied the file footage of that horrible day with care. He had every detail right, even to the cut on her forehead, except for two things. One was Nimitz, who'd been sitting on her desk in the Chamber while she waited but had somehow been translocated from there to the statue's shoulder. That much, at least, she was willing to grant as legitimate artistic license, for if Nimitz hadn't been on her shoulder, he'd still been with her, and far more intimately than the sculptor could ever have guessed. But the other inaccuracy, the nobility and calm, focused tranquility he'd pasted onto her alloy face . . . *That* she had a problem with, for her own memories of that day, waiting for the duel to the death with the treasonous Burdette, were only too clear in her own mind.

She realized Henke was still staring at her in stupefaction and cocked her head with a quizzical expression. Several more seconds passed, and then Henke shook herself.

"Four *meters* tall?" she demanded in hushed tones.

"On top of an eight-meter column," Honor agreed. "It's really very imposing, I suppose . . . and when I saw it, I was ready to cut my own throat. At least then I really would be decently dead!"

"My God!" Henke shook her head, then chuckled wickedly. "I always thought of you as tall myself, but twelve meters may be just a bit much even for you, Honor!"

"Oh, *very* funny, Mike," Honor replied with awful dignity. "Very funny indeed. How would *you* like to walk past that . . . that *thing* every single time you attended the Keys?"

"Wouldn't bother me a bit," Henke said. "After all, it's not a statue of *me*. Now, you on the other hand . . . I suppose *you* might find it just a little, ah, overwhelming."

"To say the least," Honor muttered, and Henke chuckled again. There was a bit more sympathy in it this time, but her eyes still danced with wicked amusement as she pictured Honor's face when she'd first seen Benjamin IX's "surprise."

"And they won't take it down?"

"They won't," Honor confirmed grimly. "I told them I'd refuse to use the main entrance ever again if they left it there, and they said they were very sorry to hear it and pointed out that there's always been a private entrance for steadholders. I threatened to refuse to accept my Key back from Faith, and they told me I wasn't permitted to do that under Grayson law. I even threatened to have my armsmen sneak up on it some dark night and blow it to smithereens . . . and they told me it was fully insured and that the sculptor would be more than happy to recast it in case any accident befell it!"

"Oh, dear." Henke seemed to be experiencing some difficulty keeping her voice level, and Honor reminded herself, firmly, that she had too few friends to go around killing every one of them who found her predicament hilarious. Especially, she acknowledged, since that seemed to include every single one of them.

"My, my, my," Henke murmured finally. "Coming back from the dead does seem to be a little complicated, doesn't it?" She shook her head. "And what was that business about your having violated the Grayson Constitution?"

"Oh, *Lord!*" Honor moaned. "Don't even *mention* that to me!"

"What?" Henke blinked. "I thought someone told me it had all been settled?"

"Oh, certainly it was 'settled,'" Honor groused. "Benjamin decided the best way to deal with it was to take the 'Elysian Navy' into Grayson service and give it a place in the chain of command. So he did."

"And this is a problem?" Henke asked quizzically.

"Oh, no!" Honor replied with awful irony. "All he did was create a special 'Protector's Own Squadron' of the Grayson Space Navy, buy in all the captured ships for service as its core elements, and make me its official CO."

"Did you say 'core elements'?" Henke repeated, and Honor nodded. "And precisely what, if I'm not going to regret asking, does that mean?"

"It means Benjamin has decided to offer slots in the GSN to any of the Cerberus escapees who want to take them, and he's established a special unit organization for them. He's calling it a 'squadron,' but if he gets a fraction of the number of volunteers I think he's going to get, it's going to be more like a task force . . . or a bloody fleet in its own right! Anyway, he's planning to swear them all on as his personal vassals, then make me, as his Champion, the permanent CO. He's starting out with the ships we brought back with us, but he'll be adding to them, and he and Matthews are already making gleeful noises about pod superdreadnoughts and proper screening elements."

"My God," Henke murmured. Then she cocked her head. "Does he have the authority to do something like that? I mean, I'd hate to think how Parliament would react back home if Beth even *thought* about establishing a force like that!"

"Oh, yes," Honor sighed. "The Grayson Constitution gives the Protector the right to do it. He's the only person on Grayson who does have the right to organize full-scale military units out of his personal vassals. It was one of the little points Benjamin the Great wrote into the Constitution to emphasize the Sword's primacy. Of course, he'll place it under the authority of Wesley Matthews, as Chief of Naval Operations, which should soothe any ruffled feathers, but people on Grayson take their personal oaths even more seriously than most Manticorans. If push ever came to shove between the Protector and the regular Navy—God forbid!—it would almost certainly come down on Benjamin's side. And the fact that virtually all the personnel for it, initially, at least, will be foreign-born and that 'That Foreign Woman' will be its CO, at least on paper, has the conservatives in the Keys unable to decide whether to drop dead of apoplexy or scream bloody murder. Except, of course, that they can't possibly afford to raise a stink over it at the moment because of all the whooping and hollering going on over my return. Which is exactly what that stinker Benjamin is counting on."

"Counting on?" Henke wrinkled her nose, and Honor laughed briefly.

"Service in the Grayson Space Navy automatically confers Grayson citizenship after a six-year hitch, Mike. Benjamin rammed that little proviso through right after they joined the Alliance. He was one of the first people on the planet to recognize that the GSN was going to have to recruit from abroad to man its units, and he was determined to give anyone who signed on a stake in the planet they'd be fighting to defend. Of course, once everyone else figured out the same thing, there was a lot of resistance to the notion of offering citizenship to job lots of infidels. But Reverend Hanks signed on in strong support, and it came soon enough after the Maccabean coup attempt and 'the Mayhew Restoration' that no one in the Keys could put together an effective opposition. It doesn't apply to Allied personnel serving on loan from their own navies, even if they hold rank in the GSN, but these won't be Allied personnel. Which means every person he enlists for his 'Protector's Own' will eventually become a Grayson citizen, assuming she survives, and there are almost half a million escapees . . . most of whom have no planet to go home to. I'd be surprised if at least a third of them didn't jump at his offer, and that means he'll be adding something like a hundred and sixty thousand 'infidels' to his population in a single pop."

Including Warner Caslet, she thought. *I'm not sure he'll accept, but I know Benjamin is going to make the offer to him. And I think I'd certainly accept it in his place. No matter what I or anyone else from Hell says, there'd be a lot of resistance to giving him a commission in the RMN, but the GSN's already recruited at least one ex-Peep . . . and made out very well on the deal!*

She smiled in memory of her first "Grayson" flag captain, but then her grin faded just a bit. Caslet was also a passenger aboard *Saganami*. The cruiser's crew had taken its cue from its captain and treated him as an honored guest, despite his insistence on so far retaining his People's Navy uniform, but she knew he wasn't looking forward to his arrival in the Star Kingdom. Nor would she have looked forward to it in his place. No doubt everyone would be exquisitely polite and correct, especially in light of what she and Alistair McKeon had had to say about his actions aboard *Tepes* and on Hell, but ONI must be rubbing its hands together and cackling with glee at the thought of his upcoming debrief. He *had* been Thomas Theisman's ops officer in Barnett, after all. And even though he'd been out of circulation on Hell for the better part of two T-years, he still represented a priceless intelligence windfall. They were going to wring every detail they could out of him, and while the commander had made peace with his decision to defect to the Alliance, Honor knew his stubborn sense of integrity was going to make the process both painful and difficult. His commitment to the defeat of the Committee of Public Safety was absolute, but his entire world had been the People's Navy for too many years to make "betraying" the people still in it anything but an agonizing ordeal.

And even when it's over, no one is really going to trust *him in Manticoran uniform,* she thought sadly. *They can't—not when they can't taste his commitment the way Nimitz and I can. But the Graysons can trust him. Or give him an honest chance to prove they can, at least. The Church of Humanity Unchained has always embraced the concept of redemption through Grace and good works . . . and been pretty darned insistent on the penitent's responsibility to "meet his Test." So unlike us cynical Manticorans, we Graysons are preprogramed to give people like Warner the chance to work their passages.*

Nimitz bleeked in amusement at the split-personality aspects of her last thought, but both of them had grown accustomed to such moments, and she only shook her head at him.

"But even if every one of them volunteers, that still doesn't sound like all that huge a number," Henke argued, pulling her attention back to the discussion at hand. "After all, Grayson already has a population of around three billion. So a hundred and sixty thousand would only be—what? A five-thousandth of a percent increase or so?"

"Sure they would, but they're only a part—the biggest lump so far, maybe, but only a part—of the total he's hoping this will add to the Grayson population. And they all have prolong, they'll all be highly visible, and they'll all have their own ideas about the proper place of women—and religion—in society. And they'll be *citizens,* Mike. Unlike all the Allied personnel passing through, they'll be staying on, and the conservatives can't even pretend they won't. In fact—" she smiled thinly "—the vast majority of this particular batch will probably be staying on in Harrington Steading. As will quite a few of those who don't have a naval background or choose not to take service. I'd already gotten Benjamin to agree to that before he sprang this 'Protector's Own' business on me."

"Um." Henke frowned and rubbed her lower lip. "I hadn't considered all of that," she admitted after a moment. "But it still doesn't sound like the end of the world for the Grayson way of life to me!"

"It's not," Honor agreed. "If it were likely to be that, Reverend Sullivan would never have followed Reverend Hanks' lead in supporting the idea so strongly, which he has. But it *can* serve Benjamin as one more wedge for his reforms. More to the point, it's a deliberate smack in the face to the Keys who've been complaining most loudly about foreign influences since McQueen first started hitting back so hard."

"They're not the only ones who've been complaining," Henke said sourly. "The Opposition's been howling about the Government's 'inexcusable mishandling of the military situation' ever since Giscard hit Basilisk! Leaving that aside, though, just how does Benjamin's decision constitute smacking down complaining steadholders?"

"I don't doubt the Opposition's tried its best to make capital out of it back on Manticore," Honor said, "but I doubt they've been quite as insidious about it as some of the Keys have. Benjamin's steadholders have to proceed more carefully than the Opposition in the Star Kingdom does because the Constitution gives him so much more power than Elizabeth enjoys. If they irritate him too badly, there are all sorts of ways he can punish them—ways that are perfectly legal, now that the written Constitution is back in force—and they know it. So they never attack him directly, and they never attack his policies head-on. Instead, they nibble around the edges by viewing with concern and voicing those concerns as 'remonstrances to the Sword,' always as the stewards of their steaders' interests and guardians of the Grayson way of life and never out of anything so unworthy as ambition of their own." The living side of her mouth twisted in distaste. "Ever since McQueen's first campaign, a bunch of them've coalesced around Mueller and his cronies and argued that the reverses she handed us are evidence Grayson ought to consider whether or not it wants to continue to defer to the inept *foreign* leadership which made those reverses possible. They've all but openly called for Grayson to go it alone. To withdraw from the Alliance, pull its units out of the consolidated chain of command, and become a mere 'associated power' rather than a full ally."

"Jesus, Honor." For the first time, Henke looked genuinely concerned. "I hadn't heard anything like that! Is there any possibility that they could pull it off?"

"Not a chance," Honor said flatly. "Benjamin would never allow himself to be stampeded into anything remotely like it, and for all intents and purposes, Benjamin Mayhew *is* Grayson. I don't think anyone in the Star Kingdom truly appreciates the extent to which that's true, Mike. We persist in seeing everyone else through the lenses of our own experience, but powerful as Elizabeth is, she doesn't begin to approach Benjamin's personal authority on Grayson." She shook her head.

"No, no one's going to succeed in dictating foreign or military policy to Benjamin, but that's not really what they're after. They may not like it, but they've had to accept that Benjamin is clearly ascendant. They're not going to be able to face him directly and win for a long time, so they've dug in for the long haul. All they're trying to do right now is nibble away at his popular support, plant doubts and questions and worries in the minds of as many Graysons as possible. They know as well as Benjamin does that his true authority rests on the support of his subjects, so they're trying to weaken that support and push him into acting more circumspectly against them. As they see it, that's the first step in a steady downward spiral of the Sword's authority. Each time he fails to respond forcefully to their provocations, they chip away a tiny piece of his ability to respond forcefully the *next* time, and that's all they're really after at this point."

"I see." Henke shook her head again. "I seem to remember a time when you didn't understand politics. Or like them very much, for that matter," she observed.

"I still don't like them," Honor replied. "Unfortunately, as one of the Keys myself, I haven't had much option but to learn how they work . . . Grayson style, at least. And if I had to learn about something I detest, at least Howard Clinkscales and Benjamin Mayhew were probably the best teachers I could possibly have had."

"I can see that. But I still don't see exactly where Benjamin's offering citizenship to your fellow escapees smacks down his opponents."

"It doesn't do it directly. In fact, in a way, he *can't* do it directly as long as they don't attack *him* directly. But what it does do is to make his ongoing commitment to opening Grayson to outside viewpoints abundantly, one might almost say brutally, clear. And without providing his version of the Opposition a target they can attack without seeming to attack him." Honor shrugged. "It's all a game of indirection and flanking maneuvers, Mike, and I just got tossed right back into the middle of it as the Protector's Own's official CO. I have no idea who's going to wind up actually commanding the force, though I wouldn't be surprised if they picked Alfredo Yu for the slot. But *I'll* be carried on the record as its permanent commander, which is Benjamin's not-so-subtle way of throwing another brick into the conservatives' teeth. They're upset enough just to have me back at all, whatever they have to say for public consumption. Naming me as the official CO will only rub their nose in the message Benjamin is sending them . . . and given the excitement over my return, they don't dare do or say anything that might be considered a personal slight to me."

"Jesus," Henke repeated in a very different tone, and produced a crooked smile. "I always thought our political bloodletting was bad back home! But I *am* impressed to hear Honor Harrington rattling off an appreciation of enemy intentions that readily."

"Yeah, sure you are," Honor grumped. "What you mean is that you're grateful *you* don't have to put up with it!"

"Probably. But speaking of complicated situations, and not to change the subject or anything, you did get your finances straightened out again, didn't you?"

"In a manner of speaking." Nimitz and Samantha slid off the chair back, crowding down to completely fill Honor's lap with the insistence on physical contact which had become even more a part of them since Nimitz had realized he'd lost his mental voice, and she caressed Nimitz's ears gently.

"Getting them fully straightened out is going to take considerably longer," she went on, looking back up at Henke. "Willard did wonders in the time he had, but a month and a half simply wasn't long enough to sort out a situation that complex. Unfortunately, Her Majesty was just a bit insistent on my returning to the Star Kingdom as soon as I could 'spare the time,' as she put it." She shrugged, deciding—again—not to mention the dispatches which had passed back and forth between Mount Royal Palace and Harrington House before Elizabeth's formal "invitation" arrived. "From the looks of things, it should all come out reasonably straight in the end," she said instead.

" 'Reasonably straight'? I hope you won't mind if I say that sounds just a bit casual for someone worth thirty or forty billion dollars, Honor!"

"It's only about twenty-nine billion," Honor corrected her testily. "And why shouldn't I be 'casual' about it?" She snorted. "Remember me? Your yeoman roommate from Sphinx? I've got more money than I could possibly spend in the entire rest of my life, even allowing for prolong, Mike! It beats heck out of being poor, but after a certain point, it's only a way to keep score . . . in a game I'm not all that interested in playing. Oh, it's a valuable tool, and it lets me do all sorts of things I never would have been able to do without it, but to be perfectly honest, I think I would have preferred leaving it just the way my will left it. *I* don't need it, and Willard, Howard, and the Sky Domes board were making perfectly good use of it before I came back."

"Honor Harrington, you are an unnatural woman," Henke said severely. "Anyone who's that cavalier about that much money should be locked away somewhere she can't do herself a mischief!"

"That's approximately what Willard said," Honor acknowledged with a sigh. "But the clincher was when he pointed out that all my will had actually done with the bulk of my fortune was leave it in trust for the next Steadholder Harrington. Which is me, if you want to look at it that way. Or you could say that since I was never actually dead, the will never really came into effect." She rolled her eyes. "I can just see me dealing with *that* part of it! 'Excuse me, Mac, but that bequest of mine? I need it back, I'm afraid, since it turns out I had the bad taste not to be dead after all. Sorry about that!' "

She did not, Henke noticed, mention the beloved ten-meter sloop on Sphinx, which she had left to Henke herself.

"But you aren't dead," she pointed out, and Honor snorted.

"So? All the surprise gifts I'd tucked away wound up given out when everyone *thought* I was dead, and even with their disbursement, the estate still gained something like eleven-point-five billion in value while I was away. Obviously, my fortune can survive perfectly well without them, and there's no point taking them back now just so my executor can hand them back over to everybody when I finally do shuffle off."

"Um." Henke was a first cousin of Elizabeth III on her mother's side, and her father was the Earl of Gold Peak, the Cromarty Government's Foreign Secretary and one of the wealthier members of the Manticoran peerage. Henke never had to worry about money, although the allowance her father had put Michelle on until she graduated from the Academy had been well on the miserly side by the standards of her social peers. Not that Henke had any objections in retrospect. There'd been times when she'd felt pinched for funds as a girl, but she'd had too much opportunity since then to see what had happened to childhood acquaintances whose parents *hadn't* seen to it that they realized money didn't exactly grow on trees.

Despite that, her observation had been that very few of the truly wealthy, for all that they regarded the availability of money as an inevitable part of their day-to-day lives, could have matched Honor's lack of concern. But that, she realized slowly, was because for so many of those wealthy people, fortune and the power that went with it were what defined their lives. It made them who they were, and created and established the universe in which they existed.

But not for Honor Harrington. Her wealth truly was incidental to who she was, what she did, and where her responsibilities lay. A useful tool, she'd called it, but only because it helped her discharge those responsibilities, not because it had any overwhelming impact on her own, personal life.

"You *are* an unnatural woman," Henke said after a moment, "and thank God for it. We could probably use a few more like you, now that I think about it. Not that I'd want you to get a swelled head or anything."

"Spare my blushes," Honor said dryly, and this time they both chuckled.

"So," Henke said after several moments, in the tone of one turning to a fresh, neutral subject, "what, exactly, do our lords and masters have in mind for you when you get back to the Star Kingdom?"

"You don't know?" Honor sounded surprised, and Henke shrugged.

"They just told me to go and get you, not what they were going to do with you once I delivered you helpless into their hands. I feel quite sure Beth personally instructed Baroness Morncreek to send *Eddy* to fetch you, and just this once, I decided I had no quarrel with naked nepotism. But no one told me what was in those dispatches I brought you. And while I am, of course, far too dutiful a servant of the Crown to poke my nose into affairs which are none of my concern, if it just happened that you were willing to let fall a few morsels of information . . ."

She let her voice trail off and raised both hands, palm upwards, before her, and Honor laughed out loud.

"And you called *me* 'unnatural'!"

"Because you are. And *do* you know what they plan to do with you?"

"Not fully, no." Honor shook her head and hid another twinge of worry. *And, really, there's probably no reason I should worry, when you come right down to it. Elizabeth may have sounded a little . . . irritated there at the end, but she didn't really sound angry. Or I don't think she did, anyway.*

"For one thing, though, I strongly suspect Her Majesty of wanting to play the same 'Let's surprise poor Honor!' game Benjamin's having so much fun with," she went on darkly after a moment, "and that scares me. She's got a lot bigger toy box."

"I imagine you'll survive that part of it," Henke reassured her.

"I'm rapidly discovering that it is not, in fact, possible—quite—

to die of simple embarrassment," Honor observed. *Not if you put your foot down firmly enough, at least.* "This is not always a fortunate thing, however, as it seems to challenge those about me to keep pushing the envelope to find out if someone can die of *advanced* embarrassment, on which point the jury is still out."

"Quit feeling sorry for yourself and tell me the rest!" Henke scolded.

"Yes, Ma'am." Honor leaned further back in the chair, wrapping her arm around Nimitz while she considered the parts that she felt comfortable discussing with someone else, even Henke. Samantha laid a wedge-shaped chin on her left shoulder to help her consider, and she smiled as silken whiskers brushed her cheek just above the line of nerve deadness.

"I would have been returning to the Star Kingdom fairly soon anyway, of course," she went on after a moment in a more serious voice. "They want to check all of us out at Bassingford, and Daddy will be heading this way in the next couple of weeks to oversee my repairs." She took her hand from Nimitz's pelt for a moment to gesture at the dead side of her face. "Grayson's hospitals are building up to Manticoran standards surprisingly quickly, and the neural center Daddy and Willard put together to match Mom's genetic clinic is really good, but they just don't have the support structure yet for a rebuild job quite as, um, *extensive* as my own. We're going to fix that as quickly as we can—I did mention that money is a useful tool at times, didn't I?—but for now, the Star Kingdom's the best place short of the Solarian League to handle something like this.

"I also ought to drop by Admiralty House, I suppose," she went on, and Henke hid a smile. Honor might not realize how much she'd changed over the last ten years, but the casual way she'd just referred to Admiralty House, the *sanctum sanctorum* of the Royal Manticoran Navy, was a dead giveaway to Henke. Honor was only a commodore in the RMN, but she thought and acted like the fleet admiral she was in Grayson service . . . and did it so naturally she wasn't even aware of it. "Among the other things you brought me was a very politely phrased 'request' to make myself available as soon as possible for an ONI debrief. And I'll want to talk to Admiral Cortez about the ways he can make best use of the non-Allied military personnel who came back from Hell with us . . . and don't get scooped up by Benjamin's new project.

"On top of that," she said with a little moue, "I feel depressingly certain I'm going to be spending entirely too much time talking to newsies. I'm going to insist on holding that sort of thing to an absolute minimum, but as you suggested earlier, I did see the recordings of the funeral Duke Cromarty and Her Majesty laid on for me. In the wake of all that hoopla, I don't suppose it's even remotely possible for me to avoid the spotlight."

"I'd say that was a fairly generous understatement," Henke agreed.

"After that—" Honor shrugged. "The only thing I know for certain from the Admiralty is that, assuming I plan on returning to Manticoran service while I'm in the Star Kingdom for medical reasons anyway, they'd like me to consider spending some time at Saganami Island. I'll be on limited duty while they design and build my new arm, so I guess a stint in a classroom might not be a terrible idea. I don't know exactly what they have in mind, but I'd rather keep busy than just sit around." She shuddered. "I remember the last time we went through all this neural implant business. Not having anything to do between bouts of surgery and therapy just about drove me crazy!"

"I can imagine. For that matter, I remember what it was like when they finally let you go back on active duty and gave you *Nike*." The two women smiled at one another, and if Honor's smile was just a bit bittersweet as that shared memory brought back Paul Tankersley and the agonizing pain of his loss, it was a pain she'd learned to bear.

"Well, then!" Henke said briskly, glancing at her chrono and then pushing herself to her feet. "I've pounded your ear long enough, and we've got about two hours before dinner. How would you like to make a start on that guided tour I promised you?"

"I'd love to," Honor replied. She rose in turn, and Henke helped her get Nimitz into his carrier and settled on her back. Samantha supervised from the back of the chair, and then accepted the forearm and elbow Henke offered her, and the four of them stepped out through the cabin hatch.

"I think you'll like her a lot, Honor," Henke said after acknowledging the salute of her Marine sentry. She led the way down the passage towards the lift, and her smile was proprietary and proud. "I know you're already familiar with the basic parameters of the design, but they went right on refining it up to the moment they actually laid *Eddy* down at *Hephaestus*, and a lot of the features that ended up in the *Har*—I mean, in the *Medusas*—were incorporated into her, as well. Not just the automation to reduce crew size, either. We got a lot of the new electronics goodies, including some major fire control updates, the brand new generation of ECM and stealth, *and* a little surprise for the Peeps the next time they take a down-the-throat shot at us."

She grinned evilly, and Honor returned the expression with equally wicked anticipation.

"I thought we'd start with the command deck," Henke went on, "then drop by CIC. After that . . ."

Chapter Six

The stumpy stone spire of King Michael's Tower was as old-fashioned and unimpressive-looking as Honor remembered, but this was her second visit to it. She was well aware of how misleading appearances could be, because this time she knew whose private retreat it was, and she felt a small, undeniable edge of trepidation as she watched it grow higher before her while she followed her guide through the grounds of Mount Royal Palace. Michelle Henke walked beside and half a pace behind her, and Andrew LaFollet and Simon Mattingly brought up the rear. Samantha rode on Henke's shoulder, keeping a watchful eye on Nimitz in the carrier on Honor's back, and Honor suspected their cavalcade looked more than a little ridiculous.

She nodded in acknowledgment of the sharp salutes from the uniformed personnel of the Queen's Own Regiment and Palace Guard Service as she passed. Their outward miens were professional, alert and almost expressionless, and they'd been briefed on her scheduled arrival over a month ago. That meant there was little of the astonishment and sudden bursts of excitement she'd had to deal with back on Grayson, which was a vast relief, although at least all the practice Grayson had put her through had helped her learn—finally—how to tune down the volume on her emotion-sensing ability. She chuckled mentally at the thought. Someone back on Old Earth—Samuel Johnson?—had once observed that the knowledge that someone was to be hanged concentrated one's thoughts wonderfully. Honor had discovered the bitter truth of that sitting in a brig cell aboard PNS *Tepes*, but she'd also discovered a variant on the theme since her return. The sheer intensity of the emotional storm which had lashed at her so often and so violently from so many minds had forced her to concentrate on her own empathic ability as never before. She still didn't know how she'd done it, but she'd managed (out of simple self-preservation) to acquire a far finer degree of control. She could no more have described the learning process, or even how she did whatever it was she'd learned to do, than she could have described how she'd first learned to walk or talk, but she'd heaved a vast sigh of relief when she realized she'd developed something which must be very like Nimitz's own ability to adjust the gain. She still couldn't avoid tasting the emotions of those about her, but for the first time she'd gained sufficient control that she could hold the "volume" down to a level at which she no longer had to worry about looking and feeling dazed by the clamor no one else about her could even perceive. That, she felt certain, was going to prove to be a very valuable talent in the future—like the next time she found herself unable to completely tune out Hamish Alexander's emotions—and she was vastly relieved to have it, although she could have wished for a less . . . tumultuous way to acquire it.

For now, it also helped that the Queen's Own and PGS were professional outfits whose personnel spent their careers in close proximity to their Queen, which gave them all a certain degree of familiarity with the movers and shakers of the Star Kingdom. However unnatural it still seemed to her, Honor had been forced to accept that the PR impact of her return after her very public execution and funeral had at least temporarily elevated her to that sort of stature. Which made the security people's matter-of-fact acceptance of her presence a far more soothing balm than they could possibly suspect.

Honor had deliberately answered her Queen's summons in civilian dress, and, after a little consideration, she'd chosen to appear in a Grayson-style gown and wearing, as always in civilian garb, the Harrington Key and the Star of Grayson. Partly that was because, aside from a few outfits better suited to the Sphinx bush than Mount Royal Palace, she didn't even *own* any Manticoran civilian clothing. And, if pressed, she would also have to admit that she'd long since decided she liked the way she looked in the utterly impractical Grayson garments. But there were other factors. Queen Elizabeth had requested her presence, not commanded it as she had a right to do in the case of a serving officer of the Manticoran military or a member of the Star Kingdom's nobility. Her restraint had not escaped Honor's notice, and she'd wondered how much of it had to do with the one thing she'd so far steadfastly refused to allow Elizabeth to do. It was possible that the Queen had decided, either out of tact or (though Honor hoped not) pique, to handle her with long-handled tongs. If that were the case, it might be a very good idea for Honor to put some extra distance between herself and her Manticoran persona, so she'd come as a Grayson steadholder, answering the invitation of an allied head of state, not as one of Elizabeth's subjects.

She *could* have done that and still appeared in uniform as Admiral Harrington, but that might have sent the wrong message to her (many) surviving critics in the Opposition. However temporarily quelled they might be, they knew that she knew as well as they did who'd blocked the promotion the RMN would otherwise have granted her long ago. If they saw her in Grayson uniform now, with her Grayson rank, they would almost certainly decide she was mocking their efforts to deny her advancement in Manticoran service. And, she'd been forced to admit to herself, a nasty little part of her had longed to do just that . . . and for precisely that reason. But the Queen probably didn't need her to go pumping any fresh hydrogen into that particular fire when all the publicity associated with her return from Cerberus seemed to have given her the whip hand. Besides, if she'd worn uniform, she would have had to formally return all the salutes coming her way.

Her lips twitched at the thought, and then she banished the smile as the guards at the tower's entrance ushered her and the Honorable Michelle through it. A stiffly professional captain of the Queen's Own rode up with them in the old-fashioned, straight-line elevator, and Honor frowned very slightly at him as she sensed the strong strand of disapproval winding through his emotions.

She knew what had waked it. Grayson law required any steadholder to be accompanied by her personal armsmen at all times, and the people responsible for the Queen of Manticore's security were unhappy, to say the least, at the thought of *anyone* entering her presence with a weapon. They had no reason to distrust Graysons in general, and still less to distrust anyone in Honor's service. But this was their bailiwick, and their finely honed professional paranoia was at work.

She could understand that, because she didn't much like the thought of bringing weapons into Elizabeth's presence herself, but she didn't have any choice. More than that, she'd already reduced her normal three-man detail to the minimum Grayson law would permit. If she'd tried to exclude Andrew or Simon as well, it might have seemed like an expression of distrust, and she would die before she did anything which might conceivably be construed in such a fashion.

Besides, Elizabeth's clearly considered the matter herself. If she hadn't, she wouldn't have made a point of informing me—and her security people—that Andrew and Simon were to keep their guns.

The elevator sighed to a stop, and she and Henke followed their guide down a short hall to the same sitting room in which Elizabeth had received the two of them once before. Mattingly peeled off at the carved and polished wood of the sitting-room door, standing to the left of the doorway while the Army captain took up his own post to its right, but LaFollet entered the room at her heels.

Elizabeth Adrienne Samantha Annette Winton, Queen of Manticore, sat in an overstuffed armchair across the same thick, rust-colored carpet, and she was not alone. Her own treecat, Ariel, lay across the back of the chair, and his head came up as he gazed intently at Nimitz and Samantha. Honor felt the familiar surge as he reached out to the two newcomers . . . and his quick concern as only Samantha answered. He rose to regard Nimitz even more intently, and Honor tasted his sudden shocked understanding and the sympathy and welcome he projected to her companion on its heels.

There were two other humans in the room. One was completely familiar to Honor, and her living eye twinkled as she saw her cousin Devon, Second Earl Harrington. He looked—and was; she could taste his emotions as well as anyone else's—extremely uncomfortable. It was a sensation she remembered only too well from her own first visit here, and she supposed it must be still worse for Devon. At least Honor had been a naval officer, and one who'd met her Queen before, at that, before the visit. From the flavor of his emotions and the expression on his face, Devon was still coming to grips with the fact that he was now a peer of the realm, and she felt him wondering if she secretly wanted to snatch her title back from him.

She smiled at him as reassuringly as the crippled left side of her mouth allowed, but the second man in the sitting room drew her attention from her cousin. He was slightly built and silver-haired, with a worn and weary-looking face which, in person, was disconcertingly similar to a face she'd once seen across forty meters of grass on the Landing City dueling grounds. That face, too, had belonged to a man named Summervale. But Denver Summervale had been a disgraced ex-Marine turned professional assassin; *Allen* Summervale was the Duke of Cromarty . . . and Prime Minister of the Star Kingdom of Manticore.

"Dame Honor!" Elizabeth III pushed up out of her chair with a huge smile. Honor was immensely relieved to taste the genuine welcome behind that smile, but, Steadholder Harrington or no, she was not sufficiently far removed from her yeoman origins not to feel a quick spasm of uncertainty when Elizabeth held out her hand. Yet she *was* Steadholder Harrington, and so she took the Queen's hand in a firm clasp and made herself meet Elizabeth's dark brown eyes levelly. It was hard. Far harder than she'd expected, and a tiny corner of her brain marveled at just how much her world had changed in the nine T-years since she'd last stood in this room. She wasn't at all certain she liked all those changes, but she found, as she stood face-to-face with her monarch, that it was impossible to deny them any longer, even to herself.

"Your Majesty," she said quietly, and inclined her head in a small, respectful bow.

"Thank you for coming so promptly," Elizabeth went on, waving Honor towards the armchair which faced her own across the coffee table. She nodded a far more casual greeting to her cousin, and Henke parked herself comfortably in another chair, leaving the couch to Devon Harrington and Duke Cromarty.

"I know you must still have a million things to deal with on Grayson," Elizabeth went on, waiting for Honor to seat herself before she sank back into her own chair, "and I deeply appreciate your putting them on hold for me."

"Your Majesty, I was your subject long before I became Steadholder Harrington," Honor replied, unlatching Nimitz's carrier and moving it around in front of her. Nimitz flowed out into her lap, and Samantha hopped down from Henke's chair to patter across the carpet and join her mate.

"I'm aware of that," Elizabeth said. Then her voice darkened for just a moment. "But I am also aware of the Crown's failure to protect your career, as you so amply deserved, in the face of your shameful treatment following your duel with Pavel Young."

Honor winced at the name of the man who'd hated her for so long and hurt her so cruelly before she finally faced him one rainy morning with a pistol in her hand. But that, too, had been nine T-years ago, and she shook her head.

"Your Majesty, I knew going in what was going to happen. That you and His Grace—" she nodded courteously to Cromarty "—would have no choice but to act as you did. I never blamed either of you. If I blamed anyone—besides Young himself—it was the Opposition leaders."

"That's very generous of you, Milady," Cromarty said quietly.

"Not generous," Honor disagreed. "Only realistic. And in all fairness, I can hardly claim that packing me off to Grayson in disgrace was the end of my life, Your Grace!" She smiled ironically and touched the golden Harrington Key where it gleamed on her chest beside the glittering glory of the Star of Grayson.

"But not because certain people didn't try to *make* it that," Elizabeth observed. "You've attracted the hatred of far too many fanatics over the years, Dame Honor. As your Queen, I'd like to request that you try to cut down on that in years to come."

"I'll certainly bear that in mind, Your Majesty," Honor murmured.

"Good." Elizabeth leaned back and studied her guest for a moment. Elizabeth would feel better when Bassingford Medical Center had confirmed that, other than the loss of her arm, Honor had indeed survived her ordeal intact. But she looked better than the Queen had feared she might, and Elizabeth felt her own worry easing just a bit.

She gave Honor one more searching glance, then turned to her cousin.

"And good morning to you, too, Captain Henke. Thank you for delivering Dame Honor in one piece."

"We strive to please, Your Majesty," Henke replied with a certain unctuousness.

"And with such deep and heartfelt respect, too," Elizabeth observed.

"Always," Henke agreed, and the cousins grinned at one another. They really did look remarkably alike, although Henke showed the outward signs of the original, modified Winton genotype far more strongly. Elizabeth's rich mahogany skin was considerably lighter than her cousin's, yet Honor rather suspected Elizabeth had even more of the less obvious advantages Roger Winton's parents had had designed into their progeny. The exact nature of those modifications, while not precisely classified, was unknown to the general public, as was the very fact that any Winton had ever been a genie. In fact, the Star Kingdom's security people took considerable pains to keep it that way, and Honor knew only because Mike had been her Academy roommate and closest friend for just under forty T-years . . . and because Mike had known she was a fellow genie for almost all that time. But whichever of them had more of the original modifications, both had the same, distinctive Winton features, and there were barely three years between their ages.

"I believe you know Earl Harrington," Elizabeth went on, turning back to Honor, and it was Honor's turn to grin.

"We *have* met, Your Majesty, although it's been some time. Hello, Devon."

"Honor." Devon was ten T-years older than Honor, although his mother was Alfred Harrington's younger sister, and he looked even more uncomfortable than before as all eyes turned to him. "I hope you realize I never expected—" he began, but she shook her head quickly.

"I'm perfectly well aware that you never wanted to be an earl, Dev," she said reassuringly. "In fact, that's something of a family trait, because *I* never wanted to be a countess, either." She smiled briefly at Elizabeth, then looked back at her cousin. "Her Majesty didn't give me a great deal of choice, and I doubt she gave you any more than she let me have."

"Rather less, in fact," Elizabeth affirmed before Devon could respond. "There were several reasons. One, I'm a little ashamed to admit, was to revitalize general support for the war by cashing in on the public fury over the Peeps' decision to execute you, Dame Honor. By very publically supporting your cousin's right to replace you, I managed to refocus attention on your 'death' quite effectively. Of course, I did have some motives which were less reprehensible than that, though I'm not sure they were very much less calculating."

"Ah?" Honor's single word invited further explanation, and she was too focused on Elizabeth to notice the grins Michelle Henke and Allen Summervale exchanged. Elizabeth's lips quivered ever so briefly, but she managed to suppress her own smile. There were—perhaps—twenty people in the Star Kingdom, outside her immediate family, who would have felt comfortable enough with her to cock an interrogative eyebrow in her direction with such composure.

"Indeed," the Queen said. "One was that I had a certain bone to pick with the Opposition." Her temptation to smile vanished, and her eyes were suddenly cold and hard. It was said Elizabeth III held grudges until they died of old age and then sent them to a taxidermist, and at that moment, Honor believed every story she'd ever heard about her Queen's implacable, sometimes volcanic, temper. Then Elizabeth gave her head a little shake and relaxed in her chair once more.

"The decision to exclude you from the Lords after your duel with Young upset me on several levels," she said. "One, of course, was the slap in the face to you. I understood, possibly better than you can imagine, exactly what you felt when you went after Young."

She and Henke exchanged a brief look. Honor had no idea what lay behind it, but she shivered inwardly at the shared sudden, icy stab of old, bitter anger and grief that went with it.

"I might have wished you'd chosen a less public forum in which to issue your challenge," Elizabeth went on after a moment, "but I certainly understood what forced you to choose the one you did. And while the Crown's official position, and my own, is that dueling is a custom we could very well do without, it was your legal right to challenge him, just as his life was both legally and morally forfeit when he turned early and shot you in the back. For the Opposition to make the fact that you 'shot a man whose gun was empty'—because he'd just finished emptying his magazine into *you*—a pretext for excluding you infuriated me both as a woman and as Queen. Particularly when everyone knew they were doing it, at least in part, as a way to strike back at Duke Cromarty's Government and myself, as Queen, for forcing the declaration of war through Parliament.

"In all fairness, I suppose I ought to confess that that last point weighed rather more heavily with me than I'd really like to admit," she confessed. "I'd prefer to be able to say that it was all outrage over the wrong they'd done you, but as you yourself have undoubtedly discovered as Steadholder Harrington, allowing them to get away with baiting either myself or my Prime Minister is never a good idea. Each time they do it, they chip away, however slightly, at my prerogatives and my ministers' moral authority. Very few people realize that, even now, our Constitution exists as a balance between dynamic tensions. What the public perceives as laws and procedures set in ceramacrete are, in fact, always subject to change through shifts in precedent and custom . . . which, come to think of it, is how the Wintons managed to hijack the original Star Kingdom from the Lords in the first place." She gave a wolfish smile. "The original drafters intended to set up a nice, tight little system which would be completely dominated by the House of Lords so as to protect the power and authority of the original colonizers and their descendants. They never counted on Elizabeth the First's sneaking in and creating a real, powerful, centralized executive authority for the Crown . . . or enlisting the aid of the Commons to do it!

"*My* family, however, is fully aware of how the present system came to be, and we have no intention of allowing anyone to hijack *our* authority. The Peep threat has lent added point to that determination for seventy T-years now, and I see no sign of that changing any time soon. Which is one major reason I never had any intention of allowing your exclusion to stand. Unfortunately, you'd been killed—or so we all believed—before I got around to correcting the problem. So I decided to make certain your proper heir—" she nodded to Devon "—was confirmed as Earl Harrington, *and* provided the lands commensurate with his title, *and* seated in the Lords as soon as possible. What was more, I made certain the leaders of the Opposition knew what I was doing, and why, at a time when they no longer dared express their true feelings for you because of what public opinion would have done to them." She gave another of those wolfish smiles. "I trust you won't be offended to learn that I had such an ignoble motive, Dame Honor."

"On the contrary, Your Majesty. The thought of your whacking certain august members of the House of Lords gives me a rather warm feeling, actually."

"I thought it might." For a moment, the two women smiled at one another in perfect accord, but then Elizabeth drew a deep breath.

"Now that you've returned from the dead, as it were, the situation has changed rather radically, however. If they want to see it that way, I've actually outmaneuvered myself by having Devon confirmed as Earl Harrington, since I now have no choice but to allow him to remain earl, thus neatly depriving *you* of any legitimate claim to his seat in the Lords, or else initiate steps to deprive him of the title in your favor. Legally, of course," she gave Devon a brief, almost apologetic smile, "there would be no problem with the latter. You aren't dead, after all, and there are plenty of legal precedents to cover the return of your property, including your peerage. But there would be a certain amount of embarrassment for the Crown in jumping through all the legal hoops, particularly after how, um, quietly but . . . *forcefully* Duke Cromarty and I made the case for confirming him in the first place."

"I see." Honor ran her hand gently down Nimitz's spine, then nodded. "I see," she said in a rather firmer tone. "And I also suspect that you're working your way up to something with all this explanation, Your Majesty."

"I told you she was a sharp one, Beth!" Henke chuckled.

"I hardly needed to be told, Mike," the Queen replied dryly, but her eyes remained on Honor, who felt a sudden tingle as she realized Elizabeth wasn't quite ready to give up her initial idea after all. "Unfortunately, she's also a stubborn one," Elizabeth went on, confirming her fear. "May I ask if you've reconsidered your position on the Medal of Valor, Dame Honor?"

From the corner of her eye, Honor saw Henke snap upright in her chair, but she kept her own gaze fixed on Elizabeth's face.

"No, Your Majesty, I haven't." Her soprano voice was tinged with a hint of respectful regret but also unwavering, and Elizabeth sighed.

"I'd like you to think about that very carefully," she said persuasively. "In light of all you've accomplished, it—"

"Excuse me, Your Majesty," Honor interrupted, courteously but firmly, "but with all due respect, every reason you and His Grace have given me has been a bad one."

"Dame Honor," Cromarty spoke up in his deep, whiskey-smooth baritone, "I won't pretend to deny that there are political considerations involved here. You wouldn't believe me if I did, and, frankly, I'm not particularly ashamed that they exist. The Peeps attempted to use your execution as a political and morale weapon against the Alliance. That was the sole reason for the dramatic way in which Ransom and Boardman went about announcing it to their own people, to us, and to the Solarian League. The fact that they'd utterly misread the reaction it would provoke throughout the Alliance doesn't change their intent, and they actually did score some points with certain segments of the Solarian League by portraying you as a convicted, out-of-control mass murderess without bothering to explain the details. Of course, it had already blown up in their faces to some extent, here in the Star Kingdom and in the Alliance, at least, even before you returned so inconveniently from the dead. Now it has all the earmarks of a first-class diplomatic catastrophe for them *everywhere*, and as the Prime Minister of Manticore, it's my job to see to it that their catastrophe is as complete as I can possibly make it. Awarding you the Parliamentary Medal of Valor and just incidentally rehearsing the details of your escape in the citation for public consumption is one sure way to help accomplish that goal."

Honor started to speak, but his raised hand stopped her.

"Let me finish, please," he said courteously, and she nodded a bit unwillingly. "Thank you. Now, as I was saying, the political considerations are, in my opinion, completely valid and appropriate. But they're also beside the point. Whether you care to admit it or not, you've already earned the PMV several times over, as the Graysons clearly recognize." He flicked a graceful gesture at the Star of Grayson glittering on her breast. "Had it not been for the aversion in which the Opposition holds you, you probably would have received it after First Hancock . . . or after Fourth Yeltsin. And whether you earned it in the past or not, you *certainly* did when you organized, planned, and executed the escape of almost half a million prisoners from the Peeps' most secure prison!"

"I'm afraid I can't agree with you, Your Grace," Honor said firmly. Henke squirmed in her chair, holding herself in it by main force of will, but Honor ignored her to concentrate on the Prime Minister.

"The PMV is awarded for valor above and beyond the call of duty," she continued, "and nothing I did was beyond the call of duty." Cromarty's eyes widened in disbelief, but she went on calmly. "It's the duty of any Queen's Officer to escape, if possible. It's the duty of any officer to encourage, coordinate, and lead the efforts of any of her subordinates to escape from the enemy in time of war. And it's the duty of any commanding officer to lead her personnel in combat. More than that, I should also point out that I, personally, had very little to lose in attempting to escape from Hell. I'd been sentenced to death. For me, that made whether or not to risk my life in an attempt to escape a rather simple decision."

"Dame Honor—!" Cromarty began, but she shook her head again.

"If you want to reward people who truly demonstrated valor above and beyond the call of duty, you ought to be giving any medals to Horace Harkness," she said flatly. "Unlike myself, he faced only incarceration, not execution, when we reached Hell, and he knew it. But he also chose, entirely without orders, to pretend to defect. He knowingly risked virtually certain execution if he was caught in order to break into the central computers of Cordelia Ransom's flagship, arrange all the critical details of our escape to the planetary surface, *and* completely destroy *Tepes* to cover our escape. I submit to you, Your Grace, that if you and Her Majesty want to award a PMV to anyone, Harkness is the most deserving individual you could possibly find."

"But—" Cromarty began again, and she shook her head once more, more firmly than before.

"No, Your Grace," she said, and there was no give in her voice at all. "I will not accept the PMV for this."

"*Honor!*" Henke burst out, unable to restrain herself any longer. "You never mentioned anything like *this* on the trip from Grayson!"

"Because it wasn't important."

"The hell it wasn't! They're talking about the *Medal of Valor*, for God's sake! You don't just tell Parliament 'Thanks but no thanks' when they offer you the Star Kingdom's highest award for valor!"

"I'm afraid Dame Honor doesn't agree with you, Mike," Elizabeth said. Her tone was on the tart side, but there was respect in it, as well, and she gazed at Honor with measuring eyes even as she spoke to her cousin. "In point of fact, when we first sent her word that Allen was planning to move the award, she was quite firm about rejecting it."

"Firm?" Henke echoed. "What d'you mean, *firm?*"

"I mean she offered to resign from my Navy if I persisted," Elizabeth said in a dust-dry voice. Honor felt Henke's shock, and her own cheekbones heated just a bit as she met her Queen's eyes, but Elizabeth chuckled after a moment. "They do say Sphinxians are stubborn," she murmured, "and I've heard the same about Graysons. I suppose I should have known what would happen if anyone was crazy enough to combine the two in one package!"

"Your Majesty, I mean no disrespect," Honor said. "And I'm deeply honored to know that you and Duke Cromarty truly believe I deserve the PMV. The fact that you do is something I'll always treasure, truly. But I *don't* deserve it. Not for this. And the PMV is too important to me for me to do anything that might, well . . . cheapen it, if you'll forgive my choice of words. It . . . wouldn't be right."

"Dame Honor, you are an unnatural woman," Elizabeth III said severely, unaware her cousin had used exactly the same words. "Or perhaps you're not. Perhaps I've simply spent too much time surrounded by politicians and power mongers. But I doubt very much that there are two women in the Star Kingdom who would turn down the PMV when both her Queen and her Prime Minister insist she take it." She snorted. "Of course, it might be wiser for me not to bet any money on that belief. After all, up until last month, I would've said there wasn't *one* woman who'd turn it down!"

"Your Maj—"

"It's all right, Dame Honor." Elizabeth sighed, waving a hand. "You win. We can hardly march you out into the Crown Chancellery at pulser point and *make* you accept it. Think of what a PR disaster *that* would be! But you do realize that if you persist in turning down the PMV we're not going to let you overturn our other plans, don't you?"

"Other plans?" Honor repeated cautiously, and Elizabeth grinned like a treecat in a celery patch.

"Nothing too complicated," she reassured her guest. "It's just that, as I explained, my slap on the Opposition's wrist over your exclusion from the Lords lost much of its point when you turned up alive. So since I was the one who took your title away, I thought I should be the one to replace it . . . and—" her eyes glittered "—give those self-serving cretins a kick in the ass they'll be *years* recovering from!"

"I don't understand, Your Majesty," Honor said, and her tone showed true alarm for the first time. There was too much glee in the Queen's emotions, too great a sense of having found a way to simultaneously drub the Opposition and mousetrap Honor into accepting what Elizabeth clearly considered to be her "due."

"As I said, it's not complicated." Elizabeth's 'catlike grin intensified. "You're no longer Countess Harrington, and now that I've become more familiar with Grayson, I realize that creating you that in the first place was really a bit inappropriate, considering the difference in the precedence of a countess and a steadholder. Protector Benjamin has never complained about the unintentional insult we offered one of his great nobles by equating the two titles, but I'd be surprised if he doesn't harbor at least a little resentment over it, and it's never a good idea to risk potential friction with one's allies in the middle of a war. So I've decided to correct my original error."

"Correct—?" Honor gazed at her Queen in horror.

"Absolutely. The Crown has seen fit to urge the House of Commons, and the House of Commons has seen fit to approve, your creation as Duchess Harrington."

"*Duchess?!*" Honor gurgled.

"Correct," Elizabeth assured her. "We've carved a rather nice little duchy out of the Westmount Crown Reserve on Gryphon for you. There aren't any people living there right now—it *was* part of the Reserve, after all—but there are extensive timber and mineral rights. There are also several sites which would be suitable for the creation of luxury ski resorts. In fact, we've had numerous inquiries about those sites from the big ski consortiums for years, and I imagine several of them will be quite eager to negotiate leases from you, especially when they remember the role you played in the Attica Avalanche rescue operations. And I understand you enjoy sailing, so we drew your borders to include a moderately spectacular stretch of coast quite similar to your Copper Walls back on Sphinx. I'm sure you could put in a nice little marina. Of course, the weather on Gryphon can be a bit extreme, but I don't suppose you can have everything."

"But . . . but Your Majesty, I can't— That is, I don't have the time or the experience to—"

"Now that, Your Grace, will be quite enough," Elizabeth said, and for the first time, her voice was stern, the voice of a monarch. Honor closed her mouth with a click, and Elizabeth nodded.

"Better," she said. "Much better. Because this time, you're wrong. You do have the experience for the job. My God, Honor," it was the first time she'd ever addressed Honor solely by her given name, but Honor was too stunned even to notice, "you've got more experience than most of the people who are *already* dukes or duchesses! There's not a single Manticoran noble who's ever enjoyed the sort of authority and power a steadholder wields—Elizabeth the First saw to that four hundred years ago!—and you've been handling that job for ten T-years now. After that, *this* should be a piece of cake!"

"Perhaps so, but you know I'm right when I say I won't have time to see to my responsibilities properly," Honor rejoined. "I've been more fortunate than any woman deserves to have Howard Clinkscales to rely on back on Grayson, but now you're talking about piling a second set of responsibilities on top of my duties as Steadholder Harrington! No serving officer has the time to handle responsibilities like this the way they should be handled!"

"Ah?" Elizabeth cocked her head. "Should I take that up with Earl White Haven?"

"No! I didn't mean—" Honor chopped herself off and inhaled deeply. Elizabeth had no right resorting to that particular argument, she thought, but there was no way she cared to explain why that was to her Queen.

"I know what you meant, Honor," Elizabeth said quietly. "And, frankly, I'm not at all surprised you feel that way. It's one of the things I like about you. And it *is* customary for the great peers to devote their full attention to overseeing their lands. But there have always been exceptions, just as there have been in Earl White Haven's case. Hamish Alexander is far too valuable to the Navy for us to have him sitting around gathering dust running his earldom, and that's why he has a steward—like your Clinkscales—to execute his policies in his absence. The same arrangement can certainly be made for you. Indeed, I thought your friend Willard Neufsteiler might do nicely, if you can spare him from Sky Domes."

Honor blinked, surprised that Elizabeth was sufficiently well informed to know about her relationship with Neufsteiler, but the Queen continued with calm assurance.

"Whatever it takes, we'll work it out. Of course, it will probably help that you're going to be stuck here in the Star Kingdom for at least a T-year for medical treatment. That should keep you close enough to oversee the initial organization of a new duchy . . . and the experience you had organizing Harrington Steading should prove very valuable to you, I'd think. For that matter, the fact that there's no one living there at the moment will also alleviate some of the immediacy in getting it organized. But like White Haven, you're too valuable to the Navy for us to keep you sitting at home." Elizabeth smiled crookedly. "The time will undoubtedly come, and sooner than I'd like, when I have to send you back out to be shot at for me again. And this time you may not be as lucky. So if you won't accept my medals, you will *damned* well let me give you this while I still have the chance! Is that clear, Lady Harrington?"

"Yes, Your Majesty." Honor's soprano was more than a little husky, but she tasted the Queen's complete intransigence on this topic.

"Good," Elizabeth said quietly, then shoved back in her chair, stretched her legs out before her, crossed her ankles, lifted Ariel into her lap, and grinned.

"And now that we've gotten *that* out of the way, Your Grace, I intend to insist on a command performance. I know perfectly well that you're going to do your damnedest to avoid the newsies, and that even if you fail, they're bound to get the story's details wrong— they always do!—when they report it. So instead of reading about it in the 'faxes, I want every detail of your escape in person!"

CHAPTER SEVEN

"So what do you think of her, Commander?"

Commander Prescott David Tremaine turned towards the voice and felt his spine straighten as he recognized Rear Admiral of the Red Dame Alice Truman. He'd expected her yeoman to collect him when she was ready to see him, but she'd come in person. She stood in the open hatch between the waiting room and her private briefing room aboard HMSS *Weyland*, as golden-haired, green-eyed, and sturdy as he remembered, and he started towards her, but she waved a hand before he took a step.

"Stay where you are, Commander. Don't let me take you away from the view," she said, and crossed the compartment to where he stood beside the enormous view port. That view port was a rarity aboard *Weyland*, where exterior hull space was always at a premium and most people had to be content with HD wall screens . . . assuming they got even that. Which was silly, perhaps, since the wall screens came with a zoom capability no unaided eye could achieve, but it was also very human. There was something innately satisfying about knowing one was seeing the actuality, not an image, however faithful it might be. Even hardened starship officers who *never* saw the cosmos directly from their command decks seemed to share that craving for a front row seat on God's jewel box, and the fact that Truman had snagged such a prize said interesting things about the favor in which The Powers That Be currently held her.

Not that Truman's manner showed any particular awareness of that. Many officers of her seniority would have been far more formal with a newly promoted commander, not yet thirty-seven T-years old, just reporting to her for duty, and he warned himself not to refine too much upon the fact that she wasn't. Or wasn't starting out that way, anyway. He and Truman had served together under Lady Harrington twice before, yet he scarcely expected her to remember him. The first time, Truman had been a commander herself, CO of the light cruiser *Apollo* when Lady Harrington had commanded the heavy cruiser *Fearless* and Tremaine had been a very junior officer indeed aboard the destroyer *Troubadour*. Still, a certain sense of us-against-the-universe clung to everyone who had been a part of that small squadron. *Not that there are as many of us as there used to be*, Tremaine reminded himself with a touch of grimness, then took himself sternly to task.

The second time had been only four T-years ago, when Tremaine had been Lady Harrington's boat bay officer aboard the armed merchant cruiser *Wayfarer*. Truman had been a captain of the list then, and once more she'd been Lady Harrington's second-in-command, the senior captain of her Q-ship squadron. But once again they'd served on different ships, and the second time around, their paths had never crossed at all.

We may have served together, sort of, he reminded himself, *but she's a rear admiral now. That makes her about two steps short of God; vice admirals and full admirals have to fit in there somewhere. And that doesn't even count the trick she pulled off on Hancock Station last year . . . or the knighthood she got out of it. So answer the question, dummy!*

"I like her a lot, Ma'am," he said. "She's—" Despite his resolve to maintain decorum, his hands waved as he sought exactly the right word. "She's . . . wonderful," he said finally, and Truman smiled at the simple sincerity which infused his tone.

"I thought pretty much the same thing the first time I saw *Minotaur*," she admitted, feeling her own remembered excitement in the echo of Tremaine's enthusiasm. She treasured that feeling even more now that she was a flag officer and would never again directly command a Queen's ship, and she stepped up beside the view port and clasped her hands behind her as she and Tremaine turned to gaze out it together.

The port's lack of magnification limited what the human eye could pick out of something as endless as space, but for all its immensity, space also offered the needle-sharp clarity of hard vacuum, and the nearest space dock was barely thirty kilometers away. That was more than close enough to see the huge, two-kilometer hull floating at the center of the dock, and five more identical docks, each cocooning its own hull in progress, could be made out beyond it. The nearer ship was clearly all but ready to commission, for crews were completing the fusing of her paint while a steady stream of lighters trundled up to her cargo bays with loads of ship's stores, environmental supplies, missile pallets, and all the other million-and-one items a ship of war required.

The five docks beyond hers dwindled rapidly with distance, curving away in their orbits around the blue-and-white beauty of the planet Gryphon, but if one looked very closely, one could see still another cluster of docks reflecting the distant light of Manticore-B beyond *them.*

"Quite a sight, isn't it?" Truman murmured, and Tremaine shook his head. Not in disagreement, but with a sense of wonder.

"You can say that again, Ma'am," he replied softly. "Especially when you remember that every slip aboard *Weyland* is already full."

"And aboard *Hephaestus* and *Vulcan*," Truman agreed, and turned to smile at him. "Ever expect to see Grayson-style space docks here in the Star Kingdom, Commander?"

"No, Ma'am, I didn't," he admitted.

"Well, neither did I." Truman returned her gaze to the port. "Then again, I never thought I'd see the building tempo we're starting to hit." She shook her head. "It just never seemed possible that we'd completely fill every slip aboard every space station the Navy owns and then start throwing together stand-alones like that." She nodded at the dock, and her voice turned grimmer. "But you're probably going to see even more of them in the next few T-years," she told him. "The way the Peeps have been pressing the pace, we're going to need every ship we can get . . . and soon, unless I'm mistaken. And losing two brand new yards in Alizon and Zanzibar last year doesn't help a bit."

It was Tremaine's turn to look at her. He hadn't been back all that long, and Bassingford Medical Center had turned him loose with a clean bill of health less than two months ago. He'd been eligible for a full month of liberty, since he and everyone else who'd been sent to Hades were entitled to survivor's leave, but he'd used only three weeks of it. He'd loved every minute he got to spend with his mother and his two sisters, and his older brother's admiration—verging on sheer awe, actually—had done marvelous things for his ego, but he'd been simply unable to take longer than that.

A great deal of what had happened since Esther McQueen became the Peeps' secretary of war was still classified, but there was more than enough in the public record, especially coupled with what the escapees from Hell had learned about the Peeps' side of events from the data bases of their captured ships, for Tremaine to know it hadn't been good. Indeed, the more he'd seen, the more convinced he'd become that the Navy needed every person it had. Besides, he was constitutionally incapable of sitting on the sidelines when he ought to be pulling his weight. He'd always been a bit that way, he supposed, but he'd also been blessed, if that was the word, with the examples of senior officers like Lady Harrington and Alistair McKeon—or Alice Truman—and a man didn't serve under officers like that without developing a sense of duty. It could be an uncomfortable gift, but all things considered, he much preferred it to the reverse.

And I sleep better at night, too, he told himself, all the time concentrating on making his questioning gaze properly respectful. Truman studied his face for several seconds, then smiled again, crookedly, this time, and took pity on him.

"We've managed not to completely lose control of any really critical systems, Scotty," she told him, and he felt a glow of pleasure at her use of the nickname he hadn't even known she knew, "but McQueen's hit us hard." She grimaced. "The one thing a lot of us have always been afraid of was that eventually someone who knew her ass from her elbow would wind up running the Peep Navy. It had to happen eventually, but we could at least hope that StateSec would keep on shooting anyone competent enough that she might seem to be a threat to the regime. Unfortunately, they haven't shot McQueen, and she's an even tougher customer than most of us were afraid they'd turn up to face us."

She gestured to the space docks beyond the view port.

"We've taken heavier losses in the last T-year than in the previous *three*," she said quietly, "and that doesn't even consider the damage to our infrastructure in Basilisk, Zanzibar, and Alizon. Seaford—" she waved a dismissive hand "—wasn't all that valuable. Oh, there was a lot of prestige and a sense of vengeance on the Peeps' part at having taken the system back. That wasn't good, but, even so, we wouldn't have minded its loss all that much . . . if that idiot Santino hadn't managed to get his entire task group wiped out while inflicting virtually no damage on the Peeps."

Her mouth twisted, but she made herself smooth it back out and inhaled deeply.

"It would be bad enough if McQueen were all we had to worry about," she went on after a moment, "but she's managed to put together a first-rate team to turn her strategy into reality. I believe you've met Citizen Admiral Tourville?" She crooked an eyebrow at Tremaine, and he nodded.

"Yes, Ma'am, I have," he said with feeling. "He's got all the affectations of a true hot dog, but underneath that, he's sharp as they come. As good as just about any Allied officer I've ever heard of."

"Better, Scotty," Truman murmured. "Better. And Giscard may be even better than Tourville. We already knew Theisman was good, of course." She and Tremaine exchanged tight smiles, for both of them had met Thomas Theisman during their first visit to Yeltsin's Star. "I don't think any of the others are really up to their weight, but it doesn't matter very much. McQueen has those three out in the field running her ops, and it looks like she's giving them the cream of the crop as squadron and task group commanders. And if those people aren't up to their standards when they report for duty, every operation they execute also lets them teach their captains and tac officers just a little bit more. So if the war goes on long enough—"

She shrugged her shoulders, and Tremaine nodded slowly. His expression must have been more anxious than he'd thought, because she smiled reassuringly.

"Don't panic, Commander. Yes, they're getting better, but we've still got a few people, like Earl White Haven and Duchess—" they grinned at one another once more, this time broadly "—Harrington, who can kick their butts. And now that I think about it, Admiral Kuzak, Admiral Webster, and Admiral D'Orville aren't that bad, either. But there's no point denying that the opposition is starting to get better, and that's not good when they already have the edge in numbers and their tech transfers from the Sollies are starting to close the gap between their ships' capabilities and our own.

"At the moment, they're not trying to move in and take any of our core systems away from us. They're not even making that big a push to take back the major systems that we've taken away from *them* over the last few years. What they're doing is sniping at us, running in to damage or destroy a handful of our warships or secondary bases wherever they think they see a weakness. And, unfortunately, there are a lot of places where we *are* weak, largely because of the 'citadel' defense the politicians insist on."

" 'Citadel,' Ma'am?" Tremaine repeated, and she snorted.

"That's only my personal term for it, but I think it's appropriate. The problem is that McQueen caught us at the worst possible moment. We'd worn ourselves and our ships out in an effort to maintain our offensive momentum, and no one can get away with that forever. At the moment she hit us, our strength had been heavily drawn down because of how many ships we'd finally been forced to hand over to the yard dogs for refit, and we were screwed." She shrugged. "In hindsight, we should have pulled them back sooner, when we could refit them in smaller numbers, even if it meant slowing our operational tempo. But that's the beauty of hindsight: it always has a lot more to go on than you did when you had to make the decision the first time around.

"At any rate, McQueen obviously understood perfectly that we'd been forced to reduce our strength in what we thought were safe areas in order to maintain our forward concentrations, but no one on our side had dreamed she might be able to convince Pierre and his butchers to let her strike that deep into our rear. So when she did, she caught us with our trousers around our ankles and hit us hard. She took losses of her own, but she could have lost every ship she committed to *all* of her initial ops and still come out ahead just from the physical damage Giscard did in Basilisk. Not to mention Basilisk's political consequences, both foreign and domestic."

She shook her head, and her green eyes were somber.

"Did you hear much from the civilians about that during your leave?"

"More than I wanted to," Tremaine replied grimly, remembering the one true low point of his time at home. His father had taken the entire family out to dinner and insisted he wear his uniform. Personally, Tremaine had suspected his dad hoped someone would recognize *his* son from the newscasts and 'faxes. What none of them had expected was to end up seated next to a man who had lost a lifetime's investment—and a brother who'd stayed behind, trying to make sure all of their employees had evacuated their orbital warehouse complex in time—when Citizen Admiral Giscard hit Basilisk. Worse, the man in question had clearly had too much to drink, and the scene which resulted would live forever in Tremaine's memory. It had started with muttered imprecations and escalated into full-scale screaming before the police arrived to take the man in for disturbing the peace. But worse even than his screamed obscenities and insults had been the tears running down his face . . . and the irrational sense of guilt Tremaine had felt. He'd known at the time that it *was* irrational, but that hadn't made it bite any less deeply.

"I'm not surprised you have." Truman sighed. "Hard to blame them, really. Giscard wiped out sixty T-years of investment, though at least the loss of life was a lot lower than it might have been. Thanks to Giscard's basic decency, really; he waited until the last minute to fire, and there was damn all *we* could have done to stop him if he'd wanted a massacre! But the physical damage was catastrophic enough. White Haven kept him from taking out the Junction forts in Basilisk or retaining permanent control of the system, but that was about all. And truth to tell, I very much doubt Giscard ever planned to keep the system. What he had was a raiding squadron from Hell, not the tonnage to move in and hang onto an entire star system that he and McQueen must have known we'd move Heaven and Hell, not to mention Home Fleet, to take back.

"But once the extent of the damage sank in, the entire Star Kingdom went into a sort of state of shock. We're supposed to do things like that to the *Peeps*, not the other way around, and the fact that we hadn't shook public confidence more severely than I would have believed possible. I won't go so far as to call it panic, but it was ugly, Scotty. Really, really ugly, and all of a sudden, for the first time since the declaration of war, we found political imperatives driving military operations, rather than the reverse."

"I've heard the Opposition's side of it, Ma'am." Tremaine's tone mirrored the disgust in his expression. "Especially from the Palmer Institute and that son-of-a— Uh, I mean that *jackass* Houseman."

"No, you meant 'son-of-a-bitch.'" Truman's eyes twinkled, despite her earlier bleakness. "And you were right, although, personally, I prefer 'unmitigated, fatheaded, self-serving, vindictive bastard,' myself."

"If you say so, Ma'am. After all, far be it from me to argue with a flag officer!"

"Wise of you, Commander. Very wise," she said, but then the twinkle faded and her voice turned serious once more. "But if you've heard them, you know what the Government was up against. People were scared, and the Opposition chose to play on that fear. I try to remind myself to be fair, because it probably really is true that a lot of them actually believed what they were saying, but people like High Ridge and Descroix were definitely playing it for political advantage and hang the consequences for the war."

"What consequences were those, Ma'am?" Tremaine asked quietly.

"The citadel defense, of course," Truman said sourly. "The Government didn't dare risk getting hit that hard in another core system, so they demanded that the Admiralty redeploy to make sure we wouldn't be." She waved both hands, the gesture rich with frustration. "Don't get me wrong, Scotty. We probably would have done a lot of what they wanted, in the short term, anyway, with no pressure at all, because a lot of it made sense, at least until we'd had time to analyze what McQueen had done to us and get a feel for what she was likely to try next. But we had to redeploy much more radically than anyone at the Admiralty wanted, and any offensive action of our own has been paralyzed ever since."

"But—" Scotty cut off his incipient protest. She'd been far more open than he'd had any right to expect, and he warned himself not to abuse her frankness. But she only gestured for him to go on, and he drew a deep breath.

"I understand what you're saying, Ma'am," he said, "but what about Eighth Fleet? Surely that's an offensive force, isn't it? And Admiral White Haven certainly seemed to be just about ready to go when we were in Trevor's Star."

"I'm sure he did," Truman conceded. "And, yes, Eighth Fleet is our primary offensive force . . . *officially*. But while I'm certain White Haven, Admiral Caparelli, and the Prime Minister would all just love to turn him loose, they're not going to do it."

"They're not?" Surprise betrayed the question out of Tremaine, and Truman shrugged.

"No one's told me so officially, but it's pretty clear what they're really doing, Scotty. Of course, I've got access to some information you don't, which probably makes it a little more obvious to me. But think about it. Home Fleet hasn't been materially reinforced. The Basilisk forts have been beefed up, and the unfinished ones have been brought on-line to cover the Junction terminus there. In addition, the system picket is about twice as strong as it was, and the Gryphon Squadron's been upgraded to a heavy task group. But that's all that's changed here in the Star Kingdom, because we've been forced to send every ship we possibly could to strengthen our *allies'* defenses. They got their own shock treatment out of Zanzibar and Alizon, and the Government's been forced to do a lot of reassuring the only way it could: with ships of the wall.

"But we also need to be ready to meet any threat to the Star Kingdom itself, and that's what Eighth Fleet is really doing. White Haven demonstrated the strategic advantages of the Junction when he beat the Peeps to the Basilisk terminus all the way from Trevor's Star. So what we're trying to do is shake Eighth Fleet as threateningly as we possibly can under McQueen's and Theisman's noses by looming ominously over Barnett while what Eighth Fleet *actually* is is the strategic reserve for the Star Kingdom."

"Um." Tremaine scratched an eyebrow, then nodded slowly. "I can see that, Ma'am. And I can see why we can't exactly tell the public not to worry because Eighth Fleet is covering the home systems. I mean, if we told our people that, we'd also be telling the Peeps they don't have to worry about its coming after them, wouldn't we?"

"We would. Of course, McQueen is more than smart enough to figure it out for herself. At the same time, she has to honor the threat, because she might be wrong. But what's really disturbing to me about it, aside from the fact that letting the other side pick its own time and place to hit us is the strategy of weakness, is that I feel quite sure the Opposition has had it explained to them in confidential briefings." She saw the question in Tremaine's eye and shrugged. "It's traditional to keep the Opposition leadership informed in time of war. In theory the Cromarty Government could fall at any moment, in which case we might find the Opposition parties being forced to form a government. I spend the odd sleepless night praying it will never happen, but if it did, any lost time while they figured out what was happening could be disastrous."

"I know that, Ma'am. I don't especially like the thought, but I understand why it has to be done. I was just a bit confused as to why you found that disturbing?"

"Because even though they have to know what the PM and the Admiralty are doing, no one could possibly guess it from their public statements. Have you actually read any of the Opposition 'faxes? Seen their editorials?"

"No, not really. I suppose I ought to, but—"

It was Tremaine's turn to shrug, uncomfortably, and Truman snorted.

"I don't blame you for avoiding them. In fact, I tend to do the same. But if you skim them, you'll find they're going right on viewing with alarm. They're being careful to avoid language which could too obviously be called scare-mongering or alarmist, but they're still gnawing away at public confidence in the Cromarty Government just as hard as they can. In my own opinion, they're doing it purely for political advantage . . . and they know the Duke can't publically rebut their charges or explain what he's really doing with Eighth Fleet without telling the Peeps, as well."

"But surely they have to realize they're also undermining confidence in the war itself!"

"Some of them undoubtedly do. But they—or their leadership, at least—don't care. They're completely focused on the political front, so completely that actually fighting the war is secondary. Besides, *they* don't have to take responsibility for what happens at the front; Duke Cromarty and the Admiralty do."

"That's . . . disgusting," Tremaine said quietly.

"I suppose it is," Truman agreed, but her tone was thoughtful. "On the other hand, it's also very human. Don't misunderstand me, Scotty. I'm not saying these people are inherently evil, or deliberately trying to lose the war. Some of them, like High Ridge, Janacek, and a couple of New Kiev's advisers do fall into the category of 'evil' as far as I'm concerned . . . and you don't want to get me started on Sheridan Wallace! They're the manipulators who don't give a good goddamn about anything but their own personal interests. Most of the rest are like Houseman, only less so, thank God! They're genuinely uninformed about military realities, but they think they know all about the subject, and their military advisers aren't exactly what I'd consider the best available. No doubt said advisers would feel the same way about me if our roles were reversed, however, and the fact that I think they're stupid doesn't make them evil. Nor does it make the people who rely on their advice evil. But if New Kiev genuinely believes that Cromarty is handling the entire war wrongly and that his commitment to a clear-cut, military resolution of our differences with someone the size of the Peeps can lead only to ultimate disaster, then she has a moral responsibility to do something about it. As she sees it, that's exactly what she's doing, and while I've never been much of a fan of the notion that the end justifies the means, she clearly accepts it."

The golden-haired rear admiral shook herself, and her tone changed.

"But be that as it may," she said briskly, "it's the Navy's job to get on with fighting the war, not to sit around and complain over the way the politicians are running it. Which is what this is all about."

She jutted her chin out the port at the space docks, and Tremaine nodded. When an admiral decided to change the subject, lesser mortals followed her lead. Expeditiously.

"What we're hoping," Truman went on, "is that whether or not Eighth Fleet succeeds in holding McQueen's attention, she'll go on pecking at peripheral systems long enough for us to get ready to go back over to the offensive ourselves. We've made a lot more progress on bringing our maintenance cycles back up to snuff than the Peeps know—or than we *hope* they know, anyway—and our critical-system pickets are much stronger than they were even four or five months ago. At the same time, the Graysons are building ships like maniacs, and between us, we've produced a solid core of *Harring*—I mean *Medusas* that we hope the Peeps don't know about. And the Admiralty's moving right ahead with plans to shut down Junction forts here in Manticore, which is releasing hundreds of thousands of personnel from Fortress Command to Fleet duty. And while all that's going on, we're building the ships for those people to crew and rushing them through their working up periods as quickly as we can. In fact, we're probably pushing them through a bit more quickly than we ought to, and I'm more than a little concerned about soft spots and green units. That's one reason I was so delighted to discover you were available for assignment here."

Tremaine straightened. It sounded as if she meant she'd specifically asked for him, and if she had, it was one of the highest professional compliments he'd ever been paid.

"I take it you've been briefed on the new carriers?" she asked, and he nodded.

"Not fully, Ma'am. They told me I'd be receiving my detailed brief when I reported for duty. But they certainly told me enough to whet my appetite for more!"

"I thought it would have that effect," she told him with a smile. "I remembered Lady Harrington bragging on what a hot-shot boat bay officer and pinnace pilot you were back when I commanded *Parnassus*, and I knew you'd worked closely with Jackie Harmon." Her eyes darkened, and Tremaine's mouth tightened. He had worked with Commander Harmon closely, and liked her a lot, and the news that she'd been killed in action under Truman's command in Hancock had hit him hard.

"At any rate," Truman went on more briskly, "I knew you were familiar with the first generation of the new LACs, and when I put all that together, you were at the very top of a very short list of officers who have that sort of background. You're still a bit junior for the slot I want to put you into, but I think you can hack it. Especially with the command experience you picked up in Cerberus with Lady Harrington."

"Thank you, Ma'am . . . I think." Tremaine couldn't keep himself from adding the last two words, but Truman only smiled.

"I hope you still feel that way after the next couple of months, Commander," she told him, and pointed once more at the ship in the nearest space dock. "According to the yard dogs, that ship will be ready for acceptance trials next week. If they're right, you'll be aboard her when she runs them."

"I will?"

"Indeed you will, Scotty. And once she commissions, I will personally run you, and everyone else aboard her, until you drop. And when you do, I'll jerk you back up by the scruff of the neck and start running you all over again, because you and I, for our sins, are going to be the cutting edge of the offensive we're planning on launching."

"We are, Ma'am? I mean—"

"I know exactly what you mean," Truman assured him, "and don't worry about it. You're a bright young fellow, and I know from experience that you're motivated, hardworking, and quite a bit more disciplined than you care to appear. In fact—" she smiled lazily "—now that I think about it, you're also quite a bit like Lester Tourville yourself, aren't you, Commander? All the affectations of a real hot dog . . . but with the ability to back it up."

Tremaine only looked at her. There was, after all, very little he could say in response, and she chuckled.

"I hope you are, anyway, Scotty, because that's exactly what I need. 'Fighter jocks,' Jackie called them. That's what we need for LAC crews . . . and as the new CO of HMS *Hydra*'s LAC wing, it's going to be your job to build them for me!"

CHAPTER EIGHT

"**D**uchess Harrington is here, Sir Thomas," the Admiralty yeoman announced, and stood to one side, holding the old-fashioned manual door wide. Honor stepped through it with an expression she hoped concealed a certain inner trepidation, and the barrel-chested man behind the landing pad-sized desk rose to greet her.

"Your Grace," he said, holding out his hand, and she hid a small smile as she crossed the bright, wood-paneled office to take it. The protocol was just a *bit* complicated, and she wondered if Admiral Caparelli had consulted the experts on how to handle it or if he was simply feeling his way along as he went.

In every way but one—well, two, actually—she was now this man's superior. In Yeltsin, of course, where she was Steadholder Harrington, that had been true for years. But now she was Duchess Harrington here in the Star Kingdom, as well. Her good eye gleamed with pure, unadulterated gloating as she recalled the stifled expressions on quite a few noble lords and ladies as the woman they had excluded from their midst was seated among them as the most junior duchess of the Star Kingdom . . . who just happened to outrank ninety-plus percent of the rest of the peerage. Despite lingering doubts over the wisdom of creating her new title, she had to admit that the looks on the faces of Stefan Young, Twelfth Earl of North Hollow, and Michael Janvier, Ninth Baron of High Ridge, were going to remain two of her fondest memories when (or if) she reached her dotage.

Another treasured recollection would be the speeches of welcome from the Opposition leadership. She'd listened attentively, her expression grave, while Nimitz lay in his awkward curl in her lap and both of them tasted the actual emotions behind the utterly sincere voices. It wasn't particularly nice to know how much the people doing the talking hated her, and the way they'd gushed about her "heroism" and her "courage, determination, and infinite resourcefulness" had been faintly nauseating, but that was all right. She and Nimitz had known precisely what the speakers actually felt, and she'd been faintly surprised when High Ridge hadn't fallen down and died in an apoplectic fit. Countess New Kiev hadn't been much better, although at least her teeth-gritting rage had seemed more directed at the obstacle Honor presented to her plans and policies and less tinged with the personal hatred radiating from High Ridge and North Hollow.

And it's not like there weren't at least as many—heck, a lot more!—people who were genuinely pleased over it, she reminded herself.

But she'd been Duchess Harrington for barely three weeks, and her new dignities were still an uncomfortable fit.

They were probably just as big a problem for some of the people around her as they were for her, however, and Sir Thomas Caparelli had every right to be one of them. He'd been First Space Lord since the first day of the war, when Honor had been merely one of his more junior captains of the list. Even now, she was only a commodore in Manticoran service, and the last time she'd been in the Star Kingdom, she'd been no more than the designated commander of a heavy cruiser squadron . . . which hadn't even been formed yet! She was relieved to taste no resentment from him over the heights to which she'd risen since, but there was an undeniable awkwardness, as if he were still in the process of adjusting his thinking to allow for her latest, unwanted elevation.

But there was also a genuine sense of gratitude for her survival, and his handclasp was firm. Nor had it been inappropriate for him to initiate the handshake, although some of the more supercilious sticklers among her fellow nobles (like High Ridge) would undoubtedly have looked down their aristocratic noses at him for his presumption. A *proper* greeting would have been a small, courteous bow, preferably with a respectful click of the heels . . . and a little scraping to go with the bow. When all was said and done, after all, Thomas Caparelli was a mere commoner who'd won his lowly knighthood for service to the Crown rather than inheriting it as a *true* noble would have.

But that was all right with Honor. Those were the sorts of nobles who represented what she had always considered to be the greatest flaw in a generally satisfactory society and system of government, and she could scarcely have cared less for their good opinion, whereas she valued that of Caparelli. And as far as she was concerned, the two ways in which he continued to outrank her were at least as important as any elevations which had come her way.

Like her, he was also a knight of the Order of King Roger, but while Honor had risen to the rank of Knight Commander following First Hancock, Caparelli was a Knight Grand Cross. Even more importantly, particularly in this office and under these circumstances, every single uniformed member of the Royal Manticoran Navy answered directly to him ... including Commodore Honor Harrington.

"It's good to see you," he went on now, regarding her measuringly. "I understand Bassingford has signed off on your fitness to return to limited duty?"

"Not without a fair amount of hemming and hawing, I'm afraid," Honor agreed with a small smile. "They've finished their exams, and my med records have been duly reactivated from the dead files, but I think the fact that I don't regenerate and do reject nerve grafts bothers them more than they want to admit. What they really want to do is keep me wrapped up in cotton until they get the new nerves installed and the new arm built ... and they're not too happy about the fact that I'm going to have the work done outside Navy channels."

"I'm not surprised." Caparelli snorted. Unlike too many people, Honor was pleased to note, he felt no need to shy away from a frank evaluation of her injuries. Of course, he'd been scraped up with a spatula himself when he was only a captain. Unlike her, he'd been able to take advantage of regeneration, but he'd put in his own time in the doctors' and therapists' clutches along the way.

"Bassingford Medical Center is probably the finest single hospital in the Star Kingdom," the First Space Lord went on conversationally while he guided Honor towards the comfortable chairs grouped around a polished crystal coffee table to one side of his desk. "The Navy's tried to make it that, anyway, and it's certainly the biggest. But that can be both a plus and a minus, since BuMed clearly hates to admit that no one can be the best there is at *everything*. I suspect they probably also feel just a little piqued with themselves for losing your father to civilian practice. Still, once they calm down, they'll realize only a lunatic would fail to avail themselves of his expertise if it was available."

There was a strange undertone to his emotions, and Honor cocked her head as she sank into the indicated chair with Nimitz while Caparelli seated himself facing her.

"Excuse me, Sir Thomas, but that sounded rather like a personal observation."

"Because it was." The First Space Lord smiled. "Your father was Chief of Neurosurgery at Bassingford after that little misadventure of mine in Silesia, and he did a far better job of reassembling all my bits and pieces than anyone expected. He cut way down on the amount of regen I had to survive along the way, and I rather doubt that he's gotten anything but better since." He shook his head firmly. "You go right ahead and ignore anyone at Bassingford who tries to talk you into letting them do the work, Your Grace. They're good, but 'good' is no substitute for the best there is."

"Why, thank you, Sir Thomas. I never knew Daddy was one of your physicians, but I'll certainly tell him what you just said. I'm sure it will mean a great deal to him."

"It's no more than the truth. And no more than what I said to him at the time, for that matter," Caparelli said with a chuckle. "Of course, I imagine people in his line of work hear a lot of that sort of thing from the patients whose lives they put back together."

He leaned back in his chair, eyes focused on something Honor couldn't see for several seconds, then shook himself.

"But I didn't ask you to visit me to talk about that, Your Grace," he said more briskly. "Or, at least, not to talk about it beyond being certain you've been cleared to return to duty. What I actually wanted was to offer you a job. Two of them, really."

"Two jobs, Sir Thomas?"

"Yes. Well, there was one other point I wanted to address, but we can get to that later. First, I'd like to tell you what I had in mind for letting us get the most good we can out of you while you're stuck here in the Star Kingdom anyway."

He leaned still further back, crossed his legs, and interlaced his fingers across his raised knee, and Honor could feel the intensity of his thoughts. She was rather surprised by some of what she sensed, for Caparelli had never had a reputation as a thinker. No one had ever accused him of stupidity, but he'd always had the sort of direct, shortest-distance-between-two-points, linear approach that went through obstacles, generally rather forcefully, rather than around them. It was a personality which went well with his weight-lifter's torso and wrestler's arms, but there had always been those who felt he was just a little short of . . . finesse for a flag officer of his seniority.

Now, as she sampled his emotions and as he marshaled his thoughts, she knew his critics had been wrong. It was possible he'd changed since becoming First Space Lord and finding himself responsible for directing the Star Kingdom's and, for all intents and purposes, the entire Manticoran Alliance's combat operations, but she felt very little of the bull in a china shop he was supposed to be. He might not be a supporter of an indirect approach to many problems, and he would never, she suspected, be the intellectual equal of someone like Hamish Alexander. But there was an almost frightening discipline behind his dark eyes, and a toughness and tenacity—an unwavering determination—which she suddenly realized might just make him a perfect choice for his present position.

"What I had in mind, Your Grace," he began after a moment, "was to use you at Saganami Island. I realize that's not very conveniently placed for access to your father's hospital on Sphinx, but it's only a few hours away, and we would, of course, make Navy transport available and coordinate your schedule around your treatment's timetable."

He paused, looking at her questioningly, and she twitched a small shrug while she stroked Nimitz's ears.

"I feel sure we could work around that, Sir Thomas. Daddy may be a civilian now, but he was an officer for twenty-odd T-years. He's well aware of how even 'limited duty' can complicate a course of treatment, and he's already told me he'll do everything he can to eliminate scheduling conflicts. For that matter, he and Doctor Heinrich, one of his colleagues here on Manticore, have already discussed the possibility of his using Doctor Heinrich's facilities rather than my shuttling back and forth between here and Sphinx."

"That would be an excellent arrangement from the Service's viewpoint," Caparelli said enthusiastically. "At the same time, your health and recovery come first. If it turns out that you need to return to Sphinx, even full time, until you're fit to return to full, active duty, I would expect you to tell us. I trust you understand that."

"Of course I do, Sir," Honor replied, and to her surprise, he snorted.

"Easy for you to say, Your Grace, but I've talked with several of your ex-COs, including Mark Sarnow and Earl White Haven. Even Yancey Parks. And every one of them warned me that I'd have to have someone watch over you with a club if I really expected you to put your health above what you fondly conceive to be your duty!"

"That's a bit of an overstatement, Sir." Honor felt her right cheek heat and shook her head. "I'm the daughter of two physicians. Whatever anyone else may think, I'm not foolish enough to ignore doctor's orders."

"That isn't exactly what Surgeon Captain Montoya told me," Caparelli observed with what the uncharitable might have called a grin, and she felt his fresh amusement as her blush darkened. "But that's neither here nor there . . . as long as I have your word that you *will* inform us if you need additional down time for medical reasons?"

"You do, Sir," she said, just a bit stiffly, and he nodded.

"Good! In that case, let me explain what Admiral Cortez and I have in mind."

Despite herself, Honor's eyebrow quirked at that. Sir Lucien Cortez was Fifth Space Lord, in charge of the Bureau of Personnel. In many respects, his was the hardest Navy job of all, for it was his responsibility to manage the Service's enormous manpower demands, and he'd shown a positive genius for making the available supply of bodies stretch. As BuPers' CO, the Naval Academy on Saganami Island fell within his sphere for rather obvious reasons, but she was surprised that he'd gotten personally involved in deciding how the Academy might best make use of a simple commodore. But her surprise passed quickly, because, of course, she *wasn't* a "simple commodore" anymore, whether she liked it or not.

"As you know," Caparelli went on, "we've been steadily increasing the size of the Saganami student body since the war began, but I doubt that anyone who hasn't spent some time there could fully realize how much its composition has changed. A bit less than half our total midshipmen are now from out-kingdom, from various Allied navies, and probably thirty percent of those allied personnel are Graysons. We've graduated well over nine thousand Grayson officers since Protector Benjamin joined the Alliance."

"I knew the number was high, Sir, but I hadn't realized it was quite *that* high."

"Few people do." Caparelli shrugged. "On the other hand, there were about eighty-five hundred in our last graduating class, and eleven hundred of them were Graysons. In addition, we've accelerated the curriculum to run each form through in just three T-years . . . and this year's first form will have well over eleven thousand in it."

Both Honor's eyes widened. There'd been only two hundred and forty-one in her own graduating class . . . but that had been thirty-five T-years ago. She'd known the Academy had expanded steadily over most of those three and a half decades, and that its expansion had become explosive in the last ten or eleven T-years, but still—

"I never imagined we were turning out that many ensigns every year," she murmured, and Caparelli shrugged again.

"I wish the number were twice as high, Your Grace," he said bluntly. "But one of the core advantages which have let us take the war to the Peeps despite the numerical odds has been the difference in our officer corps' training and traditions. We're not about to throw that edge away, which means we can't cut the training time any shorter than we already have. We've called up a lot of reservists, and we're running even more mustangs through the Fleet OCS program, of course, but that's not quite the same. Most of the reservists require at least three or four months of refresher training to blow the rust off, but they already have the basic skills. And the mustangs are all experienced enlisted or noncoms. We've adjusted our criteria a bit to reflect the realities of our manpower requirements, and we make some exceptions in the cases of truly outstanding candidates, but on average, they've all got a minimum of at least five T-years of experience."

Honor nodded. For all its aristocratic traditions, the RMN had always boasted a remarkably high percentage of "mustangs," enlisted personnel or petty officers who'd chosen (or, sometimes, been convinced) to seek commissioned rank via the Fleet Officer Candidate School program. The FOCS cycle ran a bit less than half as long as that of the Academy, but that was because its personnel were already professionals. There was no need to instill in them the platform of basic military skills, and their lower deck origins gave them a tough, pragmatic view of the Navy which the "trade school" graduates often needed surprisingly badly.

"But the core of our officer corps," Caparelli went on, "is still the supply we graduate from Saganami, and we are absolutely determined to preserve its quality. Moreover, there are very compelling reasons for us to graduate as many Allied officers from the Academy as possible. If nothing else, it's one way of making sure we and our allies are on the same page when we discuss military options, and the fact that they're completely familiar with our doctrine helps eliminate a lot of potential confusion from joint operations.

"Unfortunately, maintaining quality while steadily increasing quantity leaves us chronically short of teaching staff, especially in the Tactical curriculum. The Star Kingdom produces plenty of qualified teachers for most areas—from hyperphysics to astrogation to gravitics to molycircs—but there's only one place to learn naval tactics."

"I can see that, Sir," Honor agreed.

"Then I suspect you're also beginning to see where we want to make use of you. Without wanting to embarrass you, you've demonstrated rather conclusively that you're one of our better tacticians, Your Grace." Honor made herself meet his gaze levelly, and he went on calmly. "You've also, Lucien tells me, shown a particular knack for polishing the rough edges of junior officers. At my request, he pulled the jackets on several officers who've served under you, and I was most impressed with the professionalism, dedication, and skill you seem to have instilled into them. I was especially impressed by the way Captain Cardones and Commander Tremaine have performed."

"Rafe and Scotty—I mean, Captain Cardones and Commander Tremaine—were very junior when they first served with me, Sir," Honor protested. "Neither of them had yet had the opportunity to show his full capabilities, and it's hardly fair to say that they've performed so well since then because of anything *I* may have done!"

"I said I was particularly impressed by them, Your Grace, not that they were the only ones who seem to have responded to your touch. In point of fact, however, Lucien ran an analysis, and there's a clear correlation between the time officers spend under your command and the subsequent improvement in their efficiency ratings."

Honor opened her mouth once more, but he waved a hand before she could speak.

"I said I didn't want to embarrass you, so let's not belabor the point, Your Grace. Instead, let's just say Lucien and I think you could be of great benefit to Saganami's Tactical Department and let it go at that, all right?"

There was nothing she could do but nod, and he smiled with an edge of sympathy that echoed even more strongly through her link to Nimitz.

"Actually, the large number of Grayson midshipmen was another reason we wanted you," he told her. "Some of them have problems making the transition from such an, um, traditional society to the Star Kingdom's. It helps that they're disciplined and determined to succeed, but there have still been a few incidents, and one or two have had the potential to turn ugly. We've imported as many Grayson instructors as we can to try to alleviate that, but the supply of qualified Graysons is limited, and the GSN needs them on active fleet service even worse than we need their Manticoran counterparts. Having you available, both as an advisor to the faculty and as a role model for Grayson and Manticoran midshipmen alike, will be very valuable to us."

That much, at least, Honor could accept without quibbles, and she nodded again.

"Good! In that case, what we'd like to do is assign you two slots in Introductory Tactics. It's a lecture course, so class size is large, but we'll also assign you three or four teaching assistants, which should let you keep your office hours within reason. I hope it will, anyway, because we've got a couple of other things we'd like you to do for us while we've got you."

"Oh?" Honor regarded him suspiciously. There was something going on behind those eyes, but even with her link to Nimitz, she couldn't figure out exactly what.

"Yes. One of them will be to make yourself available for an occasional conference with Alice Truman. You heard about her action at Hancock?"

"I did," Honor agreed.

"Well, she was already on the short list for flag rank, and Hancock accelerated the process, so she's now Rear Admiral of the Red Truman. And she's also Knight Companion Dame Alice Truman. I was quite honored when Her Majesty asked me to dub her into the Order."

"Good for her!" Honor said.

"Agreed. And well deserved, too. But in addition to her new rank, she's also in charge of training and working up our new LAC carriers. She and Captain Harmon did wonders with *Minotaur*'s original wing, as they amply demonstrated in action. But Captain Harmon's death was a tragedy in a lot of ways . . . including the loss of her experience and perspective. Especially since we've made some major modifications to the *Shrike* design, based on experience in Hancock. We're still working out what that means in terms of doctrine, and since you wrote the final WDB specs for the original *Shrike*-class LACs, not to mention your experience creating LAC doctrine in Silesia with your Q-ships, we think you could be of major assistance to Dame Alice, even if it's only by acting as a sounding board for her own concepts. She's going to be nailed down to *Weyland*, where we're building the carriers, but you could certainly correspond, and she'll be here on Manticore fairly often for face-to-face discussion."

"I'm not sure how much help I could actually be, but of course I'd be delighted to do anything I can, Sir."

"Good. And, now that I think about it, you'll probably be in a better position than most to game out and evaluate new doctrine," Caparelli said, in an offhand sort of tone which was a very poor match for the sudden peak of anticipation in his emotions, and Honor looked up sharply.

"I will?" she said, and he nodded. "May I ask why that might be, Sir?" she asked when he failed to volunteer anything more.

"Certainly, Your Grace. You'll be well positioned because of your access to the ATC simulators."

"Access?" Honor frowned.

The Advanced Tactical Course, otherwise known (to its survivors) as "the Crusher," was the make-or-break hurdle for any RMN officer who ever hoped to advance beyond the rank of lieutenant commander. Or, at least, to advance beyond that rank as a line officer. A handful of officers, including Honor, might have commanded destroyers without first surviving the Crusher, but no one who failed the Crusher would ever command any starship bigger than that. Those who washed out were often retained for nonline branches and even promoted, especially now that the long-anticipated war with Haven had arrived, but they would never again wear the white beret of a hyper-capable warship's CO. Even those who, like Honor, had commanded DDs before passing ATC were few and far between . . . and they'd become even fewer over the last ten or twelve T-years. Being selected for ATC was the coveted proof that an officer had been picked out for starship command. That her superiors had sufficient faith in her abilities to entrust her with the authority to act as her Queen's direct, personal representative in situations where she might well be months of communication time away from any superior officer.

And because that was so, the Crusher was, and deliberately so, the toughest, most demanding course known to man . . . or as close to that as the Royal Manticoran Navy had been able to come in four T-centuries of constant experimentation and improvement. The ATC Center was also on Saganami Island, attached to the Academy campus, but it was a completely separate facility, with its own faculty and commandant. Honor's own time there had been among the most exhausting and mind-numbing of her career, but it had also been one of the most exhilarating six T-months of her entire life. She'd loved the challenge, and the fact that ATC's commandant at the time had been Raoul Courvosier, her own Academy instructor and beloved mentor, had only made it better.

Even so, she was at a loss to understand what Caparelli was driving at. Any Academy tactical instructor could request time on one of the ATC's smaller simulators or holo tanks, but they had access to almost equally good equipment right there in Ellen D'Orville Hall. And if the Navy was punching out new officers—and, presumably, new *commanding* officers—at the rate Caparelli had just described, then no one outside the ATC itself was going to have much access to the big, full-capability simulators and tanks reserved for the Crusher and the Naval College.

"Well, I certainly *hope* you'll have access," Caparelli told her. "It would be most improper for the staff to refuse to allow sim time for their own commandant!"

"For—?" Honor stared at him, and he grinned like a naughty little boy. But then his grin faded, and he raised one hand, palm uppermost before him.

"I've already said you're one of our best tacticians, Your Grace," he said quietly, "and you are. If it hadn't been for how badly we needed you in the field—and, of course, for the political fallout after your duel with North Hollow—we'd've dragged you back to teach tactics years ago. Unfortunately, we've never been able to spare you from front-line command . . . until now. I would certainly prefer for you to abandon this habit of getting yourself shot up, but if you're going to be stuck here in the Star Kingdom for a while anyway, then we intend to make maximum possible use of you!"

"But there's no way I'd have time to do the job properly!" Honor protested. "Especially not if you've got me lecturing at the Academy!"

"In the prewar sense, no. You wouldn't have time. But we've had to make some changes there, as well. The staff is much larger now, and in addition to your regular XO, you'll have several very good deputies. We'd obviously like as much hands-on time as you can spare, but your primary responsibility will be to thoroughly evaluate the current curriculum and syllabus in terms of your own experience and propose any changes you feel are desirable. We've reduced the normal tenure for the commandant to two T-years, largely because of our desire to cycle as many experienced combat commanders through the slot as we can. We're aware that your medical treatment shouldn't take much more than a year, however, and as soon as the medicos sign off for your return to full, active duty, we'll find a replacement. But you have a great deal of experience to share with the prospective commanders of Her Majesty's starships, paid for in blood, more often than not. We cannot afford to let that experience escape us . . . and you owe it to the men and women passing through ATC, and to the men and women they will command, to see to it that they have the very best and most demanding training we can possibly give them."

"I—" Honor began, then stopped. He was right, of course. She might argue about whether or not she was the best woman for the job, but he was right about how important the job itself was.

"You may be right, Sir," she said instead, trying another approach, "but ATC has always been an admiral's billet, and if you've expanded it as much as it sounds like, I'd think that would be even more true now than when *I* went through it." Caparelli listened gravely, then pursed his lips and nodded. "Well, I realize I carry an admiral's rank in the Grayson Navy, but ATC is a *Manticoran* facility. I'd think there'd be an awful lot of stepped-on toes and out-of-joint noses if you brought in a Grayson to command it."

"That might be true of any other Grayson, Your Grace. We don't expect it to be a problem here. And if you're concerned about it, we could always put you in command as an RMN officer, instead."

"But that was my point, Sir. I don't have the seniority for the post as a Manticoran: only as a Grayson. As a Manticoran, I'm only a commodore."

"Oh, I see what you're getting at now," Caparelli said, and once again his thoughtful tone was completely at odds with the bubbling mischievousness behind his sober expression. He sat there for several seconds, rubbing his chin, then shrugged. "That may be a valid concern," he admitted. "I doubt it would be the problem you seem to be assuming it could, but it *might* cause some friction. I suspect, however, that there are countervailing considerations of which you are, as yet, unaware."

"Countervailing?" Honor repeated, and his sobriety vanished into a huge grin as he heard the suspicion in her voice. Yet he didn't answer immediately. Instead, he reached into the pocket of his tunic and withdrew a small case.

"I believe I said there was one other matter I meant to discuss with you, and I suppose this may be as good a time as any." He held the case out to her. "I think you'll find the explanation of those countervailing considerations in here, Your Grace," he said.

She took it gingerly. It was a fairly typical jeweler's case, with two thumb notches for a magnetic lock. Like many routine tasks whose performance two-handed people took for granted, opening it presented a daunting challenge for a woman with only one, but Nimitz reached out an imperious, long-fingered true-hand. She smiled and handed it over, and his busy fingers did what she could not.

The lid sprang open, and Nimitz peered into the case, then bleeked in profound satisfaction. Honor's eyebrows went up as she tasted his pleasure, but she couldn't see past his prick-eared head until he looked up and passed the case back to her.

She glanced into it . . . and her breath caught.

Nestled into a bed of space-black velvet were two small triangles, each made up of three nine-pointed golden stars.

She recognized them, of course. How could she not recognize the collar insignia of a full admiral of the Royal Manticoran Navy?

She looked up, her expression stunned, and Caparelli chuckled.

"Sir, this— I mean, I never expected—" Her voice broke, and he shrugged.

"In point of fact, Your Grace, I believe this is the first time in the Star Kingdom's history that an officer has been jumped straight from commodore to admiral in one fell swoop. On the other hand, you've been an admiral in Grayson service for years now, and performed in exemplary fashion in that role. And you did spend two years in grade as a commodore, you know . . . although I understand you chose to act in your Grayson persona for most of that time in an effort to defuse certain seniority problems."

His voice turned darker with the last words, and Honor understood perfectly. Rear Admiral Harold Styles had been allowed to resign his commission rather than face trial on the charges of insubordination and cowardice she'd laid against him, but not everyone felt that was sufficient punishment.

"We've decided you shouldn't have to face that particular problem again," Caparelli told her. "Besides, you and I both know that only political considerations delayed your promotion to commodore as long as we had to wait. Those considerations no longer apply, and we *need* flag officers like you."

"But *three* grades—!"

"I think it likely you would have made vice admiral before your capture but for the caliber of your political enemies," Caparelli said, and she tasted his sincerity. "Had that been the case, then an additional promotion out of the zone would certainly have been appropriate after your return, given the nature of your escape and the multiple engagements you fought in the process." He shrugged. "I won't deny that there's an element of politics in jumping you quite this far in a single leap, Your Grace. I understand you turned down the PMV, and Baroness Morncreek passed along the reasons you gave Her Majesty and Duke Cromarty. I respect your decision, although I also think you've amply demonstrated that you deserve that award. This promotion, however, is quite another matter. Yes, it will offer political advantages to Cromarty and the Foreign Office. Yes, it will make Grayson happy—not a minor concern in its own right. And, yes, it's a way to punch the Peeps right in the eye by showing how we regard their charges against you. But it's also something you have absolutely and demonstrably earned, both in the Queen's service and as the woman who won at Fourth Yeltsin and Cerberus in someone else's uniform."

"But, Sir—"

"The discussion is closed, Admiral Harrington," Sir Thomas Caparelli said, and there was no mistaking the command in his voice. "The Promotions Board, the General Board of Admiralty, the First Space Lord, the First Lord of the Admiralty, the Prime Minister of Manticore, and the Queen have all reached the same conclusions; the chairman of the Military Affairs Committee assures Duke Cromarty that the promotion will be duly approved; and you are *not* allowed to argue with us. Is that understood?"

"Yes, Sir." The live side of Honor's mouth quivered just a little, and Caparelli smiled.

"Good! In that case, why don't I take you over to Cosmo's for lunch? I understand a few dozen or so of your closest friends are waiting to help you celebrate your promotion—I can't imagine who could have let the 'cat out of the bag to them about it—and after that, we can hop out to Saganami Island and let you meet your new staff."

CHAPTER NINE

"This just gets worse and worse," Rob Pierre sighed as he skimmed Leonard Boardman's synopsis of his latest gleanings from the Solarian League reporters covering the PRH. "How can one person—*one* person, Oscar!—do this much damage? She's like some damned elemental force of nature!"

"Harrington?" Oscar Saint-Just quirked an eyebrow and snorted harshly at Pierre's nodded confirmation.

"She's just happened to be in the right places—or the wrong ones, I suppose, from our perspective—for the last, oh, ten years or so. That's the official consensus from my analysts, at least. The other theory, which seems to have been gaining a broader following of late, is that she's in league with the Devil."

Despite himself, Pierre chuckled. The jest, such as it was, was bitterly ironic, but that didn't deprive it of its point. Especially from someone as dour and emotionless as Saint-Just. But then the Chairman sobered and shook his head.

"Let's be honest with ourselves, Oscar. She's managed it in no small part because *we've* fucked up. Oh, I have no doubt she's at least as capable as the Manties think she is, but her effect was pretty well localized until we decided to tell the universe we'd hanged her! Aside from a few stories buried in the back files of one or two of the Solly 'faxes, no one in the Solarian League had ever even heard of her. Now everyone, with the possible exception of a few neobarbs on planets no one's gotten around to rediscovering yet, knows who she is. And what she's done to us."

"Agreed." Saint-Just sighed. "And in the name of honesty, we might as well admit it was my people who did the major share of the fucking up. We can't do much about punishing Tresca, of course, but Thornegrave survived his share of the fiasco."

Pierre nodded. Brigadier Dennis Tresca had been the StateSec commander of Hades, and Major General Prestwick Thornegrave had been the officer, also in StateSec, who'd lost an entire transport fleet and its escorts to Harrington. Which had provided her with the warships to completely destroy Seth Chernock's task force and capture its ground combat component's transports. Which, in turn, had provided the additional personnel lift she'd needed to pull out every single prisoner who'd opted to join her.

"We could always shoot him for his part in letting her escape," Saint-Just went on. "Politically, he's as reliable as they come, or he wouldn't have been a sector commander in the first place. His prior record was excellent, too, but God knows he deserves a pulser dart or a rope over this one. And I suppose it wouldn't hurt the rest of my people to know they can be held to the same standards as anyone else if they screw up spectacularly enough," he added, grudgingly but without flinching.

"I don't know, Oscar." Pierre pinched the bridge of his nose. "I agree he blew it, but in fairness to the man, he had no reason to expect anything until it was far too late. And while I know she's not one of your favorite people, McQueen has a point about the downside of shooting people whose real crime was simply that they got caught in the works. If he'd done anything outside procedure, or if he'd been given any prior clue that the prisoners had taken over the planet and its defenses, then, yes, the decision to shoot him would be a slam dunk. But he didn't do any of that, and he *hadn't* been given any clues. So if we shoot him, we tell every other SS officer that he's likely to be shot for anything that goes wrong, even if it resulted from elements totally outside his control."

"I know," Saint-Just admitted. "At the very least, we'll encourage cover-your-ass thinking when and where we can least afford it. At worst, there'll be even more pressure to cover up mistakes by not reporting them or even actively conspiring to conceal them. Which is how you get blind-sided by problems you didn't even know existed until it was too late to do a damned thing about them."

"My point exactly," Pierre agreed. Privately, he was, as always, rather amused by how clearly Saint-Just could see the detrimental consequences of a rule of terror when they might affect his own bailiwick even while McQueen's efforts to eliminate them from hers only fueled his suspicion of her "empire building."

"But he still has to be punished," Saint-Just went on. "I can't afford not to come down on him after something like this."

"I agree," Pierre said. "How about this? We've already agreed there's not much point in our pretending the other side doesn't know where Cerberus is now, but there are still too many prisoners on the planet for us to move them, right?" Saint-Just nodded, and Pierre shrugged. "In that case, we may as well tell our own Navy where it is, too. I know Harrington blew the old orbital defenses to bits when she pulled out, but the main base facility and the farms are still there on Styx. So we put a Navy picket squadron into the system, under the local StateSec CO's overall command, of course, and keep the prison up and running, and we send our friend Thornegrave to one of the camps. We'll even give him a cover ID so his fellow inmates don't know he was a StateSec officer. They may lynch him anyway if they figure it out, but *we* won't have done it. So we get the effect of punishing him, and seeing to it that everyone in StateSec knows we did, plus the benefit of having shown mercy by not shooting him ourselves."

"That's an evil thought, Rob," Saint-Just observed, then chuckled. "And appropriate as hell, too. Maybe you should have my job."

"No, thank you. I have enough trouble with mine. Besides, I'm not stupid enough to think I could do yours half as well as you do it."

"Thanks. I think." Saint-Just rubbed his chin for a moment, then nodded. "I like it. Of course, there's nothing to keep the Manties from coming back in strength and taking everyone else off the planet, I suppose. I doubt very much that McQueen would agree to divert a big enough force to protect the system against any sort of raid in strength. For that matter, even if she would, it would probably be unjustifiable." The last sentence came out in a tone of sour admission, and Pierre smiled without humor.

"I don't see any reason for the Manties to come back. For one thing, it seems pretty obvious that everyone who had the guts and gumption to leave already went with Harrington. They might be able to make a little more propaganda capital out of going back and 'liberating' everyone else, but not enough of it to justify the effort on their part. And it's not as if they really *need* any more propaganda capital out of it." He shook his head wryly. "They're doing just fine as it is, now aren't they?"

"It seems that way," Saint-Just agreed sourly. Then he brightened just a bit. "On the other hand, my people are putting together a four-month summation on the Manties' domestic front, and their preliminary reports suggest that the Manties may just need all the good propaganda they can get." Pierre couldn't quite keep a hint of incredulity out of the look he gave the StateSec chief, and Saint-Just waved a hand in a brushing-away gesture. "Oh, I know anything they're reporting to me now is behind the curve. And completely out of date, in a lot of ways, since none of the information they had when they made their analysis allowed for any of the news out of Cerberus. But that doesn't invalidate its reading of base-line trends, Rob. And let's face it, what Harrington did to us at Cerberus, or even what Parnell may be doing in the League, are short-term spikes as far as domestic Manty morale is concerned. Sure, they can hurt us a hell of a lot in the short term, and if Cromarty and his bunch capitalize properly on it, they can build some long-term advantage out of it. But the really important factors are the ones that can't be fudged or spin-doctored. If anyone knows that's true, we do. Look at all the problems trying to put the best face on that kind of thing's given *us*, for God's sake, even when Cordelia was around to turn disaster into glorious triumph for the Dolists." He shook his head. "Nope. The Manty government still has to deal with its public's response to things like ship losses, the capture or loss of star systems, casualty rates, tax burdens, and the general perception of who has the momentum militarily."

Pierre nodded with a guarded expression, and Saint-Just's eyes gleamed with brief humor, but he declined to bring McQueen back into the conversation . . . yet.

"It's that kind of factor my people have been looking at, and according to what they've found, they actually believe *we* may have the long-term morale advantage."

"And how much of that is because they know you and I would really like to hear it?" Pierre asked skeptically.

"Some, no doubt," Saint-Just acknowledged, "but most of these people have been with me a long time, Rob. They know I'd rather have the truth . . . and that I don't shoot people for telling me what they think the truth is just because I don't like hearing it."

And that, Pierre mused, *actually is true. And you go to some lengths to make sure it stays that way, don't you, Oscar? Which, I suspect, is one reason you're so concerned over the possibility of your upper echelon people developing cover-your-ass mentalities after Cerberus. But the fact that the people at the* top *genuinely want to produce accurate reports may or may not mean they manage to pull it off.* "Garbage in-garbage out" *is still true, and there's no way to be sure agents lower down in the chain aren't "sweetening" the reports they send up to their superiors, who may not be quite so understanding as you are. Nonetheless . . .*

"All right," he said aloud. "I agree that your senior analysts know better than to lie to keep us happy. But I fail to see how they can feel *we* have the morale advantage!"

"I didn't say they did," Saint-Just said patiently. "Not just at the moment. I said they believe we may have the advantage in the *long term*." He paused until Pierre nodded acceptance of the correction, then went on. "The way they see it, our morale started at rock bottom when our initial offensives got hammered into the ground and the Manties seized the initiative . . . and held it for five damned T-years. And people in general haven't been any too happy with StateSec's policies, either," the SS CO went on, his tone calm but not apologetic, "and the financial hardships of the war only made that worse."

It was Pierre's turn to nod unapologetically. The Dolists' Basic Living Stipend had been frozen by the Legislaturalists at the outbreak of hostilities. Indeed, the war had begun when it did largely because the Harris Government couldn't afford the next scheduled round of BLS increases and had needed an outside threat to justify delaying them. Nor had the Committee been able to find the money for the increases. Possibly the most useful single thing the late, otherwise unlamented Cordelia Ransom had managed was to convince the Dolists to blame the Manticoran "elitists" and their "aggressive, imperialist war" (*not* the Committee) for the threadbare state of the Treasury. But the Mob's acceptance that it wasn't Rob S. Pierre's personal fault that its stipends hadn't gone up hadn't made it any happier with what that meant for its standard of living. And he supposed he ought to admit that his economic reforms had made the situation far worse in the short term. But he and Saint-Just both knew they'd been essential in the long run, and even the Dolists seemed to be coming, grudgingly, to accept that they had.

"But in a way," Saint-Just continued, "that actually works to our advantage, because when you come right down to it, the only way *our* morale could go was up. The Manty public, on the other hand, started the war terrified of how it might end, only to have its confidence shoot up like a counter-grav shuttle. As far as their man-in-the-street could see, they beat the snot out of us for three of four T-years without even working up a good sweat, and there didn't seem to be very much we could do to stop them.

"But the war hasn't *ended*, and they expected it to. No one's fought a war this long in two or three centuries, Rob. I know a lot of Sollies probably think that's because we and the Manties both are a bunch of third-class incompetents, but you and I know that isn't true. It's because of the scale we're operating on and, much as we may hate to admit it, because the Manties' tech has been so good that their quality has offset our advantages in quantity. Which is pretty depressing from our side, of course. But it's also depressing from *their* side, because their public knows as well as we do that they hold the tech advantage, and up until Icarus they were winning all the battles, but they hadn't won the *war*. In fact, they weren't even in sight of winning it. Every year their taxpayers have been looking at higher and higher naval budgets as both of us keep building up our fleets and investing in new shipyards and hardware. Their economy's stronger and more efficient than ours, but it's also much smaller, in an absolute sense, and every bucket has a bottom. The Manty taxpayers would be more than human if they didn't worry that the bottom of theirs was coming into sight after so long, so they're feeling the economic strain—less of it than we are, but more than they've ever felt before—and their casualties, low as they are compared to ours, are much higher as a percentage of their population."

He shrugged.

"They want the war to be *over*, Rob. Probably even more than our own people do, since the civilian standard of living here in the Republic is actually stabilizing after the last couple of T-years' roller-coaster ride. And then along came Operation Icarus and hammered *their* morale with a series of major military reverses." He shrugged again. "I'm not saying they're on the brink of imminent collapse or anything of the sort. I'm simply saying that Manty support for the war is nowhere near as monolithic as we tend to think it is, and my people are suggesting that Cromarty and his government are under more strain holding the war effort together than any of our previous models indicated."

"Hmmmm." Pierre cocked his chair back and toyed with an antique letter opener which had once belonged to Sidney Harris. It actually made sense, he reflected, and only the fact that he was so busy pissing on his own forest fires had kept him from giving the possibility the consideration it probably merited. But still . . .

"I'd have to agree that all that sounds reasonable," he admitted finally. "But I don't see where it's going to have a major effect on our immediate position even if it's true. Manty war weariness isn't going to cause them to collapse any time soon, and unless something like that happens, Cromarty will stay in power and he and Elizabeth III will go right on pounding us. And whatever Manty morale is like, the worst effects of Parnell's 'revelations' are going to be felt here at home and on *Solly* attitudes."

"I know that." Saint-Just flicked the fingers of one hand in agreement. "But that's one reason I want to keep the pressure on them as much as possible. And why I'd like you to reconsider your position on Operation Hassan."

Pierre bit off a groan. In fact, he managed to stop it before it even reached his expression, but it wasn't easy. Aside from McQueen, Operation Hassan was the point on which he and Saint-Just were in the most fundamental disagreement. Not because Pierre couldn't accept the basic logic behind Hassan, but because he doubted its chances of success . . . and feared the consequences if it failed. For that matter, even its success might not come anywhere near producing the results Saint-Just's planners anticipated.

"I still don't like it," he said after a moment, his voice flat. "Too much can go wrong. And even if it succeeds perfectly, remember that InSec tried exactly the same trick thirty-three T-years ago. Pulled it off, too. And look what *that* got us. Besides, think of the PR consequences if something like Hassan blows up in our faces!"

"It's not the same thing at all," Saint-Just said calmly. "Oh, the basic concept is the same, but we're at war now. The impact on the Manties would be immeasurably greater, and even if we wound up being blamed for it, no one could possibly say we weren't striking at a legitimate military objective!"

Pierre grunted skeptically, and Saint-Just shrugged.

"All right, forget that. But InSec managed to set it up so that no one knew we'd been behind it thirty-three years ago, and I can do the same today. I swear I can, Rob," he said earnestly. "None of the people I'd use in the action teams would have the least idea who they were actually working with, and my planners have come up with cutouts at all levels to keep any Manty investigator from tracing it back to us. And even if it doesn't have exactly the effect we're hoping for in a best-case scenario, it would *have* to hurt their coordination and determination. I don't happen to share the most optimistic of my people's expectations, but if we pull Hassan off, I can guarantee you that people like New Kiev, High Ridge, and Descroix and Gray Hill would turn the Manty Parliament into a dogfight to end all dogfights. They'd be so busy squabbling for power among themselves no one would have the time to spare for something as minor as a *war*."

His voice and expression were earnest and persuasive, and Pierre felt his instinctive opposition to the plan waver before his security chief's conviction.

But Oscar is a spymaster at heart, he reminded himself. *He's preprogrammed to think in terms of clandestine ops, and hard as he tries to avoid it, I know he can sell himself on an operation just because it has all the "secret agent" bells and whistles. And there's at least a little empire-building at work here, too, because if he pulls off something like Hassan, he could very well win the war, or at least end it, which is something the entire People's Navy hasn't come close to accomplishing this far.*

"Do you really think there's a chance of success?" he asked after a moment, and Saint-Just frowned at his serious tone.

"Yes," the StateSec CO said after a long moment of obviously hard, careful thought. "Depending on where the operation is finally mounted, the chances could range from excellent to poor or even very poor, but even in a worst-case situation, it *could* work. And as I say, if it fails, all we've lost is some cat's-paws."

"Um." Pierre rubbed his chin some more, then sighed heavily.

"All right, Oscar. You can set it up. But only if you can assure me the operation will *not* be mounted without my specific authorization." He raised a hand to fend off Saint-Just's slightly pained expression. "I'm not afraid *you* might go off half-cocked," *or not, at least, against my specific orders,* "but, as you say, we'd be relying on cat's-paws for the actual dirty work. I want to make damned sure one of them doesn't drag us into something we don't want to do."

"I can do that," Saint-Just said after another moment's thought. "To be honest, the biggest risk would be with Hassan Two, in Yeltsin's Star, because the people we'd use there are a bit harder to control. On the other hand, our cutouts are actually cleaner there than they are in Manticore. And, to be honest, Hassan One doesn't stand very much chance of success. Not up against domestic Manty security. I've thought from the beginning that Hassan Two is our best chance—we'd've had a clean shot for a partial Hassan there year before last, if the pieces had just been in place—and I think we ought to be willing to accept a little more risk of premature action to set things up there."

"Hmpf." Pierre closed his eyes in consideration of his own, then sighed once more and nodded. "All right. Set it up, but I'm serious about giving the final okay myself, Oscar. And I'm trusting you, personally, to see to it that any 'accident' in this particular case is just that, and not a case of someone further down the chain deciding to act on his own initiative just because a target strays into his sights!"

"I'll see to it personally," Saint-Just promised, and Pierre nodded in approval. When Oscar Saint-Just gave him his word, it could be relied upon.

"But Hassan has to be a longshot," the StateSec man went on. "If it works, it can be decisive, but we can't do a thing to create the circumstances which would let us mount it, because there's no way we can assert control over them. Unlike military operations."

Pierre sighed again, inwardly this time, but with feeling. He'd known this was coming from the moment Saint-Just arrived, but he'd allowed himself to hope the discussion of domestic Manticoran politics, civilian morale, and Operation Hassan might have diverted his chief spy from it.

Silly me. I wonder if the energy death of the universe *could divert Oscar from this particular subject?*

"All right, Oscar," he said finally. "I know you're unhappy about McQueen in general, but I thought we'd already been over that. Is there something specific—and new—you wanted to discuss about her? Or is there something you just want to revisit?"

Saint-Just looked most uncharacteristically sheepish. It was not an expression anyone but Rob Pierre had ever seen on his face, but given the Chairman's tone, and the number of times they'd been over the same ground, it was inevitable. Despite that, however, his voice was calm and collected when he replied.

"Yes and no," he said. "Actually, I wanted to discuss the misgivings you already know I have in context with these latest reports from the Sollies." He nodded to the holo display of the memo pad Pierre had been perusing when he arrived, and the Chairman nodded. He might be weary unto death of hearing Saint-Just's reservations about Esther McQueen, but he was far too intelligent to simply ignore them. Saint-Just's track record at ferreting out threats to the New Order was too impressive for that.

"Actually," the SS man went on, "I think Parnell and his lot are going to do us a lot more damage than Harrington's return. Much as I hate to admit it, it was particularly clever of the Manties to send him on to Beowulf without any major medical treatment. And it was particularly *stupid* of Tresca to have recorded his sessions with the man."

Pierre nodded again, but this time more than a trace of sick fascination hovered in the back of his brain. Saint-Just's conversational tone was completely untouched by any horror or even any indication that he saw any reason to feel so much as a mild distaste for his subject matter. Which, given that the "sessions" to which he referred had been neither more nor less than vicious physical and mental torture, was more than a little appalling. Pierre was well aware that the ultimate responsibility for anything Saint-Just or any of the security man's minions did was his. He was the one who'd brought about the fall of the Legislaturalists, and he was Chairman of the Committee. More than that, he'd known from the beginning what StateSec was doing, and he would not pretend even to himself that he hadn't. But the knowledge bothered him. There were times it bothered him a very great deal indeed . . . and he suspected Oscar Saint-Just slept like a baby every night.

I need him, Pierre thought, not for the first time. *I need him desperately. More than that, horrible as he is, the man is my* friend. *And unlike Cordelia, at least there's never been anything personal about the things he does. They're just . . . his job. But that doesn't make it any less horrible. Or mean the universe wouldn't be a better place without him in it.*

"I have to agree that Tresca's judgment was . . . questionable," he said, allowing no trace of his thoughts to color his tone. "But so was our decision— No, be honest. It was *my* decision not to simply shoot Parnell along with the others."

"Maybe. But I supported it at the time, and, given what we knew then, I still think it was the correct one. He knew things no one else knew. Especially about the Navy, of course, but also about the inner dynamics of the core Legislaturalist family connections. Given that the purges had hardly begun, and how much internal resistance still existed in some sectors of the Navy command structure, we'd have been fools to blow all that knowledge away with a pulser dart."

"Then, I suppose. But that was years ago . . . and he never gave us very much, despite all the 'convincing' even someone like Tresca could come up with. On balance, we certainly ought to've gone back and cleaned up the loose ends long before any of this had the chance to happen."

"Hindsight, Rob. Pure hindsight. Oh, sure. If we'd shot him two or three years ago, none of this would've happened, but who in his right mind would have expected a mass breakout from Hades? We'd tucked him away in the safest place we had, and he should have just quietly rotted there without making any problems for us at all."

"Which, unfortunately, is certainly *not* what he's doing," Pierre observed dryly.

"No, it isn't," Saint-Just agreed.

The Secretary of State Security's tone showed commendable restraint, Pierre reflected, considering what the testimony of the Hades escapees and, even worse, the HD records Harrington had pulled from Camp Charon's supposedly secure data banks, were doing in the Solarian League.

The fact that PubIn had lied about Harrington's death was bad enough. Having an entire series of witnesses, beginning with Amos Parnell, the last Legislaturalist Chief of Naval Operations, turn up to denounce the Committee of Public Safety in general and Rob Pierre and Oscar Saint-Just in particular as the true instigators of the Harris Assassination was worse, much worse. The fact that many of those witnesses, including Parnell, obviously had been tortured (and the Manties had been smart enough to send all of them to Beowulf, where physicians from the League itself could determine they truly had been) was worse yet. And having recorded imagery of Dennis Tresca personally, gloatingly, overseeing that torture *and* confirming that Pierre and Saint-Just had planned the entire coup was worst of all.

The damage was going to be catastrophic, and all Saint-Just's analysts and their very probably correct new models of *Manticoran* politics and attitudes couldn't begin to mitigate that damage's impact where the League was concerned.

However vital and all-consuming the war between the People's Republic and the Manticoran Alliance might have been for the inhabitants of what was still known to the Solarian League as the Haven Sector, it had been distinctly secondary news to the Sollies. The League was the biggest, wealthiest, most powerful political unit in the history of humankind. It had its own internal problems and divisions, and its central government was weak by Havenite or Manticoran standards, but it was enormous, self-confident, and almost completely insulated, as a whole, from events in Pierre's neck of the galaxy. Specific components of the League, like merchants, arms makers, shipping lines, and investment firms, might have interests there; for the Solly man on the street, the entire sector lay somewhere on the rim of the universe. He felt no personal concern over events there, and his ignorance about the sector and its history was all but total.

Which, Pierre admitted, was the way Haven had preferred things.

The Solarian League had its own share of oligarchies and aristocrats, but the ideal to which it hewed was that of representative democracy. In fairness, most of the core worlds actually did practice that form of government, and every single member of the League embraced at least its facade, whatever the reality behind the outward appearance. And that had played neatly into the hands of the Office of Public Information, for Manticore was a monarchy.

Half of the Star Kingdom's allies were also monarchies, for that matter. Places like the Protectorship of Grayson, or the Caliphate of Zanzibar, or the Princedom of Alizon all boasted open, hereditary aristocracies and were, or could readily be made to appear to be, autocracies. Actually, as Pierre knew, most of them were closer in practice to the mushy Solarian ideal than the PRH was . . . but the Solly public didn't know that. Which had given PubIn's propagandists a clear track at convincing that public that the Republic was just like them. It must be, after all, since it was a *republic*—it said so right in its name, didn't it?—fighting against the intrenched, despotic, and hence evil forces of reactionary monarchy. The fact that at least half of the out-colonies (and, for that matter, many of the planets which were now core worlds of the League itself) had gone through their own monarchical periods was beside the point. The exigencies which had all too often faced colony expeditions, especially before the Warshawski sail, had provided fertile ground for strong, hierarchical forms of government in the interests of survival, but the core world populations had forgotten that. After all, many of them had been settled for almost two millennia. They took their current, comfortably civilized status for granted and tended to forget (if it had ever occurred to them at all) that the Star Kingdom of Manticore, for example, had been settled for barely five centuries.

The societies of this entire sector were much younger than any of Old Earth's older daughter worlds, and some of them, especially in systems like Yeltsin's Star and Zanzibar, had faced particularly brutal struggles for survival. Although continued social evolution tended to undermine the autocratic systems such worlds had developed once the problems of clinging to survival yielded to security and prosperity, that process took time. Many of the regimes colony worlds had thrown up had been at least as despotic as popular prejudice could ever have imagined, and some remained that way still in many sectors, like the Silesian Confederacy, for example. But those worlds were the exceptions, and those who had joined the Manticoran Alliance were not among them.

Except that the Solly public hadn't known that, and Public Information had gone to great lengths to keep it from finding out. With, Pierre thought sourly, a remarkable degree of success, once again proving it was always wisest to bet on the side of ignorance and intellectual laziness.

But the testimony and evidence of men and women like Parnell had broken through PubIn's shield, and the SS personnel Harrington's Cerebus court martials had tried and convicted for particularly vicious violations of the PRH's own laws only made it still worse. It was difficult for anyone on Haven to make a comprehensive assessment of how bad the actual damage was because of the lengthy communications lag between the People's Republic and the League. The Manticoran Alliance's control of both the Manticoran and the Erewhon wormhole junctions meant the Star Kingdom's capital was mere hours away from the Sigma Draconis System and Beowulf, the second-oldest human colony world, and barely a week from the Sol System itself. But Haven was a six-month round trip away even for a dispatch boat, which meant the only real information Pierre or Saint-Just had was that which was carried to them aboard the neutral vessels still allowed through either junction to the People's Republic. Any additional information would be badly out of date by the time they heard about it.

Most of what they knew had thus come from the Solarian news agencies' feeds, since the Manties had been very careful not to interfere with any of the newsies' courier boats or with any third party's diplomatic traffic. And, as Pierre had feared, most of the reporters for those agencies were pursuing an aggressive style of journalism which had not been seen in the PRH in decades. They were using their better information sources to bully still more information (or admissions, at least) and more open interviews out of PubIn by doling out their own tidbits on a *quid pro quo* basis, and the fact that Pierre *needed* that information strengthened their hands.

Fortunately, however, they were not (for the moment, at least) his sole sources of information. The PRH had arrangements with half a dozen League member worlds who let its diplomatic pouches and couriers travel aboard their diplomatic vessels. It was an invaluable connection to Haven's embassies and intelligence nets in the League, but at its best, it was slower than the finely polished courier networks the news services maintained and the information it provided was always somewhat dated. That hadn't been a problem when PubIn controlled the only information gates the newsies had been interested in opening, but it certainly *was* one now that PubIn desperately wanted to know what was happening somewhere else.

Worse, there was no way to know how much longer that arrangement would hold. They'd already received rumblings that at least two of the worlds they'd counted among the PRH's friends were seriously rethinking their relationships in light of the disturbing revelations coming from Parnell and his companions. Pierre felt certain others would soon be engaged in the same process, especially if, as seemed likely, Parnell was invited to testify before the Solarian League Assembly's Committee on Human Rights. It was unlikely that anything as fundamentally unwieldy as the League would actually get around to formally declaring the PRH an outlaw state, but the inevitable mass coverage of Parnell's testimony could only make the PR disaster worse, and public opinion wasn't something any Solarian world's government could safely ignore.

Of more immediate concern, Pierre had no idea how the situation would affect Haven's arrangements with certain Solarian arms firms. Legally, any Solly firm which traded weapons technology to either the Manties or the PRH faced formidable penalties for violating the embargo the Assembly had enacted shortly after the outbreak of hostilities. In fact, the central government had always lacked the muscle or the will to make that embargo fully effective. Even if the Assembly had possessed the police power to enforce it, the Star Kingdom had used the economic clout the Manticore Wormhole Junction gave it too openly to secure it, and a great many people and firms who'd stood to make unreasonable amounts of money from supplying the belligerents (or cutting into the enormous Manty merchant marine's carrying trade) resented it enormously. Given the Assembly's official acceptance of the embargo, none of those outraged parties had been in a position to demand their government force the Manties to allow them to trade openly with the PRH, however, which meant the Manties had been able to close their wormholes to any direct, rapid transfer of actual hardware and had made even technology or information transfers difficult.

Difficult, but not impossible. It had taken a depressingly long time to establish the contacts and make the arrangements, given the time lag built into any communications loop, yet Saint-Just's people had managed it in the end. The heavy combat edge the Manties' superior technology had given the RMN and its allies had provided all the incentive anyone could have asked for from Haven's side, and those at the Solarian end had incentives of their own. Greed was undoubtedly the greatest one, for there were huge profits to be made, even from a government as close to bankruptcy as that of the PRH, but there were others.

Many Solarian shipping lines deeply resented the near monopoly the Star Kingdom had enjoyed on shipping to and from the Haven Sector *and* the Silesian Sector thanks to the astrographic accident of the Manticore Junction. There were other, wealthier sectors, but very few outside the League itself which were as heavily populated or which offered as potentially rich pickings as the regions to which Manticore controlled rapid access. Worse, the pattern of wormholes extending from Manticore covered over half the League's total periphery, with advantages in transit times whose value was almost impossible to overstate. As a percentage of the total commerce of the Solarian League, the sums involved were barely even moderate; as a percentage of the bottom lines of individual shipping lines and corporations, they were enormous, which meant the individuals in question had reasons of their own to want to see the Star Kingdom . . . diverted from nurturing its merchant marine.

Another form of greed helped explain the interest of several Solly arms makers, of course. The League in general had an invincible confidence in its technology's superiority to that of any lesser power. By and large, that confidence was probably justifiable, but there were individual instances in which it was much less so than the Sollies believed. The Star Kingdom of Manticore's R&D talent, in particular, compared favorably with that of any League world, whether the League knew it or not. The PRH's did not, but once the People's Republic realized how completely current Manticoran technology outclassed *its* technology (most of it purchased from the same people who built the Solarian League Navy's warships), it had hastened to share that fact with its suppliers. While those suppliers had felt that Solarian hardware in Solarian hands would undoubtedly prove far superior to that same hardware in the hands of a Navy whose personnel came from a ramshackle education system like the PRH's, they could not overlook specific items, such as the Manties' development of the first, practical short-range FTL communication system in history, reported by their Havenite customers. They couldn't seem to get the League Navy itself interested in sending competent observers to the front of what the League persisted in regarding as a squabble between minor, third-rate foreign powers, but the combined allure of profitable sales and access to the information the People's Navy could provide from sensor readings and occasional examination of Manty wreckage had proved irresistible.

Yet those arrangements, like everything else, now stood jeopardized by Amos Parnell's escape to the League. If he was believed, and Pierre felt dismally certain he would be, the PRH was about to stop being the "good guys" in the eyes of Solarian public opinion. It was possible, even probable, that the longstanding acceptance of the Star Kingdom and its "autocratic" allies as the heavies of the piece would prevent any fundamental, long-term swing of public support in the Manties' favor, but that wasn't the same thing as saying that it wouldn't provoke a swing *against* the PRH. If Pierre was lucky, it would generate a feeling of "a pox upon both your houses!" and lead to a general disgust with both sides, and Leonard Boardman and Public Information would certainly do their utmost to bring that about. But even that attitude would intensify public support for the embargo. Which, in turn, would inspire certain League bureaucrats to look more closely at their legal responsibility to enforce it . . . and to publically slap the wrist of anyone caught violating it. Since one thing they could slap those wrists with was a temporary or even permanent bar against bidding on Navy contracts, the PRH's suppliers were about to become much more skittish about doing business with them.

None of which was going to do anything good for the People's Navy's combat efficiency.

"Well," the Chairman said finally, "there's not much we can do about the situation in the League right now. We'll just have to ride it out, I suppose. And Boardman's right in at least one respect. The official communications lag between here and Sol really does work in our favor right now."

"For what it's worth," Saint-Just replied. "But let's not fool ourselves, Rob. We can delay sending official government responses to inquiries from the League by claiming that the Manties' control of the wormholes means we have to send them the long way around, but that's not going to help us when it comes to their newsies' questions. *They* don't have that problem, and anything we say to them is going to get back to the core worlds almost as quickly as anything the Manties say."

"Thank you for pointing that out." Pierre's tone was sour, but there was a slight, weary twinkle in his eye. He wouldn't have shown it to anyone but Saint-Just, and the StateSec CO snorted.

"You're welcome. It's my job to bring you the bad news even more than the good, after all. Which is why I mentioned Parnell in context with McQueen."

He cocked his head, eying his superior expectantly, and Pierre surrendered to the inevitable.

"Go on," he said.

"We're not going to be able to completely control the Solly version of events even here in the Republic," Saint-Just said. "So far, our existing censorship is containing its open dissemination, and the Solly agencies understand that we *will* retaliate if they violate the Information Control Act or the Subversive Agitator statutes. But bootleg versions of Solly stories are going to get out. Hell, we've never been able to fully suppress the *Manty* 'faxes dissidents keep smuggling in!"

"I know that," Pierre said patiently. "But I think Boardman is right about our ability to at least mitigate the damage. Unconfirmed, 'bootleg' reports have always been with us, but they've never been able to offset the full weight of the official information system. Not even people who automatically take anything PubIn says with a grain of salt are immune to the saturation effect over the long term. They may reject our version of specific events, but the background noise still shapes the context in which they view the rest of the universe."

"I'm not disputing that, although I think Boardman is overconfident about his ability to spin this particular story. But I'm also not worrying about *public* opinion, Rob. Not in the short term, at least. I'm worrying about how the *Navy* is going to react once the full extent of Parnell's charges sinks in."

"Um." Pierre cocked his chair back and ran one hand's fingers through his hair.

" 'Um,' indeed," Saint-Just said. "You know how popular Parnell was with the Legislaturalist officer corps. We may have had the better part of ten T-years to build our own cadre of officers, but every single senior member of it started out under the Legislaturalists. They may've been lieutenants and even ensigns, but they *started out* with Parnell as their CNO. As long as he was safely dead, especially after being executed for his part in the Harris Assassination, he was no threat. In fact, branding him with responsibility actually helped undermine any lingering loyalty to the old regime. After all, if someone they respected that much had been part of the plot, then *everything* they'd respected about the old system suddenly looked far less certain than it ever had before.

"But now he's back, and alive—which absolutely proves that at least part of what we told them about him was a lie—and he's telling the universe *we* engineered the Harris Assassination. Which means everything we thought we'd accomplished by making him one of the fall guys is now likely to turn around and bite us right on the ass."

"Are you seriously suggesting we could be looking at some sort of spontaneous general military revolt?" Pierre asked, and his tone was less incredulous than he could have wished it were.

"No." Saint-Just shook his head. "Not a spontaneous one. Whatever else is happening, they're in the military and the Republic is fighting for its life, with dozens of its star systems still occupied by the other side. They may not like us much—in fact, let's be honest and admit that they've *never* liked the Committee—but that doesn't change the larger picture, and they must realize what the Manties could do to them if the chain of command falls apart or we split into factions that start fighting among themselves. They certainly saw enough of that when we were still securing our own control and the Manties were picking off frontier systems we were too disorganized to reinforce.

"But what *is* going to happen is that we're about to lose a lot of the legitimacy we've slowly built up in their eyes. We've done our best to promote people who had bones to pick with the old order, of course, and most of those officers won't feel any great nostalgia for the Legislaturalists even if Parnell has come back from the dead. But not all of them are going to fall into that category, and even some of the ones who do are going to remember that at least the Legislaturalists never shot officers in job lots for failure to perform. So if the people who *have* shot them suddenly turn out to have seized power by having lied to them, they're not going to feel any great loyalty to *us*, either."

He paused, eyebrows raised, until Pierre nodded.

"I expect inertia to be on our side," he went on then. "We've been the government for ten T-years, and they've seen too much chaos. The Levelers aren't that far in the past, and the natural tendency is going to be to shy away from any course of action which is likely to encourage the Mob's more extreme efforts or provoke new power struggles at the top. But that's why I'm so concerned about McQueen and the degree of loyalty she's managed to evoke by winning battles."

"We'd have that problem with anyone who won battles, Oscar!"

"Agreed. And I also realize, although you must sometimes think I've forgotten, that we have to have someone who *can* win battles. I'm fully aware that it would be just as fatal—to you, me, and the Committee, at least—to lose the war as it would be for someone to stage a successful coup against us. But the person who's winning for us right now is Esther McQueen, and she's as ambitious and smart as they come. Worse, she's a member of the government . . . and one who only came on board well after all the things Parnell is accusing us of had already happened. She's in a position to claim all of the advantages of the incumbent, if you will, without having to shoulder any of the *dis*advantages. And worst of all, perhaps, she's the one woman in the Navy who's in a position to have a realistic chance of delivering a shot to the brain of the Committee. She's right here, on Haven, with direct access to you, me, and the rest of the Committee. And she's already the civilian head of the Navy. If the officer corps decided to follow her lead, there wouldn't be any factional struggles. Not immediately, at any rate. And you can bet anything you want that she's smart enough to make that point to them."

"But there's no evidence she's done anything of the sort," Pierre pointed out.

"No, there isn't. Trust me, if I'd picked up even a whisper of anything like that, you would have been the first to know. But there wasn't any evidence that she'd done anything out of the ordinary before the Leveler coup attempt, either, Rob."

Pierre nodded unhappily. It had been fortunate for the Committee that McQueen was in a position to act when the Levelers managed to completely paralyze the normal channels of command. She'd been the only senior navy officer with both the quickness to grasp what was happening and the guts to act on her own initiative, and that was all that had saved the lives of Rob Pierre and Oscar Saint-Just. But she'd been able to act with such decisiveness only because her flagship's entire company had been prepared to follow her without orders, despite the knowledge that such a display of initiative might well get them all shot for treason even if the Committee survived. Worse yet, she'd obviously managed, completely undetected, to set up her own contingency plans with her immediate staff and the senior officers of her flagship.

And those plans most definitely had *not* been directed against the Levelers, however they might have worked out in practice.

"What are you suggesting, Oscar?" he asked finally. "Do you seriously think we can remove her?"

"Not without running serious risks, no. As you say, we need someone who can win battles. But we only need her until the battles are won, and she's smart enough to know that, too. That's why I'm so antsy about her delays in launching Operation Scylla. And about the way she keeps harping on the Manties' supposed 'new weapons.' I think she's playing for time while she makes her own arrangements."

"I'm not sure I can agree with you," Pierre said. "She's kept us much more fully informed on the status of operations than Kline ever did. Granted, she could be doing that in part to convince us to leave her alone while she polishes up her plans to shoot us both, but she's right when she points out the sheer problems of scale. Hell, you referred to them yourself just a few minutes ago! It takes months to concentrate task forces and fleets, train them to carry out an operational plan, and then launch them at an enemy a hundred light-years from their own bases."

"I know it does. But I also think she's harping on the arguments in favor of caution more than the situation justifies." Saint-Just raised a hand as Pierre opened his mouth. "I'm not saying I know more about naval operations than she does, Rob. I don't. But I do know about the ways an expert can use his expertise to confuse an issue, especially when he—or, in this case, she—knows she was put in charge specifically because the people who put her there didn't have that expertise themselves. And I also know what my own analysts are telling me about the technical plausibility of things like these 'super LACs' of hers. I've been through their arguments very carefully and double-checked their contentions with people still active in our own R&D, and—" his tone changed ever so slightly "—with four or five of the Solly tech reps here overseeing the technology transfers. And they all agree. The mass requirements for a fusion plant capable of powering both a LAC's impeller nodes and a graser the size of the one McQueen says she believes in are completely incompatible with the observed size of the vessels. And McQueen *is* a professional naval officer, so she has to have sources at least as good as mine. That's one reason I think we have to look carefully at the possibility that she's deliberately overstating the risks to slow the tempo of operations still further and give herself more time to organize her own network against us."

Pierre rocked his chair slowly from side to side, lips pursed while he considered Saint-Just's argument. It was clear the StateSec CO had been headed in this direction for months now, but this was the first time he'd laid out his fears in such concise and unambiguous terms. And as he considered what Saint-Just had said, Pierre found himself wishing he could reject those fears out of hand.

Unfortunately, he couldn't. Still . . .

"Do you have any specific evidence?" he asked. "Not that she's plotting anything—I know we've just agreed we don't have any evidence of that—but that she's exaggerating the military risks?"

"Not hard and fast," Saint-Just admitted. "I have to be careful who I ask. If she is up to anything, asking anyone in her own immediate chain of command would risk letting her know what we were asking about. But as I say, I've had my own people looking at both the analyses she's presented to us and the raw data on which those analyses are based, and their conclusions are quite different from hers."

"Hardly conclusive," Pierre objected. "Any group of analysts is going to differ with any other. God knows you and I both see enough of that, even when the people doing the analyses are scared to death of us and know exactly what we want to hear!"

"Granted. That's why I said I don't have any hard and fast evidence. But this fixation of hers on the 'new weapons' the Manties used during Icarus really worries me. I know her official rationale for why they might be sitting on new hardware, but they haven't launched a single offensive action since Icarus, aside from a few local counterattacks, every one of which was executed without any new mystery weapons! And why is she so quick to dismiss the argument that we ought to be pushing the pace to take the Manties completely out before they can get their supposed new weapons into mass production? For that matter, why hasn't their Eighth Fleet moved against Barnett, if they're not fully on the defensive? They spent the better part of a year organizing it in the first place, then diverted it to Basilisk against Icarus, and now it's been sitting in place in Trevor's Star for *another* damned year! Everyone knows it was supposed to be their primary offensive force. That's why they put White Haven in command of it. So why is it just sitting there . . . unless they're afraid to attack us?"

"Have you asked her that?"

"Not in so many words, no. You've seen how she responds to the questions I *have* asked, and I've certainly given her plenty of openings to explain why she thinks White Haven is just sitting in Trevor's Star. All she ever does is trot out the old arguments about how critical the Trevor's Star terminus of their wormhole junction is to them. But even she has to admit they've finally gotten their fortresses on-line to cover the terminus . . . not to mention the fact that their Third Fleet is still permanently on station there. No, Rob. There has to be another reason to hold White Haven on such a short leash, and the only one I can think of is that they're afraid of us. Of her, if I want to be fair, I suppose."

"I don't know," Pierre said slowly. "That's all awfully speculative, Oscar. You have to admit that."

Saint-Just nodded, and Pierre scratched an ear while he frowned in thought. The problem, of course, was that it was part of Saint-Just's job description to *be* speculative where possible threats to the Committee's security were concerned.

"Even if you're right," the Chairman said at length, "we still can't just summarily dismiss her. For one thing, and particularly in light of the whole Parnell mess, it would look like another put-up job, especially to anyone who's already inclined to support her."

Saint-Just nodded once more, his expression sour, and Pierre felt his mouth quirk in a wry twist of its own as he thought of all the work he and Saint-Just had done on McQueen's StateSec dossier. It had been such a lovely job, complete with all the evidence anyone could ever ask for to "prove" she was guilty of plotting treason against the People with none other than colleagues of that arch-traitor Amos Parnell, himself. And now the fact of Parnell's survival meant it was effectively useless for its intended purpose of satisfying the military that they'd had no choice but to shoot her.

"I don't know that there *is* anything we can do about her, immediately," Saint-Just said aloud. "We're both in agreement about how good she is at her job. If I'm wrong about what she's doing, it would be a stupid waste to deprive ourselves of her abilities. For myself, my natural inclination is to dispense with her services rather than risk the possibility that my suspicions are justified, but that's part of the nature of my job. I'm supposed to look for internal threats to the state first, and I realize that sometimes I have to rein myself in before I let that carry me away."

"I know you do," Pierre said, and it was true. Which, unfortunately, lent more weight to his concerns, not less.

"The only thing I can see to do is to leave her where she is but press her even harder to move ahead on Scylla," Saint-Just told him. "She's agreed it's the next logical step and that we should execute it as quickly as possible, so she can hardly object to our pushing for its early execution. If she turns obstinate, that would not only indicate my worries may be justified but also provide us with a completely legitimate difference over policy to justify her removal. On the other hand, if we launch the operation and the Manties give ground the way my analysts expect them to, we'll have evidence that a generally more aggressive policy is in order, and we can demand she pursue it. In the meantime, I'll keep as close an eye on her as I can in hopes that if she actually is planning something we wouldn't like, she'll slip up and give herself away."

"And if she does slip up?"

"If she does, then we eliminate her, however fast and dirty we have to do it," Saint-Just said simply. "We won't have any choice, no matter what fallout may result. A dead, martyred McQueen will be a hell of a lot less threat to us than a live McQueen organizing firing squads of her own!"

"Agreed." Pierre sighed heavily. "But if push comes to shove and we have to remove her, we'll need someone on hand to replace her. Someone who could pick up where she left off against the Manties without picking up where she left off plotting against *us*. And someone we're fairly certain wasn't part of whatever she may— or may not, God help us—be planning."

"You're certainly right about that. I wouldn't want to put any money on Giscard or Tourville or any of their crowd. We've discussed that before, and my concerns about their loyalty to us are only heightened by the success they've achieved under McQueen. They'd almost have to be feeling more loyal to her than they were before Icarus." He rubbed his chin again. "I don't know, Rob. I can think of a half dozen admirals whose loyalty I'd feel confident about, but I'm afraid most of them fall well short of McQueen's military competence. Then, too, if *I* feel sure where their loyalties lie, I'm quite sure the Navy does, too. Which means they'd almost certainly be seen as our creatures, whereas McQueen's been seen as one of their own. I could live with that, but I'd rather not provide any incentive for her replacement's new subordinates to start right out feeling disloyal to him." He grinned mirthlessly. "Clearly what we need is an outstanding commander, outside McQueen's circle, who was never so loyal to us as to make the rank and file immediately suspicious of him but who has no ambitions of his own."

"And Diogenes thought he had trouble looking for an honest man!" Pierre snorted. "Just where do you expect to find this paragon?"

"I don't know." Saint-Just chuckled. But then his face hardened, and there was no humor at all in his voice when he spoke again. "I don't know—yet. But I've already started looking, Rob. And if I find him, then I think my estimate of Citizen Secretary McQueen's indispensability will undergo a small reevaluation."

CHAPTER TEN

"It looked pretty good to me, Scotty." Captain (Junior Grade) Stewart Ashford leaned over Scotty Tremaine's shoulder to study the tac simulator's display. It showed only the results of the exercise, not the "attack" itself, but the number of "dead" LACs was depressingly high, and he winced as he contemplated it. "I certainly thought it was going to work when we discussed your attack plan. So what happened?"

"I got overconfident, Stew." Scotty Tremaine sighed. "That's what happened."

"How?" Ashford demanded. He tapped keys, then pointed almost accusingly at the plot as it obediently altered to a static display of the situation just before the start of the attack. "They didn't have a sniff of you to this point, or the escorts would've already opened fire. You were in clean within—what? A hundred and eighty k-klicks? And closing with an overtake of over ten thousand KPS. *And* an accel advantage of almost five hundred gees over the merchies! They were dead meat."

"Yep." Tremaine gazed dolefully at the icons of the simulated freighters which had been his LAC wing's objectives, then gave Ashford a crooked grin.

There were only a few T-years' difference in their ages, but Ashford, part of HMS *Minotaur*'s original LAC wing and now the COLAC of HMS *Incubus*, had already enjoyed almost a year of hands-on training with actual hardware. *Incubus* was officially carried on the Ship List as CLAC-05, and she was rather closer to the original *Minotaur* in design than *Hydra* was. Not that the

146

differences were pronounced, although *Hydra*, on a bit less tonnage, actually carried twelve more LACs. She paid for it with somewhat lower magazine capacity for her shipboard launchers, but given the fact that a LAC carrier had no business getting close enough to other starships to shoot at them (and be shot at *by* them), that was a trade-off Tremaine was perfectly happy to accept. But *Hydra* would be CLAC-19 when she finished working up in another month or so, and her own LACs were only beginning to arrive. Which meant that unlike Ashford, Tremaine and his wing had been forced to do almost all of their training in simulators.

And it didn't help any that Stew and his friends poached the entire first production run of the new birds, either, Tremaine reflected. But there was no rancor in the thought. The COLACs for all six of the first group of carriers had served as squadron commanders under Jackie Harmon. They were, in fact, the only squadron COs to survive Second Hancock, and they'd paid cash for their promotions. Less than half of HMS *Minotaur*'s wing had survived the battle, but they'd massacred the Peep battleships once the enemy's formation came unglued. Ashford's own LAC crew had a confirmed total of three battleship kills, and his squadron as a whole had killed five.

If anyone in the Service had earned the right to trade in their original *Shrike*-class LACs for the new *Shrike-A*s, they were the ones.

Besides, Tremaine gloated, *they may've gotten the* Shrike-A*s, but my people got the first* B *models, and we got the* Ferrets *at the same time* Incubus *and her people did. And even if we hadn't, Stew's a nice guy. He's saved me a hell of a lot of grief by taking me under his wing, so to speak, too.*

"They were dead meat, all right. Except for one little detail the Admiral neglected to mention to us." He tapped the play key, and watched with that same crooked grin as the sim unfolded.

Everything went exactly as planned—right up to the moment his LACs reached graser range, turned in to attack . . . and four of the eight "merchantmen" dropped their ECM. Three superdreadnoughts and a dreadnought opened fire simultaneously, and not even the powerful bow-walls of the *Shrike-B* or the *Ferret* could stave off the devastating effects of a ship of the wall's energy batteries. Sixty-three of Tremaine's LACs "died" in the first broadsides, and the remaining forty-five, squadron organizations shot to hell, scattered wildly. Thirty of them managed to roll ship and yank the throats of their wedges away from the capital ships, but one of the SDs was a *Medusa*-class, and she was already rolling pods. Not even the *Shrike-B*, with her aft-facing laser clusters and countermissiles could stave off that sort of firepower, and only thirteen of Tremaine's LACs had managed to escape destruction. Seven of *them* had been so badly damaged that they would have been written off on their return to *Hydra* (in real life, at any rate).

"Hoooo, boy!" Ashford shook his head in sympathy . . . and sudden wariness. "The Old Lady's always been on the sneaky side, but this is the first time she ever did something like *that*. No warning at all?"

"None," Tremaine replied with a sort of morbid pride. "Of course, as she was happy to point out *afterward*, not a one of us— including me—ever bothered to make a specific, *visual* confirmation on the targets. We trusted out sensors, instead, and we shouldn't have relied solely on them. After all, she did warn us that we were going up against Manticoran 'merchies,' so *someone* in the wing should have reflected on what that meant in terms of EW upgrades for any possible escorts she *hadn't* warned us about. We didn't. And before you ask, yes, I specifically got her permission to show this to you. Permission, I might add, which I received with somewhat mixed emotions."

"Mixed?" Ashford looked up from the display and crooked an eyebrow.

"Well, misery loves company, Stew. It was embarrassing as hell to get handed my head this way, and I think I would have taken a certain comfort from having it happen to all the rest of you, too." Ashford chuckled, and Tremaine's eyes twinkled as he went on. "But then I thought about it, and something else occurred to me. If she went to such lengths to swat my wing in such an abundantly nasty way, and if she doesn't mind if I warn you about how she did it ahead of time, then what does that say about the nastiness she must have in mind to surprise *you*? I mean, after all, you're forewarned now, so she's going to have to come up with something *really* wicked for you, don't you think?"

His smile was beatific, but Ashford's vanished abruptly. His expression was absolutely blank for several heartbeats, and then he glared at Tremaine.

"You are a sick, sick man, Commander Tremaine."

"Guilty as charged. But I'll be looking forward to seeing what she does to you."

"Yeah? Well this is all your fault anyway, you know."

"*My* fault? And just how do you figure that? I'm the one she did it to first!"

"Uh-huh. But she wasn't doing this kind of stuff at all before she went back to Saganami Island for that conference last week.

You and I both know who she spent all that time conferring with, now don't we? And if not for you and those other jokers on Hades, Duchess Harrington wouldn't have been available to help her think up this sort of thing, now would she?"

"Um." Tremaine scratched an eyebrow. "You know, you're right. I hadn't thought about it, but this is exactly the sort of thing Lady Harrington would've done. Heck, I've seen her do it, for that matter!" He gazed back down at the display for several seconds, then nodded. "And I know exactly why she and Admiral Truman did it, too."

"Naturally evil and sadistic natures?" Ashford suggested, and Tremaine laughed.

"Hardly. Nope, they wanted to remind me—all of us, actually, because I'm sure this was only the first whack—just how fragile these birds are. I figure we can mix it up with screening units, including battlecruisers, at just about any range, and we can probably go in against battleships with a good chance of success. But against proper ships of the wall?" He shook his head. "Unless we've got an absolutely overwhelming numerical advantage, there's no way we could realistically hope to take out a dreadnought or a superdreadnought. And even then, there'd be an awful lot of empty bunks in flight crew territory afterward! Which is one of the points they wanted to make."

"One of the points?" Ashford looked at him quizzically, and Tremaine shrugged.

"Yep. I feel confident that we'll be hearing about several others when the Admiral drops by for our debrief, but I can already tell you what at least one of them will be." He paused, and Ashford made a little "go on" gesture. "Lady Harrington's said it a million times, Stew: there are very few true 'surprises' in naval combat. 'Surprise' is what happens when someone's seen something all along . . . and thought it was something else. Which is a pretty fair description of what happened here, don't you think?"

"Yeah, I suppose it is," Ashford said after a moment. "Then again, how likely is it that *Peep* ECM could fool us at that short a range?"

"I don't know. Maybe not very . . . but it'd be even less likely if we were watching for it, now wouldn't it? And come to think of it, I know at least one Peep tac witch who probably *could* fool us."

Ashford looked up from the display, eyes bright with curiosity, but he reined himself in quickly. Tremaine could almost feel the intensity with which the captain longed to ask him just which Peep tactical officer he'd managed to strike up a personal acquaintance with. But he didn't ask . . . and Tremaine chose not to tell him. In fact, he rather regretted having said a thing about it. Like the other survivors from *Prince Adrian*, he'd made a point of not saying a word to anyone about the efforts Lester Tourville and Shannon Foraker had made to see to it that they were treated decently. By now, ONI knew Tourville was one of the Peep admirals who'd trounced the Allies so severely in Esther McQueen's offensive, and it looked like Foraker was still his tac officer. Given that, Tremaine supposed it would have made sense, in a cold-blooded, calculating sort of way, to see if they couldn't convince State Security to shoot the two of them. But the survivors had decided, individually and without discussion or debate, to keep their mouths shut. The newsies had crawled all over every escapee from Hell they could find—indeed, Scotty was amazed that Dame Honor and Nimitz (or Andrew LaFollet) hadn't killed or even crippled a single reporter, given how relentlessly they'd hounded "the Salamander"— but not one report had mentioned Tourville or Foraker.

"In any case, it won't hurt a bit for us to be on guard against this kind of thing," he said after a moment, nodding at the display. "And truth to tell, I'll bet she and the Admiral saw it as an opportunity to work on anti-LAC tactics of their own."

"You don't really think the Peeps are going to be able to match our birds, do you?" Ashford failed to keep the incredulity entirely out of his voice, and Tremaine chuckled.

"Not anytime soon, no. On the other hand, don't get too uppity about the differences in our hardware. I had an opportunity to look at a lot of their stuff up close and personal, and it's not as bad as you might think. Not as good as ours, in most cases, but better than most of our people seem to assume." He paused, then grimaced. "Well, better than *I'd* ever assumed, anyway, and I doubt I was unique."

"Then how come they keep getting their ears pinned back?"

"I said their stuff wasn't as good as ours . . . but most of it's probably as good as anything anyone else has. Their real problem is that they don't know how to get the best out of what they've already got. Their software sucks, for instance, and most of their maintenance is done by commissioned personnel, not petty officers and ratings. Oh—" Tremaine waved both hands "—they don't have anything like the FTL com, and they haven't cracked the new compensators, the new beta nodes, or any of that stuff. But look at their missile pods. They're not as good as ours, but they go for a brute force approach to put enough extra warheads into a salvo to pretty much even the odds. And think about Ghost Rider. It's going to be years before they can match our new remote EW capability, but if they wanted to accept bigger launchers and lower missile load-outs, they could probably match the extended range capabilities of Ghost Rider's *offensive* side. Heck, build the suckers big enough, and they could do it with off-the-shelf components, Stew!"

"Hmph! Have to be *really* big brutes to pull it off," Ashford grumbled. "Too big to be effective as shipboard weapons, anyway."

"What about launching them from a pod format for system defense?" Tremaine challenged. "For that matter, put enough of them in single-shot launchers on tow behind destroyers and light cruisers, even if they had to trade 'em out on a one-for-one basis with entire pods of normal missiles, and they could still get a useful salvo off. I'm not saying they can meet us toe-to-toe on our terms. I'm only saying that a Peep admiral or tac officer who knows how to get maximum performance out of his hardware can still do one hell of a lot of damage, however good we are. Or think we are."

"You're probably right," Ashford admitted slowly. "And they can afford to *take* more damage than we can, too, can't they?"

"That they can . . . at the moment. Of course, that could change with the new designs and—"

The hatch to the sim compartment slid open, and Tremaine broke off as he turned towards it. Then his face lit with an enormous smile as a sandy-haired man with a prizefighter's build and a battered face stepped through it.

"Chief!" the commander exclaimed, stepping forward quickly, then paused as the newcomer held up one hand in a "stop" gesture, pointed at his collar insignia with his other hand, and gave a huge, toothy grin.

"Whoa! I mean Chief *Warrant Officer* Harkness!" Tremaine said with a grin of his own, and finished throwing his arms around the older man in a bear hug.

Stewart Ashford blinked at the sight, for commissioned officers did not normally greet their subordinates quite that enthusiastically. But then the name registered, and he gave the warrant officer a sudden, eagle-eyed second look.

Tremaine had eased up on the hug, though he still held the older man by the upper arms, and Ashford nodded. The crimson, blue, and white ribbon of the Parliamentary Medal of Valor could not be mistaken, even if this was only the third time he'd ever actually seen it on anyone. Besides, he should have recognized the man who wore it instantly. That battered face had certainly looked out of enough HDs and 'faxes once the newsies got hold of the details of PNS *Tepes'* destruction.

"Captain Ashford," Tremaine began, turning back to face him, "this is—"

"—Chief Warrant Officer Sir Horace Harkness, I believe," Ashford finished. Harkness came to attention and started a salute, but Ashford's hand beat him to it. As was only fitting. Anyone who'd won the PMV was entitled to take a salute from anyone who hadn't, and that was one tradition for which the captain felt no resentment at all.

"I'm very pleased to meet you, Mr. Harkness," the captain said as the warrant officer returned his salute. "I won't belabor the reasons—I imagine you're well and truly tired of hearing about them anyway—but I do have one request."

"Request, Sir?" Harkness repeated cautiously, and Ashford grinned.

"It's only a small one, Sir Horace, but you see, some time ago, someone dropped a little surprise into my LAC's computers. It was a legitimate trick, I suppose, under the circumstances, since, as Commander Tremaine here was just reminding me, the object is for us to learn to expect the unexpected. But as he was also just reminding me, misery loves company, and it just occurred to me that doctoring the computers could be the sort of tradition I should be passing on to some poor bast—er, I mean some *deserving soul* in my own wing. And since I understand you have a certain way with computers . . . ?"

His voice trailed off suggestively, and Harkness grinned.

"Now, Sir, that would hardly be a nice thing to do. And I've sort of promised the Navy I'd swear off playing with computer systems in return for a certain, ah, lack of scrutiny where a few of my records over at BuPers are concerned. And maybe one or two minor files at the Judge Advocate General's office, too. And then there was that— Well, never mind. The point is, I'm not supposed to be doing that kind of thing anymore."

"But it would be in a very good cause," Ashford pointed out persuasively.

"Sure it would," Harkness agreed with a snort. "You just go right on telling yourself that, Sir. Me, I can't help thinking what you really want is to see to it that you're not the only one it happens to."

"Oh, there's some of that in it," Ashford admitted cheerfully. Then his expression sobered just a bit. "But as Commander Tremaine just discovered, surprise actually is a legitimate teaching tool, and better my boys and girls get some egg on their faces from something *I* do to them than sail all fat and happy into something the *Peeps* do to them."

"There's something to that, Chief. I mean Chief Warrant Officer," Tremaine said.

"Chief's just fine, Sir," Harkness told him, then shrugged. "Well, I guess if the Captain really wants it, I'll just have to see what I can do for him. Assuming that's all right with you, anyway, Sir."

"Me?" Tremaine raised an eyebrow, and Harkness nodded.

"Yes, Sir. Seems like I'm your new senior flight engineer, Mr. Tremaine. I know it's supposed to be a commissioned slot, but I guess BuPers decided that under the circumstances, seeing as how I've already spent so much time keepin' an eye on you and all, you'd just have to make do with me. Unless you'd rather not, of course?"

"Rather not?" Tremaine shook his head and slapped the older man on the upper arm. "Do I *look* like I'm crazy?" Harkness grinned and opened his mouth, but Tremaine cut him off in the nick of time. "Don't answer that, *Sir* Horace!" he said hastily. "But in answer to your question, no. There's no one I'd rather have."

"Well, good," Chief Warrant Officer Sir Horace Harkness, PMV, CGM, and DSO said. " 'Cause it looks like you're sorta stuck with me, Sir." He paused. "Until the shore patrol turns up, anyway!"

CHAPTER ELEVEN

Honor was buried in paperwork when a hand rapped gently on her Advanced Tactical Course office door. She didn't notice the quiet sound in her preoccupation . . . until it rapped again, harder, and a throat cleared itself with pointed firmness.

That got her attention, and she looked up.

"Commander Jaruwalski is here, Ma'am," James MacGuiness said in the tone he reserved for those private moments when his wayward charge required chiding, and Honor chuckled. His eyes twinkled back ever so slightly, but the look he gave her was stern, and she composed her own expression into a properly chastened one.

"Yes, Mac," she said meekly. "Would you show her in, please?"

"In a moment, Ma'am," he replied, and crossed to her desk. It was littered with data chips, the remnants of her working lunch, a sticky-looking cocoa mug, the crusty rim of a slice of Key lime pie, a two-thirds-devoured bowl of celery, and an empty beer stein. As she looked on in faint bemusement, MacGuiness caused all that clutter—except the data chips—to teleport itself neatly onto the tray on which he'd delivered lunch in the first place. It couldn't possibly be as easy as he made it appear, Honor thought, and then smiled as his brisk fingers twitched and flipped even her data chips into seeming order. He took another second to straighten the flower arrangement on the credenza, check Nimitz and Samantha's perch, and scrutinize Honor's uniform. A speck of fluff on her right shoulder earned an ever so slight frown, and he flicked it off with a tiny sniff.

154

"*Now* I'll show her in, Ma'am," he said then, and departed with his tray in austere majesty, leaving the large office magically neat and tidy behind him.

Nimitz bleeked quizzically from his place beside Samantha, and Honor smiled as she tasted their shared delight. She couldn't be certain whether they were more amused by the arcane fashion in which MacGuiness created order out of chaos or by the firm manner in which he managed *her*, but it didn't really matter.

"No, I don't know how he does it either," she told them, choosing to assume it was the former, and both 'cats radiated silent laughter into the back of her mind.

She shook her head at them, then tipped back in her chair to await her guest.

It was odd, she thought. Or she supposed many people would find it so, at any rate. James MacGuiness had to be the wealthiest steward in the history of the Royal Manticoran Navy. If he was still *in* the Navy, that was. She'd left him forty million dollars in her will, and he'd known better than even to try to give it back when she turned back up alive. Most people with that kind of money would have been out hiring servants of their own, but MacGuiness had made it quietly but firmly clear, without ever actually saying so, that he was, and intended to remain, Honor's steward.

She'd tried, in rather half-hearted fashion, to convince him to remain on Grayson as Harrington House's majordomo. He'd shown a pronounced gift for managing the staff there (which, in Honor's opinion, was far too large . . . as if anyone cared what *she* thought about it), and she'd known how badly Clinkscales and her parents would miss his unobtrusive efficiency. More than that, Nimitz and Samantha had left their 'kittens behind. The kids were old enough now to be fostered, and they would certainly suffer no shortage of 'cat parenting with Hera, Athena, Artemis, and all the males prepared to keep a wary eye on their mischief making. The normal pattern, in the very rare instances in which a female 'cat who had adopted a human also produced a litter of 'kittens, was to foster them at two or three T-years of age. Samantha's need to remain at the side of her mate while he grappled with the loss of his mental voice had simply added a bit more urgency than usual to the fostering arrangement.

But MacGuiness had been the 'kittens' *human* foster parent for over two T-years. Honor knew how hard it had been for him to leave the cuddly, rambunctious, loving, chaos-inducing balls of downy fur behind, and she'd tasted the 'kittens' wistful sadness at his departure, as well. And it wasn't as if he'd *had* to follow her back off Grayson. At her own "posthumous" request, the RMN had allowed him to resign in order to remain permanently at Harrington House. And, she admitted, she hadn't asked the Service to do so simply because of his role in her Grayson establishment. She'd dragged him into and—barely—out of far too many battles, and she'd wanted him safely on the sidelines.

Unfortunately, that was an option she didn't appear to have. She still wasn't sure how he'd gotten his way . . . again. They'd never argued about it. There'd been no need to. By some form of mental judo which put her own skill at *coup de vitesse* to shame, he'd simply avoided the entire discussion and appeared aboard the *Paul Tankersley* for the trip to the Star Kingdom. Nor had the Navy been any more successful at imposing its own, institutional sense of order on the situation. MacGuiness had never reenlisted and showed no particular desire to do so . . . yet no one in the Service seemed aware that he hadn't. Honor was positive that, as a civilian, he must be in violation of about a zillion regulations in his current position. The security aspects of the ATC materials to which he had access alone must be enough to drive a good, paranoid ONI counterintelligence type berserk! But no one seemed to have the nerve to tell him he was breaking the rules.

Which, if she were going to be honest, was precisely how she preferred things. There'd been a time when the mere thought of a permanent personal servant had seemed preposterous and presumptuous. In many ways, it still did . . . but MacGuiness was no more her "servant" than Nimitz was. She didn't know precisely how to characterize their actual relationship, but that didn't matter at all. What mattered was that commodore, admiral, steadholder, or duchess, she was still James MacGuiness' captain, and he was still her keeper and friend.

Even if he *was* a multimillionaire civilian these days.

She chuckled again, then banished her fond smile as MacGuiness returned with a dark, hawk-faced woman in an RMN commander's uniform. It wasn't hard to assume a more solemn expression, for the dark cloud of the other woman's emotions—a wary bitterness and dread, only slightly lightened by a small sense of curiosity— reached out to her like a harsh hand, and it was all she could do not to wince in sympathy.

I think my suspicion must have been right about on the money. And I wish it hadn't been. But maybe we can do a little something about this after all.

"Commander Jaruwalski, Your Grace," MacGuiness announced

with the flawless formality he saved for times when company was present.

"Thank you, Mac." Honor said, then rose and held out her hand to Jaruwalski. "Good afternoon, Commander. Thank you for arriving so promptly on such short notice."

"It wasn't all that short, Your Grace." Jaruwalski's soprano sounded very much like Honor's own, but with a washed-out, beaten down undertone. "And to be honest, it wasn't as if I had a lot of other things to be doing anyway," Jaruwalski added with what was probably meant to be a smile.

"I see." Honor squeezed her hand firmly, for just a moment longer than was strictly necessary, then broke the handclasp to gesture at the chair which faced her desk. "Please, be seated. Make yourself comfortable." She waited until Jaruwalski had settled herself, then crooked an eyebrow. "Are you a beer drinker, by any chance, Commander?"

"Why, yes. I am, Your Grace." The commander was clearly surprised by the question, and that surprise seemed to cut through a bit of her enshrouding gloom.

"Good!" Honor said, and looked at MacGuiness. "In that case, Mac, would you bring us a couple of steins of Old Tilman, please?"

"Of course, Your Grace." The steward glanced courteously at Jaruwalski. "Would the Commander like anything to go with her beer?"

"No, thank you. The beer will be just fine . . . Mr. MacGuiness." The brief pause and her hesitant use of the civilian address echoed Honor's earlier thoughts, but her confusion over MacGuiness' status was definitely a secondary concern for her at the moment. It was obvious from the taste of her emotions that no flag officers had been in the habit of inviting her to drop by for a beer over the course of the last T-year.

"Very good, Ma'am," MacGuiness murmured, and withdrew with a silence any treecat might have envied.

Jaruwalski gazed after him for a moment, then turned resolutely back to face Honor. There was something very like quiet defiance in her body language, and Honor hid another wince as she tasted the bitterness behind the other woman's dark eyes.

"No doubt you're wondering why I asked you to come see me," she said after the briefest of pauses.

"Yes, Your Grace, I am," Jaruwalski replied in a flattened voice. "You're the first flag officer who's wanted to see me since the Seaford Board finished its deliberations." She smiled and gave a slight, bitter toss of her head. "In fact, you're the first senior officer who hasn't seemed to be going out of her way to *avoid* seeing me, if you'll forgive my bluntness."

"I'm not surprised to hear that," Honor said calmly. "Under the circumstances, I suppose I'd be astonished if it had been any other way." Jaruwalski's nostrils flared, and Honor tasted her instant, inner bristling. But she gave no sign of it as she continued in that same deliberate tone. "There's always a temptation to shoot the messenger if the news is bad, even among people who ought to know better than to blame her for it. Who *do* know better, when all's said."

Jaruwalski didn't—quite—blink, but Honor tasted a sudden watchful stillness at the commander's core. She'd answered Honor's summons unwillingly and come to this office wary and defensive, trying with forlorn pride to hide her inner wounds. It was clear she'd expected those wounds to be ripped open once again, but Honor's response had robbed her of that expectation. Now she didn't know just what Honor *did* want, and that made her feel uncertain and exposed. However much the contempt with which she'd been treated had hurt, at least it had been something she'd understood. And she dared not let herself hope this meeting might produce anything except more of the same.

Not yet, at any rate, Honor thought, and looked away as MacGuiness reappeared with two frosty steins of dark amber beer. He'd taken time to put together a small tray of cheese and raw vegetables, as well, and she shook her head with a smile as he set his burden on the corner of her desk and whisked out a snowy napkin for each of them.

"You are entirely too prone to spoil people, Mac," she told him severely.

"I wouldn't say that, Your Grace," he replied calmly.

"Not in front of a guest, anyway," she teased. It was his turn to shake his head at her, and then he withdrew once more and she looked back at Jaruwalski.

The commander had smiled, almost despite herself, at the exchange. Now she pushed the smile off her lips, but without quite the same wariness, and Honor waved at the stein closer to her.

"Help yourself, Commander," she invited, and took a deep swallow of her own beer. It was all she could do not to sigh as the rich, crisp brew slid down her throat. Of all the things she'd missed on Hell, she often thought she'd missed Old Tilman most. The StateSec garrison had imported Peep beer (most of which could have been poured back into the horse and left the universe a better place, in Honor's opinion) and some of the SS personnel and prisoners had tried their hands at brewing. But none of them had managed to get it right. For that matter, Honor had come to suspect that some subtle mutation in the hops or barley grown on Sphinx was responsible for the unique and outstanding products of the Tilman Brewery.

Jaruwalski seemed to hear the sigh Honor didn't permit herself, and her mouth twitched. Then she settled back in her chair and took a slow, appreciative swallow of her own.

Honor was careful not to show the deep satisfaction she felt as the commander relaxed. It was unusual for a flag officer to offer a subordinate beer, or anything else even mildly alcoholic, during "business hours." On the other hand, the circumstances of this meeting were hardly usual, and Jaruwalski had obviously faced more than her fair share of excruciatingly formal meetings since the Second Battle of Seaford.

Honor gave the other woman a few more moments, then leaned forward and set down her beer.

"As I said, I'm sure you wondered what it was I wanted to see you about," she said quietly. Jaruwalski stiffened back up just a little, but said nothing. She only gazed back at Honor, waiting. "You probably had a few suspicions—none of them pleasant, I imagine—about why someone from the Admiralty might want to see you, but you couldn't imagine why *I* should ask you to come by my office. Unless, of course, I intended to use you as some sort of 'horrible example' for Crusher candidates, since it must have become obvious to you that you had no hope of further promotion after Seaford."

Her voice was conversational, almost mild, and it hurt Jaruwalski even more because it lacked the vitriol she must have heard from so many others.

"I did wonder, Your Grace," she said after a moment, trying very hard to keep the hurt and bitterness from showing. "I rather doubted that you intended to offer *me* a shot at the Crusher," she added in a gallant attempt at humor.

"No, I don't," Honor told her. "But I may able to offer you something you'll find equally interesting."

"You may?" Surprise startled Jaruwalski into the cardinal sin of interrupting an admiral, and her dark face grew still darker as she realized it had.

"I may," Honor repeated, and tipped her chair back. "Before we go any further, Commander, I should perhaps tell you that I once served under Elvis Santino," she said, and paused. This time she obviously expected a response, and Jaruwalski cocked her head to one side and narrowed her eyes.

"You did, Your Grace? I didn't know that."

And you don't know just where I'm headed, either. But you will, Commander.

"Yes. In fact, I first met him on my middy cruise. We deployed to Silesia in the old *War Maiden*, and he was assistant tac officer." Jaruwalski's face twisted ever so slightly at that, and Honor smiled with no humor at all. "You may, perhaps, begin to suspect why I was less surprised than many to hear about what happened at Seaford," she said in a kiln-dry tone.

"I take it he was . . . less than stellar in that role, Your Grace?" The commander's soprano was as dry as Honor's own, hiding the hatred which had welled up within her at the mention of Santino's name, yet it also held an echo of something like humor.

"You might say that," Honor allowed. "Or you might say that, as a tac officer, he needed four astro fixes, a hyper log, approach radar, and a dirtside flight controller with full computer support just to find his backside with both hands. On a good day."

This time Jaruwalski found it impossible to hide her surprise. Her eyes widened at the scathing condemnation of Honor's tone, and she sat very still.

"I've read the Board's report on Seaford," Honor went on after a moment, in a more normal voice. "Having known Santino, I suspect I have a better grasp than many of what went on—or didn't, as the case may be—in his head. I've never understood how he managed to scrape through the Crusher himself, or how even someone with his family connections could get promoted so high with such a dismal performance record. But I wasn't a bit surprised by the fact that he clearly panicked when it hit the fan."

"Excuse me, Your Grace, but I was under the impression that many senior officers felt he *ought* to have 'panicked' . . . and didn't. Or I thought the consensus was that he should have been cautious enough not to close head-on with the enemy when they outnumbered him so heavily, at least."

"There's panic, and then there's panic, Commander. Fear of the odds, of the enemy, even of death is one thing. All of us feel that. We'd be fools if we didn't. But we learn not to let it dictate our responses. We can't, if we're going to do our jobs.

"But there's another sort of terror: the terror of failure, of being blamed for some disaster, or of assuming responsibility. It's not just the fear of dying; it's the fear of living *through* something like Seaford while everyone laughs behind your back at what an idiot you were to allow yourself to be placed in such a disastrous situation. And the fact that Elvis Santino really *was* an idiot only made that fear worse in his case."

She paused, tilting her head to study Jaruwalski with her working eye. The commander met her gaze steadily, but she was clearly uneasy. She agreed completely with Honor's assessment of Santino, yet she was only a commander . . . and one whose career had come to a crashing halt. A commander had no business criticizing any admiral, and given her situation, anything she said would have to sound self-serving.

"I was particularly struck by three points in the Board's report, all relating more or less directly to you, Commander," Honor continued after a few heartbeats. "One was that a flag officer about to face the enemy in an extremely uneven battle deprived himself of an experienced tactical officer who'd obviously been on the station long enough to have a much better grasp of local conditions than he did. The second was that having done so, he went to the length of having that tac officer removed from his flagship *and* took time to dictate a message explaining her relief for 'lack of offensive-mindedness,' 'lack of preparedness,' and 'failure to properly execute her duties.' And the third . . . The *third* point, Commander, was that you never defended yourself against his charges. Would you care to comment on any of those points?"

"Ma'am— Your Grace, I *can't* comment on them." Jaruwalski's voice was frayed about the edges, and she swallowed hard. "Admiral Santino is dead. So is every other member of his staff and any other individual who might have heard or seen what actually happened. It would . . . . I mean, how could I expect anyone to believe that—"

Her voice broke, and she waved both hands in a small, helpless gesture. For just a moment, the mask slipped, and all the vulnerability and hurt she'd sought so hard to hide looked out of her eyes at Honor. But then she drew a deep breath, and the mask came back once more.

"There was a time in my life, Commander," Honor said conversationally, "when I, too, thought no one would believe me if I disputed a senior's version of events. He was very nobly born, and wealthy, with powerful friends and patrons, and I was a yeoman's daughter from Sphinx, with no sponsors, and certainly with no family wealth or power to back me up. So I kept quiet about his actions . . . and it very nearly ruined my career. Not once, but several times, until we finally wound up on the Landing City dueling grounds."

Jaruwalski's mouth opened in surprise as she realized who Honor was talking about, but Honor went right on in that same casual tone.

"Looking back, I can see that anyone who knew him would have recognized the truth when they heard it, if only I'd had the confidence to tell them. Or perhaps what I really needed was confidence in myself—in the idea that the Navy might actually value *me* as much as it did a useless, over-bred, arrogant parasite who happened to be an earl's son. And, to be honest, there was a sense of guilt in my silence, as well. A notion that somehow I must have contributed to what happened, that at least part of it truly was my fault."

She paused and smiled crookedly.

"Does any of that sound familiar to you, Commander?" she asked very quietly after a moment.

"I—" Jaruwalski stared at her, and Honor sighed.

"Very well, Commander. Let me tell you what *I* think happened on *Hadrian*'s flag deck when Lester Tourville came over the hyper wall. I think Elvis Santino hadn't put himself to the trouble of reviewing the tactical plans he'd inherited from Admiral Hennesy. I think he was taken totally by surprise, and I think that because he hadn't bothered to review Hennesy's—and your—contingency plans, he didn't have a clue about what to do. I think he panicked because he knew the Admiralty would *realize* he hadn't had a clue when it read his after-action report. And I think that the two of you argued over the proper response. That you protested his intentions and that he took out his fear and anger on you by relieving you . . . and taking the time on the very edge of battle to send along a message with no specifics at all, only allegations so general you couldn't effectively dispute them, which he knew would finish your career. And, of course, just incidentally make you the whipping girl for anything that went wrong after your departure, since it would clearly have been *your* lack of preparedness, not his, which had created the situation. Is that a fairly accurate summation, Commander?"

Silence hovered in the office, hard and bitter, as Jaruwalski stared into Honor's one good eye. The tension seemed to sing higher and higher, and then the commander's shoulders slumped.

"Yes, Ma'am," she said, her near-whisper so quiet Honor could scarcely hear her. "That's . . . pretty much what happened."

Honor leaned back once more, her face no more than calmly thoughtful, while she and both of her friends strained their empathic senses to assay that soft reply. It would be very easy for someone who truly had been guilty of Santino's allegations to lie and agree with her, but there was no falsehood in Andrea Jaruwalski. There was enormous pain, and sorrow, and a bitter resentment that no one before Honor had bothered to reach the same conclusions, but no lie, and Honor drew a breath of mingled relief and satisfaction.

"I thought it might have been," she said, almost as quietly as Jaruwalski had spoken. "I reviewed your scores from the regular Tactical Officer's Course, and they didn't seem to go with someone who suffers from a lack of offensive-mindedness. Neither did the string of excellent efficiency evaluations in your personnel jacket. But someone had to take it in the neck over Seaford, and Santino wasn't available. Not to mention the fact that even people who'd met him had to wonder if this time he might not have had a point, since surely not even *he* would dismiss the officer he most desperately needed if she hadn't screwed up massively. But you knew that, didn't you?"

She paused, and Jaruwalski nodded jerkily.

"Of course you did," Honor murmured. "And you didn't defend yourself by telling the Board what actually happened because you thought no one would believe you. That they'd assume you were trying to find some way—*any* way—to defuse the serious charges Santino had leveled against you."

"No, I didn't think anyone would believe me," the other woman admitted, face and voice bleak. "And even if someone had been inclined to, as you say, he was dead. It would have been my unsupported word against that of an officer who'd been so disgusted by my lack of nerve that he'd taken time to make my cowardice and incompetence a part of the official record even as he headed into battle against hopeless odds."

She shrugged with hard-edged helplessness, and Honor nodded.

"That was what I thought. I could just see Santino's face as he dictated that message, and I knew a little too much about *his* 'lack of offensive-mindedness.' And his laziness. *And* his habit of looking for scapegoats."

It was her turn to shrug, with a very different emphasis, and silence stretched out between them. It radiated from Honor's desk like ripples of quiet, flowing over them both, and she tasted the relief, almost worse than pain, as Jaruwalski realized there truly was one person in the universe who believed what had actually happened.

The commander picked up her stein and took a long swallow, then inhaled deeply. Her face was closed off no longer, and in its relaxation it lost its masklike discipline. Now it was almost gaunt, sagging with the weariness and pain its owner had hidden for so long, and her eyes were intent as she studied Honor's expression.

"Your Grace, I can never tell you how much it helps to hear you say what you've just said. It's probably too late to make any difference where my career is concerned, but just knowing one person understands what really happened, is—" She shook her head. "I can't begin to say how important that is to me. But grateful as I am, I can't help wondering why you've bothered to take the time to tell me."

"Because I have a question for you, Commander," Honor said. "A very important one, actually."

"Of course, Ma'am." There was a faint edge of fresh fear in the taste of the commander's emotions, a worry that whatever Honor wanted to know would destroy her sense of understanding. But even though she waited with inner dread for the second shoe to drop, her voice was steady and she met Honor's gaze without flinching.

"What advice *did* you give, Admiral Santino?" Honor asked very quietly.

"I advised him to withdraw immediately, Your Grace." Jaruwalski never hesitated. She knew Honor's reputation, and Honor felt her fear as if it were her own—the fear that the one person who'd guessed what had happened would decide that perhaps the admiral's allegations had been accurate after all. That Jaruwalski *had* given in to the counsel of her own fears. The fact that Honor had obviously considered Santino a feckless incompetent didn't necessarily mean the woman the newsies called the Salamander wouldn't have looked for some *intelligent* form of offensive action rather than supinely surrender her command area. But Honor had asked a question . . . and Andrea Jaruwalski had answered it honestly, despite her dread that her honesty would cost her the only sympathetic ear she'd found in almost a T-year of bitter humiliation.

"Good," Honor said softly, and smiled crookedly as the commander twitched.

She didn't know whether she would have called Jaruwalski's answer "good" if not for her link to Nimitz and her ability to experience the commander's emotions and honesty directly. She liked to hope she would have, yet her own nagging honesty made her wonder if she really would have been able to look at the reply with sufficient dispassion for that. But it didn't really matter at the moment.

"I'm glad to hear you say that," she went on after a moment. "Glad because it was the right decision, given the value—or lack of value—of Seaford Nine's facilities and the weight of metal you faced. And glad because you didn't waffle when I asked. I rather suspected what sort of person would make Elvis Santino feel so small he would overcome his own terror long enough to ensure the destruction of her career. Now I've had an opportunity to see for myself, and I'm glad I have."

"You are, Your Grace?" Jaruwalski sounded stunned, as if she were unable even now to fully credit what she was hearing, and Honor nodded.

"We assume a certain level of physical courage in a Queen's officer, Andrea," she said. "And usually, by and large, we find it. It may not say great things for human intelligence that our officers are more concerned with living up to the Saganami tradition, at least in the eyes of their fellows, than of dying, but it's a very useful foible when it comes to winning wars.

"But what we ought to treasure far more deeply is the moral courage to shoulder *all* of an officer's responsibilities. To look *past* the 'Saganami tradition' and see the point at which her true responsibility as a Queen's officer requires her to do something which may end her career. Or, worse, earn her the contempt of those whose good opinion she values but who weren't there, didn't see the choices she had to make. I ordered one of my closest friends to surrender his ship to the Peeps. He was fully prepared to go out fighting, just as I suppose I might have been in his place. But *my* responsibility was to see to it that his people's lives weren't sacrificed in a battle we couldn't possibly win.

"That was hard. One of the hardest things I've ever done, and it almost got me hanged. But even knowing what the Peeps planned to do to me, personally, my responsibility, in the same situation, would be to give the same order again."

She looked deep into Andrea Jaruwalski's eyes, and her own softened with approval for what she saw there.

"I believe you advised Admiral Santino to withdraw, and I believe you did it for the right reasons. Not out of fear, but out of common sense and sanity. And that was no easier for you than ordering Alistair McKeon to surrender was for me, because it *does* cut against the tradition. But there comes a time when we have to look past the form of a tradition to the reason it came into existence in the first place, and throwing away a task force, and all the lives that go with it, in a futile gesture of defiance is not what Edward Saganami did or would have expected those who followed him to do. If there's even the remotest chance of victory, or if other, over-riding considerations, like the honor of the Star Kingdom or the risk of losing an ally's trust, make it necessary, that's one thing. But to take a force that badly outnumbered into the teeth of that much firepower in defense of a star system that was of absolutely no use to us in the first place...?"

She shook her head firmly.

"You saw that, and you advised your admiral to see it for himself. He failed because he lacked the moral courage you displayed in advising him, and his failure killed him and every man and woman aboard his flagship... and most of the people aboard all the other ships of his command. When it comes to choosing between two people who demonstrate those patterns of behavior, I know which one *I* want in the Queen's service. Which is why I asked you to come see me."

Jaruwalski's eyebrows rose in silent question, and Honor smiled.

"I've been in command of ATC for less than two weeks now," she said. "I've got three very capable deputies, plus my own experience with the Crusher, and despite the extra load Admiral Caparelli saw fit to assign me as a Tactics 101 lecturer, I've already identified several changes I want to make. Places I want to tweak the program just a bit, or change its emphasis slightly. And I want you to help me do that."

"*Me*, Your Grace?" Jaruwalski was obviously certain she'd misunderstood, and Honor chuckled.

"You. I need an aide, Andrea. Someone whose judgment I trust, who'll understand what I'm trying to do and see to it that the effort gets organized effectively. And someone who can stand in for me in the simulators, and in the classroom sessions, when I can't make it myself. And someone, if you don't mind my saying so, who can serve as a living example of how to do it right... despite the price they may have to pay afterward."

Jaruwalski's dark face had paled, and she blinked hard, lower lip trembling ever so slightly.

"Besides," Honor went on in a deliberately lighter tone, "I've got at least one much less laudable reason to offer you the slot."

"Y-you do, Ma'am?" The commander's soprano was husky, and it stumbled just a bit over the first word, but Honor pretended she hadn't noticed.

"Of course I do!" she said, and her smile was her best 'cat-in-a-celery-patch grin. "Just think of it—this gives me the opportunity to poke that jackass Santino right in the eye even after he's gone by 'rehabilitating' the officer whose career he tried to wreck out of sheer spite and spleen. Heavens, woman! How could I possibly pass up an opportunity like *that?*"

CHAPTER TWELVE

"Who did they say they were?" Samuel Mueller asked his steward. "They *said* they were investors looking for sites for new farming domes, My Lord," Crawford Buckeridge replied. The steward had been with Mueller for over thirty years, and the steadholder did not miss the slight emphasis he'd placed on the verb.

He gave no sign of it, however. He often wondered what Buckeridge thought of his own . . . extracurricular activities. The Buckeridges had been in the service of the Muellers for generations, so whatever the steward might think, Mueller had no fear of his mentioning anything to anyone else. But Buckeridge was also a deeply religious man who'd been badly shaken by the murder of Reverend Julius Hanks and the proof that William Fitzclarence had been behind both that and the deaths of dozens of school children right here in Mueller Steading. While the steward disapproved of Benjamin Mayhew's reforms as severely as Mueller could have asked for, he'd been horrified that a steadholder could stoop to such actions, which probably meant it was fortunate that he'd never realized Mueller had been Fitzclarence's silent partner.

But not for that insane assassination plan of his, Mueller reminded himself. *I still can't imagine what got into his so-called brain to inspire him to that. Brother Marchant had a lot to do with it, no doubt, but could even Marchant have been so stupid as to* deliberately *kill Reverend Hanks?*

He shook his head, brushing aside a familiar sense of bemusement. It wasn't as if it really mattered. Marchant and Fitzclarence were both dead, and no one had tied him to either of them. Besides, he'd been out of his mind to get involved in something so crude, and he was just as happy to be rid of such incompetent allies. Violence, whether open or covert, was not the answer. Not because he had any particular moral objections—indeed, one of his fondest dreams was of Honor Harrington and Benjamin Mayhew in the same air car as it blew up in midair—but because killing either of them at this point would probably be counterproductive. Especially since Harrington had come back from the dead and added *that* accomplishment to her Grayson hagiography.

Too many people were prepared to carry on if anything happened to her or Mayhew these days, and the only way to deal with that was to build a counterorganization, one openly dedicated to slowing the "reform" process . . . although only through legal, constitutional channels, of course. Since Mayhew had succeeded in institutionalizing his reforms, dismantling them would require an institutional framework of its own, and that was what Mueller had dedicated himself to building. At the same time, he'd retained some of his old clandestine connections. Most of them were pure information conduits these days, but he still had a few contacts tucked away that were a bit more action-oriented. He had to be particularly careful about those contacts, but he *was* a steadholder. And the leader of what had emerged as the equivalent of the loyal opposition, at that, which meant even Mayhew had to be very careful when dealing with him, lest it appear he were attempting to smear someone simply because that someone disagreed with him.

Mueller snorted at the thought. No one on Grayson had had any experience in running a system of government based on a division of powers eleven T-years ago. If they'd *had* that experience, they might have been able to hold Mayhew in check and prevent the entire damned "Mayhew Restoration." But they hadn't, and when Mayhew reasserted the written Constitution during the Masadan Crisis, he'd gotten away with resurrecting an autocratic system which the Keys, individually and collectively, lacked the strength to break.

Since they couldn't break it, they'd had to learn to work within it, and that took time. Whatever else he might be, Mayhew was a student of history and an extremely astute politician. He'd taken ruthless advantage of the Keys' temporary paralysis and overturned *their* autocracy and secured near total ascendancy for the Sword while they were still dithering and trying to remember what the ancient procedures had been. But they'd learned eventually, and the degree of autonomy they enjoyed within their own steadings had helped. At least they still possessed solid local bases of support, plus control of the organs of government and law enforcement in their home steadings. And Mueller, in particular, had emerged as a master of parliamentary tactics. He and his allies could only nibble away at the Protector's power at the moment, but he was patient. Benjamin IX's attention was being drawn more and more completely to fighting the war. No one could have the energy or time to do that effectively and keep a keen watch on all the domestic aspects of his government, and Mueller had convinced his fellow opposition leaders to work quietly and carefully in the shadows to which Benjamin could no longer pay close attention. It wasn't glorious or spectacular, but, in time, it would prove to be something much more important than either of those things: effective.

Still, his position as the clear leader of those opposed—respectfully, of course—to the Mayhew reforms put him in a somewhat exposed position. Every crackpot who had any hope of working within the system, and quite a few perfectly content to work outside it, saw him as a logical rallying point. The strangest people seemed to spring out of the very ground to bring him their plans and suggestions, and as he reflected on his steward's response to these two, he wondered how odd *they* were going to turn out to be.

On the other hand, one never knew when even the most unlikely tools could turn out to be just what one needed, could one?

"Show them into my office—the formal one. And have someone keep an eye on them. Hmmmm . . . Hughes, I think."

"Yes, My Lord," Buckeridge replied, and turned to sail majestically off.

Mueller smiled after him. Buckeridge didn't much care for Sergeant Steve Hughes. Not because of anything the armsman had ever done, but because, unlike the steward, Hughes was the first of his family in Mueller Steading. But that was all right with Mueller. For certain sensitive duties, he relied on people Buckeridge would have approved of, whose families *had* served his for decades or centuries. He could trust those people to keep their mouths shut and their thoughts to themselves, assuming they thought about his instructions at all rather than simply obeying. But Hughes was part of the new breed. A tall, lanky fellow, especially for a Grayson, he was far more comfortable than his more traditional fellows with the new technology gushing into Grayson. He was particularly good with computer software, and he'd been very useful to the Mueller Steadholder's Guard (and to Samuel Mueller personally) in that area.

More importantly, he was virulently conservative and almost

rabidly religious, with an oppressive personal piety which was a rarity even on theocratic Grayson. Those character traits went a bit oddly with his fascination with the new technology pouring into his home world from the off-worlders he hated, but that didn't bother Hughes. And they did make him particularly valuable to Mueller. It was good to have someone who was reliable and intelligent (those two qualities, alas, did not always go together among his more traditional retainers) *and* technologically sophisticated.

Sergeant Hughes had only been with the Mueller Guard for about five years, and Mueller had been very cautious about him initially. As the man had proved his reliability and demonstrated his conservative bent, however, he had been gradually tapped for increasingly sensitive duties. Nothing *seriously* illegal, of course. Mueller didn't do much of that sort of thing anymore, and he knew precisely which of his armsmen to rely upon for the rare instances in which something a little . . . irregular had to be accomplished. But Hughes had amply demonstrated his fundamental reliability, and Mueller had come to depend on him in matters which were merely shady.

He chuckled again at the thought, then pushed back his chair. The office from which he actually ran his steading was far less grand than the formal one to which Buckeridge had just shown his guests. It was also more comfortable and much more efficiently arranged . . . and he had no intention of allowing anyone he did not know and trust absolutely anywhere near it.

He tucked a few record chips and several pages of old-fashioned, handwritten notes into a secure drawer of the desk, closed it, and spun the ancient but still effective combination lock. Then he shrugged into his jacket, straightened his tie, and walked slowly down the hall towards his waiting visitors.

The two men sat patiently in the armchairs to which Buckeridge had ushered them, and Mueller smiled as he noted the coffee cups on the low table between their chairs. They were from the everyday set, not one of the more formal china patterns. Obviously Buckeridge considered these people to be of sufficient potential worth to his master that they merited the rites of hospitality; equally obviously, he didn't much approve of what he clearly considered to be their devious, probably dishonest way of approaching his steadholder.

Poor Crawford. If he only knew, Mueller thought, but he allowed his expression to show no trace of it as he walked briskly into the room.

Sergeant Hughes stood just inside the door, imposing in Mueller red-and-yellow, and Mueller nodded to him as he passed. The strangers heard him enter and rose quickly, turning towards him with courteous expressions.

"Good morning, gentlemen." The steadholder sounded breezy, like the confident, busy, *honest* man he was. "I'm Lord Mueller. What can I do for you this fine day?"

The strangers glanced at one another, as if taken a bit aback by such cheerful gusto, and he hid an inward, catlike smile. It wasn't strictly necessary in this case, of course, but he *did* enjoy playing with people's minds.

"Good morning, My Lord," the older of them finally said. "My name is Anthony Baird, and my friend here is Brian Kennedy. We represent an investment cartel interested in agricultural expansion, and we'd appreciate a few moments to discuss it with you."

His eyes flicked meaningfully towards Hughes as he spoke, and Mueller allowed just a trace of his smile to show as he shook his head amiably.

"That worked fine to get you past my steward, Mr. Baird," he said cheerfully, "but I very much doubt that you or Mr.—Kennedy, was it?—have any particular interest in farmland. In which case, we should probably get down to your real reason for being here, don't you think?"

Both visitors were *definitely* taken aback by that, and they turned to look at one another much harder than before. Then, as one, their gazes swiveled back to Hughes.

"The sergeant is one of my personal armsmen, gentlemen," Mueller said, putting a cooler edge on his voice, and Baird and Kennedy—assuming those were their real names, which Mueller doubted—pulled themselves quickly back together. Casting doubt on an armsman's loyalty had once been a swift way to a most unpleasant end . . . and it was still nothing a prudent man wanted to do in the presence of the armsman in question.

Accidents, after all, happened.

"Of course, My Lord. Of course!" Baird said. "It's just that, well, we weren't quite prepared— I mean . . ."

"You mean, I imagine, that you expected to have to beat around the bush and work your way gradually up to whatever actually brought you here," Mueller supplied helpfully, then chuckled at Baird's expression as he sank into the comfortably padded chair behind his huge desk.

"Forgive me, Mr. Baird. I shouldn't let my levity get the better of me, but my position among the Keys uncomfortable with the

Protector's so-called 'reforms' has made me a logical rallying point
for others who are . . . uncomfortable with them. And since the
'Mayhew Restoration,' quite a few of those others have felt a need
to avoid attracting the, ah, *official* attention of the Sword."

Baird started to speak, but Mueller waved a hand and *tut-tutted*
him back into silence.

"I regret the fact that they feel that way, Mr. Baird, and I personally feel an honest man has nothing to fear from the Sword
simply because he does not agree with Protector Benjamin in all
things. The Test still calls us to take our stands for what we believe
to be right and true, after all. Sadly, however, I can understand
why not everyone would agree with me, and so I mean no disrespect if you and Mr. Kennedy are among those who prefer not to
put my opinion to the test in that respect. My time is in short
supply, however, so I'd prefer not to waste time on cautious, circumspect approaches."

"I . . . see," Baird said. He cleared his throat. "Well, in that case,
My Lord, let me come to the true point of our visit." He nodded
to Kennedy, and the two of them sank back into their chairs. Baird
reached for his coffee cup once more and crossed his legs, obviously working hard to project an aura of relaxation.

"As you alluded to, My Lord, your position among the Keys who
are distressed by the changes here on Grayson is well known. In
our own way, my colleagues and I share that distress and have
labored as best we might in the same cause. But while we have
many friends and a degree of funding which might surprise you,
we lack the prominence and position to make our efforts effective. You, on the other hand, lack neither of those things and are
widely respected as an astute and thoughtful leader. What we would
like to propose is an association between our organization and you."

"Your organization," Mueller repeated, swinging his chair ever
so slightly from side to side. "And just how large would this
'organization' of yours be, Mr. Baird?"

"Large," Baird said flatly. Mueller looked a question at him, and
he shrugged.

"I would prefer not to be very specific about numbers, My Lord.
As you suggested earlier, most of us are more than a little uncomfortable about letting the Sword know our identities. While I would
never criticize your own faith in the safety of honest men, I've also
seen how many of our ancient rights and traditions the Protector has trampled underfoot in the last eleven years. The Sword has
never been so powerful, and we fear it seeks more power still. If
our worst fears should be true, then those of us less prominent

than the Keys would be well advised to be cautious in openly opposing the 'Mayhew Reforms.' "

"I don't agree with your conclusions," Mueller replied after a moment, "but, as I said, I can sympathize with your concerns, and I respect your decision." He rubbed his chin. "Having said that, however, what does this 'large' and anonymous organization of yours propose?"

"As I said, My Lord, an association. An alliance, if you will. Many of us have been active in the picketing and protest movements. We have many friends among the hardcore members of those movements. They bring us information which could be very useful to someone in your position, and they also provide a visible and powerful medium for transmitting your positions to the public at large. We can also offer a useful infusion of campaign workers for the next elections, and we're quite good, if I do say so myself, at getting out the vote among those who share our views. And—" he paused for just a moment "—our members are as generous with their money as with their time. We are not, by and large, wealthy individuals, My Lord. Few of us are among the rich or powerful. But there are a *great* many of us, and all of us give as we may for the Lord's work. I realize that campaign finance sources are being looked at more closely than ever before, but I'm sure we could devise a . . . discreet means of contributing to your political war chest. To the tune, let us say, of ten or eleven million austens. Initially."

Mueller managed to keep his shock from showing, but it was hard. That was a substantial sum, equivalent to seven and a half to eight and a half million Manticoran dollars, and Baird seemed to be suggesting that it was only a beginning.

Wheels whirred behind the steadholder's eyes. He was too wily a conspirator not to recognize the skill with which Baird had trolled the hook before him. But his initial confidence that Baird was overstating both the numbers and power of his "organization" had just taken a severe blow. It would *take* an organization of considerable size to produce that sort of money from its members' contributions, especially if, as Baird was suggesting, they came from the middle and lower-middle classes.

What was most tempting was Baird's suggestion that the contributions would be slipped to him secretly. There was no legal ban on contributions from any source—any such ban would have been considered a restriction of free speech—but there was a very strong tradition of full disclosure of donors. In fact, the Sword *required* such disclosure for any election which crossed the borders of more than one steading, which meant for any race for the Conclave of Steaders, the planetary government's lower house.

And therefrom hung a large part of the emerging Opposition's problems. They were strongest in the Keys, where the defense of power and privilege against the Sword's encroachments naturally strengthened opposition born of principle. In the Conclave of Steaders, the reverse was true. The lower house had been reduced to total irrelevance before the power of the great Keys prior to the Mayhew Restoration. Now it had reemerged as the full equal of the upper house, and the majority of its members, even many uncomfortable with Benjamin's reforms, were staunch Mayhew loyalists. It was there that the Opposition most needed to make electoral gains . . . and also where open campaign contributions from conservative sources would do a candidate the most harm.

But if no one needed to know where the money for those contributions had come from in the first place . . .

"That's a most interesting proposition, Mr. Baird," Mueller said after a moment. "It's sad but true that even the Lord's work requires frequent infusions of capital. Any contributions would be most gratefully accepted, and, as you, I feel sure we could find an unobtrusive way for us to accept your generous support. But I believe you also mentioned information sources and campaign organizations?" Baird nodded, and Mueller leaned back in his chair.

"In that case, gentlemen, let's take this discussion just a little further. For example, what about . . ."

Several hours later, Sergeant Samuel Hughes, Mueller Steadholder's Guard, ushered Baird and Kennedy from his steadholder's office and showed them back out of the sprawling, ancient stone pile of Mueller House. He'd said nothing while he stood post in Mueller's office, and he said nothing now—a taciturn fellow, Sergeant Hughes—but the teeny-tiny camera whose lens was hidden in the uppermost button of his tunic had caught the two visitors and their earnest discussions with Lord Mueller.

Lord Mueller didn't know that, however. Nor would he . . . until the proper time.

Unfortunately, nothing which had been discussed this morning was—quite—illegal. Not yet, at any rate. Once campaign money actually changed hands without disclosure of its sources a crime *would* have been committed. The best that anyone could hope for out of what had been said in Mueller's office was a conspiracy conviction, and even with the camera footage, convicting a man like Mueller in open court of conspiracy would be extremely difficult.

That was disappointing, or should have been. Yet Hughes felt no disappointment, for he sensed an opening. For the first time of which he was aware, an outside organization, not just an individual nut or a small cluster of them, had reached out to *initiate* contact with Mueller. Always before it had been the other way around, with Mueller very carefully approaching allies of his own selection. That had been one of the steadholder's greatest strengths, for he'd built his own contacts and alliances as a spider built its web, weaving the strands cautiously and artfully and always making certain they would bear the weight he chose to put upon them.

But if he accepted the offers Baird and Kennedy had made, and it looked very much as if he would, then he would have allowed an unknown into his web, and it would begin to generate strands of its own, whether it meant to or not. The steadholder's entire organization would become more porous and easily penetrated, and the number of potential witnesses against him would go up geometrically.

And that, Sergeant Hughes thought fervently, was a consummation greatly to be desired. Because Sergeant Hughes, who was also Captain Hughes, of the Office of Planetary Security, had spent the better part of five years worming his way into Mueller's confidence, and he still had very little to show for it. But if this morning's meeting was headed where he thought it was, that was about to change.

Chapter Thirteen

"**W**ell it's about time . . . I think," Citizen Vice Admiral Lester Tourville observed. He'd tilted back his chair at the briefing-room table, and his eyes glittered as he studied the star-spangled hologram above it. He'd seen it before, many times, during the preliminary planning stages, but then a plan was all it had been. Now it was an actual operation, waiting only for the proper concentration of assigned forces to become reality.

"Qualifications from you always make me nervous," People's Commissioner Everard Honeker replied dryly, and Tourville chuckled. The citizen vice admiral often wondered what StateSec thought it was doing leaving Honeker as his political watchdog. It seemed too much to hope that none of the citizen commissioner's SS superiors had realized that a certain strain of corruption through association had crept into their relationship. Since that entire disgraceful business with the decision to execute Honor Harrington on what everyone knew had been trumped up charges, Honeker's corruption had increased apace. By now, it had come perilously close to outright disaffection, and Tourville was willing to bet that the citizen commissioner's reports to Oscar Saint-Just bore only a passing acquaintance with reality.

For a time, both Tourville and Honeker had tried very hard to pretend nothing had changed between them. It had seemed safer that way, especially since they could never know when some other informer might be in a position to see or guess what was actually happening. But things had changed since Operation Icarus. Indeed, Tourville had noticed without comment, even to Honeker, that there seemed to have been a general thawing of the relationships between the people's commissioners and the Twelfth Fleet officers whose political reliability they oversaw. He doubted that it was anything remotely universal, but Twelfth Fleet had accomplished something none of the rest of the People's Navy, with the possible exception of Thomas Theisman's Barnett command, had managed to achieve: it had defeated the Manties in battle. More than simply defeated them. Twelfth Fleet had *humiliated* the Royal Manticoran Navy and it allies. In the process, it had obviously shaken the entire Manticoran Alliance—a man only had to look at the Allies' current total lack of offensive action to realize that— and simultaneously given the Republic's civilian morale its first real boost since the war began.

And the men and women of Twelfth Fleet, Navy and people's commissioners alike, knew precisely what they'd achieved. The pride and solidarity which came from something like that, especially after so many years of defeat and humiliation of their own, was impossible to overestimate. A man like Honeker, who'd been fundamentally decent to begin with, almost had to succumb to it . . . and not even a cold fish like Eloise Pritchart, Citizen Admiral Giscard's commissioner, was completely immune to it.

Surely the people back at StateSec GHQ had to realize something like that was inevitable. But they seemed not to have. Or, at least, they weren't reacting as they would have reacted to such a realization earlier in the war. Saint-Just's minions had made a few changes, but not the ones Tourville would have anticipated. Oh, he was more than slightly suspicious about StateSec's sudden generosity in reinforcing Twelfth Fleet with units of its private navy, but none of the citizen commissioners had been relieved or removed. And so far as Tourville could tell, no new watchdogs had been appointed to keep an eye on the commissioners, as well as the admirals . . . which he would have considered the most rudimentary of precautions in Saint-Just's place.

Of course, the fact that he'd seen no evidence of new watchdogs proved nothing. StateSec had effectively unlimited manpower, and Saint-Just had been setting up domestic spy networks for decades, first for Internal Security and the Legislaturalists and now for StateSec and Rob Pierre. No doubt he could manage to avoid detection while he set one up here if he put his mind to it. But Tourville genuinely believed he hadn't, and he wondered how many other people realized what a monumental realignment in the power balance between Saint-Just and Esther McQueen that represented.

But one of the more mundane and enjoyable side effects of the changes had been a general loosening of the frigid formality and distance the people's commissioners had previously maintained. Honeker had begun loosening up sooner than most, but a year ago, not even he would have joked about the possible risks of an ops plan. Not when it had been his job to ensure that the officer with whom he shared his jest drove the plan through to unflinching success despite any risks it might entail.

Of course, the fact that Lester Tourville had carefully built a reputation as the the sort of gung-ho, bloodthirsty officer who could hardly wait for his next fight had given Honeker a set of priorities which differed somewhat from those of his fellow watchdogs. All to often, he'd found himself maneuvered into the position of being forced to restrain Tourville's enthusiasm, and as he'd realized long ago, that had given the citizen admiral and Citizen Captain Yuri Bogdanovich, Tourville's chief of staff, a pronounced advantage when it came to maneuvering him into doing things *their* way.

Which lent a certain added point to his jest. And probably meant it was Honeker's way of posing a sincere question.

"I suppose I'm a little surprised to hear myself adding qualifiers, too, Everard," the citizen vice admiral admitted after a moment. The use of Honeker's first name was something neither of them would have dared contemplate before Icarus; now neither of them turned a hair. "And I'm not at all sorry we're actually getting Scylla organized. I just wish we knew more about whatever buzz saw Jane Kellet walked into at Hancock."

He pulled a cigar from his breast pocket and played with it without unwrapping it while he swung his chair back and forth in minute, thoughtful arcs.

"NavInt is still contradicting itself at regular intervals trying to explain what happened to her," he went on in a musing tone. "I guess I can't blame them for that, given the dearth of hard tactical data and the absolute confusion and trauma of her survivors, but I think its obvious the Manties have *something* we don't know about."

"Citizen Secretary McQueen's 'super LACs'?" Honeker's voice held an ever-so-slight edge of whimsy, but his eyes were somber, and Tourville nodded.

"I read Citizen Commander Diamato's— No, he's a citizen captain now, isn't he?" Tourville shook his head. "Damned hard way to win a promotion, but, by God, the man deserved it! I'm just glad he got out of it alive." The citizen vice admiral shook his head again, then inhaled sharply. "At any rate, I read his report, and I wish he'd been in shape to produce it before McQueen convened the board of inquiry."

"I do too. For the technical data it contained, at any rate." Tourville quirked an eyebrow, and Honeker chuckled humorlessly. "I've read it, too, Lester. And, as I'm sure you did, I rather suspected there'd been a few excisions. He said remarkably little about his task force's command structure, didn't he?"

"Yes, he did," Tourville agreed. Even now, neither he nor Honeker was prepared to comment openly on the fact that the Hancock Board had proved that despite any other changes, Esther McQueen was not fully mistress of the Navy. Citizen Admiral Porter's idiocy was excruciatingly obvious to any observer, yet no one on the Board had commented on his arrant stupidity. His political patrons remained too powerful for that, and nothing could be allowed to taint the reputation of an officer famed for his loyalty to the New Order. Which meant that despite all McQueen could do, the Hancock Report had lost two-thirds of its punch and turned into something suspiciously like a whitewash rather than the hard-hitting, ruthless analysis the Navy had really needed.

"But like you, I was thinking about the hardware side of his report and wishing the Board had been given a chance to see it before it issued its official conclusions," the citizen admiral went on. "Not that it would have convinced the doubters . . . or even me—fully, I mean—I suppose. It just doesn't seem possible that even the Manties could squeeze a fusion plant, *and* a full set of beta nodes, down into a LAC hull and then find room to cram in a godawful graser like the one Diamato described, as well!"

"I've never really understood that," Honeker said, admitting a degree of technical ignorance no "proper" people's commissioner would display. "I mean, we put fusion plants into *pinnaces*, and isn't a LAC just a scaled-up pinnace, when all's said and done?"

"Um." Tourville scratched an eyebrow while he considered the best way to explain. "I can see why you might think that," he acknowledged after a moment, "but it's not just a matter of scale. Or, rather, it *is* a matter of scale, in a way, but one in which the difference is so great as to create a difference in kind, as well.

"A pinnace has a far weaker wedge than any regular warship or merchantman. It's enormously smaller, for one thing, not more than a kilometer in width, and less powerful. The little hip-pocket fusion plants we put into small craft couldn't even begin to power an all-up wedge for a ship the size of a LAC. Which is just as well, because they use old-fashioned mag bottle technology and laser-fired fusing that's not a lot more advanced than they were using back on Old

Earth Ante Diaspora. We've made a hell of a lot of advances since then, of course, in order to shoehorn the plants down to fit into pinnaces, but the way they're built puts a low absolute ceiling on their output.

"Even the biggest pinnace or assault shuttle comes in at well under a thousand tons, though, and a worthwhile LAC has to be in the thirty- to fifty-thousand-ton range just to pack in its impellers and any armament at all. Remember that courier boats in the same size range don't carry *any* weapons or defenses and just barely manage to find someplace to squeeze in a hyper generator. A LAC may be smaller than a starship, but it still has to be able to achieve high acceleration rates (which means a military grade compensator), produce sidewalls, power its weapons— and find places to mount them—and generally act like a serious warship, or else people would simply ignore it. Which means that, like any starship, LACs need modern grav-fusing plants to maintain the power levels they require. And there are limits on how small you can make one of those."

The citizen vice admiral twitched a shrug.

"Of course, the designers can cut some corners when they design a LAC. For one thing, they don't try to build in a power plant which can meet all requirements out of current generating capacity. Ton-for-ton, LACs have enormous capacitor rings, much larger than anything else's, even an SD. They're a lot smaller in absolute terms, naturally, given the difference in size between the ships involved, but most energy-armed LACs rely on the capacitor rings to power their offensive armament, and a lot of them rely on the capacitors even for their point-defense clusters. And not even a super-dreadnought has enough onboard power generation to bring its wedge up initially without using its capacitors. Just maintaining it once it is up, even with the energy-siphon effect when it twists over into hyper, requires a huge investment in power, and initiating the impeller bands in the first place raises the power requirement exponentially. So even when they're not doing anything else, most warships tend to have at least one fusion plant on-line to charge up their capacitor rings . . . and, of course, a LAC only *has* one power plant, and just keeping it up and running requires its own not insubstantial power investment.

"And that's why so many of our own shipyard people will tell you that anything like Diamato's 'super LACs' is flatly impossible. Either the damned things have to be bigger than Diamato thought they were, or else there's some serious mistake in his estimate of the destructiveness he claims they were capable of handing out."

"I'm a bit confused, Lester," Honeker admitted. "Are you saying Diamato was right? Or that he must have been wrong?"

"I'm saying that by every logical analysis I can come up with, he must be wrong . . . but that what happened to Jane Kellet argues that he must be *right*. That's what worries me. Javier Giscard is good, and with all due modesty, I'm not exactly a slouch myself when it comes to tactics. And I've got Yuri and Shannon to help me think about them. But none of us has been able to come up with a way to really defend against the 'super LAC,' because none of us can make any rational, useful projections as to what its real capabilities are. And, frankly, I'm almost as worried by what Diamato had to say about the range and acceleration on those damned missiles someone kept shooting up their wakes while the LACs—or whatever—were shooting them from close up and personal. LACs or no LACs, the kind of range advantage *that* suggests is enough to keep a man from sleeping very soundly at night."

"So you think McQueen is right to be cautious," Honeker said flatly.

"I do," Tourville replied, and his tone was equally flat. Then he shrugged. "On the other hand, I can also understand why some people—" he carefully refrained from mentioning Oscar Saint-Just by name, even now and even with Everard Honeker "—keep asking where the Manty secret weapons are. We've hit them several times since Icarus. Not in any more of their critical systems, granted, but all along their northern frontier, without seeing a sign of anything we didn't already know about. So if they've got them, why haven't they used them? And if they haven't got them, then we ought to be beating up on them as hard and as fast as we can. And if they're in the *process* of getting them, but don't have them yet, then we *really* ought to go after them hammer and tongs."

"I see." Honeker regarded the citizen vice admiral speculatively. It must be like pulling teeth for Lester Tourville to even appear to agree with Oscar Saint-Just about anything. Not that Honeker blamed Tourville a bit for that. For that matter, Honeker had come to share a lot of the citizen admiral's reservations about the soundness of StateSec's commanding officer's military judgment.

But one thing Honeker had learned about Tourville was that there was an extraordinarily keen brain behind the wild man facade he was at such pains to project. And if Lester Tourville was genuinely worried by his inability to reconcile the apparently contradictory aspects of the reports from Hancock, Everard Honeker was certainly not prepared to dismiss his concerns.

Whether he understood their technical basis or not.

"So I take it that you approve of the basic Scylla plans," he said after a moment. "Given your desire to get in and beat up on the Manties hard and fast, I mean."

"Of course I do. There's room for us to get hurt, but that's true of almost any operation worth mounting. And the only way we could get hurt too badly would be for the Manties to figure out where we plan to hit them and concentrate everything they can scrape up to stop us. That would require them to be a lot more daring in their deployments than they've been ever since we hit them with Icarus, and I don't see any sign of that changing just yet. Which, of course, gives added point to hitting them now, before they *do* get around to regaining their strategic balance.

"But McQueen was also right about the need to concentrate our own forces and drill them before we commit them. You know as well as I do how much Twelfth Fleet has expanded since Icarus, and we *still* don't have all of our assigned order of battle. An awful lot of our people have some frighteningly rough edges, especially in the new-build units that haven't fully completed their working-up process. And the expansion in new hulls is spreading our trained engineering people still thinner . . . not that we were exactly over-supplied with them to begin with!"

He shook his head with a sardonic grin.

"Typical, isn't it? We finally start to get on top of our short-age of competent onboard technicians, and that's when the yards start producing enough new ships that we have to thin them out all over again!" He chuckled. "Oh, well. I suppose we're better off having too many ships and not enough techs than when we had too few of *either* of them.

"But the point I was making was that McQueen's insistence on taking time to prepare adequately makes a hell of a lot of sense. We'll commit as soon as we possibly can—in fact, I think McQueen is probably pushing too hard and fast, if she seriously intends to make the execution date she's specified—but it's going to take time. Just to get all of our units here, given the sheer distances over which they'll have to travel, and then to get them all up to effective com-bat standards once they arrive."

And, he did not add aloud, *just to teach those cretins StateSec's palmed off on us which hatch to open first on their damned air locks!*

He might not have said the words aloud, but Honeker heard them anyway. Like Tourville, Honeker had been astonished by StateSec's ongoing failure to make wholesale replacements among Twelfth Fleet's people's commissioners. Partly, he knew, that reflected Saint-Just's complete faith in Eloise Pritchart's judgment and coldly analytical intelligence. But for all that, he rather doubted Saint-Just was anywhere near as comfortable as he tried to appear about Twelfth Fleet's personnel relationships. He couldn't be—not when the stability of those relationships could only serve (in his judgment) to strengthen Esther McQueen's hand. Which obviously explained the "reinforcements" StateSec had provided to Twelfth Fleet.

Officially, it was only an effort to help the Navy overcome the shortage in the hulls required for the proper execution of Operation Scylla and its follow-on ops. Clearly, if the Navy was short of ships, it was the duty of State Security, as the People's guardians and champions, to make up the shortfall.

It had come as something of a shock to Honeker to discover that StateSec actually had dreadnoughts and even superdreadnoughts in its private fleet. Not a great many of them, it appeared, but Honeker had never suspected that the SS had *any* ships of the wall. From Tourville's expression, he suspected the existence of those ships had come as an even greater shock to the citizen vice admiral . . . and not a pleasant one. True, there didn't seem to be a great many of them, but still—!

Both Tourville and Giscard clearly regarded the SS units' arrival as a mixed blessing. No officer about to embark on a high-risk offensive could help feeling at least a little grateful when the equivalent of an entire, oversized squadron of the wall appeared out of the woodwork to reinforce his order of battle. At the same time, the crews of those ships were among the most fervent supporters of the New Order generally and of Oscar Saint-Just in particular. None of them really trusted regular officers, and they weren't shy about showing it. Which meant that the sense of unity and pride which lay at the core of Twelfth Fleet's achievements was threatened by the divisive inclusion of the SS ships, their companies, and—especially!—their officers. Those ships had also required a much greater amount of drilling than Navy ships would have in order to attain Twelfth Fleet's standards, and the graphic proof of their initial deficiencies hadn't done a thing to sweeten relationships between their crews and the PN regulars.

Honeker had no doubt that Esther McQueen had been less than thrilled to have the StateSec units palmed off on her, but she could hardly object to what everyone knew was their real reason for being there without appearing to be guilty of the very subversive attitudes Saint-Just clearly believed she harbored. Even if that hadn't been true, turning them down would have made it harder to argue in favor of delaying Scylla. If she were truly that short of hulls, she should be jumping at such a powerful reinforcement, after all! So if she'd objected to it instead, regardless of her official reasoning, it could only be because she wanted to drag her feet for nefarious reasons of her own, right? Or that, at least, would be StateSec's interpretation.

And the fact that they're specifically split between the squadrons which just happen to contain Lester's and Giscard's flagships hasn't passed unnoticed, the citizen commissioner thought grimly. *I doubt* that *was McQueen's idea, either, and I know Lester would just love to "adjust" fleet organization a bit to get rid of them, but neither he nor Giscard dare do such a thing any more than McQueen would have dared to turn down Saint-Just's "reinforcements" in the first place.*

He sighed. In a perfect universe, the revolution would long since have been brought to its successful and triumphant conclusion. In the one in which he actually lived, men and women he liked and admired, like Lester Tourville and Shannon Foraker, were in at least as much danger from the people who were supposed to be running the Republic they served as from the people who were *supposed* to be trying to kill them. Had those men and women truly been enemies of the People, that would have been one thing. But they weren't. And for that matter, Honeker was no longer as certain as he once had been that he—or Rob Pierre or Oscar Saint-Just—actually knew what the People truly wanted!

And so he'd found himself forced to choose between people he knew were fundamentally decent, honorable, and courageous enough to risk their lives in the thankless task of defending the Republic and people who could be guilty of the ghastly excesses being reported by the escapees from Cerberus and Camp Charon. He shouldn't have had to do that . . . and the fact that he'd been forced to do it after all shouldn't have put his own life in danger. But he had, and it had, and he sometimes wished he could come right out and tell Lester where he stood. Yet he couldn't quite do that, even now. And it didn't matter, for he was quite sure Lester had figured it out for himself.

He just hoped Oscar Saint-Just hadn't!

CHAPTER FOURTEEN

"**O**h, what a *clever*, marvelous, disgusting little girl you are!" Allison Harrington told the baby in her lap enthusiastically. "Now if only you were equally clever in ways that *didn't* make messes, you'd be the perfect daughter. As it is—" she leaned forward, pressing her lips to the little girl's stomach and blowing to produce a fluttering sound that made her daughter squeal with delight "—you're still just *almost* perfect!"

Faith gave a delighted squeal and did her level best to grab her mother's hair and pull, but Allison avoided the pink, chubby fist and distracted her with a shrewd tickle. Faith squealed again and produced a duplicate of the splendid bubble of drool which had prompted her mother's original compliment, and Allison laughed and reached for a cleansing tissue. An arm in a jade-green sleeve reached over her shoulder to offer one, and she looked up with a smile of thanks. Corporal Jeremiah Tennard, already assigned, despite Allison's vehement protests, as Faith's personal armsman responded with a smile of his own, but it didn't do much to offset the harried look in his eyes.

Which only made Allison smile even more sweetly at him before she turned back to the task of mopping up Faith's handiwork.

She'd just finished that task when an air car settled into one of the VIP terminal lounge's parking slots just a bit more rapidly than the traffic regs truly approved. A musical tone and a subdued flash of green light indicated that the car's owner's account had been debited for the appropriate use fee, and a boarding tube extruded itself from the slot's outer wall to the car's starboard hatch.

185

A moment later, the car door opened and another man in the green-on-green of Harrington Steading stepped out of it.

"Hello, Simon!" Allison greeted the newcomer cheerfully. Simon Mattingly had been promoted from corporal to lieutenant when the Steadholder's Own section of the Harrington Guard was expanded to provide Faith and James with their own, dedicated security teams. It hadn't changed his duties as second-in-command of Honor's personal team—or, rather, it hadn't kept him from being reassigned as Andrew LaFollet's second-in-command as soon as Grayson discovered LaFollet (and Honor) were still alive—and Allison was happy for his advancement.

Mostly.

Her happiness would have been completely unflawed but for the reason the Steadholder's Own had been expanded. It was absolutely ridiculous, in her calmly considered opinion, for a child barely ten months old to already have no less than four trained, lethally competent, armed-to-the-teeth, omnipresent bodyguards. James was luckier; he had only two armsmen assigned to *his* security detail, since Grayson law regarded him primarily as a spare, albeit a welcome one.

For once in her life, however, not even Allison Chou Harrington's intransigence had been enough. The fact that the Conclave of Steadholders had accepted Faith as Honor's heir, formally named Howard Clinkscales her regent, determined the composition of her Regency Council (which had *not*, as originally structured, included the Steadholder Mother), and transferred the Harrington Key to her as the second Steadholder Harrington had represented an enormous concession on the Conservatives' part. Of course, all those arrangements had come tumbling down when Honor turned out to be alive after all, but Faith remained her legally designated heir, and Allison was well aware that most of the steadholders, even those who belonged to what passed for the Keys' liberal wing, would really have preferred for her to be clever enough to have made sure James was born first. Since she'd been so inconsiderate as to produce a girl child first, however, and since Protector Benjamin had insisted, they had grudgingly agreed that it was time to allow female children to inherit their fathers' keys. They'd insisted on grandfathering in a stipulation to guarantee the succession of the sons of those among them who'd already produced male heirs, even if, as most Grayson men did, those sons had older sisters, and they'd specifically exempted the protectorship itself, despite Benjamin's best efforts, but they'd accepted yet another of his reforms.

And blamed it on "those Harrington" women just like the others, too! Allison chuckled a bit sourly in the depths of her mind. *Gave in more gracefully than I'd expected, though. But, then, that was when everyone knew Honor was dead, and none of them wanted to risk their steaders' fury by seeming unreasonable about the succession of her steading. Not to mention the fact that they had another twenty T-years before Faith would be old enough to carry the Harrington Key in her own right. Now Honor's back, and half of them seem to think she deliberately arranged to get herself sent to Hell as some fiendishly clever stratagem to "sneak" a female heir in on them! And, of course, I must have been the Machiavellian mastermind behind the whole plot because—for some reason only they could possibly come up with—Alfred and I intend to keep Harrington Steading under our despotic thumbs. Howard and Benjamin's insistence that Alfred and I both had to hold seats on the regency council only proves we do.*

She shook her head. It wasn't as if their acceptance had done her, her husband, or their younger daughter any tremendous favors, and if she had anything to say about it, Faith Katherine Honor Stephanie Miranda wasn't going to grow up thinking they had, either. Bad enough Grayson had dumped the job of steadholder on *one* of Allison's daughters without Mueller and his pompous old farts patting themselves on the backs for their generosity in saddling poor Faith with the same job! Not that a single one of them seemed capable of stretching his atrophied little mind around the concept that not everyone in the universe was driven by a desire for power over the lives of others.

Still, Allison supposed she might have been just a teeny-tiny bit more tactful about her response to Mueller's fatuous, gushing insincerities over her "heroic daughter's tragic murder" at the formal dinner which had followed Faith's succession to Honor's Key. It was remotely possible, she conceded, that Hera would never have considered climbing the steadholder's back unannounced if she hadn't caught the spike of Allison's emotions when Mueller made his way over to admire Faith and James after delivering his speech. And it could be that Nelson wouldn't have somehow gotten himself tangled up in Mueller's feet when the steadholder squeaked and tried to leap away from the completely unexpected weight and needle-sharp claws scurrying up his spine. Not that Hera had hurt him in the least. She'd been very careful and clever, never breaking the skin even once, despite the havoc she'd "accidentally" wreaked on his formal attire's expensive tailoring. But they were only 'cats, after all. Allison had heard more than enough about Mueller's comments to cronies about the foreign "animals" with which Honor had seen fit to contaminate Grayson, but for some reason he'd seemed mildly irritated when she smiled sweetly and pointed out that one could scarcely expect such simple little *foreign* creatures to understand all the nuances of civilized behavior.

Or perhaps it hadn't been her smile that upset him, she reflected. Perhaps it had been the involuntary gust of laughter none of the other guests, most of them his peers and members of their families, had been able (or willing) to stifle. Despite anything Mueller and his intimates might say among themselves while they vented their ire over the changes "those foreign women" had wreaked on Grayson, everyone on the planet knew that whatever else treecats might be, they were scarcely "simple little creatures" who had "accidents" of that sort at formal gatherings.

Allison heard later that Mueller had chosen to inform one and all that he put no faith whatsoever in the rumor that the Steadholder Mother had deliberately set the vicious beasts on him. As for her frivolous behavior after they escaped her control, that had undoubtedly been a consequence of *post partum* depression and so must be excused by any true gentlemen. It was even possible that one or two of the most brain-dead of his conservative henchmen had believed his version of the reason Allison had been "out of sorts," but no one else had, and she knew there'd been intense speculation about just why the 'cats had taken him in such disfavor. And why the Steadholder Mother shared their loathing for him. For the most part, the speculators seemed to have concluded that Allison must have had an excellent reason, and the whispered debates over what he could have done to her (or her daughter) to deserve such public humiliation continued.

Not that anyone would ever dream of asking Allison directly. Which was just as well, since she wouldn't have told them. Or she *thought* she wouldn't have, at any rate, for she wasn't absolutely positive. She knew she shouldn't, for the information had been privileged, and there was no proof in the legal, courtroom sense. But unlike most people on Grayson, neither Howard Clinkscales nor Benjamin Mayhew had ever been satisfied that William Fitzclarence had acted alone in hatching the plot to assassinate Honor which had come so close to succeeding . . . and *had* succeeded in killing Reverend Hanks and ninety-five Harrington steaders. Each of them, without mentioning it to the other (or to Honor), had used his own security forces to keep a quiet investigation going, and each of them had independently concluded that Mueller had been involved right up to his neck.

If there'd been even a speck of hard proof, Allison knew, Samuel Mueller would have been a dead man, steadholder or no. But he had a very clever, calculating brain behind that genial and bombastic facade. And because he did, there was only a handful of circumstantial evidence which was highly unlikely to stand up in court, especially against one of the Keys. And the fact that Mueller had emerged as the clear leader of the Opposition within the Keys made it unthinkable for the Protector or the Regent of Harrington Steading to make public accusations which *wouldn't* stand up in court and could all too easily be construed by a defense counsel (or a politician) as nothing more than a partisan attempt to blacken a political opponent.

Allison understood that, just as she understood why Benjamin and Clinkscales forced themselves to treat Mueller as if no suspicion of his treason had ever so much as crossed their minds. No doubt they were watching like hawks, praying he would stray into similar territory once more so they could bring the hammer down properly, but that would be then, assuming the happy day ever actually arrived, and now was now.

Fortunately, Allison was under no such constraint to be pleasant, and she rather hoped the man would be foolish enough to give her another opportunity to humiliate him. And she also had to wonder if he even began to suspect how fortunate he was that Hera and Nelson had settled for demolishing only his clothing and his dignity.

Still, satisfying as it had been, it had also been an open declaration of war between her and Mueller. Under the Grayson code of conduct, he was required to treat her with exquisite courtesy, in public, at least, despite how livid he must be. For once, Allison had found the constraints of Grayson's quaint, antiquated sexism rather enjoyable, and she occasionally entertained herself with the hope that enough concentrated bile would finish off the miserable, small-souled cretin once and for all. The thought of him perishing in a purple-faced, frothing fit was one to warm the cockles of a mother's heart, and she'd taken shameless advantage of the rules which gave her the advantage.

But Mueller was no slouch at fighting dirty, either. Everyone in the Keys had known Allison was prepared to wage a spirited battle against the creation of dedicated security teams to haunt Harrington House's nursery. Mueller certainly had . . . and he'd made himself the point man in insisting that the letter of the law be observed where Honor's heirs were concerned. After all, he'd pointed out, everyone on the planet had suffered a bitter personal loss in Lady Harrington's tragic and brutal murder. It therefore followed that Grayson as a whole had a responsibility to protect and cherish the tiny baby girl upon whom Honor's titles and responsibilities had devolved and in whom so many hopes reposed, and no chances at all could be taken with the infant steadholder's safety.

Allison doubted she would have won the argument anyway, but she might at least have gotten by with the assignment of a single armsman to each of the twins. Mueller would have none of that, however, and even some of her closer Grayson friends had agreed with him, if not for the same reasons. And, truth to tell, she'd found it appallingly easy to become accustomed to the intrusion of no less than six bodyguards into the household which had consisted for so long only of her and Alfred during Honor's long absences. She hadn't *accepted* it, precisely, but the day-in, day-out persistence of the situation had given her no real choice but to develop a sense of toleration.

It helped that Jeremiah and Luke Blacket, the senior armsman assigned to James, were both pleasant individuals. They were soft-spoken, unfailingly courteous, helpful, genuinely attached to their infant charges . . . and very, very dangerous. Allison had spent too much time with her own daughter not to recognize the wolves behind the gentle exteriors those tough, lethal youngsters presented to the rest of the universe, and she was not immune to the effect of knowing either or both of them would unhesitatingly die to protect her children. Or her, although it was still hard for her to accept the possibility that anyone might want to hurt *her* as any-thing other than some intellectual possibility on a par with per-sonally experiencing the energy death of the universe.

But Samuel Mueller hadn't gotten behind and pushed so hard because he felt nice. He'd done it because he'd known how hard Allison was resisting the notion, and she'd made a mental note to add that to the debt he'd already incurred with her, for, in the words of the ancient Terran song, she had a little list. Oh, she had a little list . . .

Knowing why he'd worked so hard to bring the situation about also made it even harder for her to tolerate the restrictions the twins' status (and guardians) had imposed on her own life. It simply wasn't done for the mother of a child steadholder to go shopping on a whim or an impulse. Nor did she decide to change any other part of her schedule without warning people ahead of time so that all the security arrangements could be put in place, usually in triplicate. Allison was too intelligent to doubt the necessity of those arrangements. God knew people had tried hard enough to kill her *older* daughter over the years, usually for what they considered excellent reasons, and there were more than sufficient cranks, eccentrics, and outright loonies who might take it into their heads to kill the first female steadholder's female heir. Nuts didn't need religion to make them nuts, Allison had long since decided, but it did seem to give them a certain added sense of commitment to whatever goals their nutdom decided to embrace.

So, yes, she understood why Jeremiah and Luke got so politely exasperated with her from time to time. She meant to be good—usually—but there were limits to how far she was prepared to go in becoming a prisoner of her own or her children's bodyguards. Every so often it became necessary to point out once again where those limits lay, and the Steadholder's Own had quickly learned that the Steadholder Mother, as seemed to be the case with *all* Harrington women, had a whim of steel.

Which explained Mattingly's resigned expression. Allison didn't need Honor's ability to sense others' emotions to know exactly what was going on behind the fair-haired armsman's gray eyes.

"Hello, My Lady." His response to her greeting was pleasant and courteous . . . and it, too, carried more than a hint of affectionate resignation. "I got here as quickly as I could," he added just a tad pointedly, and Allison's smile turned into a grin.

"I'm sure you did, Simon," she said, patting him on the arm with a fond, maternal air. He took it much better than some other Grayson males might have. Unlike most of them, he'd fully adjusted to the notion that the youthful, beautiful woman before him was several years older than any of his own grandmothers. But, then, he'd spent more time with Honor than most Graysons, and Honor looked even younger than Allison did.

"Was the traffic very bad?" she went on, and he shook his head.

"No worse than usual, My Lady. As I'm sure you anticipated." Another air car slid into the slot on the far side of the one in which Mattingly had parked and disgorged four more men in Harrington green. They nodded very respectfully to the Steadholder Mother and somewhat more casually to Tennard, and then fanned out, joining Blacket and the other four members of the twins' joint security team.

The lounge, Allison observed, had begun to seem distinctly over-populated with pleasant young men with green uniforms and guns, and she watched an expensively dressed Manticoran couple ease away from them. She doubted the man and woman even realized they were doing so, but they responded on an unconscious level to the politely alert guard-dog mentality of the Harringtons.

"You brought them along to make a point, didn't you?" she asked Mattingly in a tone of laughing accusation.

"Make a point, My Lady? Whyever would I want to do something like that? For that matter, what point could I possibly be trying to make?"

"I suppose I ought to have called it a *counter*point," Allison conceded pleasantly.

"Well, it would have helped if you'd warned us ahead of time of your travel plans," Mattingly agreed. "Or if you'd sent a com message ahead when the *Tankersley* came out of hyper. Or, for that matter, if you'd even commed when the shuttle picked you up to deliver you to the port, now that I think about it. Comming us after you're already down in a public place with only the children's travel team for coverage comes under the heading of what we security people consider A Bad Thing, My Lady."

"Goodness, you *are* ticked!" Allison murmured so wickedly Mattingly laughed despite himself. She patted his arm again, and her voice softened. "I know I can be a trial, Simon. But all of these guards and guns and no privacy at all . . . It's a bit much for a girl from Beowulf, you know."

"My Lady, I'm not 'ticked,' " Mattingly told her. "If I thought it would do any good, or that there was even a remote possibility of changing you, I probably *would* be ticked with you. But you're your daughter's mother, and Andrew and I have had plenty of experience trying to make *her* security conscious. We got to her when she was younger than you, too. And since we haven't seemed to make a great deal of progress with her, I don't see why we should be surprised when we don't make any with you when you're so much more . . . um, *mature* and set in your ways. Which, of course—" he flashed her a blindingly white smile "—doesn't mean that either Andrew or I—or Jeremiah or Luke, I'm sure—have any intention of abandoning the effort."

"Oh, I'd be disappointed if you did!" Allison said earnestly.

"I know you would, My Lady. It would take all the fun out of it," Mattingly observed, and looked across at Tennard. "Baggage, Jere?"

"Checked through the diplomatic section. The LCPD and Port Security have two men on the storage area to back up the electronic surveillance. They'll ship it out to us when we com for it."

"Good. In that case, My Lady—" the lieutenant turned back to Allison "—your air car awaits. The Steadholder is out on Saganami Island right now. She would have cleared some time to greet you if she'd known you were arriving," he couldn't quite resist adding, "but she asked me to tell you she'll join you at home for a late lunch. And your husband is also on-planet at the moment. I understand he'll be joining you at the new house this evening, though he may not make it before supper."

"Good!" Allison might find all the security constraining, but she had to admit that her life ran far more smoothly now that someone else was in charge of her schedule. Partly that was because security personnel liked how much easier their own lives were when things ran without hiccups and went to considerable lengths to make sure that they did. But she also knew it didn't all happen that way simply because it made guarding her and her children easier. All these fit young men in green were so happy to run errands and see to all the irksome details of travel because they were deeply and personally devoted to her daughter and her daughter's family, as well.

"In that case," she said, scooping Faith back up, "let's be going. Ready, Jenny?"

"Yes, My Lady," Jennifer LaFollet replied, and climbed out of her chair with James.

Allison had fought to the last ditch against the imposition of a proper Grayson maid, but, like the battle against personal armsmen, it had been one she was doomed to lose. That had become abundantly clear when she became pregnant and even Katherine and Elaine Mayhew began dropping pointed hints about how useful a maid would be as a nanny, especially with twins, since her and Alfred's persistent monogamy deprived her of sister wives to help carry the load.

She knew Honor had put up the same dogged resistance and suffered the same ultimate defeat, and she also knew how well Honor's relationship with Miranda LaFollet had worked out in the end. That being the case, she'd decided to keep the position in the family, as it were, and selected Miranda's cousin Jennifer for the role. Jennifer was more than ten years younger than Miranda. Indeed, at twenty-six T-years she'd received the original, first-generation prolong treatments, which Miranda had been just too old to physically accept when Grayson joined the Manticoran Alliance, but she shared a great deal of her cousin's quietly determined, competent personality. She looked a lot like Miranda and Andrew, as well, with the same auburn hair, although her eyes were green, not gray, and she was a bit taller than Miranda.

And, as Katherine and Elaine had suggested, she'd proved a godsend with the twins. Especially, Allison had discovered, when Alfred had accompanied Honor back to the Star Kingdom and left her to cope with both babies.

Now Jennifer glanced one last time around the terminal lounge, making sure they hadn't forgotten anything—*as though this bunch of armed-to-the-teeth adolescents would* let *me do anything as normal as forgetting something in a terminal!*—and joined Allison at the tube to Mattingly's car. Yet another Harrington armsman looked across from his place at the controls and smiled a greeting, and Allison sighed while the oversized cavalcade got itself organized around her.

I seem to recall thinking, once, how grateful I was that Honor's armsmen were so much less intrusive about guarding Alfred and me than they'd been about guarding her. She looked around the lounge at the eleven uniformed men surrounding her and laughed out loud. *I guess God was listening. I always did figure He had a peculiar sense of humor!*

Mattingly glanced questioningly at her, but she only shook her head and made a little shooing motion with her free hand. He smiled and obeyed the gesture, and Allison Harrington—and friends—filed into the two outsized air cars and headed for the modest little fifty-room mansion the Crown had deeded over to Duchess Harrington as a sign of its high regard.

Chapter Fifteen

"The Prime Minister is here, Your Majesty. He wonders if he might have a moment of your time."

"He does?" Elizabeth III looked up from the cards of her hand. "Oh, good! I mean, *shucks*, it looks like I'll have to go take care of business, Justin."

"Oh, really?" Justin Zyrr-Winton, Prince Consort of the Star Kingdom of Manticore, leaned back and regarded his wife from under lowered brows. "I have to say this sudden urgent affair of state—I assume it *is* an urgent affair of state, Edward?" He glanced at the liveried servant who'd entered the card room with the announcement, and a suitably serious-looking Edward nodded solemnly. "Thank you." The Prince Consort returned his gimlet gaze to his wife. "As I say, I find this sudden urgent affair of state just a tad suspicious, Beth. Don't you, Roger?"

He turned to Crown Prince Roger . . . who looked back as solemnly as Edward.

"I don't know, Dad," the seventeen-T-year-old prince said in a considering sort of tone. "It *could* be a genuine matter of state, I suppose. They do happen from time to time, or so I've been told. But the timing is just a little suspicious."

"Oh, come on, Roger!" His younger sister, Princess Joanna, looked up from her book viewer. "I'll admit Mom has all the sneaky Winton genes. And I'll admit she doesn't like to lose. I'll even admit the Opposition may have a point when they accuse her of being 'devious.' But even granting all that, how could she have known ahead of time that she'd need an interruption to save her? I mean, she'd have to be psychic to know Dad was going to be dealt a double run this hand!"

"Ha!" Her father's lordly disdain could not have been bettered by the pampered scion of the most nobly born family of the Star Kingdom, despite the fact that, by law, Elizabeth had been required to marry a commoner. "You're forgetting the security systems, Jo. Do you really think someone as underhanded as your mother would fail to have the systems on-line during a crucial operation like a pinochle game? She's probably wearing an earbug right now so that her sinister minion in the PGS can use the security cameras to read Roger's and my cards to her! And no doubt those *same* sinister minions commed the Prime Minister and told him to hurry right over before I trounced her."

"That, my dear, is carrying paranoia and suspicion of those in power entirely too far." Elizabeth managed to make her tone admirably severe despite the smile hovering on her lips. "Besides, if it were *that* important to me to win—which, of course, it isn't, the drive to win in all ways and at all costs being foreign to my sweet and compliant nature—I wouldn't use Allen to get me out of the game. I'd simply have you arrested for high treason or some other trumped-up charge and flung into the Citadel to languish miserably in some cold, dark, dank cell."

"I don't think so!" Justin told her with spirit. "First, the Citadel is climate controlled; it doesn't *have* any cold, dark, dank cells. And second, even if it did, we live under a Constitution, we do, and it specifically limits what tyrannical monarchs can do to their subjects on a whim!"

"Of course it does," his wife purred, while the treecat on the back of her chair bleeked laughter at the one on the back of Justin's. "The problem, oh feckless one, is that before your lawyer can apply for a writ of *habeas corpus* and protest my tyrannical ways, said lawyer has to know you're in prison in the first place. And for all the skill with which we Wintons have played the benevolent, law-abiding monarchs for so long, there have actually been whole generations of secretly held prisoners, victims of our evil autocracy, who lingered wretchedly until their miserable deaths, forgotten and alone in the unhallowed cells of our tyrannical rule."

"That was *very* good, Beth!" Justin said admiringly. "But I doubt you could get it all out in order again."

"I don't have to," she told him, elevating her nose disdainfully. "I'm the Queen, and that means I can do anything I want," she said snippily, then grinned broadly. "It's good to be the Queen, you know."

"It's better to be Prince Consort," Justin told her, reaching up and back to rub his own 'cat's ears. Monroe buzzed a happy purr and slithered bonelessly forward over his shoulder and into his lap to demand more serious petting.

"And why might that be?" Elizabeth asked suspiciously.

"Because while you go deal with whatever it is that brings Allen here, *I* can stay here, basking in the esteem of our devoted children and scratching Monroe's chest . . . while I stack the cards for the next deal."

" 'Esteem of our devoted children'? Yeah—right!" Elizabeth hooted with laughter, and the aforementioned devoted children grinned at her. "Actually, they're both in my pay," Elizabeth went on, rising and reaching for Ariel. "They'll inform me instantly if you try to stack *my* deck. And if they don't, I'll just have PGS run the imagery from the security cameras and prove all three of you are conspiring against your monarch. With—" her tone lowered ominously "—fatal consequences for the conspirators!"

"Curses, foiled again," Justin murmured, and his wife leaned over to kiss him before she turned back to the servant.

"All right, Edward," she sighed. "Lead me to the Duke."

"Of course, Your Majesty. He's waiting in Queen Caitrin's Suite."

A neatly bearded man of medium height stood outside Queen Caitrin's Suite. He was dark-complexioned and a bit on the stocky side, and he wore the uniform of a Palace Guard Service major. He wore a red-and-white aiguillette that indicated his assignment to the Prime Minister's office, the name plate above his breast pocket said "Ney, Francis," and his expression did not encourage familiarity. It was hard to say whether that was deliberate, or simply the way nature had put his face together, although there were those among his acquaintances who knew which *they* thought it was. But however grim and focused he might look to others, Elizabeth smiled as she saw him.

"Hello, Frank," she said, and Ariel twitched his whiskers in greeting.

A very small twinkle showed at the backs of the major's eyes as the 'cat bleeked a welcome to him, but the twinkle never touched his expression. Elizabeth didn't mind. She'd known Frank Ney since she was a child, and she was not among those who called him antisocial. He was certainly . . . prickly, with opinions that had been cast in battle steel. That much she was willing to concede. But he was also from Gryphon's Olympus Mountains, whose yeomen had a long history of friction with their local aristocracy, which explained a lot of his taciturn personality and general distrust of those in authority. Which might seem odd in a man who'd volunteered fifty years before to protect the monarch and senior members of her government, but made perfectly good sense to anyone who knew him. And truth to tell, the Crown had a long history of supporting Gryphon's commoners against Gryphon's nobility, which produced a fierce loyalty to the current monarch. It also explained why half of Gryphon's aristocrats were card-carrying members in good standing of the Conservative Association. (The percentage probably would have been higher, but the Association was far too liberal and namby-pamby for the *truly* conservative members of the Gryphon peerage.)

At any rate, Elizabeth knew better than most that Ney certainly wasn't antisocial. Cantankerous, stubborn, overly focused, and often infuriating to those who collided with his inflexible principles, yes. But not antisocial. Besides, he was very good at his job, and she'd been delighted when the Prime Minister tapped him to head his own security force.

"Hello, Your Majesty," the major replied to her greeting, and a smile—a small one perhaps, and fleeting, but incontrovertibly a smile—flickered on his lips.

"Is he keeping you busy?" She twitched her head at the closed door, and Ney chuckled.

"Not as busy as I try to make him think, Your Majesty. I'm managing to make him slow up at least a little by making him feel guilty over how hard he drives the rest of us. Pity I can't convince him to do the same thing to go a little easier on *himself* sometimes."

"I know." Elizabeth sighed, then reached across and patted the major on the shoulder. "Keep trying though, Frank. And I hope he realizes how lucky he is to have someone like you around to nag him."

"Please, Your Majesty!" Ney's discouraging expression was back in full force. "Not '*nag*'! I prefer to think of it as offering . . . ah, *directed encouragement*."

"That's what I said: nag," Elizabeth replied. Ariel bleeked laughter from her shoulder, and the major chuckled and reached back to press the door button for her.

Allen Summervale, Duke of Cromarty and Prime Minister of Manticore, rose, courteously but without haste, as Elizabeth entered Queen Caitrin's Suite with her 'cat.

"Hello, Allen." The Queen smiled warmly and walked across to give him a hug. That wasn't exactly protocol, but she and her Prime

Minister had known one another a long time. Indeed, he'd been a member of her regency council when she ascended the throne as a grief-stricken teenager following her father's untimely death, and in many ways, he had become a surrogate father to her. He was also the man who'd run the Star Kingdom in her name, working in partnership with her to overcome, circumvent, buy-off, or bully all opposition to the naval buildup her father had begun . . . and which had, so far at least, prevented the Star Kingdom's destruction.

"And what brings you calling on a Sunday afternoon?" she asked as she released him and waved him back into his chair. "I assume it's not all that urgent, or you would have commed to save time. On the other hand, you obviously regard whatever it is as being at least a bit out of the ordinary, or you would have let it wait till Monday."

"Actually, it *is* a bit urgent, although not in the sense of requiring an immediate response," he told her. "But it does have a certain potential to complicate our lives in a major way. Especially when the Opposition gets wind of it . . . assuming their spies haven't already alerted them."

"Oh, my." Elizabeth flopped into her own chair and hugged Ariel to her chest. "Why do you persist in bringing me news like this, Allen Summervale?" she demanded. "Just once I'd like you to come to the Palace, poke your head in, and say 'Just dropping by for a visit, Your Majesty! Nothing at all new to worry about. Have a nice day!' "

"That *would* be nice, wouldn't it?" Cromarty agreed wistfully. But then he shook himself. "Nice, but not likely to happen any time soon, I'm afraid."

"I know." Elizabeth regarded him with a fond smile, then sighed. "Go ahead and let me have the bad news."

"I'm not certain it *is* 'bad' news," he said judiciously. "In fact, it could be very good news, in the long run."

"But if you don't get to the point, not even Major Ney will be able to keep it from being *very* bad news for *you* in the short run," Elizabeth said pointedly, and he chuckled.

"All right, Your Majesty. In a nutshell, we've just received a formal request from the President of San Martin."

"Formal request?" Elizabeth frowned, and Ariel cocked his ears at the Prime Minister. "What sort of formal request?"

"It's a *bit* complicated, Your Majesty."

"It always is on San Martin," Elizabeth pointed out dryly, and the Duke smiled in rueful agreement.

San Martin was one of the heaviest-gravity worlds ever settled by humanity. In fact, at 2.7 standard gravities, it might well be *the* heaviest. The planet was so massive its colonists had been restricted solely to its mountainous peaks and plateaus despite the fact that virtually all of them had been descended from people genetically engineered for high-grav environments centuries before San Martin was settled. Fortunately, San Martin was a very large planet which had a *lot* of mountain ranges, several of which put Old Earth's Himalayas and New Corsica's Palermo Range to shame.

There had to be something about mountains that put its own impression on the human genotype, Elizabeth reflected wryly. Even here in the Star Kingdom, people from places like the Copperwalls or the Olympus Range seemed to be stubborner and stiffer-necked than their lowland friends and relations. And since San Martin had the most spectacular mountains known to man, it was no doubt inevitable that its inhabitants would be among the most fractious people in the history of mankind.

Which they were. In point of fact, they made Major Ney seem downright malleable and easily led, which was no doubt the reason they'd fought so stubbornly—and hopelessly—when the PRH moved in on Trevor's Star thirty-three T-years before.

Some had reached accommodations with their conquerors in the intervening decades, of course. Some had been outright collaborators, and some, as on any conquered planet, had actually found their spiritual home in the ranks of their conquerors. But the vast majority of the population had regarded anyone who had anything to do with the Peep occupiers with contempt, and they hadn't been shy about making their . . . displeasure with such souls known.

As a result, both the old Office of Internal Security and its StateSec successors had been forced to maintain a large presence on the planet. Worse, from the Peeps' viewpoint, thirty-odd years was nowhere near as long a time for a planet to be occupied as it had been in pre-prolong days, and far too many San Martinos for the Peeps' peace of mind had very clear, adult memories of what life had been like before the Peeps arrived to rescue them from the twin curses of prosperity and independence.

Since Admiral White Haven had taken the system away from the Peeps, it had been the Alliance's turn to deal with the stubborn mountaineers, and the process had been . . . interesting. It wasn't that the San Martinos were fond of the Peeps or wanted StateSec back, because they certainly weren't, and they certainly didn't. But the provisional government which had been set up under the aegis of the Allied occupation had encountered its own difficulties, because, having endured occupation by the PRH for so many years, the people of San Martin had no desire to be dictated to, even gently, by *anyone*, including the people who'd liberated them. They wanted control of their home world back, which was only reasonable, in Elizabeth's opinion.

The Alliance had no problem with that, but the San Martinos themselves and their constant internal bickering had created endless difficulties. Observers from Zanzibar and Alizon had been particularly dismayed by the liveliness of the exchanges, and even the Grayson delegates to the commission overseeing San Martin's return to self-government had experienced reservations about turning the planet back over to its owners. It might be their world by birth, but most of the commissioners seemed to feel the Allies had a responsibility to protect them (and their helpless planet) from their own excesses.

The Manticoran and Erewhonese commissioners had been less worried, mostly because they had rather more experience at dealing with energetic electorates of their own. The fine old art of political hyperbole, viewing with alarm, and vilifying one's political opponents had been a part of Manticoran political life almost since the Star Kingdom's inception. Erewhon wasn't far behind, and for all their enthusiasm, the San Martinos were scarcely in the same league as Manticoran or Erewhonian machine politicians out to demonize their foes. As long as no one was actively shooting at anyone else, the Manticorans and Erewhonese were reasonably content to adopt a wait-and-see attitude, and they'd concentrated their prophylactic efforts on providing transport off planet for any of the old regime's sympathizers who preferred to be somewhere else when their somewhat irritated friends and neighbors resumed self-government. No one had used any threats to compel Peep sympathizers to refugee out, but the Allies' San Martin Reconstruction Commission had found a great many people who'd been downright eager to accept their transportation offer.

In the event, that waiting attitude had proven the wiser course, if not precisely for the reasons the commissioners had thought it might. The provisional government had just started wrangling about the details for arranging the first planetwide election when Honor Harrington was captured by the Peeps, and they'd still been wrangling when she returned from the dead. That much hadn't surprised anyone in the Alliance. Indeed, what had almost stunned those who'd become accustomed to the debates, arguments, shouting matches, and occasional fistfights which formed the bone and sinew of the San Martin political process had been the screeching

speed at which those debates had come to an end with the return
of Commodore Jesus Ramirez from Cerberus.

No one, including Ramirez, could possibly have predicted the
effect of his return. In some ways, the San Martinos had been even
more infuriated than the Allies by the Peep claim to have executed
Harrington. Perhaps it was because it resonated so painfully with
their own memories of what it was like to live under StateSec's
heel, Elizabeth reflected. But whatever the cause for it, San Martin had been the scene of spontaneous, planetwide celebrations
when the Elysian Space Navy sailed into the Trevor's Star System.
Not even the fact that their world had been forced, temporarily
at least, to somehow absorb, house, and feed the better part of half
a million strangers with literally no warning at all had damped
the San Martinos' jubilation.

Then they'd discovered exactly who the "Commodore Ramirez"
who'd served as Harrington's second-in-command was. He was *Jesus*
Ramirez, nephew of the last preconquest planetary president and
the last uniformed commander of the San Martin Space Navy. The
man who'd forced the People's Navy to pay at a rate of three to
one for every San Martin ship destroyed, and who had successfully covered the final evacuations to Manticore (and, everyone
thought, died in the process) as the Peeps closed in at last.

The Ramirez family had not fared well during the occupation.
President Hector Ramirez had been "shot trying to escape" within
a month of being forced to sign the planet's capitulation. His
brother Manuel, Jesus' father, had been convicted of "terrorist
activities" and shipped off to Haven. InSec apparently had intended
to use his immense popularity to encourage his countrymen to
behave themselves and stop blowing up InSec Intervention HQs,
but the plan had backfired when he died within two years. Given
the fact that a dead hostage wasn't particularly useful, it was
probable that in this instance the Peeps had told the truth about
a prisoner's death being due to natural causes. Unfortunately, no
one on San Martin, least of all Manuel's surviving uncles, cousins, nieces, nephews, in-laws, and acquaintances, had believed a
word of it. Manuel and his brother had become martyrs, and their
surviving family members had been at the heart of the local resistance movement.

And the Ramirezes had paid for it. The Legislaturalists had
stripped them of their bank accounts and property as part and
parcel of the process of looting the San Martin economy to shore
up PRH's finances. InSec had hunted and harried them. One by
one, most of the family's men and many of its women had perished.

Some had been picked up by InSec, or later by StateSec, and simply disappeared. Others had been killed leading guerilla attacks, or in Peep raids on Resistance camps. By the time the Alliance took the planet, the family had been all but wiped out, and in the process, it had acquired an almost mythic stature in the eyes of all San Martin opponents of the Peep regime.

And then the Ramirezes had returned. First in the person of Brigadier General Tomas Ramirez, Royal Manticoran Marine Corps, who, in a rare instance of slipping a round peg neatly into a round hole, had been selected to serve as the executive officer of the Allied occupation force. That had been a sufficiently emotional experience, especially for San Martinos who remembered Tomas' family, even the boy Tomas himself, from before the occupation. But then Tomas' father had returned, as well, literally from beyond the veil of death, and the effect upon the rest of San Martin's population had been . . . profound. Hysterical hero worship was not a San Martino vice, but the staunchly individualistic mountaineers had come perilously close to it when they realized one of *the* Ramirezes, one of the icons of the Resistance, was still alive.

The squabbles over electoral processes ended overnight, and Jesus was drafted, almost without being consulted, to run for the presidency of the new government. All but one of his opponents withdrew when they realized who they faced, and the one woman who stayed the course was trounced at the ballot box, receiving barely fourteen percent of the vote and conceding defeat even before the polling closed. The last president of the old Republic of San Martin had been a Ramirez; so was the first president of the *new* Republic of San Martin, and the Allies—and especially Manticore, for whom the stability of San Martin was of particular concern—had all heaved a vast, collective sigh of relief.

Which might have been just a mite premature after all, Elizabeth thought, studying her Prime Minister's expression.

"All right, Allen. Just what, exactly, are they up to now?"

"Well . . ." Cromarty tugged on one of his earlobes, then shrugged. "In simplest terms, Your Majesty, President Ramirez has instructed his ambassador to explore the possibility of San Martin's requesting annexation as our fourth planetary member."

"He *what?*" Elizabeth stared at the Prime Minister, and Cromarty nodded.

"That's essentially what I said when Ambassador Ascencio broached the possibility, Your Majesty. It came out of absolutely nowhere."

"Is he serious?" Elizabeth demanded. "And even if he is, what in the world makes him think he could pull off something like that? I know he's popular, but if he's going to run around making offers like that one, the man must have delusions of godhood!"

"In answer to your first question, I think the answer is that he's extremely serious," Cromarty said. "The letter he sent along via Ascencio certainly reads that way, and his analysis of the benefits and advantages such an arrangement might bring to San Martin is both persuasive and well reasoned. As, I might add, is his analysis of the advantages the arrangement would offer the Star Kingdom and our desire to insure the security of the Trevor's Star terminus. And he's apparently done a surprising amount of research into the legal precedents created by your father's annexation of Basilisk. Your uncle is on Gryphon this weekend, but I had some of the Foreign Office's senior legal specialists look over his conclusions, and their preliminary consensus is that he's quite right about the Crown's authority, with advice and consent of Parliament, to add worlds to the Star Kingdom."

"But what about the rest of the San Martinos? Does he honestly think they'll stand for being sold down the river to Manticore?"

"I doubt he thinks anything of the sort, Your Majesty," Cromarty said sternly. "But I also doubt that he expects them to feel they've been 'sold down the river,' either. Apparently, the initial idea wasn't his alone. According to his letter, it had occurred independently to several of the more prominent members of their new Senate more or less simultaneously. They'd still been talking around the point with one another without anyone's quite having the nerve to propose it seriously, when a casual remark of his led them to believe he shared their interest. That was enough to get them moving, and the authorization to formally explore the possibility with us seems to have been proposed, debated before the Senate in closed session, and voted upon in less than two weeks."

"You mean he has official Senate sanction for this?"

"That's what his letter says, Your Majesty. And if their own Senate is backing at least an exploration of the matter, clearly a real possibility of pulling it off exists."

"My God." Elizabeth sat back in her chair, cradling Ariel in her arms, while she pondered the possibilities suddenly opening before her.

The question of what to do, ultimately, with the one-time Peep planets presently occupied by Allied troops had been a vexatious one from the beginning. She knew some members of Parliament, especially among Cromarty's own Centrists and the Crown Loyalists, secretly yearned for annexation as a simple resolution . . . and one that would increase the Star Kingdom's size and population base substantially, which was nothing to sneeze at when engaged in a war against the largest star nation in the vicinity. But none of them had dared to suggest it when they knew every Opposition party's leaders would trample one another trying to be the first to leap upon the idea and strangle it at birth.

The Liberals would be horrified by the very notion that the Star Kingdom might become an old-fashioned, brutal, imperialist power. They'd raised enough hell over the annexation of Basilisk, whose sole habitable planet was peopled only by a batch of aliens about as primitive as any star-traveling race might ever hope to encounter. The idea of annexing other *human*-inhabited worlds would offend every ideological bone in their bodies.

The Conservative Association would have been even more horrified. They were isolationist to the core, and the thought of adding huge numbers of new subjects who had no experience of an aristocratic society (and hence could scarcely be expected to bow and scrape properly before their betters) would be intolerable to them.

The Progressives probably wouldn't care a great deal . . . as long as they were allowed to set up their own party organizations and electioneering machinery. The fact that the inhabitants of those planets would already have their own political factions and parties, however, would stick in even the Progressives' craws, since it would inevitably lessen their ability to seize upon new sources of strength at the polls.

And even many Manticorans not blinkered by ideology or the calculus of electoral advantage would be dismayed by the thought of adding huge chunks of foreigners to the Star Kingdom. They would worry that adding so many foreign elements would dilute or even destroy the unique amalgam which had allowed the Star Kingdom to come so far and achieve so much with such a relatively small population.

Elizabeth could understand all of that, and even sympathize with the last bit. But she also knew that the Star Kingdom's unique balance and accomplishments rested in no small part upon the steady stream of immigrants it had always attracted. There'd never been an overwhelming flood of such newcomers, but there'd always been *some*, and far from weakening the Star Kingdom, they'd added their own strengths to it. Elizabeth had always believed, firmly, that the continuation of that inflow was crucial to her kingdom's ongoing prosperity, and the thought of adding whole new planets held no dismay for her.

Not that she expected selling the idea to Parliament to be easy.

"Do you think we should support Ramirez, Allen?" she asked quietly, and the Prime Minister nodded.

"I do, Your Majesty. First, we need the manpower. Second, Trevor's Star is absolutely essential to us in a strategic sense. And third, I think that ultimately the San Martinos', um, *liveliness*, let us say, would be of great benefit to our own society. Moreover, it would establish a precedent for annexing other worlds that request it . . . and give us an excuse *not* to annex those who *don't* request it. And, frankly, Your Majesty, it would bolster public morale. The incredible lift Duchess Harrington's return gave it is starting to wear off, and the new emergency Navy appropriations—and the taxes they entail—are starting to sink in. And, of course," his lips twisted sourly, "our 'friends' in the Opposition see absolutely no reason not to take advantage of either of the above."

He gave himself a little shake.

"Under the circumstances, the knowledge that another entire planet chooses voluntarily to join the Star Kingdom and share our risks and the burden of supporting the war would do wonders. After all, who would choose to formally join what he expected to be the losing side of a war like this one? If that thought doesn't occur naturally to the electorate and our public policy think tanks, I assure you we'll bring it to their notice!" He chuckled. "The Opposition isn't the only bunch who can play the public opinion game, Your Majesty!"

"I like your argument, Allen," Elizabeth mused, cuddling Ariel and pursing her lips while she considered all he'd just said. "Of course, it's all very preliminary, possibly even a little premature to speculate about, right now. But if it works out . . ."

Her voice trailed off, and Cromarty watched her face as she stared into the empty air at something only she could see. He'd seen that expression on her face before, and as he saw it now, he felt a vast certainty that, preliminary and premature or not, yet to be ratified or rejected by public opnion, Parliament, and the voters though it might be, the actual decision had already been made by the slim, mahogany-skinned woman sitting across from him.

And once that *young woman makes a decision, the rest of the universe had better resign itself to the inevitable and get out of the way,* he thought cheerfully. *Because if it doesn't, it's going to get hurt.*

Chapter Sixteen

"**I** think your Graysons think I'm a bad influence on you, dear," Allison remarked as she and Honor walked down the third-floor hall of Honor's new mansion on their way to the ground-floor dining room. They turned a corner, and Allison paused at a sitting room's open door to properly admire the huge swath of ankle-deep carpet that stretched luxuriously from the door to an entire wall of one-way crystoplast and a breathtaking view of Jason Bay. It was the fourth such door she'd paused at, and each sumptuously furnished room had boasted its own, unique color combination and decorating style.

"Not too shabby," she approved in a deliberately blasé tone. "Still," she went on just a bit critically, "if I were you, I think I'd have the bay dyed a deeper blue."

"Very funny, Mother," Honor said severely, and pressed the door plate. The panel slid shut, and she turned to her unrepentant parent with a stern expression.

"And just what, horrible person that you are, have you been doing to my poor Harringtons now?"

"Why, nothing, dear!" Allison lowered long, dark lashes (one of many features Honor had deeply envied during her gawky, pro-long-extended adolescence) and peeped innocently up through them at her towering daughter. "Nothing at all. It's just that they seem to have this fixation on schedules and message traffic. In fact, I believe 'fixation' is probably too pale a word for it. 'Obsession' would be better, and on more mature consideration, I'm not at all certain it might not properly be described as a pathological condition. Hmmmm . . . I didn't find anything in their genotype to explain it, but I'll bet that only means I missed something in the survey, because now that I think about it, it appears to be a nearly universal condition. Every single Grayson I meet seems to suffer from it, in fact, and—"

"You are a wicked and unnatural creature, Mother," Honor told her diminutive parent, "and all this babbling is *not* going to distract me from the fact that you've been bedeviling my Harringtons. I knew you'd been up to something from the way Andrew and Miranda were very carefully not mentioning your arrival this afternoon. And, clever soul that I am, I deduce from your otherwise incomprehensible comments that you deliberately declined to inform Andrew or Simon of your intended arrival time. Would it happen, perchance, that my chain of reasoning is sound?"

"It must come from your father's side of the family," Allison informed her with severe disapproval. "You never got that sort of dreary, plebeian logic from *my* genes, dear! Beowulfans' cognitive processes rely far more on the creative and intuitive manipulation of concepts without the drudgery of applying *reason* to them. Don't you realize how badly you can damage a perfectly good preconception or assumption if you insist on *thinking* about it that way? That's why I never indulge in such a vice."

"Of course you don't," Honor agreed affably. "And you're evading the question again. Which was something you never let *me* get away with as a child."

"Of course I didn't. A most unbecoming habit in a well-behaved child."

"*Mother!*" A gurgle of laughter spoiled the severity of Honor's look, and Allison giggled.

"Sorry. I just had to get it out of my system after spending the entire trip from Yeltsin aboard *Tankersley* with the twins' bodyguards, Jennifer, Mistress Thorn, and enough baggage for a six-month sojourn in the Sphinx outback. They're all very nice people, and I like them a lot, but do you realize how small the *Tankersley* really is? *I* didn't . . . until I discovered there was no place I could go where I didn't have to be on my best behavior."

"You never spent a day in your life on your 'best behavior'!" Honor snorted. "Um." She cocked her head. "Unless you wanted to charm something out of some poor unsuspecting male with your winsome smile and dimples, that is," she amended.

"Oh, I can think of one or two times I behaved myself to get something out of a female, too," Allison said, then sighed. "That was before you were born, of course," she added pensively.

"Two or three? Are you sure you wanted something out of that many females? That sounds like an excessive estimate, considering how relentlessly heterosexual you are. You're not even a hundred years old yet, you know."

"I'm certain there were at least two, and I *think* there were three." Allison wrinkled her nose in thought. "I'm almost sure there were three," she announced. "My second-year teacher in grammar school was a woman, and I must have wanted *something* out of her before the year was over."

"I see." Honor leaned back against the closed sitting room door and smiled down at her mother. "Feeling better?" she asked genially.

"Oh, *lots* better!" Allison laughed, then shook her head. "Do you have any idea how your Graysons would react if I went on with one of them that way, Honor?"

"Oh, I think Miranda might surprise you. And I know Howard and Andrew would."

"Not a fair sample selection," Allison objected. "You've been breaking those three in gradually for years now!"

"Agreed." Honor shrugged and the two of them started down the hall once more. "On the other hand, it was probably a good thing that I had a decade or so to 'break in' the entire planet before you washed up there."

"It did help," Allison agreed with a small chuckle, then shook her head in fresh amazement as they started down the huge, sweeping grand staircase to the mansion's enormous foyer. "I think this is even worse than Harrington House," she mused. "And Mistress Thorn has already discussed the distance from the kitchen to the dining room with me. She Does Not Approve, Honor. Rather vocally, as a matter of fact."

"I'm not surprised. As a matter of fact, people seem to be developing a nasty habit of giving me houses that are entirely too magnificent for my taste. Not that *they* see it that way, of course. They seem to think the problem is simply that my taste is insufficiently magnificent for one of my high station and general all round demigoddess status." She made a rude sound, and the live side of her face grimaced. "Actually, of course, it's all your fault for failing to instill a proper desire for the finer things in life into me. I told Mike that if her cousin were anyone but the Queen of Manticore I would've handed this oversized docking slip straight back to her. It'd take an entire battalion of servants to keep up with something this size back on Grayson, and even with all the remotes and the house AI, the staff here on Manticore is still over thirty!"

She shook her head and led the way down the staircase.

"It takes a good half hour to walk from one end of the place to the other," she went on, exaggerating only slightly, "and I feel like I need an inertial navigation box and way points just to get from the library to the bathroom. At least Harrington House has the excuse that it's also an administrative center, but this thing is pure ostentation!"

"Calm down, dear," Allison advised. "Her Majesty just wanted to give you a shiny new toy to show everyone how much she likes you. And you must admit she really did manage to come up with something you'd never have thought to buy for yourself."

"Oh, you hit that one right on the head," Honor agreed feelingly. "Mac loves it, of course. He feels it offers the proper setting for an individual of my towering stature." The living side of her face grimaced one more. "And Nimitz and Sam like it, too, because it's big enough they'll be able to spend years exploring before they find all its 'cat-sized nooks and crannies. And I suppose *I* actually like the two or three rooms I'll actually ever use. The view really is tremendous, too, and I don't have any real objection to comfortable surroundings. Maybe it's just that I've spent so much time aboard ship. Even the admiral's quarters on a superdreadnought are downright minuscule compared to this place, so maybe I just feel guilty about using up so much cubage."

"I don't see any reason to feel guilty," Allison said as they reached the bottom of the staircase and headed across the statue and holo tapestry-decorated foyer's endless expanse of black-and-green marble. She paused to admire the water feature splashing at its center while the black, gold, and green darts of Sphinxian koi (which actually did favor the Old Terran species of the same name, allowing for the absence of scales, the extra fins, and the horizontal flukes of the tail) sailed about in the polished granite basin's forest of water plants and artistically placed cobbles.

"*You* didn't build it or squander the money on space you don't really need," she went on after a moment. "And if someone else did, it's not like the planet is going to run out of living volume anytime soon. Besides, Honor—all kidding aside, the Queen really did give this place to you more to show the public how much she values you than because she ever imagined you'd need anything like it. From that perspective, it was as much a political move on her part as that statue of you outside Steadholder's Hall was on Benjamin's. But that doesn't mean she didn't really want to give you something special."

Honor made an uncomfortable little gesture, and her mother laughed softly.

"So that's the real reason for all this heat! You're feeling all embarrassed again."

"I am not," Honor protested. "It's just—"

"Just that you hate being 'turned into' some sort of hero."

Allison stopped and touched her daughter's elbow, halting her until she turned to face her.

"Honor, I love you very much," she said then, her voice unwontedly serious. "You know I do, even though I probably haven't told you so as often as I should have. And I'm also your mother—the one who changed your diaper, watched you learn to walk and talk, sent you off to school, bandaged your skinned knees, hauled you and Nimitz down from picketwood trees, talked to your teacher after that fistfight in fifth grade, and put up with all the mess a twelve-year-old and a treecat can generate without even breaking a sweat. I know you, dear—know *you*, not the PR image—and I understand exactly why you're so uncomfortable with the thought that people think of you as a 'hero.' But Elizabeth III didn't 'turn you into' one, and neither did Benjamin Mayhew, or even the newsies and the 'faxes. *You* did it, by your own actions and your own accomplishments.

"I know, I know." She waved a hand when Honor tried to edge in a protest. "You didn't do it so people would admire you, and most of the time you were doing all those 'heroic' things you were scared to death. I told you I know you, Honor, and how could I know you without knowing that, as well? I've seen you grit your teeth each time some newsie or vote-grubbing politician calls you 'the Salamander,' and I know all about the nightmares—and worse—you went through after Paul's death. But do you really think all those people who came to your funeral when we thought the Peeps had killed you don't understand that too? They may not know you as well as your father and I do, but they know you better than that! And truth to tell, I think that's one reason so many of them do think of you as heroic. Not because they expect you to be so stupid or so arrogant that you think you're invulnerable or because fear never enters your thoughts, but because you've demonstrated that you know you're *not* invulnerable—" her tiny wave indicated Honor's missing arm and the dead side of her face "—and they're smart enough to realize you *are* scared . . . and you do your job anyway."

Honor felt her face heating, but Allison only smiled and squeezed her elbow.

"I realized, when I thought you were dead, that I'd never told you often enough how very proud I was of you," she said quietly. "I know it makes you uncomfortable when someone praises you for doing something you considered to be your 'job,' and I'm your mother, so there are times I wish to heaven that you'd picked some safer career. So I probably won't embarrass you again by harping on this. But you've made me a very proud woman, Honor Harrington."

Honor blinked eyes that stung suddenly. She opened her mouth, but no words came out, and her mother smiled again, more normally, and gave her arm a little shake.

"And as for the size of your house—piffle! If the Queen of Manticore wants to give you a present, then you darned well accept it. If I have to put up with all the ruffles and flourishes on Grayson, then you can take your medicine here in the Star Kingdom and *smile* about it, by God! Is that clearly understood, young woman?"

"Yes, Momma," Honor said submissively, with only the tiniest quaver to betray her own emotions.

"Good," Allison said smugly, and smiled brightly at James MacGuiness as the steward opened the dining room door to greet them.

CHAPTER SEVENTEEN

Several hours later, Honor and her mother were comfortably ensconced on one of the mansion's several terraces. As part of its ostentatious luxury the estate sat atop the coastal cliffs of the Eastern Shore section of Jason Bay and boasted just over two full kilometers of pristine, completely private beachfront. That was by straight-line, aerial measure; allowing for the indentations of the rugged shoreline, it was more like three and a half kilometers, by Honor's estimate. Of course, all of the Star Kingdom's planets were sparsely populated compared to someplace like Haven or one of the Solarian League's older daughter worlds. All three together had barely half the population that Old Earth alone had boasted in the last century Ante Diaspora, so land ownership was scarcely restricted to the ultrarich as it was on more densely peopled planets. For that matter, the estate was far smaller than the Harrington homestead back on Sphinx. But it was also less than twenty kilometers from the exact center of Landing City's business district, and the East Shore was considered the second or third most desirable residential site on the entire capital planet. That meant that even in the Star Kingdom, those hectares of dirt would have brought a fantastic price on the open market. Especially with the spectacular view available from the top of the craggy palisade of the cliffs.

Manticore-A balanced on the western rim of the bay, and Manticore-B was a bright, brilliant star, clearly visible in the darkening eastern sky. The breeze off the bay gathered strength slowly but steadily, ruffling the fringes on the umbrella shading their loungers, and just a hint of a cloud bank hovered to the north, harbinger of the overnight rain the weather people were calling for. A blizzard of scaled, twin-tailed, gray-and-green lizard-gulls lifted and dove above the cliffs, or bobbed like corks on the swell beyond the surf line, singing to one another in the high, clear trills of their kind, and the scent of tidewater mingled with those of crown blossom, Old Earth roses, and the brilliant banks of mixed native and Terran flowers which softened the terrace's gray, flagstoned severity.

"I suppose," Allison remarked from behind her dark glasses, "that I could grow accustomed to this sort of decadent luxury if I really put my mind to it. Difficult, of course, for one of my naturally puritanical bent, but possible. Possible."

"Sure." Honor reached out a long arm, snagged another choco-late-chip cookie from the plate on the table between them, and bit into it blissfully. Her mother, she reflected, might have a point, for there were a few luxuries she would have hated to give up herself, like Susan Thorn, her Grayson cook.

"Mistress" Thorn was another member of the LaFollet Clan—an aunt by marriage, if Honor had managed to pick her way successfully through the complex Grayson clan structure. Her native formality preferred the old-fashioned mode of address, and she would *never* have felt comfortable being addressed by her Stead-holder by her Christian name. But that was all right, because she also was firmly of the opinion that no kitchen had been properly consecrated to its sacred calling until it had produced its first trays of cookies and fudge. Given the sort of cookies (and fudge) she produced, Honor wasn't about to argue with her, and she rather suspected that her own genetically modified, heavy-world metabo-lism was one reason Mistress Thorn so enjoyed cooking for her. It took a lot of calories to stoke her internal furnace, and Mis-tress Thorn was delighted to have an employer she could stuff to the eyebrows without having her worry about her weight or her figure, two subjects of enormous importance to any old-style Grayson lady.

For all that, however, Mistress Thorn had been scandalized the first time Alfred Harrington wandered into the Harrington House kitchen. The kitchen was *her* domain, and no mere male had any business mucking about in it. Even those of them who claimed they liked to cook actually only played at it, in her experience, and even the best of them cheerfully left the mess and clutter behind for someone else (and female) to clean up.

There hadn't been anything she could do about it, short of

quitting, however, and so she'd gritted her teeth and put up with it . . . only to discover that Alfred was, quite possibly, just as good a cook as she. She had the edge in pastries, cakes, and breads, but he had a better touch with meats and soups, and they ran a dead heat with vegetables. Within weeks, Alfred was the only denizen of Harrington House, including the Steadholder, who was not only permitted unlimited access to her kitchen but to address her by her first name. He was even, in a shocking breach of all precedent, allowed to teach *her* how to prepare his own patented spinach quiche. As one who was not and never would be a charter member of the Society of Cooks, Bakers, Chefs, and Wine Snobs, Honor had been perfectly happy to let him plan menus and discuss differences between Sphinxian and Grayson cuisine with Mistress Thorn to his heart's content. Her mother had always been content to let him rule the kitchen when Honor was a child, after all, and all Honor really cared about was the quality of the end product. Which had been good enough when either Alfred or Mistress Thorn were left to their own devices and had become still better once the two of them started collaborating.

She bit into the cookie and looked over to where Nimitz and Samantha snored gently on the perch above the low wall of rough rock which guarded the terrace's seaward side. James MacGuiness had personally overseen the installation of the multibranched perch even before Honor moved into the mansion, and both 'cats loved it. She could taste their sleeping contentment, hovering on the surface of their dreams as if they were purring in the back of her brain.

"Do you remember that awful sunburn you got your first week at Saganami Island?" her mother asked in tones of drowsy content all her own, and Honor snorted.

"Of course I do—and so does Nimitz. I hope you're not planning on administering another 'I told you so' at this late date, Mother!"

"Not I," Allison averred. "I figure that if the burned hand teaches best, then the entire scorched epidermis simply has to get its point across. Even to you, dear."

She turned her head to give her daughter a seraphic smile, and Honor chuckled. Her mother's birth world was dry and dusty by the standards of most human-inhabited worlds. It had enormous continents and few but deep seas. While it lacked the mountains and extreme axial tilt which made Gryphon's weather so . . . interesting, it also lacked the climate-moderating effect of Gryphon's extensive oceans. That meant she'd grown up accustomed to a pronounced "continental" climate, with long, hot summers and extremely cold winters, but Honor was a child of Sphinx. For her, the long, slow seasons of her chilly home world, with their rainy springs, cool summers, blustery autumns, and majestic winters would always be the norm, which had left her completely unprepared for the climate she'd encountered at Saganami Island. Manticore was much closer than Sphinx to the primary they shared, and Saganami Island, only a few dozen kilometers from where Honor and her mother sat at that very moment, was barely above the capital planet's equator. Allison had warned her about what that meant, but she'd been only seventeen T-years old, out on her own (or that was how she'd thought of the Academy's highly structured environment at the time, at least) at last, and too busy enjoying Manticore's lesser gravity and bone-deep warmth to pay much heed. Which had ended, inevitably, with one of the more spectacular sunburns in human history.

"And why, O revered parent, did you bring the subject up, if not to engage in one of your homilies on the horrid fates which await daughters who ought to listen to their revered parents—especially their *female* revered parents—and don't? Are you dusting off your skills for use on Faith and James?"

"Heavens, no. It's far too early for that." Allison chuckled. "You know how it is, Honor. If you go into training for anything too early, your skills are likely to peak prematurely. I figure I'll wait at least until they're walking before I start practicing proper parental judo on them. After all, that worked fairly well with you, didn't it?"

"I like to think so." Honor helped herself to another cookie and offered the plate to her mother, but Allison shook her head. Her genes lacked the Meyerdahl modification which produced Honor's accelerated metabolism. There were times, as she watched the gusto with which her daughter and husband shoveled in anything edible that crossed their paths without the least concern about calories, when she rather regretted that. On the other hand, she could go considerably longer between hunger pangs . . . and took a certain pleasure in sweetly reminding them of that point when they woke her up rummaging noisily through cabinets or refrigerators in the middle of the night.

"Of course," she said now, just a bit provocatively, "I suppose you might be just a little biased about how well it worked out, mightn't you?"

"I might be. But I'm not, of course."

"Oh, of course!"

They chuckled together, but then Allison rolled over on her side and lifted her sunglasses to regard her daughter with unwonted seriousness.

"Actually, Honor, there was a reason I brought it up, but it concerns Nimitz more than it does you."

"It does?" Honor's eyebrow quirked, and her mother nodded.

"In a way. I was thinking about how miserable Nimitz was while he endured the experience with you, and in turn, that got me to thinking about the nature of the link you two share." Honor cocked her head, and Allison shrugged.

"I haven't had a chance to do more than screen your dad and tell him I'm on-planet, so I certainly haven't been able to discuss anything about your case or Nimitz's with him. On the other hand, I don't have to discuss anything to see that Nimitz is still limping almost as badly as ever. May I assume your father and the 'cat docs have decided to move more cautiously than usual because of the loss of his mental voice?"

"That's about right." Honor spoke quietly, and her gaze was troubled as she glanced at the 'cats. She was just as glad they were asleep, because she couldn't stifle a bite of resentful grief over Nimitz's handicap. *No, not his handicap: his* mutilation. *Because that's what it is—even more than what happened to my arm.* She gritted her teeth and fought off a murderous stab of rage before it reached the surface. It got close enough to make Nimitz shift uneasily, but she managed to throttle it before she woke him completely, and he settled back down. Besides, there was no one on whom she could take vengeance. Both Cordelia Ransom and the StateSec thug whose pulser butt had actually done the damage had died aboard *Tepes*, and however much she might long to do it, she couldn't bring them back so she could personally kill them all over again.

"They're about ready to start work on both of us, actually," she went on after a moment, her voice calm. "They've mapped the damage to my face—" she brushed her fingers over her dead cheek "—and it's as bad as Fritz's original examination suggested. We're looking at total replacement, and there's additional damage to the organic-electronic interface, thanks to the power surge that burned out the artificial nerves. It doesn't look as bad as Daddy was afraid it might be, but it isn't good, especially with my history of rejecting implants and grafts alike. At the moment, he's estimating about four T-months for the surgery and grafting, assuming we don't go through another complete round of rejections. But the training and therapy sessions should be shorter this time, since I've been through them once before and already know the drill, so we're probably looking at about seven months, total, for the face.

"The eye is a little simpler, since the optic nerve was never damaged the way my facial nerves were. Even better, the surge when the Peeps burned it out seems to've been weaker. It damaged the electronic side of the interface, but the fail-safes and circuit breakers protected the organic side almost completely, so it's basically just a matter of plugging in the new hardware. But since I'm already going to be stuck in the shop for so long with the face, Daddy's decided to build a few extra capabilities into the new eye. It'll mean I have to learn how to activate and control the new features. Heck, after all the time my old eye's been down, I'm going to have to *re*learn all the old ones! But he managed to convince me it'll be worth it in the long run. Of course—" the living side of her face crinkled into a smile "—I think it's probably a bit unfair for a physician to take advantage of the fact that he's also your father when he starts in on convincing you of something. I almost expected him to say 'Because I'm your *father*, that's why!' "

"I can't imagine why he'd say something like that," Allison murmured. "It never worked when you were ten, so why in the world should he expect it to now?"

"He shouldn't," Honor agreed. "Which didn't keep me from thinking for a minute that he was going to try it anyway."

"And the arm?"

"That's going to be both easier and harder than the face. The good news is that, despite the primitive facilities he had, Fritz did a really good job when he took it off."

Allison nodded, but her serene expression didn't fool Honor. It couldn't have fooled anyone who could taste her jagged emotional response, even now, to the thought of her daughter, lying more than half-starved and wounded almost to death, while a doctor worked with frantic haste to amputate the shattered ruin of her arm with nothing but an assault shuttle's emergency med kit for equipment and supplies.

"He took particular care with the nerves," Honor went on, her voice as serene as her mother's face, "and Daddy says we shouldn't have any trouble at all with the interfaces there. As I say, that's the good news. The *bad* news is that, unlike the face and the eye, I'm going to have to start from scratch with the arm."

Allison nodded once more, this time with a grimace of sympathy. Despite the best the technical types could do, an artificial limb remained just that: artificial. The designers could do many things with their prostheses, but not even the Solarian League's medical establishment could make one which obeyed exactly the same nervous impulses, and in exactly the same way, as the natural limb it replaced had obeyed. There were too many idiosyncratic differences from individual to individual. It would have been possible to chart the unique impulses whoever was to replace the limb had used, after which modifying the software to obey them would have been fairly simple and straightforward. But doing that would have taken months and required the recipient to put her missing natural arm—and hand, *and* fingers—through every aspect of their full range of movement for the sensors recording the neural commands. In practical terms, it made more sense to build the limb with a software package that emphasized heuristic functions that learned from doing and then simply let the recipient (and the software) learn to use it. Even then, however, a certain sense of the alien or the once-removed about the new limb would always remain, however well she learned to control it, which was the real reason such prostheses weren't simple "plug and play" devices.

Honor had learned to adjust for the fact that the artificial nerves in her face simply did not report sensory data the same way live ones did. At the moment, she felt nothing at all on her left cheek. Had her implants been working properly, however, she would have "felt" the pressure of the growing sea breeze quite differently on the two sides of her face . . . and even after so many years, the sensations from the left side would have felt artificial. Which was fair enough, since that was precisely what they would have been. She sometimes wondered if it would have been easier to adjust if they'd had to replace the nerves in both cheeks, but she had no intention of experimenting to find out.

That artificiality was the main reason so many star nations, including the Star Kingdom, had no extensive market in bio enhancement. Some nations did, of course. The rogue bio-modifiers of Mesa came to mind almost automatically, but her mother's native Beowulf had also supported a lucrative enhancement market. In one way, Honor could understand the temptation, for there had been features to the eye the Peeps had burned out that she missed sorely, like the low-light vision and telescopic and microscopic functions. But even there, what she saw had never seemed quite as alive—as "real"—as what the unenhanced vision of her right eye had reported. It was something that probably could never be fully described to anyone who hadn't experienced it directly. For that matter, she supposed it might well be purely psychological, although it was reported with near total unanimity by everyone who'd received similar implants. The closest she'd ever been able to come to defining the difference even for herself was to think of what she saw through her left eye as a very, very good, three-dimensional flat screen presentation. Again, she'd often wondered whether or not replacing both eyes, so that she no longer had the "distraction" of her natural eye's input, would have ameliorated the problem in time. And, again, she had no intention of ever finding out.

But there were people who'd made the opposite choice. Indeed, in some of humanity's far-flung cultures, like Sharpton, where the cyborg was a sort of cultural icon, it was as routine for an individual to replace limbs and eyes with artificial improvements as it was for someone on Manticore to have her teeth cleaned and straightened. Or her ears pierced, for that matter. Personally, Honor couldn't imagine doing such a thing. In fact, the very thought made her uncomfortable—probably because she'd spent so much of her life in space. After so many years in an artificial exterior environment, she felt no temptation whatsoever to turn her own body into an artificial *interior* environment, whatever advantages over mere flesh and blood it might have brought with it.

Although the Star Kingdom didn't practice that sort of casual enhancement, it wasn't out of any horror of "cyborgian monstrosities." Honor had met a few people, mostly from places in the Solarian League, whose enhancement had been so obvious and extreme as to make her feel actively ill at ease, but those were exceptions. Most people who had themselves enhanced went to some lengths to make the enhancements appear as much like natural (albeit as perfectly *developed* natural) limbs, as possible, and the same held true for the minority of people who couldn't regenerate.

She had no qualms over how her new arm would look or feel to anyone else, and she and her father had visited the firm which would build it to discuss the enhanced features they wanted, since if she had to have a prosthesis, it would have been stupid not to build in as many advantages as she could. The techs who would produce it had been given access to her BuMed records, and she felt confident that, externally, they would reproduce her original arm perfectly, right down to the small mole on the inside of her left elbow. The synthetic skin covering it would have precisely the right texture and coloration. It would even tan or sunburn exactly as her natural skin, and it would maintain exactly the same skin temperature as her right arm did.

Internally, it would be far stronger and tougher than the limb it replaced, and she'd thought of several other small features she wanted incorporated into it, while her father had suggested a couple that hadn't occurred to her on her own. But marvelous as it would be, it would also be a totally inert, dead lump hanging from the stump of her natural arm, initially, at least. She would have to learn to use it all over again, from scratch, the way an infant learned to use her arms. Worse, she would have to *unlearn* the way her natural arm had once worked, because none of the old nerve impulses or commands would evoke precisely the same responses they once had.

She'd never had to do that with her facial nerves. There, it had been a simple matter of learning to interpret new passive data and match it with old information files. And even with her eye, there'd been relatively few new control functions to learn, for the muscles of her eye socket had been untouched by the damage to the eye itself. They'd moved the new eye precisely as they had the old, and focusing and automatic adjustment for natural light conditions had been built into the software. All she'd really had to learn was a pattern of specific muscle contractions which activated or deactivated any of the special functions she wanted to use.

But it wouldn't work that way for the arm, and she was honest enough to admit that she felt a certain dread whenever she thought of what this therapy was going to be like. And the fact that she'd spent so many years training in *coup de vitesse* was only going to make it still worse, because she'd spent so much time programming muscle-memory responses into herself, and every one of them would have to be deleted and reprogrammed. She would probably be able to retrain herself with the prosthetic well enough to fool most people into believing she'd fully mastered it within no more than nine or ten T-months, but it would take years of hard, unremitting work to completely reintegrate her control of it. For that matter, she never would have quite the same degree of fine motor control she'd once had.

"Anyway," she went on, pulling herself back up out of her thoughts and returning her attention to her mother, "given the time we're going to be down for the arm anyway, Daddy and Doctor Brewster don't see any reason to rush Nimitz. Nor did he and Sam when I discussed it with them. They've done some preliminary work on his midlimb and straightened the ribs, but they've stayed away from the pelvis itself so far, which is why he still can't walk on that hand-foot properly. He's still got some constant, low-grade pain, too, and I know he'd like to be able to get around better, but he and Sam agree with Daddy that there's no point in risking more damage to his 'transmitter site' until Daddy and Brewster feel confident about what they're dealing with." She chuckled suddenly. "Both Nimitz and Sam, and a couple of dozen of other 'cats, as well, are helping out with the study, and we're making pretty rapid progress, now that we know what we're looking for. The 'cats actually seem to enjoy it, like the tests are some sort of game. *Something* certainly appears to have them more fired up than usual, because they're responding much more successfully to Brewster's tests than they ever did to anyone else's."

"Oh, come now, Honor!" her mother chided. "Don't try to fool me, dear. I've always suspected, just as I'm sure you have, that the 'cats were deliberately blowing off half the intelligence tests they were given!" Honor's eyes narrowed, and Allison chuckled. "I never blamed them for it, just as you didn't. Heavens, Honor! If I were as small as they are and some huge, hairy bunch of high-tech aliens moved in on my world, *I'd* certainly want to appear as small and innocent and lovably furry as I could! And it helps a lot that they *are* small and lovably furry," she added in judiciously. "Even if anyone who'd ever seen what they can do to a celery patch—or to any human they decide needs to be put firmly into his place— would know they aren't exactly 'innocent.'"

"Well . . . yes," Honor admitted. "I've always suspected something like that myself. I don't know why, exactly. I just had a feeling that they wanted to be left alone. Not poked and prodded at, or dragged out of their own chosen way of living, I suppose." She shrugged. "I never knew exactly why they felt that way, though I imagine you've probably put your finger on how it started. But it didn't really matter to me, either. If that was the way they wanted it, *I* didn't see any reason to insist they change."

"Of course you didn't. And I doubt very much that Nimitz, or any other treecat, would be drawn to adopt a human who *would* try to change them. It may be because I wasn't born in the Star Kingdom and didn't grow up 'knowing' how intelligent 'cats were— or weren't, as the case may be—but I've always believed that native Manticorans and Gryphons, even most Sphinxians, tend to under-estimate the 'cats largely out of a sense of familiarity. And the people who get themselves adopted, like you and the Forestry Service rangers back home, do their dead level best to divert any inquiry that would intrude on them or violate their own wishes."

"You're right," Honor agreed. "We do, and I suppose that if I'm honest about it, a part of me wishes we could go right on doing just that. I guess it's sort of like a parent feels when she sees her children growing up. She's proud of them, and she wants them to stand on their own and fly as high as they can, but she can't help feeling nostalgic when she remembers them as little kids, all bright and shiny and new and dependent on her." She smiled crookedly. "Oh, I never thought of Nimitz as *dependent* on me, of course! But you know what I mean. And I think I may feel even a bit more bittersweet over it because, in a way, they never really were quite as 'young' as we all thought they were."

"Not you," Allison corrected gently, and waved down Honor's protest before she could utter it. "I saw you with Nimitz from the day you met, Honor. You thought he was a wonderful new discovery, but you never thought he was a toy, or a pet, or anything but another person who just happened to be shaped a bit differently from you. I think you were surprised by his capabilities, but you adjusted to them without feeling as if you somehow had to assert your seniority in the partnership. And let's face it. However intelligent they may be, they really do need human guides if they're going to survive among other humans, and in that sense, Nimitz truly was dependent on you. Still is, in some ways—not least when someone else's emotions get him all jangled and upset. Do you think I haven't seen the way you calm him down at times like that? Or the way *he* calms *you* down when you start beating yourself up inside?" She shook her head. "It's a partnership, Honor. That's what it always has been, and like any partnership that lasts, each of you takes turns being there for the other one. Sort of like a mother and her adult daughter," she added with a gentle smile.

"I suppose that's true," Honor said after a moment, and chuckled. "You're really rather perceptive for an antiquated old fogy of a parent, did you know that?"

"The thought had crossed my mind. As has the sad conclusion that I didn't beat you often enough as a child. Which was probably Nimitz's fault, now that I think about it. It would have been more than my life was worth to try!"

"Oh, no. There were a couple of times when you or Daddy were chewing me out as a kid that Nimitz would cheerfully have *helped* you beat me! Fortunately, there was no way he could tell you that."

"Ah?" Allison cocked her head, and something about her tone made Honor look at her sharply. "Odd you should mention that," her mother went on, "but convenient. It provides a neat bridge to where I was headed when this conversation started."

"I beg your pardon?" Honor blinked at her, and she snorted.

"Have another cookie and listen carefully, dear," she advised. Honor regarded her with a certain suspicion, but then she picked up another cookie and settled back obediently.

"Ah, if you'd only been that biddable as a child!" Allison sighed.

Then she sat completely upright and looked at her daughter much more seriously.

"You and I have never discussed this, mainly because there was no need to," she began, "but as I say, I've watched you and Nimitz together from the very first day. And because I have, I realized years ago that your relationship had begun changing. I've seen enough other bonded pairs to know your link was always a bit different, and I went back and looked over the Harrington medical records very carefully when you were just a little girl. On the basis of my study, I think there's a specific reason so many Harringtons have been adopted over the years."

"You do?" Honor had forgotten the cookie in her hand, and her good eye was very intent as she gazed into her mother's face.

"I do. I started out by looking at precisely what was involved in the Meyerdahl genetic mods. Most people don't realize it, but there were actually four different modification sets within the single project. By this time they've intermingled enough to lose some of their original differentiation, but like a lot of other 'locked' mods, they've managed to stay remarkably stable and dominant over the generations.

"You and your father are direct descendants of the Meyerdahl Beta mod. I won't go into all the specifics, which wouldn't mean a great deal to you, anyway, but most of what it gave you is exactly what all the Meyerdahl recipients got: more efficient muscles, enhanced reaction speed, stronger bones, tougher cardiovascular and respiratory systems, and so on. But the Meyerdahl Betas also got what they used to call an 'IQ enhancer.' We've learned enough more about human intelligence since then that reputable geneticists refuse to tinker with it except under extraordinary conditions. For the most part, you can only enhance one aspect of the entire complex of attributes we think of as 'intelligence' at the expense of other aspects. That isn't an absolute, but it works as a rule of thumb, and it's one reason I never mentioned my research to you or your dad. There was no reason to—and the . . . less successful efforts at engineered intelligence were one reason Old Earth's Final War was as bad as it was. And one reason humanity in general turned so strongly against the entire concept of engineering human genes at all."

"I take it," Honor said very carefully, "that your research didn't indicate that we were one of those 'less successful efforts'?"

"Oh, heavens, no! In fact, the Meyerdahl Betas and the Wintons have quite a lot in common. I don't have as complete a degree of access to the Winton records, of course, but even from the incomplete data in the public files, it's obvious that whoever designed the Winton modification for Roger Winton's parents was remarkably successful. As was the team that put together the Meyerdahl Beta package. I'd like to say they succeeded because they were so good at their jobs, but I rather doubt that was the case, particularly in light of their relatively primitive understanding of just what they were tinkering with. I think that, as we geneticists like to put it when discussing the vast evolutionary sweep of upward human development, they lucked out.

"The really unsuccessful efforts, on the other hand, tended to show very high levels of aggressiveness, like the 'super soldiers' on Old Earth, and weed themselves out of the genotype. As a matter of fact, that aggressiveness was the most common nasty side effect of intelligence modification projects. Some of the recipients verged uncomfortably closely on sociopathic personalities, without the sort of moral governors people need in a healthy society. And when you coupled that with an awareness that they were designed to be (and usually were) quite a lot 'smarter,' at least in certain, specific ways, than the normals around them, they started acting like a pride of hexapumas quarreling over who should boss all those inferior normals about until they got around to picking out lunch."

She shrugged and ran the fingers of both hands through her hair, combing the long strands the sea breeze had begun to whip back from her face.

"Then too, a lot of the IQ enhancements, in particular, simply tended to fade into the general background of the unmodified without showing any special advantages," she went on. "As I said, it usually worked out that the designers wound up enhancing one aspect of intelligence at the expense of one or more others, and what happened most often was that those who succeeded simply learned to use their enhanced abilities to compensate for the areas in which they'd taken a loss in ability.

"In the case of the Meyerdahl Betas, however, the effort actually worked, by and large. One thing you should remember, Honor, is that evolution always wins in the end, but it does it by conserving the designs that happen to be able to survive, not by going out and deliberately creating leaps forward. In fact, I've always disliked using the word 'forward' in terms of evolution at all. We assign an arbitrary valuation to the changes we consider positive and call those 'leaps forward,' but nature doesn't care about that, except in the statistical sense that more individuals with Mutation A survive than those with Mutation B or C. In many circumstances, however, the enhanced aggressiveness we see as a destructive side effect could be a positive survival trait. In a high-tech society, with high-tech weaponry, and surrounded by vast numbers of people who didn't share that aggressiveness—and who were seen as inferior by many who did—it had . . . negative implications, let us say. Under other circumstances, like a colony on a world with serious external threats against which it could be focused, it might mean the difference between survival and extinction.

"But even assuming we can all agree on what does constitute a natural 'leap forward,' those sorts of things happen only very occasionally. And we only know about the instances in which it happened and *was* conserved . . . which is approximately what happened in the case of your ancestors.

"I ran the Harrington intelligence test results against the base norms for their populations, both here and back on Meyerdahl, and the evidence is very clear. So far, I've found only three Harringtons who placed below the ninety-fifth percentile in general intelligence, and well over eighty-five percent of those I've been able to check placed in the ninety-nine-plus percentile. You tend to be very smart people, and if I hadn't wound up in the same select company according to my own test scores, I'd probably come all over inferior feeling or something of the sort."

"Sure you would," Honor said dryly, but her eye was still wide as she considered what her mother had just told her. And especially what she'd said about "undesirable levels of aggressiveness."

"At any rate," Allison went on briskly, "I've come to suspect that an unintended consequence of the IQ enhancer effort, both in the Harrington line and, quite possibly, in the Winton line, was something that makes you more attractive, as a group, to treecats. Given that we know the 'cats are empaths, I'm inclined to think that the confluence of the IQ package as a whole makes you . . . call it 'brighter' or 'tastier' to the 'cats. As if your 'emotional aura' were stronger or more pronounced. Possibly more stable." She shrugged. "I can't explain it any better than that, because I'm shooting blind. This is one area in which there is absolutely no existing body of data, to the best of my knowledge, and we don't even begin to have the tools to define or explain it. As a matter of fact, I feel like a woman trying to describe how a sound smells or a color feels.

"But I've also come to suspect, over the last few years, that the changes in your link to Nimitz are also linked to the Meyerdahl Beta mods. Whatever it is that seems to make all Harringtons so much tastier to the 'cats is even more pronounced in you, and it may be that there are some unique aspects to Nimitz's abilities, as well. At any rate, for the first time in human-'cat history, you two have actually managed to establish a genuine, two-way bond. Or I think it's for the first time. Even if it is the result of the Meyerdahl Beta mods, the possibility has to exist that at least one or two totally unmodified humans could have developed the same ability. But it definitely exists for you and Nimitz," she said softly, "and, God, but I envy you that."

The eyes hidden behind her sunglasses stared off into depths of time and space and imagination that only she could see, and then she shook herself.

"I envy you," she repeated more naturally, "but tell me this: am I also right in believing that *your* link to Nimitz hasn't been impaired by whatever keeps him from making Samantha 'hear' him?"

"I think you are," Honor said cautiously.

"And is it only emotions you feel?" Allison asked intently. "What I mean is, can you two communicate more than feelings or broad impressions?"

"Yes, we can," Honor said quietly. "Whatever's happening, it's still in a state of change, and we seem to get bigger changes in moments of extreme stress." She smiled without humor. "If stress is a factor in its development, I suppose it's not surprising that there've been changes over the last ten or twelve years!"

"I'd say that was probably at least a two or three thousand percent understatement," her mother said wryly.

"At least," Honor agreed. "But what I meant to say was that it started out as simple, raw emotion, but we seem to have learned how to use the emotion as a carrier for more complex things since. We're still a long, long way from the sort of things two 'cats can communicate to one another. I know we are, because I can just feel the edges of it when Nimitz and another 'cat 'talk' to each other. Or I could," she added bitterly, "before that bastard crippled him."

She paused and drew a deep breath, then squared her shoulders and returned resolutely to her mother's question.

"What we seem to be able to communicate most clearly, after emotions, are mental pictures. We're still working on that, and getting better at it. We can't seem to get actual words across the interface, but visual images are something else, and we've gotten a lot better at reading what the other one wanted to get across from the images."

"Ah! That's exactly what I hoped to hear—I think!" Allison

announced, and wrinkled her nose as Honor cocked her head once more. "Sorry. I didn't mean to sound cryptic. It's just that I think I may have come up with a way for Nimitz to be able to communicate more than just emotions to Samantha."

"You have?" It was Honor's turn to sit fully upright. She turned to face her mother squarely, and it was hard to keep her inner tumult out of her own expression. She could taste Allison's concern over how she might react. She knew Allison would never have broached the subject if she hadn't genuinely believed she might have an answer, but she also knew Allison was fully aware of how terribly it would hurt if she raised Honor's hopes and then was unable to carry through to success.

"I have. Back before we learned to correct things like deafness and myopia on a routine out-patient basis—for that matter, it was before we ever even got off Old Earth—there was something called the sign language of the deaf. There was more than one version of it, and I'm still researching it. That was one reason I wanted to come home to the Star Kingdom, to take a look in the archives here. Even if I can manage to find a complete dictionary for it, we'd have to modify it a good deal, I suppose, given that 'cats have one less finger on each true-hand than we do. But I don't see any reason we couldn't work out a system that would work for Nimitz and Sam."

"But—" Honor began, and then bit her lip as the precursor of bitter disappointment flowed through her.

"But no one has ever succeeded in teaching a 'cat to read," Allison finished for her, and chuckled. "We've just finished discussing the fact that the 'cats may have been a bit less than fully forthcoming with us as to the extent of their abilities, dear! And, no, I don't think that was the only problem. I can't quite picture a race of telepaths using language among themselves the way we do, and without some form of communication which would be at least a close analog to the language we use, I'd think the concept of an organized, written version of it wouldn't make a lot of sense to them. And, unfortunately, ours is the only one we can teach them, since we're not telepaths and don't have a clue as to how to 'speak' theirs.

"On the other hand, no one's tried to teach a 'cat to read in over two hundred T-years, Honor, because everyone agrees that it's been conclusively demonstrated that you can't. That's been one of the sticking points for the minority which continues to insist that treecats aren't truly 'intelligent'—in the human sense, at least.

"But none of the people who tried earlier had your sort of link.

And unless my impression is completely wrong, the 'cats' ability to understand spoken English has improved dramatically since Stephanie Harrington's day. They have to have mastered at least the rudiments of semantics, syntax, and the rules of grammar, because if they hadn't, anything we said to them would still just be mouth noises as far as they were concerned, and that clearly isn't the case, now is it?"

"No," Honor admitted.

"What I'm hoping is that the 'cats' increased facility in understanding spoken English indicates a fundamental improvement in their ability to understand the *concepts* of a spoken—or written—language . . . and that the unique nature of your link with Nimitz may give you an edge that will let you take those concepts that tiny bit further needed to teach him to sign."

"I don't know, Mother," Honor said slowly. "It sounds logical . . . assuming your basic read on the process is accurate. But even if you're right about Nimitz and me, I'd have to be able to teach it to *Sam* for it to do any good."

"No doubt. But I'd be extremely surprised if Nimitz is the only 'cat in the universe who could tap into whatever it is the two of you do. I don't mean you could get the idea across easily or completely, but neither Nimitz nor Sam is stupid, Honor. In fact, I suspect they may be brighter than even you and I would be ready to believe, even now. More to the point, they're a mated pair, and they both know you very well indeed. Success certainly isn't guaranteed, but I think you'd have a shot at it. Probably a good one, especially once the two of them figure out what you're trying to do. Even I can see how badly it hurts Sam to be unable to 'hear' anything Nimitz says. If she catches on to the notion that you're trying to teach them a way to fix that, however imperfectly, compared to outright telepathy, I think you'll find she's as motivated a student as you could hope for."

"It *would* be wonderful to find a way for him to actually talk to her again," Honor agreed almost wistfully, and her mother laughed.

"Honor, you ninny!" she said as her daughter looked at her in surprise. "You're not thinking clearly," she scolded. "Of course the immediate object is to give Nimitz and Sam a way to talk to one another, but hasn't it occurred to you that if you teach them to sign, *you*'ll have to learn how, too? And that if they can communicate with each other that way, they can also communicate with *you*?"

Honor gawked at her, and Allison laughed again, eyes dancing.

"Not only that, but they're *telepaths*, Honor . . . and there's nothing at all wrong with *Sam's* 'transmitter.' So if you teach her, I imagine she'd have an excellent chance of teaching other 'cats. And if she does that, while you and I teach their humans . . ."

Her voice trailed off. She pulled off her sunglasses, and the two of them stared at one another as Manticore-A began to slide finally and completely below the horizon.

CHAPTER EIGHTEEN

"Good morning, My Lord."

"Mr. Baird." Samuel Mueller nodded to the dark-haired, dark-eyed man in his study and then waved at a chair.

"Please be seated," he invited, with much more congeniality than he showed most people who visited him in the middle of the night. Of course, most people hadn't managed to pump nine million traceless austens into the Opposition's war chest. He had to be careful how he spread those funds around lest too much money in any one spot get questions asked, but it freed up his legitimate contributions enormously. It was too early yet to predict the full impact of the media blitz he and his fellows were planning, but so far their closely coordinating candidates were on a pace to outspend their less organized opponents by a margin of almost two to one.

"Thank you." Baird settled into the indicated chair and crossed his legs. He seemed to have become considerably more comfortable with Mueller since their first meeting. Indeed, he hadn't even turned a hair over Sergeant Hughes' presence.

"You said it was important we meet," Mueller noted, and Baird nodded.

"Yes, My Lord. First, I wanted to discuss additional funding arrangements with you. My organization has just come into a small windfall—one which would allow us to contribute another three-quarters of a million austens to your campaign funds, assuming we can do so without attracting the Sword's attention."

"Three-quarters of a million?" Mueller scratched his chin

thoughtfully, managing to keep the elation from his expression. "Ummm. I think we can handle that. We have a mass rally in Coleman Steading week after next. It's an outdoor picnic, with entertainment, and we're expecting several thousand people. Most of them wouldn't be able to contribute more than a few austens under normal circumstances, but enough of them are members of our team that I think we could pass the money through them. It would have to be in cash, though. As long as it's in cash, they can always tell anyone who asks that they were keeping it at home under the mattress because they didn't trust banks, and no one can prove they weren't. Electronic trails are much harder to hide."

"I believe we can make it in cash," Baird agreed. "Actually, we'd prefer that ourselves. As you say, breaking the transfer trail protects all of us."

"Good!" Mueller beamed, and Baird smiled back. But then his smile faded, and he uncrossed his legs to lean forward in his chair.

"In the meantime, My Lord, there's another point which needs to be considered. Were you aware that the Protector intends to introduce an additional bundle of reforms and associated measures before the next Conclave of Steadholders?"

"I've heard some talk of it," Mueller said a bit cautiously. "No details, I'm afraid. The Protector's become much too good at keeping secrets for my peace of mind. Unfortunately—" he shrugged "—he and Prestwick have almost completely replaced the appointees the Keys had installed before the 'Restoration.' While they remained in place, and remembered who they owed their positions and loyalty to, we still got occasional but valuable peeks inside the Protector's Council and the Sword ministries. Since then—"

He raised one hand, palm uppermost, then made a throwing away gesture.

"I understand, My Lord," Baird said sympathetically. "But while we never had the access the Keys originally had, we haven't lost as much of it since the 'Restoration,' either. We still get fairly frequent reports, and while they're from considerably lower in the chain than the sorts of sources you and your fellow Keys might have counted on earlier, combining them gives us a reasonably accurate picture of what Benjamin plans. And what he plans this time around we find particularly disturbing."

"Ah?" Mueller sat more upright, and Baird smiled without humor.

"You've heard about San Martin's petition to join the Star Kingdom, My Lord?"

"Yes," Mueller said slowly but with a hint of asperity. "Yes, of course I have. It's been in all the 'faxes for several weeks now."

"I know it has, My Lord." Baird sounded almost apologetic. "My question was a way of introducing the topic. I didn't intend to suggest you aren't alert to such events."

Mueller grunted and nodded for him to continue, and Baird settled back again.

"As I'm sure you know from those 'fax accounts, My Lord, both houses of the San Martin Congress have requested admission as the Star Kingdom's fourth world. The vote in favor of seeking annexation was much higher than most outsiders would have expected, I think, especially given how strenuously the San Martinos had demanded a return to local autonomy. But when you look carefully at the exact language of their request, it becomes evident that they aren't really giving up that autonomy. As we understand the proposed arrangements, San Martin would become a member world of the Star Kingdom, with a planetary governor proposed by the Queen and approved by the San Martin Senate. The governor would head a Governor's Council, with members selected in equal numbers by the Queen and by the Planetary Assembly. The planetary president would automatically be the chairman of the council—in effect, the Prime Minister of San Martin in the Crown's name—and the citizens of San Martin would elect two sets of legislators: one to sit in the Assembly, working with the governor and his council as the local legislative body, and one to sit in the House of Commons back on Manticore. Several questions still require attention, like whether or not the Queen will create a peerage for San Martin, but essentially what they're proposing is a relationship in which the planet would be integrated into the Star Kingdom, but only with several layers of insulation designed to protect San Martin's existing domestic institutions and prevent them from simply disappearing into the Manticore's maw, as it were."

Mueller nodded. He'd already known all of that, but he felt no impatience at being told over again. Mostly because of how impressed he was with Baird's summation. It was unusual for most of Mueller's allies, even (or perhaps especially) among the Keys, to look beyond domestic politics, since it was the threat to their traditions and way of life which had motivated them in the first place. Even those who ever got their noses out of Grayson tended to restrict themselves to matters which concerned their own world's position in and obligations to the Manticoran Alliance and the waging of the war against Haven. Very few of them had any attention to spare for matters further afield than that, and the fact that Baird, whose organization, by his own admission, was composed mainly of members of the lower classes, had analyzed the San Martin proposals in such depth came as a considerable surprise.

"I apologize for restating things I'm certain you already knew, My Lord," Baird told him, "but there was a reason for my redundancy. You see, according to our sources, San Martin is likely to figure rather largely in the 'associated measures' the Sword plans to submit to the Keys. Which is because Chancellor Prestwick and certain other members of the Protector's Council are urging the Protector to seek similar status for Grayson."

"*What?!*" Mueller came half-way to his feet. He froze there, staring at Baird in complete shock, and the other man nodded soberly.

"We have similar reports from several sources, My Lord," he said quietly. "There are minor differences between them. There always are. But the core information is the same in all of them. Apparently the Chancellor and his allies believe that if the Star Kingdom can annex San Martin under an arrangement which guarantees that the planet's local institutions will remain largely untouched, it can do the same in Grayson's case."

"That's preposterous! *Lunacy!*" Mueller shook himself like an enraged bull. "The Alliance and our forced association with its members already threatens all our most sacred institutions. Surely even that idiot Prestwick has to see that any closer association would spell the death knell of our entire way of life! We would be secularized, dragged into the same sort of degenerate society and lax morals as the damned Manticorans!"

And the Keys' power and authority would also be drastically curbed, he thought furiously. Benjamin Mayhew's "reforms" had already immensely bolstered the power of the Sword to intervene in matters which ought to be left to the control of the steadholders. Always in the name of fairness and uniform, universal application of those reforms rather than to encompass the gradual, systematic destruction of the Keys' historic autonomy, of course . . . not that Mueller or any of his allies were fooled. But if the accursed Manticorans were given an open invitation to poke their devil-spawned noses into domestic affairs which were none of their damned business, things would only get worse. And the forced association of Grayson's steaders, and especially Grayson's youth, with the corrupt society of Manticore, with all its material wealth and temptations, would have catastrophic effects on the stability of the planet's social order.

"My friends and I certainly agree with you, My Lord." Baird's voice was far calmer than Mueller's. "But I think that may be the entire point. The Chancellor *does* know what it would mean for our traditional institutions . . . and that's precisely what he actually wants. All the assurances of local autonomy and the inviolability of our religion and institutions would be no more than camouflage for his true intention: to 'reform' our world right into a slavish duplicate of the Star Kingdom of Manticore."

"Damn him," Mueller hissed. "*Damn* his soul to *Hell!*"

"Please, My Lord. I realize this has come as a shock to you, and I, too, am dismayed and angered by the potential for our way of life's destruction, but the Tester and Comforter tell us we must not lose our own souls to hate."

Mueller glared at the other man for several tense seconds, then closed his eyes and sucked in an enormous breath. He held it for another five or ten seconds, then exhaled noisily, opened his eyes, and nodded choppily.

"You're right, I suppose," he said, and actually managed to sound as if he meant it. "And I'll try to to remember that I ought to be able to hate the consequences of another's acts without letting that drive me into casting curses upon another child of God's immortal soul. But it won't be easy, Mr. Baird. Not this time."

"I know, My Lord," Baird said almost gently. "And my initial reaction was much the same as yours. But we must not allow anger, however justified, to cloud our thinking. It's far more important to prevent such things than to rail at them after they've come to pass, and preventing them will require us to approach them rationally, without passion."

"You're right," Mueller repeated, this time with true sincerity. And Baird *was* right. In fact, Mueller was deeply impressed by his ability to step back from the anger he must also feel and remember where his true duty lay. The steadholder was discovering yet more depths to the man, and he felt a sudden surge of gratitude that Baird's organization had approached him.

"Since we've known about this longer than you have, My Lord, we were able to give it a great deal of thought before I asked to see you. It seems to us that the first and most important thing to do is to confirm the accuracy of our reports. Once we know for certain that the Chancellor and his allies are, in fact, suggesting that we join the Star Kingdom, we can publicly denounce the idea and begin to warn and arouse the people. But it's also remotely possible the Protector and his advisors have deliberately fed us a false rumor. That they *want* us to denounce their plans when, in fact, they have no intention of suggesting anything of the sort. Not openly or immediately, at any rate."

"In order to discredit us by making us look like hysterics who see plots where there are none," Mueller murmured. "Yes. Yes, I can see the possibilities. On the other hand, I doubt Mayhew or Prestwick would make the attempt. Their efforts so far have been aimed at manipulating the common steaders into believing in and supporting their reforms, not at manipulating us into taking false public positions." The steadholder snorted harshly. "And it's been working," he admitted bitterly. "They haven't *needed* to manipulate us into false steps as long as they can lie to our steaders effectively and deceive them into believing the Sword truly cares what happens to them. Or their souls."

"It would be a new strategic departure for them," Baird agreed. "And, over all, we share your analysis. But we need to be *positive* before we speak openly, and if we can secure any proof of how cynically they're maneuvering to bring this about, so much the better. The more specific and pointed we can make our warnings, the more difficult the Sword will find it to deflect the people's justifiable anger. What we need, My Lord, is what they used to call 'a smoking gun,' *proof* that the Sword truly intends to betray the faith the people have placed in this so-called 'Mayhew Restoration'!"

"You're right," Mueller agreed again, and it never crossed his mind to consider how completely Baird, the man who had been supposed to be no more than a source of funds and a tool to dance to *his* piping, had dominated the entire conference. "But how can we confirm it?" the steadholder wondered aloud. "As I already said, Mayhew and his ministers have gotten altogether too good at keeping secrets."

"We're working on it, My Lord. One reason my associates asked me to speak to you was in the hope you might think of some way to acquire that proof. It never hurts to put as many brains as possible to work upon any puzzle the Tester lays before us."

"No, it doesn't." Mueller sat fully back in his chair and rubbed his lower lip. "I'll certainly put my mind to it. And I have sources of my own who might be in a position to hear anything Prestwick or his crew drop in the wrong places. In the meantime, however, I think we ought to give some thought to the best way to proceed once we find that proof. Or, for that matter, how best to deal with the situation if we can confirm Prestwick's plans but can't provide the common folk with the sort of 'smoking gun' you mentioned."

"Agreed. Agreed." Baird rose. "As always, My Lord, you raise a valid point. And with your permission, I'd like to suggest that we stay in somewhat closer contact for the immediate future. Obviously, it remains important that we be . . . discreet in our contacts, but this latest possible move requires all who would oppose it to pool our information and coordinate our planning more fully than before, I think. Especially with the Keys scheduled to convene in little more than five months. If they do mean to introduce such a scheme, the new session would be the time for them to do it."

"You're right," Mueller said positively, rising and walking Baird to the study door almost as if they were social equals. "Our usual means of arranging meetings is a bit clumsy for the sort of coordination we need to achieve," he went on. "Screen my steward, Buckeridge, tomorrow afternoon. By that time I'll have been able to have Sergeant Hughes here set up a secure channel no one with Planetary Security can trace."

"I'm not certain there is such a thing," Baird said with a thin smile, glancing sideways at Hughes as he spoke.

"I'm not either, really," Mueller replied. "But I intend it only as a way for us to reach one another to set up face-to-face meetings. I would neither ask nor want you to say anything on a com line, however secure I thought it was, which might compromise our plans, your organization, or myself."

"In that case, My Lord, please do set it up. I'll screen your steward sometime late tomorrow afternoon to see what arrangements have been made. And in the meantime, I'll see if our sources have been able to learn any more about the Chancellor's plans."

"An excellent idea," Mueller said, and paused in the hall outside the study. "Thank you very much, Mr. Baird," he said, and extended his hand. The other man clasped it firmly, and the steadholder gave him a grim smile. "Our Test may be a difficult one," he told Baird, "but I believe the Tester has seen fit to bring us together for a purpose, and we must not fail Him."

"No," Baird said softly, squeezing his hand even more firmly. "No, we mustn't. And we *won't* fail Him, My Lord. Not this time."

CHAPTER NINETEEN

Vice Admiral of the Green Patricia Givens checked her chrono, then looked up with a small smile as the First Space Lord stepped into the Pit.

The Pit was known to the rest of the universe as the Central War Room of the Royal Manticoran Navy, but no one who had spent time in it ever called it by its official name. The Pit was kept permanently on the cool and dim side, the better to encourage alertness among watch standers and to enhance the visibility of their displays. Most of the time, as now, the vast chamber actually was as calm and orderly as the dim lights and chill air might suggest to the casual observer. And, truth to tell, the Pit had never been able to match the frenzy which must, for example, have gripped the Western Alliance's war room under what had once been a huge chunk of granite called Cheyenne Mountain back on Old Earth during the Final War. Then again, no enemy had ever successfully invaded the Manticore Binary System, even on a high-speed, hit-and-run basis, so no one in the Pit had ever had the doubtful pleasure of seeing a deep penetrator, two-hundred-and-fifty-megaton warhead headed directly at them.

And, Givens thought dryly, *it's to be hoped we never will, I suppose. Of course, it was also to be hoped that no one would ever hit Basilisk.*

Unless that unthinkable (but carefully considered, here in the Pit, as part of its endless contingency planning) event occurred, the Pit never would be the site of split-second decisions. The sheer scale of interstellar combat precluded that sort of thing, for the speed at which messages and fleets moved through hyper, while starkly unimaginable in absolute terms, was scarcely a crawl beside the distances they must cross. There was always time to consider decisions here in the Pit, because no matter how quickly one made a decision, days or even weeks would go by before one's orders could reach their recipients and be acted upon.

Yet that very leisure created a different and perhaps even more corrosive tension for the Denizens of the Pit, as the watch crews termed themselves with a certain morbid pride. It was very difficult for most human beings to avoid a sense of helplessness when they reflected on their responsibilities and considered the delay built into the information loop. It was their job to collate all available data, to make the best possible analyses and, on that basis, project the enemy's options and probable intentions for the handful of men and women charged with devising the Royal Manticoran Navy's responses and strategy. Yet the information which reached them was *always* out of date, and they knew it. Knew that the Allied fleets and task forces whose icons burned so steadily in the Pit's huge holo tank might no longer even exist. Might not have existed, in some cases, for weeks, or even longer.

Even worse, perhaps, they knew their information on enemy deployments, ship movements, industrial mobilizations, diplomatic initiatives, propaganda, domestic unrest, and all the billion-and-one details which underpinned their appreciations of Peep capabilities at any given moment was even more out of date than the data on their own units' positions. It had to be that way, because even the reports of their own scouting units had to first be passed back to the scouts' local HQs before they could be collected and dispatched to Manticore by courier boat. Information from other sources, ranging from those as sinister as covert ops networks maintained on Peep worlds to those as innocuous as simple listening watches on PubIn or clipping files from neutral news services, took even longer to reach them, and it was those other sources which frequently gave them their best look inside their enemies' thoughts.

And because all that was true, they all too often felt like ground car drivers on glaze ice, knowing that however orderly things looked at any given moment, slithering chaos might burst upon them in the next. As had happened when Esther McQueen struck so deep into the Alliance's rear, for example. That event had been particularly traumatizing for the Denizens of the Pit, because they'd been so universally of the opinion that it would never happen, and had so advised their superiors.

Superiors like Patricia Givens, who'd shared their view, and Sir Thomas Caparelli, upon whose broad shoulders rested the greatest burden of all: that of making decisions based on the data every one of them knew was out of date. Givens felt a special kind of terror whenever she thought about that burden. Not only was she, as head of the Office of Naval Intelligence, the officer specifically charged with providing the data Caparelli needed, she was also Second Space Lord. In the event that anything happened to him, it would be *her* job to make decisions until the civilians got around to appointing a new First Space Lord, and it was a job she hoped passionately to avoid. Permanently.

There'd been a time, in the long-ago days of peace, when Caparelli's entry would have brought everyone in the Pit snapping to attention. That, however, had been one of the first casualties of the Havenite War. It also happened to have been one that Givens strongly approved. Neither her dignity nor Caparelli's were so in need of bolstering as to make all that formality and saluting necessary, and both of them worked day in and day out with the people who crewed the Pit. Better to let those people get on with their jobs rather than worry about properly abasing themselves.

Caparelli obviously agreed, for he had officially ordered that no one was to interrupt his or her duties just because the uniformed commander of the Manticoran military had entered the room. Which was not to say that Rear Admiral of the Green Bryce Hodgkins, commanding the current watch, didn't immediately hustle over to greet the First Space Lord in quiet tones.

Givens followed Hodgkins rather more sedately, and Caparelli nodded to her. She nodded back, and hid a small smile at the utter predictability of it all. He couldn't possibly read all the reports she and her ONI analysts provided every morning. No one could. Hell, *she* couldn't, because there simply weren't that many hours in a day. But she also knew he did read every word of the digest of précis which accompanied each day's data chips, and that he somehow made time to read all the reports which the digest suggested to him were truly critical. Of course, that process relied on his personal judgment, but that, too, was part of the massive weight of his job. In the final analysis, *someone* had to decide what were the truly critical elements, the threats which must be countered and the opportunities which must be seized, and whatever the official flowcharts might indicate, that someone was Sir Thomas Caparelli. If his civilian bosses disagreed with his decisions, or their results, they could always replace him. Until they did, *he* was the one who had to call the shots.

It was not a pleasant prospect, yet whatever some of Caparelli's prewar critics might have had to say about his intellectual stature, he'd demonstrated what Givens considered to be several priceless talents since the shooting started. High on the list was the ability to rely on the judgment of the people who prepared his daily intelligence summaries and *not* bury himself trying to read every single report. She supposed some might argue that he managed that only because he was such a stolid, unimaginative, *boring* sort of person. Of course, *some* people could argue that Gryphon had a pleasant and salubrious climate.

In fact, Givens was convinced, he managed it through iron self-discipline. His truly was a stolid, plugger's personality, yet he'd shown plenty of imagination and a few flashes of what could only be called genius since the war's start. He'd also learned to delegate, and to trust the people to whom he delegated a responsibility . . . and how to bring the ax down on any unfortunates who proved unworthy of the trust he reposed in them. The fact that his subordinates knew he relied upon them and could be relied upon, in turn, to back them to the hilt, had built a loyalty to him which Givens had seldom seen equaled. It also allowed his staffers and the staff of the Pit to polish off prodigious workloads with the efficiency of a beautifully designed machine which had worn away every rough spot.

And along the way, a few traditions had developed. One of which was that every Tuesday and Thursday, at precisely ten hundred hours, Sir Thomas Caparelli would just happen to walk into the Pit while Patricia Givens just happened to be there. They'd been doing it every week for years now, yet it never showed up on the official agendas their yeomen and flag secretaries meticulously maintained. Not because there was any reason they shouldn't put their heads together, and certainly not because they thought anyone would fail to notice they were doing it. It was simply one of those things that had grown up so naturally that neither had felt any need to make it official.

"Morning, Pat," Caparelli said quietly as Hodgkins returned to his duties and Givens took his place.

"Good morning, Sir."

She waved one hand in a small, inviting gesture towards the master tank, and Caparelli walked to the console reserved for his use whenever he visited the Pit. He seated himself, and Givens stood by his right shoulder. She had her own console, a few meters from his, but she seldom used it during their regular "unscheduled" meetings, and she folded her hands behind her while she watched him tap keys and study the results.

He brought himself up to date on the shipping movements and deployment orders which had been executed since his last check, then leaned back and rubbed his eyes wearily. He'd been doing a lot of that since the Peeps hit Basilisk, Givens reflected, keeping her own expression serene. It wasn't particularly easy. Thomas Caparelli was the bedrock upon which the Navy rested, and she didn't like the thought that that rock might be eroding under the strain.

"Anything special come in overnight?" he asked, still rubbing his eyes, and she nodded, even though she knew he couldn't see her.

"Several items, actually," she replied. And that, of course, was the real reason for their "coincidental" meetings. Caparelli had developed a special trust in her and in her feel for which straws in the wind might be truly important. It was one thing to read digests and summaries, but the First Space Lord wanted her input, personally and directly, so he could listen for the tone of voice or watch for the flicker of expression which no summary could possibly communicate. Moreover, he knew ONI was a bureaucracy. Givens was its head, and he knew she kept a firm hand on the reins, yet the analyses handed to him represented the consensus of a bureaucracy (or as close to a consensus as ONI's sometimes fractious analysts could come), which might or might not be identical with the views of its head. At their twice-a-week meetings, he could pick her brain, be sure he had *her* views on a given subject, and give her the opportunity to tell him what she, personally, believed to be of special importance.

And he could do it without stepping on the toes of her section chiefs by officially asking her to second-guess their reports. It would have been entirely appropriate for her to critique them, however officially he wanted it done, but she believed he was right about the way in which the informality of the method they'd actually worked out contributed to the smoothness with which the entire machine ran. It was probably a small point, one of those "minor details" people brushed aside, but that was another of Caparelli's strengths. He recognized the importance of details and had a positive knack for dealing with them without letting them bog him down in minutiae.

"Ah?" He lowered his hand and quirked an eyebrow at her.

"Yes, Sir. For one thing, we've got more reports of units being withdrawn from secondary Peep systems near the front. I know." She made a brushing motion with the fingers of her right hand. "We've been hearing a lot of those sorts of reports, especially since the Basilisk raid. And I know there are *always* ship movements in any navy. I even know that analysts—like me—have a tendency to look on the pessimistic side in evaluating routine movements, especially after McQueen hit us so hard. And," she admitted, "after I supported the view that the Peeps would be institutionally incapable of giving her the authority to use her talents so effectively against us. But I honestly don't think I'm being influenced by a need to cover my backside because I screwed up once before."

"I didn't think you were," Caparelli said mildly. "And you were hardly alone in doubting that Pierre and Saint-Just could or would risk easing their own grip on the Navy to let her run her own war plans. I agreed with you, for that matter. Although—" he smiled crookedly "—Admiral White Haven didn't, as I recall. Worse, he specifically warned me that we were all going off the deep end. A bad habit of his, being right."

"He's been wrong a time or two himself, Sir," Givens pointed out. She liked and respected Hamish Alexander. But as she'd watched Caparelli bear up under his responsibilities, she'd come to the conclusion that, for all his brilliance, White Haven would have been a poorer choice than Caparelli as a wartime First Space Lord.

She'd been surprised when she realized she'd come to feel that way, but reflection had only strengthened the feeling. White Haven was brilliant and charismatic, but he had no patience with fools, he was far less accustomed to (or possibly even capable of) delegating important tasks, and sometimes he became a victim of his own brilliance. He was *accustomed* to being right, and people around him also became accustomed to it. Partly, Givens knew, because that was the normal state of affairs . . . but it also happened because he was so self-confident, he simply overwhelmed everyone else. And because he entered so passionately and completely into any debate. He enjoyed stretching his mind and wrestling problems into submission, and he expected his subordinates to feel the same. But not everyone's brain worked that way, and some inevitably felt intimidated or threatened by the vigor with which he required them to defend their conclusions. They shouldn't have. They were supposed to be adult, responsible officers of the Queen's Navy, after all. But that was an ideal which all too often failed of attainment in the real world, and while Givens knew he would never punish someone simply for disagreeing with him, not all his subordinates shared her assurance of that. It was a brave staffer who openly challenged his views, and that, coupled with his confidence in his own judgment, created an occasional case of tunnel vision. Like his initial resistance to the new LAC carriers and superdreadnought designs. He hadn't even realized he was being doctrinaire and closed-minded, because no one junior to him had possessed the gall to tell the man universally regarded (even, albeit unwillingly, by Sonja Hemphill and the rest of the *jeune ecole*) as the RMN's premier strategist that he was being an idiot.

But no one was afraid to offer a divergent viewpoint to Thomas Caparelli. He might or might not agree with it, but Givens had yet to see him brush a differing view aside. And if he lacked White Haven's brilliance, he also lacked the earl's occasional abrasiveness. Coupled with his unflinching integrity, self-discipline, and determination, that made him, in her opinion, the best possible choice for his present duties.

"I know he's been wrong on occasion," the First Space Lord agreed now. "But they're rather *rare* occasions. And this wasn't one of them."

"No. No, it wasn't," she admitted.

"Oh, well." Caparelli turned his chair to face her, cocked back comfortably, and folded his arms. "Tell me why these new Peep movements seem particularly significant."

"For several reasons," Given said promptly. "First, we're seeing ships of the wall being pulled in this time, not just battleships from their rear areas. They're still coming from *secondary* systems, yes, but this time around some of them are systems where one would expect them to worry seriously about the possibility that we might pounce with raids of our own, not just ones where they'd left a couple of battleships on station to depress any local temptation towards civil unrest or disloyalty to the New Order.

"In addition, my latest reports indicate that they've actually pulled at least one squadron of superdreadnoughts out of Barnett." Both of Caparelli's eyebrows rose at that, and she nodded. "Given how hard McQueen's worked at *reinforcing* Barnett, that represents a major change of policy.

"There are also some indications that units of StateSec's private navy are being diverted to regular fleet duty. There could be several reasons for that, including a desire to have a few politically reliable ships positioned to watch the flagships of admirals whose accomplishments might be beginning to make them look like threats to the Committee. But it's also possible that it represents a rationalization and concentration of their total strength, whether it's officially SS or People's Navy, as a preliminary to a major operation somewhere. I, for one, think that's something they ought to have done years ago. Of course, I also thought it was stupid to let their security service build a navy of its very own in the first place, so I may not be the best judge in this instance. But whatever their thinking, we've got confirmation from three separate sources—including one ONI has been nursing for years inside their naval communications structure—that StateSec capital ships are being assigned to Tourville and Giscard. Neither of whom," she added dryly, "appears to have been properly appreciative of the reinforcement.

"Finally, I got a report yesterday from another of our sources in Proctor Three."

Caparelli cocked his head and pursed his lips. Proctor Three was one of the three main naval shipyards in the Haven System—which, by definition, made them the three largest yards in the entire PRH.

"According to our source," Givens went on, "the Peeps have made a major, and successful, effort to clear their repair and refit slips. Our source—" even here, and even with Caparelli, she was careful to give no clues to that source's identity, including even his (or her) gender "—isn't highly placed enough to be privy to the reasons for that effort. But our source's personal observation confirms that they seem to've gotten an awful lot of capital units off the binnacle list and back to the fleet over the past few months. That sort of surge must've required a major commitment of time, manpower, and resources, which suggests that they must have skimped somewhere else to get it done. And if they've sent that many ships back to active duty and they're still pulling even more ships in from less critical systems, then my feeling is that they have to be concentrating a powerful force somewhere for a purpose. And," she added dryly, "I didn't much care for what they did the *last* time they managed to assemble a striking force like that."

"Um." Caparelli unfolded one arm to rub his chin, then nodded. "I can't fault you there," he said. "But how reliable is your data?"

From some people, that might have sounded challenging, or like a dismissal of her argument. From Caparelli, it was only a question, and she shrugged.

"All of our data is weeks, even months, old," she admitted. "It has to be, over such distances, and the fact that agent reports have to be transmitted clandestinely slows things even more. And there's always the possibility of disinformation. We've done that to the *Peeps* a time or two, you know, and however heavy-handed and brutal State Security may be, the people running it have a lot of experience dealing with internal security threats. Like spies.

"Having said all that, I think it's basically reliable. There are going to be some errors, and it's seldom possible to conclusively confirm or deny the reliability of any given report. Taken as a whole, though, I think the picture that's emerged is pretty solid."

"All right." Caparelli nodded. "In that case, what do you think they—or McQueen, at least—is planning to do with them?"

"That, of course, is the million-dollar question." Givens sighed. "And the only answer I can give you is that I don't know. Before they hit Basilisk and Zanzibar, I'd have felt a lot more confident predicting that they were thinking in terms of something along the frontier, but now—?"

She shrugged, and Caparelli snorted.

"Let's not double-think ourselves into indecision, Pat. Yes, they hit us with a deep, rear-area operation and got away with it . . . once. Actually, when you look at it, they took fairly heavy losses, especially at Hancock, and the physical damage to our infrastructure wasn't really all that bad except at Basilisk. The morale and diplomatic consequences were a whole different kettle of fish, of course, and I'm certainly not trying to minimize them. They were bad enough to throw us back on the defensive, after all. But we have to remember the way things probably look from their side of the hill, not just the way they look to us. They have to be nervous over what we did to them at Hancock, and they also have to know we've redeployed to make similar deep raids *extremely* risky in the future."

"I can't argue with that, Sir. Not logically, anyway. But I think we have to allow for the possibility that they might try a similar operation again, despite the risks."

"Agreed. Agreed." Caparelli nodded briskly, then turned his chair back to his console and waved out over the tank's huge holo display. "On the other hand, though, they've got all that area out there to pick from, and the further they get from our core systems, the greater their operational freedom and the lower their risks.

"If they wanted the lowest-risk operations, they'd stick to the frontier systems like Lowell or Cascabel," he went on. "That would continue to push the pace, but in a way that let them concentrate against relatively weak picket forces if they pick their spots with even a little care. It wouldn't hurt us much, but it would let them blood their new units and build experience and confidence without facing the likelihood of major losses. And it would let them continue to inflict a nagging little stream of losses on *us*.

"If they're feeling a little more adventurous but still want to avoid major risks, they could go for something closer in to Trevor's Star, like Thetis or Nightingale or Solon. That would nibble away at Trevor's Star's periphery—almost a mirror image of the way White

Haven nibbled at *them* to pull them out of position when he took Trevor's Star in the first place—but without exposing the rear of any forces they commit. And they have to know how sensitive we are about the system, so they could reasonably anticipate that an open threat to it would rivet our attention even more firmly to defending ourselves there rather than attacking *them* at some spot of *our* choosing.

"Or they could get really frisky and strike somewhere between Trevor's Star and here. The most logical target would be Yeltsin, but they'd have to feel extremely nervous about committing to an attack there, given what's happened to every force which has attacked the Graysons in the past. I doubt McQueen's particularly superstitious, but she has to've come to the conclusion that something about that system is just plain bad luck for the People's Navy." He showed his teeth in a thin, ferocious grin then went on.

"Failing that, they might swing way down on the flank and go for Grendelsbane or Solway. Losing the satellite yard at Grendelsbane, in particular, would hurt worse than anything they've done to us except Basilisk. Hell, in terms of actual impact on our warmaking ability, losing the yard there would hurt *worse* than Basilisk. More importantly, taking out either of those systems would also represent another major defeat for us that they could trumpet to their public—and ours—as 'proof' we're losing the war. Not to mention the fact that it would also let them begin cutting in between us and Erewhon, and Erewhon is damned near as important to the Alliance as Grayson.

"What they're *not* going to do is go to all the effort and strain of assembling a major striking force and then throw it straight at one of the systems where we've reinforced most heavily." He shook his head. "Nope, if they're smart—and smart is one thing Esther McQueen most certainly is, unfortunately—they'll be looking for a target they can hit without incurring an unreasonable risk and sill ratchet up the pressure on us again. And if their intelligence types are still groping trying to figure out what Truman did to them in Hancock like we hope, that should encourage them to be even more cautious."

"It could also encourage them to probe more aggressively, instead," Givens pointed out. "They may not know what happened, but they know they ran into *something* out of the ordinary. If I were McQueen, I'd want to find out what that something was as quickly as possible. And I'd be willing to spread my effort wider in hopes of drawing a fresh attack from whatever it was, even at the risk of substantial losses to my probes, because until I had positive data on its capabilities, I wouldn't dare contemplate any operations on a decisive scale."

"I considered that, and you may be right," Caparelli agreed. "On the other hand, if they were going to probe aggressively, they should already have started, and so far they've restricted themselves to going after targets that aren't important enough that we would have been likely to station our 'secret weapons' to protect them. That's one reason I've insisted so strongly on holding the carriers back and not using the full capabilities of the *Har*—uh, *Medusa*-class ships unless we had no choice. The more uncertainty we can generate, the better, and White Haven was right: we need those weapons available in sufficient numbers to be *decisive* before we commit them at all."

"Which is why I'm still worried about probing attacks by the Peeps," Givens countered. "McQueen has to suspect that that's exactly what you're up to. Or what you *could* be up to, at any rate."

"Agreed."

Caparelli gazed into the tank for several silent seconds, then shook himself.

"What I really want to see is whether or not she changes her pattern," he said slowly at last. "She won a big dividend by splitting her forces for her first offensive, but she also ran the risk of defeat in detail . . . which is exactly what happened at Hancock, actually. Overall, it worked out for her by letting her hit us in so many places at once. Even without the Basilisk damage, the sheer astrographic scale of her ops area would have created enough consternation on our side to make all her losses worthwhile. If nothing else, she won months to continue to build up her forces and train her crews without heavy losses defending against *our* attacks.

"But she knows we've redeployed extensively. If she's content with hitting only low-priority, frontier systems, she can still operate spread out and split into smaller forces without too much risk. If she's willing to come further into our yard and go for more important real estate, though, she's going to have to concentrate and pack a lot more punch into each attack.

"Frankly, I think seeing which way she jumps in that regard would be almost as important as seeing *where* she jumps. More of the buckshot pattern, with smaller forces spread over broad but strategically less vital areas would probably indicate she's still feeling her way, not yet ready to commit to a serious offensive. But concentrated forces, hitting deeper behind the frontier—" He shook his head. "That could be a bad sign, an indication that she's confident enough, or that Pierre and Saint-Just are pushing her hard enough, to be getting ready for an offensive they intend to be decisive."

"And if they are?" Givens asked quietly.

"If they are, I'd expect to see them hit us in at least two or three places," Caparelli said flatly. "Not core systems, but important enough to have serious pickets. That would give them the opportunity to inflict worthwhile attritional losses, and if they picked systems that really were important, we'd have to respond by counterattacking, assuming we lost control of them, or at least by reinforcing even further if we managed to beat off the attack. And I'd want spots far enough apart that we couldn't respond by establishing a local response force at some central node. I'd look for targets spread out too far to make offering one another mutual support against future attacks practical. More important, I'd want the Alliance thinking in terms of multiple axes of threat—to put our strategists between Scylla and Charybdis if we try to redeploy to cover them all."

"Makes sense," Givens acknowledged after a moment, and inhaled deeply. "Care to place any bets either way?"

"Not me." Caparelli shook his head again. "I think you're right, that they are planning some sort of fresh offensive. That's the only explanation for the movement reports you've received that really makes sense. I'll want to look at your best estimate of the hard numbers, but it sounds to me like they're probably thinking in terms of one or two heavier attacks. I'm not about to start trying to redeploy on a 'hunch,' and I'm certainly not psychic enough to predict their specific targets, but I'm leaning towards operations down Grendelsbane way. I doubt they'll hit the fleet base directly— not unless they've pulled in a hell of a lot more of the wall than you seem to be suggesting—but I won't be at all surprised if they try to make us nervous about our access to Erewhon. And even if they're really planning on going after Trevor's Star from Barnett sometime soon, drawing our attention around to the southeast first could only help them out there. At the very least, it would have us looking over our shoulder at the fresh threat."

He paused, rubbing thoughtfully at a craggy chin, then nodded firmly, as if settling an inner debate.

"Of the various things they can do, I think hitting us in the southeast is probably the most dangerous from our viewpoint. On the other hand, if we can get them to concentrate *their* efforts there while we look elsewhere, we could turn that around on them, now couldn't we? In the meantime, though, I suppose we should take a few precautions. Let's see if we can't shake loose a squadron or two of our *Medusas*—or the Graysons' *Harringtons*—" he added with a small, wicked smile "—and reinforce the flank. Even a couple of them in the right place at the right time could be a rude surprise to a Peep attack force, but they won't look so overwhelming, especially if the local system COs are sneaky about their firing patterns, as to scare the Peeps back into their shells."

"Back into their shells?" Givens repeated with a quizzical smile, and cocked her head as he looked at her. "Everyone else in the Alliance is sweating what the Peeps are going to do to us next, and you're worrying about scaring them back into their shells?"

"Of course I am." Caparelli sounded almost surprised, as if whatever he was thinking ought to have been as blindingly obvious to her as it was to him. "If they're really worried about what our new hardware can do to them, then they'll probe, but they'd have to be planning on probing across a hell of a broad front to be pulling in the tonnage you're talking about. No, this sounds a lot more like the preliminary for a narrow-focus operation of some sort, not a scattergun series of small probing actions."

"And?" Givens prompted in a respectful tone when he paused.

"And if I'm right, if this *isn't* just the preliminary to a spread out series of small-scale probing attacks, then Esther McQueen is about to screw up by the numbers," Caparelli said, with an evil smile, "and I don't want to scare her into doing the smart thing, instead. She *ought* to be probing until she knows what happened to her. If she comes in full bore, then that suggests a certain degree of . . . overconfidence, shall we say? And I want to encourage that overconfidence just as much as I can right now. Whether it's on her part or on the part of her political superiors doesn't really matter, either, in this instance. What matters is that the Peeps may be about to come rushing in where angels fear to tread . . . and our carrier groups and pod SDs are just about ready. All I really want is for her to stick her neck out, put herself badly enough off balance and concentrate her forces sufficiently in one ops area that I can capitalize properly when I pull the trigger someplace else. Oh, I *do* want one other thing. I want her to wait just long enough for us to completely finish working up the current group of carriers and for the Ghost Rider EW platforms to reach full deployability. If she'll just give me both of those things, as well, then I will die a happy man, because before I do, I will by God kick the Peeps' worthless asses all the way back to Haven!"

CHAPTER TWENTY

"**E**xcuse me, Milady. The lawyer you were expecting is here."
"He is?" Honor looked up from the chessboard as James MacGuiness entered the library to make his announcement. Andrew LaFollet had followed him in from the hall, and she smiled broadly at both of them. "Thank God!"

She looked back at her mother.

"I'm afraid business calls, Mother," she said with exquisite politeness. "Much as I deeply regret the interruption, it seems I have no choice but to concede the game. Although, of course, I would have won if not for the way duty has called me away."

"Oh?" Allison cocked her head, and her eyes glinted. "And precisely what aspect of the endless chain of defeats you've suffered at my hands over the years gives you the least cause for such airy optimism?"

"As a mature and reasonable woman, I decline to enter into such a petty debate," Honor declared, and Nimitz bleeked a laugh as she lifted him from his perch. Samantha laughed as well, but more quietly. She was curled up in the crib with Faith, resting her chin on the baby's chest and sending the subliminal, soothing buzz of her purr deep into the child. Over the centuries of 'cat-human bonding, the two-legged side of the process had discovered that 'cats made superlative babysitters. They might be too small to pick a child up, but that didn't mean they couldn't cuddle, and no human could be as sensitive to an infant's moods and needs. Then, too, for all its diminutive size, a 'cat was formidably armed and perfectly willing to use its weaponry in defense of its charge.

Besides, they loved babies, whether they had six limbs and fur, or only two legs and no fur at all, and babies actually seemed to be able to "hear" the 'cats in a way adults could not.

Now Honor paused, waiting to see if Samantha wanted to accompany her and Nimitz, but the female 'cat only flicked an ear, radiating a gentle sense of contentment, and then closed her own eyes once more, as if to share Faith's slumber.

"Goodness," Allison murmured respectfully. "I was never able to keep a child that quiet. And I don't remember Nimitz's managing it with you, either. Although," she added thoughtfully, "that was probably because he got to you too late, after you were already set in your obstreperous ways."

"Obstreperous, is it? I'll remember that."

"Small minds fixate on small things, dear," Allison said airily.

"Indeed they do," Honor replied with deadly affability, and her mother laughed. "Would you care to sit in on this?" Honor went on. "I don't know how interesting it would be, but you're welcome to come along."

"No, thank you. Actually, if Sam is going to keep an eye on Faith, I think I'll just leave James with Jenny, grab my suit, and spend a few hours down on the beach."

"Your 'suit'?" Honor snorted, and glanced at LaFollet. The major looked back, with an equanimity he would never have displayed if he'd found himself trapped in the middle of such a conversation a few T-years earlier, and she grinned. "Mother, I've seen you swim, and I don't recall any suits being involved. In fact, I seem to remember certain comments of yours on backward, barbarian, repressive cultures."

"That was before I found myself forced to associate with an entire household of Graysons, my dear." Allison grinned wickedly at LaFollet. The armsman's eyes twinkled back at her, and she chuckled as he made the gesture a Grayson sword master used to indicate a touch in the fencing salle. "And I've seen you swim, too, you know," she went on, "so don't get snippy with me, young lady! I happen to know the suits you introduced to Gryphon were a lot more, um, modest than anything you ever wore back home or at Saganami Island!"

"But at least I always wore *something*," Honor replied serenely.

"So did I—exactly what God issued me at birth. And if it's good enough for Him, then it ought to be good enough for anybody else. Especially—" Allison drew herself up to her full diminutive height and preened comfortably "—when it looks so good on me."

"I don't know how Sphinx survived you, Mother," Honor said

mournfully. "And when I think of the effect you're bound to have on Grayson now that you've been unleashed on my poor Harringtons, my blood runs cold."

"We'll survive, My Lady," LaFollet assured her. "Of course, I understand that since your mother arrived, Lord Clinkscales has been insisting on cardiovascular exams for any visitors to Harrington House. Something about liability concerns, I believe."

"I know," Allison said wickedly. "Isn't it wonderful?" LaFollet smiled and both Harringtons laughed, then Allison made shooing motions. "Go on—get! Never keep a lawyer waiting. They have friends in low and infernal places."

"Yes, Momma," Honor said obediently, and turned to follow MacGuiness from the room.

The man who turned towards her as she and LaFollet entered her office had a face which might charitably have been called "rough hewn," although some might have been tempted to use a less complimentary phrase. He was on the small side, little more than six or seven centimeters taller than her mother, and impeccably groomed. Indeed, he was a little on the dandyish side, and obviously sufficiently well off that he could have had his face biosculpted into surpassing handsomeness. That he had not so chosen said interesting things about his personality, and what Honor tasted of his emotions only confirmed that first impression. He radiated an air of self-possession even a 'cat might have envied and carried himself like the high-priced courtroom specialist he was, yet anyone who mistook him for a soft, citified type would undoubtedly learn to regret it. There was a toughness behind the brown eyes at odds with the manicured, well-groomed exterior, and Honor liked the taste of his emotions as he regarded her calmly.

"Good afternoon, Mr. Maxwell." She crossed the office, set Nimitz on her desk, and turned to hold out her hand. "I'm Honor Harrington."

"So I see," he said, smiling as he clasped the offered hand. She cocked an eyebrow, and he chuckled. "I've seen you often enough on HD since your return, Your Grace," he explained. He tilted his head back to gaze up at her and pursed his lips. "It's odd, though," he murmured. "Somehow I thought you'd be taller."

"You did, did you?" Honor moved behind her desk, waving him into a facing armchair as she went. She seated herself and waited until he'd followed suit, then tipped her chair back. "Willard warned me you had a sense of humor," she remarked then.

"Did he?" Maxwell smiled. "Well, he's told me quite a few things about you, as well, Your Grace. None, I hasten to add, confidential. I'd say you've impressed him quite favorably, over all. Especially after that business at Regiano's."

"He was impressed with the wrong person then," Honor said uncomfortably, the live side of her face tightening as she recalled a crowded restaurant and the shouts and panic as pulser darts screamed across it. "Major LaFollet—" she gestured briefly to the Grayson "—and my other armsmen were the ones who actually saved Willard and me both," she said, and her face tightened a bit more, for of the three men who had saved her life that dreadful day, only Andrew LaFollet was still alive.

"He told me that, too. I think it was your *sangfroid* he admired, actually. And the way you finally settled the account. I don't really approve of dueling, Your Grace, but in that particular case, I was happy to make an exception. I once represented a young woman who— Well, never mind. Let's just say Pavel Young was not a nice person, and it stuck in my craw to have to negotiate an out-of-court settlement with someone like him."

His tone was light, conversational, but the emotions behind it weren't, and Honor nodded mentally. This was a man who did what he did because he believed in it, and she liked the taste of his determination and passion.

"I hope to avoid involving you in anything quite so dramatic as all that, Mr. Maxwell," she told him with one of her crooked smiles. "I believe Willard said he was going to bring you up to speed in his letter. May I assume he did so?"

"You may, Your Grace. And I'm flattered that he thought of me, although I'm not certain I'm actually the best person for the job. I've been practicing almost exclusively before the criminal bar for the last twenty or thirty T-years. Although I've handled a few business matters for Willard, primarily when he wanted someone he'd known for years and knew to be discreet, my commercial law is actually fairly rusty."

"Does that mean you're not interested?" Honor asked, although she suspected she already knew the answer from the taste of his emotions.

"No, Your Grace. It simply means I believe in informing a potential client when I know there are weaknesses to compensate for as well as when I have strengths to offer."

"Good," Honor said firmly, "because that's exactly what I need."

"What you *need*, Your Grace," Maxwell corrected calmly, "is a complete legal staff of your own. Failing that, you certainly ought to put one of the major firms on retainer and let them provide the staff. With Willard more or less anchored to Grayson these days, and particularly in light of all the details and complications your new title involves, I shudder to think of the state your affairs must be in just now."

"I do miss Willard's touch. A lot," Honor confessed. "On the other hand, things may not be quite as bad as you assume. The Queen was gracious enough to have her own legal staff handle all the details concerning the duchy, to this point, at least, and Klaus and Stacey Hauptman have been keeping an eye on my business affairs. Actually, unraveling those was a lot more complicated than creating a brand new duchy!"

"I'm not surprised. I'm certainly glad to hear the Crown has been looking after matters related to your new title and lands, but Willard gave me some idea of what was involved in untangling your other affairs. I'm just as happy he was able to take care of so much of it under Grayson law from the Grayson end, and I was a bit surprised to hear that the Hauptman Cartel had gotten involved as your agents here in the Star Kingdom. That's some high-powered talent to have in your corner, Your Grace."

"I know it is." *And it wasn't always in my corner, either. But we won't go into that just now.* "My point, however, was that while you're undoubtedly right about the size and scope of the staff I'm going to need eventually, the situation as it stands is probably less dire than you thought. Assuming you accept the position, I'd expect you to assemble a staff of your own and tailor it to fit the requirements as you see fit."

"Um. That's a flattering offer, Your Grace. Very flattering. And I'm certainly tempted to say yes. I suppose most of my hesitation stems from how much I love the practice of criminal law. It would be hard for me to give up the courtroom. Very hard."

"I imagine so," Honor agreed. "I know how hard it was for me to give up the captain's chair when they promoted me to flag rank." He cocked his head at her, and she tipped a little further back. "Willard told me about your military career, Mr. Maxwell. I hope you won't be offended to learn that I looked into your record just a bit before I asked you to come see me."

"I'd have been surprised—and disappointed—if you hadn't, Your Grace."

"I thought you'd feel that way. But I was interested to discover that you and I share something in common, and I was rather impressed when I read your citation. It isn't every Marine second lieutenant who wins the Manticore Cross for bravery under fire. And not many lawyers have that on their résumés, either, I imagine."

"More may than you think, Your Grace," Maxwell replied, apparently oblivious to the considering look LaFollet had turned upon him. "And the MC may or may not be something you need in a lawyer. But I do take your point, and you're right. In many respects, a legal career is like a military one. The higher the level of responsibility, the less time there is for the hands-on side of it that brought you into it in the first place."

"Exactly," Honor said. "And people use the same sneaky argument to get you to accept that responsibility, too: we need you. I always thought it was an unscrupulous button to punch when someone did it to me, but now I'm going to do it to you, because it's true. I do need you, or someone like you, and the strength of Willard's recommendation makes me disinclined to go looking for anyone else."

"I couldn't be available immediately, Your Grace. Not on a full-time basis," Maxwell warned her. "I've got two cases to argue at the common bar, and an appeal before the Queen's Bench right now. It would be at least two months, probably three or four, before I could give you the sort of hours you'll really need out of me."

"That's fine. I wouldn't expect you to abandon criminal cases in which you were involved. Frankly, if you were willing to hand them off to someone else and simply walk away it would be proof you weren't the man I wanted for the job in the first place! Nor is time pressure all that compelling just yet. The Crown has everything neatly tied up on Gryphon for right now, and things can stay just the way they are until you're free and able to deal with them. I've already heard from two of the major ski consortiums, but Clarise Childers over at Hauptman's has agreed to handle the preliminary negotiations there for me. Aside from that, there's nothing urgent, because I don't have any tenants at the moment. For the foreseeable future, the Duchy of Harrington is basically just a big, unpopulated swatch of mountains and trees. A nice swatch, you understand, but not anything that needs human attention at the moment."

"I see." Maxwell's lips quivered a bit at her last sentence, and he drew a deep breath. "In that case, Your Grace, I suppose I don't have much choice but to accept."

"And the terms Willard suggested in his letter to you are acceptable?"

"More than acceptable, Your Grace. Willard has always understood how to build business arrangements that are equitable to all parties. I imagine that's why he's been so very successful at it."

"The same thought had occurred to me," Honor agreed.

"Yes." Maxwell gazed at something only he could see for several moments, then gave himself a small shake. "I realize you just said there was no great rush, Your Grace, but I would like to make at least a modest start, as time permits, as soon as possible. Will you be available if I need an hour or so of your time here and there?"

"Probably," Honor said a bit cautiously. "My schedule is fairly hectic at the moment. The Navy has me thoroughly busy at the Advanced Tactical Course, and my lecture courses at the Academy are eating up more of my time than I'd anticipated. On top of that, I'm scheduled for the first surgery on my face day after tomorrow. We'll probably install the new eye at the same time, and the replacement arm they've been designing for me is just about ready. It should be delivered in time for surgery for *it* late next month. I imagine I'll be out of action for a week or so following each round of actual surgery. And then there'll be the physical therapy, of course. And we're about ready for the corrective surgery on Nimitz, as well, so that'll—"

"Stop! Stop, Your Grace!" Maxwell laughed and shook his head. "What you're saying is that, yes, you can make yourself available to me, but I should let you know a day or two—or three—in advance so you can adjust your schedule. Is that about it?"

"I'm afraid so," Honor admitted a bit sheepishly, and shook her own head. "You know, until you asked, I hadn't really thought about just how much I really do have on my plate right now."

"And this is your idea of a 'convalescence'?" Maxwell asked quizzically.

"Well, yes, I suppose." Honor's good eye twinkled, but her tone was serious. "Actually, people seem to forget that I've had over two years to get accustomed to what I lost. A lot of them seem to feel a lot more urgency about fixing everything than I do after so long. I'm actually more concerned over Nimitz than I am over me, I think."

"I believe most people are more concerned over people they love than they are over themselves," Maxwell agreed, his voice suddenly soft, and Honor looked up quickly. There was something behind that, something even more than a surprisingly keen perception of the bond between her and Nimitz, but she couldn't tell what it was. Only that it was very deep . . . and that the pain of it would never fully heal.

An odd stillness hovered between them, but only for a moment before Maxwell gave himself another little shake.

"Willard also said something about your having to return to

Grayson, I believe," he observed, "but I wasn't clear on how soon that was. Is it likely to take you back to Yeltsin's Star any time immediately? And do you know how long you'll be there?" She cocked an eyebrow at him, and he raised one hand. "If I'm going to require your signature or personal authorization for anything, it would be good to know if there's a time block when you absolutely won't be available."

"I see." Honor frowned as she considered her calendar. "I won't be going anywhere at least before the end of the next semester at the Academy," she said after a long moment. "Protector Benjamin has asked me to come home—I mean, return to Grayson—for the opening of the new session of the Keys. Of the Conclave of Steadholders, that is. That would fall during the long holiday, which comes at the end of this semester anyway. So I'd probably be off Manticore for at least two or three weeks—more probably a couple of months—about then."

"That's—what? Five months from now?"

"About that, yes."

"And you'll be taking the *Tankersley*, I assume."

"Actually, not this time around." Honor wasn't surprised that he knew about her private starship. The small, fast vessel had been one of the best investments she'd made, and Willard Neufsteiler was the one who'd nagged her into buying it. But Maxwell looked a bit puzzled.

"I expect I'll be traveling commercial for this visit," she explained. "I'll have a sizable piece of cargo to take home, and *Tankersley* is designed for speed, not cubage."

" 'A sizable piece of cargo'?" Maxwell repeated.

"Well, actually—" Honor blushed slightly "—I've decided to spoil myself a bit. I mean, thanks to Her Majesty I hardly need to buy a place to live here in the Star Kingdom—" she gestured to the splendid office about them "—and it's almost as bad back on Grayson, but everyone's been pushing me to 'relax' and 'enjoy' myself. So—"

She shrugged, and Maxwell chuckled.

"And might one ask just how you've decided to spoil yourself, Your Grace?"

"Her Majesty gave me this place, she said, because it wasn't something I'd think of buying for myself," Honor said a bit obliquely. "So I decided to buy something no one else would think of giving me. I mean, all this money has to be good for something, doesn't it?"

"I'm sure it does, Your Grace."

"So I bought myself a new ten-meter sloop for my parents' boat-house on Sphinx, another one for the marina here on Manticore, and a third for Gryphon. I'm keeping that one in a commercial marina until we get the duchy up and running. But Grayson was a bit harder, because no one in her right mind goes boating there. Not with all the interesting things dissolved in Grayson's oceans. So I decided to buy myself a runabout."

"A runabout?"

"Something to let me keep my hand in at the controls," Honor explained. "I laid out what I want over at Silverman's three months ago." Maxwell's eyebrows rose. Samuel Silverman & Sons was the oldest, most prestigious supplier of private space yachts in the Star Kingdom. HMS *Queen Adrienne*, the current, hyper-capable royal yacht, had come from Silverman's, and so had all three of her predecessors. Honor read his expression and laughed. "Oh, it's nothing quite that big, Mr. Maxwell! Not hyper-capable. I've got *Tankersley* for that, and it's not likely I'd have the time to go haring off into hyper on my own, anyway. No, this is a little sublight ship, only about eleven thousand tons. Sort of a cross between a pinnace and a LAC, but without the guns and with a lot more creature comforts. I tried one like her in the simulators, and she should be exactly what I want. Small and lively enough to let me play, but big enough to be comfortable and have the intrasystem range for anywhere I might need to go."

"I see." Maxwell thought for a moment, then nodded. "I imagine that *is* something no one else would have thought to buy you, Your Grace. But I can see why it would appeal to you, I think. I hope you enjoy it as much as I suspect you will."

"I'll certainly try, as time permits, anyway," Honor said, and then grimaced as her chrono beeped all too appropriately from her wrist. "And speaking of time," she went on regretfully, "I'm afraid I'm due over at ATC for a conference in twenty minutes."

"I understand, Your Grace."

Maxwell rose, and Honor came to her own feet to escort him to the door. Nimitz curled in the crook of her arm, and LaFollet brought up the rear, as usual.

"Thank you again for coming. And for accepting the job," Honor told him seriously as they headed across the echoing foyer of her preposterous mansion.

"You're very welcome. I look forward to the challenge, and to working with you and Willard," Maxwell replied. "I'll write up my acceptance and send it to Willard with a copy routed to you."

"That sounds fine," she agreed, and paused at the door. She

couldn't offer him her hand with an armful of treecat, and he smiled as he recognized her problem.

"I see who really runs this household," he murmured, and Honor laughed.

"You only think so. You won't see who really runs it until you meet his wife!"

"Indeed?" Maxwell cocked his head, then chuckled. "I look forward to meeting her . . . and their children." He shook his head. "I must say, Your Grace, this looks like it may turn out to be even more interesting than I'd thought it might."

"Oh, it will, Mr. Maxwell. I feel quite sure it will . . . in the ancient, Chinese sense of the word."

"I beg your pardon?"

"An ancient Chinese curse," Honor explained. " 'May you live in interesting times.' Think about it."

"I don't have to," Maxwell said. "And with all due respect, Your Grace, I think I speak for a lot of people when I say that we wish you'd try to find something just a little less 'interesting' to do with yourself for the next decade or so."

"I'll try. Really I will," she assured him. "It's just—"

She shrugged helplessly, and Maxwell laughed.

"I imagine I'll get used to hearing that sort of thing from you, too, Your Grace," he observed, and nodded farewell as MacGuiness opened the door for him.

Andrew LaFollet watched the door close behind him, then chuckled softly. Honor turned to him, one eyebrow raised, and he shrugged.

"I was just thinking how nice it was that you were able to hire a prophet for your chief counsel, My Lady," he explained.

"A prophet?" Honor repeated in a slightly puzzled tone.

"Yes, My Lady. It's obvious he must be one."

"And why, though I'm sure I'm going to regret asking, might that be?"

"Because he *is* going to get used to hearing you promise to try to be good, My Lady," LaFollet said innocently.

"Are you suggesting my promises are less than sincere?" she demanded.

"Oh, no, My Lady! They're as sincere as they could possibly be . . . when you make them."

Honor gave him a very old-fashioned look, but he only gazed back innocently, and she heard MacGuiness trying, almost successfully, not to chuckle behind her.

"It's all right, My Lady," her armsman said soothingly. "We know you try."

CHAPTER TWENTY-ONE

Citizen Captain Oliver Diamato punched the button to adjust the captain's chair on the bridge of the brand-new battlecruiser PNS *William T. Sherman*. The chair assumed the angle he wanted (or, rather, that his aching back and shoulder demanded in the wake of yet another physical therapy session), and he swiveled in a slow circle to contemplate his new domain.

In some respects, he rather regretted being elevated to his new rank and given his splendid, shiny toy. Not that he was tempted to give it back. Navies, even revolutionary ones, tended to agree that an officer who felt he was incapable of command was undoubtedly right. That being so, his superiors wouldn't dream of arguing with him . . . or ever offering him a command, or any other worthwhile duty, again. There were probably some exceptions to the rule, but Diamato couldn't think of a single one.

Besides, he knew *Sherman* was a sign the Navy in general, or at least Citizen Secretary McQueen in particular, approved of him, and he was honest enough to admit that his own ambition was gratified by it. But he remembered his own last captain, and he knew he still had a long, long way to go before he could hope to match Citizen Captain Hall's worthiness to command a warship in the Republic's defense.

He was good, with a better technical background than usual in the People's Navy and a natural gift for tactics. He fell short of Citizen Captain Hall's stature as a tactician, but Citizen Captain Hall had been a natural herself, one who'd spent decades honing her inborn talents, and she'd showed him the way to hone his own.

He would miss her tutelage, but she'd given him the critical guidance which would let him someday match her ability as a tactician.

He knew that, too. But he also knew that when it came to motivating a crew, to melding the individuals of its human material into one finely whetted weapon, he fell even further short of her stature. Mostly, he told himself as honestly as he could, because, like so many of the PN's officers, he'd been forced up the rank ladder too quickly by the joint pressures of internal revolution and external war. He simply hadn't had time to amass the experience Joanne Hall had amassed . . . and *she* had not had sufficient time to pass that experience along to him, although God knew she'd tried in the time she'd had!

But because he was self-honest, Diamato also admitted doubt he ever would have that magic touch. He hoped, someday, to learn to imitate it well enough that others would be impressed by his command presence, but he would never have that . . . something. That ability to reach out to her subordinates even as she clung to all the old, outmoded, elitist formalities of naval command, ignoring all of the egalitarian changes which the New Order had wrought, and inspire them to follow her straight into the fire.

Of course, that may *be because not all of those "outmoded" formalities and concepts are quite so outmoded after all,* Diamato thought very quietly, in a hidden corner of his mind, and carefully did not glance at the man standing beside his command chair. It wouldn't do to let Citizen Commissioner Rhodes know what dangerous, counter-revolutionary ideas might be flowing through his brain. On the other hand, Rhodes might yet turn out to be another Citizen Commissioner Addison and actually end up supporting a more traditional discipline structure aboard *Sherman*, much as Addison had for Citizen Captain Hall. The problem was that he hadn't yet given any indication that he might, and Diamato dared not come right out and ask.

Which was the final reason the citizen captain was less than completely delighted with his own promotion and new ship, for command of one of the People's battlecruisers was not the best imaginable job for someone whose faith in the Revolution—or its *leaders*, at least—had taken a pounding in the eighteen months since Operation Icarus.

It wasn't something Diamato allowed himself to contemplate often, even in the privacy of his own thoughts, but it was there. Indeed, it was the reason he hadn't been more aggressive in sounding out Rhodes' attitudes. And try though he might, Diamato still couldn't eradicate the festering doubt that haunted him.

Nothing had happened to change his commitment to the ideals officially espoused by the Committee of Public Safety. Or, for that matter, his sense of personal loyalty to Citizen Chairman Pierre. But he'd discovered too much about the empire building, and the mutual suspicion and hostile camps, which divided the people who should have been the New Order's paladins. And he'd seen too much—too terribly, ghastly much—of what that empire building could cost.

He closed his eyes and shuddered again as he recalled the dreadful final phase of the Hancock attack. Citizen Admiral Kellet had been killed early in the action, but her second-in-command, Citizen Rear Admiral Porter, had been a near total incompetent. Worse, though Diamato hadn't realized it before the battle, he'd also been a coward. Yet the citizen rear admiral had possessed impeccable political credentials and enjoyed patronage from the highest levels. In fact, although Diamato had not been able to confirm it, the citizen captain had picked up strong hints that Porter's most powerful patron had probably been Oscar Saint-Just himself.

That sort of direct connection between a member of the Committee of Public Safety and an officer of the People's Navy, while uncommon, wasn't exactly unheard of. That was especially true among the Navy's higher ranks, and everyone knew it. Before Icarus, even Diamato would have endorsed the necessity, or at the least the propriety, of such arrangements. It was (or ought to be) only fitting for the civilian leaders charged with directing the People's struggle at the highest level to support the careers of those they felt were best suited to leading that struggle in open battle. And if a member of the Committee believed an officer was both capable and loyal, then it only made sense to see to it that such a person was put where he could do the most good in the People's struggle.

The problem was that by any standard, *except* his loyalty to the Committee of Public Safety (or, at least, to Oscar Saint-Just), Porter had been utterly unqualified to command anything more important than a garbage scow . . . on its way to the breakers. It was always possible Diamato was being too harsh on the dead officer, and he attempted, from time to time, to make himself grant that possibility. But Citizen Admiral Kellet and Citizen Captain Hall had clearly considered Porter an incompetent, and even Citizen Commissioner Addison had shared their view. If he hadn't, he wouldn't have supported Citizen Captain Hall when she pretended Kellet was still alive and issuing the orders that actually came from Hall rather than passing command to Porter as regulations required.

That was one incident from the Second Battle of Hancock which

Diamato had not included in any of his reports, and he doubted either of the other two survivors from PNS *Schaumberg*'s command deck had volunteered it either. Both of them were petty officers, not commissioned, and no doubt they both felt it was safer to let sleeping dogs lie, but in Diamato's case there had been an added incentive in the form of a direct, personal hint from no less than Citizen Secretary McQueen herself.

Diamato had heard the rumors about McQueen's ambition. What was more, he suspected those rumors were true. Yet not even that had been enough to immunize him against her personal charisma. And even if it had been, her sheer competence, and the fact that she was obviously a voice of sanity—and, he'd come to fear, an *isolated* voice—on the Committee of Public Safety would probably have silenced any qualms.

When it came right down to it, Diamato felt certain McQueen was the only member of the Committee who believed a word he'd said about the LACs which had massacred TF 12.3. Worse, he hadn't been as surprised to discover that fact as he should have been. To be sure, the lack of any but the most fragmentary sensor data, plus the fact that he had been unable to make any coherent report for weeks, had undoubtedly contributed to the skeptics' rejection of the idea. But there were other factors.

For one thing, that incompetent, cowardly, self-serving, panic stricken, gutless *idiot* Porter had thrown away all Citizen Captain Hall had died to achieve with a single, unforgivably stupid order. The Manties had been about to break off. Diamato knew they had, knew their mounting losses, inflicted, in no small part, by one Oliver Diamato and PNS *Schaumberg*, had finally convinced them there was no point in continuing to smash headlong into the shattered task force's massed defenses. Task Force 12.3 had been crushed, driven off in defeat, but if its offensive capability had been shattered, its defensive firepower had remained formidable. There was absolutely no reason for anything as fragile as LACs—even *those* LACs—to keep expending themselves harrying an obviously broken foe when that foes' units retained enough mutually supporting defensive fire to kill their attackers if they persisted in closing for kills of their own.

Citizen Captain Hall's iron-nerved tactical command had brought that about. She'd saved the majority of TF 12.3's battleships, gotten them (and all the people aboard them) to the very threshold of safety—battered, bleeding, and desperate, but alive—before what Diamato *knew* would have been the Manties' last massed attack broke through to savage *Schaumberg*'s bridge and kill her.

With her death, and Citizen Commissioner Addision's, Diamato had had no option but to pass command to Porter. To be honest, he'd never even considered not passing it . . . but he should have. Oh, yes. He should have, and he cursed himself after each night's nightmares for failing to.

His jaw clamped as he recalled Porter's incredulous, panic-stricken response to the news that he was now in command. And his jaw clamped tighter still as his memory replayed the citizen admiral's frantic order for the task force to scatter and proceed independently for the hyper limit.

That order had been an act of suicide. One which had, unfortunately, killed thousands of people besides the single, incompetent political appointee it damned well *ought* to have killed.

Diamato doubted the Manties had been able to believe their good fortune as the tight formation to which Citizen Captain Hall had clung so tenaciously abruptly disintegrated into individual units. Yet worse even than the physical separation which had opened vulnerable chinks in the umbrella of the battleships' defensive fire had been the panic Porter had communicated to his captains. Even the most levelheaded of them had realized their commanding officer lacked the first clue as to what to do and that any hope of their own ships' survival lay in their own, individual efforts. Those whose nerve had been worst shaken before the scatter order had lost their courage completely and concentrated solely on putting the greatest possible distance between themselves and the enemy.

And when the formation unraveled, the Manty LACs which had just turned away instantly reversed acceleration and bored in for the kill.

Diamato remembered the unending succession of disasters, the helplessness with which he had watched other battleships being clawed down, blown apart by those incredible LACs' impossible grasers or—possibly even worse—fired into just until they lost an alpha node or two. With even one alpha node down, it was impossible to generate a Warshawski sail, and Hancock lay directly in the path of a grav wave. Which meant no one without Warshawski sails could maneuver in hyper at all . . . and that, in turn, meant there would be no escape from the vengefully pursuing Manty superdreadnoughts of the system's inner picket. The SDs *could* cross the hyper wall and maneuver freely, which meant they would run the battleships down with absurd ease no matter what normal-space velocity they might have attained, and once a true ship of the wall brought a mere battleship to action, there could be only one outcome.

Whenever their sensors told them a Republican ship had lost an alpha node, the LACs instantly dropped their attacks on her, swinging away to go after one of her sisters who could still run, and the gaps opening between the battleships as they obeyed Porter's order had made the Manties' murderous task immeasurably simpler.

When they finally got back around to *Schaumberg*, the battleship had been as completely on her own as any of the others. Diamato had done his best, and that best had included killing two more LACs, but his ship's own damage had already been too great for a truly effective defense. A single screaming pass had crippled *Schaumberg*'s Warshawski sails. A second had scored yet another hit on the battleship's command deck and ended Citizen Commander Oliver Diamato's participation in the Second Battle of Hancock with brutal finality.

He was alive, he knew, only because the savagely wounded heavy cruiser *Poignard* had been close enough, and her skipper, Citizen Captain Stevens, had been gutsy enough to close with *Schaumberg*'s crippled wreck right at the hyper limit. *Poignard* had come alongside long enough to take off the battleship's worst injured (including an unconscious Oliver Diamato) before making her own alpha translation. Very little of the cruiser had been left, aside from her hyper generator and Warshawski sails, but that had been enough for her to run.

Schaumberg, with three alpha nodes shot out, had been less fortunate. Citizen Lieutenant Commander Kantor, her assistant engineer, had become her senior officer when Diamato went down, and, according to Stevens' after-action report, he'd believed there was at least a chance he could get his damaged nodes back on-line before the Manties caught up with him.

Obviously, Kantor had been wrong. Six of Citizen Admiral Kellet's thirty-three battleships had trickled home after the battle; PNS *Schaumberg* had not been one of them. Nor had Porter's flagship, *Admiral Quinterra*. And those which had made it out had been so mauled that much of their tracking data had been either lost completely or scrambled beyond recovery.

Even so, it should have been possible for the Board of Inquiry to have formed *some* proper conclusions about what TF 12.3 had run into. Diamato had been too badly injured to be called as a witness, but the tactical officers aboard the handful of surviving ships had to have seen what had happened, and their reports about the new LACs and the godawful missiles which had come screaming up the task force's wake just as the LACs attacked ought to have alerted the Navy that it faced a new, deadly threat.

Except that Citizen Admiral Porter's patrons had demanded (and gotten) a report which avoided the scathing posthumous condemnation Porter's stupidity so amply deserved. Diamato was no longer so innocent as to believe they'd done so to protect Porter's reputation. Nor did he believe, as some people pretended to, that it was because Operation Icarus' success was too important to civilian and Navy morale to allow any hint that its success had been less than total tarnish it in the People's eyes. No, he'd seen enough by now to know it had been their own reputations and the dismal depths of their misjudgment in having supported and nourished the career of such an incompetent that Porter's patrons had been protecting. But it hadn't mattered. The only way to protect the admiral, and thus themselves, had been to suppress the entire inquiry, because any accurate report would have been a blistering indictment of Porter's ineptitude and cowardice.

And Diamato's surviving fellow tac officers had taken the unveiled, threatening hint. They'd volunteered nothing when they faced the Board, and their responses to the questions the Board's members had asked had been limited to an absolute, self-protecting minimum. Furious as he'd been when he heard about it later, Diamato could scarcely blame them. Not a one of them had been above the rank of citizen lieutenant commander, and the board members, the most junior of them a citizen rear admiral, had been even more careful about the questions they'd asked (or hadn't) than the tac officers had been about how they'd answered.

And the whole thing had been conducted with unseemly haste, as well, as if all involved were ashamed and wanted it over and forgotten as quickly as possible. By the time Diamato emerged from the hospital, the deed was done, the report was written, and no one wanted to hear from one furious, heartbroken, embittered citizen commander.

He'd tried to tell them anyway, driven by his agonizing need to discharge his duty as an officer . . . and to atone for his failure to fulfill Citizen Captain Hall's dying plea to get her people home. She'd counted on him for that, clung to life to charge him with their safety literally with her dying breath. She'd *trusted* him to get them out . . . and he hadn't. It wasn't his fault, and he knew it, just as he knew whose fault it *had* been, but that did nothing to silence the demons of conscience when they came to him in his dreams.

And so, even knowing it was futile, he'd mounted his single-handed effort to storm the battlements of the official, politically imposed whitewash. He'd filed reports, and they'd been set aside unread. He'd demanded to be heard, and been turned down by his immediate superiors. He'd drafted a personal letter to the commander of the Capital Fleet, and it had been returned unread (officially) with a terse note reminding him that the inquiry had been completed . . . and that no further communications on the subject were desired or would be received. The warning had been clear, but duty and guilt had refused to accept it. Unable to stop, he'd prepared to go as far up the ladder as it took, a move which undoubtedly would have ended with his own destruction, except for Citizen Secretary McQueen.

He didn't know how the Citizen Secretary of War had heard about his hopeless crusade, but she'd personally summoned him to her office, and in the presence of Ivan Bukato, the senior uniformed officer of the People's Navy, listened to every word he'd had to say. And unlike the Board of Inquiry, she and Bukato had asked incisive, probing questions. Indeed, they'd managed to wring things out of him that he hadn't even realized he knew, although the lack of hard scan data or tac recordings to support his recollections had limited the reliance which could be placed upon them. At the end, McQueen had sent him to an office at the Octagon and had him write out a fresh, formal report for her eyes only.

Diamato had sensed McQueen's initial dislike for him. Only later had he realized that it resulted from the fact that she'd perused his personnel jacket before the interview and that, in the process, she must have come across the StateSec evaluations which no doubt stressed his loyalty to the New Order. She must have feared he was another Porter in the making, seeking to curry the sort of patronage which had allowed that incompetent to kill so many thousands of his fellow Navy personnel. It would have been stupid of Diamato to seek it by deliberately antagonizing the people who'd supported Porter, but it must also have seemed possible to her that he was too naive or too foolish to realize that was what he was doing. She might even have believed that he thought the whitewash had been the *Navy's* idea, and that he viewed attacking it as a way to win the approval of the Navy's StateSec watchdogs.

But his outrage and determination to get the truth across had been enough to erase her dislike. If he'd needed any proof of that, the assignment to command *Sherman* while his rehab therapy was still considerably short of complete would have wiped them away. Perhaps even more to the point had been the way in which she'd urged him, without ever explicitly saying so, to abate his charge at the windmill of the Hancock whitewash. It had been weeks before he discovered what had actually produced that report . . . and realized McQueen's veiled warning was probably all that had prevented his disappearance as "an enemy of the People." After all, if Porter's patrons were prepared to go as far as suppressing critically important tactical data to protect themselves, they were undoubtedly capable of using the full power of State Security and a set of trumped-up charges to eliminate a single, troublesome citizen commander.

So instead of being disappeared, here he sat on the bridge of his splendid new ship, watching on the tactical display as the other units of a new task force gathered for a fresh offensive against the Manties. It was a proud moment, as well it ought to have been, but he could not suppress a shiver whenever he remembered the blazing madness of Second Hancock.

At least Citizen Vice Admiral Tourville had shown an interest in what Diamato could tell him about the battle. Diamato had been rather more circumspect than he had in his conversation with McQueen, but he'd gotten the essentials across, and Tourville had listened. Nor had he scoffed, although he hadn't exactly announced that he believed them. And Diamato had no idea whether or not Tourville had passed that information further up Twelfth Fleet's chain of command. He hoped the citizen vice admiral had, but all he knew for certain was that he had never been invited aboard the superdreadnought *Salamis* to recount his experiences for Citizen Admiral Giscard. Obedient to McQueen's warnings, he hadn't spontaneously volunteered them at any of the conferences he'd attended, either. He was, after all, a very new citizen captain in command of his very first starship. Even though the starship in question was one of the PN's newest, most powerful battlecruisers, he remained one of the junior men on Twelfth Fleet's totem pole, and his betters would tell him when they wanted to hear from him.

But he hoped—oh, *how* he hoped!—that Tourville had believed him . . . and that Giscard had seen the report he'd written for Citizen Secretary McQueen and read it very, very carefully.

"All right, citizens." Citizen Admiral Javier Giscard pinched the bridge of his nose in an unconscious effort to ease his fatigue, then looked around the briefing room table. Only six officers—and, of course, their people's commissioners—were present, including himself, and he smiled tiredly at the others as he asked, "Are there any questions or points we need to consider before we get to the main reason for this briefing?"

"I'm sure there must be," Lester Tourville replied, mustache bristling as he returned Giscard's smile with a much fiercer one of his own. "Unfortunately, I'm not sure what they might be. BJ?"

He looked across the table at Citizen Vice Admiral John Groenewold, known to his intimates as "BJ," and flicked one hand in a questioning gesture. Groenewold was the newest member of Twelfth Fleet's senior command team, replacing Citizen Vice Admiral Shallus, who had been recalled to Haven to serve as Citizen Admiral Bukato's deputy at the Octagon. An intense, dark-complexioned officer, Groenewold had a reputation for aggressiveness in action which almost matched that of Tourville himself, and the two men had known one another for years.

"I guess my only real question is whether or not we should be putting much stock in the rumors of new Manty secret weapons," Groenewold said, and Tourville hid a wince. Trust his old friend to jump right in with both feet, he reflected. BJ never had been known for his tact, but Tourville had hoped he'd at least become sensitive enough to political realities not to charge blindly into a minefield like the Hancock Board's report. Or not, at least, in front of witnesses.

Tourville glanced at Everard Honeker's profile from the corner of his eye. Honeker seemed no more than politely attentive, with no indication that he might consider Groenewold's question the slightest out of line. Groenewold's commissioner, Citizen Commissioner Lasrina O'Faolain, was a bit more demonstrative. Her mouth tightened, and the corners of her eyes quivered, as if she'd been forced to override a reflex to close them in resignation, but she seemed almost more apprehensive for her charge's sake than angry at him for broaching the forbidden.

Which left Citizen Admiral Giscard's people's commissioner, and Tourville couldn't prevent himself from turning to look in her direction. Citizen Commissioner Eloise Pritchart had a short way with enemies of the People, and there were rumors that her icy, perpetually controlled exterior was a mask for a very different internal personality—one which hunted down the People's foes with a zealot's vengeful passion. Whatever the truth of those rumors, it was well known that Pritchart stood high in the esteem of Oscar Saint-Just, who had personally picked her to ride herd on Giscard. And since certain other persistent rumors insisted that the late, unlamented Citizen Admiral Porter's personal patron had been that same Oscar Saint-Just . . .

"I'm not sure exactly what you mean by 'putting stock' in them, Citizen Admiral," Giscard said after only the slightest glance at Pritchart's beautiful, coldly composed features. "I think it's evident that Jane Kellet ran into something out of the ordinary. I'm sure you've read the Board of Inquiry's report, of course. But while I'm certain the Board considered all the information available to it—" he actually sounded, Tourville thought admiringly, as if he truly believed a single word of that, "it's also true that the Board was under a great deal of pressure to issue its report quickly. The strategic situation demanded that we disseminate its findings as rapidly as we could to all interested COs and their people's commissioners. It's entirely possible that the speed with which it discharged its duty, while otherwise admirable, prevented it from considering every scrap of information as fully as might, perhaps, have been merited under other conditions."

My God, but he's good! Tourville's mustache hid another smile as he drew a cigar from his breast pocket and unwrapped it. Citizen Commissioner Pritchart had quietly but firmly arranged for his assigned place to be directly under one of the enviro plant's air returns whenever he was summoned aboard *Salamis*. It rather amused the citizen vice admiral, but it also constituted an unstated permission to indulge himself in the vice he had cultivated purely as a matter of image. *And it also suggests to me, like Javier's response to BJ, for that matter, that perhaps the accuracy of the rumors about her might leave just a teeny-weeny bit to be desired. Not that I intend to run any risks to find out. Ms. Tourville's little boy Lester may be aggressive, eager, bloodthirsty, hard-charging, and other clichés to that effect, but he ain't stupid!*

But whatever the innermost truth about Eloise Pritchart might be, she chose not to make an issue of Giscard's response to Groenewold's question. There was nothing in his actual words to which she could have legitimately objected anyway, but that wouldn't have deterred some people's commissioners for a moment.

O'Faolain seemed to relax just a bit at Pritchart's silence, and Groenewold (predictably, to those who knew him) plowed on as if there'd never been any reason he should have worried in the first place.

"I know the report came out in a hurry, Citizen Admiral. And I suppose that could explain its failure to address the points that worry me. But I've heard some disturbing reports since then. Rumors, really, I suppose. I can't say I believed half of 'em . . . but even if they were only half true, they still sounded alarming."

"I take it you're referring specifically to the reports about new

Manticoran LACs," Giscard said with admirable aplomb, and Groenewold nodded. "Well," Twelfth Fleet's CO went on, "I have to admit there have been such reports. There hasn't been any confirming evidence, one way or the other, really, since the great bulk of TF 12.3's sensor data was lost along with its ships. As to the import of what the techs did manage to recover from the surviving units—" he shrugged slightly "—opinion is divided. Some of NavInt's analysts seem to feel the Manties have come up with something considerably better in the way of LACs, while others are of the opinion that the claims about new levels of LAC performance are exaggerated. Those who hold with the theory that they're exaggerated point out, reasonably, in my opinion, that the officers making the reports were undoubtedly badly traumatized by what happened to their task force. While their reports were doubtless made in good faith, it's certainly possible that what they'd been through had warped their impressions of whatever the enemy actually had."

Groenewold looked less than satisfied, and Tourville restrained an impulse to kick him under the table. If BJ really wanted the lowdown on the rumors, all he needed was to get Tourville alone and ask *him*, in front of fewer (and less official) witnesses. There was, after all, a reason Tourville had specifically requested that the *William T. Sherman* be assigned to his task force. Any *Warlord* was a powerful and desirable unit, but he'd been much more interested in *Sherman*'s captain than in the ship's firepower, and after talking to Citizen Captain Diamato, he was glad he had. He'd been impressed by the citizen captain, and he regretted the circumstances which made it inadvisable to tell the man so. But he'd also recorded a carefully worded memo, summarizing what Diamato had told him as circumspectly as possible, and sent it off to *Salamis*.

"On the off chance that the initial reports on the new LACs were somewhat less inaccurate than the Hancock Board was able to determine during the brief period in which it had to consider them, however," Giscard went on, "my staff and I have been working on possible responses. Lack of hard data on their capabilities—assuming, of course, that they actually exist at all—means we can't suggest a great deal about the best way to deal with them, but I assure you that we'll pass on any inspirations that strike us, or any new information that comes our way, before we conclude our training exercises and move on our objectives. Will that be satisfactory, Citizen Vice Admiral?"

"Completely, Citizen Admiral." Groenewold made no effort to hide his satisfaction that his fleet commander was alert to a possible threat, and the temperature in the briefing room seemed to rise considerably.

And isn't it a hell of a note when task force and fleet command-ers have to tiptoe around a perfectly legitimate military or intelli-gence issue like little kids scared of ghosts just because some fucking politician *has decided to deny the sky is blue?* The dispassion of his own mental tone took Tourville slightly by surprise. He wasn't at all sure he liked being sufficiently cynical to accept the situation so readily, but he supposed it was a survival tool in the new, improved People's Republic of Haven.

"In that case," Giscard went on, "let's look at the final list of objectives." He nodded to his chief of staff, and Citizen Captain MacIntosh input commands at his terminal. Tourville felt Yuri Bogdanovich shift slightly in the chair to his left, prepared to enter notes into the memo board plugged into his own terminal. Citi-zen Commander Bhadresa, Groenewold's chief of staff, apparently preferred to dictate her notes, and she positioned the hush mike of her own memo board to take down her comments as the dis-play above the table blinked to life.

"Citizens," Giscard said formally, "this is where we're going. I will command the attack on Treadway. Citizen Vice Admiral Groenewold, your force will be tasked to attack Elric, and Citi-zen Vice Admiral Tourville will command the Solway attack. We've only got two months to complete the assembly and training of our forces, so we're all going to have to hit the ground running, but I have complete faith in our people's ability to pull the op together and carry it through successfully.

"Now, as the first stage in our exercises, I intend to begin with some time in the simulators for ourselves and our task group and squadron commanders. We can bring the individual ship COs aboard once we've polished off most of the flag officer's rough edges. Since Citizen Admiral Tourville and I have worked together before, but you and I haven't, Citizen Admiral Groenewold, I intend to make him the op force commander for our first sims while you and I command Twelfth Fleet and Citizen Rear Admiral Fawcett stands in for Citizen Admiral Tourville. I trust you won't have any problems taking 'orders' from a citizen rear admiral for the duration of the sim?"

"Certainly not, Citizen Admiral," Groenewold assured him. "Besides, I know Sue Fawcett. She's a good woman and a fine offi-cer. Ought to have another star of her own by now, anyway."

"I'm glad you feel that way, Citizen Admiral," Giscard said. "In that case, let's look at some specifics of what I hope to accomplish.

First, of course, I want to be sure you and I, and all our other senior officers, all understand the basic ops plan. Second, we're short of time and we've got a lot of new squadron COs who need to be brought up to speed and made familiar and comfortable with and confident in Twelfth Fleet's combat doctrine and standards, both of which are somewhat different from the rest of the Navy's in general. Third, I'd like—"

His voice went on, crisply outlining his intentions, and Lester Tourville leaned back and listened approvingly while Citizen Commissioner Pritchart listened with matching approval, or at least with acceptance, and no expression at all.

Now if only the Manties will be as obliging as Pritchart seems to be feeling today, this whole thing may actually come off as planned!

CHAPTER TWENTY-TWO

"It's an interesting challenge, Your Grace. An exciting one, really. But you do realize the chances of success may not be very good, don't you?"

Doctor Adelina Arif sat in the armchair in Honor's home office, a teacup and saucer in her lap. Nimitz and Samantha sat upright on their perch before the French doors onto the terrace, very quiet and intense, and Miranda and Farragut had joined the discussion at Honor's specific invitation. Her Grayson maid had proven just as useful here in the Star Kingdom as she'd ever been at home, and not just with Honor's wardrobe, grooming, or social schedule, either. Whether she wanted to or not, Honor had been forced to accept that her days were simply too busy for her to keep track of all she had to do herself. The acceptance process had begun on Grayson when she was first forced to grapple fully with her duties as Steadholder Harrington, but the "restful" schedule of "limited duty" the Admiralty had arranged to help with her recuperation had completed it. She'd come to the conclusion that it would have required two of her (or at least one and a half) to tend to everything she was supposed to be tending to, and MacGuiness and Miranda had stepped even more completely into the gap. And not simply as her assistants. In many ways, the two of them combined were becoming her alter ego, making decisions and taking the actions they knew she would want taken and seeking her approval afterwards, exactly like a good XO aboard a warship. And like a good captain, Honor treasured their initiative as much as their ability.

More importantly in this case, however, Miranda and Farragut had just as much interest in this project as Honor and Nimitz did. And Miranda's first-class brain was just likely to have something very valuable to contribute to the conference.

"I think you can safely assume that I recognize the challenge implicit in the concept, Doctor Arif," Honor said now, her tone dry. "It was my mother who thought it up, of course, and even she doubted that it would be easy. But we have a few advantages no one else ever had, and I doubt you could hope for more motivated students."

"I realize that, Your Grace. And I apologize if it sounded as if I didn't think you'd considered the concept in detail. I suppose I was really throwing out a sheet anchor of my own to be sure no one expected me to perform miracles."

"No one expects miracles. All anyone can ask for is your best effort. What I'd really like to do would be to have you teach *me* to sign and let me teach Nimitz and Samantha, capitalizing on how well we already understand one another. Unfortunately, that simply isn't going to work. Or not in any reasonable time period, anyway. I'm afraid this—" she raised her artificial left hand "—still has a long way to go before it's up to anything delicate and coordinated, and from my understanding of what's involved, it would be difficult, if not impossible, to sign effectively with only one hand. Worse, perhaps, I simply don't have the time to put in the hours I'm sure it's going to take. Miranda is in a better position to steal the time from all the other things *she* ought to be doing, but she doesn't have any more background in this sort of thing than I do. That's why we decided to call in a specialist, and one reason we specifically asked for you was the part you played as a member of the contact team assigned to Medusa."

"I guessed as much," Arif said with a small smile. She sipped her tea, then set the cup on the saucer. "You do realize I was a rather junior member of Doctor Sampson's team, I hope."

"I do. But I've also read the first contact report and Baron Hightower's report on his initial negotiations with the Medusan chiefs." Arif looked surprised, and Honor smiled. "Resident Commissioner Matsuko is a friend of mine, Doctor Arif. When I wrote her to describe what I hoped to accomplish and asked her for some background on how communication had been opened with the Medusans, she was kind enough to give me full access to her archives. Which is how I happen to know a 'rather junior member' of the team was the one who made the breakthrough suggestion to Doctor Sampson."

Arif blushed but said nothing, and Honor's smile broadened.

"Given your record there and the glowing commendations Hightower attached to his report, I feel confident we have the best woman for the job. Which, as I say, doesn't mean we expect miracles. Only that we believe you honestly have a shot at it."

"I hope you're right, Your Grace, and you'll certainly get my best effort. But the problem of opening communication with the Medusans isn't really a very good parallel to this one." She paused, one eyebrow raised, and Honor nodded for her to continue.

"The Medusans, like every other sentient species we've encountered, except the 'cats, at least use a means of communication we can perceive and analyze, Your Grace. In the Medusans' case, it's a combination of spoken sounds, body language, and scent emissions. We can duplicate the sounds, although we require artificial assistance to reach some of the higher frequencies, but the body language and scent emissions were much more difficult. Partly, of course, that's because they have six limbs, not four, and they're radially symmetrical. More to the point, because Medusan faces are immobile, they don't use facial expressions, which makes the body language even more important, since their gestures have to carry the weight of both body language *and* expression. Fortunately, their gestures are mostly confined to their upper limbs. They're . . . vigorous—that's why Doctor Sampson described them as 'berserk semaphore machines' in one of his early reports—but the restriction to just the upper limbs greatly reduces the total signal set. On the other hand, they still have three arms to our two, and no human could possibly duplicate the range of motion possible for a Medusan."

"I know," Honor put in as Arif paused, and grinned. "That was why I was so impressed with your hologram suggestion."

"Well, I have to admit that I think it was one of my better notions myself," Arif acknowledged with an answering smile. "Of course, it scared the hell out of the local chieftains when it suddenly appeared. I think they thought it was some sort of demon, although they were never willing to admit it if they did. And figuring out how to put three arms on a human torso was a lot tougher than I'd anticipated, too. Not to mention how weird it looked to anyone who saw it. But at least we were able to program the holo's arms to mimic the Medusans' gestures, and from there we worked out a pidgin version a human can produce with only two arms. And we were really fortunate that their scent emissions are used primarily for emphasis, not for information content."

"The holo you built and your development of the 'pidgin' version, as you call it, was one of the strongest reasons for calling you in," Honor said. "I hope it won't be as difficult in this case—at least 'cats only have two true-arms—but there are obvious parallels between what you accomplished there and what we hope to manage here."

"I know. And in many ways, I agree that it should be more straightforward. I've been back into the archives, looking over the families of sign language your mother dug up, and the small physical differences, like the fact that the 'cats have one less finger than we do, shouldn't be a problem.

"What's going to be more difficult in simple mechanical terms is the extent to which all of the really flexible signing languages also relied on body language and, especially, expression, since we're dealing with a situation in which the two sides of the conversation, as it were, can't possibly duplicate the full range of one another's expressions. Or even a partial range, for that matter."

"I can see where that would be true," Honor agreed, rubbing her nose in thought. "On the other hand, anyone who's ever been adopted knows 'cats are just as physically expressive as humans. They simply use different sets of movements—their ears carry an awful lot of the weight, for example—and we get to recognize them fairly quickly."

"I'm counting rather heavily on that. Unfortunately, *I'm* not familiar with treecat body language or expression, so the first thing I'll have to do is spend time observing them, interacting with them, and generally compiling a list of expressive techniques. And once I've done that, we'll have to devise a system in which we can relate a very specific gesture or movement on their part to a human expression or gesture . . . and vice versa.

"That, unfortunately, will be the easy part. Because once we've devised the hand signs, and figured out the 'code' for 'cat–human expressions, we'll have to get across the notion that they compose a real language."

"I think Nimitz and Samantha have grasped the notion already." Honor nodded to the two intently watching 'cats. "They certainly understand that all this effort is designed to give them a means of communicating with one another again, at any rate."

"I don't doubt they do, Your Grace, and the link you and Nimitz share will undoubtedly help." Honor nodded again, this time in agreement. She hadn't really wanted to advertise the existence of that link, but there'd never been any question about whether or not whomever they enlisted would have to know about it.

Fortunately, Arif took her professional responsibilities seriously, and she'd readily agreed to keep the full nature of Honor's bond with Nimitz confidential.

"Nonetheless, and despite the extra 'channel' you two have," Arif went on, "there are some potentially serious obstacles. And, frankly, they loom a bit larger in light of the fact that my research has uncovered at least two previous attempts to teach 'cats to sign."

"It has?" Honor shot a glance at Miranda. "I wasn't aware of that."

"Few people are," Arif said. "The first was by a xenobiologist by the name of Sanura Hobbard. She was one of the first out-kingdom specialists to study the 'cats in detail, and she spent the better part of fifteen T-years trying to teach them to sign without success. The second attempt was about a hundred T-years later, also without success. I've been unable to find the records on precisely what sort of signs they tried to teach, but I wouldn't be surprised if they worked out something very much like what we're talking about. But whatever format they tried, the fact that neither attempt even came close to success didn't do wonders for my optimism when I came across them, I'm afraid."

"I notice you used the past tense, Doctor," Honor observed, and Arif nodded.

"I still wouldn't pretend to be wildly optimistic, Your Grace, but I do think there's at least a chance of succeeding where they failed. Assuming we can overcome those obstacles I mentioned."

"Exactly what sorts of obstacles do you envision?" Honor asked intently, and Arif shrugged.

"The greatest is the fact that telepaths simply do not use spoken language. The standard references on the 'cats all indicate that they do use aural signals, but they're just that: signals. Or, to put it another way, they're communication but not *language*."

"Excuse me?" Miranda LaFollet leaned forward, one hand resting on the treecat in her lap. "I always assumed that language and communication were synonymous."

"Many people do, but they aren't," Arif told her. " 'Communication' can be used to identify a lot of activities, from the way animals relate to one another, to a deep philosophical discussion between humans on the Meaning of Life, to the way electronic devices transfer information from one location to another. They're all communication, of a sort, at least. But *human* communication—language—is the means by which two sentient beings exchange value-laden symbols. Feelings and ideas have no physical substance, Ms. LaFollet. We can't just hand them back and forth the way we would an apple or an orange or a brick, so we devise symbols which carry their weight, and we call those symbols words. A child, immersed in a language-saturated environment and motivated by the need to express its own desires and needs to those upon whom it depends, learns to associate certain patterns of sound with certain meanings, but that's only the beginning of truly acquiring a language.

"In addition to acquiring associations between sound and symbol, learning a language also requires one to deduce—or, in the case of children, absorb—the rules for the way the sounds are put together. Each sound can be thought of as an individual building block or sound bit. What we call a 'phoneme' is the smallest bit of sound that may change or alter meaning, which usually means a vowel or a consonant, and phonemes vary from language to language. Let's take Spanish and English as an illustration, since San Martin's been in the news so much of late. In Spanish, the 'sp' phoneme *never* begins a word; in Standard English, however, that's quite a common beginning sound. So natives of San Martin, where Spanish is the common language and Standard English is essentially a second tongue, frequently have problems pronouncing English words—like *Spanish* itself, for example—which begin with the 'sp' sound, because their birth tongue simply doesn't put that sound in that location.

"On its own, a phoneme usually has no meaning, but groups of them combine in strings or patterns which *do* have meaning. We call the smallest string of sound which does have meaning a 'morpheme,' which is a sound—it may be a word on its own, or only a part of a word—which can't be broken down any further. Take 'biker,' for instance. 'Bike' is a morpheme. It can't be broken down any further and retain its meaning. But by adding an additional phoneme—'er' to it—we tell our listener that we're talking about someone who rides a bike. We can go further and add yet another phoneme, 's' to it, in which case we create the plural form and tell our listener we're speaking of more than one person, all of whom ride bikes. And to complicate things still further, 'bike' can be either a verb or a noun, and our listener has to determine which we intend for it to be from the way in which we position and use the word. 'He bikes' means the person we're speaking of rides a bike. 'His bikes' means the person owns more than one bike. As you can see, the very tiny difference—the use of 'he' instead of 'his'—makes an enormous difference in the concept being communicated, and that doesn't even begin to get into verb tenses, temporal and spatial references, stress and emphasis patterns, or any of the other enormous number of shared conventions which go into a true language."

She paused, and Miranda nodded slowly, her expression thoughtful.

"What you might think of as a 'full-blown' language isn't the only way to communicate, of course. As I said, it's well established that treecats use at least some vocal signals, but signals don't necessarily equate to language. For example, if I scream as a hexapuma leaps on me, that's a signal. It's not *language*, however. Most probably, anyone who hears me will know I'm very unhappy over something, but I haven't communicated anything more than that, nor can I with a signal that simple and crude.

"The main problem here, however, is that 'cats don't *use* phonemes or morphemes. So far as we can tell, they don't use a spoken language *at all*. From Her Grace's explanation of her link with Nimitz, it's clear the people who theorized that the 'cats were telepaths were right all along, and the tests Doctor Brewster and his people have conducted over the last several months confirm it, conclusively, in my opinion. But *we* aren't telepaths. We don't have the least idea what the ability to communicate directly, mind-to-mind, without the intrusion of a secondary interface like language, means to the way they think and receive and process information. In my opinion, it's not only possible but probable that they've never developed the sort of 'bit-based' format we humans have had no option but to use, and that could be a very serious problem."

"Because they won't have any inbuilt referent for what we're trying to teach them?" Miranda asked, her expression still intent, and Arif nodded firmly.

"Exactly. All humans rely on some physical form of language to communicate, and so, with the exception of the 'cats, does every other sentient species we've encountered. That means anyone we've ever tried to teach a language, or learn a language from, at least shared certain utterly basic concepts and mental tools. But the 'cats almost certainly *lack* those mental tools, and that puts us in the position of someone who has to go back and invent the wheel all over again. Actually, inventing the wheel would be easy compared to what we have to do here, because at least we could physically demonstrate our invention for someone who'd never thought of it before."

"I understand what you're saying, Doctor," Honor said, "but I think you may be overly concerned. Anyone who's been adopted knows the 'cats understand us when we talk to them."

"Forgive me, Your Grace, but we *don't* know that," Arif replied. "I'll certainly grant that the evidence strongly suggests you're correct, but we haven't got any proof you are because no one has ever successfully established true two-way communication."

"Yes, someone has," Honor replied, her tone nonconfrontational but firm. *Very* firm. "Nimitz and I have. Not through the sort of interface you're talking about, of course, but I *know* when he understands me. Confusion is a very distinctive 'tasting' emotion, I assure you. There are times when I have to pick words carefully, especially when I start dealing with concepts 'cats simply haven't had to develop, like heavy-metal toxicity," she said, flashing a smile at Miranda. "But he usually understands me at least as well as most human adolescents I've tried to explain things to."

"I don't doubt he does, Your Grace. And I didn't say he didn't; I only said we can't *prove* it . . . yet. And while I hope your analysis is correct, I also have to point out that you do have a special link to Nimitz. One which no one else, to the best of our knowledge, has ever shared. It's possible that at least a part of what you believe you're communicating to him with your words is actually reaching him over that link. It's even possible that a part of what *all* 'cats 'hear' from *all* humans is enhanced by an ability on their part to perceive the thoughts behind our words. For purposes of applied cognitive effort, humans tend to think in language, to organize the syntax of our thought processes in the fashion in which we're accustomed to receiving information, so perhaps what's actually happening is that we're putting words together to communicate with them, but what they're actually 'hearing' is the mental organization behind the words."

"I suppose that's possible," Honor acknowledged with a frown. It was odd, but the possibility Arif was suggesting had never occurred to her, and it should have. "I don't think it's what's happening, but I can't dismiss the possibility out of hand."

"As I say, I hope it isn't what's happening," Arif said, "because it's clear Nimitz's injuries have completely silenced his ability to send thoughts to Samantha. Or, put another way, she can't 'hear' anything from him, which means she wouldn't be able to 'hear' the thoughts behind the signs we might teach him to make.

"My personal belief is that the 'cats *have* grasped the concept of human language, at least at its most basic level. But that's *only* my belief. It hasn't been demonstrated yet, and until we do demonstrate it, I don't want anyone assuming we're home free."

"I can appreciate that," Honor said, and Miranda nodded.

"Actually," Arif went on in a more thoughtful tone, "in many ways, I'll be deeply surprised if it turns out the 'cats haven't grasped the concept. I know I just finished arguing that a race of telepaths would have no need to develop a language interface like our own, but they do communicate, and they obviously know we do. More to the point, they can *hear* us communicate, even if we can't hear *them*, and they've been watching and listening to us for hundreds of T-years. The fact that they're empaths and we know they can detect and correctly interpret human emotions is another hopeful sign, in my opinion. They've been able to hear us speaking to one another, and to them, while they simultaneously tracked the emotions behind the words, which you could think of as sort of the ultimate in paralanguage. And the fact that two previous attempts failed might not mean a thing in relation to that long a period. It's been a tad over three hundred years since the last try was made, and if the concept of a spoken language was as alien to them as I believe it almost certainly was, it could very well have taken them considerably more than a century of contact with humans to make the sort of mental leap forward required to grasp the concept at all.

"But given the fact that Doctor Brewster's tests have demonstrated that the 'cats are at least as smart as most of their champions have claimed from the beginning, and given that learning to understand their humans would certainly be high on their list of things to do, I'd think there's an excellent chance they truly have learned to understand us when we speak to them *since* the last failure to teach them to sign. I don't think it would have been easy for them, mind you, but they've certainly had plenty of time to work on the problem!"

"That's true enough," Honor said wryly, and all three treecats bleeked laughter. Honor paused at the sound and turned to cock an eyebrow at Nimitz. "You know, Stinker, it just occurred to me that we've been sitting here and trying to reason our way through this when there was a much simpler solution. Come over here a minute."

Nimitz bleeked cheerfully and jumped from his perch to the back of Honor's chair with much of his old agility. His tail flirted airily as he flowed down over her shoulder to the chair arm and from there to her desk, then parked himself upright on his rearmost limbs, cocked his head at her, and twitched his whiskers.

"I believe we may be able to settle this right now, Doctor Arif," Honor said, with a smile whose crookedness was the product of wry humor and no longer imposed by dead nerves, then looked back at Nimitz.

"*Do* you understand us when we talk to you, Stinker?" she asked softly.

There was a moment of complete silence while all three humans stared at the silken-coated, six-limbed creature on the desk, and then Nimitz bleeked softly and his head moved in what could only have been a slow, deliberate nod.

Honor exhaled, slowly and deeply, then looked at Arif and raised both eyebrows. The linguist gazed back for several seconds, and then dropped her eyes to the 'cat.

"Nimitz?" she said, and the 'cat turned to face her. "Do you understand *me* when I speak to you?" she asked, and he nodded once more. "Do you listen to my words and understand them and not just the thoughts behind them?" Again he nodded. "And do you and Samantha understand that I'm going to be trying to teach you and Her Grace a way to let you talk to people, and each other, in a way that doesn't use words?"

He nodded yet again, and Arif sat back in her chair, her dark eyes glowing.

"It's still not conclusive, Your Grace. Until we've established a way for him to tell me more than simply yes or no, we won't be able to know we aren't losing an enormous amount of information in transmission—or, for that matter, that he truly is hearing and understanding us without a telepathic 'overlay.' But I think you're right. I think he and Samantha—and Farragut," she added, smiling at Miranda "—really do understand spoken English. I don't know how well yet, but I think you and Nimitz have just demonstrated the basic ability. And if that's the case, my job just got enormously easier, because all I'll really have to do is design a nonverbal interface through which someone who already understands what I'm saying can 'talk' back to me. And your mother is right. The old sign languages for the speech and hearing impaired are definitely the place to begin."

Honor's mental ears pricked at the emphasis Arif had placed on the last word, and she tipped back her own chair and gazed thoughtfully at the linguist.

" 'Begin,' Doctor?" she repeated, and Arif grinned.

"Well, if I'm right about your having demonstrated that they understand human language, I'm already past the single greatest hurdle. But the next logical question for any linguist to ask herself is obvious, I think. If 'cats can grasp the concept of a *spoken* language, can they make the next jump and grasp the concept of a *written* one? We invented it as a way to record the symbols—the sounds—we use in language. Obviously, the 'cats have never needed a means to record sounds, but it doesn't necessarily follow that they haven't devised some means of recording whatever they use in the place of our symbols. No one has ever identified anything remotely like the means *we* use, but they obviously have a fully functional society with a deep continuity, which means they must have developed some substitute for writing to pass ideas on. My own theory is that it would have to be something like an oral history tradition, similar to those of preliterate human societies, although even the limited amount I've already learned about 'cat clan structures and group social behavior suggests that it's a bit more than that.

"But assuming that we're right about the 'cats' preexisting grasp of the concept of language, teaching them to sign shouldn't be all that difficult. Teaching them to read and write, however, require them not only to grasp the concept of words but also the concept that 'the map is the territory.' They'd have to grasp the association between inanimate symbols and living ones, but if they can . . ."

"If they can, then the bandwidth for communication with them just expanded enormously," Honor said, and Arif nodded.

"Absolutely, Your Grace." She looked back at Nimitz, her expression now that of someone eager to dive into a task, and her eyes were brighter than ever. "Only a tiny handful of linguists have ever had the opportunity to learn to communicate with an alien species," she said softly, almost reverently. "I've already had that chance once with the Medusans. Now you've offered it to me all over again, Your Grace, and I promise you this much: if it *can* be done, then it *will* be done."

CHAPTER TWENTY-THREE

Honor sat back in her chair with a sense of simple pleasure and looked down the lengthy expanse of snow-white linen at the wreckage of an excellent meal.

She'd spent most of the morning at Silverman & Sons, discussing her newest baby with their engineering staff and Wayne Alexander (no relation to the Alexanders of White Haven), her new flight engineer. She'd just about decided to call the fleet, little craft the *Jamie Candless*, though the decision had been a bittersweet one. She seemed to be making a habit out of naming ships for dead people, and she wished she had a smaller supply of names. But there was nothing bittersweet about her delight in the ship.

She was lucky to have someone of Alexander's caliber watching over the project for her, too, and she knew it. Just as she knew the engineer was delighted to have been offered the position.

Alexander had escaped with her from Hell. According to the Camp Charon records, he had enjoyed the distinction of having spent more time on Hell than any other escapee. It was an honor he would willingly have declined, but since he hadn't been offered a choice, he'd decided to take a certain pride in his status as the "oldest" escapee in the planet's history.

He'd also been a "political," not a military POW: a civilian spacecraft design specialist who'd been packed off to Hell for criticizing the Technical Conservation Act of 1778 P.D. The Act had been almost seven decades old at the time, but Alexander had made the serious mistake of claiming that "nationalizing" the expertise of all research and production engineers (like himself) had been a bad idea. It had, he pointed out, created layer upon layer of bureaucratic oversight that stifled individual creativity quite handily. Worse, it had put government appointees, with zero real-world experience, in charge of selecting R&D goals to "steer" the Republic's technological development most effectively. Which, of course, accomplished nothing of the sort.

His arguments had been self-evident, but he really shouldn't have made them at a Republic-wide professional conference, where the very people Internal Security had least wanted to share his sentiments—his fellow engineers—had been certain to hear about them.

After over seventy years on a prison planet, he held an understandable hatred for the PRH, whoever was running it, yet he remained remarkably unembittered otherwise. He had, however, had enough of fighting the system, and as a civilian, he'd had few skills to offer the Allied military. And while he'd been on the cutting edge of the Republic's R&D before his sojourn on Hell, he was far, far behind the curve now. But his background had made him perfect for his present job when he chose to settle in Harrington Steading and accept Honor's offer of employment. Now he was a permanent fixture over at Silverman's, where he was overseeing every detail of the *Candless'* construction, and it was obvious to Honor that he thought of the runabout as "his" ship . . . which she might be allowed to play with from time to time if she was very, very good and ate all her vegetables.

She chuckled at the thought and wiped her lips with a napkin. MacGuiness and Mistress Thorn had done their usual outstanding work, and one advantage of being unreasonably wealthy and possessing a dining room large enough to hangar a Fleet pinnace was that one could afford to entertain on a lavish scale.

Not that "entertaining" was precisely what Honor had in mind. She'd always found that dining regularly with subordinates was an excellent way to cement the sort of personal relationships that made a merely good command team into an outstanding one. It was a custom she'd pursued throughout her career, and she'd seen no reason to stop since her assignment to the Academy and to ATC, although there'd been a hiatus over the last several weeks while she and Nimitz both underwent surgery. Without quick heal, the interval would have been much longer, too. Given the amount of time Honor had spent in the doctors' hands over the last ten or fifteen T-years, she'd decided not to brood over her inability to regenerate. It would have been nice to be able to grow a new arm or eye, or new facial nerves, but at least quick heal let her recover from surgery with a rapidity no pre-Diaspora surgeon would have believed possible.

Of course, it doesn't do much to help with therapy time—except to let me get started a little faster. And thank God *Daddy was right about how much easier it would be to get used to the nerves and eye this time!*

Her mouth quirked at the reflection, and for the first time in thirty-four standard months, she felt the *left* side of her mouth move and her left cheek dimple. The sensation seemed decidedly unnatural after so long, and the contrast between the reports of the newly replaced artificial nerves and the natural ones on the other side only made it more so. But at least her face was *alive* once more . . . and this time around, she hadn't had to spend weeks with the muscles jerking and twitching uncontrollably at random intervals. She still had to concentrate on what she wanted her face to do when she chewed or changed her expression deliberately, but that was fine. The naturalness of expression would return soon enough, and she was profoundly grateful to have been spared the dreary task of learning how to control her own face from scratch all over again.

Despite her brave words to her mother, she hadn't really allowed herself to fully believe her father when he assured her that would be the case. Her memories of the first time around were too clear, and she hadn't dared risk the potential disappointment if she read too much into his assurances. But he'd been right, and now she felt a bit guilty for having doubted. Even the new eye was working smoothly, although she was still experiencing a bit of visual disorientation. The programmers hadn't hit the software exactly right, and the self-correcting features were still zeroing in on controlling image brightness and contrast and coordinating those qualities with her natural eye's acuity properly. It was getting better, though, and while she hadn't even begun mastering the eye's new features, all the old ones had been programmed to use the same muscle commands as her old eye had used. For the present, the new features were simply switched off until she felt comfortable with the old ones and with the control of her face. There would be time enough to bring the new capabilities on-line . . . and at the moment, she needed no extra distractions, because her new arm had been attached, as well.

Her small smile turned into something much more like a grimace at the thought of the new limb. She was delighted to have at least started learning to use it, of course. In fact, she told herself that almost hourly . . . every time the unwieldy thing swung wide and smacked into a door frame as she went by, or flicked side-ways suddenly in response to some neural command she'd never meant to give it. Her sheer clumsiness (except that it wasn't really "her" clumsiness) was maddening, especially for a woman who'd spent decades training in the martial arts. But at least the soft-ware contained programmable overrides. She had to leave them off-line most of the time, not just during scheduled therapy and practice sessions, because she needed to get used to the fact that the arm was there again and gain control of its unintentional jerks and movements. But the override software let her lock the arm down completely, allowing her to carry it in a sling, neatly out of the way and without endangering any unfortunate passerby, for public occasions. The next level up restricted the arm to a series of limited movements that the arm's built-in AI recognized as ones she had mastered on a conscious level. The basic package was more flexible than she'd expected, offering her several intermediate levels of override, but she wasn't sure she liked having them. No, that wasn't accurate. What she wasn't sure of was that having them was a good idea, however convenient it might be in the short term. She half-feared she would be tempted to overuse them. In fact, she'd already caught herself doing just that, and justifying it on the basis of how much she had to do and the need to keep the limb under control while she attended to it all. But at least she *had* caught herself, and she was working hard on avoiding that particular temptation. The possibility she was actually more afraid of in the long run, however, was that she might settle for less than the best degree of control she could obtain, and rely on the software to let her get by with an agility and coordination that were merely "good enough."

But for tonight, at least, she had no qualms about using the override. It would never have done for the hostess' left arm to go flailing about amid the glassware and silver, after all! That would hardly contribute to the impression of the calm, capable senior officer she wanted to project. And considering the mix of whom she was inviting to her current round of dinners, it was particu-larly important that she project the image of someone who knew what she was doing . . . and what she was talking about.

She sipped her after-dinner cocoa and studied this evening's guests as she pondered on why that was true.

Andrea Jaruwalski, her strong features no longer a haunted mask, sat to her left. Jaruwalski had made enormous strides in regain-ing her self-confidence since Honor had chosen her as her ATC aide. The fact that she'd been allowed hands-on participation in

Honor's reshaping of the Crusher and that she'd gained the rueful respect of the current crop of ATC students for her cunning and nastiness as the opposition force commander hadn't hurt, of course. The biggest factor, though, appeared to be that she knew the rest of the Navy was coming around to Honor's view of what had really happened in Seaford Nine. She seemed to give Honor complete credit for that, although Honor felt that that was overgenerous of her. In either case, what really mattered was that the Navy wasn't going to shoot itself in the foot by depriving itself of one of its better tactical officers.

Nimitz and Samantha, of course, sat to Honor's immediate right, sharing a special, double-perch highchair MacGuiness had designed for them, but Rear Admiral of the Red Jackson Kriangsak, Honor's executive officer at ATC, sat just beyond them. If the somewhat plump, dark-haired admiral had any problem with sitting "one place down" from a pair of silken-furred arboreals, he'd given no sign of it. More to the point, Honor had sensed nothing but amusement from him when he discovered the seating arrangements, and he was fascinated by Samantha. He'd made a point of speaking directly to her during the meal, a courtesy even many Sphinxians often failed to extend to 'cats. Honor had noticed him slipping her an extra stick of celery from his own salad plate, and the admiral had also made a point of congratulating Nimitz on his rapid recovery from his own latest round of surgery.

Six more officers and eighteen midshipmen stretched down either side of the long table beyond Kriangsak and Jaruwalski, and Mike Henke, whose ship was back in the Star Kingdom, attached to Home Fleet while she awaited assignment to one of the forward fleets, sat facing Honor from its foot. Now Honor let her eyes linger on those midshipmen—who, in a very real sense, were the true reason for this entire dinner—and saw Midshipman Theodore twitch as if someone had just kicked him under the table. Which someone almost certainly had, Honor thought cheerfully as she saw Midshipwoman Theresa Markovic frown at Theodore and then cut her eyes meaningfully to his almost untouched wineglass.

Theodore looked at her blankly for a moment, and then his face turned an interesting shade of magenta as understanding struck. He was the most junior officer present, even if a midshipman was no more than a larva in the cycle that turned civilians into Queen's officers, and that carried certain traditional obligations. One of which he'd obviously forgotten until someone bruised his kneecap. Now he rose abruptly and grabbed at his glass. It almost spilled, which darkened his blush still further, but then he drew a deep breath and visibly got a grip on himself. As a third-generation prolong recipient, he looked about thirteen T-years old, and his voice cracked just a bit as he cleared his throat, raised his glass, and announced the toast.

"Ladies and Gentlemen, the Queen!"

"The Queen!" the response rumbled back, and Honor raised her own wineglass and sipped. The burgundy tasted a little strange on the heels of hot cocoa, and she felt Nimitz's laughing amusement in the back of her brain as he shared the experience.

Wineglasses were lowered around the table, and side conversations began once again, but the formalities weren't quite finished, and Honor glanced at Midshipwoman Abigail Hearns. The young woman looked back for a moment, then stood, drawing a deep breath of her own, if less obviously than Theodore had, and raised her own glass.

"Ladies and Gentlemen," she announced in a soft, foreign accent, "I give you Grayson, the Keys, the Sword, and the Tester!"

There was a moment of consternation before the other glasses rose once more, and Honor hid a wicked smile as the other officers and midshipmen stumbled through the response. One or two got it right; the rest clearly hoped their imperfect efforts were lost in the general mumble, and she found it hard not to giggle at the emotions flowing back to her from her guests. With the exception of Mike Henke and, she suspected, Andrea Jaruwalski, none of the others had ever heard the Grayson loyalty toast, and it was darned well time they did. Honor's other Navy had paid for its equality with the RMN in blood and courage, and she was determined to see that it received it.

She let Hearns see just a small smile of approval, and the young woman sank back into her seat. Honor could taste the youngster's vast relief, and she set her own wineglass back down and reached over to rub Nimitz's ears, partly to give Hearns a chance to settle completely back down. The midshipwoman was a good two T-years older than Theodore, but in many ways, what she'd just done had been even harder for her than it had for the younger midshipman, and Honor was proud of her.

In fact, she was proud of young Abigail Hearns for a lot of reasons. She'd been astonished, the first day she'd called the roll at the beginning of this quarter's Intro to Tactics classes, to hear a soft, unmistakable accent respond to the name Hearns. Her own head had snapped up in a surprised movement she'd been unable to prevent, and her one good eye had widened as she saw the blue-on-blue Grayson uniform sitting amid a sea of Manticoran black-and-gold. It wasn't the only Grayson uniform scattered about the large room, but it was the only one which contained a midship*woman*. The very *first* midshipwoman in the history of the Grayson Space Navy, in point of fact.

Honor had gotten her surprise under control almost immediately and proceeded briskly with the roll with no other sign that Hearns' presence was anything out of the ordinary, but she'd made a point of asking the young woman to visit her during her D'Orville Hall office hours. She'd hesitated about doing it. Lord knew Hearns' unique status was likely to make problems enough for her without the added risk of becoming known as a "teacher's pet"! But her curiosity had gotten the better of her. Besides, it was likely the young woman would need all the moral support she could get.

To her astonishment, young Abigail was not only a Grayson female, but a highly born one, the third daughter of Aaron Hearns, Steadholder Owens. She was also, Honor had quickly come to suspect, Lord Owens' *favorite* daughter, which helped explain her presence on Saganami Island in one way, but made Honor even more astonished Owens had agreed to let her come in another.

She'd managed, eventually, to piece together the details of how it had all happened, although Abigail herself had been on the reticent side. The tall (for a Grayson; she was only of middling height by Manticoran standards), attractive, willowy brunette was nineteen T-years old. That meant she'd been around eight when Honor first visited Grayson, and from the taste of the young woman's emotions, it was obvious she'd been smitten with a severe case of hero worship for one Commander Harrington. Some of that still lingered, though it had eased with time and she had it under firm enough control that no one who lacked Honor's special advantages would have known it was there. What had not eased with time was the fact that she'd been Navy mad from the moment she stood one night on a balcony of Owens House, watching the terrible, pinprick flashes of nuclear warheads glare defiantly in the endless depths of space, and known a single, brutally outmatched heavy cruiser was locked in a death duel with a battlecruiser full of fanatics in defense of her planet and all its people.

The very idea of her doing anything about it had, of course, been out of the question. Decently raised Grayson women did not serve in the military. Foreign women from less civilized cultures might join the Navy, or even the Army or Marines, and it would no doubt be wrong to hold their career choices against them. Their actions were quite in accord with the lower standards of their own birth societies, and *they* could scarcely be blamed for the deficiencies of those societies' standards. And they were both brave and, yes, in their own ways, even noble to have elected to face the enemy in combat. And, yes again, many of them *were* serving in the frantically expanding GSN, helping meet its desperate need for trained officers. But they were not Grayson women, and *Grayson* women were needed right where they were, at home, where they could be properly protected and live the lives the Tester had intended. End of story, end of argument, end of hope.

Except that Abigail had been disinclined to accept that it was the end of anything. She'd obviously been her father's darling, but if he'd tried his best to spoil her, he'd managed to do it without turning her into a brat or making her petulant when she failed to get her way. Instead, she'd simply been convinced that if she worked at it hard enough, she could get or accomplish anything she put her mind to . . . a belief her present uniform certainly seemed to validate.

She'd politely but firmly continued to request permission from her father (one could scarcely have called such reasoned approaches *nagging* . . . exactly) to join the Navy at every opportunity. And in the meantime, she'd taken advantage of the new educational climate Benjamin Mayhew's reforms and one Honor Harrington's example had opened up on Grayson. She'd signed up for every hard-science and math course in the curriculum, and she'd added some phys-ed courses which were scarcely normal for a "proper" young Grayson woman. And, most insidious of all, she'd taken every chance to trot the example of Steadholder Harrington back out for her father's edification. The fact that Lord Owens was one of the more open-minded and liberal of the Keys (where other men's daughters and wives were concerned, at least) had helped, as had the fact that he'd met Honor, that he liked her, and that he respected her. But the fact had remained that in his mind, and especially where his own daughter was concerned, Honor had been both an off-worlder by birth and a larger-than-life, heroic figure. One could hardly expect *other* women to attain such standards or endure such suffering. And even if one could, he had no intention whatsoever of exposing his beloved Abigail to even the faintest risk of the wounds and personal loss Honor had experienced . . . or to something even worse.

For all that, Abigail's persistence had begun undermining his adamant resistance, rather like a mountain stream slowly and patiently washing away one tiny fragment of a boulder at a time.

It might still have come to nothing in the end (although Honor suspected that Lord Owens might have gotten a most unpleasant shock, steadholder or no, when his daughter turned twenty-two, the legal age of majority on Grayson) if not for Honor's own capture and supposed execution. Owens had been no more proof against Grayson's planetary grief and outrage than anyone else, and his daughter, even more impassioned over it than he, had caught him at exactly the right moment and *demanded* the right to help avenge Lady Harrington's murder.

Honor often wondered how High Admiral Matthews had reacted when Lord Owens approached him to request a midshipman's warrant for his *daughter.* Knowing Matthews, she felt confident that he'd managed to maintain his usual decorum. But she also knew that what he must really have wanted to do was to turn cartwheels of sheer joy. He'd been reared with just as much of the spinal reflex need to protect women as the next Grayson male, but he'd had far more exposure to the foreign-born female officers serving in the GSN. And he also knew how strained Grayson's manpower was becoming. He'd certainly discussed the need to figure out how to usefully mobilize some of his home world's huge, untapped store of womanpower with Honor and Benjamin Mayhew often enough, although Honor doubted that he'd actually expected to get any of them into naval uniform in his own lifetime.

There had, for obvious reasons, been no problem with the approval of Saganami Island. And by the time Honor turned back up alive, it had been too late for Lord Owens to rethink his position. From the few things Abigail had said—and the emotions which had bubbled up behind them—Honor suspected Owens was both proud of, terrified for, bemused over, and baffled by the willful, determined young woman he'd somehow raised. But despite that, he'd managed to smile as he sent her off as if the entire idea had been his own from the start, which probably said good things about his mental flexibility.

Since the initial shock of discovering her presence, Honor had gone out of her way to show Abigail no special favor. It was hard, because the young woman was everything Honor believed a middy should be. And she was, in the words of the Grayson cliché, cute as a button, too. But Honor had known that hovering in the background would have done Abigail no favors in the long run, and so she'd made herself maintain a public stance of no more than distant watchfulness. In private, she'd kept a rather closer eye on her, and she knew that at least some of what Abigail had encountered in the Star Kingdom had shocked or even dismayed her.

It could not have been easy for the daughter of a Grayson steadholder, however Navy mad, to go from the pampered, genteel, over-protected environment of her father's home to that of Saganami Island. RMN midshipmen were deliberately kept harassed and harried for their entire first form. The sort of hazing by upperclassmen which was the norm in some military academies was strictly prohibited in the Star Kingdom, but the level of discipline demanded, the workloads assigned, and the energy with which instructors and senior midshipmen . . . *encouraged* one to meet the Navy's standards compensated quite nicely. Physical and mental exhaustion became familiar companions for first-form middies, and the students were deliberately run till they dropped, then yanked back up and made to run all over again. It wasn't nice, and some people questioned its necessity, but Honor agreed with the philosophy. Especially now. These young men and women would go straight from their classrooms into a shooting war. Coddling them would do neither them nor the men and women they would someday command any favors. Pushing, bullying, and demanding until their instructors and, far more importantly, they themselves knew how much they were capable of would be *far* more useful.

But however much she might have approved, she knew it had been even harder for Ms. Midshipwoman Hearns than for almost anyone else in Academy history. And the sudden exposure to Manticoran ideas about sexual equality, mixed gym classes, mixed hand-to-hand combat classes, and lord only knew what else must also have been a shock to her system. And even if that hadn't, the invitations someone with her looks and natural poise must have attracted from her male classmates had to have been shocking enough to curl a properly raised Grayson girl's hair . . . among other things.

Yet Abigail had weathered the storm. Honor had made it quietly clear to her that, as the only steadholder within light-years, she felt a certain special responsibility to make herself available as counselor and mentor to all Grayson midshipmen. Which was true, but which (as she had not said) was particularly true in the case of the single Grayson midship*woman* on the island. Abigail had thanked her and, once or twice, availed herself of the offer, seeking advice or guidance, particularly in social situations. But she was scarcely alone in that, and none of her classmates had felt it was any sign of a "teacher's pet" mentality.

Honor was glad, and not just for Abigail's sake. The young woman had turned out to have a pronounced flair for tactics, and unlike Honor, she was a whiz at math. She was a bit hesitant about exerting her authority in training situations, which was hardly surprising in a young woman reared in the Grayson tradition. But her performance was acceptable even there, and it helped that she was a *steadholder's* daughter. Traditional Grayson women might not compete in what custom had hallowed as male occupations, but a steadholder's daughter was accustomed to wielding an authority few less nobly born women could expect to possess.

Pleased as Honor was to see a female Grayson at the Academy, however, that wasn't the reason she'd invited Abigail tonight. Invitations to Duchess Harrington's thrice-a-week dinners were handed out on two bases. *Every* student in any of her classes would receive at least one invitation, which was one reason the number of midshipmen present at any dinner hovered at around twenty and sometimes rose as high as twenty-five. Additional invitations had to be earned on the basis of academic performance, however, and Abigail Hearns was well up in the top third of repeat attendees.

It still bemused Honor that there was such fierce competition for places at the Admiral's table. She was quite prepared to take advantage of it to inspire her students to greater heights, but her own Academy experience had been that most middies would go to considerable lengths to avoid being trapped alone with any flag officer. In the infrequent instances in which beings of that exalted rank also taught (which was more common in the RMN than in almost any other navy, but remained vanishingly rare), the old adage about "out of sight, out of mind" operated powerfully in a middy's thought processes. But the jockeying for the relatively low number of slots in the sections Honor had been assigned had been intense from the outset, and that clearly carried over to the winning of her dinner invitations.

Even knowing what they would face after the dishes were cleared away.

She suppressed a fresh grin at the thought. It was unheard of for mere midshipmen to find themselves face-to-face with instructors from the rarified heights of the Advanced Tactical Course. Aside from the middies themselves, Andrea Jaruwalski, a full commander, was the most junior officer in the room, and those hectares of gold braid and gleaming planets and stars had not been invited solely for their dinner conversation. In fact, Lady Harrington's dinner parties were some of the most rugged instances of small group instruction in Saganami Island's history, and the surprising thing was the eagerness she sensed around her as the youngsters braced themselves for what they all knew was about to come.

MacGuiness reappeared to check her cocoa mug, and she smiled up at him.

"I think we're about done, Mac. Please tell Mistress Thorn her dinner was as delicious as always."

"Of course, Your Grace," he murmured.

"And I think we'll move this into the game room," she went on, pushing her chair back and rising. The prosthetic arm still felt heavy and unnatural on her left side after all this time, but it was becoming steadily less so, and her students had grown accustomed to seeing it. They were used to its occasional random twitches during her lectures, but they also seemed to have boned up on the prosthesis enough to know about the software overrides. None of her guests had turned a hair at the obvious mobility limits she'd set for the evening, at any rate, and she suppressed a small chuckle at the thought of their tact as she slipped the arm from its sling long enough to lift Nimitz very carefully with both hands.

His surgery had been even more successful than hers—where simple muscle, bone, and tendon were involved, at least—and he was rapidly regaining the smooth, flowing mobility of old as long-disused muscles built back up. The taste of his simple joy as he regained his full natural range of movement had almost brought tears to Honor's eyes, and she knew how much pleasure he took from *using* that movement. But he shared with her a very deep and even more profound joy in her ability to pick him up with two hands once more, and his muzzle pressed firmly into her left cheek and his purr vibrated into her very bones as she set him properly upon her shoulder once more.

Samantha hopped down to trot beside them, then looked up with a happy, buzzing purr of her own as Jaruwalski stooped and scooped her up.

Honor smiled her thanks at the commander and, followed even here by Andrew LaFollet, led the way into the mansion's enormous game room. It had become the center for her post-dinner confabs, and she'd had some rather different "gaming" equipment moved in. Four compact but complete simulator stations had been constructed, each duplicating a scaled-down command deck. Compact though they were, they put a decided squeeze on the space of any room, even one this size, but none of her guests complained. Those simulators were the real reason for their visit here, and those who'd been here before hurried to claim favorite seats among the chairs and small couches crowded together to make room for the simulators. None of them went anywhere near Honor's personal chair beside the huge stone hearth (which had probably never had a fire on it in its entire existence, given the semitropical climate), but every other place was up for grabs. Not that a midshipman was going to argue with a captain or an admiral who had his or her eye set on a given seat, of course.

"So, Ladies and Gentlemen," she said to the middies after everyone had settled. "Have you given some thought to the point I posed in class?"

There was silence for a moment, then one midshipman raised his hand.

"Yes, Mr. Gillingham? You wished to start the ball rolling?"

"I guess so, Ma'am," Midshipman Gillingham said wryly. His voice was surprisingly deep for someone of his physical age and wiry build, and he spoke with the flattened vowels of a strong Alizon accent.

"Someone has to," Honor agreed, smiling at his tone. "And you get extra points for courage for volunteering so eagerly."

Several of Gillingham's classmates chuckled, and the young man grinned back at her . . . respectfully, of course.

"Thank you, Ma'am," he said. Then his grin faded into a more serious expression and he cleared his throat. "The thing that bothered me just a little, Ma'am," he went on diffidently, "was when you said there's no such thing as a real surprise in combat."

"That's a slight oversimplification," Honor corrected. "What I said was that given modern sensor capabilities, the possibility that anyone can slip one starship into combat range of another undetected is remote. Under those circumstances, 'surprise' usually means not that one opponent truly failed to see what was coming, but rather that she simply misinterpreted what she saw."

"Yes, Ma'am. But what if one side really *doesn't* see it coming?"

Another hand went up, and Honor glanced at its owner.

"Yes, Ms. Hearns? You wanted to add something?"

"Yes, My Lady." No one raised an eyebrow at Hearn's form of address, despite the tradition that any senior officer was simply "Sir" or "Ma'am" to any middy. Knighthoods and peerages were important, but no one expected mere midshipmen to keep who was what straight. The tradition wasn't ironbound, however, and there wasn't a Grayson on Manticore, middy or not, who would have dreamed of addressing Honor by any other title.

"It sounded to me," Hearns continued, "that what you were actually talking about was the need to *generate* a surprise, My Lady. To use deceptive maneuvers or EW or anything else to convince your opponent to see what you *want* him to see until it's too late, sort of like you did with your electronic warfare systems at Fourth Yeltsin."

"That was what I was getting at, yes," Honor said after a brief pause. She could hardly fault Hearns for her choice of example, but her students had a tendency to seek examples from actions in which she'd fought. It wasn't sycophancy—in most cases, at least. It was more a case of their looking for an example which felt "real" to them . . . and one which they knew she could address from first-hand experience.

"And Fourth Yeltsin would certainly be one example of it," she went on. "Another would be *Third* Yeltsin, when Earl White Haven managed to mislead Admiral Parnell about his true strength until after Parnell had accepted action."

"I understand that, Ma'am," Gillingham said. "But at Third Yeltsin, Earl White Haven used his stealth systems and low-powered wedges to keep the Peeps from seeing his additional units at all. They were a surprise because no one on the other side had detected a trace of them until it was too late."

"Not exactly," Honor countered, and looked at Jackson Kriangsak. "Would you care to address that point, Admiral? You were there, after all."

Several midshipmen's eyes widened at that, and they turned to give the portly Kriangsak much closer looks.

"Yes, I was, Your Grace," Kriangsak agreed, managing not to break a smile at the sudden intensity of his audience's regard, and then turned to look at Gillingham.

"What I believe Her Grace is getting at, Mr. Gillingham, is that when the Peeps detected our additional units it was too late for Admiral Parnell to avoid action entirely. But go back and review Earl White Haven's and Admiral D'Orville's after-action reports. For that matter, ONI interviewed Admiral Parnell to get his side of the battle, as well, before he left for Beowulf. If Parnell's account is still classified—it shouldn't be, but there's no telling what the red-tape types have been up to—drop me an e-note and I'll get you cleared for it." Gillingham nodded wordlessly, and Kriangsak shrugged.

"What I believe you'll find from all three sources is that even with the best EW we had, and despite the fact that Admiral Parnell had convincing intelligence to suggest that our forces were far weaker than they actually were, he still correctly identified our extra ships of the wall early enough to avoid a *decisive* action. He was forced to withdraw and suffered heavy losses, but had he been even fifteen or twenty minutes slower in reacting, he would have lost virtually his entire fleet. Personally, I suspect that his faulty intelligence made it even closer than it would otherwise have been. He saw, as is far too often the case, what he *expected* to see. Initially, at least."

"Absolutely," Honor agreed. "But one mark of a superior officer—and Amos Parnell is one of the best tacticians you will ever encounter, make no mistake about that, Ladies and Gentlemen—is her ability to overcome her own expectations. Parnell did that. Too late to avoid suffering a defeat, but much too soon for Earl White Haven to completely envelop him and destroy his forces entirely."

"That's certainly true, Your Grace," Kriangsak said, nodding his head vigorously. "And we tried hard, too. My battlecruiser and her squadron were probably the best placed to get around on his flank, and he avoided us easily. Especially—" the rear admiral grinned wryly "—with the amount of fire a wall of battle can hand out. Which is nothing any battlecruiser squadron ever wants to tangle with."

"All right, Sir, I can see that," Gillingham agreed. "But Earl White Haven clearly *tried* to achieve complete surprise. Are you and Admiral Harrington saying we shouldn't do the same thing?"

His voice and expression were thoughtful, not challenging, and Honor rubbed the tip of her nose while she considered how best to encourage his willingness to question received wisdom while still making her own point.

"What Admiral Kriangsak and I are saying," she said after a moment, "is that it would be a mistake to fall in love with one's own cleverness in attempting to manipulate one's enemy. The most dangerous tactical surprise of all is the one *you* suffer when you suddenly discover that your opponent has seen through your own deception and turned the tables on you. One of the most outstanding examples of that happened near a place called Midway back on Old Earth in the middle of the second century Ante Diaspora. In fact, I'd like you to pull up the Battle of Midway, Admiral Raymond Spruance, Admiral Chester Nimitz, Admiral Chiuchi Nagumo, and Admiral Isoroku Yamamoto on the Tac Department's data base—you'll find them in the historical, wet navy archives—and give me a short analysis of just how the Imperial Japanese Navy fell prey to that overconfidence. And be prepared to share it briefly with the rest of the class, as well, please."

"Yes, Ma'am." Gillingham's respectful response sounded less than thrilled, but that was about the worst anyone could have said. Partly because her pleasant-voiced order came as no surprise—all of

Honor's students quickly discovered her penchant for handing out such individual assignments—but also because she had a reputation for making those assignments *interesting*.

"To continue, however," she went on, "what I wanted to suggest is that while it's always worthwhile to convince your opponent to underestimate you or to misinterpret what she's seen, you should never *rely* on having done that. Work for every advantage you can provide yourself, but base your planning on the assumption that the enemy will make one hundred percent correct deductions from her sensor readings."

"Excuse me, My Lady, but that wasn't what you did at Fourth Yeltsin," Midshipwoman Hearns said quietly. Honor tasted a ripple of surprise from a few of the other middies, seasoned with just a trace of trepidation, at Abigail's polite contradiction, but she only cocked her own head and gazed at the midshipwoman, silently inviting her to continue. "You used EW to disguise your super-dreadnoughts as lighter units in order to draw the enemy into your engagement range," the young woman went on obediently. "Your after-action report, or the part sufficiently declassified for me to access, at least, doesn't say so in so many words, but weren't you really counting on the Peep admiral to see exactly what you wanted him to see?"

"Yes, I suppose I was," Honor said. "On the other hand, my battle plan reflected the fact that I had no choice but to offer action and that my SDs' acceleration was too low to force a close engagement if the Peeps chose to evade. It was imperative to keep the enemy out of powered missile range of the Grayson orbital farms, but it was equally vital to prevent them from simply withdrawing to extreme range and sending their missiles in ballistic at cee-fractional velocities. Under those very special circumstances, I had no choice but to adopt the plan I did. Which, I might add, wasn't a very good one. It was, in fact, a plan of desperation . . . and I wasn't at all certain it was going to work."

Or that any of my ships were going to survive the experience if it did work. Not that I have any intention of worrying the lot of you with that particular aspect of it. Yet.

"But what about the Battle of Cerberus, Ma'am?" Theresa Markovic asked politely. Honor turned her gaze to the red-haired midshipwoman, and Markovic raised one hand, palm uppermost. "You actually came in under reaction thrusters at Cerberus," she said. "And modern sensors or not, the enemy never *did* see you coming until you actually opened fire on them."

"Um." Honor cocked her head. "I wasn't aware my after-action report had been released to the general data base, Ms. Markovic," she observed rather cooly, and smiled inwardly at the young woman's sudden total lack of expression. Then she glanced at Kriangsak. "I see the backdoor into the ATC second-tier tac base is still open."

"Yes, Ma'am. We keep meaning to close it, but we never seem to get around to it," Kriangsak said blandly, and Honor felt a ripple of relief run through the midshipmen at the admiral's calm tone. It was interesting. From their emotions, virtually all of her current guests had discovered and made surreptitious use of the backdoor, and they were obviously relieved that Markovic (and so, by extension, themselves, if *they* got caught) would not be blasted to cinders. That was reasonable enough of them, but she wondered how long it would be before they realized that particular backdoor had been left for a purpose. Although it was moved every year and the modes of access changed each semester, it was always there, and the Academy made careful note of which students were enterprising and interested enough to find it.

"In answer to your question, however," she told Markovic now, "Cerberus is certainly not an example I'd choose as a model for teaching someone how to plan a battle."

"But . . . but it worked perfectly, Ma'am!" Gillingham protested, apparently unaware that to do so confirmed that he, too, had been peeking where he had no official business poking about. "Like Terri said, the Peeps never even saw you, and you wiped out their entire fleet without taking a single hit! I haven't been able to find another battle in the last three or four hundred years where that was true!"

"Then I suggest you take a look at what Citizen Rear Admiral Lester Tourville did to Commodore Yeargin at Adler, Mr. Gillingham," Honor said grimly. "I believe the Board of Inquiry's report is available to all of you in the Department data base. Tourville managed to take our picket commander at least as much by surprise as anything I managed at Cerberus, and pulling it off was a lot harder. Or should have been."

Gillingham's face smoothed into nonexpression at the bite in her voice, and Honor made herself draw a deep breath.

"Not that it was the first time something like that happened to a picket force that ought to have been anticipating attack," she went on. "For example—" She considered the middies, then nodded at a dark-eyed blonde on the couch beside Theodore.

"Ms. Sanmicheli," she said pleasantly. "Since Mr. Gillingham is going to be busy looking into the Battle of Midway for us, I'd appreciate it if *you* would look up the Battle of Savo Island from the same war and compare and contrast what happened to the Western Allies in that battle to what happened to Commodore Yeargin at Adler. And you might also look up the Battle of the Farnham System and look for parallels—and differences—between Savo, Midway, Adler and what happened to Baoyuan Anderman when someone tried a 'sneak attack' on him there."

"Yes, Ma'am," Sanmicheli acknowledged the order, and Honor smiled crookedly at her, then turned back to Gillingham.

"But to return to Cerberus. My method of approach was made possible only by certain very special circumstances no reasonable admiral can expect to encounter. First, I knew exactly where the enemy was likely to translate out of hyper, which let me predict his most likely approach vector for Hell—I mean, Hades. Second, using that information I was able to position my own fleet so that we had Cerberus-A at our backs. And third, Mr. Gillingham, was the fact that no sane fleet commander would even have considered such a maneuver for a moment, which helped immensely in surprising the Peep fleet commander, who, so far as I know, was quite sane. You will find, however," she added dryly, "that while acts of insanity have the advantage of unpredictability, that doesn't normally make them good ideas."

"I realize conditions were unusual, Ma'am." Markovic came to Gillingham's aid—courageously, Honor thought, given how thick and fast the extra assignments had been falling. "But your plan didn't look 'insane' to me. And it certainly worked!"

"Yes, it did. But have you looked past what went right to the appalling number of things that could easily have gone *wrong*?" Honor asked her reasonably.

"Wrong, Ma'am?"

"Very wrong," Honor said, and glanced at Michelle Henke. The two of them had discussed the Cerberus action at some length, and she saw Mike's small smile as they both remembered her horrified reaction to Honor's battle plan. "Captain Henke," Honor said now, "would you care to comment on the potential flaws in my battle plan?"

"Certainly, Your Grace. Respectfully, of course." Amusement bubbled just under the surface of Henke's contralto, and Honor saw her more senior guests exchange smiles of their own. Most of the Navy knew about Honor's friendship with Henke, and Rear Admiral Kriangsak sat back and crossed his legs with a cheerful grin.

"The first and most glaring weakness of Her Grace's battle plan, Ms. Markovic," Henke said calmly, "was that it left no margin at all for error. She effectively drained her reactor mass to zero with a burn of that duration and power. If the enemy *had* detected her approach and maneuvered radically against her, she would have lacked the fuel for more than a few hours of maneuvers under impeller drive. Which means she could easily have found herself completely without power at the moment the enemy closed for the kill . . . and not one of her ships had the fuel reserves to reach another star system if they'd been forced to run for it.

"The next weakness was that her plan counted on the Peeps' sensor techs to be effectively blind. By using thrusters, she avoided the sensors which most tactical officers tend to rely upon—the Peeps' gravitics—but she was mother naked to everything *else* in their sensor suites. In fairness—" Henke's tone turned judicious, her expression serious, though her eyes twinkled at Honor "—it was reasonable enough to at least hope the Peeps, who don't usually maintain as close a sensor watch as we do, wouldn't think to look for her in the first place, but if they had looked, they would have found her.

"In line with the second weakness," the captain continued, "was the fact that even though a reaction thruster approach allowed her to avoid the enemy's gravitics, the plume of ejecta it produced must have been quite spectacular . . . and energetic, and Peep stealth fields, which were what Her Grace had to work with herself, you will recall, aren't as good as ours. Again, Her Grace had taken the precaution of placing herself with the local star at her back. Had she not possessed 'inside information' on Peep movement patterns at Cerberus, she would have been unable to do that, of course. In this case, as she mentioned, she knew her enemy's probable approach vector well in advance, which let her give herself the advantage of attacking 'out of the sun,' as it were. If the enemy had failed to appear where she anticipated him, the entire maneuver would have been out of the question, and I'm certain she had a more, ah, *conventional* fallback plan for that situation. As it was, however, Cerberus-A's emissions were sufficiently powerful to greatly reduce the effectiveness of any sensor looking directly at it, and by the time Her Grace's vector had moved her clear of the star, she'd shut down her thrusters and other active emissions. Nonetheless, the circumstances only made it *difficult* for the Peeps to have picked up her approach; they didn't make it *impossible*, and an alert sensor crew could have given the enemy warning in plenty of time.

"Finally, while I could continue to point out other potential weaknesses, I'll simply add that if the admiral in command of the

Peep task force *had* picked up Her Grace's units, the smart thing to do would have been to pretend he hadn't. Once he'd spotted her, he could have run a track on her with passives alone, and she was coming in without any wedges at all. If he'd timed it right, he could have fired full broadsides of missiles into her, with flight times just too short for her to have gotten her units' wedges up, when all she would have had would have been her countermissiles and laser clusters. Those defenses alone, without sidewalls or wedges for passive interdiction, would never have prevented the destruction of her entire fleet."

Henke paused for a moment, then cocked her head at Honor before she looked back at Gillingham.

"All things considered," the captain told the midshipman judiciously, "Her Grace's plan may not have been the single rashest, most foolhardy, do-or-die, all-or-nothing throw of the dice in the history of the Royal Manticoran—or Grayson—Navy. If it wasn't, however, I have so far failed to find the plan that *was*."

Gillingham and Markovic looked at one another, then blinked and turned their gazes half-fearfully to Honor. But there was no thunder in Honor's expression. In fact, she smiled at the captain before she returned her own attention to Gillingham.

"Captain Henke may have employed just a *little* hyperbole in her analysis, Mr. Gillingham," she said pleasantly. "But not very much. In fact, I adopted that plan because it *was* a 'do-or-die, all-or-nothing' situation. I couldn't disengage and run without abandoning over a hundred thousand people on He—Hades. At the same time, my forces were badly outnumbered, I had only skeleton crews, almost all my personnel were extremely rusty, and we'd had no more than a few days to shake down our captured vessels and begin smoothing off our roughest edges. Any conventional battle plan would inevitably have resulted in the destruction of my own forces in return for light enemy casualties. It was possible I might have been able to trap them between my mobile units and the planet's fixed defenses, but that seemed most unlikely, since I estimated, correctly, as it transpired, that they'd come expressly because they feared the prisoners had managed to take Camp Charon. If that was true, there was no way they would allow themselves to come into effective range of the orbital defenses, which meant I could scarcely hope to 'catch them between' those defenses and my ships. So I used a tactic which was a one-time-only, high-risk–high-return proposition. If it worked—as it did—I should have been able to win the battle quickly and at relatively low cost. If, however, it had *failed*, then, as Captain Henke has so admirably pointed out, the inevitable result would have been the destruction of my entire command. Only the fact that, in my judgment, my entire force would have been destroyed anyway if I failed to win quickly and decisively inspired me to adopt such a risky plan. Or could possibly have justified me in doing so."

There was silence for several moments while she tasted the middies absorbing the starkness of the alternatives she'd just described, and then Markovic cleared her throat.

"I don't suppose we ought to use your Cerberus tactics as a pattern for our own then after all, Ma'am,"she observed diffidently.

"Hardly!" Honor snorted. "And if I should happen to see them turning up in as a response to a test problem, whoever used them will think Captain Henke was downright kind compared to the comments *I'll* make!"

A ripple of laughter ran around the room, but then Gillingham spoke up again, his voice thoughtful.

"So what you seem to be saying, Ma'am, is that at both Fourth Yeltsin and Cerberus, you felt you had no choice but to fight anyway, despite an unfavorable force balance. And because you did, you tried to generate any advantages you could. But while the fact that they worked fully was critical to what happened at Cerberus, the success of your plans didn't depend as heavily on them at Yeltsin because, in a sense, it didn't matter if they worked *completely* there or not. You still had to fight, but at Yeltsin the real problem was simply to get into range in the first place. The balance of firepower was a lot closer to equal once you did get there, and the fact that you were able to fool the Peeps and encourage them to weaken their forces by dividing them was simply gravy, in a way. Is that what you're saying, Ma'am?"

"Pretty much," Honor agreed. She looked around at the other senior officers present and made her selection. "Andrea? You and I discussed this the other day. Would you care to respond to Mr. Gillingham?"

"Of course, Ma'am." It was Jaruwalski's turn to turn a thoughtful expression on Gillingham. "Tactics are an art, Mr. Gillingham," she told him, "not a science. There's no way to absolutely quantify them, no way to define secret formulas for victory. There are rules a good tactician follows, but they aren't absolutely binding on her . . . and certainly not on her opponents! The 'secret' to winning lies, in my opinion, not in trying to manipulate the enemy, but in creating general situations in which you know the available menu of maneuvers and the balance of firepower will favor your force. The concept is really that simple. It's in the *execution* that things get tricky, and the ability to execute effectively is what sets a good tactician apart. But successful execution often depends on knowing when to break the rules—to take, to use an overused phrase, a 'calculated risk'—because you have no choice or because you 'feel' an opportunity." She paused. "Was that about what you'd have said, Ma'am?" she asked Honor.

"In its essentials, certainly," Honor agreed. "But you should always bear in mind," she went on, meeting Gillingham's eyes as she took the thread of the conversation back into her own hand, "that that feel for when to break the rules is not something most of us are issued at birth. It's a talent and an ability we develop first by study, and then by doing, starting with lecture courses like Intro to Tactics, progressing to actual exercises in the simulators, and finally—if we're lucky enough to survive the event—to actual experience in combat. Your instructors at the Academy are here to teach you doctrine and the capabilities of your hardware. We also offer you a distillation of what we consider the best from past military thinkers, from Sun-Tzu to Gustav Anderman, as background, and we'll break down and analyze actual engagements, both from the current war and from wars past. We'll try our very best to teach you what *not* to do, based on the institutional wisdom of the Royal Manticoran Navy. We'll run you through sims in which you'll be everything from the junior officer of the watch on a destroyer in a single-ship duel to the one sitting in the admiral's chair on a superdreadnought flagship in a fleet action, and we'll critique your performance every step of the way.

"If you're wise, you'll listen to everything we tell you and learn from it. But you will also remember this, Ladies and Gentlemen. When it finally comes down to it, when you *are* the officer in the hot seat and the missiles and beams flying straight at you are real, nothing we can possibly teach you will truly matter. Hopefully it will all be there in the back of your mind, as the platform of knowledge you'll need, but what will *matter* will be the decisions you make based on your read of the situation *you actually face*.

"Some of you will not survive those situations."

She let her eyes sweep her youthful audience, tasting their mingled soberness and youthful sense of immortality. That belief in their own invulnerability was inevitable in people so young, she knew. All she could do was try to prepare them for the hideous moment of shock when they felt their own ships' bucking and heaving to the enemy's fire and realized death *could* come for them as easily as for anyone else.

"Even if you do every single thing right, you may find yourself in a situation where all the tactical genius in the universe is insufficient to balance the odds against you," she went on quietly. "It happened to Edward Saganami and Ellen D'Orville, and if it could happen to them, it can certainly happen to any of *us*. Indeed, I suppose I'm living proof that it can, because that was exactly what happened to *Prince Adrian* in Adler.

"But whatever you face, you will have three things to support you. One is the tradition of the Royal Navy—and when you graduate from Saganami Island—" she let her eyes sweep all of the middies once more "—that tradition *will* be yours, whatever the uniform you wear. Listen to it. Strip it down to get rid of all the holodrama heroics and the hagiography and learn what it truly expects of you, and you will have a guide that never fails you. It may get you killed," she smiled wryly, "but it will never leave you trying to guess where your responsibilities lie.

"And the second support you will have will be your own confidence in yourself. In your training, in your hardware, and more importantly, in your people. But most importantly of all, in your own judgment. It won't always be perfect. Sometimes, despite all we can do here at Saganami and in ATC, it will be execrable. But you must have faith in yourself, Ladies and Gentlemen, because *there will be no one else*. You will be it. Your ship, your people, will live or die on the basis of *your* judgments and *your* decisions, and even if you get it all absolutely right, some of them will die anyway."

Her smile had vanished, and her face was stern, almost cold.

"Accept that now, because it *will* happen. The enemy wants to live as badly as you do, and like you, the way for her to do that is to kill the ones trying to kill her. Which will be *you*, Ladies and Gentlemen. You and the people under your command. And I can assure you that there will be nights your dead will haunt you. When you ask yourselves if you could have saved a few more lives if you'd only been faster, or smarter, or more alert. Sometimes the answer will be yes, that you *could* have saved them. But you didn't. You did your best, and you did your job, and so did they, but they're still dead, and whatever the rest of the universe thinks, you will go to your own grave convinced you ought to have done better, should have found the way to keep them alive. Worse, you'll think back to what happened, replay it in your head over and over, with the invaluable benefits of hindsight and all the time in the world to think about the decisions you had only minutes to make at the time, and you'll see *exactly* where you screwed up and let your people die."

She paused, and beside her, Kriangsak and Captain Garrison, the senior simulation programer for ATC, nodded, their faces as still as her own.

"Accept that now," Honor repeated quietly after a moment. "Accept it . . . or find another line of work. And I warn you all now, as Admiral Courvosier, my own Academy mentor, warned me, that even if you think you understand exactly what I'm telling you, you'll discover in the event you weren't really prepared for the guilt. You can't be, not until it's your turn to shoulder it. But that will be the third thing that supports you in battle, Ladies and Gentlemen: the knowledge that your people will die uselessly if you screw up. It's not your job to keep them alive at all costs. It's your job to be certain they don't die for nothing. You owe them that, and they expect it of you, and that need to keep the faith with your people is what will keep your brain working and the orders coming even while the enemy blows your ship apart around you. And if you don't believe it will, then the command chair on the bridge of a Queen's ship is not the proper place for you."

There was complete and utter silence in the game room, and Honor let it hover there for several seconds. Then she leaned back in her chair with a small smile.

"On the other hand, your careers aren't going to consist solely of desperate battles to the death. I assure you that you'll find the odd moment of relaxation and even pleasure in the Queen's uniform—or that of your own worlds' navies," she added, nodding at Hearns and Gillingham. "Unfortunately," she went on, her tone turning droll, "tonight won't be among them."

Another ripple of laughter answered her, and she nodded to Kriangsak.

"Admiral Kriangsak, with Captain Garrison's able assistance, has very kindly constructed a small tactical problem for you, Ladies and Gentlemen," she informed them, and several apprehensive glances flickered towards Kriangsak, who simply smiled benignly. "We'll be dividing into three teams. Admiral Kriangsak will serve as the adviser to one team, Captain Garrison will advise the second, and Captain Thoma—" she nodded to the red-haired woman whose tunic, like Honor's own when she was in uniform, bore the bloodred ribbon of the Manticoran Cross "—will advise the third. Captain Henke and Commander Jaruwalski will play the role of referees and umpire the exercise."

"And you, Your Grace?" Jaruwalski asked, as innocently as if she didn't know already.

"And I, Commander," Honor told her with unconcealed relish,

"will command the op force." One of the midshipmen groaned, and Honor gave them all a wicked smile. "This one is pass–fail, Ladies and Gentlemen. If you still have a ship left at the end, you pass. Otherwise . . ."

She let her voice trail off menacingly, then bestowed another smile upon them.

"And on that note, people, let's be about it!" she told them briskly.

CHAPTER TWENTY-FOUR

"**W**ell *that* certainly went much better. In fact," Scotty Tremaine said judiciously, gazing at the scores for CLAC Squadron Three's latest engineering inspection, "one might even say that it went quite well, mightn't one, Sir Horace?"

"One might," Sir Horace Harkness growled back. "I guess. Sort of."

Unlike the youthful commander, the burly warrant officer's expression was not a happy one. Indeed, an objective observer, if asked to describe it in one word, would have been hard-pressed to choose between disconsolate, surly, or just plain disgusted. The less charitable might even have suggested "petulant."

Despite the fact that the Book said the senior engineer in any LAC wing was supposed to be a commissioned officer, an awful lot of engineers, at both the squadron and wing levels, held warrants rather than commissions. Normally, a warrant was offered to a noncom who, because of his special knowledge or depth of expertise, or because he was needed for duties normally assigned to an officer, had to be placed on a footing of equality with at least the more junior of the commissioned officers with whom he dealt. Warrant officers stood outside the executive line of command, for the WOs might actually be thought of as the non-commissioned equivalent of staff officers. Even the design of their uniforms indicated their unique status, for their tunics were tailored like those of officers, but they carried sleeve stripes (although in silver, not gold) similar to those of petty officers and silver or gold crowns, depending on grade, as collar insignia.

311

In addition, each WO's sleeve carried the insignia of his specialty above the stripes.

A WO-1 was equivalent to a junior-grade lieutenant in a nonline specialty, while a chief warrant officer, or WO-3, like Sir Horace Harkness, was equivalent to a senior-grade lieutenant. A master chief warrant officer, or WO-5, was actually equivalent to a full commander . . . and had reached the highest rate any member of the Navy could attain without a formal commission. Given the basis on which they were offered their warrants in the first place, a WO was usually somewhat older than the average commissioned officer of his equivalent rank. On the other hand, the more youthful commissioned officers who found themselves warrant officers' legal superiors knew those WOs had been given their warrants expressly because they were so good—as in, much better than any wet-behind-the-ears, fresh-out-of-Saganami-Island, young whippersnapper could hope to be, though he might someday approach their abilities, *if* he worked really hard and listened to the voice of experience when it deigned to share its wisdom. As a result, the RMN's warrant officers carried far more clout than most civilian observers would have expected.

Nonetheless, BuPers really had wanted commissioned engineers for any slot above the individual LAC squadron. BuPers, however, had been disappointed, and the reason its desires had never been more than a rather wistful hope was simple enough. The sudden, explosive expansion of the Royal Manticoran Navy's light attack craft strength after decades of steady build down had simply caught the Fleet short of LAC engineers. Severely short, as a matter of fact.

It was certainly true that LACs allowed enormous reductions in manpower on a per-weapon basis as compared to regular, hyper-capable warships. By the same token, however, the manpower they *did* require tended to be more than a bit specialized. Nursemaiding one of the new fission plants, for example, was just as complex a job as running one of the far larger fusion plants aboard a hyper-capable combatant. The engineer running it might have instrumentation that was at least as good, and a lot more (and more sophisticated) remotes, proportionately speaking, but he was still one man, with only a single human assistant, running an entire fission plant, two impeller rooms, environmental, not just two but *three* sets of sidewall generators—four, actually, on the even newer *Ferret*-class LACs—*and* handling all power allocation and repairs (if needed) for at least one revolver missile launcher and magazine, point defense, sensors, ECM, and one humongous graser. The tac officer and captain had similarly outsized workloads, and their remotes and AIs weren't the same as having real live assistants to help spread the burden. To be sure, their instrumentation and computer support set new standards for capability and user-friendliness, but it was still one hell of a load to carry. It was also one which required high and consistent skill levels, since LAC crews were too small to rely on someone else catching a mistake, and the manning requirements for each bird were repeated over a hundred times per wing.

All of which meant the Navy had discovered it had no choice but to reach down into the ranks of its noncoms to find the warm and, especially, competent bodies it needed. At least BuPers had been able to keep up with the demand so far without diluting skill levels, and the shutdown of so many forts should ease much of the pressure shortly. But it hadn't eased it *yet*, and the fact that the petty officers BuPers was tapping for the new slots and offering warrants to tended to be older and more experienced than the commissioned officers junior enough to be assigned to the LACs also offered a useful leavening of seasoned judgment to rein in the youthful exuberance that was part of the emerging "LAC jockey" mentality. That was good, but some of the purists among the commissioned officers deeply resented the sudden mass elevation of senior chiefs, chiefs, and even a few PO 1/cs to fill slots that ought properly to have been filled by lieutenants and lieutenant commanders.

That attitude, in Sir Horace Harkness' considered opinion, was stupid. Actually, he usually appended a few colorful adverbs to his opinion, if only to himself. It was also hurting the acceptance of the new LACs and their carriers—or, at least, the notion that "real" officers should associate with the jumped-up riffraff who crewed them.

The RMN's officer corps, as a whole, was among the most capable in space, but that didn't mean it wasn't riddled with its own careerists. And in those careerists' view, nothing so minor as a war for survival should be allowed to interfere with the appointed unfolding of God's plan for the universe . . . otherwise known as the seniority system. They'd always hated officers like Honor Harrington for their meteoric rises and the way they kept jumping the zone, leapfrogging those ahead of them on the basis of mere achievement and, in the process, pushing back the regular, seniority-based promotions on which any good careerist relied. But now they had something even worse to worry about—a situation in which noncommissioned peons were receiving warrants in job lots in order to occupy slots in which their more deserving (and com-missioned) betters could otherwise have been accruing the seniority which would lead to the promotions they so earnestly desired. Even worse, a lot of those ex-noncom warrant officers were almost certain, eventually, to wind up exchanging the warrants they ought never to have been offered in the first place for regular commis-sions. Not only that, the miserable wretches and their irritating LAC carriers were going to be in the thick of the new offensives, if the tea leaf-readers had gotten it right, which meant they would also be the ones picking up the medals, being mentioned in dis-patches, and generally acquiring all the other career-enhancing benefits of combat experience. (Of course, they would also be getting shot at—a lot—while zipping around in the most fragile warships in the RMN, so perhaps, on more mature consideration, that last point could be considered a wash.)

Among the undeserving souls, who, strictly on the basis of their unfair advantages in experience, training, and ability, had received warrants, however, was a surprisingly large leavening of men and women like Sir Horace Harkness. Individuals who would have been happier to cut their own throats than accept regular commissions. Who'd seen the world of the officers' mess from the outside and much preferred a slot that let them get their hands dirty, tinker with the hardware they loved, and avoid the increasing levels of executive responsibility that were part of the commissioned seniority track. It wasn't that they were afraid of responsibility per se so much as that they preferred to remain with the type of respon-sibility they understood and stay well clear of the threat of ever commanding an entire starship and finding themselves in the hot seat, responsible for hundreds or even thousands of other lives, when it all fell into the crapper.

Sir Horace Harkness had many friends among that particular group of individuals, including one Warrant Officer Scooter Smith. WO-1 Smith had been only a petty officer first before the Second Battle of Hancock, and he was considerably younger than Harkness, but he was also very good at his job. Which was the problem. Smith's ability and willingness to dig in and heave when the going got rough accounted for how much Harkness liked him. Those same qualities, however, also helped explain how Captain Ashford's wing readiness rate had just edged Harkness' by exactly three per-centage points. Which meant *Incubus* had won the competition Admiral Truman had organized to see which LAC-carrier would be the senior ship of CLAC Squadron Three. Ashford's seniority to Tremaine had given his ship the inside track for the job, but

Hydra's captain was senior to *Incubus'* by over six T-months. Had *Hydra*'s wing—which meant Sir Horace Harkness' wing—aced the competition, Admiral Truman might well have decided (as the outraged traditionalists insisted she ought) to go on the basis of the seniority of the two CLACs' skippers rather than that of the commanders of the LAC *wings*.

"Oh, come on, Chief!" That was another thing that tended to confuse outsiders to whom the Navy's inexplicable customs remained a foreign language. There were chief warrant officers, and there were chief *petty* officers. Properly speaking, a CWO was always addressed as "Chief Warrant Officer" and a CPO was addressed as "Chief Petty Officer" or "CPO" to avoid confusion. In fact, the Navy tended to be much more informal in practice. Besides, Harkness would always be "the Chief" to Scotty Tremaine, and although Captain Adib, *Hydra*'s CO, was known as a stickler for correct etiquette, not even she would have protested in this very special case.

"Stew and Scooter beat us fair and square . . . and *we* beat everyone else!"

"They don't give out anywhere near the same prizes for secondbest, Sir," Harkness grumbled, "and if that beta node on Twenty-Six just hadn't—"

He made himself stop and breathe deeply, then grinned at his youthful boss.

"All right, Skipper. Guess I was venting just a bit much. But it really frosted me to lose over a component that passed every preinspection test and was supposed to have another three thousand hours on its clock! I swear, I think Scooter *bribed* the damned thing to fail just when it did."

"That, Sir Horace, is because you are a devious and unscrupulous soul. I, on the other hand, as the trusting, honest, and open sort I am, rather doubt Mr. Smith would stoop so low. And even if he would have stooped so low—which," Tremaine admitted thoughtfully, "upon more mature consideration, I don't suppose we can *quite* rule out—I don't see how he could have pulled it off. Besides, we're still the senior ship for Division Two, and that's nothing to sneeze at!"

"No, Sir, it isn't." Harkness gazed at the results for one more second, then shook his head and turned away with an air of resolution. "And now that that's outta the way," he went on more crisply, "what do you want me to tell Commander Roden?"

"I don't know." Tremaine rubbed his nose in a gesture uncannily like one Harkness had seen scores of time from Lady

Harrington. "I can't fault his eagerness, but I'm not sure what Dame Alice would think of the idea. Or if this is the right time to be tinkering with it in the first place."

"Never gonna know if we don't ask, Sir," Harkness pointed out reasonably. Then he cocked his head. "You want me to write up a proposal?"

Tremaine's eyebrows rose. Harkness must feel pretty strongly about Roden's suggestion if he was actually volunteering to write a proposal which he knew was certain to end up on at least one flag officer's desk. And which, under the circumstances, might go all the way up the chain to Vice Admiral Adcock, the Fourth Space Lord, at the head of the Bureau of Weapons.

And he may have a point, Tremaine mused. *Besides, I sort of think I may be waffling because of the rarified heights to which any such suggestion is likely to ascend.*

He grinned at the thought, then folded his arms and leaned back against the bulkhead while he replayed the idea once more.

At twenty-seven, Lieutenant Commander Robert Roden was even younger for his rank than Scotty Tremaine. And he didn't exactly look like an HD writer's concept of the steely-eyed, courageous warrior, either. He was a bit on the plump side, stood just under a hundred and seventy-six centimeters, and wore his dirty-blond hair quite a bit on the long and shaggy side by current RMN standards. Thanks to the fact that he was third-generation prolong, he looked a lot like a pre-prolong sixteen-year-old, and his guileless eyes and innocent expression contributed to an impression of youthful diffidence.

Appearances, however, could be deceiving, which was how Lieutenant Commander Roden had come to command the 1906th LAC Squadron, the sixth squadron of Tremaine's own Nineteenth LAC Wing.

The organizational structure of the new carrier forces had been worked out by Alice Truman and Captain Harmon, and its nomenclature sounded a bit odd to those accustomed to traditional Navy designations. The number designator of each wing matched that of its mother ship. Hence the wing assigned to CLAC-19, HMS *Hydra,* was the Nineteenth Wing. In turn, each LAC squadron was numbered to indicate both its parent wing and its own place within the wing, which meant that Roden's squadron, the sixth of the nine squadrons *Hydra* carried, was designated the 1906th. Orderly as the system was, it resulted in squadron numbers which seemed preposterously high to people accustomed to numbering squadrons of *starships* rather than sublight parasites, but it got even worse, because a LAC's hull number was based on its slot in its wing, not on the original builder's number by which BuShips tracked its maintenance and service history, and was subject to change whenever the vessel was reassigned. For example, Tremaine's own *Shrike-B* was officially LAC-1901, indicating that it was the number-one LAC of the Nineteenth Wing. Roden's personal bird, on the other hand, was LAC-1961, and the last unit of the 1909th Squadron was LAC-19108. The system broke down just a bit at the very end, because the twelve spare LACs aboard each carrier *were* designated by their builder's numbers until they were put on-line to replace one of the birds from the regular squadrons . . . at which point they assumed the number of the LAC for which they were substituting. The full number of any LAC was too cumbersome (and, with so many digits, too likely to be misheard or misunderstood in the heat of combat) so each bird was also assigned a call sign: *Hydra One* in the case of Tremaine's own ship, since he was both *Hydra*'s COLAC and skipper of the 1901st LAC Squadron, and *Hydra Six* in the case of Roden's ship. The other units were assigned alpha designators within their squadrons to build their call signs, so that the second ship of the 1906th was *Hydra Six Alpha* to the controllers, while the third was *Hydra Six Beta*, and so on.

Of course the LAC crews were a bit less formal in the unofficial names they assigned their ships. In *Hydra One*'s case, Harkness' bid to immortalize his wife, Sergeant-Major Iris Babcock, by naming the vessel the *Iris B* had come to naught—not without vigorous campaigning and a certain degree of somewhat threatening moral persuasion on his part. Instead, Ensign Audrey Pyne's nomination had carried the day. Ensign Pyne, Tremaine's tac officer, was a bit of a romantic and a pronounced history nut, and she'd dug back into Old Terran history in search of ancient parallels to her new duty slot. Like Jackie Harmon, she'd found inspiration in the fragile, old-fashioned, downright quaint pure air-breathers of the last two centuries Ante Diaspora, and it was largely thanks to her efforts that the Nineteenth Wing had begun a new tradition, already spreading to the other wings (with Admiral Truman's support, despite the disapproval of certain other senior officers), of embellishing their LACs with distinctive "nose art." She was also something of an optimist, and her crewmates had decided her suggested name—*Bad Penny*—carried hopeful connotations which certainly ought to be encouraged. Lieutenant Commander Roden's crew, on the other hand, had opted for the rather more colorful suggestion of its engineer, PO 1/c Bolgeo, and decided to go with *Cutthroat*.

At the moment, however, what mattered more than the internal organization of the RMN's LAC force was what Roden and Bolgeo had come up with.

The original *Shrike*-class LACs had suffered from the fact that they were still an experimental design. The concept's basic soundness had been demonstrated conclusively at Second Hancock, but it would have been remarkable if their first battle hadn't demonstrated a certain number of flaws in the initial execution.

The worst weakness had been the absence of any after-point defense. The ability of the new LACs' missiles to accept radically off-bore firing solutions theoretically let countermissiles fired from their bow-mounted launchers cover most of their rear threat arc. But *only* in theory, because the designers had been overconfident. They had assumed that *Shrikes* would be such elusive targets that "overs" would be unable to attack from astern, and, in order to save mass and internal volume, they'd included no countermissile control links to guide long-range intercepts, and CM sensors were too myopic to do the job without the links. That had been bad enough, but even worse, perhaps, they had also failed to provide aft-firing laser clusters for close-in defense . . . and their assumptions had proven far too optimistic. Most of the *Shrikes* lost at Second Hancock had, in fact, been killed by "up-the-kilt" laser head snap shots at close range—exactly the sort of attack the designers had believed would be impossible. But while the firing solutions for that sort of attack against something as small and agile as a *Shrike* were, indeed, difficult to generate, the odds of success were much better than prebattle analyses had projected, and it took only a single one of them to kill an LAC.

BuWeaps' and BuShips' response had been the *Shrike-B*, which exchanged the original *Shrike*'s internal hangar for its own small cutter/lifeboat for four more countermissile launchers, a half dozen fire control links, and six more laser clusters designed to cover its stern. In addition, total countermissile magazine space had risen from fifty-two to one hundred, evenly divided fore and aft. Unlike larger, hyper-capable ships, the *Shrike-Bs* lacked transfer tubes, so each point defense battery had its own magazine, and the forward launchers could not use the after-launchers' birds or vice versa. That was a fairly minor concern, however, and all of the sims (whose parameters had been heavily updated on the basis of actual combat experience at Hancock) indicated that the new LACs would be considerably more survivable than the original *Shrike*.

In addition, however, Vice Admiral Adcock's BuWeaps was finally getting the entire Ghost Rider missile and drone family into full production. Because Ghost Rider's components had initially been conceived of as something to be carried only by hyper-capable combatants, BuWeaps had faced a severe challenge in engineering the same capabilities into something a LAC could carry, but they'd met it. The LAC-sized specialist missiles and drones were less capable than the full-sized versions, but the LACs were also far harder for enemy fire control to lock up in the first place, so the trade-off in *effectiveness* was virtually a dead heat. Where the LACs came up shortest was that they didn't have much internal capacity for *any* missiles, and each electronic warfare bird they carried was one less shipkiller they could have fitted in.

BuShips' solution, designed in close cooperation with BuWeaps, was the *Ferret*-class LAC. The *Ferrets* dropped all offensive energy armament to provide the maximum hull volume for missile magazines and an even more powerful electronic warfare suite. The enormous squeeze the *Shrikes'* massive graser put on their internal volume was obvious when the missile numbers on the *Shrike-B*—twenty shipkillers and a hundred countermissiles—were compared to the same numbers for the *Ferret:* fifty-six shipkillers and no less than one hundred and fifty countermissiles. That was particularly impressive given that EW volume requirements had grown by over twelve percent at the same time.

Doctrine called for the *Ferrets* to operate in a support role for the *Shrike-Bs* in alpha strikes on heavy warships. Against light combatants or merchantmen, the *Ferret* would be lethal from well outside the *Shrike-B's* energy-attack range, but LAC-sized missiles would be much less effective against anything bigger than a heavy cruiser. Against heavy units, the *Ferret's* job was to accompany the *Shrike-B* to provide EW support and as an antimissile escort, relying on its heavy countermissile load for active intercepts, and with its main magazines stuffed with electronic warfare birds rather than with shipkillers. Each LAC wing was assigned two squadrons of the missile boats, and despite a certain initial skepticism, the "Bird Boats" of the missile squadrons had quickly earned the respect of anyone who exercised with them. Or against them.

But the *Ferrets* also had one more innovation which the *Shrike-Bs* lacked. Because they had no offensive energy armament, it would have been foolish for them to accompany the graser-armed LACs all the way in on an alpha strike, so doctrine called for them to break off before the strike entered the enemy's point-blank energy range. That protected them from the fury of heavy shipboard lasers and grasers to which they could not reply, but it also meant enemy missiles were far more likely to get a clean shot at their after-aspects as they broke off and away. Accordingly, BuShips had used the last scraps of the internal volume freed by removing the graser to shoehorn in an additional sidewall generator. Just as powerful as the new "bow-wall" that closed off and protected the front of a *Shrike*'s wedge as it bored into energy range, the *Ferret*'s "stern-wall" closed off the rear of the wedge. Power requirements and the physics of the wedge meant only one aspect, bow or stern, could be closed at any given moment, but it gave a *Ferret*'s skipper a much more flexible choice of breakaway vectors.

What Roden and Bolgeo wanted to do was build the same capability into a *Shrike-B*. BuShips had already considered the possibility and pronounced against it because the designers had no more internal volume to work with. They couldn't put the additional generator *in* without taking something else *out*, and they were disinclined to start pulling the additional systems BuWeaps had just bullied them into putting in in the first place.

They were no doubt correct about that, but Roden and Bolgeo had a notion of their own. They were both natives of Liberty Crossing on Gryphon, and until Bolgeo went into the Navy, ten years before Roden headed for Saganami Island, he and Roden's older brother had spent most of their free time in the machine shop of Bolgeo's engineer father. They'd done a lot of tinkering with spacegoing hardware, and Bolgeo had come up with an interesting solution to BuShips' objections. If the generator wouldn't fit inside the hull, why not mount it *out*side?

Personally, Tremaine was a bit surprised Roden and his crew had been able to find time to even consider such an original approach. The new LAC wings had already demonstrated a propensity for attracting the oddballs and the colorful (himself excluded, of course), but *Cutthroat*'s crew was more offbeat than many. Bolgeo, *Cutthroat*'s engineer, for example, had a record almost as distinguished as Horace Harkness' had been in his more adventuresome days. Then there was PO 2/c Mark Paulk, *Cutthroat*'s helmsman. Paulk had a well-deserved reputation as a hot pilot . . . and he'd once been a chief petty officer before a certain incident involving an admiral's pinnace, a pair of young ladies of negotiable virtue, and a case of really good Hadrian's World scotch. *Cutthroat*'s astrogator, Lieutenant (jg) Kerry Gilley, was younger than the others, but old in sin, with eyes which tried (generally unsuccessfully) to look innocent as the newborn day . . . as they had the day after he and CPO Paulk had taken the admiral's pinnace for its unauthorized spin. There were PO Sam Smith and his buddy PO Gary Shelton, *Cutthroat*'s electronics warfare specialist and com officer respectively. Both of them were lifers—Smith had over thirty-six T-years in, and Shelton wasn't far behind—and there were persistent rumors that before the war, they had made themselves very helpful to Logistics Command in the disposal of redundant electronics. Of course, LogCom hadn't *known* the parts were redundant, but that was only because Smith and Shelton hadn't wanted to bother the Navy by cluttering up the proper channels with the paperwork on them. Or the profit from their disposal.

The rest of *Cutthroat*'s crew were almost mundane in comparison. Lieutenant (jg) Olivia Cukor, the LAC's sensor officer, and Lieutenant Kirios Steinbach, the executive officer, actually didn't have a single blemish on their records. How long that would remain true, given the company they were now keeping, remained anyone's guess, of course. PO 3/c Luke Thiele, the assistant engineer, was too brand, squeaky new to have earned the same reputation as his older crewmates, but the way he followed Bolgeo around with puppylike devotion boded ill for his future record. As for the final member of the crew, Lieutenant Joe Buckley, the tac officer, the jury was still out. He was very good at his job, and had demonstrated a positive genius for tweaking and modifying his weapon systems' software, but the consensus in the squadron was that he could not possibly be as innocent as his earnest expression and manner seemed to indicate. He was, after all, assigned to *Cutthroat*, and everyone knew what *that* meant.

Actually, Tremaine admitted to himself with an inner smile, Roden had managed to hammer his personal collection of misfits into exactly the sort of "LAC jocks" Captain Harmon had envisioned. Their record in sims and drills was second to none, *Cutthroat*'s engineering readiness was the second best in the wing, and they had that swaggering confidence, verging on arrogance, which was the mark of an elite small-craft crew. Indeed, Tremaine was often bemused by how well they performed, since they never seemed to have the time to waste on things like practice. That would have dragged them away from their true passion, for the lot of them seemed addicted to cards, and particularly to the ancient game of spades, which they played with special fervor and bloodthirstiness. As a rule, they seemed to resent the intrusion of anything so ephemeral as an interstellar war on *important* things like setting the high-bidder in a hand of cutthroat, and Bolgeo and Paulk, the two who'd actually come up with the idea for locating the sternwall generator, were the worst of the lot.

Of course, it *was* an . . . offbeat approach, which was probably no more than was to be expected of those two. Indeed, it was hardly surprising that the more orthodox thinkers at BuShips had never considered such an *outré* notion, no matter how much sense it made once someone actually suggested it.

Sidewall generators were too fragile and too valuable to expose to damage. Everyone knew they *had* to be put safely behind armor, where a freak hit would be less likely to destroy them and open a deadly chink in a warship's defenses. That meant they always went inside the hull, since the armor, by definition, was on the *outside* of the hull. But as Bolgeo, Paulk, and Roden pointed out, a LAC *had* no armor. There was no point in it, since no one could armor a ship that small to stand up against heavy weapons fire while still having the internal volume to carry a worthwhile weapons load of its own. So if there was no armor to put the generator behind in the first place, there was no logical requirement to put the generator inside the ship, either.

Harkness and Tremaine had checked their numbers, and it certainly looked as if the three of them were on to something. The problem of interference with the after beta nodes would require some careful number crunching, but it was the matter of power supply which seemed likely to pose the real difficulties. Nice as the new LACs' fission plants were, they simply couldn't produce the power out of current generating capacity for everything that had to be done in the heat of combat . . . especially in a *Shrike* or *Shrike-B*, with its battlecruiser-sized graser mount. The bow-wall, like the graser itself, was actually fed from a massive superconductor capacitor, and one of the flight engineer's jobs was to see to it that any of his pile's output not being used for anything else was diverted into maintaining the charge on the capacitors. To make the sternwall work, one of the other capacitors would have to be tapped (with the potential for draining it doing one job just at the moment it was urgently needed for its originally intended purpose), or else yet another dedicated capacitor of its own would have to be crammed into (or *onto*, possibly) a hull that was already packed like an e-rat can.

"They really think they've got the node interference and wedge deformation problems solved?" Tremaine asked Harkness finally.

"Tim says so," the warrant officer replied, and shrugged. "He's the one with the hands-on experience. Commander Roden's more into the theory and enthusiasm, but Tim's the one who's run up the actual schematics, and he says he's confident."

"Um." Tremaine rubbed his nose again. "And the power feeds?"

"They're talking about running two taps, one to the graser ring and one to the ring for the bow-wall. That way they could siphon off power from either of them and balance the load rather than have to choose between draining one of the other systems completely or doing without the sternwall."

"Or they could end up draining *two* critical systems."

"Yep." Harkness nodded, then shrugged. "Other way to look at it, though, Skip, is that if the shit's so deep they're draining both the other capacitors just trying to cover their asses while they bug the hell out, it ain't real likely they're gonna need any power for *offensive* action, now is it?"

"You could just have a point there, Chief." Tremaine thought another moment, then shrugged. "All right. Go find Bolgeo, and tell him to round up Roden and Paulk. I want to talk to all three of them and go over their numbers in person. After that, I'll write up the memo and route it to Captain Adib and Admiral Truman. In the meantime, I'll authorize you and Bolgeo to start building the thing out of the wing's own resources."

"Good enough," Harkness said with obvious satisfaction, then grinned. "You know, Sir, I think the thing I may like best about this job is the machine shops. I got all those gorgeous new toys to play with, and the Navy actually *pays* me to do it! It don't get a lot better than that, Skipper."

"If you're happy, *I'm* happy, Chief," Tremaine told him expansively. "Just don't get too carried away. This monster of Roden and Bolgeo's isn't going to be cheap, and if it doesn't work, I'm going to have a real hard time explaining to the LogCom people where all the parts for it went."

"Don't worry, Sir. If I build the thing, it'll damned well work. And if it don't, I'll personally take Bolgeo's spades' deck away from him until he *makes* it work!"

CHAPTER TWENTY-FIVE

"**A**nd it's been one thing after another for months now," the slender, dark-faced woman on the display groused. "We're *still* catching flak from the attack on Zanzibar. The Caliph's ambassador was in here just yesterday to see Dame Elaine and press for 'clarification' on the status of the reinforced picket. Which really meant he wanted her to swear a blood oath to leave it there forever. Which she couldn't, of course. They needed to talk directly to the Earl, not to one of the permanent undersecretaries. And even if Dame Elaine had the authority to make official policy commitments, the Duke's made it clear to everyone in the Alliance that something like that is a military decision, which means Ambassador Makarem ought to have one of his attachés sounding out *your* bosses' staff over at Admiralty House, not us!"

Rear Admiral Aristides Trikoupis, GSN (who had been a captain junior-grade in the Royal Manticoran Navy just over three years before) reclined on the couch in the admiral's day cabin aboard GNS *Isaiah MacKenzie* and wiggled his sock toes in shameless luxury as he viewed the letter from his wife. Mirdula Trikoupis was a senior-level member of the Foreign Office's permanent staff, and the expression on her lively face was just a tad on the disgusted side.

"And then certain individuals who shall remain nameless started trying to pressure us for details of privileged communications between the Earl and the Graysons—and hinting at all sorts of dire consequences the next time the government changes hands if we didn't cough up what they wanted!" She grimaced with more than a hint of true anger. "I swear, Aristides, sometimes I want to run out into the street and strangle the next three politicians I meet with my bare hands!"

Trikoupis chuckled aloud at that. Not because he didn't share her longing to permanently remove certain of those "nameless" individuals—*I wonder if they were staffers for High Ridge, New Kiev, or Descroix? Had to be one of them*—but at the image that flashed through his brain. Unlike most of the Manticoran officers on loan to the Grayson Space Navy, Trikoupis, at just a hair over a hundred and seventy centimeters, did not tower over the native Graysons of his crews . . . but he looked downright tall next to his diminutive wife. Mirdula was fourteen centimeters shorter than he was, and the thought of her strangling politicians—preferably one with each hand, simultaneously, while holding their toes well clear of the ground—appealed mightily to him.

Strictly speaking, Mirdula had no business sharing that sort of information with anyone outside her office, but she'd been careful to use their private encryption (which was supplied by the Foreign Office), and her letters to him traveled only aboard high-security Navy courier boats. Besides, he'd spent three prewar years as a naval attaché on Haven, and his Foreign Office and ONI clearances remained in force. Still, he made a mental note to suggest that she might want to tone down the inside info in her next letter.

"I really don't know how the Earl puts up with it, even with us to run interference for him," Mirdula went on more seriously. "I suppose he must be used to projecting a pleasant mood even when he wants to shoot people. And he has to be used to people trying to buttonhole him for personal favors, too; he *is* the Queen's uncle, after all. But this place has been a madhouse, and he and Lord Alexander are taking the brunt of it."

Trikoupis grunted, his humor souring as he contemplated the truth of yet another of his wife's observations. His Grayson commission had taken him out of the mainstream of the Star Kingdom's political life, but Mirdula's insights and a thoughtful study of the 'faxes (plus the analyses Grayson Naval Intelligence circulated to its senior officers) kept him abreast of what was happening, and he didn't like some of what he was hearing.

Trikoupis had met Countess New Kiev during his stint assigned to the FO, and he hadn't much enjoyed the experience. He was willing to accept that she held her beliefs sincerely, and honest enough to admit he'd met Centrists and Crown Loyalists who were just as officious and nearly as strident. But her towering faith in her own rectitude was so sublime as to elevate her to a status all her own. No doubt the fact that he shared so little of her view of the universe made it seem even worse, but she reminded him irresistibly of the witch-hunters of ancient Terra who had dragged their victims out, tortured them into confessing, then burned them alive . . . all strictly for the good of the sinners' immortal souls. The Countess had that same zealous streak, and she was just as determined to do what was "best" for people whether they wanted it done for—or *to*—them or not.

Given the uproar over the Peeps' resumption of the offensive, it was probably inevitable for New Kiev and her allies to gain more credence with the electorate. Less because they'd done anything right where the war was concerned (because even the stupidest voter knew they hadn't), but because they led the opposition to the government on whose watch things had gone *wrong*. Human nature's desire to find someone upon whom to blame disasters had operated faithfully and efficiently . . . and in their favor.

Much of the furor had faded when the Peeps failed to follow up with more deep raids, and Duchess Harrington escaped from Cerberus. But the public wanted the Navy to do more than just *stop* the Peeps. It wanted the Navy to resume the offensive—without running any risks, of course, or exposing any more core systems to attack—and push the Peeps back where they belonged so the Allies could end the war once and for all. Worse, the military budgets were beginning to bite truly deep, and the taxpayers who felt that bite failed to understand that their increased tax burden was actually a good sign.

Trikoupis switched off the viewer, puffed his cheeks, and swung into a sitting position. This was his third time through Mirdula's letter, and he knew he'd view it several more times before he recorded his response. Just at the moment, though, the direction of his own thoughts had soured his enjoyment of it, and he rose to pace, still in his sock feet, on the carpet covering his day cabin's decksole.

Isaiah MacKenzie (known to her crew as *Izzie* when they figured no spies from the Office of Shipbuilding might overhear) was part of the taxpayers' pain, although the taxpayers in her case were Graysons and not Manticorans. Despite an exponential increase in effective firepower, *Izzie* actually had only about forty percent as much crew as her older consorts, thanks to the sophistication of her automation, and the same trend towards lower crew numbers obtained across the board in all the new classes being designed by BuShips and the Grayson Office of Shipbuilding. Trikoupis rather doubted that the average Manticoran civilian would have understood what that meant even if the Government had been in a position to share such sensitive information with anyone. But what they did know about the Navy's new ships was quite simple enough for the voters to grasp: they cost a lot.

But there was more to it than that. In fact, there was a great deal more to it, and Trikoupis wished it were possible to tell the people paying for the new designs just how much they were actually getting for their money.

The most obvious advantage of the new designs—and especially the SD(P)s, as the new *Harrington/Medusa* class was being designated—was a huge increase in offensive capability. Whether or not the new defensive systems could match that increase remained to be seen, but until the Peeps had equivalently armed classes, that hardly mattered. Trikoupis had commanded Battle Division Sixty-Two from the *Izzie* for over a T-year now and run innumerable exercises with her and her division mate, GNS *Edward Esterhaus*, so he knew exactly how devastating the Peeps were going to find her and her sisters once the new class was employed en masse.

Perhaps even more important than the increase in offensive power was the huge *decrease* in crew requirements. With one exception, the bottleneck for the RMN's expansion had always been more about manpower than the cost of hulls. That exception had been the Junction forts in the Manticore Binary System itself, where a large number of units had been a strategic necessity, whatever the cost. That commitment *had* put a squeeze on available peace-time funding, and manning the forts had only made the personnel problems worse. But the capture of Trevor's Star had alleviated that particular requirement, and two-thirds of the forts had been transferred from active to reserve status. Even with the need to fortify the Basilisk and Trevor's Star ends of the Junction, that had still released enough personnel to man a hundred and fifty *old-style* SDs. With the new automation, that gave the Navy the manpower for almost *two* hundred and fifty, which was a third again more than the RMN's entire prewar superdreadnought strength.

The junction fortress reduction was the most enormous windfall BuPers had ever experienced, and while the new LAC wings about which Trikoupis had heard endless rumors seemed to be skimming off a lot of junior officers and senior noncoms, the vast bulk of that manpower pool remained untouched. Which meant that for the first time since Roger III had begun his Navy's buildup against the Peep threat, the RMN literally had the crews to man as many vessels as it could physically build.

And it was building a lot of them.

No one had experienced a true revolution in naval design or weaponry in over half a millennium, and the sheer expense of carrying one through in the midst of a shooting war was enough to stagger the most avid militarist. According to Trikoupis' latest classified briefing on the subject, the Navy had close to two hundred new ships of the wall under construction simultaneously. At roughly thirty-five billion a pop, that came to the tidy sum of seven *trillion* Manticoran dollars, and that was an enormous bite out of anyone's budget. Nor did it include the price tag on all the escorts those ships would require, or the new carriers (and the LACs to go on them), or the new missiles, or the R&D to support all of the above.

The Cromarty Government had borrowed heavily, and the Star Kingdom's record of stable financial growth, coupled with how well the Allied navies had done up until the Basilisk Raid, had helped sell a lot of bonds in places like the Solarian League. Increased Junction use fees had also helped, but ultimately there'd been no choice but to raise taxes. More, for the first time in the Star Kingdom's history, Parliament had, with much trepidation, adopted a graduated income tax rather than the Constitutionally-mandated flat rate. The new tax would automatically expire at the next general election or within five years, whichever came first, but it had still come as a profound shock to the taxpayers and sent a massive ripple through the financial and investment markets, and there were sinister signs of a steadily rising inflation rate, all coupled with a far more intense, government-imposed rationalization of the entire industrial sector.

Trikoupis could scarcely blame the electorate for its dismay. The Star Kingdom had gotten by without such measures for almost five T-centuries, and experiencing them now seemed like a reversion to the Dark Ages of the last century or two Ante Diaspora. Or, even worse, to the ruinous policies which had transformed the once prosperous Republic of Haven into an interstellar appetite that could never be sated.

And New Kiev, North Hollow, High Ridge, and Lady Descroix had all voted for the new taxes out of "patriotic duty." Of course, they'd done so only with profound, eloquently expressed personal reservations, and only because the Cromarty Government had assured them it was essential to ultimate victory. They'd made certain the electorate *knew* how reluctant they'd been . . . and how Lord Alexander, Cromarty's Chancellor of the Exchequer, had twisted their arms to make them cooperate. Which had been shrewd of them, Trikoupis acknowledged. Not nice, but certainly effective. They'd not only garnered the benefits of having put aside their own agendas in the interest of the Star Kingdom's security in a time of emergency, but managed to stick the Cromarty Government with full responsibility for imposing such a painful burden. And they'd taken great care, throughout the process, to never, ever mention the fact that the new ships coming off the ways would win the damned war and so, ultimately, get the entire Alliance out from under its crushing economic burden.

At the moment, the three most unpopular men in the entire Star Kingdom were probably Cromarty, William Alexander, and the Earl of Gold Peak. They were the senior members of the government, and so the inevitable targets of public resentment and unhappiness. Given the Queen's unflinching, iron support for her senior ministers, there was little the Opposition could do in the short term to capitalize on that unhappiness, and Trikoupis hoped fervently that the anticipated turn in the war's military momentum would hurry up and arrive. Once the Allies were again winning victories, a lot of the—

His thoughts chopped off as his com terminal sounded the strident, two-toned warble of an emergency message, and he reached the acceptance key in two strides.

"Yes?" he said sharply, even as the display lit.

"Sensor One reports unidentified hyper footprints at nineteen light-minutes from Zelda, bearing one-one-seven, zero-one-niner true, Admiral." Captain Jason Haskins, *Isaiah MacKenzie*'s skipper, was grim-mouthed, and his normally soft Grayson accent was crisp, almost staccato. "Admiral Malone has ordered the task force to readiness state one. The FTL buoys make it at least thirty-five of the wall, Sir."

"Not just a raid this time, I see," Trikoupis said much more calmly than he felt.

"I think that's probably a safe assumption, Sir." Haskins' tight mouth relaxed into a quirky grin for just a moment. "They're headed in-system now at three hundred and twenty gravities, which suggests they're heavy with pods. Current velocity is thirty-five hundred KPS, so assuming a zero-zero intercept with the planet, a least-time course would make it just over five and a half hours with turnover at two-point-six hours—call it a hundred and fifty-six minutes. Except that I doubt that's what they have in mind."

"I share your doubts." Trikoupis' tone was wry, and he gave a small grin of his own. The planet Zelda was the Elric System's only more-or-less (and rather less than more) habitable planet. It had a thoroughly unpleasant atmosphere: dank, muggy, and heavily flavored with volcanic outgassing. As if that weren't enough, Zelda was home to a microscopic, airborne plant that contributed to the fuzziness of planetary vistas, added its own piquant flavor to the methane, sulfur, and other objectionable smells of Zelda's many volcanoes, and generally clogged up every air filter in sight, including the human lung. And, as a sort of *pièce de resistance*, the planet had an axial inclination even more extreme than Manticore-B's Gryphon, which produced a seasonal climate shift which had to be seen to be believed.

It was, in short, one of the most worthless pieces of real estate Aristides Trikoupis had seen in his entire life. Its sole value was that its marginally breathable atmosphere had made it a logical place for the Star Kingdom's engineers to camp while they built (as quickly as possible, considering the incentives) the much nicer orbital habitats to which they had moved as soon as humanly possible. And since their superiors had decided they had to use Zelda as their local support base while they built the habitats, they'd also used the planet as the gravitational anchor for the Alliance's presence in Elric.

Some people might have questioned that decision, since it put the smelters and repair yards so far from the asteroid belt which was the source of their raw materials, but it actually made a sort of sense—militarily, if not necessarily economically. By putting their bases well inside the hyper limit, the Allies had ensured plenty of warning time if anyone came calling with hostile intent. In this case, for example, the picket had five and a half hours of response time before the bogies (whoever and whatever they were) could reach the base structure. And Elric Station wasn't really all that important in terms of its support facilities, anyway. The RMN had established the station only to fill a hole in the outworks of the far more important satellite yard at Grendelsbane. Squarely between Treadway and Solway, two of the forward bases the RMN had taken from the Peeps early in the war, it helped cover the approaches to Grendelsbane by supporting a "picket force" large enough to pose a threat to the rear of any raiding force.

But thirty-five ships of the wall was a bit more of a raiding force than the planners had intended Elric to stand off, even with Trikoupis' *Harringtons* in support. Which meant the Alliance was about to lose yet another system to the Peeps.

The thought was not a palatable one, but it was hardly unexpected. No one had ever expected Elric to resist a major attack, and Trikoupis knew Admiral Malone's instructions were clear. He'd even surmised the strategy upon which those instructions rested, and while he liked giving ground no more than the next man, he rather approved of what he suspected Sir Thomas Caparelli and High Admiral Matthews had in mind. But that was for the future. For now, the evacuation order must already have gone out, and the transports held in-system for just this eventuality would already be filling up while the demolition charges were armed. It was a pity that so much investment—in time and effort more than in money—was about to be blown into very tiny pieces, but the Peeps would receive absolutely nothing of value for their efforts.

And in the meantime, the Elric picket force, and Rear Admiral Aristides Trikoupis, had a little something to *show* them. . . .

"Wake up the tactical section, Jason," he told Haskins. "I'll be on Flag Deck in fifteen minutes."

Citizen Admiral Groenewold stood beside the master plot on the flag deck of the superdreadnought PNS *Timoleon*. Citizen Commissioner O'Faolain stood beside him, her hands folded behind her back, and watched him study the display intently.

There wasn't much for him to see just yet. Like everyone else in TF 12.3, O'Faolain knew the Manties' long-range sensor net had to have detected them. More to the point, its FTL transmission capability meant the Manties must already have a breakdown on TF 12.3, at least by type. Without similar technology, all *Timoleon* could expect to pick up at this range were active impeller drives, and even those would be invisible if the Manties chose to hold their accel down and use their EW properly.

Under the circumstances, Groenewold couldn't actually expect to learn much from his intense scrutiny. With some admirals, O'Faolain would have written his intense concentration off as nothing more than an effort to impress his people's commissioner with the depth of his thought, but she'd come to know Groenewold too well to think anything of the sort here. The dark, intense admiral didn't have a devious bone, or even a politically circumspect one, in his entire body, and it never even would have occurred to him to worry about impressing his State Security watchdog. That made it very hard not to like him—a lot—and O'Faolain had to keep reminding herself that it was her job to *watch* the officers assigned to her charge, not to like them.

Groenewold gave the display one last look, noting the rate of advance of TF 12.3's recon drones. Assuming nothing happened to them, they would start getting close enough to what Tactical estimated to be the most probable locations for Manty forces in another twenty minutes or so. Until then, he'd undoubtedly seen all he was going to see, and he rubbed his nose thoughtfully as he turned to walk back to his command chair. O'Faolain tagged along beside him, but he was barely even conscious of her presence while he contemplated the situation. It certainly never occurred to him to ask her opinion on how to proceed. This was an admiral's job, and all he really needed from her was for her to stay out of his way and see to it that the other people's commissioners aboard the ships of his task force did the same. As far as BJ Groenewold was concerned, that was an equitable division of labor, and he'd never actually considered how fortunate he was that O'Faolain was prepared to recognize the narrow intensity with which he focused on the task at hand rather than take offense at being ignored.

Now he waved Citizen Lieutenant Commander Bhadressa and Citizen Lieutenant Commander Okamura closer and leaned back in his chair.

"Don't see any sign of LACs out there, Fugimori," he murmured to his ops officer. Citizen Commissioner O'Faolain stepped up beside Okamura, and Groenewold nodded a welcome to her without ever taking his attention from the ops officer.

"I'd be surprised if we did, Citizen Admiral." Okamura's voice was deep, rumbling up out of an immense chest. Despite his name, the blue-eyed citizen commander stood almost two meters tall, and his golden beard gave him the look of a Viking gone adrift in time. But there was nothing of the berserker about Okamura. Indeed, Groenewold had chosen him for his job in large part because the citizen vice admiral was aware that his own aggressive nature predisposed him towards rashness. Okamura was no coward, but his was a much more deliberative, thoughtful personality.

"According to Citizen Captain Diamato, the first they saw of them at Hancock was when they opened fire from within graser range," Okamura went on calmly. "We're keeping the sharpest sensor watch we can, but if they got in that close against Citizen Admiral Kellet, I doubt *we'll* catch them a lot further out, however hard we look. Assuming Citizen Captain Diamato's memory of events is correct, of course."

"Of course," Groenewold agreed, but despite the qualification, there was no doubt in his own mind. Lester Tourville had slipped him a copy of Diamato's report, and Groenewold had promptly shared it with his staff and all of his COs. Nor had he left any doubt in anyone's mind as to whether or not he expected them to give credence to the report's contents. He was no more able than anyone else to explain how anyone could squeeze so much nastiness into so small a package, but he wasn't about to put *anything* past those never to be sufficiently damned Manticoran R&D types. The overly clever bastards had hit the People's Navy with one unpleasant surprise after another, and while BJ Groenewold was not about to decide all Manties were three meters tall, covered with curly hair, and routinely walked on water, he had no intention of underestimating them, either. PN flag officers who did that had a nasty habit of not coming home again.

"Our sources haven't said a word about LACs having been shipped in to any of these systems, Citizen Admiral," Ellen Bhadressa put in diffidently. The slender, chestnut-haired chief of staff shrugged. "I'm not suggesting that they couldn't have done it anyway, but our intelligence has been pretty impressive on this op. And LACs aren't exactly pinnaces. If any freighters big enough to deliver them in worthwhile numbers had been in the area, our friends would have had an excellent chance of spotting them."

"Um." Groenewold nodded, but only in acknowledgment, not in agreement. The intelligence for the op had been *extensive*—he was more than ready to grant that—but he wasn't prepared to call it "impressive" until after the fecal matter hit the fan and he had a chance to see how close to right the spooks had come *this* time. And experience had taught him that not expecting great things from them was usually the path of wisdom. Especially given that most of the intelligence in this case came from neutral merchant spacers who'd passed through the region running supplies for the Erewhon Navy and then sold their information to StateSec's agents on Erewhon. Groenewold had a pretty shrewd notion of what had inspired them to be so forthcoming. After all, if he'd needed a few credits and known who the local spymaster was, he might've been tempted to do a little business with said spymaster himself. Which was not to say that he would have sold him *accurate* information . . . only that he would have sold a lot of it to someone who obviously wanted all he could get.

It was a reservation he knew Tourville and Giscard shared, and even though the reports came from the NavInt section of Citizen Commissioner O'Faolain's own StateSec, she'd made her own reluctance to unhesitatingly accept them quite clear. But it was also the only recent information they had.

"All right," he said after a moment. "You're probably right about how soon we'd see anything, Fugimori. And the people who don't believe in 'super LACs' may have a point, as well. But we'll proceed on the assumption that they exist and that they're out there. Check?"

"Check, Citizen Admiral."

"Good. In line with that, screen Citizen Captain Polanco. If any LACs turn up, I want her ready to respond instantly, without waiting to pass any questions on to me."

"Yes, Citizen Admiral. I'll get right on it."

Okamura headed for his own station and Groenewold leaned further back in his chair and pursed his lips. Diamato's report had made it clear that the new Manty LACs had been hellishly difficult targets. At anything above point-blank range, energy weapons had been largely useless against them, but a laser or graser was a precision weapon that required precise fire control because it lacked the area-attack capability of a laser head. After a lot of careful thought, Groenewold had decided that the most effective way to deal with something like Diamato's LACs, even at what was normally energy range, would be with heavy shipboard missiles. If he got the opportunity, he was quite prepared to flush entire missile pods at the elusive little bastards, but he rather doubted he could pick them up far enough out for that. It was much more likely to be a matter of close-in—*very* close-in, compared to normal missile ranges—combat, with each ship or division taking snap shots whenever they were offered, and he'd trained for just that. Citizen Captain Bianca Polanco, *Timoleon*'s skipper, had been involved with that training from the outset, and Groenewold had taken the highly unusual step of designating Polanco as the tactical commander of TF 12.3's anti-LAC defenses. She was specifically authorized to coordinate all of the task force's missile fire expressly to kill LACs, even if that meant ignoring hyper-capable units. A ship of the wall had a higher priority; nothing else did.

Okamura and Bhadressa had dug in and worked hard to turn his ideas into reality, even though Bhadressa was one of those who seriously doubted that even Manties could build the sort of LACs Diamato claimed to have faced. Against normal LACs, even the improved Manty models NavInt had hard numbers on from Silesia, Groenewold's precautions were certainly excessive, and he knew it. But if Diamato was right about what the Manties actually had, the People's Navy was going to require a whole new defensive doctrine, and he saw no reason not to start formulating it right now.

No doubt some of his fellow flag officers would think he was jumping at shadows, but Groenewold didn't especially care about that. For that matter, he himself doubted that even Diamato's super LACs would be capable of destroying properly handled ships of the wall without suffering murderous and prohibitive losses. But he might be wrong, and he could stand a little mockery if that was the price of covering his crews' backs against a threat whose parameters had yet to be fully determined.

It was simply his misfortune that all of his laudable precautions had been directed against the wrong threat.

CHAPTER TWENTY-SIX

"They don't seem very interested in letting us set up any ambushes, do they, Aristides?" Vice Admiral of the Red Frederick Malone's smile was wintry on Trikoupis' com screen.

"No, Sir, they don't," Trikoupis agreed.

Whoever was in command over there was obviously anxious about something. Trikoupis doubted it was *Izzie* and *Esterhaus*, since there was no way for the Peeps to know they were even here, much less what they were capable of, but if it wasn't BatDiv 62, he didn't know what else it could be, either.

"I suppose they *might* be afraid we'd try to pull off the same sort of thing Admiral Harrington tried at Cerberus," he suggested, and Malone snorted.

"I'll be delighted to take your money if you want to put down a bet on *that*! Or are you suggesting their intelligence people have some reason to question my sanity?"

"Perish the thought, Sir." Trikoupis grinned, but then the moment of humor faded, and he shrugged. "It does make sense for them to come in cautiously, even with that sort of numerical advantage, Sir. I doubt they have any idea what we actually have waiting for them, but jinking that way is certainly complicating our intercept calculations."

"Um." Malone nodded in agreement, but his expression reflected a certain contempt. "I can see that, I suppose. But all that dancing around wouldn't help them much against any serious defensive force. They've still got to come into weapons' range of *Zelda* . . . unless they really *like* stooging around the outer system

336

while we do whatever we want in the inner system. That means all we'd have to do is sit right there in orbit until they had to commit to their actual approach vector, then come out and smash into them head-on before they ever got into attack range of the base."

"Agreed." It was Trikoupis' turn to nod, but he went on in a respectful tone. "But that assumes we've got the strength to meet them toe-to-toe. And at the very least, they've already forced a half-dozen course changes on us and managed to slow our closure rate considerably. Which will also slow our *breakaway* rate when the time comes. And they've got recon drones out, Sir. Every course change they force and every minute they add to our intercept time gives their drones one more chance to get a sniff of us."

"I know." Malone sighed, and rubbed his eyes. "You know, I really enjoyed my job more when things were simple and straightforward. I'm sure all the new toys people insist on giving us have their place, but each of them seems to make everything more complicated in some sort of geometric progression. Worse, some of the Peeps seem to be figuring that out."

"That they do, Sir." Trikoupis glanced down at one of the displays deployed about his command chair. *And they're getting slicker about their maneuvering, too. ONI was right; that* does *look more like an Allied formation than anything I'd expect a bunch of Peeps to put together. Look how tight those suckers are.* "At least it looks like they may finally be steadying down for their final run in," he observed aloud.

"Sooner or later they had to," Malone agreed, and his voice was crisper as he studied his own displays. "My tac people are suggesting we come to zero-zero-niner, zero-three-one at two hundred gravities. Does that sound good to you?"

"Just a moment, Sir." It was unusual for a vice admiral of the Royal Manticoran Navy to ask someone who hadn't even made list in the RMN for advice on a fleet intercept, but Malone's entire force consisted of only five superdreadnoughts and a screen of battlecruisers and cruisers, and three of those superdreadnoughts— BatDiv 62's own *Izzie* and *Esterhaus* and HMS *Belisarius*, one of the RMN's *Medusas*—were under Trikoupis' command. They were also the only reason Malone hadn't already retired at his top speed. Adler, Basilisk, and Alizon had taught the Allies not to take Peep missile pods lightly, and it was obvious from the oncoming attackers' relatively low acceleration rate that they'd brought a copious supply of pods to the party.

But Trikoupis' command made the difference. Or so he and

Malone hoped, at any rate. In many ways, Malone's own flagship and her division mate were only along to thicken the antimissile defenses while *Izzie, Esterhaus,* and *Belisarius* did the fighting.

"Zero-zero-niner, zero-three-one looks good to me, Sir," Trikoupis said as the projected vectors appeared in his own plot. "Assuming constant accelerations on both sides, that would bring us into launch range in about seventy-five minutes."

"You don't think it'll take us too deep into their envelope?" Malone asked. There was no hesitation in the vice admiral's tone, only a note of professional question.

"Worst case, assuming they alter and go to maximum accel on an intercept course, they could stay just in their extreme missile range of us for about fifty minutes, Sir," Trikoupis replied. "If they break directly away from us immediately and we do the same, their engagement window drops to barely ten minutes. And frankly, when they see what we've got for them, I doubt very much that they're going to want to close any more heroically than they have to in order to look good in their after-action reports."

"You're probably right." Malone gazed down at his display for several more seconds, then nodded. "All right, Aristides. You're the lead element for this attack, so you call it for the run in. The rest of the task force will conform to your movements."

"Thank you, Sir," Trikoupis said, and nodded to his ops officer. "You heard the man, Adam. Let's do it."

"Citizen Admiral, we're beginning to pick up something on two of the drones," Citizen Lieutenant Commander Okamura reported. Groenewold looked up quickly from a side discussion with Citizen Commander Bhadressa, and Okamura frowned. "We're not sure what it is, Citizen Admiral. Their EW is obviously playing tricks on the drones, and even our position fix isn't all that positive, but it looks like they're coming in from starboard and high. If CIC's target track is accurate, they'll close to about six million klicks fifty-two minutes from now. Assuming constant accelerations, the range will start to open again almost immediately at that point."

"Any idea at all what it could be?"

"CIC says it *looks* like a couple of ships of the wall, Citizen Admiral."

"I see."

Groenewold frowned into his plot as the icons of the new contact—assuming it was a real contact and not just a case of sensor ghosts—appeared. He sensed someone beside him and glanced up to find Citizen Commissioner O'Faolain at his side.

"What to do you think it is, Citizen Admiral?" she asked quietly.

"Could be a lot of things, Citizen Commissioner, but I don't think it's Diamato's LACs. If Fugimori's vectors are right, whatever it is obviously doesn't want to get any closer than extreme missile range, and that doesn't sound like LACs with big, nasty energy weapons. They'd want to close, get into knife range and hit us hard."

"Could the capital ships be planning to support a close-in LAC attack with long-range missile strikes?" O'Faolain asked, and Groenewold looked at her with respect.

"It's certainly possible, Ma'am. But, again, I don't think it's what's happening. If they were going to commit to a LAC strike, it would probably indicate they meant to mount a serious defense of the system. In that case, their SD element shouldn't be on a vector that would make it all but impossible for them to stay in range if we break off sharply. They'd want to bring it in closer to their LACs and keep it in engagement range to cover the close-in strike." He shook his head. "No, I think those are SDs with missile pods out there. If NavInt was right about Manty forces in this area, there can't be more than six to eight of them, though, and their pods aren't good enough to even the odds against the greater number we have on tow. If these people want to close into missile range of us, they're dead meat.".

"All right, Adam. Let's start rolling pods," Rear Admiral Trikoupis said, and Commander Towson nodded.

"You heard the Admiral," he said, his Grayson accent just a bit crisper than usual as he turned to his assistants. "Plan Bravo Three. Execute now."

Responses came back, and Trikoupis watched his repeater. A sparkle of diamond dust began to decorate it, each small cluster of gems a clutch of missile pods. They weren't launching yet. Instead, each cluster of pods went spilling out astern of one of the missile superdreadnoughts' wedges to be grabbed by the tractors of one or more of her consorts. With a *Harrington* along, a task force commander could accelerate at his maximum rate, without worrying about towed pods' drag on his compensators, because he could deploy any pods he needed from the missile ships just before the action opened.

As Trikoupis watched, HMS *Belisarius* replenished the EW drones. There were only four of them, each pretending to be a superdreadnought trying unsuccessfully to hide under stealth, and Trikoupis smiled as he looked at them. Some might have assumed those four false SDs were there in an effort to bluff the Peeps into breaking off, but they were there for a very different purpose, and he wished he could have deployed even more of them. Unfortunately, four were all they could fit into their intended deception.

Trikoupis watched the sprays of light a moment longer, reassuring himself that each pod's intended recipient was spearing her charges with her tractors as planned, and then looked back at the Peep formation. The enemy clearly had a hard fix on at least some of the picket force, and he was altering course to close with it. But Admiral Malone was also altering course, holding the range open, and it would be some minutes yet before anyone was in range for a normal missile exchange. Of course, the Peeps were in range of *Trikoupis'* missiles now, but he was under strict orders not to demonstrate the enormous reach advantage of the Ghost Rider birds.

But that was all right. The goodies from Ghost Rider *he* was allowed to play with today would make the missile exchange far less profitable for the Peeps than they could possibly anticipate . . . assuming they worked as well in action as they had in the exercises. And given what he'd surmised about the strategy Admiral Caparelli and High Admiral Matthews had put together, losing control of Elric would probably be a *good* thing, in the long run . . . and as long as the Peeps didn't take it too cheaply. Which they wouldn't, he thought grimly. He didn't know how many of Malone's ships the Peeps might have spotted, but his own tactical people had iron locks on the Peep SDs. The ones their onboard sensors couldn't see had been plucked from concealment by the improved recon drones which were also part of the Ghost Rider cornucopia. Those people were naked to his fire control solutions, and that changed them from warships into targets.

Hmmmm . . . The more he studied that formation, the more it looked downright Manticoran. That was unpleasant. Closing up on one another that way gave each unit a much more restricted maneuver envelope when it came to rolling ship against incoming missile fire. There was simply less room—a *lot* less room— for the edges of their impeller wedges to clear one another. But it also brought them in closer under one another's point defense umbrellas, and the formation was tight enough that if the enemy managed to roll it simultaneously, its wedges would form a huge picket fence. Some missiles would penetrate the gaps between pickets, but not very many. Even a missile's wedge would be too wide to fit through the openings between the ships's wedges unless it hit at precisely the correct angle, which could only be the result of pure good luck. And any wedge that *didn't* clear the vastly stronger wedges of its targets would blow immediately, vaporizing the missile which had generated it in the process.

Still, there was something a little odd about the intervals. No, not the intervals. About the relative attitudes of the super-dreadnoughts at the center of the formation.

"Have you taken a close look at the intervals in their wall, Adam?" he asked Towson, and the Grayson commander looked at him with raised eyebrows.

"What about them, Sir?"

"Look at the way they've got their units staggered," Trikoupis suggested, tapping keys to highlight selected units. "See the center of the wall? It actually extends out to starboard, almost like a cone with the closed end pointed straight at right angles to us. The *vertical* separation is the same for the ships in the cone as for any of the rest of their formation, but they're definitely extended perpendicular to our approach vector."

"I see what you mean, Sir," Towson replied, but his voice was puzzled. "I don't think I understand it, though. It may help their sensor efficiency a little bit by clearing the interference of the ships between them and us, but it won't give them any advantage once they turn away to open their broadsides. In fact, it actually hurts their tactical flexibility, now that I think about it. With those ships pushed out to their port and our starboard that way, they don't have any choice but to turn to their starboard to bring their broadsides to bear. Swinging the other way would mask the fire of several of the units in the cone."

"I'd think so," Trikoupis agreed, his tone thoughtful. "But that formation is far too tight for it to be an accident or something they just strayed into. That means whoever's in command over there has a reason for it."

"But what kind of reason, Sir?"

"I don't know," Trikoupis said slowly, but then his tone firmed up. "Unless—" He pondered for another few seconds, then nodded. "I think that may be the first effort to develop a new anti-LAC doctrine."

"Anti-LAC?" Towson looked back at his own plot. "I suppose that could be it, Sir."

"Frankly, I've been a bit surprised we haven't seen something like it before this," Trikoupis said. "Given what happened at Hancock, I'd be terrified of the new LAC classes in their place. I'd assumed the absence of any apparent precautions against them in engagements since Hancock meant they'd taken such heavy losses there that they genuinely didn't know what happened to them. But now . . ."

"I can see some advantages, if that's what they're doing," Towson agreed. "It brings the sensors of the displaced ships clear of the fore-and-aft interference of their consorts, on one side of the wall, at least. And look at their screen, Sir." The tac officer touched a control, and the Peep battlecruisers and cruisers blinked brighter. "See how they have the bulk of them pulled further back and spread further to the sides? Spreading them that wide has to hurt their mutual support capability, and it cuts down on the screen's ability to support the wall's point defense, but look at the way it expands their sensor envelope to the flanks and rear. And it extends their total missile envelope, too. They can't get as much density at any given locus, but they can put at least *some* missiles into a much wider volume. That might make sense if they were hoping to pick LACs up early and then lay fire down on them while they close."

The tac officer frowned and scratched meditatively at an earlobe.

"Assuming you're right and it's an attempt to come up with an effective anti-LAC screen, though, Sir, why bulge out the heavy ships on only one flank? It gives them better sensor coverage, and probably more effective missile fire, *on that side* of the wall, but it doesn't do a thing on the other."

"I don't know," Trikoupis admitted. "My best guess would be that they still don't feel confident enough of their ship-handling skills. If they have to reform on a radically different axis, just bulging one side will give them problems enough. Displacing the wall's plane on *both* sides at once?" He shook his head. "I'd hate to try that with Grayson or Manty units. No, I think what this represents is a compromise between what they'd really like to do and what they realistically believe they *can* do. Which only makes me respect whoever came up with the idea more. It must have been tempting to try to squeeze in every possible refinement, and he was smart enough to settle for what he figured would work rather than risk losing it all by trying for too much too soon."

"I see what you mean. On the other hand, it's going to hurt them once the actual missile exchange begins. Unless they tighten up again between then and now, of course."

"I don't think they're going to. If they were, they'd already have— Look! They're altering to port now."

Towson nodded but did not reply to his admiral directly. He was too busy passing instructions over his tactical net, and Trikoupis left him to it. At this point, there was very little an admiral could do to influence the outcome. The training, planning, deployments, and opening maneuvers were all behind, the options for both sides stark and simple, defined by the closing range and the numbers of missiles on either side, and Rear Admiral Trikoupis and Admiral Malone were little more than high-ranking spectators while they relied upon their subordinates to get things right.

Towson was right about how that unorthodox formation was going to affect the Peeps' point defense, Trikoupis reflected. It pushed the displaced ships closer to the Allied formation as the two walls altered heading to clear their broadsides. In so doing, it both made them easier targets and gave their more distant consorts' point defense poorer firing angles to help cover them. But it was a marginal difference, and Trikoupis felt another moment of respect for whoever had come up with the idea. The ideal time for LACs to jump a wall would be when their own capital ships were punching missiles into it. The incoming fire would confuse the enemy's tracking data and, more importantly, force his tac officers to decide whether to fire their close-in defensive weapons at LACs or missiles. Which meant it was just as critical to keep an eye out for stealthed LACs *now*, and that was precisely what the Peeps were doing.

"We're coming up on our firing bearing now, Sir!"

"Engage as instructed, Commander," Trikoupis said formally for the record.

"Their acceleration's stopped dropping, Citizen Admiral," Okamura reported. "It's holding steady at five hundred and ten gees. Call it five KPS squared."

"Um." Citizen Vice Admiral Groenewold plucked at his lower lip. Allowing for the apparent efficiency of the Manties' new inertial compensators, that was about right for an SD with pods deployed outside her wedge. So if the Manties were dropping their accel now, that would indicate they were, indeed, deploying their pods. But it also meant none of their light units had full pod loads. They couldn't have, because, unlike superdreadnoughts, they lacked the tractor capacity and room to tow full loads *inside* their wedges, which meant they couldn't have stayed with the ships of the wall on the approach run. And since Tactical reported that his ships of the wall outnumbered the Manties by almost three to one and his screening elements *were* towing full pod loads, it looked like things were about to get messy for the Manty CO.

But he has to know that as well as I do, which means either he's an idiot—which they've proven is possible but still seems pretty unlikely—or else he figures he's got an edge to compensate for his missile inferiority. Which means we may just see Diamato's LACs popping out of stealth any time now.

"Pass the word to the screen. I want an even closer scan watch. If they've got some sort of 'super LAC,' this is the time *I'd* be producing it against us."

"Coming up on firing position . . . *now!*" Adam Towson snapped, and the Elric picket force flushed its pods.

All of its pods . . . including the full loads that had been passed to every single ship of the screen by *Isaiah MacKenzie, Edward Esterhaus,* and *Belisarius.* Between them, the three SD(P)s were also able to deploy enough additional pods to account for the four extra "superdreadnoughts" on the Peeps' tracking displays, and their crews rolled the extras off the internal rails with glee.

The Allied chiefs of staff had been firm in their instructions: the new ships were not to go about flaunting their ability to roll waves of pods from their hollow-cored central magazines. If the Peeps didn't know about them yet, this was not the time to alert the enemy to their existence. But that didn't mean they couldn't pass those same pods on to their consorts. The Peeps' point defense tracks would amply demonstrate that the incoming fire had originated with the units actually towing the missiles at the moment they launched. What it *wouldn't* tell them was that all of those missiles were under the fine-meshed, carefully honed fire control of GNS *Isaiah MacKenzie,* with her two division mates poised to assist if they were needed.

Admiral Malone had five superdreadnoughts, sixteen battlecruisers, ten heavy cruisers, twelve light cruisers, eight destroyers . . . and four electronic warfare drones. When BatDiv 62 finished distributing its gifts, those ships (and drones) had a total of four hundred and four pods, each containing ten missiles. Adding the internal launchers brought the total number of missiles in that first, massive salvo up to forty-nine hundred.

It could have been higher still, but BatDiv 62's internal launchers were busy firing something besides shipkillers. They were firing more electronic warfare drones that took station on the formation and began to thresh the Peeps' targeting systems with jamming, and others that took on the appearance of more superdreadnoughts, more battlecruisers, more heavy cruisers, all beckoning to the Peep's sensors.

Such decoys had always been available, but only in limited

numbers. The power required to sustain a convincing false sensor image of a warship in engagement range was so high that a drone required direct power transmission from the ship it was protecting. That meant standard practice had always been to deploy decoys only on tractors and in low numbers. But the same technology which had provided the power plants for the RMN's FTL recon drones had been brought to bear on the decoy problem by the R&D types responsible for Project Ghost Rider, and the result—*one* of the results—was a completely independent unit with an endurance of up to twenty minutes from internal power alone, depending on the strength of the sensor image it had to duplicate. And one that could be fired from one of the new capital missile tubes, at that. Now BatDiv 62's internal launchers went to rapid fire, spewing them out, multiplying the Peeps' targets catastrophically with each broadside.

Rear Admiral Aristides Trikoupis felt his lips skin back in a cold, predatory grin as his plot blossomed with waves of false targets.

It was not, he thought, going to be pleasant afternoon in Elric for the Peeps.

"Holy Mother of God!" someone whispered. BJ Groenewold wasn't certain who it had been, but whoever it was had summed up his own emotions quite well.

The Manties *couldn't* have fired that many missiles at him, not with the approach accelerations his tac teams had monitored! It simply wasn't possible.

But it had happened, and he felt a ball of ice in his belly as the avalanche of fire soared towards his own force. Okamura had to be just as stunned as he was, but the tac officer wasn't letting it rattle him, and despite his disbelief, Groenewold was pleased with the citizen commander's self-control. Manticoran fire control and missile sensors were better than the People's Navy's. To compensate, Okamura was holding his own launch, refining his firing solutions up to the very last moment. He had to get his birds off before any of the incoming got close enough to target his own pods or score proximity soft kills on them, but every second he waited improved his hit percentages by a small yet possibly significant amount. Given his druthers, Groenewold would have launched at the very edge of the missile envelope, but Manticoran EW was too good for that. It had been impossible to get hard locks at that range, and having come this deep into the enemy's envelope, neither Okamura nor Groenewold had any intention of launching with less than the very best solutions they could generate.

Okamura gave his displays one final glance, then grunted in satisfaction.

"Launch," he said, and TF 12.3's missile pods belched return fire. The missiles streaked out, charging towards their meager number of targets, and—

The plot shifted again, and Groenewold's jaw tightened at the sudden, ridiculous increase in targets. He swore, silently but bitterly and with feeling, as the tide of false target sources danced and capered. He'd never seen so few ships produce so many decoys, and even as he watched, the plot began to fuzz with strobes of jamming far more powerful and widespread than anything Groenewold had ever seen before.

TF 12.3's thirty-five superdreadnoughts and their escorts had over eight hundred pods on tow, with twelve missiles per pod. The salvo it had produced had more than thirteen thousand missiles in it, nearly three times the weight of incoming fire, and ought to have been able to achieve a far heavier concentration on the much smaller number of targets which faced it. By any rational prebattle calculation, even allowing for the acknowledged superiority of Manticoran missiles and fire control, the result should have been the virtual extermination of the Elric picket force.

But that would have been before the People's Navy had met Project Ghost Rider, and BJ Groenewold—who had done everything right—was about to discover just how wrong his calculations had been.

"Initial tracks look very good, Sir," Commander Towson reported. "Telemetry from the birds indicates half already have internal lock."

"Very good, Adam!" Trikoupis allowed himself a full-fledged smile. Another of Ghost Rider's gifts had been an increase of almost eighteen percent in the sensitivity of the new capital missiles' onboard seekers, coupled with almost as great an increase in their onboard computers' ability to discriminate between genuine and false targets. R&D was still working on enhancing both those areas—a practical necessity, once the Fleet was allowed to begin using the full, extended range of the new missiles—but what they had now was already showing marked dividends. *Izzie* and her sisters were able to hand off from shipboard to missile fire control much sooner, which let them spend longer on the more difficult targeting solutions and should substantially increase the percentage of hits.

✧   ✧   ✧

Range at launch was six-and-a-half million kilometers, with a closing speed of three hundred and twenty kilometers per second, which gave TF 12.3's missiles a nominal flight time of a hundred and seventy-two seconds. Terminal velocity would be just over 75,700 KPS, and Citizen Vice Admiral Groenewold's birds would have a bare eight seconds left on their drives for terminal attack maneuvers. At their attack velocity, eight seconds ought to be enough . . . assuming the active defenses didn't zap them all short of their laser heads' 30,000-kilometer stand-off range. Of course, Manty missiles had marginally higher accelerations. Flight time for *their* birds would be ten seconds shorter, giving them even more time for attack maneuvers and a terminal velocity over two thousand KPS higher, but Groenewold had no choice but to accept the disadvantage.

Had he and his captains known it, even at those numbers, the performance of Vice Admiral Malone's missiles had been deliberately degraded. The new multiple-drive missiles Ghost Rider had produced could have made the entire attack run at 96,000 gravities rather than stepping down to the 47,520 KPS^2 at which they actually bored in. At that acceleration, they would have made the crossing in barely a hundred and eighteen seconds and come in with a terminal velocity of over 110,000 KPS . . . and well over a minute left for terminal maneuvers. At that velocity, and with that much time on their clocks, they would have slashed through TF 12.3 like thunderbolts, but the Alliance high command had decided those capabilities were also to be held in reserve.

Still, what TF 12.3 actually got was bad enough. Every fifth missile in that massive salvo was either a jammer or a decoy pretending to be an entire pod's worth of missiles all by itself. Both sides had used jammers and electronic warfare birds before, of course. It was routine. But the People's Navy had never imagined EW missiles with so much power to burn, and the raw ferocity of the jamming and the blazing strength of the decoys' false signatures surpassed anything Groenewold or Okamura could possibly have anticipated. Their point defense was less than half as efficient as it ought to have been, and the incoming missiles obviously had far better seekers than anything the Manties had previously employed.

The Elric picket had launched fifty seconds ahead of TF 12.3, and its missiles reached their targets over a full minute before Groenewold's began their own final attack maneuvers. Countermissiles sped desperately to meet them, and Groenewold watched in disbelief as countermissile after countermissile was sucked off by the decoys or blinded by the jammers. The last-ditch laser clusters opened fire, spitting coherent light at the oncoming laser heads, but they, too, suffered from the jamming and spent all too much of their effort engaging harmless decoys. Barely twenty percent of the incoming were picked off by the missiles, and the laser clusters got only another eighteen percent.

And then twenty-four hundred Allied laser heads detonated almost as one, and a massive tide of destruction broke over Task Force 12.3.

Every single one of those missiles had been fired at a mere five ships, and the chosen victims staggered in agony as almost five hundred missiles attacked each of them. Superdreadnoughts were tough almost beyond comprehension. Even capital ship missiles were seldom capable of doing truly critical damage against their massive armor and powerful active and passive defenses. They could be killed with missiles, certainly, but normally only as part of a long, painful pounding match in which they were literally battered to bits one centimeter at a time.

The reintroduction of the missile pod and the enhanced lethality of its missiles had not changed that calculation. It *still* took scores—or hundreds—of individual hits to kill any SD, but the long, brutal pounding matches were no longer required to put those missiles on target. Now it could be done in a single broadside, and Task Force 12.3 writhed at the heart of a vortex of bomb-pumped lasers. No one would ever know how many hundreds of individual lasers wasted themselves uselessly on the impenetrable gravity bands of their targets' impeller wedges, or how many more were twisted aside at the last minute by the sidewalls shielding their victims' flanks. For that matter, no one would ever know exactly how many lasers actually got through to their targets' hulls.

And it didn't matter. One moment TF 12.3 had a solid core of thirty-five ships of the wall; a moment later, it had thirty-one. The terrible glare of failing fusion bottles lit the heart of the Havenite formation, lighting the graves of what had been multimegaton superdreadnoughts mere seconds before, and there were no survivors at all from any of Rear Admiral Trikoupis' targets. Twenty-five thousand men and women died in those incandescent pyres, and among them was Citizen Vice Admiral BJ Groenewold, who had prepared his task force against every threat he could imagine, only to encounter one only a psychic could have anticipated.

Aristides Trikoupis watched his victims vanish from his plot, and then it was the turn of the Peeps' missiles. There were far too many of them for the outnumbered picket force's active defenses to destroy, but Ghost Rider's children were waiting, and his eyes flashed with triumph as missile after missile veered off to engage one of the decoys, or wandered suddenly aside, blinded by jamming, or simply streaked straight past, unable even to *see* its intended target through the warships' own jamming and the remote Ghost Rider platforms. Of the thirteen thousand missiles sent back at the picket, over ten thousand were spoofed or blinded. Two or three thousand of those streaked in to obliterate the four EW drones masquerading as additional superdreadnoughts, and the three thousand which actually attacked genuine targets were spread over every ship in the picket. Given the sheer number of incoming missiles, that had actually made sense, since that weight of fire was certain to overload the active defenses. All the Peeps had really needed to do was lame or cripple the ships of Admiral Malone's command, leaving them unable to accelerate clear and escape the follow-up attacks of the far more numerous raiding force, and that should have been relatively simple once the active defenses were suppressed and beaten down.

But the active defenses were up to the challenge they actually faced, countermissiles in the incoming missile storm, and then the laser clusters began to track and fire with cold, computer-controlled efficiency.

Vice Admiral Malone and Rear Admiral Trikoupis watched with narrow eyes as the ragged survivors of the initial Peep launch continued to close, and then, at the very last minute, the order flashed out from the flagship and every ship of the picket force rolled ship simultaneously, presenting only the bellies of their wedges to their attackers.

Some of the missiles got through anyway. There were simply too many of them for any other result, and *Isaiah MacKenzie* and *Edward Esterhaus* shuddered and jerked as they took hits. The SD(P)s bow-walls, copied from the new LACs, helped reduce their damage enormously, and *Belisarius* actually escaped without a single hit. But she was the only superdreadnought who could make that claim, and the battlecruisers *Amphitrite* and *Lysander* bucked in agony as lasers blasted into their far more fragile hulls. *Amphitrite* shook off the blows and continued to run, streaming atmosphere from her mangled flanks but still under full command. *Lysander* was less fortunate. Three separate hits went home in her after impeller ring, destroying two alpha nodes and at least four beta nodes, and more ripped into her midships section, gutting her starboard broadside, destroying CIC, her flag bridge (the latter thankfully unoccupied), and two of her three fusion plants. A third of her crew was killed or wounded, and she staggered, lagging as her acceleration fell.

She was doomed, but the Peeps had clearly been stunned by the magnitude of the blow they'd just taken. Their own acceleration dropped suddenly, and *Lysander* was able to continue pulling slowly away from them.

Vice Admiral Malone assessed the situation quickly. There was no way to get *Lysander* out of the system with her after Warshawski sail completely disabled, but at least he could get her people out. His superdreadnoughts, none of them seriously injured, slowed to the best pace the crippled battlecruiser could maintain, rolling to open their broadsides once more and thundering defiance back at the Peeps while *Lysander*'s squadron mates closed. It was a risky decision, for without the full pod capability of the *Harrington/Medusas*, the balance of power still favored the Peeps heavily, and he was forbidden to use that full capability.

But the Peeps had had enough. It was as if the force which had driven them had disappeared—as perhaps it had, Trikoupis thought grimly, for he'd concentrated his fire on the volume of the enemy wall that should have contained the Peep flagship—and their initial determination wavered. They allowed the range to continue to open slowly, showering the picket with a desultory spatter of missiles that were utterly ineffective against targets protected by Ghost Rider, and Trikoupis and Malone were more than happy to accept that.

They completed the recovery of all of *Lysander*'s personnel and then continued their withdrawal, as per their orders from Sir Thomas Caparelli and Wesley Matthews. Behind them, the survivors of TF 12.3 watched them go and settled sullenly into the possession of the system which, had they but known, their enemies' high command *wanted* them to have.

CHAPTER TWENTY-SEVEN

"I'll be damned. It actually works."

Commander Scotty Tremaine sat in his command chair aboard *Bad Penny* and shook his head. On the display before him, *Hydra Six*'s icon flashed the bright, strobing green that indicated a unit shielded by an active sidewall. Which was very interesting, since *Bad Penny* was directly astern of Lieutenant Commander Roden's LAC.

"Yep." Sir Horace Harkness tapped a query into the auxiliary terminal to the left of his own chair at the Engineer's station. He studied the numbers, then frowned. "Still got some interference with the after nodes," he announced. "Nothing big, but it could be a problem if a hit came in on it just wrong. There's a grav eddy here." He tapped a command into the touchpad and dumped a large-scale schematic of *Cutthroat*'s after aspect to Tremaine's main display, and a cursor blinked, indicating a shaded patch where the sternwall should have merged flawlessly with the roof of the LAC's wedge.

"See it, Sir?"

"I see it," Tremaine confirmed. He studied it carefully, then input a command of his own. The computers considered his order and obediently overlaid the schematic with a gridded readout on the sternwall's density. The shaded area Harkness had indicated grew slightly as the numbers came up, and the commander grunted.

"Got a seventy percent drop in wall strength all along the eddy," he told the CWO, "and it drops almost to zero right along the edge of the seam. Not good, Chief."

"But it's not all that terrible, either, Skipper," Ensign Pyne put in from Tactical. "The eddy's not that big," she pointed out, "and the bad guys'd have to hit it dead on at exactly the right angle to get through it. Compared to a wide open kilt, that's one hell of an improvement in my book!"

"Oh, there's no question about that, Audrey. But if we're going to build this thing, we might as well get it right. And we know it *can* be done right, because the *Ferrets* don't have any chinks like that."

"No, they don't," Harkness said. "On the other hand, BuShips has got a shit pot of engineers and computers to model the thing. And they got to put the generator inside the hull, too, so they had a lot more leeway on where to place it. Hate to say it, but I think Bolgeo did a pretty damned good job, all things considered."

"For God's sake don't let *him* hear you say that, Chief!" Pyne cautioned. "He and Smith and Paulk got half-snockered last night over at Dempsey's and nearly put their arms out of joint patting themselves on the back as it is."

Harkness gave a deep, grunting laugh, and the rest of *Bad Penny's* crew joined in. HMSS *Weyland*, like *Hephaestus* and *Vulcan*, had its own branch of the popular restaurant chain. Since the Admiralty's decision to turn Manticore-B into its own private playground as a place to test its newest toys, *Weyland's* civilian traffic had all but vanished. Dempsey's had more than made up the loss from the tremendous upsurge in naval personnel staging through the space station, but not without the occasional unfortunate incident which ended in the arrival of the SPs. The arrival of Admiral Truman's LAC wings and their obstreperous personnel had increased the rate of those incidents by a power of two. The LAC crews' decision to turn Dempsey's into *their* watering hole and club house, which, naturally, *required* them to physically expel any outsider who dared poke his or her nose into their lair, hadn't helped, but at least it gave them a place where they could talk shop over copious quantities of beer. Tremaine hoped ONI was keeping a close eye on the restaurant's staff, since there was no possible way to keep details the Peeps would have loved to know from popping out in such conversations. The good news was that Nikola Pakovic, the manager, and his people appeared to have adopted the LAC wings, one and all. They fussed over them, made allowances for them, and didn't even pad the (frequent) bills for repairs which Dempsey's presented *to* them, and more than once Tremaine had heard Nikola or Miguel Williams, the bartender, quietly suggest to someone that they might be straying into matters they ought not to be discussing in public. Still . . .

"Were they actually talking about it in public?" he asked, and Pyne chuckled.

"Oh, no, Skip! As a matter of fact, they'd gotten Lieutenant Gilley and Shelton to sucker some poor ensign from the Sixty-First into playing spades with them. For fifty cents a point, no less." She shook her head. "Fleeced the poor sucker like a sheep, too. But they had this entire side conversation going—wouldn't have meant a thing to anyone who didn't know about their project—the whole time. They never actually said a single word about *what* they were working on, only about how well they were doing whatever it was. Cryptic as hell, and confused the crap out of their victim, too, but the more beer they got outside of, the more pleased they were with themselves."

"Over the cards, or the sternwall?" Lieutenant Hayman, *Bad Penny*'s EW officer inquired.

"Both . . . I think. It's hard to be sure with those characters. Bolgeo, especially. He's downright insufferable whenever he sets *anyone*, and he was snarfing so loudly over a busted nil the ensign bid that I thought he was going to drown in his own beer."

"All right," Tremaine said. "In that case, I agree with you, Audrey. We definitely don't need to be giving Roden's happy crew any more reason to feel full of themselves. In fact, Chief, I want you to write up this grav eddy in detail. We'll give 'em a problem to fix right along with the attaboys to keep their heads from getting too big."

"Too late for Bolgeo," Harkness sighed, then flashed a grin. "Still, Sir, I 'spect I can phrase it so's to make 'em feel just a *little* humble if I put my mind to it."

"Well, well, well, well . . ."

First Space Lord Sir Thomas Caparelli sat at his console in the Pit and frowned pensively. He'd just finished reading the after-action report on Elric from Vice Admiral Malone and Rear Admiral Trikoupis. It had taken two standard weeks to reach him by courier boat, and it was quite similar to reports he also had from Solway and Treadway. The Solway picket, with no *Medusas* to thicken its missile fire, had inflicted lower losses, but the Ghost Rider systems had passed their first comprehensive test with flying colors in all three actions. Some of the new hardware had been tested in isolation in earlier engagements, but this was the first time entire task groups had been able to put *all* the defensive applications to the test simultaneously, and Allied losses had been absurdly low. Not a single ship of the wall had been lost, and only three battlecruisers. The Treadway picket had lost five destroyers out of a single squadron, but that had been sheer bad luck. The squadron had been conducting independent maneuvers, and the Peeps' arrival translation had just happened to put the entire attack force right on top of them. The squadron CO had shown great presence of mind and skill in getting any of her ships out, and Caparelli deeply regretted that her own ship hadn't been one of them.

But painful as the Allies losses might have been, they were much lower than the *Peeps'*. Of course, they probably didn't realize that. It was fairly evident from the Elric report, for example, that the Peeps' fire control had been completely fooled by the EW drones generating superdreadnought signatures. Given the confusion which was always part of any battle, and especially one so short and intense and in such a heavy EW environment, it was likely the PN believed the disappearance of the drones marked the destruction of actual ships of the wall. A really close, critical look at their scan data might cause them to question that conclusion, but Caparelli rather doubted anyone would look that closely. It was only human to need to believe one had scored at least *some* success against an opponent, especially when that opponent had killed fourteen percent of one's own ships of the wall. If the Peeps did believe they'd killed four or five SDs, however, then the losses at Elric became almost even by their reckoning, and Elric was where they'd gotten hurt worst.

So the Peeps were now in possession of three strategically important (but not critically so) star systems, at a cost which certainly wasn't extravagant considering the amount of real estate they'd retaken, and *probably* believed they'd inflicted roughly equal ship losses on the Alliance. Moreover, it appeared Trikoupis and his fellows had used their Ghost Rider technology and the *Medusas'* capabilities as intelligently as Caparelli could have asked, and it seemed unlikely the Peeps had any clear notion of what had been done to them. They had to know the Allies' EW capabilities had been far more effective than usual, but they couldn't be certain exactly why that was so. Not yet.

All of which meant there was going to be a lot of pressure for McQueen to push boldly ahead. For that matter, it was possible she herself would read the outcome of her latest operation as an indication the Allies were on the ropes. He doubted she would let her euphoria overcome her common sense, but she didn't operate in a vacuum, and Pierre had to be desperate for military victories in the wake of what Amos Parnell's testimony before the Solly Assembly was doing to the PRH's diplomatic relations. It was clear from the reports of Pat Givens' sources within the Republic that the Peep pipeline to Solly technology had taken a heavy hit, and it looked like it was getting worse for them quickly.

The loss of that pipeline, or even a moderately serious constriction in its flow, could only put even more pressure on the PN's strategists and planners. And not just because anyone on the civilian side was getting hysterical, either. If Caparelli were in McQueen's shoes and had a fistful of reports which even hinted at the capabilities of Ghost Rider, the potential loss of his link to the League's military R&D types would be downright terrifying to him. The need to push ahead quickly, while the Allies were still on the defensive and before they could get enough of the new hardware, whatever it was, to their front-line battle squadrons, would become even greater. Even if he was afraid of the losses he would take, he would realize losses would be even higher later if he delayed long enough for his enemies to fully deploy their new systems, and his immediate response would be to charge ahead—hard.

And the place he'd do it, Caparelli thought, gazing into the tank, would be where he'd already kicked in the Alliance's front door, had the shortest distance to go to reach a really important Allied base and shipyard, and had his best command team in place and ready to go. He'd round up every hull he could free from other duties and send it forward to support his Twelfth Fleet, and then he would drive straight for Grendelsbane. Of all the targets within his reach, that was the one which would hurt the Allies worst, and putting pressure on it would compel the Alliance to redeploy to meet *his* attack, thereby retaining the initiative in his own hands.

The First Space Lord cocked his chair back, whistling soundlessly through pursed lips while he contemplated the icons of Elric, Treadway, and Solway. It was dangerous to try to read an enemy's mind. If you guessed right and acted on the guess, you might score a huge success. But if you guessed wrong . . . Worse, it was hellishly easy *to* guess wrong, to decide the enemy was going to do something because you needed so very badly for that to be the thing he decided to do. Or to assume he saw something as clearly as you did when he didn't, or when what he actually saw was something *you* hadn't even noticed way over at the other edge of the strategic picture.

Yet this time Caparelli was prepared to play a hunch. The Peeps *were* going to keep pushing in from their new conquests and driving on Grendelsbane. It was what he'd hoped for, and he knew that probably predisposed him to conclude that it was what they would do, but he felt totally confident anyway.

The only bad thing about it was that it was too soon. The turn-around time for dispatches would be even longer for the Peeps. McQueen wouldn't be finding out about Elric for at least another twelve or thirteen standard days, for instance, and it would take almost another full month for her to get her forces their fresh orders and begin moving any reinforcements into the area. But that didn't help *his* problems very much.

He'd wanted another month—two or three, if he could get them—for the new LAC wings to finish working up in Manticore-B space. Alice Truman's reports were encouraging, and Caparelli was beginning to think the new *Shrike-Bs* and *Ferrets* might end up surpassing the predictions of even their fiercer partisans, but it was obvious they hadn't yet attained full readiness. Some were closer to combat ready than others, but he wanted desperately to give them at least several more weeks of drills and exercises.

Unfortunately, he didn't have those weeks. Or, rather, he *might* not have them . . . and dared not wait to find out if he did. It would take at least two weeks to get the more combat-ready CLACs ready for their first war deployment, and they'd need at least two or three weeks to integrate themselves into the more conventional forces which would have to operate with them. Which meant that if he meant to take advantage of the Peeps' most recent attacks, he had to give the order almost immediately.

He swung his chair gently from side to side, staring into the holo tank and listening to the quiet, hushed efficiency of the Pit, and the weight of his responsibility crushed down on him. He could have called in his fellow space lords to discuss the situation. Yet he also knew that, in the end, the decision would be his. Or, rather, his and Baroness Morncreek's. But the First Lord had always been guided by the advice of her First Space Lord, which meant it was *his* call, whatever the official tables of organization might say.

And it was better that way. Better that the responsibility for the decision was so clear cut. That there would be no question about who'd made it, or why.

He gazed down into the tank for another silent, endless clutch of seconds, then nodded sharply and looked up. He waved to a communications lieutenant, and the young woman trotted over to him.

"Yes, Sir Thomas?"

"Record a dispatch for Rear Admiral Truman," he told her.

"Yes, Sir." The lieutenant tapped controls on the recording unit she wore and shifted position very slightly, making certain that the lens and microphone were both trained properly on Caparelli. "Recording, Sir," she said crisply.

"Admiral Truman," the First Space Lord told the recording unit, "this message is to be regarded as a first-stage alert for Operation Buttercup. Please place your squadron and ship COs on standby and prepare for immediate redeployment. I would appreciate latest readiness reports soonest, and you are instructed to compile a list of all needs for LogCom within six hours of receipt of this message." He paused, then smiled. "On my authority as First Space Lord, you will also consider this message notification of your brevet promotion to vice admiral. No one else is as well equipped to command your component of the operation, and I have no desire to break up your chain of command at this late date. I will advise Admiral White Haven, and the official paperwork from BuPers will follow as rapidly as possible."

He paused, and his smile faded.

"I realize this is sooner than any of us expected to put Buttercup on-line. If my evaluation of the Peeps' probable course of immediate future action is accurate, however, we're looking at a window of opportunity which is unlikely to present itself again any time soon. I anticipate approval of the operation from Baroness Morncreek within the next twenty to thirty hours. Assuming approval is forthcoming, you and your personnel will be expected to shoulder a heavy responsibility with less training and preparation time than anyone at the Admiralty had hoped to give you. I regret that, but I know I can depend on you and your people to come through for us anyway.

"If Buttercup is approved, I will inform you immediately. Good luck, Admiral."

He stopped speaking to the pickups and nodded to the lieutenant.

"Get that out immediately, Lieutenant. And have me informed as soon as receipt is acknowledged."

"Aye, aye, Sir!" The lieutenant came briefly to attention, then turned and headed for the com section with her message.

Caparelli watched her go, then leaned back and rubbed his eyes with the heels of his hands. There ought to be ominous music in the background, he thought. The sort HD producers used to tell the viewer monumental doings were afoot. But there was only the quiet hum of the Pit and the measured thump of his own pulse in his ears.

How strange. How quiet when I've just committed so many

*thousands of men and women to battle . . . and condemned all too
many of them to death.*

He lowered his hands and smiled crookedly into the tank one
more time, then pushed himself up and stretched. Despite the
message he'd just recorded, he still had com calls to place and
people to see, starting with Pat Givens, proceeding through the
other space lords, and ending up with Baroness Morncreek and
(probably) the Prime Minister. Given that he proposed *not* to
reinforce Grendelsbane's approaches to the maximum, he might
even find himself required to explain the risks he was deliberately
courting to the Queen in person. It was all dreadfully official and
efficient seeming . . . and none of it meant a damned thing.

The decision had already been made. All the rest was only window dressing, and Sir Thomas Caparelli turned and walked slowly
from the Pit, spine straight as a sword, while the weight of the
entire Alliance's war effort pressed down upon his broad and
unbowed shoulders.

CHAPTER TWENTY-EIGHT

Crawford Buckeridge appeared as if by magic, sailing through the study door with stately dignity, and paused with an expression of polite enquiry for his Steadholder.

"Yes, My Lord?"

"Mr. Baird and Mr. Kennedy are leaving now, Buckeridge. Please see them out."

"Of course, My Lord." The steward turned to Baird and Kennedy and bowed majestically. "Gentlemen," he invited.

"I'll look forward to our next meeting, gentlemen," Mueller said, reaching out to shake hands with both men in turn. "And I should have the details for the demonstration in Sutherland settled by then."

"That sounds good, My Lord." Baird, as always the spokesman for the duo, gripped Mueller's hand firmly.

Neither he nor Kennedy mentioned the well-stuffed briefcase they'd left under Mueller's desk or the thick envelope of reports from Mueller's own sources which they'd received in return. To date, Mueller had been unable to confirm Baird's suspicions about any annexation proposals, but all involved had decided to treat their existence as a given until and unless it could be disproved. The result had been an even heavier flow of money from Baird's organization, coupled with carefully orchestrated demonstrations and protests against Benjamin's reforms in several good-sized cities. Mueller had been a bit disappointed in the degree of support Baird's people had been able to give in organizing those protests. In his opinion, a properly run mass-based party ought to be more

359

capable of turning out manpower for a grassroots protest. On the other hand, all the protests were on the northern continent of New Covenant, where they could enjoy physical proximity to Austin City and Protector's Palace, and Baird had explained that his own organization was strongest in the south and the west.

"Good evening, then," Mueller said, and the two organizers followed Buckeridge out. The steward, Mueller knew, would see to it that the two of them got off Mueller House's grounds discreetly, and he stood a moment in thought, running back through the points covered in their discussion. It was odd, he thought. Only a few months ago, he hadn't even known Baird and Kennedy or their organization existed. Now he had them woven firmly into his net and dancing to his piping along with everyone else under the Opposition's umbrella. And they paid him so *well* for producing the music.

He chuckled at the thought, then turned to the armsman who'd stood post silently just inside the study door throughout the meeting.

"Thank you, Steve. I think that will be all, and I'll need you fresh in the morning, so go get a good night's sleep."

"Thank you, My Lord. I will." Sergeant Hughes bowed to his Steadholder and left the study. His heels clicked on the stone floor as he headed down the hall towards the east exit and the walkway to the armsmen's barracks, and no one could have guessed from his erect, military bearing or stern eyes the thoughts which were passing through his brain. Then again, no one in Mueller Steading would have believed those thoughts for a moment if they *had* known what they were. Not from Sergeant Hughes, with his well-known religious conservatism and intolerance for all of Protector Benjamin's "reforms."

There were times when Hughes felt more than a little uncomfortable with his assignment. He'd volunteered for the duty, and he believed in it. More, he knew someone *had* to do it, and he was proud to answer his Protector's call. But the oaths a personal armsman swore were stark and unyielding, and whatever his duty or the need to play a part, Hughes had sworn those oaths before Samuel Mueller, his fellow Mueller Armsmen, and Brother Tobin, the Mueller Steading chaplain. All too often late at night, like tonight, the thought of violating them weighed heavily on his soul.

It shouldn't. Mueller was in gross violation of his own oaths to the Protector, and the law of both the Sword and Father Church was clear on what that meant. No one could be held to an oath sworn to an oathbreaker. By the law of God and the law of Man alike, Steve Hughes owed Samuel Mueller no true allegiance. More than that, Hughes had been taken by Brother Clements, the Mayhew Steading Chaplain, to Deacon Anders' office in Mayhew Cathedral, before he ever reported to this assignment. There, with the approval of Reverend Sullivan, under the seal of the Sacristy and the provisions of a Sword finding of possible treason on the part of a steadholder, Anders had granted him a special dispensation, absolving him from the terms of his oath to Mueller.

All of that was true, but Hughes was a man who took his sworn word seriously. If he hadn't been, he would never have been selected for this assignment. Yet those very qualities made him acutely . . . uncomfortable with lying in such solemn and sanctified manner to one of the great feudal lords of his home world.

But not uncomfortable enough to reconsider having volunteered. It had taken him years to get this close to Mueller, to be so trusted, and that effort and dedication were finally beginning to pay off. His contacts with his Planetary Security superiors had to be circumspect, but he knew Colonel Thomason and General Yanakov were more than satisfied with the intelligence he'd developed and the evidence he'd secured for them. The recordings Hughes had made of Mueller's meetings with Baird and Kennedy, coupled with the duplicates he'd made of the various blind fund transfers Mueller had ordered him to set up, were utterly damning. Campaign finance law violations were scarcely high treason, and certainly didn't rise to the level of the crimes Planetary Security was convinced Mueller had already committed, but they were a beginning. Moreover, Mueller had personally planned them, personally received the illegal funds, and personally ordered Hughes to disburse them. There were no intermediaries to take the fall for him or for him to hide behind when his appointment with the Sword's justice came around. And as more and more money flowed through the web of illegal transfers, more and more of Mueller's cronies implicated themselves by accepting his illegal largesse. When the trap finally sprang, it would net an appalling number of highly placed individuals, and it was possible that someone among them would know enough about Mueller's other acts, and be desperate enough to turn Sword's Evidence and talk about them, to bring the rogue steadholder down once and for all.

And if no one is, we may get him anyway, Hughes reflected. *I don't like this Baird fellow a bit. Kennedy—pfffft! A lightweight who's just along for the ride and to provide Baird with a sidekick, but Baird now . . . Baird knows what the hell he's doing, and I don't like how much money he's throwing around. Where the hell is he getting it all? There's no way—no way at all!—anyone should be able to move funds around on that level without Security catching even a whiff of it. But it's as if the money just materializes in his hand the instant before he hands over the newest bag of it. Like it doesn't leave any traceable trail because it doesn't even exist until that moment. Which is stupid, but damned if I can come up with another explanation for it.*

He chuckled mirthlessly and paused under one of the old-fashioned globe lights illuminating Mueller House's landscaped grounds to consult his chrono. He'd told Mueller he would get a good night's sleep, and that was precisely what he intended to do, but first he had a little errand to run. His piety was not at all feigned, although no one who'd known him before this assignment would have recognized the narrow, straitlaced, intolerant version of it he'd assumed here in Mueller Steading. Coupled with the persona he'd chosen to project, that gave him the one excuse he could rely on to make contact with his superiors when he had to, and he headed for Mueller House's main public entrance.

If he cut through the back courts and alleyways, Mueller Cathedral was barely five blocks from the Steadholder's mansion, and Hughes made a point of visiting the church at least twice a week. Brother Tobin was not party to his assignment and, as far as Hughes could tell, *was* a hundred percent loyal to his Steadholder, but he was also a good man and a true priest of Father Church. Hughes didn't believe for a moment that Tobin knew what Mueller was up to . . . and the captain was *positive* Tobin had no idea Mueller had been implicated in Reverend Hanks' murder. If the chaplain had suspected that for even an instant, he would have resigned his post and left Mueller Steading so quickly the sonic boom would have demolished half the buildings along his exit route. Tobin certainly was a conservative, but he was too good a man to let it go completely to his head, and he'd often gently remonstrated with Hughes over his own assumed intolerance. He was also an excellent chess player, and he and Hughes looked forward to their twice-weekly games and the slow, wandering theological discussions which went with them.

And it just happened that Hughes' message drop for his reports to his superiors was a bookstore on the direct route to Mueller Cathedral.

The sentry at the main entrance recognized him and waved casually, without the snap he would have displayed had anyone else been present or the hour earlier.

"Out late, Steve," he observed as Hughes paused beside the guard box. "Brother Tobin know you're coming?"

"I told him I'd be late this evening," Hughes replied with a small smile. "He told me to come on whenever I got free—said he'd be up until all hours, anyway, working on Sunday's sermon, so I might as well come by and keep him company. Personally, I think the real reason he's so cheerful about the hour is that he thinks he's got checkmate in three more moves. Unfortunately, he's wrong."

"You and your chess games." The sentry shook his head. "Too intellectual for me, boy. Anything more complicated than a deck of cards makes my head ache."

"You mean," Hughes corrected with a broader smile, "that anything that doesn't give you the opportunity to fleece your hapless fellow children of God mercilessly doesn't pay enough for you to learn the rules."

"Ouch!"

The sentry's laugh held just a hint of discomfort, for none of Hughes' fellows were certain how much of his condemnation of cards and gambling in general was meant in humor and how much of it carried the bite of true conviction. Father Church had no problem with games of chance, as long as he who gambled chose to do so, the games were honest, and a man's losses weren't such as to deprive his family of the means for a decent life. Not all of Father Church's children shared that tolerance, however, and Hughes' assumed conservatism made the sentry suspect he was one of those who did not. But Hughes only shook his head and clapped him on the shoulder.

"Don't worry, Al. I won't tell Brother Tobin he needs to aim that sermon he's writing at your gambler's ways. I'm sure he's got more important sinners to bring to task. Besides, I happen to know you tithe even more than Father Church expects."

"Well, I do try," Al agreed. "And I do like a good game of poker—for cash," he admitted.

"No reason you shouldn't, as long as you don't get carried away," Hughes assured him. "And now I really should be on my way. Brother Tobin may've said 'any time,' but I doubt he'll really be pleased to see me if I get there after midnight!"

"Somehow I kind of doubt he would be," Al agreed, and waved him through the gate.

Hughes stepped out onto the ancient, stone-slab sidewalks of the City of Mueller. Moonlight slanted down across narrow, twisting streets almost a thousand years old and beamed into wider thoroughfares which had been driven through the Old City in more recent times. Modern lighting had been added, but Mueller was a Grayson city, not a Manticoran one. It was a warren of low buildings, few more than eight or nine stories tall and none more than thirty, spread out in a sprawling, anachronistic confusion of streets and alleys and roadways. The Old City, in particular, had never been planned for modern lighting, and its constricted, twisty streets and lanes produced unexpected puddles of darkness at odd intervals.

But it was also an orderly place, like most Grayson cities. Street crime wasn't unknown on Grayson, but it was vanishingly rare compared to most urbanized planets. Besides, Hughes was armed and wore his Mueller Guard uniform, and he walked confidently along the sidewalk, cutting through the maze of alleys towards the cathedral—and the back door of the bookstore—and whistling tunelessly.

"That's him," the man who called himself Baird whispered to the two men who flanked him in the alley. The taller of the two turned his head, watching with cold and calculating eyes as the lanky sergeant ambled past the alley mouth, whistling.

"No problem," he said, but Baird shook his head and caught the other's arm.

"It has to be done cleanly," he said flatly. "And don't forget what you're really after."

"No problem," the other repeated, and raised one arm in a beckoning gesture. Three more men blended out of the darkness, and a jerk of his head sent them moving soundlessly after the whistling sergeant. "We'll get it for you," he assured Baird.

"Good, Brother. Good," Baird replied, and released the other man's arm. "This world is God's," he said formally, and the cold-eyed man bent his head briefly.

"This world is God's," he confirmed, and then he and his final companion were out of the alley and hurrying after the others. Baird watched them go, then turned and walked away almost as silently as they had.

Hughes didn't know what had alerted him. Whatever it was came and went too quickly for him to sort it out, and there was no time to try anyway. Perhaps it was simply instinct, or perhaps his trained subconscious had picked up on something his forebrain never noticed, but he was already turning when the first knife came out of the night.

He grunted in agony as the keen-edged steel drove into his back, above and to the outside of his right kidney. The blade grated on rib, and then his own movement wrenched it out of his flesh. He staggered to one side, feeling the scalding rush of blood, and the man who'd knifed him snarled and closed for another thrust.

But Captain Steve Hughes had been chosen for this assignment for many reasons, and one of them was that he was very, very tough and very well trained. His right hand had gone to his pulser even as he turned, and despite the agony of his wound, the weapon came out of the holster with smooth, deadly speed. The knife man's eyes widened in sudden panic as his forward rush rammed the pulser's muzzle into his own belly, and then Hughes squeezed the trigger.

The burst of hypersonic darts almost ripped his assailant in two. The pulser's shrill whine rebounded from the stone buildings lining the narrow roadway, but it wasn't fueled by chemical explosives the way older-style side arms had been. There was no thunder of gunfire, and the man Hughes had shot went down without a sound, a corpse before he had time even to think about screaming.

Hughes staggered back, nauseated and suddenly weak-kneed as the shock of the wound hit him through the adrenaline rush. His hand shook, and he gritted his teeth against the white-hot pain lashing through him. He couldn't reach the wound without dropping his pulser, but he leaned heavily against the facade of a building, forcing himself to remain on his feet while he tried to press the elbow of his right arm against the dreadful, bleeding gash.

The combination of shock and pain was like a club, trying to beat him to his knees, and he shook his head doggedly. It had all happened so quickly there'd been no time to think about it, try to reason out what was happening, but instinct told him his assailant hadn't been alone.

Nor had he. Another man came out of the darkness of the alley. Dim light, spilling from a window high overhead, gleamed faintly on a steel blade, and he charged Hughes with an ugly curse, trying to close before the dazed armsman could react.

He almost made it, but another blast of pulser darts took him in the chest, and he sprawled backwards with a dull, meaty thud.

Hughes gagged as the smell of blood, ruptured organs, and voiding sphincters washed over him, and his brain told him he needed help. That the wound he'd taken was even more serious than he'd thought. That he might very well die without immediate medical attention. Even with the support of the alley wall, it was harder and harder to stay on his feet, and he raised a suddenly clumsy left hand to key his com.

And that was when the *third* man came out of the alley.

Another knife flashed, and Hughes grunted as the blade struck. He managed to throw his left arm up to intercept the blow, and steel grated on the bone of his forearm. Fresh pain exploded through him, and he felt himself going down, but his wounded arm shot out and grabbed his attacker by the front of his jacket. His muscles felt weak and flaccid to him, but the other man cried out in sudden panic as he was jerked half off his feet and yanked towards the man he'd come to murder. His knife arm flailed for balance, and then he went down with a choked, gurgling scream as half a dozen pulser darts ripped through his chest and lungs.

He and Hughes both went to their knees, facing one another on the blood-soaked sidewalk, and Hughes saw the dreadful understanding in the other man's eyes. Then there was nothing in those eyes at all, and the other man slumped to the side.

Hughes knelt alone on the sidewalk, his brain working sluggishly. Three of them. There'd been three of them, and he'd gotten them all, but—

The sudden, whiplash crack of an old-fashioned automatic pistol exploded down the alley, and the blinding brilliance of the muzzle flash flared like trapped lighting. Steve Hughes never heard or saw it, for the heavy handgun's bullet struck him squarely in the forehead, killing him instantly.

People who hadn't heard the whine of Hughes' pulser heard the distinctive crack of the gun that killed him, and voices shouted in alarm. Windows were thrown open, and people craned their necks to peer out into the night. It was too dark, and there was too much confusion, for anyone to realize—yet—what had happened. But that was going to change, and the cold-eyed man who'd listened to Baird's orders swore venomously as he rushed to the dead armsman's side.

Who the hell had this guy *been?* Taken by surprise by three trained killers, he'd still managed to kill all of them before he went down himself! The cold-eyed man had worked with Baird for over two T-years. Before that, he'd been a high-ranking officer in the Office of Inquisition on Masada, and this was far from the first sinner's death he'd overseen. But he was shocked by how quickly and completely a quiet, efficient assassination had gone wrong, and anger blazed like fiery ice in his eyes.

He knelt in the hot, sticky pool of four men's blood, and his left hand ripped the top button from Hughes' tunic even while he held the pistol ready in his right. He shoved the button into his pocket, then took a moment to check the pulses of his three fellows.

"We've got to get *out* of here!" his sole surviving henchman hissed from the shadows, and the cold-eyed man nodded curtly and shoved himself to his feet.

"*Cleanly*," he snarled, his cold eyes blazing for just an instant with raw fury, and he kicked the dead armsman savagely. "Stinking *bastard*!" he hissed, his voice softer but even more malevolent.

"Come *on*!" the other man demanded. "I can already hear sirens! We've gotta go *now*!"

"Then shut up and go, damn it!" the cold-eyed man barked, and jerked a furious nod down a side alley to where their getaway car waited. The other man didn't hesitate. He was off with the gesture, racing down the alley and already fumbling the keys from his pocket.

"*Bastard*!" the cold-eyed man hissed once more, then drew a deep breath and gazed down for one more moment at the bodies of his companions.

"This world is God's," he told them, a man swearing a solemn oath, and then he, too, disappeared down the alley.

CHAPTER TWENTY-NINE

"**W**elcome to Trevor's Star . . . finally, Dame Alice." Hamish Alexander's word choice might have been more felicitous, but he smiled broadly as he reached out to shake the golden-haired officer's hand firmly. They stood in the boat bay of GNS *Benjamin the Great*, and Alice Truman, in rear admiral's uniform but wearing a vice admiral's collar stars, grinned back at him as she returned his handclasp with interest.

"It's good to be here, My Lord."

"I'm glad you think so, because we've been waiting for you with what might be called bated breath," Earl White Haven told her. She raised an eyebrow, and he laughed. "Your arrival means we're about finished playing paper tiger for Barnett's benefit, and we've all been looking forward to that. Impatient as the public may be back home, I doubt they can even begin to match *our* impatience. For that matter, most folks back home probably don't even realize we were initially supposed to go after Barnett almost three full T-years ago!"

"Probably not," Truman agreed. "As a matter of fact, My Lord, it's hard for a lot of us in the Service to really realize how long you've been sitting out here. Maybe—" she smiled again, this time mirthlessly "—because McQueen's managed to make life so . . . interesting that we haven't really had much leisure to think about it."

"Well, leisure is one thing Eighth Fleet's had altogether too much of," White Haven said firmly, "and I'm looking forward to making things *interesting* for McQueen for a change."

He turned and gestured for Truman to accompany him, and the two of them followed Lieutenant Robards towards *Benjamin*'s central lifts.

"I think we can confidently assume we'll manage at least that much, My Lord," she said. "I know my boys and girls are ready to hold up their end of it. I just hope ONI and the First Space Lord have figured McQueen's probable responses accurately."

"Oh, I think they have." White Haven waved her into the lift car ahead of him, then joined her while Robards punched the destination code into the panel. "I've been more and more impressed with the First Space Lord's insight into the Peep operational posture, especially over the last few months," he went on. "Oh, he got caught out like the rest of us by the Basilisk raid, but between them, he and Pat Givens have predicted just about every major Peep move since then with surprising accuracy. And that little number he pulled off on the Grendelsbane approaches was nothing short of genius." The earl shook his head. "Even if they don't launch the sort of offensive down there that he's hoping for, he's certainly drawn them into a false position. They have to believe we're still not ready for a stand-up fight . . . and I'll guarantee they don't have a clue as to what Buttercup is about to do to them."

"I hope you're right, My Lord," Truman repeated. And, to be honest, she felt confident he was. Which was the reason she spent so much time and effort making herself stand back a bit from the general confidence. *Someone* had to watch out for the pseudogators lurking in the reeds to bite them all on the ass if Sir Thomas Caparelli—and Hamish Alexander—*weren't* right, and it looked like the job was hers.

And one reason I made it mine was because I know how green some of my people really are, she reminded herself grimly. *I said we can hold up our end, and we can, but* Lord *what I'd've given for just three more weeks of training!*

"Another reason I'm glad you're here now," White Haven went on in a more serious tone, "is that security on the entire Anzio project has held up much better than I ever expected it to. All my flag officers and most of my captains have received the stage one briefing, and there are lots of rumors floating about all the way down the line. But no one really *knows* anything, and people have been remarkably careful about when, where, and with whom they'll even discuss the rumors. Which is why I scheduled this conference on the very day of your arrival. I know it's rushing you a bit, but I really want my senior officers, at least, to hear about the new LACs from the horse's mouth, as it were, before the carriers actually begin arriving."

"I understand, My Lord. And at least you said 'from the horse's mouth,' rather than another portion of his anatomy." She chuckled. "Besides, I might as well admit I'd pretty much figured out that was what you had in mind when you invited me aboard. Which is why I brought this." She raised her left hand, and the chain from her wrist to the briefcase it held glittered in the lift car's lights.

"And 'this' is?" White Haven inquired politely.

" 'This' is the official holo presentation my staff put together for Admiral Adcock and BuWeaps just after our last readiness tests, My Lord. I think it will bring all of your people up to speed quite handily. And give them a realistic appreciation of the LACs' limitations, as well as their potential."

"Excellent!" White Haven beamed at her. "I've known you were a resourceful officer since that business at Yeltsin's Star, Dame Alice. I'm happy to see you've stayed that way." The lift slid to a halt, and he looked at Robards. "I see we did forget one thing though, Nathan," he said.

"We did, My Lord?" Robards frowned, and White Haven chuckled.

"It's not our fault, of course. We didn't know Admiral Truman was going to be bringing her home video. I'm sure if we *had* known, we'd have remembered to be sure everyone had lots of popcorn."

Commander Tremaine sat in the chair reserved for him in PriFly, otherwise known as Primary Flight Operations. PriFly was the nerve center of HMS *Hydra*'s LAC operations, and he let his eye flick down the long rows of steady, green lights on the master status panel. Each of those lights showed a LAC bay with its own LAC nestled into the docking arms at one hundred percent readiness for launch. Had any bay been down, or the LAC in it not ready for instant deployment, its light would have burned an angry red, not green. But there wasn't a single flicker of red, and he allowed himself a deep, well-deserved glow of pride as the big CLAC held her place in the transit queue.

He took his attention from the master status panel and looked into the repeater plot deployed from the arm of his command chair. In its own way, that plot was even more impressive than the status panel. There were almost as many lights on it, although their precisely drawn lines were spread more widely, and the ships each of those lights represented were far larger than any LAC. Especially the string of blinking green beads which stretched out ahead and astern of *Hydra*'s own light dot.

Seventeen. That was how many LAC carriers—and their wings—Admiral Truman had managed to get worked up. Each of them was the size of a dreadnought, and between them, they carried almost two *thousand* LACs.

A lot of those LACs could have used weeks or even a month or two more of working up, but that would have been true whenever the Admiralty decided to take the gloves off, he reminded himself. *Someone* would always have been the new kids in the pipeline, after all, and they were scheduled to spend almost a month integrating the carrier groups with Eighth Fleet. Most of that would be for Eighth Fleet's benefit, but they'd get in some more training of their own. And however it worked out, it was past time to commit the carriers and their broods. Past time to throw the *Peeps* back onto the defensive once more.

And this time, we finish *the bastards,* he thought grimly. As the commander of the Nineteenth Strike Wing, he'd been part of the audience when Admiral Truman's staff briefed them on Operation Buttercup. He still thought that was an idiotic codename—it sounded like the name someone might bestow on a pet pig—but he'd been awed by the sheer scale of Admiral Caparelli's brainchild.

Buttercup was going to virtually double the total number of hyper-capable hulls assigned to Admiral White Haven's Eighth Fleet. That was impressive enough, given how hard Tremaine knew the Admiralty had been forced to scratch and scrape to built White Haven's original order of battle. But Eighth Fleet's actual combat power was about to go up exponentially, not arithmetically. In addition to Truman's seventeen LAC carriers, with six more scheduled to follow within two months, it was about to receive twenty-four more of the new *Harrington/Medusa*-class SD(P)s. That would give White Haven thirty-one, and he would be the first admiral allowed to use their full capabilities in an offensive operation. With hordes of LACs to cover their flanks and sweep up lighter units and cripples, those ships were going to mow a swath right through any Peep force stupid enough to get in their way.

Tremaine cocked his chair back, watching the beads ahead of *Hydra*'s vanish through the Junction to Trevor's Star with metronomic precision.

It was funny, really, how important missiles had become for capital ships even as LACs turned into energy-range combatants. It was a reversal of all classic doctrine, for the inability of an old-fashioned

LAC to squeeze in and power a weapon like the massive graser the *Shrike-B* was wrapped around had left the designers no option but to rely on missiles. They hadn't been very *good* missiles, but they'd been the only armament a ship that size could hope to carry, and the theory had been that even crappy weapons were better than none.

Dreadnoughts and superdreadnoughts, on the other hand, had (with a few experimental exceptions) always emphasized energy-heavy armaments and skimped on missiles. Partly that was because a unit locked into the formation of a wall of battle had a very limited firing arc. Its sensors and fire control could see only a relatively small slice of any enemy formation at a time . . . and the same was true for the seekers in its missiles. Worse, each missile broadside's impeller wedges blinded the sensors of its mother ship or any follow-on missiles, at least until they were far enough out to clear the range.

The width of a missile wedge meant that even with the massive grav-drivers missile tubes incorporated, the tubes themselves had to be fairly widely spaced. Otherwise, wedge fratricide would have killed a ship's own broadside. That limited the total number of tubes in a broadside, because there was only so much hull length in which to spread the tubes. Designers had tried for centuries to come up with a way around that, but they'd failed. Staggered launches had seemed like the best bet for many years, but wedge interference with fire control sensors was the spacegoing equivalent of the blinding walls of gunsmoke old wet-navy ships had spewed out. The delay between launches had to be long enough for the missiles already out of the tubes to clear the range . . . and that would have made the intervals between launches so long that it became virtually impossible to achieve the sort of time-on-target fire that saturated an opposing capital ship's active defenses. Rather than a constant dribble of missiles coming in on the target in twos and threes, designers had opted for the maximum number of tubes they *could* cram in, allowing for mutual wedge interference, in order to throw salvos which would at least be dense enough to give point defense a challenge.

For lighter combatants, who fired lower numbers of missiles and whose ability to maneuver was not restricted by the need to maintain rigid position in a wall of battle, missiles became a much more attractive weapon. Their firing arcs were wider, and they could maneuver as radically as they wished to clear those arcs faster once a broadside was away. Not only that, their shorter absolute hull length, coupled with the lower number of tubes they had the mass to mount anyway, meant their missiles spread much more rapidly relative to their firing arcs and made tubes with higher cycle times practical, thus increasing their effective rate of fire even more.

And, of course, there was another reason capital ships had been missile light. Any ship of the wall was extremely hard to kill with missiles. ECM, decoys, and jammers made any ship harder to hit, and ships of the wall could produce more of all of them than anything else in space. Countermissiles, laser clusters, and even broadside energy weapons, could kill incoming missiles short of threat range, and ships of the wall mounted more point defense launchers, laser clusters, and energy mounts than anything else in space. Sidewalls bent and attenuated energy attacks of all types, including the lethal "porcupines" of X-ray lasers generated by bomb-pumped laser heads, and ships of the wall had heavier sidewalls and better particle and radiation shielding than anything else in space. If all else failed, armor could still limit and restrict the damage of anything which actually managed to hit a ship . . . and ships of the wall had heavier, more massive *armor* (and sheer hull size to absorb damage) than anything else in space. And when you put a couple of squadrons of them into a wall, with interlocking point defense and sensor nets, with screening units on their flanks to add to the antimissile fire (and run away and hide as the range dropped to that of the energy weapons), any single missile broadside which could have been mounted by any SD—even one of the Andermani's *Seydlitz*-class—could never hope to take out an opposing superdreadnought.

Not that missiles hadn't always been important. They were the long-ranged sparring tool an admiral used to feel out his enemy's EW and defensive dispositions. And no admiral in his right mind fought one-to-one duels between the units of his wall and those of his opponent's. An entire division or squadron of his ships would lock their sights on a single unit in the enemy wall and throw every missile they had at it, hoping, usually with at least some success, to saturate the defenses locally and get a few hits through. Besides, there was always the chance of a "golden bee-bee." Scotty Tremaine had no idea what a "bee-bee" was (or used to be, at any rate), but every tac officer knew what the ancient term meant. Even the mightiest superdreadnought might simply find itself fatally unlucky when the laser came in from the laser head. Loss of beta or alpha nodes was the most common "freak" hit, but there were others, and there had even been extremely rare cases in which a dreadnought or superdreadnought actually blew up after no more than a couple of hits. No sane strategist would dream of relying on such a one-in-a-million occurrence, but it *had* been known to happen, so it was always worthwhile to throw a few missiles at an opposing wall as you closed.

But the real killer of ships of the wall had always been the short-ranged energy duel . . . which was why, prior to the present war, so very few ships of the wall had been killed over the last few centuries. To really finish off an enemy fleet, your wall had to close through his missile envelope and get to shipboard energy range. No countermissile could stop a capital ship graser or laser. No laser cluster could kill it, and at any range under four hundred thousand kilometers, no sidewall could deflect it. And no other weapon in the universe could match the sheer, armor-smashing, hull-crushing destructiveness of a ship of the wall's energy batteries.

And that was why no reasonably intelligent admiral hung around, if he could help it, while a more powerful wall closed with his. And as it happened, he usually *could* help it. Every admiral knew when to break off and run, and by turning his wall up on its side relative to its attacker, he could completely neutralize his enemies' energy weapons while he ran for it. Which meant it was all up to the missiles once more, and that the advantage shifted decisively to the evader. Indeed, it was the fact that admirals *did* know when to run which had made the slaughter of Fourth Yeltsin so shocking to the naval community when Lady Harrington's SDs managed to close to energy range of Peep battleships.

But that had been a special case. Against an adversary who knew he faced ships of the wall—which the Peeps *hadn't* known at Fourth Yeltsin—the trick had been to pick a target the other side simply had to defend. If you could find one in whose defense he would be compelled to stand and fight, he was effectively pinned while you waded into his fire, closed with him, and finished him off with point-blank energy fire. The problem was that those sorts of targets were hard to find, especially in a war against something as big as the People's Republic of Haven. Which explained why naval warfare had been one long, weary attritional contest for so long.

But the missile pods changed that. By definition, pod missiles launched from some point outside their mother ships' wedges, and their salvos never blinded the sensors or cut the telemetry links of the launching ships' fire control. That allowed a vastly higher number of missiles to be put into space simultaneously, and the hollow-cored SD(P)s could go right *on* launching them in enormous numbers. The sheer volume of fire they could sustain was guaranteed to swamp any old-fashioned wall's defenses, and any electronic warfare more old-fashioned than Ghost Rider's would be only marginally effective against such massive, crushing broadsides.

And where any single missile, or handful of missiles, posed no threat to a ship of the wall, two or three *hundred* laser heads was another matter entirely.

Yet just when the capital ships were rediscovering the joys of long-range missile duels, the *Shrike-Bs* were designed to attack straight into an enemy's teeth. Their grasers could be stopped or at least severely blunted by dreadnought or superdreadnought armor; nothing lighter could stop them. And at close enough range, even a ship of the wall's armor could be breached. It would be suicide to take such a small, light craft in that close against a healthy ship of the wall, but cripples were another matter entirely, and so was anything *lighter* than a ship of the wall.

Which was why Eighth Fleet was about to show the Peeps what the bear did to the buckwheat, Tremaine thought with cold, vengeful anticipation as it became *Hydra's* turn to slip into the Junction. A lot of LACs were probably going to get killed along the way. Some of his would be among them, possibly even *Bad Penny* herself. But with shoals of Admiral Truman's piranha to sweep ahead of Eighth Fleet's wall and a solid core of thirty-plus SD(P)s to smash anything the LACs couldn't handle, nothing in the People's Navy could stop them.

And the Peeps didn't even have a clue what was coming.

CHAPTER THIRTY

"**A**ll right, Oscar." Rob Pierre sighed with an edge of resigned humor. "I know why you're here, so you might as well get started."

"Am I really that predictable?" Oscar Saint-Just asked wryly, and the Chairman of the Committee of Public Safety nodded.

"To me, at any rate. On the other hand, I know you just a bit better than most other people. And it's part of your job to be persistent about things you genuinely feel should be brought to my attention. So lay on, MacDuff."

Saint-Just's right eyebrow rose as the last reference sailed over his head. But literary allusions weren't high on his list of interests, and he brushed the momentary flicker of curiosity aside and turned to the matter which had brought him here.

"Not to harp too strongly on it, Rob, I think the preliminary reports from Twelfth Fleet confirm the fact that McQueen's been . . . overly cautious, let's say, where the Manties and their new weapons are concerned."

"Maybe," Pierre replied, and smiled as Saint-Just's eyes rolled ever so slightly heavenward. "All right, Oscar," he admitted. "I tend to agree with you. But that doesn't necessarily mean her caution has been the product of sinister designs on you and me."

"It doesn't *prove* it," the emphasis of Saint-Just's concession was pointed, "but the fact that she has been over cautious seems fairly evident, doesn't it?"

"It looks like it, but as you just pointed out yourself, all we have so far are the preliminary reports. And the fact that we lost five of the wall, including the task force's flagship and its commanding admiral and his commissioner at Elric to a single missile salvo from the Manties is at least a little worrisome."

"Giscard's and Tourville's reports are preliminary," Saint-Just retorted. "My own reports from the senior SS officers assigned to their task forces aren't. They set forth their own conclusions very clearly and, I think, with powerful supporting evidence."

"And Twelfth Fleet's commissioners? Have *they* expressed any reservations about Giscard's and Tourville's reports?"

"Not so far," Saint-Just admitted. "But they're part of the command structure. Honeker, Tourville's commissioner, has gotten a good bit more reticent in his reports since Operation Icarus. No—" he shook his head as Pierre's eyes sharpened "—I don't think he's covering up for anything overtly treasonous on Tourville's part. If I did, I'd yank him home in a heartbeat. But I do think he's been directly associated with Tourville in his moment of triumph and he's seen how well the man performs in action. What I'm afraid of is that that may make him less skeptical about Tourville's post-battle analyses than he ought to be. It's fairly clear—from what he hasn't said, even more than from what he has—that Honeker admires and respects Tourville, and that he also respects Tourville's military judgment. Which, in turn, might explain why he's withholding his own judgment until he feels Tourville's had time to fully consider the results of Scylla.

"And Pritchart?" Pierre watched Saint-Just carefully. Pritchart had been Oscar's fair-haired girl for years, and Pierre knew how much Saint-Just respected her instincts.

"I think it may be more of the same in her case, though for somewhat different reasons," Saint-Just admitted. "As I've said before, Eloise has never liked Giscard a bit, and that seems to have become even more pronounced over the last T-year or so. But she's always respected his military ability, and *that's* become more pronounced, too. Overall, I think it's a good thing she can overcome her personal dislike enough to consider his command decisions dispassionately, but in this instance, I think she may have bent too far over backward trying to be fair."

"And it's also possible *you're* refusing to bend far *enough* over backward because of your distrust for McQueen," Pierre pointed out. Saint-Just gazed at him for a moment, then nodded. "All right. As long as we both bear that in mind, go ahead and tell me what your superdreadnought captains have to say."

"They're pretty much in agreement with Giscard, really. Except for the need for more in-depth analysis he keeps harping on. The

Manties have demonstrated an improvement in their electronic warfare abilities and a somewhat smaller improvement in their missiles' seeking capability. Giscard certainly seems to be correct when he suggests that a higher than normal percentage of Manty missiles managed to acquire locks on their targets, but he may be overly pessimistic about how much higher the percentage was. My captains were more impressed with the improvements in the Manties' defensive EW and ECM. Their jammers and decoys both seem to have been much better than they ought to have been, and my analysts agree with Giscard and Tourville that the improvement is likely to have unpleasant implications for future missile engagements.

"At the same time, however, my captains' reports indicate that the other side's improved EW wasn't enough to overcome the disparity of throw-weight Twelfth Fleet managed to achieve. At Elric alone, we killed at least four Manty SDs. Given the difference in the sizes of the two forces, that was decisive, and the Manties had no choice but to break and run. The same thing happened at Treadway and Solway, except that the Manties ran sooner, inflicted lower losses on us, and took lower losses of their own. The implication of *that*, it seems clear, is that they're still more sensitive to losses than we are, probably because their absolute strength is still so much lower than ours and because of the way McQueen's earlier operations pushed them into redeploying the ships of the wall they have. If we move against them in strength and force combat, we're going to take heavier losses than they are. That's been a given from day one. But I think Elric also demonstrates that as long as we can balance our numbers against their tech advantage, we can push them back for an acceptable loss ratio. Which, by the way, is exactly the argument *McQueen* made when she put Operation Icarus together."

"Which does suggest she ought to at least understand what you're getting at," Pierre acknowledged, and Saint-Just nodded vigorously.

"Exactly. She was the one who trotted out that old saying about omelettes and eggs, Rob, and she was right. Which gives one furiously to think when she suddenly starts sounding so much like Kline did before we brought her in to replace him.

"But most importantly, there wasn't a single sign of any of her 'super LACs,' and while the Manties' missiles may have been a bit more accurate than usual, there was no sign of any enormously extended range, either. Those are the two things she's been most scared of, officially, at least, and our ships never saw either of them. And they never saw them, let me remind you, in a series of actions in which we broke through the Manty front to within less than sixty light-years of Grendelsbane. If they had any new weapons, surely they would have used them to protect the approaches to a system that critical."

"So you think this proves they don't have them, and that Esther's argument they may just be withholding them for the right moment is unfounded."

"Pretty much. The reports don't absolutely disprove or invalidate her arguments. Then again, nothing short of a Manty surrender ever will *absolutely* disprove them. More to the point, I don't think we can afford to let ourselves be paralyzed by 'might-be's and 'maybe-so's. If the Manties are on the ropes, even if it's only temporary, we need to slug them harder than ever, and McQueen is certainly a good enough strategist to know that. So if she keeps refusing to push the pace, I think we ought to start seriously considering the need to assume the worst about her ultimate motivations and intentions."

Citizen Secretary of War Esther McQueen sat back and puffed her lips irritably while Citizen Admiral Ivan Bukato finished reading the memo from Rob Pierre. The man who had inherited all the unglamourous portions of Amos Parnell's job got to the end, snorted harshly, deactivated the memo pad, and leaned forward to lay it on her desk.

"Short and to the point, at least."

"It is that," McQueen agreed. "I'm still not convinced that activating Operation Bagration is the right move, but orders are orders. In the final analysis, all I can do is advise the Committee—the actual decision is theirs," she added for the benefit of StateSec's microphones. "Our job is to do what we're told, so I suppose the first order of business is to start looking around for reinforcements we can send Twelfth Fleet."

"Agreed." Bukato sat back and crossed his legs. "But we also need to see about getting more repair ships moved up, as well, Ma'am. If we're going to accelerate the operational tempo, Giscard is going to need the capacity to make more temporary front-line repairs for units with minor damage."

"Good point." McQueen nodded and frowned thoughtfully. "We'll need a bigger commitment in missile colliers, too. I don't like the initial estimates of how much the Manties' EW has improved. It looks to me like it's going to take more missiles than ever to saturate their defenses, and if their fire is going to get even more accurate than it has been, we'll need that saturation badly."

"I think we can hack that part of it, Ma'am. I'm more concerned about coming up with the ships of the wall."

"I suppose we'll have to take them away from Tom Theisman." McQueen sighed. "I hate it, but it looks like the only real option."

Bukato nodded unhappily. Neither he nor his superior chose to comment, for the microphones, on *why* reducing the mobile forces defending the Barnett System was the only real option, but the answer was simple enough. Even though the People's Navy clearly held the initiative, the very politicians who demanded that that initiative be exploited were unwilling to uncover any of their own vital areas. The Capital Fleet here in the Haven System, for example, contained over seventy ships of the wall. McQueen would dearly have loved to cut that number by a third. If she'd been allowed to do that for the Capital Fleet and only two or three other fleets covering nodal systems, she could have more than doubled Twelfth Fleet's superdreadnought strength. And all without taking a single additional ship away from Barnett, which was the system most likely to draw an actual attack if the Manties did suddenly throw an offensive at her.

"Theisman won't like it," Bukato predicted after a moment, and McQueen surprised herself with a small, sharp laugh.

"No, he won't. For that matter, *I* wouldn't like it very much, if I were in his shoes. Hell I'm *not* in his shoes and I don't much like doing it! But everything we've seen suggests the Manties have more or less turned their Eighth Fleet into a scarecrow. I think NavInt is right; they're using White Haven and his ships as their strategic reserve, and their possession of the Junction lets them get away with it."

"But their stance could change, Ma'am, and that's what Theisman's going to be worried about."

"Me, too," McQueen admitted frankly. "But the Citizen Chairman is right in at least one respect. If we're going to push the offensive, we're going to have to take some risks somewhere. And let's be honest, Ivan. Barnett was mainly important because of the way Ransom turned it into some sort of 'People's Redoubt' for public morale. The fleet base is big, and losing it would hurt, but it was really designed as a jumping-off point for offensive operations against the center of the Alliance. If we're going to go around their flank instead, DuQuesne Base isn't going to be very useful to us, and losing it would hardly cripple us at this point."

"I know, Ma'am." It was Bukato's turn to grimace. "How much were you thinking about taking away from him?"

"At least a couple of more squadrons of the wall," McQueen said, and the citizen admiral winced. "I don't like it either, but he's got almost all the fixed defenses back up and running, and we've shipped in over three hundred additional LACs. They may not be all that nasty compared to Manty LACs—" she and Bukato met one another's eyes with matching humorless smiles "—but they're a hell of a lot better than nothing for inner system defense. And, frankly, I was impressed by what he's managed with the mines and pods."

"Me, too," Bukato agreed, and he meant it. Minefields were a part of almost any area defense plan, but traditional mines were little more than floating, bomb-pumped laser buoys designed to lurk until some unfortunate entered their range. Theisman had taken them a bit further, using Barnett's local yard capacity to field-modify the mines by strapping the buoys onto the noses of stealthed recon drones. They weren't very fast, and they weren't very accurate, but they had a lot of endurance and they would be hard to detect. McQueen wasn't certain that they would prove effective at sneaking into attack range, but there was always a chance, and it was the sort of innovative adaptation the People's Navy needed badly.

Longer-ranged missiles, deployed in orbit around key planets, were also a common defense. Those missiles were subject to prox-imity soft kills and always had marginally shorter powered ranges than those launched from proper shipboard launchers, and arrang-ing fire control for them had always been a problem, yet they were a useful adjunct to proper orbital fortresses or launchers on moons and asteroids.

But Theisman had made changes there, too, by figuring out how to duplicate what NavInt (or, at least, the portion of NavInt under McQueen's control) had decided White Haven must have done at Basilisk. It hadn't been easy, given the generally cruder state of the PN's fire control and cybernetics, but his techs had found a way to deploy literally dozens of missile pods for each orbital fortress. The pods' internal launchers neatly overcame the small range dis-advantage older style orbital missiles suffered from, which was nice. But what was even nicer was that the techs had come up with a cascade targeting hierarchy, one in which individual pods were designated to lead a wave of up to six additional pods in a single launch. In practice, it meant the forts' fire control "aimed" only one pod at each target. That pod then uploaded exactly the same targeting data to the six pods slaved to it, and all seven of them went after the same victim with over eighty missiles . . . and required only one "slot" of a given fort's targeting capability. None would have a firing solution quite as good as the fort might have managed had its targeting systems been linked directly to each pod, providing each with its own individual solution, but the degradation was acceptable. Indeed, given the sheer weight of fire it would produce, the degradation was much more than merely "acceptable."

"I don't think he could hold out indefinitely if the Manties really came after him," McQueen went on after a moment, "but he could certainly hurt them badly. Especially in the initial attacks, before they figure out what his pod fire control can do to them. And, like I say, we've got to find the ships somewhere, Ivan."

"You're right, of course, Ma'am. But even if we take two squadrons away from him, we're going to have to come up with more from somewhere else. Groenewold lost five of the wall, with two more damaged badly enough to require yard repairs. Giscard lost another at Treadway, with two more headed for the yard. Tourville didn't lose any outright at Solway, but he still has at least one that's going to have to head for the yard, and from my reading of his initial report, that may go up to four for him, too, once he has a chance for complete damage surveys. That's six completely destroyed, and from five to eight down for repairs, and that makes a minimum total of eleven and possibly as many as fourteen. So even if we take two full squadrons away from Theisman, Twelfth Fleet's order of battle will only be back to where it was before Scylla, and we need more than that if Bagration's going to be a serious offensive."

"I know. I know." McQueen leaned her head back and pinched the bridge of her nose. "We can probably divert another squadron or two from rear areas if we pick off single ships here and there, but they'll come as individual units, not cohesive squadrons." She thought hard for several seconds, then sighed. "Moving additional units from all over the Republic to Treadway would take too long, Ivan. The Citizen Chairman wants this expedited to the maximum—he made that clear enough—but if that's what he really wants, he's going to have to give me a little more freedom in deployment postures."

"Meaning, Ma'am?" Bukato asked. His expression was considerably more cautious than he allowed his tone to be, and McQueen gave him a faint, reassuring smile.

"We need to get concentrated reinforcements to the front as quickly as possible if we're going to comply with this directive," she said, flicking a finger at the memo pad on the corner of her desk. "The fastest way to do that would be to slice them off of

Capital Fleet. We can dispatch them directly from the capital, without having to send couriers all over Hell's back forty before the ships we're reassigning even know to begin moving, which would cut weeks off the total deployment time. And we can send experienced squadrons who've had months and years to train together, rather than singletons and doubletons from all over the damned place that Giscard will have to shake down, plug in, and train after they arrive. I know it's against existing policy, but we've got to make some hard choices to bring this off, and we can avoid being uncovered here for a couple of weeks. I can think of four or five core systems where we could easily skim off single SD squadrons and order them to the capital . . . and every one of them could be here almost as quickly as any units we detach from Capital Fleet could reach Tourville."

"Do you think the Committee will agree?" Bukato asked, and she shrugged.

"I think the military arguments are persuasive," she said, "and I know what the Citizen Chairman's just ordered me to do. Combining those two things, yes, I think the Committee will agree. Not happily, perhaps, but I think we'll get the go ahead."

" . . . think we'll get the go ahead."

Oscar Saint-Just stopped the playback, and his frown was pensive. He didn't much care for what he'd just heard. Oh, McQueen and Bukato were saying the right things, outwardly, at least, about the primacy of civilian control and the need to obey orders. But there was an . . . undertone he didn't like. He could scarcely call it conspiratorial, but neither could he avoid the suspicion that the two of them had plans of their own. No doubt Rob would remind him, probably with reason, that any smoothly functioning command team had to develop a shared mindset and a sense of solidarity. The problem was that both McQueen and Bukato knew they were speaking to his bugs, which meant they were certain to *say* all the right things. It didn't mean they were certain to *mean* them, however, and all their dutiful subservience to civilian authority sounded entirely too much like a mask for something else to his trained and suspicious ear.

Nor did he care for this notion of transferring units from Capital Fleet. Oh, it made sense in a narrow military way. That was the problem; *everything* McQueen suggested made sense, or could at least be justified, in military terms. But he'd taken a look at her preliminary list of proposed ship movements, and it seemed . . . interesting to him that the admirals commanding the squadrons

she wanted to send Tourville seemed to include such a high percentage of politically reliable officers. Of course, all of the COs
in Capital Fleet had demonstrated their reliability, or they would
have been somewhere else in the first place. But she still seemed
to Saint-Just's possibly hypersuspicious way of thinking to have
concentrated on the *most* reliable of them. The squadrons she
wanted to transfer *into* the capital system, on the other hand,
seemed to contain a remarkably high percentage of officers who
would clearly have been more comfortable in a more traditional
naval command structure. Which was to say, one without people's
commissioners looking over their shoulders.

The problem was that because the movements were so logical from a military perspective, and because McQueen was justifying them on the basis of obeying a direct order from Rob
Pierre, Saint-Just could scarcely object to them. He'd gotten his
way in the accelerated operational tempo. If he started complaining about how McQueen was doing what he'd wanted her to do
in the first place, it could only be seen as a possible indication
of paranoia on his part, which would undercut his credibility with
Pierre on the topic of McQueen in the future. But if she was,
in fact, using her new orders as a way to restructure Capital Fleet
into something which would be more . . . responsive to any plans
of her own, then it was Saint-Just's job to see to it she failed
in her objective.

He tilted his chair back and drummed the fingers of his right
hand on a chair arm while he swiveled back and forth in short,
thoughtful arcs. What he needed, he decided, was a way to defang
any plans she might have while justifying his own actions just as
amply and logically as she'd justified hers. But how?

He thought for several more moments, then stopped drumming
on the chair arm while an arrested light flickered in his eyes.

Theisman, he thought. *The man's about as apolitical as a lump
of rock, he's good at his job, and the Navy respects him. More to
the point, he's been stuck out at Barnett the whole time McQueen's
been Secretary of War. Whatever she may be up to with Bukato
and his bunch over at the Octagon, she hasn't had the opportunity to involve Theisman in it, and if he winds up commanding
Capital Fleet, she'll at least be stymied until she can bring him on
board her little conspiracy. And since she's raiding Barnett herself
on the basis that we can afford to lose it, she can hardly object
to the transfer by arguing that we need to leave him in such a
critically important post.*

He pondered the idea for a while longer, turning it in his

thoughts to examine it from all angles. It wasn't perfect, he decided, but it would at least be a step in the right direction. Besides, McQueen would know why he'd done it, and that would piss her off mightily . . . which would make it eminently worthwhile in its own right.

CHAPTER THIRTY-ONE

Honor looked around the smallish office and sighed. It was a heartfelt sound, but even she couldn't have said whether it sprang from relief or sadness. There was certainly relief in it, because the last several months had been much more exhausting than any "convalescent duty" should have implied. Which was mostly her own fault. She should have turned down at least one of Sir Thomas' requests, but she could no more have done that than she could have flown the Copperwalls without her hang glider.

It had left her with some hard decisions, though. One had been to more or less abandon the language-teaching project to Doctor Arif and Miranda. Well, the two of them and James MacGuiness. Leaving Nimitz behind for his and Samantha's "lessons" had been one of the harder things she'd done since escaping Cerberus, especially when, even at a distance, she'd been able to taste his frustration in the early days of the project. But one lesson she'd forced herself to accept years ago was that she simply *had* to turn loose when she delegated some responsibility. Hovering over the person she'd entrusted a task to only bought the worst of both worlds. She ended up spending almost as much time on it as if she'd simply done it herself from the beginning, and those she'd delegated were liable to be left with the impression that she didn't fully trust their ability. Not to mention the fact that the only way someone really learned was by doing, and trying to clear all the obstacles out of someone's path didn't do her any favors, however it seemed at the time. At the very best, it cost them the chance to learn from mistakes. At worst, it simply postponed the time when they ran into a problem they didn't know how to handle . . . and left them fatally overconfident because they thought they *did* know.

It was something she'd long ago learned to do where junior officers were concerned—her lips twitched in a small smile as she remembered an agonizingly young Rafael Cardones and a flight of improperly programmed recon platforms—but that was because she'd recognized her responsibility to teach them. It was infinitely harder to hand a job she thought *she* ought to be doing to someone she knew could do it just as well, because that felt . . . lazy. Like shirking. Which helped explain why she felt she'd never had *quite* enough time over the last T-year to spend on any given task.

But if she hadn't been able to put in as many hours in this office as she thought she really should have, she'd put in enough to discover something she hadn't known. Something she had to give up along with the office . . . which explained the sadness that was also so much a part of that sigh.

She loved to teach.

She supposed that she shouldn't have been surprised by that. After all, one of the things she'd most enjoyed about her career was stretching the minds of junior officers, sharing with them the joy *she'd* found in mastering their shared profession. And, if she was honest, she took far more pleasure from the men and women she'd watched grow and blossom into the potential she'd seen in them from the outset than she did in all her medals and titles and prize money. *They* were what the future was all about, just as they were the ones who would have to do the fighting and the dying if the Star Kingdom was to have a future, and teaching them how much they could accomplish was one of the highest callings she could imagine.

Which had made her a natural at Saganami Island. Not only that, but the empathic sense she'd developed had given her a priceless gift: that of knowledge. Of knowing her students recognized how much they meant to her, how proud of them she was.

She would miss D'Orville Hall. She would miss everything about Saganami Island, even if it was no longer quite the Academy she recalled. It was so much bigger, so much more bustling. The reality of the war which had been only a looming threat during her years here had fallen upon the Academy like a landslide and made it over into something faster and more furious, with a different, harder-edged dedication. In all too many ways, the wartime Academy had become an extension of the front lines, which was good, in some respects, she thought. She had stressed to her students that they were headed straight from their classrooms into a shooting war, and it was important they understand that. Yet along the way the "Saganami experience," she supposed she should call it, had lost something. Not of innocence, or of sleepiness. But of . . . assimilation. Of the way young men and women grew gradually into the Navy, and of the way the Navy accepted that transformation of civilians into itself.

No, that wasn't right, either. In fact, she couldn't seem to hit exactly the right way to describe it, and she doubted she ever would be able to. Perhaps there wasn't a word.

And perhaps what I'm really remembering is that golden glow of never-was that seems to hang onto everything we remember from "happier days," she thought with a wry snort, and Nimitz bleeked softly from the perch beside the door.

"All right. All right, Stinker! I'm through moping," she told him, and closed the desk drawer firmly. Her papers and record chips had already disappeared, and she made one last check for dust or forgotten possessions, and then held out her arms to the 'cat.

He launched himself from the perch with every bit of his old assurance, and she laughed, tasting and sharing his pleasure as he landed precisely in her arms and then swarmed up and around onto her shoulder. He adjusted his position with care, hooking his feet-hands—*both* feet-hands, functioning perfectly at last—into the shoulder of her tunic while the claws of his true-feet dug gently in below her shoulder blade. He balanced himself there, one true-hand resting on top of her head, and she drew a deep, lung-filling breath.

One thing a naval career taught was that nothing ever remained the same. Doors opened and closed as duties and assignments changed, she reminded herself, and stepped through the door from this one. She closed it quietly behind her, then paused to acknowledge the salutes of two third-form middies who were apparently remaining on campus over the long holiday. They went on down the echoing hall, and she watched their backs for a moment with a smile, then turned to the green-uniformed man who'd stood waiting patiently for her outside her office.

"All right, Andrew. We can go now."

"Are you sure, My Lady?" His eyes showed the gentle amusement and understanding she tasted in his emotions, and she squeezed his shoulder.

"Yes, I'm sure," she told him, and turned to follow the midshipmen down the hall.

✧   ✧   ✧

"Well, Your Grace, I have to say we got more than our money's worth out of your stay on Manticore."

Sir Thomas Caparelli and Honor sat on the balcony outside his office. Admiralty House was a modest structure, only a little over a hundred stories in height, but the First Space Lord's office was on the seventy-third floor. That turned the people on the walkways and avenues below into brightly colored specks, and the old-fashioned umbrella shading the crystoplast table flapped occasionally as an air car swooped past just a little faster than traffic regs really allowed for such low altitudes.

Honor, Nimitz, and LaFollet had arrived early, and she'd been amusing herself by cycling her new eye back and forth through the full range from normal vision to its maximum telescopic magnification while she watched the pedestrians. It made her feel a little giddy, but it was fascinating, too. Rather like playing with one of the kaleidoscopes of which Grayson children were so fond. And it had also seemed appropriate, somehow. Almost as if it were some formal proof that the physical repairs which had kept her here for so long were truly completed at last.

Oh, they weren't really *completed*, of course. She was mastering her new arm's more usual range of movement, but its fingers remained maddeningly clumsy. Sometimes it almost seemed it had been better to have only one hand than it was to have one and a fraction. And a *clumsy*, unreliable fraction, at that. But it was only a matter of practice. She kept telling herself that, kept forcing herself to *try* to use two hands for what ought to be two-handed jobs rather than simply shutting the thing down and doing them the one-handed way she'd been forced to learn.

Now she turned and smiled at Caparelli across the table.

"I'm glad you think so, Sir. I have to admit, I sometimes felt you'd given me too many balls to keep in the air simultaneously. Even now, I sort of wish you'd settled for asking me to wear a single hat. That way I could really have concentrated on just one job. As it is, I can't help thinking I could have done better at any one of them than I actually did if I hadn't spread myself so thin."

"Trust me, Your Grace. The Navy is more than satisfied . . . and Doctor Montoya was certainly right about your notion of a leisurely convalescence! If I'd realized how hard you were going to push yourself on all of the tasks I asked you to take on, I would have felt horribly guilty for asking. I'd have done it anyway, though, I'm afraid, because we really did need you."

Honor made a brushing-away gesture with her hand—her *left* hand, this time, but he shook his head at her.

"No, Your Grace. It's not something you can brush off. You did an outstanding job with your classes, despite the many other charges on your time, and those dinner parties of yours were far above and beyond the call of duty. I don't believe anyone's ever before seen midshipmen actually fighting to get invited *into* an admiral's presence. More to the point, fourteen of the top fifteen scorers—and thirty-seven of the top fifty—in the first year Tactical curriculum were your students,."

"They did the work, Sir. I just pointed them in the right direction," Honor said a bit uncomfortably, and he chuckled.

"There's some truth in that, I suppose. But that's partly because you did such a good job of pointing . . . and partly because of how motivated they were. Both before you ever got your hands on them—we set a new record for middies who requested a single instructor—and after you had a chance to put your stamp on them." He chuckled again. "I understand you're not particularly fond of the nickname, but when the student body heard 'the Salamander' was going to be lecturing, the registrar's office was almost buried under transfer slips from people trying to get into your sections."

"The 'faxes had a lot more to do with that sort of hero worship than anything *I* ever did," Honor insisted.

"Perhaps." Caparelli allowed her the last word on that topic and took a sip from his chilled glass. Honor drank from her own, then set it down and offered Nimitz a celery stick. He took it and crunched cheerfully away, and she turned back to Caparelli as the First Space Lord returned his moisture-beaded glass to its coaster.

"Even more than the Academy, however, I wanted to thank you for the job you did at ATC," he said more seriously. "For two things, really. One is the nature of the changes you made to the Crusher. The other is using the opportunity to salvage Commander Jaruwalski's career. I ought to've seen to that myself."

"You're the First Space Lord of the Queen's entire navy, Sir. You've got more than enough on your plate without dealing with individual commanders. I, on the other hand, happened to have served under Santino early in his career. I *knew* what a vindictive idiot he was, and that gave me a personal motive for looking more closely than most at what happened in Seaford. But I am glad Andrea's turned her career back around. She's good, Sir Thomas. Very good, indeed. It's only my opinion, but I think BuPers should be looking closely at the notion of promoting her to captain jaygee outside the zone."

"I think you can safely assume that's being seen to. Jackson

Kriangsak's already spoken to Lucian, and I understand she's being slipped onto the next list."

"Good," Honor said firmly, and suppressed a mental snort at her own actions.

She'd always hated the way some officers played the patronage game, and she'd always felt that such a system, by its very nature, was subject to serious abuse. Elvis Santino and Pavel Young were telling cases in point. But, then, she'd never really considered the possibility of having sufficient power to play it herself, and now, in the best tradition of rationalizers the galaxy over, she saw some advantages to it. Andrea Jaruwalski's career had been headed for the ash heap, and its salvage, which was certainly a plus for the Navy, stemmed entirely from the fact that Honor had made her own first investment in the patronage system. Perhaps those who'd played the game the way Hamish Alexander did (she scarcely even noticed the familiar little pang that name sent through her) had had a point all along. The nurturing of junior officers not because they were relatives—or the children of friends or relatives, or of people who could repay you with favors of their own—but because they were outstanding *officers,* truly was a form of payback. Not to any individual. Not even to the individual you took under your wing. It was payback to the Navy, and to the Star Kingdom at large.

"I have to admit, though," Caparelli went on, "I never anticipated what you'd do at ATC. I should have, I suppose, given your background and career track, but I didn't. Maybe we've all been suffering a bit too much from the 'not-invented-here' syndrome to see a lot of things that need doing."

"I wouldn't go that far, Sir. I do think the RMN suffers from a bit of, well, call it tunnel vision. There's definitely a sense of superiority, which is fair enough, I suppose, when we compare ourselves to the Peeps, or the thugs we keep running into in Silesia. We *are* better than they are. And, for that matter, we *do* have more experience than any of our allies as a deep-space force. But I do believe the Service needs to be more awake to the fact that there are other ways—some better, some worse—to do the same things."

"I agree entirely. And that's especially true now that we're running so many non-Manticoran officers through the Crusher. Not only do we need to be aware that we may have something to learn *from* them, but we damned well ought to be making sure we don't step on their toes by talking down *to* them. No doubt there will always be a certain inescapable edge of, um, *institutional arrogance,* perhaps. That's probably a healthy thing, and I imagine most of our allies will understand and accept it in the Alliance's senior partner. But bringing in Allied flag officers to help design and build the training programs was a stroke of genius, Your Grace. And building scenarios which require Manticoran officers to follow foreign doctrine and operate with Zanzibaran or Grayson or Alizonian hardware was another. I understand several of our aspiring COs found it a humbling experience, and forcing them to recognize that a lot of our supposed 'officer superiority' actually rests on the superiority of our hardware was a very good thing. Besides, we've already picked up several useful notions from the Graysons. I'll be very surprised if we don't pick up a few more from some of our other allies, as well . . . now that you've started us listening to them."

"I hope so, Sir Thomas," Honor said very seriously. "They *do* have things to teach us, and admitting that—to them, as well as to ourselves—seems to me to be one of the better ways to motivate them to learn from *us*, as well."

"Agreed, Your Grace. Agreed." He nodded vigorously, then leaned back in his chair and gazed out over the sun-drenched, afternoon capital.

"I understand you'll be returning to Grayson shortly," he observed, and Honor nodded at the change of subject.

"I've been here for almost a year, Sir. It's time I got back to my responsibilities as Steadholder Harrington. Besides, Willard Neufsteiler has a batch of papers I need to sign."

"I can certainly understand that, Your Grace. But I also understand the new session of the Conclave of Steadholders will begin a few weeks after you get back."

"That's another reason I need to get home," Honor agreed, then paused and smiled crookedly. " 'Home,' " she repeated quietly. "You know, that word's gotten just a little complicated for me over the last few years."

"That would seem to be a bit of an understatement," Caparelli agreed. "But I suppose the reason I asked was that I was wondering what your plans for the future are. Specifically, what your plans for returning to active duty might be."

"My plans?" Honor cocked an eyebrow. "I rather assumed that was up to the Bureau of Personnel, Sir," she said, and he shrugged.

"Your Grace, you're an admiral in the Queen's Navy, and a duchess. You're also an admiral in the *Grayson* Navy, and a steadholder. That means Grayson and the Star Kingdom can both make legitimate claims on your services, and we're both clever enough to *want* to claim them. But given your status, the decision of which of us actually gets you is going to be up to you, so I thought I'd just get my bid in early."

"Sir Thomas, I—" she began, but a wave of his hand interrupted her.

"I'm not trying to put pressure on you yet. If for no other reason, because I've spoken to BuMed and I know Admiral Mannock wouldn't even let you go back on full active duty status in our uniform for another three or four months. I just want you to think about it. And, I suppose, I wanted to be sure you realize you're at a stage in your career which gives you a great deal more control over your future and your future assignments than you may have noticed. You need to be prepared to deal with that fact."

"I—" Honor paused once more, then shrugged. "I suppose you're right, Sir Thomas. And you're also right that it hadn't occurred to me to think of it that way."

"Oh, I think you were headed in that direction, and rightly so. I just thought I'd mention it as something you should specifically consider."

It was his turn to pause, and Honor turned to look more directly at him as she tasted the turn of his emotions. They'd grown suddenly pensive, yet there was an excitement—an anticipation—and perhaps just a small edge of fear in them. He turned his head to gaze out over the city once more, then drew a deep breath.

"In addition to the points we've already discussed, Your Grace, there was one other thing I wanted to tell you when I asked you to visit me this afternoon." He turned back to her, and she raised her eyebrows in polite question.

"I activated Operation Buttercup yesterday," he told her, and she felt herself sit straight upright in her chair. She knew about Operation Buttercup. She and Alice Truman had gamed out several variant strategies for it using the main tactical simulator at ATC, and the final ops plan had Honor's fingerprints all over it.

"Alice Truman will be leaving for Trevor's Star next week," Caparelli went on quietly. "By the time you get back to Grayson, Eighth Fleet should be ready to move. At the moment, we seem to have the Peeps strongly committed to an offensive against Grendelsbane Station, and I had to divert some of the SD(P)s to bolster the station's defenses. But we managed to hit the basic force levels specified by the final ops plan. Some of the LAC wings are still a lot greener than I could have wished, but—"

He shrugged slightly, his emotions laced with the regret any good commander felt at sending his men and women into harm's way.

"I understand, Sir," Honor said, her voice equally quiet, and she thought about some of the men and women she knew in the ships committed to Buttercup. Scotty Tremain and Horace Harkness. Alice Truman. Rafael Cardones, who commanded one of Alice's CLACs, and Rear Admiral of the Red Alistair McKeon, one of her division commanders. There were dozens of others beyond those names, and she felt a momentary stab of fear, an echo of the gut-deep awareness that people died in battle.

"Thank you for telling me," she said after a moment, and forced a smile. "I never realized how much harder it is to send people off to fight when you can't go with them."

"One of the hardest lessons to learn . . . or accept, at least," he agreed, gazing back out over the city once more. "Here I sit, on a beautiful summer afternoon, and out there—" he twitched a nod at the deep blue vault of the sky "—hundreds of thousands of men and women are heading off into battle because *I* told them to go. Ultimately, whatever happens to them will be my responsibility . . . and there's not a thing in the universe I can do from this point on to affect what does happen to them."

"Whatever they pay you, Sir, it isn't enough," Honor told him, and he turned to grin wryly at her.

"Your Grace, they don't pay *any* of us enough, but if we can't take a joke, then we shouldn't have joined."

The hoary, lower-deck proverb took Honor completely by surprise coming from him, and she giggled. She couldn't help it, and his smile of delight as he startled the schoolgirl sound out of her only made it worse. It took her several seconds to get herself back under control, and she gave him a severe look once she had.

"I can think of one or two other clichés which might appropriately be applied to you, Sir Thomas. None of them, at the moment, complimentary, I'm afraid."

"Ah, well! I suppose I shouldn't be surprised. And I'm used to the abuse by now. Very few people seem to appreciate what a fine, stalwart sort of fellow I actually am."

" 'Fine' and 'stalwart' are *not* the first two adjectives which spring to mind when I think of you, Sir," she told him severely, and he chuckled again. "However, I did want to take this opportunity to invite you to a small get-together Miranda and my mother are planning for next month. I understand it will be a modest little affair—no more than two or three hundred on the guest list—to clear the decks here in the Star Kingdom before we head back to Grayson. Her Majesty has consented to attend, and I hope you will, too."

"I would be honored, Your Grace," he said seriously.

"Good. Because between now and then, I'm going to put Nimitz, Farragut, and Samantha up to devising some proper greeting for a fine, stalwart sort of fellow like yourself." She smiled seraphically at him. "And knowing the three of *them*, Sir Thomas, you may just discover that you'd have been better off in the lead wave of Buttercup!"

CHAPTER THIRTY-TWO

"**H**ow about taking a walk with me, Denis?"

People's Commissioner Denis LePic looked up quickly. Citizen Admiral Thomas Theisman's voice could not have been more casual, but LePic had known Theisman for many years, and over that time, he'd come to understand the citizen admiral as well as any of his StateSec superiors could possibly have desired.

In fact, he'd come to know Thomas Theisman rather too well for his superiors' taste . . . had they known it. But LePic had gone to some lengths to insure that they *didn't* know, and especially over the last three years. It hadn't been an easy decision, for he was a man who believed passionately in the need to reform the old system. Yet despite that, it had still been easier than it ought to have been. He'd begun to have quiet doubts, so quiet he'd almost managed to conceal them even from himself, long before Cordelia Ransom gloatingly condemned Honor Harrington to death and used the occasion to grind home her contempt for the Navy's uniformed personnel. And any concept of common decency.

The two years after that had been especially hard on LePic and his conscience. He'd tried to tell himself Ransom had been an aberration, that the rest of the Committee wasn't like her, and to an extent, that was true. Ransom had been a sadist who actually drew some sort of warped sustenance from degrading and breaking her victims before she had them killed. Rob Pierre and Oscar Saint-Just weren't like that. But Ransom had forced LePic to truly think about all the New Order's leaders, not just her, and when he looked at them with open eyes, he'd discovered he was even more terrified of Citizen Secretary Saint-Just than he'd been of Ransom. Because Saint-Just *didn't* act out of personal hatred or pique. He never even raised his voice. Yet compared to the thousands upon thousands of men and women—and sometimes children—whom he'd dispassionately blotted from the face of the universe, Cordelia Ransom had been no more than a spoiled child petulantly striking out at her classmates for not giving her their toys.

Denis LePic had looked into what passed for the soul of Rob S. Pierre's People's Republic and discovered a monster. A monster *he* had served willingly, even eagerly, since the day the old regime's Navy attempted to seize power. And the people he'd watched and guarded for the monster had too often been men and women like Thomas Theisman. Good men and women, as dedicated to the Republic and basic human dignity as Denis LePic had ever been, but more honest than he. Clearer-eyed. People who'd recognized the monster before he had, and whose discerning vision had placed them in mortal peril if the monster ever realized they had pierced its disguise.

Faced with that discovery, LePic had wanted to resign his post and return to private life. But his superiors at StateSec would have wondered why he wanted out. They would have demanded answers, and the one answer he could never have given them was the truth, for if they were savage to their enemies, they were utterly merciless when their own fell into apostasy. Besides, even if he could have resigned and lived, that would have been the easy way out. A way to walk away from the consequences of his own actions, like the ancient Pilate, washing his hands and proclaiming his personal innocence. No, there'd been only one thing a decent man, which was what he'd always hoped he was, could do under the circumstances.

He'd stayed right where he was and sent his reports in right on schedule. And over the weeks and months, he'd gradually shifted the emphasis of those reports, ever so carefully, to shield the people he ought to have been denouncing. He knew, for example, that the repugnance Citizen Admiral Theisman had always felt for the Committee's excesses had turned into cold, bleak hatred when it allowed Ransom to ordain Harrington's judicial murder. The citizen admiral and Harrington had a history, and Theisman believed he owed her a debt of honor for the way she'd treated him and his people when they'd been *her* prisoners. It was a debt he'd been unable to repay, and that had both infuriated and shamed him, but not even that, bitter though it must have been for a man like him, explained the implacable depth of his hate.

It was the hatred of a moral man for a system so twisted that it allowed someone like a Cordelia Ransom (or an Oscar Saint-Just) to practice butchery. One that shot its own officers and their families not for treason but for failing to execute orders whose authors had known they were impossible when they gave them. That drove men like Lester Tourville to the brink of open rebellion and destroyed men like Warner Caslet simply because they were decent, honorable men, and so a danger to the "New Order."

Tourville had survived, but only because Ransom had died before she could have him purged. And Warner Caslet had also survived . . . but only after the monster had driven a man who should have been—who'd tried, desperately, *to* be—one of the Republic's most loyal and skilled defenders into defecting. LePic knew Caslet's defection had hurt Theisman deeply, but not because Theisman blamed the citizen commander for it. It had hurt because he understood exactly why Caslet had done it, even knowing that it meant burning all of his bridges behind him. That even if the Committee somehow fell, he would never be able to come home again.

And then had come the stunning revelation that Harrington was alive. That she'd actually managed to escape from Cerberus with half a million other prisoners, including Warner Caslet . . . and Admiral Amos Parnell.

That had been the final straw. Like most of the Navy's pre-Coup officer corps, Theisman had respected Amos Parnell deeply. Almost as deeply as he'd respected Captain Alfredo Yu. Yet Theisman's loyalty to the Republic had managed to survive Yu's defection to the Grayson Space Navy, largely because he knew it had been the *Legislaturalists'* search for a scapegoat after the botched Masadan operation, not the Committee, which had driven Yu into exile.

It had not survived Parnell's revelations about who had actually murdered Hereditary President Harris. And who'd done so as a cold-blooded, carefully thought-out maneuver to brand the Navy, Thomas *Theisman's* Navy, as traitors in order to discredit and paralyze it while they seized power for their own ends.

Who had deliberately and premeditatedly created the reign of terror which had enveloped Theisman's entire world, destroyed so many people for whom he'd cared, and stripped him of his own honor, his own dignity.

But no one back home on Haven knew that had happened, for Denis LePic hadn't told them. It had been a terrifying decision, for he'd known what would happen if StateSec had informers he didn't know about on the planet Enki. Just one outside his own network, making solo reports to Haven, would have been enough to reveal him as a traitor to be shot right beside the no doubt treason-minded citizen admiral. Unfortunately, it had been a decision he'd had no option but to make, and while he'd been frightened to his very marrow by the risks associated with it, he had never really regretted it.

Until now.

Theisman must know LePic was covering for him. He couldn't *not* know, not and say some of the things he'd let slip in LePic's hearing, or even said directly to him, since Cordelia Ransom's death. But the look in his eye and the edge in his tone were different today, and so was the invitation to "go for a walk."

The time had come, LePic realized. The time when Theisman would invite him to take the next step, from passive concealment to active collaboration, and accepting that invitation would be an act of madness. There was no possible way Theisman could succeed in any active resistance to StateSec's merciless machinery. Any such attempt would be doomed, and so would anyone who followed him into it.

The citizen commissioner knew that, and his heart raced madly as he stared at Theisman's preposterously calm face. He swallowed hard, then drew a deep breath.

"Certainly, Citizen Admiral," he said. "Just let me get my jacket."

The wind outside DuQuesne Central's main admin block was cold and sharp. The sprawling expanse of barracks, warehouses, armories, landing pads, factories, and offices stretched as far as the eye could see in any direction, yet it was only one component, and not the largest, of what was collectively known as DuQuesne Base. Before the present war, DuQuesne had been the third-largest base of the People's Republic, conceived, designed, and built after the conquest of the Republic of San Martin as the springboard for the PRH's next wave of conquest. Aside from the base, the entire Barnett System had no true intrinsic value. Indeed, it had become a decided strategic liability. It was located all too close to Trevor's Star and, of course, remained conveniently placed for operations against that base. Unfortunately, most of the operations in the vicinity had been directed *from* Manty space and *into* Republican space, and that turned Barnett into an enormous prize for the enemy: an exposed system, with over a million permanent Marines and Navy personnel, not to mention six or seven times that many civilian support personnel, plus the crews of all the mobile units detailed to defend it.

The logical thing to do would have been to evacuate those personnel, shut down the facilities not needed for purely defensive operations, and reduce the mobile forces to something that could run for it when the inevitable attack came in. Or to a force small enough the Republic could stand to lose it, at least, if it didn't get a chance to run. Instead, even more strength had been poured into defending it, making it an even more attractive target for the Manties.

The breathing space Esther McQueen's offensives had won the People's Navy had helped, LePic thought as he turned up his jacket's collar, but it hadn't changed the basic equation. And the more recent orders transferring ships of the wall *out* of Barnett, only made DuQuesne's security more precarious. Yet he felt unhappily certain Thomas Theisman hadn't invited him outside on this cold, windy evening to discuss that.

He trudged along beside the citizen admiral, waiting. Not patiently, exactly. More with a sense of resignation. To be honest, LePic didn't really want to hear whatever Theisman had to say. He only knew he had no choice but to listen . . . assuming he wanted to be able to look himself in the mirror tomorrow.

Wonderful. I'll be able to look at myself in the mirror tomorrow. And the day after. Maybe even the day after that. But eventually someone back home is going to hear about this, and once that happens, I won't be in any position to be looking into any damned mirrors ever again!

"Thank you for coming with me, Denis," Theisman said at last. His deep, low-pitched voice was half lost in the louder voice of the wind.

"I don't know if you ought to thank me for anything . . . yet," LePic said tartly. "I'm sure this is a conversation we shouldn't be having. And you may as well know I'm not prepared to guarantee that it won't go any further than you and me, Citizen Admiral."

"It sounds as if you automatically assume I want to discuss 'treason against the People,'" Theisman observed, and the people's commissioner snorted.

"Of course you don't! You just wanted to let me know about your undying loyalty to Citizen Secretary Pierre and Citizen Secretary San-Just, who you think are the two greatest leaders in human history. But you didn't want to embarrass them with your fulsome praise. *That's* why you dragged me out on this balmy evening instead of into your office where the microphones could get every word of it down for the record!"

Theisman blinked at him, taken aback by his fear-inspired asperity. But then the citizen admiral chuckled.

"*Touché*, Citizen Commissioner! But if I may be so bold, if you assume I'm thinking treasonous thoughts, why come with me? Unless you've brought along your handy little pocket recorder to catch me in the act."

"If I wanted to do that, I could have done it any time in the last three years, and you know it," LePic said, looking away a bit uncomfortably. Theisman studied his profile, recognizing the citizen commissioner's discomfort. In many ways, it was the mirror image of his own unhappiness, for neither of them were men to whom defiance of civilian authority came easily.

"I suppose I do know that," he said after several moments of silence. "In fact, that's why I invited you on this little walk." He stopped, and LePic paused in automatic reflex, turning to face him. "What I want to know, Citizen Commissioner LePic," he asked levelly, "is what you're going to do when we get back to Nouveau Paris."

"When we *what*?" LePic's heart began to pound once more. Back to the capital? Had his superiors realized he'd been covering for Theisman and the others like him on Enki? Were he and the citizen admiral being recalled to be turned into horrible examples?

"You didn't know?" Theisman sounded surprised.

"Know what?!"

"I'm sorry, Denis." Theisman sounded genuinely contrite. "The orders came from the Octagon, but I'd assumed you'd already heard about them." LePic felt his muscles quiver with the need to reach out and *shake* a straight answer out of the other man, but the citizen admiral went on quickly. "I'm—we're—being recalled to Haven so I can assume command of the Capital Fleet, with you as my People's Commissioner."

"So you—?"

LePic stared at him. The Capital Fleet? They wanted *Thomas Theisman* to command the *Capital Fleet*? They had to be insane! That was the People's Navy's most sensitive post, the one naval command perpetually poised above the Committee of Public Safety's head like some megaton Sword of Damocles. The person who commanded it had to be totally trusted by the Committee, and Theisman was—

But then his thoughts slithered to a stop. Yes, Theisman had come to hate the Committee. But the Committee didn't know that. Oscar Saint-Just and *StateSec* didn't know that . . . because one Denis LePic had made a point of not telling them.

His shock began to fade a bit, and something very like awe replaced it.

My God, he thought. *They're putting a loaded pulser into the hands of one of their most deadly enemies and then turning their backs on him, and they don't even know it!*

And then another thought came. He'd accepted months ago that the time would come when Theisman would be found out and, by extension, when LePic would be found out right beside him. And when that day rolled around, the two of them would die. But if they were in command of the *Capital Fleet* . . .

"You want to know what *I'm* going to do?" he demanded finally. "My God, man! I ought to be asking *you* that! You're the one who's been turning steadily into a loose warhead for the last two or three years!"

"If I were a *loose* warhead, I'd already have done something stupid," Theisman replied reasonably. "In which case we wouldn't be freezing our asses off out here. As to what I'm planning to do, I honestly can't tell you. I have no more desire to die than the next man, Denis, and the admiral in me gets really pissed off at the thought of dying without accomplishing anything in the process, which is exactly what would happen if I—if *we*—went off half-cocked. But as you've obviously figured out, I'm not exactly in the mood to just keep on obeying orders like a good little boy."

"Meaning?" LePic asked nervously.

"Meaning that if an opportunity presents, or if one can be created, I might just reach for it," Theisman said flatly. LePic winced, and the citizen admiral raised one hand. "I haven't done anything yet. Haven't even breathed a word of it to anyone but you. But you need to know the way my head is working on this. You deserve to know, because I do realize you've been covering for me . . . and what that will mean for you, and possibly for your family, if I try something and blow it. But more than that, I need you. I need you to go *on* covering for me, and if the coin drops, I'll need you right there beside me."

He paused, gazing into the citizen commissioner's eyes, and his voice was very level when he went on.

"I won't lie to you, Denis. Even with me in command of the Capital Fleet, the odds against being able to accomplish anything other than getting ourselves and a lot of other people killed are high. The most likely outcome would be for StateSec to catch us and shoot us early on. Next most likely would be for us to try something and fail, in which case we either get killed in the fighting, arrested and shot afterward, or start a civil war that leaves the entire Republic wide open for the Manties. The *least* likely outcome would be for us to actually take out the Committee. On the other hand, the chance of managing that from the capital is a hell of a lot better than from here, and if we can . . ."

He let his voice trail off, and Denis LePic met his eyes in the cold and windy dark. Met and held them . . . and then nodded very slowly.

CHAPTER THIRTY-THREE

"Citizen General Fontein is here, Sir."

Oscar Saint-Just looked up as Sean Caminetti, his private secretary, ushered a colorless, wizened little man into his office. No one could have looked less like the popular conception of a brilliant and ruthless security agent than Erasmus Fontein. Except, perhaps, for Saint-Just himself.

"Thank you, Sean." He nodded permission for the secretary to withdraw, and then turned his attention fully to his guest. Unlike most people summoned to Saint-Just's inner sanctum, Fontein calmly walked across to his favorite chair, lowered himself into it with neither hesitation nor any sign of trepidation, waited while its surface adjusted to the contours of his body, then cocked his head at his chief.

"You wanted to see me?" he inquired, and Saint-Just snorted.

"I wouldn't put it quite that way. Not," he added, "that I'm not always happy to visit with you, of course. We have so few opportunities to spend quality time together." Fontein smiled faintly at the humor Saint-Just allowed so few people to see, but the smile faded as the Citizen Secretary for State Security went on in much a more serious tone.

"Actually, as I'm sure you've guessed, I called you in to discuss McQueen."

"I had guessed," Fontein admitted. "It wasn't hard, especially given how unhappy she was to move ahead on Operation Bagration."

"That's because you're a clever and insightful fellow who knows how much your boss is worried and what he worries about."

"Yes, I do," Fontein said, and leaned slightly forward. "And because I know, I've been trying very hard not to let the suspicions I know you have push me into reading something that isn't there into her actions."

"And?" Saint-Just prompted when he paused.

"And I just don't know." Fontein pursed his lips, looking uncharacteristically uncertain. It was Saint-Just's turn to incline his head, silently commanding him to explain, and the citizen general sighed.

"I've sat in on almost all of her strategy discussions at the Octagon, and the few I wasn't physically present for, I listened to on chip. I know the woman is a fiendishly good actress who can scheme and dissemble with the best. God knows I won't forget anytime soon how she outfoxed me before the Leveler business! But for all that, I think her concerns over the possibility of new Manty weapons are genuine, Oscar. She's been too consistent in the arguments she's made for those concerns to be feigned." He shook his head. "She's worried. A lot more worried, I think, than she lets herself appear at Committee meetings, where she knows she has to project a confident front. And," he added unhappily, "I think that because she's really worried, she's also very, very pissed off with you for pushing her so hard against her own better judgment."

"Um." Saint-Just rubbed his chin thoughtfully. Erasmus Fontein was, with the possible exception of Eloise Pritchart, the most insightful of StateSec's commissioners. He didn't look it, which was one of the more potent weapons in his arsenal, but he had a cold, keenly logical mind and, in his own way, he was just as merciless as Oscar Saint-Just. More than that, he'd been Esther McQueen's watchdog for the better part of eight years. She'd fooled him once, but he knew her moves better than anyone else . . . and he was a hard man for the same person to fool twice. Which meant Saint-Just had to listen to anything he had to say. But even so . . .

"Just because she's genuinely concerned doesn't mean she's *right*," he said testily, and Fontein very carefully didn't allow his surprise at his superior's acid tone to show.

It was very unlike Saint-Just to reveal that sort of irritation, and the citizen general felt a sudden chill. One thing which made Saint-Just so effective was his ability to think coldly and dispassionately about a problem. If personal anger was beginning to corrode that dispassion in Esther McQueen's case, her time could be far shorter than she guessed. Worse, Fontein wasn't at all sure *he* was prepared to dismiss her concerns, whatever Saint-Just thought. He'd had too many opportunities to see her in action, knew how tough-minded she was. And, he admitted, had seen her physical and moral courage much too close up for comfort during the Leveler revolt. He might not trust her, and he certainly didn't like her, but he did *respect* her. And if there was any basis to her fears, then however rosy things looked at this moment, the People's Republic might find in the next few months that it needed her worse than ever.

"I didn't say she was right, Oscar." Fontein was careful to keep his voice even. "I only said I think most of her concern is genuine. You asked me if I'm suspicious of her, and a part of my answer is that I think a lot of her reluctance to charge ahead with Bagration was unfeigned."

"All right." Saint-Just puffed air through his lips, then shook himself. "All right," he said more naturally. "Point taken. Go on."

"Beyond her apparently genuine concerns over her orders, I really can't say she's given me much to work with," Fontein said honestly. "She staked out her claim to authority in purely military affairs the day she took over the Octagan, and she works her staff, and herself, so hard that even I can't manage to sit in on all the meetings she has with planners and analysts and logistics people and com specialists. She works best one-to-one, and no one could fault the energy she brings to the job, but she's definitely got a firm grip on the military side of her shop. You probably know that even better than I do." *Since,* he did not add aloud, *you were the one who told me I had to* let *her* get *a grip on it.* "I don't like it, and I never did. Nor have I made any secret about how much I don't like it. At the same time, she has a point about the need for a single source of authority in a military chain of command, and the results she's produced certainly seem to have justified the decision to bring her in in the first place.

"I don't *think* she's been able to sneak anything past me, but I can't rule it out. As I say, no one could possibly keep pace with a schedule as frenetic as hers. There've probably been opportunities for side discussions I don't know anything about . . . and I still haven't figured out how she made her initial contacts before the Leveler business, when all's said. I have a few suspicions, but even knowing where to look—assuming I'm right and I am looking in the right places—I haven't been able to come up with any hard evidence. That being the case, I'm in no position to state unequivocally that she hasn't managed to do the same thing again at the Octagon.

"And let's face it, Oscar, she's charismatic as hell. I've watched her in action for years now, and I'm no closer to understanding how she does it than in the beginning. It's like she uses black magic. Or maybe it's a special kind of charisma that only works with military people. But it *does* work. She had Bukato out of his shell within weeks of taking over, and the rest of the Octagon's senior officers followed right behind him. And she managed to send Giscard and Tourville out ready to take on pseudogrizzlies with their bare hands, even though you and I both know from Eloise's reports that Giscard was suspicious as hell of her reputation for personal ambition. If anyone could inspire one of her subordinates to risk trying to do an end run around me to set up some clandestine line of communication, she's the one. I haven't seen a single trace of that, or I'd already've been in here bending your ear about it, but we can't afford to take anything for granted with a woman like her."

"I know." Saint-Just sighed and tipped his chair all the way back. "I was never happy about bringing her in and giving her such a long leash, but damn it, Rob was right. We needed her, and however dangerous she may be, she produced. She certainly produced. But now—"

He broke off, pinching the bridge of his nose, and Fontein could almost feel the intensity of his thoughts. Unlike almost anyone else in State Security, Fontein had read the doctored dossier Saint-Just had constructed when McQueen was brought in. He knew exactly how that file had been manicured to make McQueen look like the greatest traitor since Amos Parnell—indeed, to brand her as a previously undetected junior partner in the "Parnell Plot"—if it became necessary to remove her. Unfortunately, Parnell was back among the living and spilling his guts to the Solly Assembly's Committee on Human Rights, and—

The rhythm of Fontein's thoughts broke as a sudden insight struck him. Parnell. Was his escape from Cerberus an even larger factor in Saint-Just's intensified suspicions of McQueen than the commissioner had previously guessed? The ex-CNO's return to life had definitely shaken a lot of the old officer corps. They'd been careful about what they said and who they said it around, but that much was obvious. And after the victories Twelfth Fleet had produced, McQueen, for all the Navy's original wariness about her ambition, was almost as popular with, and certainly as respected by, its officers as Parnell had been. She must seem like some sort of ghost of Parnell to Saint-Just, and the neutralization of her edited dossier had hit him hard.

It was ironic, really. When the time bombs had been planted in that dossier, they'd been seen as little more than window dressing. There'd been no real need for anyone to justify her removal when StateSec had been shooting admirals in job lots for years, since no one in the Navy would have dared raise even a minor objection. The entire purpose had been to provide Cordelia Ransom's propagandists with ammunition to dress up the decision and be sure the Republic's public opinion was pointed in the right direction. But now that McQueen had become so popular with both the public and the Navy, that sort of justification for removing her had become genuinely vital. And just when it had, Parnell had escaped from Cerberus and discredited everything in her dossier.

Saint-Just's weapon had been knocked from his hand when he most feared he needed it, and perhaps that, as much as his frustration over her refusal to agree with his analysts, helped explain the way in which his habitual self-control had frayed in this instance.

"She produced," Saint-Just went on at last, "but I think she's become too dangerous for us to keep around. Someone else—like Theisman—can go on producing now that she's gotten the Navy turned around. And we won't have to worry about someone like Theisman trying to overthrow the Committee."

"Does that mean you and the Citizen Chairman have decided to remove her?" Fontein asked carefully.

"No," Saint-Just replied. "Rob is less convinced she's a danger. Or, rather, he's less convinced we can afford to get rid of her *because* of the danger she represents. He may even be right, and whether he is or not, he's still Chairman of the Committee . . . and my boss. So if he says we wait until we either know we don't need her or we find clear proof she's actively plotting, we wait. Especially since Bukato will have to go right along with her. Probably most of her other senior staffers, too, which makes it particularly imperative that we be certain the Manties are really on the run before we dislocate our command structure so severely. But I expect Bagration to pick right up where Scylla left off, and if it does, then I think we *will* have proof we don't need to hang onto a sword so sharp it's liable to cut our own heads off. Not when we've got other swords to choose from. And in that case, I expect Rob to greenlight her removal."

"I see." Despite himself, Fontein felt an inner qualm. For all his own reservations about McQueen, he'd worked closely with her for so long that the announcement that she was a dead woman, one way or the other, within months hit him hard.

"I don't want to rock the boat," Saint-Just went on. "Not now that Bagration is just kicking off, and certainly not before Theisman gets here and gives us someone reliable to hand Capital Fleet to. And above all, I don't want to do anything that will make her realize her time is running out. But I think it's time we started building a dossier to replace the one we can't use anymore. I want a nice, clean, convincing paper trail to 'prove' she was a traitor before she gets shot resisting arrest, and we can't throw that kind of thing together at the last minute. So I want you to sit down with Citizen Colonel Cleary and begin putting one together now."

"Of course." Fontein nodded. There was no chance in the world that Saint-Just would take overt action against McQueen until Pierre authorized it. The StateSec CO's mind simply didn't work that way. But it was very like him to attempt to anticipate and put the groundwork in place ahead of time. The collapse of the original "proof" of McQueen's "treason against the People" only made him more determined than usual.

"Remember," Saint-Just said firmly, unwittingly echoing Fontein's own thoughts, "this is only a preliminary. Rob hasn't authorized me to do a thing, and that means *you're* not authorized to do anything except gather information and begin assembling a file. I don't want any mistakes or unauthorized enthusiasm that gets out of hand, Erasmus!"

"Of course not, Oscar," Fontein replied just a bit cooly. Saint-Just gave a small nod in response, one with a hint of apology. One reason (among many) Fontein had been chosen for his position was that he would no more act against McQueen without Saint-Just's specific order to do so, except in a case of dire emergency, than Saint-Just would have had her arrested or shot without clearance from Pierre.

"I know I can rely on you, Erasmus," he said, "and that's more important to me and to Rob right now than ever before. It's just that waiting for the coin to drop with McQueen has stretched my patience a lot thinner than I ought to have let it. I have to keep reining myself in where she's concerned, and some of it just spilled over onto you."

"I understand, Oscar. Don't worry. Cleary and I will put together exactly the sort of file you need, and that's *all* we'll do until you tell us otherwise."

"Good," Saint-Just said more cheerfully, and shoved up out of his chair with a smile. He walked around his desk to escort his visitor out and, in a rare physical show of affection, draped one arm around Fontein's narrow shoulders.

"Rob and I won't forget this, Erasmus," he said as the door from his private office to its waiting room opened and Caminetti looked up from his own desk. The secretary started to rise, but Saint-Just waved him back into his chair and personally escorted Fontein to the door.

"Remember," he said, pausing for one last word before Fontein left the waiting room for the public corridor beyond. "It has to be *solid*, Erasmus. When we shoot someone like McQueen, we can't leave any loose ends. Not this time. Especially not when we're going to have to make such a clean sweep at the Octagon along with her."

"I understand, Oscar," Fontein replied quietly. "Don't worry. I'll get it done."

Esther McQueen was working late—again—when the door chime sounded.

She glanced at the date-time display on her desk and grinned wryly. This late at night, it had to be Bukato. No one else worked quite the hours she did, and of those who might work this late, anyone else would go through her appointments yeoman. Now what, she wondered, would Ivan have to discuss with her tonight? Something about Bagration, no doubt. Or perhaps about Tom Theisman's impending arrival to take over the reorganized Capital Fleet.

She pressed the admittance button, and her eyebrows rose as the door opened. It wasn't Bukato. In fact, it was her junior com officer, a mere citizen lieutenant. Citizen commodores and citizen admirals were a centicredit a dozen around the Octagon. No one paid all that much attention to the gold braid and stars walking past them in the halls, and a lowly citizen lieutenant was literally invisible.

"Excuse me, Citizen Secretary," the young man said. "I just finished those signals Citizen Commodore Justin gave me this afternoon. I was on my way to his office with them when I realized you were still here, and it occurred to me that you might want to take a look at them before I hand them to his yeoman."

"Why, thank you, Kevin." McQueen's voice was completely calm, without even a trace of surprise, but her green eyes sharpened as she held out her hand for the citizen lieutenant's memo board. Despite his own conversational tone, the young man's features were drawn for just a moment as their eyes met, and McQueen's breathing faltered for the briefest instant as she saw the flimsy strip of paper he passed her with the board.

She nodded to him, laid the board on her desk, keyed its display, and bent over it. Had anyone happened to walk into her office at that moment, all they would have seen was the Citizen Secretary of War scanning the message traffic her staffer had brought her. They would never have noticed the strip of paper which slipped from the memo board's touchpad to her blotter and lay hidden beyond the holo of its display. And because they would not have noticed it, they would never have read the brief, terse words it bore.

"S says EF authorized to move by SJ," it said. Only that much, but Esther McQueen felt as if a pulser dart had just hit her in the belly.

She'd known it was coming. It had been obvious for months that Saint-Just's suspicion had overcome his belief that they needed her skills, but she'd believed Pierre was wiser than that . . . at least where the military situation was concerned.

But maybe I only needed to believe that because I wasn't ready. The thought was unnaturally calm. *I needed more time, because we're still not ready. Just a couple of more weeks—a month at the outside—would have done it. But it looks like waiting is a luxury I've just run out of.*

She drew a deep breath as she hit the advance button and her eyes appeared to scan the display. Her free hand gathered up the thin paper, crushing it into a tiny pellet, and she reached up to rub her chin . . . and popped the pellet into her mouth. She swallowed the evidence and hit the advance button again.

Thirty percent. That was her current estimate of the chance of success. A one-third chance was hardly something she would willingly have risked her life upon, or asked others to risk their lives on with her, if she'd had an option. But if Saint-Just had authorized Fontein to move, she *didn't* have an option, and thirty percent was one hell of a lot better than no chance at all. Which was what she'd have if she waited until *they* pulled the trigger.

She paged through to the final message in the board, then nodded and held it out to the citizen lieutenant. Incomplete though her plans were, she'd been careful to craft each layer independently of the layers to follow it. And she could activate her entire strategy—such as it was and what there was of it at this stage—with a single com call. She wouldn't even have to say anything, for the combination she would punch into her com differed from Ivan Bukato's voice mail number only in the transposition of two digits. It was a combination she'd never used before and would never use again, but the person at the other end of it would recognize her face. All she had to do was apologize for mistakenly screening a stranger so late at night, and the activation order would be passed.

"Thank you, Kevin," she said again. "Those all look fine. I'm sure

Citizen Commodore Justin will want to look them over as well, of course, but they seem to cover everything I was concerned about. I appreciate it." Her voice was still casual, but the glow in her green eyes was anything but as they met the com officer's squarely.

"You're welcome, Ma'am," Citizen Lieutenant Kevin Caminetti said, and the younger brother of Oscar Saint-Just's personal secretary tucked the memo board under his arm, saluted sharply, and marched out of Esther McQueen's office.

Behind him, she reached for her com's touchpad with a rock-steady hand.

CHAPTER THIRTY-FOUR

"**E**xcuse me, My Lady," Andrew LaFollet said quietly into Honor's ear.

She paused in her conversation and gave the Earl of Sydon a small, apologetic smile. Sydon was a jolly, well-fed man some people were foolish enough to take at face value and write off as a gregarious gadfly who regarded his position in the House of Lords as a bothersome inheritance. Honor, however, could taste the emotions of the keen brain behind his perpetually cheerful face and knew better. In fact, he was one of Duke Cromarty's strongest supporters, and while he truly was the *bon vivant* the rest of the world knew, he was also a very astute politician who found it advantageous to be taken lightly by the Government's opponents. And one who recognized a new duchess who was just as firmly behind the Cromarty Government as he was.

"Would you pardon me, My Lord?" she asked now, and he chuckled.

"Your Grace, I've held you in conversation for a full—" he glanced at his chrono "—six minutes and eleven seconds. My social peers are undoubtedly gnashing their teeth already, and it would never do for pure envy to cause any of them to suffer a mischief. By all means, attend to whatever requires your attention."

"Thank you," she said, and turned her attention to LaFollet.

"Simon just buzzed me, My Lady," her armsman said, one finger brushing an all but invisible earbug. "PGS says the Queen's air car is about three minutes out."

"Good."

Honor looked out over the crowded ballroom of her East Shore mansion. The guest list was smaller than she'd intimated to Admiral Caparelli, but not by an enormous amount. And at the moment, all of her guests—except for the most important one—seemed to be packed into this single room.

It was the first formal party she'd hosted since her return. She hadn't been able to avoid going to a great many parties thrown by *other* people, and she'd actually enjoyed a few of them, despite the way they cut into the time available for other things. Like doing her job at ATC, or the Academy, or with Maxwell and the organization of her duchy. Or spending time with her mother before Allison's return to Grayson. Or physical therapy. Or discussing the delivery of her runabout with Silverman & Sons. Or—

She chopped the mental list short. There'd always been *something* else she should have been doing, and one or two of the galas to which she'd been dragged had been anything but "gay" for her. She'd been ambushed by newsies at Lady Gifford's ball, and that jackass Jeremiah Crichton, the Palmer Foundation's so-called "military analyst," had caught her at Duke Waltham's and tried very hard to get her to break security about the new LAC wings. He'd actually seemed to believe she *enjoyed* the way the newsies hung about her like vultures, and he'd looked astounded when she'd expressed her opinion (with rather more precision and vigor than diplomacy) of him, his "analyses," and the batch of intellectually myopic, ideologically blinkered, and ethically crippled mental defectives for whom he produced his carefully tailored version of the war's events rather than taking the opportunity to play the "woman in the know" game. His expression was a memory she would always treasure, but she could hardly say she'd *enjoyed* the evening.

Overall, though, she had to admit most of them had been at least endurable, and some had been downright fun. And she knew MacGuiness and, even more, Miranda had been wistfully disappointed by her failure to reciprocate with events of her own. Unlike them, however, Honor had always hated parties, and she hated the sort of cutthroat one-upmanship which seemed to be an inseparable part of the competition among "Society's" leading lights even more. But she knew how much Miranda loved them. Her "maid" actually seemed to enjoy all the drudgery and planning which went into coordinating the insane things, and as the Star Kingdom's newest duchess, she'd known there was no way she could get off without throwing at least one blowout of her own.

Coward that she was, she'd put it off until just before departing for Grayson . . . and since Miranda liked organizing the things, she'd gleefully "allowed" her maid and MacGuiness to shoulder the full burden of putting it together. Well, almost the full burden. LaFollet and Simon Mattingly had been responsible for coordinating with the Palace Guard Service and the Queen's Own to insure the security of the evening's most illustrious guest, and Honor had made a point of reviewing *their* plans in detail.

"You and I should go meet her," she told LaFollet now, and she and her armsman made their unobtrusive way towards the side exit to the estate's private landing pad.

Honor was in formal Grayson attire for the evening. The sweeping drape of her gown—not white, this time, but more of an opalescent pearl—and the dark, jewel-toned green of her sueded, vestlike tabard, coupled with her height, made her stand out like a Terran swan amid a flock of gaily plumed, chattering Manticoran near-jays, and Nimitz rode on her right shoulder, radiating an almost palpable aura of complacent contentment. Unlike her, he was as fond of social events as Miranda or MacGuiness at their worst, but Samantha rode on LaFollet's shoulder—logical, since he was going to be anywhere she and Nimitz might go—and Honor tasted the gently mocking amusement flowing from Nimitz's mate. She, it was obvious, came much closer to Honor's view of parties.

Both 'cats had been on their best behavior all night, however, as had Farragut, who was currently over by the punch bowl with Miranda, and she tasted their shared pleasure at the prospect of seeing Ariel again. Queen Elizabeth's companion was about Samantha's age, and both of Honor's companions had struck up firm friendships with him. That didn't take long among 'cats, and they'd seen rather more of Ariel and Prince Consort Justin's Monroe than most treecats got to, since Honor had been a fairly frequent visitor at Mount Royal Palace while her new peerage and its estates got settled. But they hadn't had the opportunity to visit with him for some months now, and there was more to their anticipation than the simple pleasure of seeing him again.

Someone else moved steadily through the crowd towards them, and Honor glanced over to note without surprise that Miranda had abandoned the punch bowl to join her Steadholder and her brother.

"I see someone passed the word to you, too," Honor remarked as the Grayson woman reached them. "Was it your earbug or a certain six-limbed cockleburr?"

"A bit of both, My Lady," Miranda admitted, then grinned. "But more the cockleburr than the earbug, if the truth be known."

The 'cat in her arms—she lacked the size and strength to carry a treecat Farragut's size on her shoulder—buzzed a happy purr of agreement, and Samantha bleeked in resigned laughter. Honor had never considered it before, but as she looked at Farragut and compared his attitude and emotions to Nimitz's, she felt a sudden suspicion. Male treecats were much more distinctively marked than females, and they were the ones who performed all the daring, attention-grabbing duties of their clans. Maybe that made it inevitable that they would also be the ones who partied hardest whenever the opportunity came their way? Come to that, just what *did* 'cats do on social occasions? She had a sudden mental image of Nimitz officiating over a treecat psych-rock concert and felt his laughter shaking his entire body on her shoulder as he shared it with her.

"Well, we're all here now," she observed, "so let's not keep Her Majesty waiting."

The three of them slipped through the door, unobtrusively but efficiently guarded by two PGS agents in plainclothes, and out into the cool, breezy night. A strong wind was setting in off the bay, and the distant murmur of surf came clearly from the beaches. A sleek luxury air car whose flowing lines did not conceal its heavy armor from knowing eyes was just settling on the pad, flanked by two stingships in the colors of the Queen's Own. A third stingship hovered silently overhead on its counter-grav, and Honor knew the Landing City Police Department and the Queen's Own, in close cooperation with her own armed-to-the-teeth Harringtons, had established a perimeter around her mansion that a battalion of Marines would have found tough to break.

There'd been a time when Honor Harrington would have found that ostentatious security mildly amusing, in an overblown, paranoid sort of way. Now she simply looked upon the quiet efficiency and obvious competence of the people guarding her monarch's life and found them good.

The air car hatch opened, and Elizabeth III stepped out with Ariel. The pad lights illuminated her clearly, and Honor heard Miranda's delighted, appreciative laugh beside her as they both saw Elizabeth's attire. It seemed Honor and her maid were no longer the only traditionally garbed Graysons at the party, and Honor felt herself chuckling evilly as she pictured the effect of Elizabeth's gown on those members of the Star Kingdom's social elite who had lifted their noses at her own failure to don the trousers, tail coat, and ruffled shirt of traditional Manticoran court dress on her visits to Mount Royal. She hadn't refused to wear it because she had any problem with the way it looked. Indeed, its elegantly severe lines would have suited her tall, slim figure far better than it did such plump unfortunates as Earl Sydon or poor Lady Zidaru. Instead, she'd worn Grayson attire as a way to emphasize her dual home worlds, and unlike the sticklers, Elizabeth had understood perfectly.

And now she'd chosen to attend Honor's party, on the grounds of what was also the Harrington Steading Embassy and hence legally Grayson soil, in Grayson attire herself. Her gown and vest were in the dusky blue and silver of the House of Winton, and very good they looked on her, too, Honor noted approvingly.

"Honor!" Elizabeth came quickly down the pad steps and held out her hand.

"Your Majesty," Honor murmured, clasping the hand and dropping a Grayson-style curtsey. Miranda produced a much deeper curtsey beside her, while LaFollet came respectfully to attention, and Elizabeth laughed.

"Very becoming, Honor, but I trust you'll pardon me if I don't reciprocate? You and Miranda make it look as simple as it is elegant, but I'm not sufficiently accustomed to this particular style of formal dress. I guess it's no wonder I never learned how to produce one though, since I suspect I'd look pretty stupid practicing it in trousers."

"Trust me, it looks a lot worse than 'pretty stupid' in trousers," Honor assured her. "Of course, it looks even worse in a dress until you get the hang of it. Miranda has an unfair advantage, though. She grew up performing that particular unnatural act."

"Only because no properly raised Grayson girl would be so lost to all propriety as to wear *trousers* in the first place, My Lady," Miranda said demurely, and Honor and Elizabeth both laughed. Then the Queen turned to Honor and made a small face.

"I thought right up to the last moment that Justin would be able to come after all, Honor, but one of us simply *had* to go to that ribbon-cutting on Gryphon, and Roger chose yesterday of all days to come down with the flu!" She rolled her eyes. "You'd think that at his age he'd be past childhood ailments that come out of nowhere, but, no."

"Actually, Your Majesty," the uniformed Army colonel who'd followed her from the air car murmured, "I suspect that his interest in Ms. Rosenfeld had rather more to do with the way that wicked bug laid him so low. You did notice she turned up speedily at his bedside to hold his hand, make sure he drank plenty of fluids, and put wet compresses tenderly on his brow, didn't you?"

"Oh, my!" Elizabeth turned to the colonel. "I knew she'd come calling, Ellen. But was she really that gooey about it?"

"I'm afraid so, Your Majesty." Colonel Ellen Shemais' blue eyes twinkled as she shook her head. "I think they'll probably start getting over the most blatant aspects of it fairly soon, but it looks a great deal like a really severe case of mutual youthful adoration in all it glorious excessiveness."

"What a wonderful thing to look forward to." Elizabeth sighed. Then she grew more serious. "Do you think it has a real potential to last, Ellen?" The colonel crooked an eyebrow at her, and Elizabeth waved a hand. "Don't look innocent at me, woman! You've headed my personal security force for over thirty years, and you know the members of my family at least as well as I do. Probably better, because you don't suffer from mother's myopia where my offspring are concerned! I know Ariel likes Rivka a lot, but I have to confess I hadn't really been thinking of her as a possible consort for Roger."

"He—and the Star Kingdom—could do a lot worse, Your Majesty," Shemais said after a moment. "She's a sweet girl, but even though their mutual mush-mindedness is turning her and Roger into unbearable adolescent goo just this moment, she's also level-headed, smart, and self-confident. Her family isn't all that wealthy, but they're well enough off they were able to get her into Queen's College without depending on scholarships, so I doubt she'd be completely overwhelmed by Palace life, either."

"Wealth is the last thing I'd worry about," Elizabeth said bluntly. "You seem to forget what they called Mother when she married Dad—'the Little Beggar Maid,' remember?" An uncharacteristic edge of bitterness colored the Queen's voice for just a moment, but it vanished almost instantly as she went on. "And Rivka would meet the Constitutional requirement that Roger marry a commoner, too. So perhaps I should be encouraging the match, even if it's a little early for either of them to be making formal commitments. I certainly don't want him to end up like some Heirs who went and fell in love with someone from their own 'class' and then had to marry someone else just to satisfy the law! Besides—" she smiled in memory "—I seem to remember someone else who met her future consort on a college campus."

"Odd you should mention that, Your Majesty," Shemais murmured. "I seem to remember the same thing myself."

"I thought you might." Elizabeth smiled at her equivalent of Andrew LaFollet for a moment, but then she shook herself and turned back to Honor. "Forgive me, Honor. I'm a guest in your home tonight. I should be concentrating on that instead of running on about domestic concerns."

"Nonsense," Honor replied firmly. "You should hear some of the conversations I've had with Benjamin and his wives. You know that their next-to-youngest—well, she was still their next-to-youngest when I left Grayson, though I understand Katherine is about to change that—is my goddaughter?"

"I'd heard," Elizabeth agreed, reaching out to slip a hand into Honor's elbow in a rare display of public intimacy as they walked back along the path towards the mansion. "I've also heard she's a lovely child."

"She is," Honor admitted with becoming modesty. "In fact, she's not even going to be stuck the way I was with an 'ugly duckling' period, thanks to prolong."

"You too?" Elizabeth laughed delightedly. "Remind me to tell you sometime about the absolute misery I put the Palace PR types through for about fifteen years by insisting they find some camera angle that would keep me from looking like a flat-chested, no hips, androgynous mannikin! I thought I'd *never* grow a bosom!" She shook her head with another chuckle. "I think I almost drove even Ariel to drink for a while. Fortunately, there was no way he could give me the kind of royal—you should pardon the expression—chewing-out he certainly thought I deserved!"

The 'cat on her shoulder bleeked an echo of her laughter, and Honor shared it, although there was more than a shadow of remembered misery in her own amusement. But then she stopped in the middle of the path, and Elizabeth paused automatically beside her, looking up at her greater height with a questioning expression.

"Excuse me, Your Majesty," Honor said in a much more serious voice. "I'd intended to wait, but your comment about Ariel is too perfect an opening to pass up."

"Opening?" Elizabeth sounded puzzled, and Honor nodded.

"Nimitz and Samantha have a surprise for you and Ariel, Your Majesty. Something they've been working on with Mac and Miranda and a Doctor Arif for the last few months." The Queen looked completely baffled by this point, and Honor smiled, then turned her head to look up at the 'cat on her shoulder.

"You had something you wanted to tell Her Majesty, Stinker?" Nimitz bleeked and nodded his head in vigorous agreement. "Well, I'm sure Miranda would be delighted to help you out," Honor told him, and turned to her maid. "Miranda?"

"Of course, My Lady," Miranda replied, but her eyes were on

Nimitz, not Honor, and the 'cat rose higher on Honor's shoulder. Elizabeth followed the direction of Miranda's gaze, and then her own eyes widened as Nimitz's hands began to move.

He brought his opened right hand, fingers spread, against his chest then raised it, folding its fingers down beside the thumb, drew it down the right side of his head from prick ear to muzzle, and then raised both hands before him and clasped them, right above left.

"My wife . . ." Miranda said, her attention fixed on the 'cat.

Nimitz's right hand moved again, as he extended his index finger and touched it to his chest.

" . . . and I . . ." Miranda said.

Again the 'cat's hands moved. Both of them opened in front of his body, palms facing him, and he drew them back towards his chest, his fingers closing in a slight grasping motion as they moved.

" . . . want . . ."

Hands moving again, while Elizabeth Winton's eyes began to blaze in disbelieving wonder. This time the fingers of both hands touched Nimitz's forehead, then swung out and down, opening fully as they reached the bottom of their motion, and the 'cat raised just his right hand to point directly at the Queen.

" . . . to teach you . . ."

His left hand rose, fingers spread, and his right thumb and index finger touched his left index finger, framing a little triangle like a flag.

" . . . and Leaf . . ."

Both hands moving again, this time to mime someone catching a ball or some other falling object.

" . . . Catcher . . ."

Right hand rising, index finger pointing left, and circling before his mouth.

" . . . to talk . . ."

Both hands moved once more, this time with all their fingers folded but their thumbs extended, right thumb down and left up, while the right circled in a clockwise motion above the left one.

" . . . to each other . . ."

He raised both hands, index fingers extended and pointing levelly outward before his chest, and brought them together three times.

" . . . like . . ."

His extended right index finger pointed downward directly in front of his right shoulder and then moved left, across his body, in a slight downward arc.

" . . . we . . ."

Miranda nodded and drew a deep breath, then looked directly at the Queen and repeated her translation quietly.

"He said, 'My wife and I want to teach you and Leaf Catcher to talk to each other like we do,' Your Majesty."

Elizabeth's eyes moved slowly from Nimitz to the auburn-haired Grayson, and her own right hand rose, trembling ever so slightly, to touch the motionless 'cat on her shoulder.

" 'Leaf Catcher'?" she said softly, her voice barely audible. "Is that Ariel's true name?"

"Not exactly, Your Majesty." Honor's voice was almost equally soft. The Queen's eyes moved to her, and she smiled. "We've been having quite a few chats with Nimitz, Samantha, and Farragut over the last few weeks. As nearly as they can explain it, any 'cat who's been adopted has two names: one given by his clan, which is something of a descriptor and often changes several times over his life, and the one his adopted human gives him, which never changes. They seem to regard the naming change as deeply significant, like a formal recognition of the bond, and it's very important to them."

Elizabeth nodded like a woman in a dream, and her gaze moved back to Nimitz. He'd stopped moving his hands, and his eyes gleamed like emeralds in the backwash of the landing pad lights as he returned her steady regard. Elizabeth stood as still as if she had been struck to stone, and Ariel seemed even more stunned than she was.

"Honor—" she said at last. But the single word came out low and husky, and she paused to clear her throat. "Honor," she went on in a more normal tone, "do you really mean you've taught Nimitz and Samantha what I *think* you have?"

"Actually, Dr. Arif did most of the teaching," Honor admitted. "I've been so busy over at the Academy and at ATC that I simply didn't have the time to do it myself. Assuming this bum wing of mine would have let me do it right anyway." She waved her artificial left arm in a tiny arc. "As a matter of fact, the reason Miranda did the translating just now is that she's put in the hours to master the signs far more completely than I have. Fortunately for Nimitz and me, most of the signs are intuitive enough, and he and I have been together for so long and our bond is so much deeper than most, that I can 'read' his signs without actually consciously having learned most of them just by concentrating on what comes with them. But, yes, Your Majesty. Nimitz and Samantha have learned how to sign, and they assure us that they—or at least Samantha, since her 'transmitter' still works—will be able to teach any other 'cat how to do it in a matter of hours. In fact, it's going to be us slowpoke humans who really slow the process down."

"My God," Elizabeth whispered reverently, her brown eyes glowing almost as brightly as Nimitz's had. "You mean that after all these years, Ariel and I will actually be able to *talk* to each other? And Monroe and Justin?"

"That's exactly what I mean," Honor said gently. "It's not like Standard English. It's more of a pidgin in a lot of ways, though it looks like the rough edges will rub off as all of us become more fluent with our hands. But I promise you Miranda and Nimitz didn't rehearse their demonstration. What he had to say came at her cold, but as I'm sure you could tell from the translation, it really works."

"My God." Elizabeth's tears gleamed under the lights. "After four hundred years, you've finally proved once and for all that the 'cats are just as sentient as *we* are!"

"This is one thing you are *not* going to give me credit for, Your Majesty!" Honor said almost fiercely. "All *I* had to do with it was to be the person whose friend had his mental voice destroyed, whose mother was brilliant enough to come up with the notion, and whose money let her find and hire the equally brilliant linguist who actually made it all work. If you want to go feeling grateful to someone, you feel grateful to my mom and Dr. Arif and leave me out of it!"

Elizabeth blinked at her vehemence, then gave her a crooked grin.

"Yes, Ma'am," she murmured demurely, and Honor heard Andrew LaFollet and Ellen Shemais smothering almost identical laughter behind them. "You do realize, however," Elizabeth went on, "that whatever I may do or feel, the *newsies* are going to smother the 'faxes with headlines like 'HARRINGTON MAKES NEW BREAKTHROUGH IN INTERSPECIES COMMUNICATION' or 'SALAMANDER STRIKES AGAIN,' don't you?"

"Oh no they are not," Honor said roundly. "Not this time! And the reason they aren't, Your Majesty, is that in response to the earnest request of one of your loyal subjects, *you* are going to have Dr. Arif make her announcement from Mount Royal Palace, and *Ariel* is going to be the one who demonstrates his newfound loquaciousness for the newsies."

"What?" Elizabeth shook her head quickly. "I couldn't possibly take credit for something like this, Honor! Not when it's going to mean so much to everyone who's been adopted!"

"You won't. Dr. Arif and my mom will get the credit. I'm sure my name will be tucked away somewhere in the small print of Dr. Arif's first few monographs on the subject, but that will be then, when the initial excitement's worn off. All I want is for you to make the original announcement and buy me the time to get off-world before the newsies hit their stride. And frankly, Your Majesty, this is an excellent opportunity to make a little down payment on that debt you keep insisting the Star Kingdom owes me. I still think you're wrong about that, you understand, but I'm prepared to take shameless advantage of your wrongheadedness in this instance."

"I see." Elizabeth studied her for a long moment, then smiled slowly. "Well given the size of the stick I've needed to beat you with to make you take anything from me, I don't see how I can possibly refuse if you feel so strongly about it that you're actually *eager* to call in a marker on it."

"Good," Honor said firmly, and started back towards the ballroom and her other guests.

"You know," Elizabeth went on thoughtfully as the two of them walked down the path side by side, "now that I think about it, there's something else I really ought to've done before this. Not for *you*, precisely, but possibly for Steadholder Harrington and all the other steadholders of Grayson."

"I beg your pardon?" Honor looked down at her in puzzlement.

"Grayson has been our most important, most loyal, and most courageous ally since this war began," the Queen said, and there was no laughter at all in her tone this time. "They started with an awful lot less than Erewhon, and frankly, they've accomplished one hell of a lot more. And if, as I confidently expect, we begin getting back reports on the success of Operation Buttercup in the next couple of weeks, we'll owe an enormous amount of that success to Grayson, both for the R&D alleys they helped point us down and for the way their Navy is fighting alongside our own."

She paused, and Honor nodded.

"I certainly can't argue with any of that, Your Majesty," she said soberly, unable to hide the pride she felt in her adopted world. "Graysons are a remarkable bunch."

"They are, indeed," Elizabeth agreed, "and I'd appreciate it if you'd carry a message from me to Protector Benjamin when you return there."

"A message?"

"Yes. Please inform the Protector that I would consider it a great honor if he would do me the courtesy of extending an invitation from the Sword of Grayson to the Crown of Manticore for a state visit to his planet."

Someone—Honor thought it was Colonel Shemais—inhaled audibly behind them, and Honor herself almost stumbled in her surprise. The last state visit by a reigning Manticoran monarch to a foreign planet had been Roger III's visit to San Martin eight T-years before the Peeps took Trevor's Star. The Queen of Manticore was simply too busy, and too important to the Alliance, to go haring off on trips away from the security of her capital and the nerve center of her communications net.

"Are you certain about that, Your Majesty?" Honor asked. "As Steadholder Harrington, I think it would be a wonderful idea. As Duchess Harrington, I have to wonder if you ought to be off Manticore that long. The voyage time alone will run to over a standard week for the round trip. And Grayson will go berserk over a visit from you. I'll be astonished it they're willing to turn you loose in less than another couple of weeks, so you're looking at at least the better part of a standard month away from the capital just when we'll all be finding out whether or not Admiral White Haven and Alice Truman can maintain their momentum after Buttercup's initial strikes."

"I'm aware of all that," Elizabeth replied. "But I think the timing makes this an even better idea, not a worse one. What I'd really like is to come after the Conclave of Steadholders convenes. It would be logical for me to visit while the Keys are in session, and having me there, where Benjamin and I can issue joint communiques as reports of additional victories come in from Eighth Fleet, would let us wring the most PR mileage possible out of them. Having me on Grayson to issue those communiques would also let me personally and directly demonstrate the Star Kingdom's deep gratitude to our Grayson allies. For that matter, the indication of confidence—the fact that I'm *willing* to be away from Manticore during such crucial military operations—would be very reassuring to our own public opinion and *all* our allies." She shook her head. "No, Honor. If Benjamin will go along, I think this may be the best possible time to schedule something like this. Besides, I'd really like to meet him in person, and if I bring Allen and Uncle Anson along, we could deal with several pressing intergovernmental matters face-to-face and probably settle all of them in a fraction of the time we'd need to do the same thing through normal channels."

"If you're sure it's what you want, I'd be delighted to carry the message."

"Good." Elizabeth tucked her hand back into her hostess' elbow and kicked one leg to make her skirt swirl. "And now that we have that unimportant little detail settled, Duchess Harrington, let's you and I—and Miranda, of course—go show these Manticoran stuck-in-the-mud snobs what the *true* fashion-conscious are wearing this season!"

CHAPTER THIRTY-FIVE

"**S**tand by for translation . . . *now*."

Captain (Junior Grade) Jonathan Yerensky announced the return to normal-space, and Hamish Alexander grimaced as the familiar discomfort and disorientation lashed through him. That was one nice thing about being a senior admiral, he thought. By the time you acquired as much rank as he had, you no longer had to worry about impressing uppity juniors with your stoicism. If crossing the alpha wall made you feel like throwing up, you could go ahead and admit it . . . and nobody dared laugh.

He grinned at the reflection, but his eyes were already flicking over his repeater plot on *Benjamin the Great*'s flag deck. At the moment, CIC was feeding him a schematic of the entire star system. Which didn't tell him a thing, of course. As soon as the scanner crews had anything besides stock projections of the system's astrography to show him, CIC would throw it on his plot.

He listened to a murmured litany of background reports without really hearing them. His staff had been with him for over three T-years. They might have spent all too much of that time floating in orbit around Trevor's Star, but it had given them plenty of time to train in exercises and sims. By now, they knew exactly what he needed to know immediately and what he expected them to handle on their own, and *he* knew he could rely on them to do just that.

Which freed Hamish Alexander to study his bland, uninformative plot and worry.

Well, uninformative from the *enemy's* side, he amended, for quite a few Allied icons burned on the display. First, there were the seventy-three superdreadnoughts and eleven dreadnoughts of his wall of battle. Then there were the traditional screening elements, already spreading out to assume missile defense positions. And last, there were the seventeen CLACs of Alice Truman's task group and *their* escorts—battlecruisers and heavy cruisers, with four attached dreadnoughts to give them a little extra weight—astern of the main formation. A blizzard of diamond chips erupted outward from the CLACs as he watched, and he smiled grimly as they began to shake down into formation even as they accelerated ahead of the main body. CIC had a tight lock on them when they launched, but their EW was already on-line, and within minutes even *Benjamin the Great's* sensors began to lose them.

A second blizzard, almost as dense, sped outward at accelerations even a LAC could never hope to match, and White Haven tipped back his command chair as the FTL-capable recon drones darted in-system.

I actually feel almost as calm as I'm trying to look, he reflected with some surprise. *Of course, that's because I can be reasonably confident the Peeps don't have a clue as to what's coming at them. Whether or not that will be true—and whether or not it will matter if it isn't—the next time around are two different questions, of course.*

He watched the drones speeding steadily inward, and he smiled.

Citizen Admiral Alec Dimitri and Citizen Commissioner Sandra Connors were in DuQuesne Base's war room for a routine briefing when an alarm buzzed. The tall, stocky citizen admiral turned quickly, trained eyes seeking the status board, and Citizen Commissioner Connors turned almost as quickly. Neither she nor Dimitri had ever expected in their worst nightmares that they would suddenly find themselves responsible for the Barnett System, but they'd served as understudies to Thomas Theisman and Denis LePic for the better part of four T-years. Both were serious about their duty, and even if they hadn't been, Theisman and LePic would have made damned sure the two of them were intimately familiar with the system and its defenses. As a result, Connors' eyes were only fractionally slower than Dimitri's in finding the fresh datum on the big board, and her frown mirrored his own.

"Twenty-two light-minutes from the primary?" she murmured, and Dimitri turned his head to give her a tight smile.

"It does seem a bit . . . overly cautious of them. Especially on that broad a bearing from Enki," he agreed, and wondered what the hell the Manties thought they were up to. Barnett was only a G9 star, with a hyper limit of just a hair over eighteen light-minutes, so why were they turning up a full four light-minutes further out than they had to? And on a bearing from the primary which added yet four more unnecessary light-minutes to their distance from their only possible objective?

The citizen admiral clamped his hands behind him and took a slow, deliberate turn around the command balcony above the enormous war room. His outermost sensor shell was seventeen light-minutes from the primary, safely within the hyper limit to at least make hit-and-run raids on it difficult, but far enough out from the gravitational center of Barnett to give the enormous passive arrays a reach of almost two and a half light-weeks, over which they could expect to pick up the hyper transit of anything much bigger than a courier boat. That range put them nine light-minutes outside the planet Enki, and the actual range to the platform closest to the Manties was about thirteen light-minutes. Which meant it would be another—he checked the time—ten minutes and twenty-six seconds before he got a light-speed report from the sensors with the best look at whatever was coming at him. On the other hand, the inner-system arrays had more than enough reach to at least detect such a massive hyper translation. They'd picked up the faster-than-light ripple along the alpha wall as the Manties made transit, and they were picking up a confused clutch of impeller drive signatures now. But they were much too far away to see anything else, which meant Tracking's reports were going to be maddeningly vague until the Manties were a lot deeper in-system. Unfortunately, Tracking had already picked up enough for Dimitri to feel certain the enemy would be coming *in* a lot deeper. The estimate blinking on the main board said there were over seventy of the wall headed for Enki, and that was no raiding force.

"It's White Haven," he rasped. "It has to be their Eighth Fleet. Maybe with their Third Fleet along to side it, judging from the preliminary numbers. Which means we're probably screwed, Citizen Commissioner."

Connors' expression turned disapproving, but only briefly. And the disapproval wasn't really directed at Dimitri. She didn't like defeatism, but that didn't change what was going to happen, and she knew the citizen admiral was correct. Their own strength had been reduced to only twenty-two of the wall. Even with the new mines and missile pod deployment Theisman had devised, plus the forts and the LACs, that was highly unlikely to stop seventy or eighty Manty superdreadnoughts and dreadnoughts. And, she reminded herself, initial estimates at this sort of range were almost always low, not high, even if the enemy wasn't using EW to conceal still more ships. On the other hand . . .

"We can still give them a fight, Citizen Admiral," she said, and he nodded.

"Oh, we can certainly do that, Ma'am, and I intend to make *them* aware of that fact, too. I just wish I knew why they made translation so far out . . . and why they're coming in so slowly. I don't object to an enemy who gives me time to assemble all my forces to meet him, but I do have to wonder why he's being so obliging."

"I had the same thought," Connors murmured, and the two of them turned as one to look out at the huge holo tank's light sculpture replica of the Barnett System.

The angry red pockmarks of a hostile fleet hung in that display, twenty-six-point-three light-minutes from Enki and headed for it at an unhurried six thousand KPS with an acceleration of only three hundred gravities. Preliminary intercept solutions were already coming up on a sidebar display, providing Dimitri with his entire menu of choices. Not that he intended to use any of the ones that involved sending his mobile units out to meet that incoming hammer. His outnumbered units would undoubtedly score a few kills if he were stupid enough to do that, but none would survive, and his fixed fortifications and LACs would be easy meat for an unshaken, intact wall of battle. Nor did he intend to waste his long-ranged mines. Those would wait until he could coordinate their attacks with those of his mobile units' missiles. Which narrowed the only numbers he really needed to think about to the ones which showed what the Manties could do to *him*.

Assuming they maintained their current acceleration all the way in and went for a passing engagement with Enki's close-in defenses, they could be on top of him in just under five hours. But they'd go ripping right on past him at over fifty-three thousand KPS. They could go for that option, but he doubted they would. It would get them to him a bit sooner, but that obviously wasn't a factor in their thinking, or they'd have made their translation further in and be coming in under a much higher acceleration. Besides, there was no point in their opting for a passing engagement. The fighting would be all over, one way or the other, by the time they reached Enki's orbital position, and if they overshot, they'd simply have to decelerate to come back and occupy the ruins.

No, the way they were coming in, they meant to go for a leisurely but traditional zero/zero intercept. Which meant, assuming they stuck with their ridiculously low accel, that they would come to rest relative to Enki (and ready to land their Marines) in six and a half hours . . . by which time, all of his units would be so much drifting wreckage.

But that wreckage was going to have a lot of Manty company, he thought grimly. That was all he could really hope for, and if he could take a big enough chunk out of those slow-moving, over-confident bastards, they might just find themselves fatally weakened when Operation Bagration went in, took Grendelsbane away from them, and started rolling them up from the southeast.

He glanced at another display and grunted in approval. This one showed his mobile units, racing from their scattered patrol positions to form up with the forts. Another one showed the readiness states on his LACs, with squadron after squadron blinking from the amber of stand-by to the green of readiness, and he nodded sharply. He'd have plenty of time to assemble and prepare his forces, and the bastards didn't know about the new mines and pod arrangements he had to demonstrate for them.

His upper lip curled, showing just a flash of white teeth, and he turned back to the main board, waiting patiently for solid enemy unit IDs to appear.

"Here comes the first info, My Lord."

Admiral White Haven looked up from a quiet conversation with his chief of staff, Captain Lady Alyson Granston-Henley, as the new data blinked onto his plot.

"I see it, Trev." White Haven and Granston-Henley moved over beside Commander Trevor Haggerston, Eighth Fleet's dark-haired, heavy-set ops officer. The Erewhonese officer was attractive, in a rough-hewn craggy sort of way, and White Haven suspected that he and Granston-Henley might be getting just a bit closer than a narrow interpretation of the Regs would have approved. Not that the earl had any intention of finding out anything that would require him to take official notice of their relationship. They were entirely too valuable to Eighth Fleet's command team for him to worry about such foolishness.

Now he and his chief of staff paused beside Haggerston, and watched with him as the FTL drones began reporting in.

There were only a spattering of additional icons at first, but the initial spray grew quickly into a wider, deeper, brighter blur of light codes, and White Haven pursed his lips as CIC began evaluating the data. Unless the Peeps were trying to be sneakier than usual, they had considerably fewer ships of the wall than he'd anticipated.

That probably indicated that Caparelli's diversionary efforts down around Grendelsbane had worked, White Haven thought, with a mental nod of respect for the First Space Lord's efforts.

Of course, there was a downside to Caparelli's success. Under normal circumstances, fewer ships meant fewer opponents, which would have been a very good thing. In *this* instance, however, fewer ships simply meant fewer *targets*.

"What do we make it so far, Trev?" he asked after a moment.

"CIC is calling it twenty-two of the wall, ten battleships—there could be a couple more of those hiding behind the wedge clutter—twenty to thirty battlecruisers, forty-six cruisers of all types, and thirty or forty destroyers. Looks like they've got forty to forty-five of their forts on-line, as well, and there's one hell of a lot of LACs swanning around in that mess. CIC figures it for a minimum of seven hundred."

"Um." White Haven rubbed his chin. Seven hundred *was* a lot of LACs . . . for a navy that didn't have *Shrikes* or *Ferrets*. Older style LACs simply weren't effective enough to build in huge numbers, and McQueen must have scraped the bottom of the barrel to put that many in one system. Unless, of course, the PN had started building the things again themselves. They'd be largely useless against hyper-capable warships, but enough of them could still inflict painful losses on the newer LAC types. The exchange rate would be ruinously in favor of the *Shrikes* and the *Ferrets*, but McQueen had already proved herself capable of playing the attrition game when that was her only option.

Not that seven hundred old-style LACs or even twice that many were going to be much of a problem for Alice Truman's boys and girls.

Assuming they had to fight them at all.

"Range to their forces?"

"We've been inbound for thirty-seven minutes, Sir. Range to zero/zero is roughly four hundred sixty-six million klicks—call it twenty-six light-minutes—and we're up to a smidge over seventy-two hundred KPS. Long way to go yet even for Ghost Rider, Sir."

"Agreed. Agreed." White Haven rubbed his chin some more. The final—or *currently* "final"—version of the long-range missiles could reach 96,000 gravities of acceleration, four thousand more than the ones Alice Truman had deployed at Basilisk. That gave them a powered attack range from rest of almost fifty-one light-seconds at maximum acceleration. By stepping the drives down to 48,000 g, endurance could be tripled, however, and that upped the maximum powered envelope to well over three and a half light-*minutes* and a terminal velocity of .83 c. That was crowding the very limits of the fire control technology available even to the Royal Manticoran Navy, however.

But given that the maximum possible engagement range from rest for the *enemy*, even at low accel, was going to be on the order of less than thirty light-seconds in *maximum* accel mode, things were about to get very ugly for the Peeps.

"I think these guys are going to get reamed, Skipper," Sir Horace Harkness observed in tones of profound satisfaction as Her Majesty's Light Attack Craft *Bad Penny* led the Nineteenth LAC Wing towards the enemy.

"Accurately, if inelegantly, put, Chief," Ensign Pyne agreed, and Scotty Tremaine nodded. His active sensors were shut completely down, but *Bad Penny* could tap the feeds from the recon drones just fine. His tactical display didn't allow for anything like the resolution and detail available to *Benjamin the Great*'s combat information center, but he could see quite enough to know Harkness had it right.

Against a conventionally armed Allied fleet, the Peeps could have put up a decent fight, he thought. They would have lost everything they had, but they would also have taken a hell of a bite out of their attackers. But that supposed their attackers had to come into their range . . . and Eighth Fleet didn't. Or its starships didn't, at least. It would be another story for the LACs, but they would be going in only on the heels of the missile strikes, and Tremaine very much doubted there'd be much left besides cripples waiting to be killed and the wreckage of ships which had already died.

He *was* just a tad concerned by all the LACs he saw out there, but not enough to lose any sleep over it. By his most pessimistic estimate, they had less than half as many of them as Admiral Truman did, and all of hers were *Shrike-Bs* and *Ferrets*. And all of the *Shrike-Bs* of the Nineteenth Wing had the new, improved, better-than-ever Bolgeo-Roden-Paulk sternwall to make them even nastier.

Citizen Admiral Dimitri accepted another cup of coffee from a signals yeoman. It was good coffee, brewed just the way he liked it, and it tasted like corrosion-strength industrial cleaner. Not too surprisingly, he supposed. Five hours and thirty-eight minutes had passed since the Manties' translation, and the bastards had come the next best thing to four hundred and sixty million kilometers in that time. They were down to just a hair over fifteen million klicks from Enki, decelerating now, and their velocity was back down to a little over ninety-three hundred KPS.

He still didn't understand their approach course, and his brain continued to pick at its apparent illogic like a tongue probing a sore tooth. No doubt they were coming in heavy with pods—*he* certainly would have been in their place!—but Manty SDs could pull a lot more than three hundred gees, even with full pod loads on tow. So why had they wasted so much time? And why hadn't they gone for a least-time course at whatever accel they were willing to use? The logical thing for them to have done would have been to translate into n-space on a heading which would have pinned Enki between them and Barnett. As it was, they'd not only come in too far out and too slowly, but they were actually approaching Enki's position to intercept at a shallow angle. At the moment, their icons and those of the mobile units positioned to intercept them weren't even on anything approaching a direct line with the blue dot that marked Enki's position.

It all looked and felt dreadfully unorthodox, which was enough to make Dimitri instantly suspicious, especially knowing that if that was Eighth Fleet out there, he was up against White Haven, who had systematically kicked the crap out of every Republican CO he'd ever faced. Which suggested there had to be *some* reason for the Manties' apparently inept and clumsy approach, except that try as he might, Dimitri couldn't come up with a single one that made any sort of sense. It was almost as if White Haven were intentionally making certain the defenders had plenty of time to concentrate their full forces to meet him, but that was ridiculous. Granted, Manty hardware was superior, but there were limits in all things. Not even *Manties* could be ballsy enough to deliberately throw away any chance of catching him before he could concentrate. Any flag officer worth his braid schemed furiously in search of some way to catch the defenders with their forces still spread out so he could engage and crush them in detail rather than facing all of them at once!

But that seemed to be exactly what White Haven wasn't doing, Dimitri thought irritably, then shrugged. In another twelve minutes it would no longer matter what the Manty CO thought he *was* doing, because the range would be down to six million klicks. Given the geometry of the Manties' approach vector, they would be in his powered missile envelope—technically speaking—for at least two minutes before that, but against Manty electronic warfare, even six million klicks against a closing enemy might be a little optimistic. Which meant he and his people were going to have to take their lumps from the Manties before any of their own birds got home. But he'd be sending the mine-armed drones out in another four minutes, and at least he ought to be able to flush all of his pods before any of the incoming arrived, and—

A shrill, strident alarm sliced through the war room's tense calm like a buzz saw.

"Coming down on fifteen million kilometers, Sir," Trevor Haggerston said quietly, and White Haven nodded.

"Anything more on those unidentified bogies?" he asked.

"We still can't be positive, but it looks like most of them are missile pods, Sir. We're a bit more puzzled by some of the others, though. They're smaller than pods, but they seem to be bigger than individual missiles ought to be. About the size of a deep recon drone, actually."

"I see." The earl frowned, then shrugged. Missiles or drones, a saturation pattern of heavy warheads should take them out with proximity kills handily enough . . . and before they could do anything nasty.

The Peeps obviously didn't know it, but they'd been in his powered missile range for well over an hour, assuming he'd been willing to go for low-powered drive settings, but even with his RDs hovering just beyond the range of the Peeps' weapons, targeting solutions would have been very poor at sixty-five million kilometers . . . not to mention that flight time would have been the next best thing to nine minutes. That was plenty of time for an alert captain to roll ship and take the brunt of the incoming fire on his wedge, and even with Ghost Rider's EW goodies along for company, it might have given the defenders time to achieve effective point defense solutions.

Besides, there was no need to do any such thing. He still had over twelve minutes before he entered the *Peeps'* effective envelope, and each of his *Harrington/Medusas* could get off sixty six-pod salvos in that time. That was over a hundred and eleven thousand missiles from the SD(P)s alone, and they *weren't* alone, and he checked his plot one last time

Between the input from his drones and the long, unhurried time his fire control officers had been given to refine their data, his ships had tight locks on most of the Peep capital ships. Of course, "tight lock" at this sort of range didn't mean what it would have at lower ranges, and accuracy was going to suffer accordingly. On the other hand, the Peeps hadn't yet deployed a single decoy, and their jammers were only beginning to come on line. Which made sense, if they wanted to avoid putting too much time on their EW systems' clocks. Unfortunately, this time it was going to be fatal.

"Very well, Commander Haggerston," he said formally. "You may fire."

Citizen Admiral Dimitri's mug hit the floor and shattered, but he never noticed. Neither the sound of breaking china nor the sudden pool of steaming coffee registered even peripherally, for he could *not* be seeing what he saw.

But the sensors and the computers didn't care what their human masters thought. They insisted on presenting the preposterous data anyway, and Dimitri heard other voices, several shrill with rising panic, as the war room's normal discipline disintegrated as completely as his broken cup. It was inexcusable. They were trained military men and women, manning the nerve center of the system's entire defense structure. Above all else, it was their primary duty to remain calm and collected, exerting the control over their combat units upon which any hope of victory depended.

But Dimitri couldn't blame them, and even if he could have, it wouldn't have mattered. No conceivable calm, collected response could have affected the outcome of this battle in the least.

No one in the history of interstellar warfare had ever seen anything like the massive salvo coming in on his ships. Those missiles were turning out at least ninety-six *thousand* gravities, launched from pods and shipboard tubes which were themselves moving at over nine thousand kilometers per second, and that didn't even consider the initial velocity imparted to them by their launchers' grav drivers. A corner of Dimitri's brain wanted to believe the Manties had gone suddenly insane and thrown away their entire opening salvo at a range from which hits would be impossible. That the incredible acceleration those missiles were cranking meant they could not possibly have more than a minute of drive endurance. That they would be dead, unable to maneuver against his evading units, when they reached the ends of their runs.

But one thing the Earl of White Haven was not was insane. If he'd launched from that range, then his birds had the range to attack effectively . . . and none of Dimitri's did.

He watched numbly as the missiles roared down on his wall. The entire front of the salvo was a solid wall of jamming and decoys, and he clamped his jaw as he pictured the panic and terror crashing through the men and women on those ships. *His* men and women. He'd put them out there in the sober expectation that their ships would be destroyed, that many—even most—of them would be killed. But he'd at least believed they would be able to strike back before they died. Now their point defense couldn't even *see* the missiles coming to kill them.

It seemed to take forever, and he heard someone groan behind him as the Manty wall belched a *second* salvo, just as heavy as the first. Which was also impossible. That *had* to be the firepower of a full pod load out for every ship in White Haven's wall. He *couldn't* have still more of them in tow! But apparently no one had told the Manties what they could and couldn't do, and yet a third launch followed.

The first massive wave of missiles crashed over his wall, and his numb brain noted yet another difference from the norm. The tactical realities of towed pods meant each fleet had no real choice but to commit the full weight of its pods in the first salvo, because any that didn't fire in the first exchange were virtually certain to suffer proximity kills from the *enemy's* fire. They were normally concentrated on the enemy vessels for whom the firing fleet had the best firing solutions, as well, because firing at extreme range rather than waiting until the enemy had irradiated your weapons into uselessness meant even the best solutions were none too good.

All of that tended to result in massive overkill on a relatively low number of targets, but that wasn't happening this time. No, *this* time the Manties had allocated their fire with lethal precision. There were well over three thousand missiles in the first wave. Many of them were jammers or decoys, but many were not, and Hamish Alexander's fire plan had allocated a hundred and fifty laser heads to each Peep ship of the wall. His targets' hopelessly jammed and confused defenses stopped no more than ten percent of the incoming fire, and Havenite capital ships shuddered and heaved, belching atmosphere and debris and water vapor as massive, bomb-pumped lasers slammed into them. Hulls spat glowing splinters as massive armor yielded, and fresh, dreadful bursts of light pocked Citizen Admiral Dimitri's wall as fusion bottles began to fail.

But even as the SDs and DNs reeled and died under the pounding, a second, equally massive wave of missiles was on its way. This one ignored the surviving, mangled ships of the wall. Its missiles went for Dimitri's lighter, more fragile battleships and battlecruisers, even heavy and light cruisers. Fewer of them went after each target, but even a battleship could take no more than a handful of hits from such heavy laser heads . . . and none of them could begin to match the point defense capability of a ship of the wall.

The third wave bypassed the mobile units completely to swoop towards Enki's orbital defenses. They ignored the fortresses, but their conventional nuclear warheads detonated in a blinding, meticulously precise wall of plasma and fury that killed every unprotected satellite, missile pod, and drone in Enki orbit.

And then, as if to cap the insanity, a tidal wave of LACs—well over fifteen hundred of them—erupted from stealth, already in energy range of the broken wreckage which had once been a fleet. They swept in, firing savagely, and a single pass reduced every unit of Dimitri's wall to drifting hulks . . . or worse. The LACs were at least close enough that his fortresses could fire on them, but their EW was almost as good as the capital ships, and they deployed shoals of jammers and decoys of their own. Even the missiles which got through to them seemed to detonate completely uselessly. It was as if the impossible little vessels' wedges had no throat or kilt to attack!

The LACs had obviously planned their approach maneuver very carefully. Their velocity relative to their victims had been very low, no more than fifteen hundred KPS, and their vector had been designed to cross the base track of Dimitri's wall at an angle that carried them away from his forts and his own LACs. A few squadrons of the latter were in position to at least try to intercept, but those who did vanished in vicious fireballs as hurricanes of lighter but still lethal missiles ripped into their faces. Then the Manty LACs—Esther McQueen's much derided "super LACs," Dimitri thought numbly—disappeared back into the invisibility of their stealth systems. And just to make certain they got away clean, that impossible Manty wall of battle blanketed the battle area with a solid cone of decoys and jammers which made it impossible for any of the surviving defenders to lock onto the fleet, elusive little targets.

Alec Dimitri stared in horror at the display from which every single starship of his fleet had been wiped without ever managing to fire a single shot. Not *one*. And as he stared at the spreading patterns of life pods, someone touched him on the shoulder.

He flinched, then turned quickly, and his com officer stepped back from whatever she saw in his eyes. But he stopped, made himself inhale deeply, and forced the lumpy muscles along his jaw to relax.

There was no more shouting, no more cries of disbelief, in the war room. There was only deep and utter silence, and his voice sounded unnaturally loud in his own ears when he made himself speak.

"What is it, Jendra?"

"I—" The citizen commander swallowed hard. "It's a message

from the Manties, Citizen Admiral," she said then. "It was addressed to Citizen Admiral Theisman. I guess they don't know he's not here." She was rambling, and her jaw tightened as she forced herself back under control. "It's from their commander, Citizen Admiral."

"White Haven?" The question came out almost incuriously, but that wasn't the way he felt, and his eyes narrowed at her nod. "What sort of message?"

"It came in in the clear, Citizen Admiral," she said, and held out a message board. He took it from her and punched the play button, and a man in the black-and-gold of a Manticoran admiral looked out of the holographic display at him. He was dark haired and broad shouldered . . . and his hard eyes were the coldest blue Alec Dimitri had ever seen.

"Admiral Theisman," the Manty said flatly, "I call upon you to surrender this system and your surviving units immediately. We have just demonstrated that we can and will destroy any and all armed units, ships or forts, in this system without exposing our own vessels to return fire. I take no pleasure in slaughtering men and women who cannot fight back. That will not prevent me from doing precisely that, however, if you refuse to surrender, for I have no intention of exposing my own people to needless casualties. You have five minutes to accept my terms and surrender your command. If you have not done so by the end of that time, my units will resume fire . . . and we both know what the result will be. I await your response. White Haven, out."

The display blanked. Dimitri stared at it for several seconds, his stocky body sagging around its bones. Then he handed the message board back to the com officer, squared his shoulders, turned to Sandra Connors, and made himself say the unthinkable.

"Ma'am," his quiet voice cut the silence like a knife, "I see no alternative." He inhaled deeply, then went on. "I request permission to surrender my command to the enemy."

CHAPTER THIRTY-SIX

"**C**itizen Admiral Theisman, report to the bridge! Citizen Admiral Theisman, report to the bridge *at once!*"

Thomas Theisman's head jerked up from his book viewer as Citizen Lieutenant Jackson's voice rattled from the speakers. Theisman had been less than overwhelmed by Jackson when he first boarded the citizen lieutenant's boat. Not that he'd thought the man couldn't handle his present duties. In fact, Jackson was, in many ways, what Theisman considered the perfect courier commander: stolid, phlegmatic, predictable, and utterly incurious. Men like that were never tempted to tamper with or snoop around among the sensitive documents in their computers. From a security perspective, that was wonderful, but it didn't exactly recommend them for any job *except* that of a postman.

But the voice jarring from the intercom was anything but phlegmatic, and Theisman didn't even think about hesitating. Aboard a ship this small he could reach the bridge almost as quickly as he could have screened it, and he dropped the book viewer and was out his cabin hatch and thundering down the passage before it hit the decksole.

What in God's name can his problem *be?* The question crackled in Theisman's brain as he pounded towards the ladder. *The passage here from Barnett was so routine, Denis and I almost died of boredom, and his translation back into n-space was obviously nominal. So what in hell is going on?!*

He vaulted up the ladder onto the bridge, and his eyes automatically darted to the main view screen. It was in tactical mode, and his blood ran cold as he saw the two battlecruisers. They were barely three million kilometers distant, and their icons radiated the vicious, strobing rays of radar and lidar while a warning signal warbled.

My God, he thought almost calmly, *they've got us locked up for missile fire!*

He felt Citizen Lieutenant Jackson behind him and glanced over his shoulder. The dispatch boat's CO was white-faced and sweating, and his hands trembled visibly.

"What is it, Citizen Lieutenant?" Theisman made his voice as deep and calm as he could, and wished he could project that calm directly into Jackson's brain without the clumsy interface of language.

"I-I don't know, C-C-Citizen Admiral," the citizen lieutenant stuttered. Then his chest swelled as he sucked in a huge breath. When he exhaled once more, it looked as if some of the calmness Theisman had tried to will into him must have taken, and he cleared his throat.

"All I know is that we made transit as usual, and everything seemed just fine, until all of a sudden those two—" he jabbed a finger at the battlecruisers on the plot "—lit us up and ordered me to cut my accel immediately or be destroyed. So I did that," he astonished Theisman with a tight, death's head grin, "and then they demanded my ID all over again. I sent it to them, and they . . . they said they didn't *accept* it, Citizen Admiral! They ordered me to leave the system! But I told them I couldn't. That I had you and Citizen Commissioner LePic aboard and I was supposed to deliver you to the capital. But they said no one—no regular Navy ships, that is—were getting through, and when I insisted my instructions came directly from the Octagon and the Committee, they ordered me to get you on the com in person, and . . . and . . ."

His voice trailed off, and he raised both hands in a gesture of helplessness. It was hardly the picture of a decisive CO, but if his account was even half accurate, Theisman could hardly fault him for that. The citizen admiral felt sweat popping out along his own hairline, but he made himself nod calmly, then turned and beckoned the com officer out of her chair. She hastened to obey, scrambling up as if to put as much distance as physically possible between her and the com station, and Theisman took her place.

It had been years since he last personally placed a ship-to-ship com request, but he hadn't forgotten how, and his fingers moved quickly while his brain tried to imagine what the hell could have happened. It had obviously been drastic, and "drastic" was a word that terrified anyone who'd lived through the massive upheavals of the People's Republic over the last decade. The part of him that concerned itself with minor matters like survival had no interest at all in comming the waiting battlecruisers. All *it* wanted to do was tell Jackson to turn and slink away, exactly as ordered, and as he worked, it occurred to Thomas Theisman that this would no doubt be an excellent time for an *ex*-naval officer to consider a lengthy vacation somewhere like Beowulf or Old Earth.

But he was an admiral of the Republic, however he'd gotten there. That gave him responsibilities he simply could not turn his back upon, and so he waited while the com link came up and steadied.

Despite himself, Theisman's lips tightened as he saw the woman at the other end. She wore the crimson-and-black of State Security, and her narrow face was cold and hard. Even across the vacuum, Theisman could feel her hatred and desire to go ahead and fire. He didn't think it was because of anything Jackson had said, or because of who Thomas Theisman was. She wanted an excuse to blow something—*anything*—apart, and a fresh wave of tension rippled through his belly.

"I am Citizen Admiral Thomas Theisman," he told that hating face as calmly as he could. "And you are?"

At three million klicks, it took more than ten seconds for his light-speed transmission to reach her . . . and another ten for her response to reach him. The delay in transit did not seem to have improved it.

"Citizen Captain Eliza Shumate, State Security," she snapped. "What business do you have in Haven, Theisman?"

"That's between myself and . . . the Committee, Citizen *Captain*," Theisman replied. He wasn't certain why he'd switched from "Citizen Secretary McQueen" to "the Committee" at the last moment, but when his instincts shrieked that loudly, he made a point of listening to them.

"The Committee." It wasn't a question the way Shumate said it, and the hate in her eyes flared higher. But Theisman didn't flinch, and a sliver of grudging respect crept into her expression as he glared back at her unyieldingly.

"Yes, the Committee. Citizen Commissioner LePic and I are under orders to report directly to Citizen Chairman Pierre on our arrival."

Something changed in Shumate's eyes yet again—a flicker of something besides hate or suspicion, though Theisman wasn't prepared to hazard any guesses on what it was instead. She stared at him for perhaps three extra heart beats, then expelled her breath in a harsh, angry grunt.

"Citizen Chairman Pierre is dead," she told him flatly.

Theisman heard someone gasp behind him, and knew his own face had turned to stone. He hadn't liked Pierre. Indeed, he'd learned to loathe everything the man stood for. But Rob Pierre had been the Titan looming over the pygmies who served with him on the Committee of Public Safety. His had been the guiding hand behind the People's Republic since the Coup, and especially since Cordelia Ransom's death had removed the one true challenge to his power from within the Committee itself. He *couldn't* be dead!

But he could, and Theisman felt a fresh stab of fear when he put that together with Shumate's hair-trigger balance . . . and apparent hatred for officers of the People's Navy.

"I'm sorry to hear that, Citizen Captain," he said quietly, and to his surprise, he meant it, if not for the same reasons Shumate might have.

"I'm sure." Shumate didn't sound anything of the sort, but at least she mouthed the words, and her tight shoulders relaxed ever so slightly. Theisman felt someone step up beside him and realized it was LePic. The people's commissioner had obviously arrived in time to hear Shumate's announcement, for his face was pale. He moved into the range of the pickup and addressed the StateSec citizen captain.

"Citizen Captain Shumate, I'm Denis LePic, Citizen Admiral Theisman's commissioner. This is terrible news! How did the Citizen Chairman die?"

"He didn't '*die*,' Citizen Commissioner. He was murdered. Shot down like an *animal* by one of that *bitch* McQueen's staffers from the fucking Octagon!"

All the hatred which had faded from her face and voice was back, redoubled, and Theisman suppressed an urge to wipe sweat from his forehead. No wonder Shumate was so antagonistic.

He started to speak, but LePic's hand squeezed his shoulder, and he made himself sit silently, leaving the conversation to the commissioner who had become his friend.

"That sounds terrible, Citizen Captain," LePic said. "Still, the fact that you and your ships are on patrol out here suggests to me that the situation is still at least marginally under control. Can you tell me anything more about it?"

"I don't have all the details, Sir," Shumate admitted. "As far as I know, no one does yet. But apparently that bi—" She stopped and made herself draw another deep breath. "Apparently *McQueen*," she went on after a moment, "had been plotting with her senior officers over at the Octagon for some time. No one knows why they moved when they did. It's obvious their plans weren't fully mature—which is probably all that saved any of the situation. But they'd still managed to put together one hell of an operation."

"What do you mean?"

"There were at least half a dozen assault teams. Every one of them was made up of Marines, and McQueen had insured that they had access to heavy weapons. Most of them had battle armor, and they went through the quick-reaction security forces like a tornado, starting with the Citizen Chairman's. One of their teams wiped out a platoon of Public Order Police, rolled right over three squads of the Chairman's Guard, and eliminated his entire StateSec protective detail in less than three minutes, and the Citizen Chairman was killed in the fighting. We *think* that was an accident. There are indications McQueen wanted him and as much of the Committee as she could capture alive, if only to try to force him to name her his 'successor.' But whatever their intentions, he was dead in the first five minutes. Citizen Secretary Downey, Citizen Secretary DuPres, and Citizen Secretary Farley were also killed or captured by the insurgents in the first half hour. As nearly as we can make out, Citizen Secretary Turner had thrown his lot in with McQueen. Apparently they intended to make themselves the core of a smaller Committee they could dominate while presenting the appearance that it was still a democratic body."

Shumate's expression didn't even flicker with the last sentence, and Theisman had to control his own face carefully. "Democratic body" was not a term he would have applied to the Committee of Public Safety, but perhaps she honestly believed it fitted. And whether she did or not, this was hardly the time to irritate her by calling her on it.

"The only one of their initial targets they *didn't* get was Citizen Secretary Saint-Just," Shumate went on, and this time her tone carried bleak satisfaction that her own chief had eluded McQueen's net. "I don't think they realized how good his security really was, but it was a hell of a shootout. His protection detail took ninety percent casualties, but they held until a heavy intervention battalion took the attackers in the rear."

"My God," LePic said softly, then shook himself. "And Capital Fleet?"

"Didn't make a move, for the most part," Shumate replied. Her distaste at having to do so was manifest, and she went right on,

"Two SDs did look as if they might be about to intervene on McQueen's behalf, but Citizen Commodore Helft and his State Security squadron blew them out of space before they even got their wedges up." She smiled with bleak ferocity. "*That* took the starch out of any other bastards who might've been tempted to help the traitors!"

And from the sound of it, the kill-happy, murderous son-of-a-bitch killed them when there was absolutely no need to, Theisman thought with sick loathing. *Nine or ten thousand men and women, wiped out as if they were nothing at all, when all the bastard had to do was order them to stand down—if they were really thinking about supporting McQueen to start with! If he caught them with their wedges still down, there wouldn't have been anything they could've done but obey him. And if they'd been stupid enough to refuse his orders,* then *he could have blown them away. But that's not what happened, is it,* Citizen Captain *Shumate?*

"The situation was pretty much deadlocked in Nouveau Paris by that time, though," Shumate went on more heavily. "The Citizen Chairman was dead, and McQueen had control of the Octagon. She probably had five or six thousand Marines and Navy regulars siding her, and she and Bukato had gotten control of the place's defensive grid. Worse, they had at least half a dozen members of the Committee in there with them, where they were effectively hostages. We tried to land intervention units on them, and the grid blew them away. Same thing for the air strikes we tried. And the whole time, McQueen was on the air to the rest of the Navy and Marine units in the system, claiming she was acting solely in self-defense against some sort of plot by the Chairman and Citizen Secretary Saint-Just to have her and her staff arrested and shot. Some of them were beginning to listen, too."

"So what happened?" LePic asked when she paused once more.

"So Citizen Secretary Saint-Just did what he had to do, Sir," she said in a cold voice. "McQueen and Bukato might've gotten control of the defensive grid, but they didn't know about the Citizen Secretary's final precaution. When it became obvious it was going to take us days to fight our way in, and with reports more and more Marine and Navy units were beginning to turn restless, he pressed the button."

"The button?" LePic asked. The citizen captain nodded, and LePic scowled. "*What* button?" he demanded with some asperity.

"The one to the kiloton-range warhead in the Octagon's basement, Sir," Shumate said flatly, and Theisman's belly knotted. "It took out the entire structure and three of the surrounding towers. Killed McQueen and every one of her traitors, too."

"And civilian casualties?" Theisman asked the question before he could stop himself, but at the last moment he managed to make it *only* a question.

"They were heavy," Shumate admitted. "We couldn't evacuate without giving away what was coming, and the traitors *had* to be stopped. The last estimate I heard put the total figure somewhere around one-point-three million."

Denis LePic swallowed. The casualties had been even worse in the Leveler Rising, he knew, but another million *civilians*? Killed simply because they happened to be too close to a building Saint-Just had decided had to go . . . and warning them *might* have warned McQueen what was coming?

"So how much of the Committee is left, Citizen Captain?" he heard himself asking, and Shumate looked at him with some surprise.

"I'm sorry, Sir. I thought I'd made that clear. The only surviving member of the Committee is Citizen Secretary—only he's Citizen Chairman now, of course—Saint-Just."

Several hours later, a silent, hard-faced StateSec major showed Thomas Theisman and Denis LePic into an office in Nouveau Paris. The major was clearly unhappy about their presence, and the daggers his eyes kept shooting Theisman's way ought by rights to have reduced the citizen admiral to ribbons. Nor was his attitude unique. Hostile, hating StateSec eyes had followed Theisman all the way from his air car to this office, and an ominous quantity of firepower, from pulsers to plasma rifles, was on prominent display.

And all of them want to rip my head off and piss down my neck, Theisman thought mordantly. *Hard to blame them, really. I'm a senior Navy officer, and they just blew up most of the command structure of the Navy and the Marines. They have to be wondering where I'd have stood if I'd been here. Or, for that matter, where I stand now.*

The major opened the office door and stood aside with one last, distrustful glare for Theisman and a curt nod for LePic. Both of them ignored him and stepped into the office, and Theisman watched the small man behind the desk rise.

Funny. I was surprised Ransom was so much shorter than her HD imagery, and here Saint-Just is, almost as short as she was. Is there some sort of overcompensation for small size going on here?

"Citizen Commissioner. Citizen Admiral." Saint-Just sounded

weary, as well he might, and there were fresh, harsh lines in his face. For all that, however, he was still the same harmless-looking little man . . . with all the emotions of a cobra. "Please," he invited, waving at a couple of chairs. "Sit."

"Thank you, Sir." By previous agreement, LePic took the lead as their spokesman. Neither of them wanted it to be too obvious that he was trying to protect Theisman, but it seemed wiser to avoid possible confrontations as much as possible.

The two visitors sat, and Saint-Just perched on the corner of his desk.

Remarkable, Theisman thought. *This man started out as the second-in-command of Internal Security and betrayed the Legislaturalists to Pierre and helped him blow them up. Then he played second fiddle to Pierre for over a decade . . . and now he's the whole show, the entire "Committee of Public Safety." And all he had to do was blow up the rest of the Committee along with Esther McQueen. What a sacrifice.* The citizen admiral snorted mentally. *Wasn't there someone back on Old Earth who once said "we had to destroy the village to save it" or something like that? Suits this cold-blooded little bastard to a "T," doesn't it?*

"We were shocked to hear about what happened, Sir," LePic began. "Of course, we'd heard rumors about McQueen's ambitions, but we never dreamed she might try something like that!"

"To be honest, I didn't expect it either," Saint-Just said, and to Theisman's surprise, he seemed sincere, even a little bewildered. "Not out of the blue like this. I didn't trust her, of course. Never did. But we needed her abilities, and she'd turned the entire military situation around. Under the circumstances, I was prepared to take a few routine precautions, but neither the Citizen Chairman nor I had any intention of moving against her without much better cause than reports about her 'ambition,' and I was certain she knew it. It's obvious now, of course, that she was plotting all along. Incomplete as her plans clearly were, she still came within millimeters of success. In fact, if Rob hadn't been killed, I don't know if I could have—"

He stopped and waved a hand, looking away from the other two men, and Theisman felt a fresh stab of surprise, this time at Saint-Just's obvious pain over Pierre's death. Thomas Theisman had been prepared to grant the commander of State Security many qualities; the capacity for close personal friendship had not been one of them.

"At any rate," Saint-Just went on after a moment, "she did act. We may never know what pushed her into it. I think it's pretty evident she wasn't ready yet, and that's certainly just as well. If she *had* been completely ready, I'd probably have been killed or captured just like Rob, and then she undoubtedly would have won. As it is . . ."

He shrugged, and LePic nodded.

"Which brings us to the reason I wanted to see you two," the man who was now the dictator of the People's Republic said more briskly, and the look he directed at Theisman was not a particularly encouraging one. "You both know McQueen had agreed to bring you two in to take over Capital Fleet. What you may not realize is that she did so only at my request and strong urging."

Theisman felt his eyebrows rise, and Saint-Just snorted.

"Don't think it was because I believe you're a fervent supporter of the New Order, Citizen Admiral," he said bluntly. "I don't. Nor do I think you're another McQueen, however. If I thought you had the same ambition, you wouldn't be sitting in this office; you'd be dead. What I think you *are*, is a professional officer who's never learned to play the political game. I don't think you loved the Committee, and I don't really care as long as you settle for being loyal to the government and to the Republic. Can you do that?"

"I believe I can, Sir. Yes," Theisman said. *Or at least half of it, anyway. I'm loyal to the* Republic, *all right.*

"I hope you can," Saint-Just's voice was bleak, "because I need you. And because I will not hesitate to have you shot if I come to suspect you *are* disloyal, Citizen Admiral." Theisman looked into the emotionless eyes and shivered. "If that sounds like a threat, I suppose it is, but there's nothing personal in it. I simply can't afford to take any more chances, and McQueen's conspiracy was built in the military. Obviously I'm going to be keeping an even closer eye on the officer corps of the Navy and the Marines."

"Obviously," Theisman agreed, and saw what might have been a flash of approval flicker across Saint-Just's face. "I can't say I'm happy about the effect it will no doubt have on military efficiency, but frankly, Sir, I'd be astonished if you felt any other way. I certainly wouldn't in your place."

"I'm glad you can understand that. It gives me some hope for our ability to work together. However, I also hope you understand why, under the circumstances, I do not intend to give any officer of the regular military the power to emulate McQueen. I intend to retain the office of the Secretary of War myself, along with StateSec and the chairmanship of the Committee. Lord knows I never wanted the top slot, mostly because I saw what it cost the people who had it, but it's mine now, and I'll do the job, finish what Rob started, however long it takes.

"But what you have to understand right now is that the Octagon is gone, and so are two-thirds of the planning staffs, virtually all of its central records, and a huge chunk of the senior officers of the Navy. More of them were killed in the fighting even before that, several of them because they sided with McQueen. It's fortunate the Manties are on the run right now, and that Operation Bagration should keep them that way, because our command structure has been pretty well pulverized, and I don't dare rebuild it out of regulars until I've had time to be absolutely certain of their loyalties. I tell you this not because I'm certain of *your* loyalty, but so you'll understand what's happening and why."

He paused until Theisman nodded, then went on.

"As I say, I will retain the office of Secretary of War. I will also be creating a new general staff whose members will be drawn primarily from State Security. I realize they have only limited combat experience. Unfortunately, they're the only people whose loyalty I *know* I can trust, and that's going to have to be the overriding consideration, at least until we're sure the Manties have been whipped.

"But I'm not foolish enough to believe I can find fleet commanders among my SS officers. We saw entirely too much of how expensive 'on-the-job training' in that slot can be in the first year or so of the war. So instead, I'll have to rely on regulars, like yourself, for that job, but with their people's commissioners' 'pre-McQueen' powers restored and, probably, augmented. As you implied, it may cost us something in military efficiency, but I'm afraid I have no choice.

"And of all the fleet commands, the one most critical to the security of the state is Capital Fleet, which brings me back to you and Citizen Commissioner LePic. Your first job will be to restore some semblance of order and morale. There's a great deal of resentment over the destruction of *Sovereignty of the People* and *Equality*. Understandable, I suppose, but something which has to go. And the fleet has to get itself back into shape to properly acknowledge and carry out orders which come down the chain of command—the *new* chain of command—from me. In addition, Capital Fleet has to be prepared for the possibility that McQueen may also have suborned fleet or task force commanders outside the Haven System. Commanders who may be headed here at this very moment with some or all of their commands to support her. That would be foolish of them, but that doesn't mean it won't happen, and I need a Capital Fleet which can deal with any such renegades. In short, it will be up to you to transform Capital Fleet from a force which is currently in a state of confusion and disarray into a disciplined fleet which will become the key to maintaining the state and its stability rather than a threat *to* the state. Do you understand that, Citizen Admiral?"

"I do, Sir," Theisman said firmly, for once in complete agreement with Saint-Just.

"And can you do it?" the new Chairman of the Committee pressed.

"Yes, Sir," Theisman told him flatly. "I think— No, I *know* I can turn Capital Fleet back into something that will protect the Republic . . . with your support, of course."

The sun had long-since set when Osar Saint-Just signed the last of the endless stack of official documents, a quarter of them death warrants, which had streamed across his desk with dreary persistence every day since the chaos and terror of McQueen's failed coup. He tilted his chair back and rested his head on the contoured head rest while he pinched the bridge of his nose wearily.

I told Rob I never wanted his job. Now I've got it, and I think I'll probably die of terminal writer's cramp. His mouth twitched slightly at the thought. Wry and bitter as it was, it was also almost the first humorous thought he'd had since the Octagon vanished in a mushroom of light and fury.

He'd hated that. But as he'd told Theisman and LePic, he'd done what he had to, unflinchingly, just as he would continue to do. He had no choice, for he was all that was left of the Committee. He had no assistants, no colleagues or backups, no one to whom he could truly delegate authority or whom he could rely upon to watch his back, and his legitimacy was very much in question. Blowing up the Octagon had also blown up his fellow Committee members, and he doubted anyone would fail to note that and wonder if he hadn't, perhaps, destroyed the Octagon as much to clear his own path to supreme power as to crush McQueen's revolt. That meant no one was going to feel any moral qualms about going after him. And the Navy—the *damned* Navy—was the biggest threat of all. It was organized, armed, and everywhere, and its officers could no doubt convince themselves they were the true guardians of the state . . . whose duty included guarding it against someone who'd blown up his only competition in order to seize control of it. Crank Amos Parnell's version of the Harris Assassination into that, and then add in the popularity McQueen had amassed as the brains behind Operation Icarus, Operation Scylla, and Operation Bagration, when it finally went in, and the Navy was probably considerably more dangerous to him right this minute than the Manties were.

His thoughts went back to Theisman and LePic. He'd handpicked the citizen admiral for his slot . . . but that was before McQueen had been seized by whatever mad impulse had driven her to act so precipitously. As things stood, Theisman might or might not be reliable, and it would be up to LePic to keep an eagle eye on him. LePic's record was exemplary, and Saint-Just felt confident he'd be just as prepared and vigilant as he could, yet the StateSec CO couldn't help wishing Erasmus Fontein had survived McQueen's putsch. He didn't know if McQueen had killed Erasmus, or if the citizen commissioner had simply been taken prisoner and died when Saint-Just blew up the Octagon, but it didn't really matter. What mattered was that Saint-Just badly missed his expertise and knowing, trained military eye.

Saint-Just had even considered calling Eloise Pritchart home to ride herd on Theisman, but in the end he'd decided he couldn't risk it. Critical as Capital Fleet was, Twelfth Fleet was just as important, at least immediately. Saint-Just was confident he and State Security could defuse the internal threat the Navy presented, but to do it, he needed the war ended. Giscard, Tourville, and their staffs would have to go as soon as the shooting ended, of course. It could be no other way, given their probable loyalty to McQueen. But he couldn't do that until after Bagration, and that meant he couldn't recall Pritchart to the capital. Not when he needed her right where she was. For that matter, as much as he knew he was going to miss Erasmus, he had to keep reminding himself Capital Fleet was right here, less than an hour away from his own office, where he could get at it quickly in an emergency. If LePic needed it, he had the full, massive weight of State Security to call upon, and Theisman appeared sufficiently cowed.

No, not "cowed," Saint-Just admitted. *The man's got too much nerve to be "cowed." But he* does *know where the line is . . . and that I won't hesitate to shoot him if he steps even a toe across it. And I believe him when he says he's loyal to the Republic, just as I believe LePic's assessment that the man doesn't want political power. Under the circumstances, that's the best deal I'm going to get.*

His mouth twitched in another almost-grin, and he folded both hands in his lap while he rocked the chair ever so gently back and forth.

He'd done about all he could, he decided. Ideal or not, Theisman was still the best choice for his job, and Eloise would keep an eye on Giscard. And while they did that, the StateSec officers who were taking over for McQueen and her cronies would build a new staff system, one which Saint-Just would *know* was loyal to him.

In the meantime, other StateSec officers had imposed martial law and clamped down on the capital system like steel. As quickly as possible, he would extend that same clampdown to all of the Republic's other core systems. And while all that was going on, he would *end* this damned war and find the time he needed to deal with the looming menace of the Navy. It was probable Bagration would do the job, exactly as he'd told McQueen it would. But he had more than one string to his bow, and he showed the very tips of his teeth in a feral smile. The first thing he'd done after the destruction of the Octagon, even before he'd sent dispatch boats to the other core systems to warn their StateSec garrisons, was to dispatch other couriers with orders to activate Operation Hassan. Slight as its chance of success might be, Hassan had just become even more important. If he could spread a little of the same internal disruption *he* had to deal with across the Allied camp, it ought to have a major beneficial impact on the course of the war.

And if Hassan failed, he lost nothing at all that mattered.

CHAPTER THIRTY-SEVEN

A fresh shout of laughter echoed from the lawn.

Honor turned her head, eyes seeking the source, and grinned broadly as she watched Rachel Mayhew leap into the air for a spectacular catch. She came back down with the Frisbee firmly clutched in both hands, and Nimitz and Hipper both jumped up and down on their rear limbs, true-hands spread as they bleeked at her. She cocked her head at them, then stuck out her tongue—at Hipper, Honor thought, though it was hard to be certain—and flipped a graceful backhand throw to Samantha. Nimitz's mate pounced on the hurtling disk with both true-hands and hand-feet. She came down with the Frisbee and looked up as Artemis and Farragut charged at her, trailed by Jason and Achilles. Her sons bleeked joyfully as they hurtled forward—keep-away was a contact sport among treecats—but Samantha avoided Artemis, leapt clear over Farragut's head, and flipped the Frisbee to Rachel's sister Jeanette just before Jason and Achilles swarmed over her.

The Frisbee sailed straight for Jeanette, but in the instant before her fingers closed on it a cream-and-gray blur shot across in front of her. Togo snatched the Frisbee out of her hands and dashed off, bleeking in triumph, with six children (two human and four treecat) and three adult treecats in hot pursuit. Shrieks of human delight mingled with ringing bleeks of 'cat laughter, and Honor heard a chuckle from one of her guests.

She turned back from the lawn to see Benjamin Mayhew shaking his head at her.

"This is all your fault, you know," he said, twitching a nod at the pandemonium rolling over the Harrington House lawn and generally wreaking havoc on the flower beds.

"Why? For bringing the 'cats home with me?"

"That, certainly. But that damned Frisbee is almost as bad," Mayhew growled. "Not just with the girls, either. The things are taking over the entire planet. It's more than a man's life is worth to wander through Austin Central Park after school these days!"

"Blame that on Nimitz, not me! *He's* the Frisbee freak."

"Oh? Then who was it I saw romping around teaching Rachel, Jeanette, Theresa, and Honor how to throw the thing? Just before you returned to Manticore, I believe it was. A one-armed woman . . . rather tall, as I recall. And this year she got back just in time for Christmas and gave each of them a Frisbee of their very own!"

"I have no idea who you could possibly be referring to," Honor said with dignity. "You're probably mistaken anyway, now that I think about it. To the best of my knowledge, there *aren't* any tall Grayson women."

"I can think of at least one, and she's been a troublemaker from Day One. This—" the Protector nodded at the lawn again, as his two older daughters finally cornered Togo, only to see him flip the Frisbee neatly to Farragut the instant before they reached him "—would give any number of conservatives apoplexy. Why, if Lord Mueller were here, sheer outrage would undoubtedly carry him off to an early grave," he added, and several of Honor's other guests chuckled.

"All very well for you shameless infidels," Benjamin told them. "*I*, on the other hand, as Lord Mueller's Protector and liege lord, am constrained by duty and tradition to regret his possibly impending demise. Unfortunately."

His voice lost much of its humor on the last word, and Honor saw one or two faces grimace. Not that she blamed them, she thought, looking back out across the lawn. Katherine and Elaine Mayhew sat at a shaded table, Katherine nursing the first Mayhew son, Bernard Raoul (who had finally supplanted Benjamin's brother Michael—much to Michael's relief—as heir to the Protectorship), while Elaine read aloud to Honor and Alexandra Mayhew. At twenty-one months, Alexandra was perfectly happy to lie in her traveling cradle and listen to her mothers' voices, but Honor's goddaughter had recently celebrated her seventh birthday, and *she* obviously would have preferred being out with the Frisbee gang. Unfortunately, she was following in her oldest sister's tracks, and the sling on her right arm had her firmly sidelined. It was a clean break, and youthful resilience and quick heal would have the cast off in another week or so, but Grayson's conservatives had been appalled to learn that the Protector's youngest daughter had broken her arm climbing the tallest tree on the grounds of Protector's Palace.

Yet another dreadful lapse to write off to my "evil influence," she thought dryly, recalling how hard and skillfully Mueller had worked at making that point without ever coming out and saying it in so many words. She frowned slightly at the reflection, and bent a thoughtful eye on Benjamin. She could taste something going on in his mind whenever Mueller's name came up. Something more serious and considerably darker than his normal way of speaking about the conservative steadholder might suggest. But whatever it was, he was determined not to discuss it. Or, to be more precise, he was determined not to discuss it with *her*, and she couldn't help wondering why that was.

"We may be shameless infidels, Sir, but we've seen enough of Grayson to know Mueller doesn't speak for most of your people," Rear Admiral Harriet Benson-Dessouix, Grayson Space Navy, said, and heads nodded around the table on the terrace.

"Not for most of us, no," Benjamin agreed. "But for an unfortunately significant number of us, judging from the polls."

"If you'll pardon an 'infidel's' input, Your Grace, I think it would be a mistake to place much emphasis on those polls," Vice Admiral Alfredo Yu said. The ex-Peep who'd been Honor's first flag captain was now the second-in-command of the Protector's Own. Since Honor was its official CO, that made him the Protector's Own's de facto commander, and it was shaping up to be an even more important post than she'd originally anticipated. In addition to the ships of the Elysian Space Navy, Benjamin and Wesley Matthews had earmarked an entire squadron of the new SD(P)s for Yu's command. The first three had already run acceptance trials and were working up at this very moment, with two more due to be released by the yard for trials within the next week or so, and the "appropriate screening elements" Mayhew and Matthews had discussed were beginning to assemble. Not only that, but the first two CLACs were also on order from the Star Kingdom's home yards.

"I don't know, Alfredo," Commodore Cynthia Gonsalves put in. "It looks like the Opposition's going to improve its representation in the Steaders by—what? I think I saw twelve seats being discussed in the 'faxes last week."

"Fourteen, by the latest estimate," Captain Warner Caslet corrected. "I think that's probably high, though. It came from

Wednesday's Cantor poll, and Cantor's in Mueller's pocket, whether they want to admit it or not. They've been pretty damned optimistic—if that's the right word—about the Opposition's chances all along."

"A lot more optimistic than the numbers will support, if you ask me," Captain Susan Phillips snorted. "Personally, I think they've got orders from someone to *keep* the numbers favorable, too. I just haven't figured out whether they're trying to encourage their supporters or *dis*courage their opponents into staying home on voting day."

"You people seem to be paying awful close attention to local politics," Benjamin commented, regarding the assembled officers thoughtfully, and Yu shrugged.

"Most of us either watched our home worlds' governments go down in flames or grew up watching Dolist managers and Legislaturalists deliver completely predictable 'honest votes,' Your Grace. Either of those experiences gives you a lively interest in the political process. Those of us whose native countries no longer exist are determined not to see it happen all over again, and those of us who grew up in the PRH are possibly even more fiercely attached to genuine free speech and free elections than they are."

"Then it's unfortunate most of you aren't eligible to vote yet," Mayhew said, "because that's exactly the sort of attitude which preserves freedom in the first place." His sincerity was obvious, and he smiled. "Which makes me look forward to the day all of you, and not just Admiral Yu, *do* have the franchise here on Grayson."

"Hey! *I've* got the vote here," Honor protested.

"True," Mayhew agreed. "But everyone knows that 'that Foreign Woman' is so firmly in my pocket—or that I'm in hers, depending on their prejudices—that you have absolutely no interest in genuine debate on the merits of my reforms. So the people who agree with you already listen to what you say, and the ones who support Mueller simply tune you out. Or, worse, listen selectively and edit anything you say to suit their bigotry."

He said it lightly, but there was a bitter aftertaste to his emotions, and Honor quirked an eyebrow. The bitterness was sharpened and intensified by whatever he was determined not to discuss with her, but she was unaccustomed to feeling such tension from him.

"Are you really anticipating serious losses in the Steaders?" she asked quietly, and he shrugged.

"I don't know. Some losses, certainly. And possibly more than just 'some' if the present trends continue."

"I don't believe they will, Sir," Yu said, and snorted a laugh when Benjamin looked at him inquiringly. "What you're seeing in the polls right now isn't a genuine, fundamental shift in public attitudes, Your Grace. It's the result of the Opposition's media blitz, and they can't go on spending money hand-over-fist that way forever."

Honor's eyes narrowed at the sudden, savage spike of rage which blazed through Mayhew at Yu's last sentence. The rage wasn't aimed at the vice admiral, and Benjamin suppressed it almost instantly, but she felt it resonating with whatever it was he wasn't going to mention. And the more she tasted it, the more she realized it was something he was specifically avoiding mentioning to *her*, not to the other members of his inner circle. Now that she thought about it, she'd tasted an echo of something very similar from her mother whenever someone mentioned Mueller.

She felt Andrew LaFollet behind her, standing at the edge of the terrace with Major Rice, and made a mental note. If anyone could figure out the reason both her mother and the Protector of Grayson had decided not to tell her something, Andrew could, and it was time she sicced him on the problem. Particularly since she was picking up a strong flavor of "for her own good" from Benjamin. It was almost as if the Protector were afraid she might do something . . . hasty if he shared whatever it was with her.

"I hope you're right about that, Admiral. I suppose even the Opposition's pockets have to have bottoms somewhere," Mayhew said a trifle sourly to Yu.

"I think Admiral Yu is probably right, Sir," Brigadier Henri Benson-Dessouix put in. "And I *know* Harry is." As always, he sat beside his wife, and his arm went around her as he spoke. "The people who tend to be the most conservative are the ones with the most to lose if the system changes, and if they're well enough off to worry about what you may lose, they're also well enough off to contribute to political campaigns. But there are limits to how much they're willing to cough up. I don't believe Mueller can maintain this level of spending indefinitely, and even if he can, the surge he's generating in the poll numbers is probably deceptive. As the elections get closer, I expect a lot of the Opposition's present apparent strength to fade in the stretch."

Honor nodded, but she was hard put to hide a smile. The speech impediment from which Harriet and Henri had suffered on Hell had completely disappeared as the result of the medical treatment Fritz Montoya had started and the Harrington Neurological Clinic had completed. Both of them had been delighted to regain clarity of speech, but it had taken longer for Henri. He'd made up for it since by turning downright loquacious, which was a bit difficult for Honor's mental image of him to adjust to. He'd seldom spoken at all back on Hell, and she'd been away from Grayson while that was changing.

Which didn't invalidate a thing he'd just said.

"I think Henri is right, Benjamin," she said now, "and especially with the way the war is turning around. I don't think Mueller can be a very happy man right now. Just when the poll numbers show he's making ground in the Steaders, Operation Buttercup starts undercutting one of the Opposition's cental themes. He's going to find it awful hard to keep carrying on about 'tying our incomparable Navy to the leading strings of incompetent foreign admiralties' now that Eighth Fleet's blown Barnett to dust bunnies."

"What in the world makes you think *that*, Honor?" Benjamin demanded, only half humorously. "As you just more or less said yourself, the man's already been able to refer to '*our* incomparable Navy' with an absolutely straight face, as if we'd built the tech base or trained enough officers to support that 'incomparable' fleet solely out of our own resources. Which," he added with a wry glance around the table, "present company would seem to indicate wasn't quite the case."

Since he was the only native-born Grayson, aside from LaFollet and Rice, on the terrace at that particular moment, Honor had to concede his point.

"But that kind of ignore-the-facts approach works best when you're talking to people who already agree with you and choose to wear the same sort of blinkers," Rear Admiral Mercedes Brigham pointed out.

"Absolutely," Caslet agreed. "The people he actually needs to convince are going to be a lot more skeptical than his true-believers, Your Grace."

"Please, Captain Caslet!" Benjamin said with another chuckle. "Here on Grayson, we reserve that particular term for those idiots on Masada! Our own intolerant, bigoted, unthinking, doctrinaire reactionaries are properly referred to as 'conservative thinkers.' "

"Sorry, Your Grace." Caslet smiled. "I suppose that's one of those fine cultural distinctions we outsiders have trouble picking up on."

"Don't feel bad, Captain. It's one most of us who *aren't* intolerant reactionaries would love to get rid of."

"Seriously, Sir, you may just have a chance for that," Henri put in. "It's clear from what happened at Barnett that Buttercup took the Peeps completely by surprise. And the new systems were more effective than I think anyone could have predicted. *I* certainly didn't expect them to prove that decisive, but then, the information most of us had on the systems was pretty limited before the offensive kicked off."

"Speak for yourself, *baudet*," Harriet told him. "You Marine types had no need to know about Ghost Rider. For that matter, it's hard to think of a Marine having any real *need* to know about anything more complicated than a club, conservative dirt-pounders that you are. We *naval* officers, on the other hand, were thoroughly briefed on Ghost Rider, and we had a pretty fair background on the new LACs, as well."

" 'More complicated than a club,' is it?" Henri murmured, cocking his head at his tall, blond wife. "Perhaps when we get home, my uncomplicated club and I will have something to say about your disrespectful attitude."

"You think so, do you?" Harriet smiled sweetly. "In that case, I think it would be wise of you to tell the Protector where you'd like to be buried before we leave, dear."

"Leaving aside threats of domestic violence," Yu said, "I think Henri is right, Your Grace. I don't want to sound too optimistic—the last thing any of us need is to fall prey to overconfidence—but I genuinely believe the new LACs and missiles are going to win this war outright. And probably a lot sooner than anyone on either side would have believed possible. And if that happens, Mueller's going to look pretty damned stupid if he goes on insisting that joining the Alliance was a serious mistake for Grayson."

"Perhaps," Mayhew agreed. "On the other hand, it's part of my job to worry about what happens *after* the war, assuming you're right and we win the thing. It's clear that the need to face a common foe and build up our own military capabilities in concert with the rest of the Alliance has been a factor in the willingness of at least some Graysons to go along with the reform programs. They may not have liked the domestic changes, but they weren't prepared to rock the boat in the middle of a war. So if the pressure of fighting the war comes off, what happens to their support?"

"You'll probably lose some of your majority in the Steaders, and I imagine Chancellor Prestwick will suffer the defection of at least a few of the Keys, as well," Honor acknowledged. "But I doubt very much that you'll lose enough to turn the clock back, or even to slow the rate of change very much. And I think there's more domestic support for the 'special relationship' between Grayson and the Star Kingdom than Mueller realizes. Look how enthusiastically most Graysons seem to be responding to the announcement of the Queen's state visit!"

"Yes, that *was* encouraging, wasn't it?" Mayhew brightened. "I think it was a wonderful idea on Elizabeth's part, and Henry is eager for the opportunity to sit down at the same table as Duke Cromarty. We got a tremendous amount accomplished when Lord Alexander was here three years ago, and Henry's staff is licking its chops at the prospect of a visit from the Prime Minister himself."

"I'm glad," Honor said. "That's exactly what she had in mind, and the timing looks even better in light of Buttercup's initial successes. In fact, I think—"

"*I* think that's entirely enough shop talk," another voice interrupted, and Honor turned with a smile as Allison Harrington stepped onto the terrace, followed by Miranda and Jennifer LaFollet. "This is supposed to be a *social* occasion," Allison went on severely. "I had my doubts when you explained you intended to invite this lot," she flipped a hand at the senior officers of the Protector's Own, "but I thought, no, she's a responsible adult. She knows better than to sit out on the terrace all afternoon talking shop with her cronies while her other guests languish unnoticed and unappreciated."

"You really shouldn't refer to the Protector as my 'crony,' Mother. Just think what would happen if some spy from the Opposition overheard you."

"Ha! Opposition spies would have to get past a whole horde of treecats, not to mention a battalion of security types. Not that it isn't just like you to come up with specious arguments in an effort to avoid my righteous wrath!"

"I'm not avoiding anything," Honor said with dignity. "I'm simply raising a completely valid point."

"That's your story, and you're sticking to it, I suppose," her mother said, then folded her arms. "In the meantime, however, Mac sent us out to tell you Mistress Thorn is going to start wreaking havoc if her lunch is allowed to get cold. Worse, she says she won't make you any more fudge—or cookies—this week if you let it happen."

"Well, goodness, Mother! Why didn't you say that to *start* with?" Honor rose and turned to her guests with a twinkle. "On your feet, people! That's one ultimatum I have no intention of rejecting!"

CHAPTER THIRTY-EIGHT

"**M**r. Baird."

Lord Mueller's voice was a bit cooler than usual as Buckeridge showed Baird and Kennedy into the office. It had been his own idea to establish closer communications with Baird and, for the most part, it had worked out quite well. But this time Baird had *insisted* Mueller see him, and the steadholder hadn't cared for that. Helpful as Baird and his organization had been, Samuel Mueller was still a steadholder, and no common steader had any business issuing demands to him, however politely phrased.

"My Lord. Thank you for agreeing to see us on such short notice. I realize it must have been inconvenient, but I'm afraid it's quite important," Baird said.

Mueller nodded curtly, but he felt a flicker of wariness. The man's words were polite enough, but something about his tone bothered the steadholder. It held an . . . assertiveness that rang faint warning bells in the back of Mueller's brain, and he suddenly found himself missing Sergeant Hughes even more than usual.

Hughes' murder had shaken the entire Mueller Guard. His fellow armsmen had taken a grim pride in the fact that he'd managed to kill three of his assailants, even though it was obvious he'd been completely surprised by the attack. But no one had the least idea what had prompted his murder. Officially, it had been written off as a botched robbery attempt, although no one really believed that for a moment. There was little random street crime on Grayson, and no street thug in his right mind would choose to rob an armed, trained armsman when there had to be less dangerous prey available.

Unfortunately, no one had been able to come up with any other explanation. Mueller's own suspicion was that Hughes had inadvertently discovered something and been killed before he could act on it or warn Mueller and his superiors. The steadholder knew he was probably overly suspicious. That, after all, was an occupational hazard of conspirators the galaxy over. But still . . .

"What can I do for you, Mr. Baird?" he asked after a moment, his tone a bit less brusque and a little more wary, and glanced at Corporal Higgins. He'd chosen Higgins to replace Hughes at these meetings because of the corporal's doglike loyalty, but he suddenly found himself wishing he'd selected someone a bit brighter. Not that he really expected any sort of physical threat to suddenly emerge, but because . . .

He didn't really *know* why, he admitted after a moment. It was pure instinct, and he tried, without success, to command his instincts to leave him the hell alone.

"My organization has become increasingly concerned by our inability to secure the proof we need of the Protector's plans to request annexation by the Manticorans," Baird said, apparently unaware of any uneasiness on Mueller's part.

"Perhaps that's because there *isn't* any proof," the steadholder pointed out. "My people have been looking just as hard as yours, and we haven't found a thing. While I certainly wouldn't put such a plan past Prestwick and Benjamin, it may be that in this case our suspicions are misplaced."

"We don't think so, My Lord," Baird said, flatly enough to make Mueller bristle. He wasn't accustomed to being contradicted so cavalierly. "We've heard too many 'rumors' from too many separate sources. And we find this state visit of Queen Elizabeth's most suspicious. Look at how public opinion is already responding to the news of it! What time could be better for the Sword to propose such an annexation, especially with the San Martin business going so smoothly. She and the Sword may well find themselves in a position to capitalize on the recent victory in Barnett and the public hysteria over her visit to ram an annexation proposal through the Keys. At the very least, they could use those advantages as a springboard for getting the idea a favorable hearing if they should decide to go public with it and present it in sufficiently seductive terms."

"Granted," Mueller agreed. "All I've said is that there doesn't seem to be any evidence to support the belief that they intend to do anything of the sort."

"Only because we haven't looked in the right places . . . or with the right determination," Baird said, and this time all of Mueller's hackles rose. There was a new note in Baird's voice. One not of simple confidence, but of triumph.

"We've looked as hard as we could," the steadholder said aloud, and anger glowed within him as he heard the temporizing note in his own voice.

"No, My Lord, we haven't," Baird disagreed, even more flatly than before. "But we will. That's why I asked to see you."

"What do you mean?" Mueller demanded, harshly enough that Corporal Higgins shifted position behind him and dropped one hand to his pulser.

"I mean, My Lord, that we require your help to obtain that proof."

"But I've already used every avenue and source I have!"

"We realize that. But we have a way to open an entirely new avenue. With your assistance, that is."

"What sort of avenue?" Mueller looked back and forth between Baird and Kennedy and felt tempted to order them to leave. He told himself it was because of their disrespectful attitudes, but there was something darker and more ominous beneath his pique. An edge, though he refused to admit it, of fear. But that was ridiculous. He was a steadholder, and they were guests in his home, present only on his sufferance.

"Our plan is simple enough, My Lord," Baird told him. "And in an ironic sort of way, Queen Elizabeth's visit is what makes it workable."

"Get to the point, please," Mueller said testily, and Baird shrugged.

"Certainly. Our logic is straightforward. Assuming, as we do, that the Sword does intend to suggest we merge with and be absorbed by the Star Kingdom, this visit would be the ideal time for Prestwick and the Protector to discuss their plan with Elizabeth and the Duke of Cromarty—in person, with no intermediaries who might leak details of their discussions' true nature. The fact that she's bringing along her foreign secretary, as well, only strengthens our suspicions, as the Earl of Gold Peak would be deeply involved in any negotiations on such a point. Would you agree so far?"

He raised his eyebrows courteously, and the steadholder gave him a choppy nod. He'd come to the conclusion that Prestwick and Mayhew had no such plans, but if they *had* been planning such a move, Baird was obviously correct that this visit would be the perfect opportunity to finalize their strategy for it.

"We also believe," Baird continued, "as you and I have discussed several times, that the entire annexation plan is no more than a ruse, a cover for the Sword's true purpose, which is to further accelerate the Protector's 'reforms,' break the power of the Keys and the truly faithful among Grayson's steaders, and make us over in Manticore's image. If that is, indeed, true, then their private discussions are certain to touch upon their actual motives. And if we were able to record those discussions, they would give us the 'smoking gun' we've sought for so long now out of their own mouths, as it were."

"*Record* their discussions?" Mueller sat up straight, staring at Baird, then he laughed harshly. "Well, certainly, recording the Protector's private conversations with the Queen of Manticore would provide no end of useful information. I have no doubt of that at all! But there's no way to plant any sort of bug to pick up that kind of conversation!"

"You're wrong, My Lord," Baird said softly. "There *is* a way . . . and we need your help to make it work."

"What are you talking about?" Mueller snapped.

"Elizabeth and Cromarty will be invited to attend a session of the Keys when they arrive on Grayson." Baird showed no awareness of Mueller's growing impatience. "No doubt there will be all sorts of flowery speeches and public relations opportunities, and you, of course, will be present as the acknowledged leader of the loyal opposition. All we need you to do is to present Elizabeth and Cromarty each with a memory stone."

"A memory stone?" Mueller blinked at Baird, taken completely by surprise at the sudden turn of the conversation.

Memory stones were an ancient tradition. Despite the relative primitiveness of Grayson's pre-Alliance tech base, the planet had maintained a presence in space for longer than the entire Star Kingdom of Manticore had existed. The systematic and steadily increasing exploitation of their star system's extraplanetary resources was all that had permitted the Graysons to sustain their population and industry, and the huge investment they'd made in relatively crude infrastructure had been instrumental in allowing them to upgrade their technical and industrial base so rapidly once they allied themselves with Manticore.

But there had always been a price for that effort. Mueller had no idea how many Graysons had died in space, whether in industrial accidents or in the wars with Masada, but the number had to be large. He knew that, and Grayson had developed its own traditions and customs for honoring their memory.

Memory stones were lumps of unrefined asteroid iron or rock, carried constantly on their persons for six days by those who wished to honor the memory of the dead in space. On each of those days, the bearer of a stone prayed briefly and meditated on the debt the living owed to all those who had been lost in space. On the seventh day, the day upon which the Tester had rested, the stones were laid to rest, as well, by being released in space on a trajectory which would drop them into the system primary. They would never actually reach Yeltsin's star, of course, for the furious energy radiating outward from the star would consume them and blow their particles outward, as the souls of the Tester's children were forever borne upward and illuminated throughout eternity by the living presence of God. It was a religious custom which every element of Grayson, from the most conservative to the most liberal, honored and treasured, and it had become even more meaningful to them since the current war's casualties had begun to roll in.

But what, exactly, memory stones had to do with the Sword's inner councils was more than Samuel Mueller could—

His thoughts broke off, and his eyes widened. No! They couldn't *possibly* mean that!

"I trust," he said very carefully, "that you aren't proposing what I think you are. I have no doubt that you could produce a remote listening device sufficiently small to fit into a memory stone, but Planetary Security or the Manticorans would spot a transmission from something like that in an instant."

"There will be no transmission, My Lord. The memory stones *will* contain bugs—you're quite correct about that—but only simple recording devices. The public gift of memory stones to Elizabeth and Cromarty will leave them no choice but to honor our customs. That means they *will* accept the stones and keep them on their persons, as tradition requires, and the newsies would never allow the moment in which the stones were released to escape unreported. You know as well as I how long it will take them to travel all the way from Grayson orbit to the sun, which will be plenty of time for us to intercept them when no one is looking."

"*Intercept* them?" Mueller's incredulity showed, and Baird shrugged.

"If we know when and where they were released, generating an intercept solution won't be difficult. And while they won't transmit while they're actually recording data, each of them will be fitted with a location beacon which we can activate from a range of a few thousand kilometers, so collecting them should present no great difficulty."

"You're far more optimistic in that regard than *I* am." Mueller snorted, once again wishing Hughes were present. The sergeant's technical expertise would have stood him in good stead when it came to heading off this insane plan.

"Our people assure me it can be done," Baird said. "I don't say it will be easy, but it *will* be straightforward. Yet to make it work, the stones must be presented as publicly as possible . . . and by someone of sufficient stature to make it impossible for the newsies to ignore the occasion. As the acknowledged leader of the Opposition, you have that stature, and the Manticorans' visit to the Keys will give you the opportunity."

"I won't do it," Mueller told him. "I don't share your confidence in your ability to recover the recorders, in the first place. And in the second, I can't risk being caught up in such a scheme. As you say, I *am* the leader of the Opposition. Can't you see how disastrous it would be—not simply for me, but for all of us who oppose the systematic destruction of our way of life—if Planetary Security were to find listening devices hidden in 'gifts' which I, personally, had given to the Queen of Manticore and her Prime Minister? Tester, man! It would destroy my credibility, and that of the entire Opposition with it!" He shook his head firmly. "No. Not for something as speculative as rumors about possible plans being suggested by the Chancellor to the Protector."

"The chance of detection is minute, My Lord," Baird replied, apparently unmoved by his vehemence. "The recording devices have been constructed using the best molecular circuitry, and since they'll be completely passive, aside from the location beacons, which must be activated by an encrypted external signal, there will be no emissions to draw attention to them. Besides, memory stones are religious objects. Even infidels like the Manticorans will be forced to treat them with due respect lest they anger the very people they want to seduce into joining their Star Kingdom. And they'll be gifts from one of the most prominent and respected steadholders on Grayson. Why in the world would they be suspicious of such a gift in the first place?"

"No, I tell you! The potential return doesn't even come close to justifying the risk you're asking me to run!"

"I'm sorry you feel that way, My Lord. I'm afraid, however, that I must insist."

"*Insist?*" Mueller half-rose, and Higgins stepped forward behind him, but neither Baird nor Kennedy as much as turned a hair.

"Insist," Baird repeated, his tone cool but inflexible.

"This conversation is over," Mueller grated. "And if you insist

on issuing such absurd demands, then so is our entire relationship! I am not accustomed to being dictated to, and I will not risk
all I've striven for years to accomplish on your. . . your *whim!*"

"It is not a whim. And you have no choice, My Lord," Baird
told him.

"Get out!" Mueller snapped, and gestured to Higgins. The corporal started forward, then stopped, more in shock than in fear,
as Kennedy produced a small pulser and aimed it at his chest.

"Are you *mad?*" Mueller demanded, as shocked as his armsman
and far too furious to feel frightened. "Don't you know the pen-
alty for bringing a weapon into a steadholder's presence?!"

"Of course we do," Baird replied. "We refuse, however, to allow
ourselves to be murdered as Steve Hughes was."

"*What?*" Mueller blinked at the complete *non sequitur.*

"Nicely done, My Lord, but your apparent surprise can't deceive
us. We know you had Hughes murdered, just as we know why. I'll
admit we were surprised you should do so in such a clumsy manner. Surely you knew that 'failed robbery' wouldn't fool us! But
it wasn't totally unexpected."

"What are you talking about?" Mueller demanded. "He was my
own armsman! Why in the Tester's name would *I* want him killed?"

"It would be much simpler if you'd stop pretending so we could
get back to the business at hand, My Lord," Baird said wearily. "We
were under no illusions about your trustworthiness before, or we
would never have placed Hughes in your service. And while some
of our people were outraged by his murder, the rest of us had
anticipated the possibility all along. As he did, when he volunteered.
But that doesn't mean we can no longer work together . . . as long
as you remember that we know exactly the sort of man with whom
we're actually dealing."

"You *placed* Hughes in my service?" Mueller stared at Baird for
a moment, then shook his head. "That's a lie! Some sort of clumsy
trick! And even if it weren't, *I* never ordered anyone to kill him,
you lunatic!"

"My Lord, you're the only one who could possibly have had a
motive," Baird said with an air of weary patience.

"*What* motive?" Mueller half-roared, and Baird sighed.

"When you discovered he was secretly recording every one of
my conversations with you, you must have realized who he was
working for." He shook his head. "Whatever else you may be, you're
an intelligent man, My Lord. Must I really draw you a detailed picture of our logic?"

"Recording?" Mueller parroted. The other man's calm assurance gnawed away at the armor of the steadholder's rage, and he sagged back into his chair, staring at the men he'd been so confident he could effortlessly dominate.

"Of course." Baird allowed a hint of asperity to creep into his own voice for the first time. "Really, My Lord! Why do you insist on pretending this way?" He shook his head again, then shrugged. "But if you insist, we'll give you proof. Brian?"

Kennedy reached into his tunic once more, without ever letting his pulser's muzzle waver from Higgins, and tossed Baird a tiny holo projector. The older man held it on his palm and punched the play command, and Mueller swallowed as he saw the interior of his study, right here in Mueller House, while he and Baird discussed illegal contributions and the names of those through whom they could be routed.

Baird allowed it to play for several seconds, then switched it off once more and slipped it into his own pocket.

"You waited too long to murder him, My Lord. We have his recordings of every earlier meeting with you. I feel confident the Sword would be more than interested in proof of your illegal activities."

"You wouldn't dare!" Mueller snapped, but his mind reeled. He had no idea who'd actually killed Hughes, and the enormity of the dead sergeant's betrayal was stunning, but the recording was obvious proof the armsman had really been working for Baird's organization from the very beginning.

"Why not?" Baird asked calmly.

"Because you're just as guilty of any crimes as I might be!"

"First, My Lord," Baird said very precisely, "that presupposes that these are the only crimes of which we have evidence. In fact, they're not, nor was Hughes the only agent we've planted in . . . strategic spots, shall we say?" Mueller swallowed, and Baird smiled faintly. "We've been keeping an eye on you for quite some time. We're well aware of your activities and alliances—*all* of them, My Lord, from the beginning of your resistance to the 'Mayhew Restoration.' I trust you'll forgive me if I don't provide matching documentation of them right this moment, however. In this case—" he tapped the pocket which held the projector "—you obviously already identified and murdered our agent. We have no intention of giving you anything which might suggest the identities of our *other* agents to you. But we would have no compunction about sharing that information with the Sword if you forced our hand.

"Secondly, you assume we'd be afraid to admit our own complicity in your illegal campaign financing schemes." Baird allowed himself a small, cold smile. "Those schemes are the least of your worries, My Lord . . . and the greatest of ours. We have far less to lose than you even if we're arrested right alongside you. Which, by the way, would be rather more difficult for the Sword to accomplish than you appear to think. Surely you must realize that Mr. Kennedy and I have constructed in-depth covers rather than meet you under our own names and identities! Moreover, neither of us has ever appeared in Planetary Security's files. We have no records, and Security has no place to start in hunting us down. You, on the other hand, are just a little too prominent to elude their net, I think. And, finally, My Lord, we, unlike you, are truly ready to face arrest, trial, even conviction. If that should be our Test for serving God's will, then so be it."

Mueller swallowed again, harder. How long *had* they been spying on him? From Baird's total confidence, it had to have been a long time. Even—the steadholder shuddered—long enough for them to have picked up some scrap of evidence linking him to Burdette and the murder of Reverend Hanks. That certainly seemed to be what Baird was implying, and it would justify the other man's obvious assurance and confidence. If there was even the faintest possibility they could connect him to Burdette's treason . . .

"I did *not* have Hughes killed," he said firmly. "As for the rest of it, any 'crimes' I may or may not have committed were in the name of all of Grayson and of God Himself."

"I haven't said otherwise, My Lord," Baird said mildly. "Honesty requires me to say that I believe ambition has played a part in your actions, but only God can know what truly lies within any man's heart, and I might well be wrong. But the fact remains that however justified your actions may be in the Tester's eyes, in the eyes of the Sword, they remain crimes. Serious crimes, I fear, to which serious penalties attach."

"You're mad," Mueller said. "Think about what you're doing, man! Are you really willing to throw away all we've already accomplished this way?"

"We have no desire to throw anything away," Baird said in that same mild tone. "We see no reason we can't continue to cooperate in the future as in the past, unless you foolishly force us to hand our information to the Sword. And before you ask, My Lord, yes. We *do* think securing proof of the Protector's annexation plans justifies the risk that you might force us to do just that. Besides—" Baird allowed himself a thin smile "—some of us believe the public furor which would be generated by going public with our evidence would actually give us the platform we require to force the steaders of

Grayson to recognize what the Sword truly intends. In which case—"
he shrugged "—we accomplish as much as we could hope to accomplish with the recordings we need your help to obtain."

Mueller sat motionless, staring at the other man, and his heart
was a stone. Baird meant it, he realized sickly. He and his allies
were genuinely ready to throw away everything, including the life
and future of Samuel Mueller, on the *off chance* that their recording
devices could be smuggled past Planetary Security and the Manticorans, capture something incriminating, *and* be recovered in a
deep-space interception afterward. And the fact that they were
insane to even contemplate such an operation meant nothing. They
had the blackmail evidence to force him to go along with them.

At least they're only recorders, he told himself, trying to pretend
he didn't know he was grasping at straws. *Even if they're found,
and tied to me, all the Sword would have would be an attempt to
obtain privileged information. That's serious, but nowhere near
evidence of complicity in murder! And I am a steadholder. And the
leader of the Opposition. Under the circumstances, they probably
wouldn't even want to go public with the charges.*

The man who called himself Anthony Baird gazed into Samuel
Mueller's eyes and watched the defiance run out of them like water.

"Thank Tester, he actually fell for it."

"Why, 'Brian,'" James Shackleton said, his voice gently mocking. "How could you possibly have doubted me?"

"I didn't doubt *you*, Jim. I just had trouble believing he'd cave
in with so little proof we had the goods on him." Angus Stone,
whom Samuel Mueller knew as Brian Kennedy, shook his head.

"'The guilty flee where no man pursueth,'" Shackleton quoted.
"The only real question was whether or not Hughes was actually working for *him*. That was always a possibility . . . up until
we got our hands on that camera button. Hughes must have been
on his way to deliver it to someone else. If he'd been working
for Mueller, he would've handed it over before he left Mueller
House that night. And we were lucky there were several days
worth of imagery stored on the chip. If Mueller'd insisted on
more proof, we could have shown him some of that footage
without starting him wondering why the only evidence we had
was recorded the night Hughes died." Shackleton shrugged. "Once
we convinced him we had *any* evidence, his reaction was completely predictable, Angus. After all, he *had* to be guilty of things
we didn't know a thing about."

"Um." Stone leaned back in the passenger seat of the air car, gazing out at the night sky, and frowned. "I wish *we* knew who Hughes had been working for."

"If it wasn't us, and it wasn't Mueller, then it almost has to have been Planetary Security," Baird said equably, "though I suppose it might be one of his fellow Keys. From all I've heard, Harrington would certainly be capable of taking direct action against him if she suspected the sort of action he was contemplating against her or Benjamin. It doesn't really matter in either case, though. The man's been dead for months. If whoever he was working for felt they had sufficient evidence to nail Mueller, they would certainly have acted by now. And if they don't have sufficient evidence to charge him, then they have no choice but to pretend nothing's happened at all."

"And do you really think this is going to work?" Stone asked much more quietly.

"Yes, I do," Shackleton replied, his own eyes on the instrument panel. "I wasn't especially confident to begin with. The whole thing seemed like such an outside shot that I was afraid to let myself hope for too much. But whatever anyone may suspect about Mueller, it would never cross Palace Security's mind that such a prominent member of the Keys would risk trying to plant elec-tronic devices on the Protector's guests. If they do—" he shrugged "—all we lose is Mueller."

"And the opportunity to strike."

"And *this* opportunity to strike," Shackleton corrected. "And I don't think we will lose it. When Donizetti came through with the weapons, I began to think it might succeed. And when he came up with the molycircs for the memory stones as well—"

He shrugged once more.

"I only wish we weren't so reliant on Donizetti in the first place." Stone sighed.

"He's an infidel and a mercenary," Shackleton agreed, "and I'm sure he's taken a bigger 'commission' off the top than he says he has. But he's also managed to come up with everything we needed. Not as quickly as I might have wished, especially on the memory stones, but he got it all in the end, and we couldn't have done it without him. And the bottom line, Anson, is that we have to remember we're about God's work. He won't let us fail Him as long as we trust in His guidance and protection."

"I know." Stone drew a deep breath and nodded. "This world is God's," he said softly, and Shackleton nodded back.

"This world is God's," he promised.

CHAPTER THIRTY-NINE

"**W**e've got a solid lock, Skipper," Audrey Pyne announced, and Scotty Tremain nodded. According to ONI, the MacGregor System lacked the enormous passive arrays which could pick up hyper transits light-days and even further out. That was why the CLACs had made their hyper translation one full light-day out . . . and why *Bad Penny* and the rest of her silent brood had been slicing in-system for over two days.

Their acceleration had been held down to a leisurely four hundred and fifty gravities to help the efficiency of their stealth systems. At that rate, it had taken them over sixteen hours just to accelerate to the eighty percent of light-speed their particle shielding could handle. Once they'd done that, they'd taken their wedges down entirely and simply coasted for twenty-one hours. They'd come swooping in out of the outer darkness at almost two hundred and forty thousand kilometers per second and blown right past the outer perimeter sensor platforms like hyper-velocity ghosts. The mid-system arrays had been a little trickier, and the destroyer screen had been trickiest of all, for they'd had to begin decelerating before they hit it, and even at a mere 4.127 KPS^2, they'd had to be careful about their EW. Their active sensor suites were down for the same reason, but the Ghost Rider teams had provided the LACs with their own FTL recon drones. Their drives had a very short endurance compared to the all-up drones, but Tremaine had deployed them hours ago and let their base acceleration carry them inward without any drive power at all. They'd come ghosting in even more stealthily than the LACs themselves, and their very weak, directional gravitic transmissions had told *Bad Penny*'s passive sensors exactly where to look.

"Have all our birds confirmed data receipt, Gene?" he asked now, and Lieutenant Eugene Nordbrandt, *Bad Penny*'s com officer, nodded.

"Aye, Skip. All ships report locked and ready to fire."

"All right, then," Tremaine said, with a nod of his own. "Put Audrey on voice."

"Me, Skip?" Pyne sounded surprised, and Tremaine grinned.

"You're the tac officer who set this up, Ensign. The shot is yours to call."

"Uh . . . yes, Sir. Thank you, Sir!"

"Thank me if it works," Tremaine advised her, and looked back at Nordbrandt.

"Ready, Gene?"

"Live mike, Skipper," Nordbrandt confirmed, and Tremaine waved a hand at Pyne, who drew a deep breath.

"All *Hydras*, Hydra One," she announced crisply into the mike. "Tango. I say again, *tango, tango, tango!*"

Citizen Commodore Gianna Ryan sat in her tipped-back command chair on the flag deck of PNS *Rene d'Aiguillon*, legs crossed, and nursed a cup of coffee. The MacGregor System was fairly important to the PRH. It had long served as a sentinel for Barnett's northeastern flank, but it also boasted a robust economy. The system population was over two billion, and despite decades of bureaucratic management, it was one of the few systems in the Republic which continued to generate a positive revenue flow every year.

Despite that, MacGregor had never received a genuine deep-space sensor net (the financially-strapped PRH was parsimonious about emplacing those *anywhere*), and its picket force had been steadily reduced over the last several years. The lengthy stalemate on the Barnett front after the fall of Trevor's Star helped explain a lot of that, but so did Citizen Secretary McQueen's decision to reinforce Barnett so heavily. The strength Citizen Admiral Theisman had received had made a flexible, nodal defense practical, and Ryan's job was not to try to stave off the Allied Hordes all by herself. Her job was to fend off raiding squadrons and serve as a distant early warning post. If the Manties came after her in strength, she was supposed to avoid action but remain in-system, shadowing and harassing the intruders, if possible, but staying the hell away from a serious fight while she screamed for help from Barnett.

Unfortunately, she reflected as she sipped at her coffee, that had presupposed Theisman would be allowed to *keep* his reinforcements. A mere citizen commodore was not, of course, privy to the inner deliberations of the Octagon, but Ryan doubted Citizen Secretary McQueen could have been very happy about the need to take away so much of the strength she'd scraped up for Barnett. If the rumor mill was correct about Twelfth Fleet's successes down on the southern flank, it was unlikely the enemy was going to feel like showing any sudden activity on the Barnett front. Even so, depleting Theisman's strength was risky. MacGregor, along with the Owens, Mylar, and Slocum Systems, represented a valuable little cluster of prizes, and Barnett, at the center of the rough square they formed, was the lynchpin of their joint survival. Ryan was confident the PRH could survive even if it lost all four of them but as her staff intelligence officer had remarked the other day, "A system here, a system there . . . keep it up long enough, and pretty soon you're talking about some serious real estate, Citizen Commodore."

Still, there'd been no sign of any—

Alarms whooped, suddenly and savagely, and Gianna Ryan threw her coffee cup aside as she hurled herself out of her command chair. That was the *proximity* alarm!

She spun to her dreadnought flagship's flag plot, and her heart seemed to stop as she saw the rash of angry red icons. There were *hundreds* of them . . . and they were less than eight million klicks out and closing at twenty-five thousand kilometers per second! How in God's name had even *Manties* gotten that close without a single one of her scanner arrays or starships spotting them?!

There was no way to answer that question, and she leaned on the rail around the main plot, hands white-knuckled with the force of her grip, and watched disaster roar down on her command. Only her ready squadron of battlecruisers and the three squadrons of picket destroyers the Manties had somehow slipped right past had hot impeller nodes. All the rest were at standby, for she'd been confident no force big enough to pose a serious threat could slip through her sensor net, even with Manty stealth systems. But these Manties could, and at their current velocity, they'd be right on top of her two squadrons of dreadnoughts and battleships in five minutes . . . and they were *already* within missile range. Had been for at least a full minute, and—

"Hostile launch! I have multiple hostile launches!" someone barked.

Tremaine's Nineteenth Wing led the assault, and he watched his *Ferrets* salvo their shipkillers. A deadly swarm of missiles streaked towards the sitting targets of the main Peep force, and the crest of that wave of destruction was heavily seeded with Dazzlers and Dragons' Teeth, two more selections from the LACs' arsenal of Ghost Rider systems. The downsized versions which could be crammed into a LAC-sized missile were far less individually capable than the versions capital missiles could carry, but they were nastier than anything any LAC had ever been able to deploy before.

The Dazzlers were an in-your-face, burn-out-your-sensors jammer of unprecedented power. They were burst emitters (no missile a LAC could carry could sustain such power loads for more than a few seconds), but before their EW warheads burned out, they produced savage strobes of jamming. They started going off like a cascade of prespace magnesium flares, beating down the fire control of any Peep ship which might manage to get her sensors on-line in the first place.

The Dragons' Teeth came behind them, and Tremaine smiled nastily as they flashed to life. Personally, he thought they might be the nastiest offensive EW system the LACs had been given, for each missile was basically a powerful decoy. As it headed for the enemy, it made itself look like a *Ferret*'s entire missile load, roaring down in a concentrated salvo which *had* to draw heavy countermissile fire. Which, of course, meant the same countermissiles couldn't go after the *real* shipkillers.

Not that either Dazzlers or Dragons' Teeth were actually going to be necessary this time, he realized. A single battlecruiser squadron appeared to have its point defense on-line, and it looked as if a couple of its ships were far enough away, and alert enough, to get their wedges and sidewalls up before the missiles arrived. The remainder of the Peep picket force had been caught almost as flat-footed as Commodore Yeargin at Adler. And with far more justification, Tremaine thought, remembering the picketing destroyers his attack force had passed on its way in. Nothing larger than a LAC, and no LAC which had lacked the *Shrikes*' and *Ferrets*' EW, for that matter, could have penetrated that screen undetected, and he allowed himself a moment of sympathy for the Peep CO.

But only a moment, for he had the Nineteenth, Sixteenth, and Seventeenth Wings under his command, and his missiles were in final acquisition. The Peeps had stopped less than three percent of his original launch, and the explosions began as twenty-seven hundred shipkillers speared into their formation.

Citizen Commissioner Halket arrived on the flag deck just as the first missiles came in, but Ryan never even noticed him. Her attention was locked to the plot, and she heard one of her staff officers groan in horror as missiles began to detonate.

They were small, the sort of missiles which might come from destroyers or light cruisers, and a corner of Ryan's mind nodded in bitter understanding. LACs. These had to be the Manty "super LACs" StateSec had assured one and all couldn't possibly exist. Well, they *did* exist, and they were about to rip the guts right out of her command.

Under normal circumstances, such light laser heads would have posed no threat to dreadnoughts. They could have hurt battleships, though it was unlikely they could have killed even a battleship outright, and enough of them could have crippled a battlecruiser easily enough. But dreadnoughts were simply *super*dreadnoughts writ small, with the same massive armoring scheme and active and passive defensive systems. Those missiles ought to have been mere fleabites to such vessels.

But the Manties had caught the deep-space equivalent of an anchored fleet. Her ships couldn't maneuver, their weapon systems were down, and the absence of wedges and sidewalls was fatal. The loss of their sidewalls was bad enough, but even that paled beside the consequences of their cold impeller nodes, for the wedges which should have protected their topsides and bellies were nonexistent. And the spine and belly of a ship of the wall was completely unarmored, because nothing could get to them to inflict damage in the first place . . . as long as its wedge was up. Which meant the designers could use all the mass devoted to its stupendous armor on its vulnerable flanks and even more vulnerable hammerheads.

And not a single one of those Manty missiles showed the least interest in attacking any of Gianna Ryan's ship's sides or hammerheads.

Tremaine's missiles streaked "across" and "under" the helpless Peep leviathans at ranges as short as five hundred kilometers, and as they crossed their targets, they detonated. Their lasers struck with lethal accuracy, knifing into hulls which might as well have been totally unarmored, and thin battle steel skins shattered under the transfer energy. Clouds of atmosphere and water vapor exploded from the hideous rents, and Tremaine's jaw clenched as he pictured the carnage aboard his targets. It was obvious no one had seen them coming, and that meant there'd been no time for the Peeps to set general quarters, evacuate atmosphere from the outer hull segments, insure internal hull integrity . . . get into their skin suits.

A wave of flame marched through the Peep formation, tearing its ships apart. Three dreadnoughts, five battleships, and at least a dozen battlecruisers and cruisers died under its pounding. One of the ships of the wall completely vanished as one of her fusion bottles failed, and the others were beaten into wreckage. Life pods spilled from their flanks, but not very many of them, Tremaine noted grimly.

Yet he had little attention to spare them. His *Ferrets* had expended their offensive missile loads. Under normal circumstances, it would have been time for them to break off and roll away from the Peeps. This time, though, they stayed tucked in tight, each *Ferret* squadron dropping back to form the apex of an inverted cone behind three squadrons of *Shrike-Bs*, as the entire formation smashed straight into the main Peep force.

Now it was the *Shrikes'* turn. Their missile loads were lighter than the *Ferrets'* had been, but there were far more of them, and they'd deliberately reserved their fire when the *Ferrets* launched. Now orders flashed across the wing command nets, from Audrey Pyne and Eugene Nordbrandt, and fresh squadron salvoes began to launch. Those salvoes were more scattered than the original, massive assault, but they were targeted with merciless precision upon the mangled survivors of the first strike, and the Peeps' confusion was now complete.

Gianna Ryan dragged herself back to her feet. Dust hung in the air, seasoned with the smell of burning insulation, and she scrubbed the back of her hand across her mouth. It came away smeared with blood from her mouth and nose, but she scarcely noticed. Her attention was on the catastrophe in her plot. She had no energy to waste wondering how *d'Aiguillon*'s CIC had managed to keep the display up after the pounding her flagship had just taken, but they'd done it. Despite their best efforts there were entire dead quadrants, yet it scarcely mattered. She felt *d'Aiguillon* buck, shuddering again and again as still more lasers slammed into the big ship's vitals, and most of the rest of her capital ships were in even worse shape.

Three of the ready duty battlecruisers, on the far side of her formation from the attacking LACs, had managed to get their wedges and walls on-line and even to roll ship before any missiles reached them. They, and the units of her so far unengaged destroyer screen, were the only relatively unscathed ships she still had, and she watched the battlecruisers accelerating out of their positions. Not that it was going to help them much. Even at maximum military power, they could never hope to stay with the Manties—not with the tremendous velocity advantage the LACs had brought with them. But at least they were accelerating to *meet* the enemy, she thought with forlorn pride, not simply panicking and trying to flee.

"Com! Order the picket destroyers to get out of here!" she heard herself snap. "Tell them they have to warn the rest of the fleet about these new LACs!"

"Aye, Citizen Commodore!"

She never turned her head. She simply watched the plot, and wondered if her com section would have time to get the order out before the Manties killed them all.

"*Hydra Six*, take the lead battlecruiser. *Three* and *Five*, you've got the trailers. All other squadrons, attack as previously briefed!"

Lieutenant Commander Roden and the skippers of Tremaine's third and fifth squadrons acknowledged their orders and veered slightly away from the main axis of the attack. He'd chosen them because they were his most experienced squadrons . . . and because they'd had the sternwall Roden's crew had devised longer than any of the others. They'd had more time to drill with it, and they were the ones most likely to take fire from surviving enemy units as the strike overflew the Peep formation.

Three hundred and twenty-four LACs, two hundred and fifty-two of them *Shrike-Bs*, slammed into the Peeps like the hammer of Thor. It was the opportunity of a LAC's lifetime, a virtually unopposed, energy-range run against capital ships who *still* didn't have wedges or sidewalls up, and the *Shrikes'* grasers began to fire. Dreadnoughts which had survived the missile storm staggered bodily as those impossible beams smashed into them. At least half the LACs were able to target their unarmored topsides and bellies, just as the missiles had . . . and with horrifically greater effect.

Other LACs found themselves shouldered aside by the crowding. Deprived of equally prestigious targets, they vented their fury on battlecruisers, cruisers, and destroyers, and beams which could disembowel dreadnoughts tore lighter units to pieces. It was a massacre, a nightmare vortex of ships ripping apart in mighty spasms of destruction, dotting the night skies of the planet MacGregor with their eye-tearing pyres, and the *Shrikes* and *Ferrets* slashed through the heart of the inferno like demons.

But it wasn't quite all one-sided, and Scotty Tremaine swore bitterly as he watched icons blink and flash on his plot. Even some of the ships which had been unable to bring their wedges up had managed to get at least a few of their weapons on-line. They were probably in local control and feeding only from the capacitor rings, but they struck back with the defiant gallantry of despair. Here and there a graser or laser got lucky and slammed its way through a LAC's sidewall or bow-wall. One actually scored a direct up-the-kilt hit on a *Ferret* that had its bow-wall, and not its sternwall, on-line.

Two of Tremaine's strike died, then a third. A fourth. Three more flashed the amber of serious damage, but they were through the Peep formation and streaking away, safe from further harm while their crews fought to make emergency repairs.

The three squadrons Tremaine had diverted to the battlecruisers swarmed over their massive foes, firing savagely. The sheer fury of their headlong attack seemed to touch them with invulnerability, and two of the Peep ships blew up in spectacular boils of light as raking graser shots slammed down the throats of their wedges and directly down their long axes. But the third survived, brutally wounded, probably dying, but still in action, and her commander wrenched his broken ship around, rolling his less-damaged broadside onto his attackers as they overflew him and receded rapidly into space's immensity.

His fire ripped at them, and the sternwalls Roden and his crew had designed proved their worth as they bent and diverted the handful of shots which struck home.

But even as relief began to flash through Tremaine, the single Peep battlecruiser got off one last broadside . . . and a single graser struck squarely on the grav eddy Horace Harkness had spotted so long ago.

Her Majesty's Light Attack Craft *Cutthroat* exploded as violently as any of her victims had, spewing herself into the void like a fleeting nova, the only casualty of the three-squadron strike on the battlecruisers.

There were no survivors.

CHAPTER FORTY

"**Y**ou'd better talk to him, Tom. Someone has to, and I can't risk making him suspicious of me."

"I see." Thomas Theisman gave his people's commissioner a long, cool look across the conference table. "So since we can't risk making him *start* to feel suspicious of you, we have to go ahead and make him *more* suspicious of me?"

"Actually, yes." Denis LePic smiled crookedly. He'd gotten just as little rest as Theisman since their return to the capital, but the lines in his face were less deeply grooved, and there was actually a faint gleam of genuine humor in his eyes. "Face it, Tom. You're a regular. That means he's automatically suspicious as hell whenever you suggest something. At the same time, you're the man he picked to command Capital Fleet, and he hasn't *un*picked you, which suggests he distrusts you less than he does most regular officers. The fact that you've been so matter-of-fact about acknowledging that he has reasons to feel suspicious probably helps with that, and I think he actually respects you a bit for standing up to him over Graveson and MacAfee. But the main point is that the one thing we can't afford is for him to decide he has to replace *me* with some commissioner who'd be . . . less disposed to protecting your confidences, shall we say?"

"Um." Theisman nodded, though his expression was sour. The problem was that Denis was right, and he knew it. Which meant he really had no choice but to yet again examine the backsides of the lion's teeth by poking his head down its throat.

He sighed and scrubbed his eyes with the heels of his hands, once more wishing Esther McQueen and Rob Pierre were still alive so he could strangle both of them with his bare hands. What in *hell's* name had those two idiots thought they were *doing?* To kill each other off and throw the PRH's entire command structure, civilian and military alike, into chaos at a moment like *this?*

He lowered his hands and made himself step back from the useless rage. Not only were its objects safely beyond his reach, but it was unfair to blame them for the exact timing of the clash between their mutually homicidal ambitions. They hadn't had any way to know the Manties were about to unveil a quantum leap in interstellar warfare. And, truth to tell, the timing probably wouldn't matter in the end. If the reports from MacGregor, Mylar, Slocum, Owens, and—especially!—Barnett were accurate, *nothing* was going to matter, because the Fleet was screwed. And the Republic with it.

His jaw tightened . He didn't like admitting that. In fact, his belly knotted every time he contemplated the Navy's helplessness. But there was no point pretending. The new Manty missiles were able to engage from far beyond any range at which the PN could return fire. On top of that, it was obvious now that the reports about their new EW hardware from Operation Scylla had, if anything, *under*stated its capabilities. Worst of all, or most demoralizing, at least, it appeared every one of Esther McQueen's fears about the much derided "super LACs" had been totally justified.

Personally, Theisman suspected that the LACs were probably the one system the People's Navy had some hope of mastering, or at least offsetting. But the preliminary reports indicated that most of the survivors had actually found the LACs more psychologically devastating than the new missiles. The fleet little craft's maneuverability, high acceleration rates, massive short-range armament, and apparent near invulnerability to defensive fire were a completely new departure. Long-range missile duels had always been part of the naval mix, and especially in the last few years as both sides deployed the updated pod technology. The PN's personnel had been given time to adjust to that fact of life, and while they might intellectually recognize the threat of the Manticoran range advantage, it hadn't come at them completely cold, as it were. The LACs had, and word of the massacre of Citizen Commodore Ryan's picket force had sent a shudder of terror through the rest of the Navy. And, Theisman admitted, the thought of *LACs* which could actually kill ships of the wall, no matter how bizarre the circumstances which had made it possible, *was* terrifying. Such tiny, relatively inexpensive craft could be built in enormous numbers, and there were those who believed the Battle of MacGregor proved traditional capital ships had been rendered obsolete overnight.

Theisman didn't think so. Ryan had been caught completely unprepared for the attack. That was hardly her fault, and Theisman was honest enough to admit that the same thing probably would have happened to *him* under the same circumstances. Certainly the defensive plan Alex Dimitri had ridden down in flames at Barnett had been the product of Theisman's own planning sessions, although that (fortunately, perhaps) seemed to have escaped Oscar Saint-Just's attention. But the burned hand taught best, and it was unlikely the Manties would be able to repeat MacGregor's devastating, close-in run on ships of the wall with cold nodes. Which meant they would be unable to get any more of those perfect, lethal shots against the unarmored portions of their targets' hulls, which meant, in turn, that dreadnoughts and superdreadnoughts would be as hard for them to kill in the future as they ought to have been at MacGregor. Besides, impressive as the new LACs were, enough old-fashioned light attack craft, operating purely defensively, should be able to considerably blunt their effectiveness. They couldn't possibly be as tough as the more panicky analysts suggested. Theisman was willing to concede that they obviously had something new in the way of sidewalls to go along with their EW, but it was also obvious that it had been possible to get through their defenses occasionally . . . and that they were no tougher than any other LAC when someone actually hit them. So if he could swamp them with old-style LACs and generate lots and lots of firing angles, he should be able to kill them. Or at least force them to operate far more circumspectly, which would be almost as good.

But nothing the Navy had was going to offset the enormous range advantage of the new Manty missiles. Or their new rate of fire. Theisman might still be in the dark about how they'd achieved such a leap forward in range, but, unlike many of his fellow officers, he'd at least realized almost instantly how they must have managed to sustain such a heavy volume of fire. Of course, he'd had the advantage of long discussions with Warner Caslet about the citizen commander's sojourn aboard Honor Harrington's armed merchant cruiser in Silesia. Caslet had long since figured out how HMS *Wayfarer* must have been modified to produce the weight of missile fire he'd observed. It was unfortunate he and Shannon Foraker had been almost completely ignored by the people running the PRH's intelligence agencies on their return, though it had probably been inevitable, given the suspicion in which they were held over the loss of their ship and the fact that they *had* been prisoners of war, after all.

But if the Manties could put some sort of pod-dispensing system inside a freighter, there was no reason they couldn't do the same thing with a superdreadnought, and if anyone had bothered to listen to Caslet and Foraker, the PN might actually have figured out how to do the same thing. He doubted it had been easy, and he shuddered at the thought of all the design and redesign studies which must have been involved in restructuring a ship of the wall's internal anatomy so completely. But difficult was hardly the same thing as impossible, and the payoff for their efforts had been a handsome one. Not only did their ships dramatically outrange the People's Navy, but their rate of fire was devastatingly superior, as well. Which meant no Republican commander was going to survive to get into effective range of a Manticoran fleet no matter *what* he did.

He sighed and looked across at LePic once more. The war was lost. It seemed obvious the Manties didn't have a huge number of their new classes, but the reason for their quiescence had become painfully obvious the instant they cut loose at Dimitri. McQueen had been right—again. They'd been waiting until they could build up a decisive strength, and they'd done so. No doubt they'd be at least a little cautious, for they couldn't afford heavy losses among their new units, but they had enough, concentrated in one spot, or at least on one front, to smash anything the PN put in their way. The only thing that could prevent them from cutting their way right through to the Haven System itself, and that in a matter of months, not years, would be ammunition constraints. The new weapons had to be in short supply, just like the ships equipped to fire them, but Theisman doubted that anyone like White Haven had been stupid enough to launch his offensive without an ample reserve of the new missiles. And, much as he hated to admit it, they were actually using *less* of the new birds than they had of the old. Their standoff range should be (and probably was) lowering accuracy, but the new EW missiles and drones more than compensated for that by blinding the active defenses. Which meant far more hits were getting through on a per-missile basis.

"We're screwed, Denis," he said now, quietly, admitting aloud what they both already knew. "I trust, however, that you don't expect me to put it to the Citizen Chairman in quite those terms, however."

"I think that would be . . . um, inadvisable," LePic agreed with another of those weary smiles. "Maybe we can bring him around to accepting that after another month or so, assuming the Manties haven't arrived here in the capital and made the point for us by then, but for now, I think we have to concentrate on lesser matters. Maybe if we can talk some sense into him on smaller issues, he'll listen more closely when the time comes to tackle the greater ones."

" 'If *we* can talk some sense into him,' " Theisman repeated, then chuckled tiredly. "All right, Denis. I'll see what I can do," he promised.

Oscar Saint-Just watched Citizen Admiral Theisman enter his office with eyes which were beginning to show the strain a bit too clearly for his own taste. He was unhappily aware that he was retreating into a bunker mentality, hunkering down as the entire galaxy prepared to come crashing down on his head. There was altogether too much desperation in his thinking of late, and he knew it was pushing him towards ever more excessive responses, but he couldn't help it. Which only made it even worse. That sense of sliding helplessly down into a pit of quicksand could either paralyze a man or drive him into a mad, senseless effort to lash out at the universe, however uselessly, before it killed him, and the strain of trying to steer a course between those two extremes was grinding away at his stability.

But he made himself step back from his desperation for a moment as Theisman crossed the office towards him. He suspected the citizen admiral resented the mandatory weapon search which had become the lot of any regular officer entering his presence, but if he did, Theisman was careful not to show it. And Saint-Just was a bit surprised by how comforting he found Theisman. The man was scarcely the dull, stolid sort, but he stubbornly refused to allow himself to be panicked, and rather than rail against his difficulties, he simply drew a deep breath and got down to overcoming them. The aura of competence he projected was almost as great as McQueen's had been, and it came without the jagged edges of ambition. At this particular moment, that was more important to Saint-Just than he would have admitted to a living soul.

"Good afternoon, Citizen Admiral," he said, waving his visitor into a chair. "What can I do for you?"

The citizen admiral inhaled deeply, then met his eyes squarely.

"Sir, I've come to request that you reconsider your intention to order Citizen Admiral Giscard and Citizen Vice Admiral Tourville home."

Saint-Just's nostrils flared ever so slightly—the equivalent, for him, of a screaming tantrum—but he made himself sit still and actually think about what Theisman had just said. He wondered how the citizen admiral had learned of his intentions. Of course, it was always possible he hadn't "learned" about anything; Giscard's and Tourville's affiliation with McQueen had to have a lot of people wondering when he'd summon them home and dispose of them. Especially now, when it was obvious to every regular officer that McQueen—and, by extension, Tourville and Giscard—had been absolutely right about the new Manty weapons while *he* had been absolutely wrong.

Whether Theisman had learned about it from some source or simply figured it out on his own, however, was less important than the fact that he felt strongly enough about it to come discuss it. He had to know that if Giscard and Tourville were under a cloud, the displeasure of the new Citizen Chairman might very well splash all over anyone who tried to stand up for them, as well.

"Why?" the Citizen Chairman asked flatly, and Theisman shrugged.

"I'm in command of Capital Fleet, Sir. As you yourself told me, my foremost responsibility is to reorganize that formation as a coherent combat force whose loyalty to the Republic I can guarantee. At this moment, I'm far from confident I can do that if you were to recall Giscard and Tourville and . . . something happened to them."

"I beg your pardon?" Saint-Just's tone was frosty. Theisman had already talked him out of executing Citizen Admiral Amanda Graveson and Citizen Vice Admiral Lawrence MacAfee, the previous CO of Capital Fleet and her second in command. Some of his senior StateSec officers had urged him to shoot both flag officers as an example to all the other senior officers who hadn't instantly declared their loyalty to the Committee when McQueen's coup started. But as Theisman had pointed out, neither Graveson nor MacAfee had moved to support *McQueen*, either, and there'd been more than enough confusion coming out of the capital, where personal orders from their direct superior, the Secretary of War, had been countermanded by the Secretary of State Security (who wasn't in their official chain of command at all), and no one had been able to reach the Citizen Chairman for confirmation of which Committee member they ought to be listening to. Under the circumstances, Theisman had argued, the only prudent course for a senior flag officer was to try to figure out who was really trying to stage the coup—McQueen or Saint-Just—before they jumped.

It had been, in some ways, a specious argument, in Saint-Just's opinion. But it had also contained at least a little truth, and Theisman had certainly been right to point out that shooting them could only make the rest of Capital Fleet's officers wonder who was next. Which, as the citizen admiral had rather dryly remarked, was unlikely to contribute to a calm and collected state of mind on their part. Or, as he carefully had *not* remarked, their ultimate loyalty to the man who'd ordered up the firing squads.

Saint-Just had been impressed, almost against his will, both by Theisman's reasonable tone and by the guts it had taken to stand up for his two subordinates when so much bloodlust hung in the air. And as he'd considered the other man's arguments, the new Citizen Chairman had come to the conclusion he might well be right. Even if he wasn't, the fact that everyone knew how seriously Saint-Just had considered shooting Graveson and MacAfee would make the point that future lack of loyalty would be fatal while the fact that he *hadn't* shot them in the end might help convince them the new master of the PRH wasn't a frothing-at-the-mouth madman after all.

But this time was different.

"I trust that admission wasn't intended as an implied threat, Citizen Admiral," he said coolly. "Even if it was, however, I think you should be aware that certain evidence connecting Tourville, at least, and possibly Giscard, as well, to McQueen's plot has been brought to my attention."

"I don't doubt it." Theisman managed to keep both his expression and his voice calm and hoped Saint-Just didn't guess how hard it was for him to do that. "I'd like to point out two things in return, however, Sir. First, I don't doubt that a great many people who are actually loyal to the Republic and the Committee have done or said things which could be construed in the wake of McQueen's coup attempt as disloyal or even treasonous. I'm not saying that's the case here," he added unhurriedly as Saint-Just's eyes narrowed ever so slightly. "I don't know one way or the other in this case. I simply wanted to point out that it *might* be . . . and that whether it is or not, other people are likely to wonder if it is.

"Which leads me to my second point, Sir. If Tourville and Giscard are brought home and . . . removed, much of the repair work I've done on Capital Fleet will be undone. For better or worse, Twelfth Fleet and its command team are regarded as the one bright spot on the horizon, especially now that the new Manty weapons are cutting such a swath. As such, Tourville and Giscard are important to the Navy's morale. Removing them without clear and

convinving evidence of complicity in McQueen's treason would do
a great deal of damage to that morale. For that matter, removing
them even if they're guilty as sin would do at least some harm.
Some officers who are in the process of settling back down might
even see it as a sign no regular officer will ever be trusted again,
which could push them into actions you and I would both regret.
I'm not saying they aren't guilty, Citizen Chairman. I'm not even
saying their removal—yes, and execution—may not be fully justifiable. I'm simply saying that to do so now, at this moment, when
everyone is more than half-panicked by new enemy weapons and
still . . . unsettled by events here in the capital, may have consequences which, as a pragmatic matter, would be far worse than
waiting. If we get through the current instability and manage to
slow the Manties back down, my opinion could well change. For
right now, however, I would be derelict in my duty if I failed to
warn you that their executions could have serious repercussions
on the loyalty and reliability *of* Capital Fleet."

He stopped and sat back in his chair, and the dangerous smoul-
dering in Saint-Just's eyes faded ever so slowly as the Citizen Chairman considered what he'd just said. Saint-Just suspected Theisman
was more opposed to executing Giscard and Tourville on a personal level than he'd just implied, but that didn't necessarily invalidate his analysis of Capital Fleet's possible reaction to it.

"So what would *you* do with them?" Saint-Just had intended for
the question to come out hard-edged. Instead, somewhat to his
own surprise, it was a genuine inquiry, and Theisman shrugged.

"If it were up to me, Sir, I'd leave them as far away from the
Haven System as I could possibly get them. The capital has always
been the true key to control of the Republic. Whatever their
ambitions may or may not be, they can't accomplish anything
against the Committee without first seizing control of Nouveau
Paris. Which they can't do if they're somewhere down around
Grendelsbane or somewhere else at the front. And they *have* demonstrated that they're one of our more effective command teams.
Under the circumstances, my choice would be to pick them as the
field commanders tasked with slowing down the new Manty offensive. I'm not certain which would be the more effective way to do
that—whether it would be better to have them redouble their efforts
in Bagration to try and draw Manty strength back down to
Grendelsbane, or to take the time to pull them out of that area
and transfer them clear across to meet White Haven head-on—
but that's certainly the proper task for them."

"And if they succeed, they'll have more prestige than ever."

"True," Theisman acknowledged, cautiously relieved by the Citizen Chairman's reasonable tone. "On the other hand, if *someone* doesn't slow White Haven down, any ambitions on their part won't really matter a great deal, will they?" Saint-Just raised his eyebrows, and Theisman shrugged. "I realize I'm only in command of Capital Fleet, Sir, which restricts my information on the general war situation under the new security arrangements, but my read of the situation is that the Manties are blowing away anything that gets in their path. If my understanding is even partly correct—" in fact, it was *completely* correct, thanks to Denis LePic, but this wasn't the time to mention that "—nothing we currently have between them and Haven is going to be able to stop them. Twelfth Fleet, on the other hand, is our most powerful, best-trained, best-equipped formation. If it can't stop White Haven, then nothing else we have can do the trick, either, and if the Manties capture the capital, we lose the war."

He held his mental breath as he said it at last, but Saint-Just only nodded slowly.

"In addition, Sir," Theisman went on, deeply encouraged by the other's response (or lack thereof), "I think there's another point you ought to consider. So far, Twelfth Fleet has lost two task force commanders in action. There's no reason why it couldn't lose a third . . . or even a commander in chief. Especially with the new Manty weapons."

Saint-Just's eyes widened ever so slightly, and he regarded Theisman for several silent seconds.

"I hope you'll pardon me, Citizen Admiral," he said at last, "if I say I find that last remark just a bit suspicious. My estimate of your character doesn't include that sort of deviousness, which forces me to wonder why you should make such a suggestion."

"I may not be devious, Citizen Chairman," Theisman replied levelly, "but I hope you'll forgive me for saying that everyone knows *you* are." He smiled thinly as Saint-Just gave him a very sharp look indeed. "I don't mean that as an insult, Sir. Merely as an observation of fact. And deviousness can be a very useful talent, even for a Navy tactician, but especially for someone who has to pick his way through the sort of factions I've seen here on Haven. I admit, however, that I did intentionally appeal to your devious side. For myself, I would simply say that in a situation as desperate as ours, my inclination is to get the most utility I can out of any resource we have. And if doing that creates a situation in which a potential threat to the State eliminates itself, or is eliminated by enemy action, then we've just killed two birds with one stone. That's something I've always preferred to do whenever possible, and if it also helps buy me time to get Capital Fleet straightened out and settled down, so much the better."

"Um." Saint-Just considered the citizen admiral for several more seconds. "You've made some convincing points, Citizen Admiral," he said finally. "And whatever lack of faith I may feel where Tourville and Giscard are concerned, I do have at least one outstanding commissioner riding herd on them. More than that, I have to admit, if somewhat against my will, that the 'evidence' against them is conjectural at this point. I don't apologize for feeling an urge to eliminate them just to be on the safe side. Not after what's happened here in Nouveau Paris . . . and what could still happen if we're unlucky. But you do have a point about jumping too quickly. And about how valuable they could be in our present situation. For that matter, my advisers and I hadn't sufficiently considered the effect removing them might have on the loyalty of Capital Fleet's officers.

"All of those are sound points, and I appreciate your courage in making them. I don't say you've completely convinced me, because you haven't. But you *have* given me a great deal to think over before I make my decision."

"That was all I really wanted to do, Sir," Theisman said, standing as Saint-Just rose and walked around his desk. The Citizen Chairman held out his hand, and Theisman shook it firmly. Then Saint-Just walked towards the office door with him.

"I trust you won't let yourself get into the habit of arguing my orders with me, Citizen Admiral," he said with wintry humor that didn't quite hide the warning behind it. "In this instance, however . . . thank you."

It came out a little grudgingly, and Theisman allowed himself a smile.

"You're welcome, Sir. And trust me. I have no intention of habitually arguing with you. Leaving aside the little matter that you're certainly Citizen Chairman Pierre's legitimate successor, I'm not foolish enough to do anything which might make *me* look like a threat. You've been honest enough to warn me my own position and continued good health depend on how well I do my job and your confidence in my loyalty to the Republic. I can understand your attitude, and I appreciate your candor. And candor also compels me to say I am sufficiently terrified to be very careful about the company I keep and the things I suggest. I'll do my best to tell you the truth as I see it, but I'll also watch my mouth and stay the hell away from *anything* that might make you think of me as another Esther McQueen."

"A straightforward declaration," Saint-Just observed, and there might actually have been a slight twinkle in his eye as he opened the office door for Theisman. "I see you have greater depths than I'd thought, Citizen Admiral. That's good. I'm not foolish enough to expect everyone to be loyal because they love me, and it's refreshing to meet someone who's honest enough to admit he's afraid of making me suspicious of him."

"I much prefer to be open and straightforward," Theisman deliberately reused the Citizen Chairman's choice of adjective. "Trying to be any other way simply invites misunderstanding, and none of us can afford that at this moment."

"True, Citizen Admiral. Absolutely true," Saint-Just agreed, shaking his hand once more, and Theisman stepped out into the waiting room. The Citizen Chairman's new secretary glanced up at him curiously, then returned to her paperwork, and the citizen admiral allowed himself to draw a deep, lung-stretching breath before he crossed to the waiting-room door and stepped into the hall.

Oh, yes, Citizen Secretary. Open and straightforward—which is not *necessarily the same thing as loyal and honest. But I hope to hell you don't figure that out before it's too late.*

He headed down the hall towards the lifts and the pinnace awaiting to return him to his orbiting flagship, and as he walked, he allowed his mind to reach out for just a moment towards Javier Giscard and Lester Tourville.

I've done what I can, he told them. *For God's sake try to stay alive a little longer. We're going to need you—both of you—soon enough . . . if not for exactly the reasons Saint-Just thinks.*

CHAPTER FORTY-ONE

Hamish Alexander stood on *Benjamin the Great*'s flag deck with his hands clasped behind him and tried very hard not to feel a sense of godlike power.

At the moment, his plot was in astrographic configuration, showing him the stars between Trevor's Star and the Lovat System. Peep-held systems sprawled across it in a leprous red rash. That much remained the same. But a few changes had been introduced over the last two months, and his lips pursed thoughtfully as he regarded them.

Lovat lay close to the center of the spherical volume of the PRH. Only forty-nine light-years from the Haven System, it was a major industrial node, which made it an important target in its own right. It was also one of the PRH's core systems, a daughter colony rather than one of its unruly conquests, whose local government had been one of the first to declare its support for the Committee of Public Safety following the Harris assassination. Yet for all its importance, it was so far behind the frontiers no prewar strategist had ever seriously contemplated the possibility of a major attack upon it.

But things change, and over the last four or five T-years most strategists, Allied and Peep alike, had come to regard Lovat as the penultimate stop on any advance to Nouveau Paris. Always well fortified, the system now bristled with defenses almost as tough as those protecting the capital system itself, not to mention a local defense fleet built around several squadrons of the wall.

All in all, Lovat was a formidable military obstacle, and after eleven years of war, it had come to seem hopelessly remote. Something, some people had joked, to make them grateful for prolong, since that was the only thing which gave them a chance of living long enough to see it taken.

But now, as White Haven gazed into the plot, a solid cone of green stars glowed amid the crimson traceries of Peep-held space. That cone's base rested on the systems of Sun-Yat, to the north-west, and Welladay, to the southeast, and its tip was the Tequila System—pointing straight at Lovat from a distance of barely 3.75 light-years.

It was incredible, he thought, contemplating the campaign he'd fought to reach this point. It had been utterly unlike the grinding, brutal slogging match for Trevor's Star. Indeed, it was unlike any campaign *any* admiral had waged in over seven hundred years, and White Haven was honest enough to admit it had been made possible only by the new ship types he'd once dismissed so cavalierly. But he'd learned his lesson, he told himself. First when Honor—his lips curved in a small, secret smile—jerked him up short, and now, especially, when Alice Truman's LAC wings had spearheaded Operation Buttercup with such power and panache.

The Peeps are done, he thought almost wonderingly. *Finished. They don't have a prayer against the new hardware, and our people are learning how to use it more effectively every day.*

His thoughts ranged back over the hectic, furiously paced series of actions which had brought them to this point. Secure in his technological and tactical superiority, he'd embraced the operational concept Truman and Honor had devised for Buttercup and split Eighth Fleet into independent, fast-moving, hard-hitting task forces. The main force, TF 81, built around a solid core of *Harrington/ Medusas*, had hammered straight up the middle, smashing the defenses of one fortified system after another with missile bombardments to which the Peeps could make no reply. At the same time, lighter forces, each based around three or four CLACs and escorts, with one or two SD(P)s to keep an eye on things, had spread out from the main axis of advance. They'd slashed into more lightly held systems, ravaging the picket forces covering the flanks of the nodal task forces TF 81 had reduced to wreckage. Even when the Peeps detected the LACs on their way in, the fleet, lethal little craft invariably managed to accomplish their missions. Partly that was because those missions were carefully planned, but it was also because of the sheer tenacity and ability of the LAC crews. They'd taken losses along the way—much heavier losses than TF 81, in point of fact—but grievous as those casualties were among the small, tight knit communities of the LAC wings, they were minute compared to the cost a conventional advance through so many systems would have exacted.

Yet for all his tactical superiority, he knew he'd accepted some serious risks to maintain the speed and fury of his advance. Caparelli and the Allied Joint Chiefs were working furiously to dig up the conventional forces to hold what he'd taken, but the Peeps were growing more ambitious as he cut deeper and deeper into the PRH. They couldn't fight Eighth Fleet head-on, but they knew that, so they were concentrating on working around his flanks, striving to threaten his rear and cut his supply lines, instead. He had too few of the new ship types to detach any for rear area security, so they could at least hope to pounce on conventional ships of the wall. On the other hand, those "conventional" capital ships were well equipped with pods stuffed full of Ghost Rider missiles, which meant even the flank attacks were producing catastrophic Peep losses.

Nonetheless, it was a mathematical impossibility for the Alliance to adequately picket and garrison all of the systems in which Eighth Fleet had blitzed the defenses. Indeed, the Allies lacked the ground troops to occupy or even take the formal surrenders of all of the inhabited *planets* in the systems through which Eighth Fleet had rampaged. But that was all right. White Haven's units had smashed the defenses and orbital infrastructure in any system he wasn't prepared to occupy and then moved on, leaving them crippled and impotent behind him. They might still serve as support bases for the raiding squadrons trying to operate against his rear, but that was all they could do, and eventually the Alliance would get around to gathering them up in a neat, orderly sort of way.

It was a sort of wild, freewheeling warfare that was downright intoxicating, and he'd had to step on his own enthusiasm more than once. He had an arrogant streak. He knew it and admitted it, and that arrogance embraced the division of his fleet with enthusiasm. Indeed, it wanted to divide into even smaller forces, taking on its enemies with a numerical inferiority no sane fleet commander of the last seven centuries would have contemplated even in an opium dream, and some of his squadron and task group commanders were even more drunk with victory than he was.

It's going too well, he told himself. *There has to be a catch somewhere!*

But even as he told himself that, he didn't believe it. It was no more than the reflex of a professional, automatically watching for the unanticipated, the unexpected.

But however heady the moment, the time had finally come when he had no choice but to call a halt. Not a long one. No more than a few weeks—a month and a half; two months at the outside—while his mobile repair ships dealt with a growing litany of minor repairs and deferred maintenance requirements. While the missile colliers labored forward from Trevor's Star, to reload his SD(P)s' pods. While other freighters came forward with replacement LACs for his CLACs . . . and, in too many cases, replacement crews. The LACs had been worked hard, and he welcomed the opportunity to stand them down for a little much needed rest. And he was determined that he would not run his maintenance cycles too far into the red this time. *This* time he would be certain he had no need to stop and send a third of his combat power back to the yards!

But it wouldn't be a long pause, he promised himself. And when Eighth Fleet advanced once more, it would be as a single, concentrated force that would reduce the defenses of Lovat to splinters.

And from there, he thought, astounded even now that he dared to so much as contemplate the possibility, *Haven and Nouveau Paris.*

"And here we are," Citizen Admiral Giscard said, and there was a universe of bitterness in his voice.

He sat in a briefing room off PNS *Salamis'* flag deck, and there were very few other people present. Indeed, aside from Citizen Captain McIntyre, his chief of staff, and Citizen Commander Tyler and Citizen Lieutenant Thaddeus, his staff astrogator and intelligence officer, respectively, the only other people in that briefing room were Lester Tourville and Citizen Commissioner Everard Honeker.

And, of course, Citizen Commissioner Eloise Pritchart.

It was dangerous for them to be here, and all of them knew it. Esther McQueen's death, the destruction of the Octagon, the disbandment of the Naval Staff and the arrest of all its surviving members, Oscar Saint-Just's emergence as the dictator of the PRH, and the replacement of both the Naval Staff and the General Staff with State Security officers—those things had riven their universe down to bedrock. None of them had even suspected such cataclysmic upheavals might be coming. Even if they'd guessed, there'd been nothing they could have done to prepare for it, and Giscard and Tourville had realized instantly that their lives, and the lives of their staff officers, hung by threads. Indeed, both admirals were amazed when they weren't summarily ordered home within days of McQueen's abortive coup and "disappeared" as a routine precaution.

Only two things had saved them. One was the sudden Manti-coran offensive, which had thrown the military front into chaos as wild as anything happening back in Nouveau Paris. And the other, to their astonishment, had been Thomas Theisman.

Giscard and Tourville both knew Theisman well, yet neither of them would ever have expected him to be picked to replace Amanda Graveson as the commander of Capital Fleet . . . or to prove so adroit at handling Saint-Just. But he had, and Tourville suspected that Denis LePic was one of the main reasons for his success. The citizen vice admiral had known LePic almost as long as he'd known Tourville, and the citizen commissioner had always seemed a bit too decent for a StateSec spy.

Rather, he thought wryly, like the commissioners in this brief-ing room.

Of all the surprises he'd suffered since McQueen's death, few had matched the impact of discovering the true relationship between Giscard and Pritchart. Tourville had begun nursing some suspicions about Pritchart. Less because of anything she'd ever said or done, for she'd played her role to perfection, than because Giscard had shown just that little bit too much independence and freedom of maneuver in exercising his command authority. But not even he had dreamed the two of them were *lovers*. He'd thought it was something else, like his own pre-Cerberus relationship with Honeker. The possibility that the two of them were actual part-ners, working *jointly* to deceive StateSec's other spies, had been a total shock . . . and explained a great deal.

Not that it seemed likely to make much difference in the long run. If it *had* been likely to, he doubted Giscard and Pritchart would ever have let him and his own people's commissioner in on the secret. As it was, they clearly had little left to lose, and there was no sense in jumping through any hoops to maintain a deception that no longer mattered. Especially not if jumping through those hoops might hamper the achievement of anything which could conceivably give them a chance of survival.

Except for Pritchart, of course, the citizen vice admiral thought, and his eyes softened as he gazed at the beautiful, platinum-haired woman. *Saint-Just obviously doesn't suspect her even now. If he did, he never would have passed on his conversation with Theisman to her . . . or let her know he still plans on shooting all of us afterward. But if he does still trust her, all she and Javier had to do was keep their mouths shut, and she, at least, might have walked away alive.*

But there was no sign Giscard and Pritchart had even contem-plated that course. Tourville doubted Giscard was happy about it, but it was clear she'd made her own decision. Live, or die, she and Giscard would fight to the last ditch together.

"And here we are," the citizen vice admiral agreed, smiling grimly at his CO. "You know, I realize Tom did the best he could for us under the circumstances, but right this minute, I find it just a *tad* difficult to feel suitably grateful."

"Do you?" Giscard managed a smile of his own. "Well, I look at it this way, Lester. Even if the Manties shoot *Salamis* right out from under me and Eloise, there are still life pods. And, frankly, the possibility of being picked up after the battle seems a whole lot more attractive than somehow winning the damned thing and going home to face Saint-Just! If he's nervous now, imagine how unhappy he'd be to have 'The Men Who Stopped the Manties' riding into Nouveau Paris on their white horses!"

"An unhappy but no doubt accurate summation," Tourville admitted.

"At least they seem to have slowed down for the moment," Honeker put in.

"Only to catch their breath, Everard," Tourville told him. "They're just refitting and resupplying before their next lunge . . . and guess who's sitting right on top of what has to be their primary target."

Several people around the table surprised themselves with weary chuckles, and all eyes shifted to the star chart above the conference table.

The Lovat System lay before them in all its glory. The space about the central star glittered with the icons of military and civilian shipyards, processing plants, deep-space factories, fortresses, minefields, old-style LACs, missile pods, and the serried squadrons of Twelfth Fleet. Against any normal enemy, that massive concentration of power would have been impregnable. Against what was going to come at them, probably in no more than a month or two, all it was likely to accomplish was to inflate the body count.

"I wish," Tourville said very quietly, even here, before people he trusted with his very life, "we could just surrender the damned place to White Haven." Eyes swiveled to him, and he twitched his shoulders uncomfortably. "I know. It goes against the grain. But, Jesus! It's not just what's waiting for us back on Haven. Think of all our people, sitting here in ships the Manties have just turned into nothing but targets. How many thousands of *them* are going to get killed just because Saint-Just is too frigging stubborn—or stupid—to realize it's over and surrender?!"

"You may have a point, Lester," Giscard conceded. "No, you *do* have a point. Unfortunately, there's no way to pull it off after Saint-Just stuck us with his fresh 'reinforcements.' " His smile was a sour grimace, and Tourville nodded. Twelfth Fleet now boasted two complete squadrons of StateSec SDs which no longer even pretended that their real job wasn't to watch Giscard's and Tourville's flagships. "Even if we didn't have to worry about Heemskerk and Salzner, we couldn't pull off a successful surrender without at least discussing it with our own squadron commanders and the local defense COs. And if even one of them disagreed with our intentions . . ." He shrugged.

"I know," Tourville sighed, gazing into the display. "I know. It just irritates the hell out of me to die so *stupidly*. And not even because of my own stupidity!"

"Me, too," Giscard admitted. He, too, gazed into the display, then inhaled. "Have you and Everard decided about telling your staff?"

"I think not," Tourville said heavily. "There's always the chance Saint-Just will decide they're too junior to deserve a pulser dart, and I know Tom will do his best for them—especially for Shannon. Besides, I'm afraid of what might happen if I told them. I'm pretty sure Yuri's figured it out, anyway, but Shannon scares me these days. If *she* found out, she might decide to do something about it. I'm sure it would be spectacular and no doubt inflict all sorts of damage, but it wouldn't change anything in the end. Except to guarantee she got shot, too." He smiled at McIntyre, Tyler, and Thaddeus. "I understand *you* three figured it out and insisted on shoving your noses into it. I respect that, but I'm going to try like hell to get at least some of my people out of this alive."

"Don't blame you, Sir," Andre McIntyre told him. "I tried to do the same thing for Franny here—" he nodded at Tyler "—but she's about as stubborn as Shannon."

"If you don't mind," Pritchart put in, "I'd just as soon concentrate on trying to get *all* of us out of this in one piece."

"All of us would," Honeker said gently. "The problem is that none of us see a way to do it."

"I don't see any great and glorious scheme for it, either," Pritchart said, "but I'd at least like us to do a little contingency planning. For instance, suppose something happens to Saint-Just back home? If he disappears from the equation, the whole situation is up for grabs. More to the point, if whoever takes over from him—assuming someone does, and the entire Republic doesn't simply dissolve into one massive dogfight among potential successors—sends us new orders, what do we do about them? For that matter, what do we do if White Haven decides to bypass Lovat and go straight for Haven?" Her smile was strained but genuine. "Maybe I just want to keep myself busy to avoid dwelling on our chances, but humor me. Let's put some thought into that kind of question . . . and see if any brilliant ideas fall out on the table in the process."

"Why not?" Tourville's grin was almost as fierce as of yore. "One thing *I've* already decided is that they're not taking me back to Haven in suitable condition for shooting after arrival. And if I can come up with a way to cause them more grief than a shootout with SS goons in my quarters, I'm all for it!"

CHAPTER FORTY-TWO

The statue was just as embarrassing as Honor remembered.

It loomed over the broad flight of stairs leading up from the sunken square, dominating the neoclassic portico of Steadholder's Hall, and this time she couldn't avoid it. She was Benjamin Mayhew's Champion. As a consequence, she was forced to stand at his side in the ridiculous thing's very shadow, the Sword of State in her hands, and look suitably stern and impressive as the Keys of Grayson greeted the Queen of Manticore.

Somehow she doubted she managed to look quite as impressive as her huge, bronze doppelganger.

The good news was that the normally reserved Graysons were so wild with enthusiasm that no one was paying the least attention to *her*. The bad news was that the tumult must be generating enough tension among the security people of both star nations to produce a battalion worth of strokes. She knew how unhappy Andrew LaFollet had been over the protocol which denied him his proper place watching her back; she could scarcely imagine how Major Rice was putting up with his own forced absence from Benjamin Mayhew's side. Then there was Colonel Shemais. She couldn't feel any too happy about being excluded from the ranks of diplomats and councilors—not to mention the mayor and city fathers of Austin City—clustered around Elizabeth as she made her way from the formal ground car up the flower-strewn steps amid a hurricane of cheers.

Of course, the security people had found ways to compensate for their exclusion, she thought, glancing up at the buildings fronting on Steadholder's Square. Even Austin Cathedral's towers had been taken over by Planetary Security SWAT teams, and there was at least one security man with a pulser, and another with a plasma rifle, and a third with a man-portable SAM launcher on every building top which offered a line of sight to the square. Not to mention the stingships drifting watchfully overhead, or the troopers waiting just out of sight in full battle armor with heavy weapons.

It was all very impressive, yet Honor suspected it was also unnecessary. Not that she'd even considered objecting. Assassination was a tactic which shocked the Grayson soul, as the public reaction to Lord Burdette's attempt to assassinate *her* had demonstrated, not to mention the planet-wide revulsion and horror produced by Reverend Hanks' death. But those murder attempts also demonstrated that it was not unheard of, and anything that protected the heads of state of both her star nations was a very good thing in Honor Harrington's eyes.

Yet the idea that anyone on Grayson might want to assassinate Benjamin or Elizabeth at this moment seemed ludicrous as she gazed out over the cheering, applauding, waving crowd filling the enormous square. There must be forty or fifty thousand people out there, all crushing together to get an eyewitness look at the Protector and his foreign ally when they could have been comfortably home watching on HD. And they were here because Grayson had always felt it owed a special debt to Elizabeth—to her, personally, not just to her government—for the warships which had saved them from Masadan conquest. And for the loans and technical assistance which had transformed their star system and their world. And now, and especially, for the steady chain of victories which had broken the back of the People's Navy at last.

The war was as good as won. For once, that was the verdict of the professionals and the pundits alike . . . and it was also the verdict of the Allied public. For that matter, it was *Honor's* view, and she felt a special swell of pride whenever she thought of the part Alice Truman, her LAC crews, and Operation Buttercup had played in bringing that to pass. And, she admitted, whenever she considered who'd commanded Eighth Fleet during its unstoppable advance. She wished passionately she could have been there herself, but if she couldn't, knowing the campaign was in the hands of Alice and Hamish Alexander, not to mention Alistair McKeon and all the others she knew so well who were serving in Alice's CLAC squadrons, was the next best thing.

And being stuck here on Grayson also meant that, unlike the

people actually fighting the battles, she got to see the public's response first hand, as it happened.

Elizabeth and her party started up the final flight of steps, and Honor drew her attention back to the present. There would be time enough to daydream about Eighth Fleet. For the moment, she had other duties, and she stepped forward with the Sword of State to greet her monarch in the name of her liege lord.

"*Tester*, I'm glad that's over!" Benjamin Mayhew groaned as he dropped into a chair. Unlike Elizabeth, he'd shed his formal, eminently uncomfortable robes as soon as possible and wore a pair of slacks and an open-necked shirt without the ridiculous, anachronistic "necktie." Elizabeth had attended in Manticoran court dress, the first time in history that a woman had appeared in the sacred precincts of Steadholder's Hall in trousers. It had no doubt shocked the more fragile souls among the Keys, but it also had the advantage of being quite comfortable. She'd taken off her tail coat, but that was all, and now she smiled as Henry Prestwick handed her a tall, cold drink.

"Your people *do* seem to be on the . . . enthusiastic side," she observed, and Benjamin laughed.

"You mean they're raving lunatics!" He shook his head. "When I think about all the INS stories about the 'dignified and reserved people of Grayson,' I have to wonder what planet the newsies were *really* covering!"

"It's hard to blame them at the moment," Honor put in from her own chair. She and Lord Prestwick were the only steadholders among the small gathering, and neither of them was present in her or his capacity *as* a steadholder. She was there as Benjamin's champion (and, at Elizabeth's request, as Duchess Harrington), and Prestwick was present as Benjamin's Chancellor, just as Allen Summervale was present as Elizabeth's Prime Minister. Now Benjamin cocked an eye at her, and she shrugged.

"INS just broke a fresh story on the chaos in Nouveau Paris," she said, and grimaced. "I can't say I'm happy at the thought of a butcher like Saint-Just running the PRH single-handed, and I doubt the public at large is, either, when it thinks about it. But people also figure that the way he got there indicates there's a lot more opposition to the Committee than anyone thought . . . and that a general Peep collapse may be the fastest way to end the war. Besides, the same broadcast released the declassified portions of Earl White Haven's latest dispatches."

"You mean you don't think it's all due to my eloquent speeches and sheer force of personality?" Elizabeth demanded plaintively, and everyone (except the armsmen and Colonel Shemais) laughed.

"Actually, I think both those factors *have* played a part," Benjamin said a moment later, his expression more serious. "This entire visit was a brilliant notion, Elizabeth, if you'll pardon my saying so. There are some on Grayson who'd managed to convince themselves, or perhaps it would be better to say comforted themselves with the notion, that you're actually just a mouthpiece. That the Star Kingdom isn't *really* run by anyone as silly and frivolous as a mere woman! Those people have built up this notion that some sort of male cabal is really hiding behind your throne, pulling the strings. Now that we Graysons have had a chance to see you in person, that idea is so obviously ludicrous that anyone who openly suggested such a thing would be laughed out of public life."

"And the timing is superb, Your Majesty," Prestwick put in. "Your arrival is associated in the public mind with the sudden turn in the course of the war. No one is foolish enough to attribute that turn to your visit. Not on an intellectual basis, at least. But the emotional impact has linked you and those victories indelibly in the impressions of our steaders. And quite a few of our stead*holders*, I suspect."

"*And* it's another nail in the coffin of the notion that women have no business getting involved in 'serious' affairs," Benjamin added, and smiled. "Katherine and Elaine made that point to me— again—over breakfast. Sometimes I suspect they wish I were an old-fashioned chauvinist so they could gloat over my discomfiture. Fortunately, they can always gloat over everyone *else's* discomfiture in front of me, and that's almost as good."

"I can imagine," Elizabeth agreed with a laugh.

She and the Protector's wives had taken to one another instantly, and Rachel Mayhew had been deeply impressed to discover that the Queen of Manticore's 'cat companion was considerably younger than her own Hipper. *And* a better signer. Like Honor, the Mayhews were still adjusting to the sudden emergence of treecat conversation at the dinner table. But at least there was only *one* 'cat in Protector's Palace, she thought enviously. Well, two, now that Elizabeth and Ariel had arrived as houseguests. With Nimitz and Samantha home, there were *thirteen* at Harrington House, and every one of them, including the 'kittens, was signing away like mad. She doubted she would ever get over the sheer joy of experiencing true, two-way *conversations* with her six-limbed friends, but watching that many 'cats signing simultaneously (and with widely varying proficiency) was like being trapped inside an old-fashioned piston engine!

Nimitz bleeked a soft laugh from the back of her chair as he picked up her emotions, and she tasted his loving mental caress.

"I'm sure you can visualize it all perfectly," Benjamin said. "Still, Henry's right. You've got the conservatives in full retreat." He smiled with intense satisfaction. "Even Mueller's 'media blitz' hasn't kept them from taking a beating in the polls. And his expression when he presented you and the Duke with those memory stones was priceless!"

"I know." Elizabeth's smile was less satisfied than Benjamin's, and he looked a question at her. She looked back for a moment, then shrugged. "There's just . . . something about him that bothers me. And Ariel," she added, and all eyes swiveled to the treecat in her lap. Ariel raised his prick-eared head and gazed back with grass-green eyes, and Shemais cleared her throat.

"Excuse me, Your Majesty, but what do you mean 'bothers' you and Ariel?" The Queen looked at the head of her security team, and the colonel frowned. "The Queen's Own learned to take 'cats' 'feelings' seriously a long time ago, Your Majesty. If there's something *we* should be bothered about, I'd like to know."

"I don't know that you should be," Elizabeth said slowly. "If I'd felt certain one way or the other, I would have told you before this. There's just . . . something. Ariel and I discussed it while Benjamin was changing, and he can't nail it down any better than that. Of course, we're still learning to sign, but I don't think that was the problem. According to him—" she ran one hand gently down the 'cat's spine "—Mueller has a lot on his mind right now. He's nervous and angry, and more than a little scared about something, and he doesn't care for *me* at all. But whatever he's angry or scared about isn't associated with me. Or, rather, it isn't *directly* associated with me. I'm mixed up in it somewhere, but more as an additional thing for him to be scared about than because of any threat he poses *to* me." She shrugged and grinned crookedly. "It's just a little humbling to discover that the 'cats aren't quite as all-knowing as some of us had imagined. Ariel can pick up a lot from other people's emotions, but he can't establish direct links between those emotions and specific individuals or thoughts unless those links are *very* strong . . . and in the forefront of the other person's mind, at that."

She looked at Honor, and it was Honor's turn to shrug.

"It's pretty much that way with me and Nimitz," she agreed, but she frowned as she said it. She hadn't really noticed it before, but now that she thought back, it struck her that Mueller had gone to some lengths to avoid her. It was almost as if he were deliberately staying away from her and *Nimitz*, and she wondered, suddenly, just how well briefed he truly was on 'cats in general . . . and on her and Nimitz in particular.

"It's a bit sharper and more specific in our case, I think," she went on, and heads nodded. Everyone in this room had been cleared for the truth about her bond with Nimitz. "But you're right. Unless it's a very strong link and one the other person is thinking about at that particular moment, specific connections are hard to make."

"Um." Benjamin sat back in his chair and rubbed his upper lip while he thought, then shrugged. "I can think of quite a few reasons Mueller would feel . . . uneasy in your presence, Elizabeth. Or yours, Honor. I'm not sure about this 'scared' business, though. Unless it's the threat to his plans your visit has proven? You *have* brought down a lot of scheming and set a huge financial investment pretty much at naught in less than a week."

"I don't know." Elizabeth sighed. "I suppose that could be it, but Ariel says he felt *scared*, not just uneasy or frustrated or upset."

"Excuse me, Your Majesty," Major Rice put in diffidently, "but it may be that he's managed to piss off—" Rice stopped abruptly, glanced apologetically at Elizabeth, Honor, and Shemais, and went beet red.

"Excuse me, please," he repeated, with a rather different emphasis, then drew a deep breath as Shemais hid a smile behind a raised hand. "What I meant to suggest," he went on doggedly, "is that we—" a wave at the uniform he wore indicated who "we" was "—have been keeping an eye on him for a lot of reasons, and it could be that certain associates are turning out to be a little nastier than he thought." He glanced at the Protector, then looked back at Elizabeth as Benjamin gave an almost imperceptible nod.

"I'd planned to brief the Prime Minister and Colonel Shemais about this later this evening, Your Majesty, but since you've brought Mueller up, it might be better to go ahead and tell you, as well. We have several domestic concerns about Mueller, and there's an ongoing investigation into some of his activities."

Honor's eyes widened. Unlike any of the visiting Manticorans, she knew what was involved in investigating one of Grayson's Keys. It was hardly something the Sword would undertake lightly, both because of the evidentiary standards required to initiate such a move and the risk of political damage if it became known. But if Benjamin had issued a Sword finding of the probability that a Key was guilty of high treason, the only legal basis for a "black" investigation of a steadholder, then perhaps there was a very good reason for those bleak spikes of hatred she'd felt coming from him whenever Mueller's name was mentioned.

"One of the things we've been looking into is the huge amount of money he's spending," Rice went on. "We have strong evidence that he's funneling illegal campaign contributions to Opposition candidates in the upcoming elections. That's a serious offense, but it falls short of the Constitutional definition of treason. The Sword can preemptively remove a steadholder for treason, unless a two-thirds vote of the Keys overrides him. But for the misdemeanors and malfeasance we can actually prove, a full impeachment hearing, where it would take a two-thirds vote to *remove* him before he could face criminal charges, would be required. We'd like to avoid that, so we've been digging along several other lines, as well, though I feel confident we'll settle for impeachment in the end if we have to.

"But despite the progress we've made, we still haven't been able to ID some of the people who've been passing funds to him in the first place. Obviously, they represent a large, well-funded organization of some sort, though, and I suspect the Steadholder has just discovered that *he* doesn't control *them* as completely as he'd thought. We don't have any hard evidence to that effect, and our best information channel was shut down rather permanently a few months ago, but I've felt from the beginning that they were a lot more dangerous than he thought they were. And if *they're* unhappy about the effect your visit is having, they may just have decided to turn the heat up on him. He might well even see them as a physical threat. I'd like to think he might, anyway. Do you think that could explain what your friend's been picking up from him?"

Elizabeth looked down at Ariel, and the 'cat sat upright in her lap to sign briefly but energetically at her. She laughed and nodded, then looked back at Rice.

"Ariel says, 'He's scared as a treehopper on hunting day,' Major."

"How sad," Rice murmured with a beatific smile.

"I must say, however," Cromarty put in, fingering the unfinished lump of nickel iron in the beautifully worked cage of golden filagree which hung from his belt, "that this 'memory stone' custom of yours is a lovely one, Your Grace. I wish we had one like it back home, though I suppose we're too hopelessly secular for it. Whatever else he may be up to, I'm grateful to Steadholder Mueller for introducing me to it."

"Even Samuel Mueller has his moments I suppose," Benjamin conceded. "And you're right. It is a deeply meaningful ritual among us, and whatever I may think of Mueller, I owe him a debt for reminding me of it, as well. It's time I cast a memory of my own into the stars, I think. Especially now, when it's so fitting to remember *all* the people who have given their lives in this war."

"Absolutely," Elizabeth agreed, gently touching the matching memory stone at her own belt. "Absolutely."

CHAPTER FORTY-THREE

"**B**leek!"

Honor looked away from her heads-up display and grinned as Nimitz registered his protest. The 'cat was curled into his own, custom-designed flight couch, mounted beside hers on *Jamie Candless'* flight deck, and his ears were half-flat as the plaintive strains of one of her flight engineer's favorite songs wafted over the runabout's speakers.

"Mommas, don't let you babies grow up to be spacers . . ."

She listened for a moment, then sent a wave of agreement back to the treecat. Wayne Alexander had settled in quite nicely on Grayson. Better in some ways, in fact, than Honor would ever have anticipated. He seemed fascinated by the tenets of the Church of Humanity Unchained, and she suspected he might well convert to the Grayson faith in the not too distant future.

Not that he didn't retain a goodly number of rough edges. The intractability and stubborn intellectual honesty which had gotten him sent to Hell in the first place were still very much a part of him, and he loved a vigorous debate. That much the Graysons found good, for it was a fundamental part of *their* natures, too, as they applied the doctrine of the Test to their lives. What drove some of his new neighbors absolutely mad, however, was his ability to argue *both* sides of any question, often in the same debate, with perfectly good cheer, just to keep things moving in suitably lively fashion.

But one part of Grayson's culture which he'd adopted enthusiastically was its classical music, which was based on something from

Old Earth which had once been called "Country and Western." Honor had been rather taken aback by it when she first met it, and it had taken her years to acquire any true taste for it. By now, she was actually quite fond of certain composers, but Alexander's allegiance was given to the Primitive School, and she'd never much cared for the Primitives.

" . . . spacers love smokey old bar rooms and clear crystal vacuum . . ."

"Sorry, Stinker," she told Nimitz under her breath, "but I did tell him he could program the entertainment banks." The 'cat gave her a pained look, and she grinned. "All right. All right! I'll talk to him about it, promise!"

Nimitz sniffed and groomed his whiskers at her, and she chuckled, then turned back to her controls.

The *Jamie Candless* had proven all she'd hoped for, though she'd had precious little time to play with her new toy. Despite her eleven thousand two hundred-ton mass, *Candless* was almost as maneuverable as a pinnace, and Silverman's had gotten permission from the Navy to build in a next-to-last-generation military compensator. They never would have gotten it if they'd been building the ship for anyone else, but this time Honor had decided to go right ahead and trade on who she was, and the result was a ship which could crank close to seven hundred gravities. Without one of the lightweight fission piles used in the new LACs, *Candless* had precious little internal volume to spare, and her maximum designed passenger load was only eight, but she was also designed with the latest system-management AIs. In an emergency, Honor could have managed the entire runabout by herself from the flight deck, but she was too experienced a spacer try it *except* in an emergency. Besides, Alexander would have had a fit if she'd tried to take "his" boat away from him!

She chuckled again, then leaned back and surveyed the jewel-speckled vista of eternity through the bubble armorplast canopy. That was a feature Silverman's—and Andrew LaFollet—had argued about. Silverman's had wanted the flight deck in its "traditional" place, which meant the approximate center of mass, because their designers were traditionalists and that was where flight decks were *supposed* to be. LaFollet, on the other hand, had wanted it there because the much smaller cockpit Honor had insisted upon was too small to cram in a flight chair for anyone but Honor and Nimitz. Which meant, of course, that there was no way he could watch her back when she sat at the controls.

Honor had actually sympathized with her armsman rather more

than with Silverman's, but she had been adamant. As she'd pointed out to Andrew, his presence could hardly affect anything which was likely to pose any sort of threat to her from inside her cockpit, so there was no real point in his standing guard over her while in flight. And much as she might have emphasized with him, she'd also pointed out rather sternly that a traditional flight deck would have restricted her view of the same displays which formed her work-a-day shipboard world. *Candless* was for her to play with, a way to get away from that same work-a-day world, and cramped as the runabout's passenger space might be, there was plenty of room for Andrew to ride along with Wayne. So she'd demanded the pinnacelike modification, and she was glad she had, even if Andrew *had* been on the grumpy side for days afterward.

The roof of *Candless'* wedge was clearly visible, stretching above and ahead of her and extending for kilometers to either side, and she watched the stars ahead of her abruptly shift position and color as the wedge's leading edge swept across them. The focused gravity of the impeller band clawed at photons with a force of almost a hundred thousand MPS^2, and stars red-shifted visibly as it interposed itself between them and Honor. It was something she'd seen countless times, but it was also something she never tired of, which was why she'd insisted on building a ringside seat for it into *Candless*.

She checked her instruments again. For her, the current trip was play time, a treat she'd decided to give herself because she'd earned it, but for others it was anything but a vacation, and she looked at the two golden icons on her small plot. They were only a few hundred kilometers clear of *Candless*, but nothing else was anywhere close to either of them, and a sphere of *Shrike-B* LACs held station on them, two hundred thousand klicks out, to make certain nothing else could be.

Queen Elizabeth had announced her desire to tour the Blackbird Yard even before she left for Yeltsin's Star. There had been lots of reasons for her to make the trip out to Blackbird, most political, but some personal. Blackbird had been the site of the battle in which Honor's small squadron effectively wiped out the Masadan Navy eleven years earlier, which made it a logical place for the Queen of Manticore to visit. It was also the place where the survivors of HMS *Madrigal's* crew had been systematically raped and murdered by their Masadan captors, and that made it a place Elizabeth Winton the woman felt a deeply personal obligation to visit. And the yard itself was a cooperative venture, encouraged by the most-favored-nation status the Crown had extended to Grayson, between the Hauptman Cartel, Sky Domes of Grayson, and the Sword's Office of Financial Development, which made it a perfect symbol of all the Alliance had accomplished. Besides, Elizabeth had heard a great deal about the Blackbird Yard from William Alexander, and she wanted to see it for herself.

The original plan had been for her to make the trip along with Benjamin Mayhew aboard HMS *Queen Adrienne*, the yacht in which she had traveled to Yeltsin's Star. That scheme had been altered, however, in light of how extremely well the ministerial-level meetings were going. Cromarty and Prestwick had corresponded often, but this was the first time they'd actually met, and they'd quickly established a congenial relationship. The Earl of Gold Peak had established an almost equally good relationship with Lawrence Hodges, Benjamin's Councilor for Interstellar Affairs, and the four of them had been closeted with their staffs virtually nonstop since the Manticorans' arrival.

Elizabeth was glad she'd insisted Cromarty and her uncle bring along complete staffs, even if doing so had packed *Queen Adrienne* to capacity. The Prime Minister had argued, at first. Few people, even at the Admiralty, had counted on how rapidly and completely Eighth Fleet was going to break the Peeps' front or how deeply White Haven would cut. And even the handful of optimists who might have predicted anything of the sort had never expected the coup (or whatever it had been) which had brought Oscar Saint-Just to absolute power. Which meant none of them had counted on the number of military and foreign policy decisions the Alliance was going to have to make very, very soon. The fortuitous timing which had brought the two rulers universally regarded as the heart and soul of the Alliance into direct, face-to-face contact at such a moment could not be allowed to slip past unutilized, and that had turned Cromarty's and Gold Peak's "vacation" into an exhausting grind of meetings, conferences, and planning sessions.

In fact, it was obvious they weren't going to get to everything that needed attention within the time constraints of Elizabeth's planned visit however hard they tried, and they, like Prestwick and Hodges, resented every distraction from their workload. Both Manticorans were scheduled to accompany Elizabeth and Benjamin to Blackbird, however, and Elizabeth was determined that they would enjoy at least a small break. Some souls might have been hardy enough to argue with her, but the Duke of Cromarty was too wise for that so a compromise had been evolved. He, Gold Peak, Prestwick, Hodges, and their staffs would make the trip aboard *Queen Adrienne*, which would let them confer to their hearts' content en route, then break for a few hours to tour the yard.

That would keep everyone more or less happy. Unfortunately, it would also pack *Queen Adrienne* to the deckheads, so Benjamin had invited Elizabeth to make the trip as his guest aboard *Grayson One*, instead. The Grayson vessel was smaller than *Queen Adrienne*, and not quite so palatial, but she still had plenty of gold plating in the heads. And despite her smaller size, she actually had more room, since she wasn't going to be cluttered with secretaries, assistant secretaries, under-assistant secretaries, and special assistants to the assistant secretaries. Elizabeth and her Aunt Caitrin, who had accompanied her husband on the trip, had accepted the invitation. Although Duchess Winton-Henke had once been Elizabeth's regent and remained an important member of her inner circle of advisers, she no longer held official office and had been fervently grateful for the opportunity to escape the ministers' crushing workload for at least one afternoon. At this very moment, Honor felt certain, Benjamin and his guests were comfortably ensconced in one of *Grayson One*'s luxurious salons enjoying themselves immensely. Elizabeth's cousin Calvin, alas, was not, for he was stuck aboard *Queen Adrienne* as his father's confidential secretary.

Honor had also been invited aboard *Grayson One*, and she'd been tempted to accept. She'd known both Caitrin and Anson Winton-Henke for decades, ever since Mike Henke had invited her home from the Academy on a visit, and she hadn't seen as much of either of them as she wished. But she'd begged off in the end. She'd had *Candless* for less than two months, and the opportunity to make the trip aboard her had been too much to turn down. One or two members of Benjamin's staff had been a bit miffed over the "insult to the Protector," but Benjamin had only laughed and shooed her off with orders to "Go play with your toy and enjoy yourself. But *don't* be late for the tour of the yard!"

She grinned now in memory. She'd done exactly as he'd told her to, like a dutiful vassal, especially the bit about enjoying herself. *Candless* was even more responsive than she'd hoped, with all the truly essential flight controls located on the military-style stick. Not only was that a configuration with which any Navy small craft pilot was intimately familiar, but it also allowed a woman whose left arm still disobeyed orders from time to time to fly her bird with her single natural (and reliable!) hand. It was also a configuration which simply *begged* any pilot to put the runabout through the same sort of maneuvers pinnaces routinely executed, and to

Honor's delight, *Candless* came very close to matching the nimbleness of the much smaller craft. She had no doubt that the bridge crews of *Queen Adrienne* and *Grayson One* had watched her antics with amusement—*and,* she thought smugly, *eat-your-heart-out envy*—as she danced and cavorted about their base course. But they were getting close to Blackbird now. She just had time for one last tango with the stars before she had to slow back down and be good again, and she watched the gauges on the holographic HUD spin upward as she fed power to the nodes once more.

Captain Gavin Bledsoe sat in his own command chair, watching the icons on his plot move steadily closer, and an odd, euphoric terror gripped him. He, too, saw the shell of light attack craft maintaining careful watch on *Grayson One* and *Queen Adrienne,* and he'd heard enough about the recently declassified craft to know how lethal they were. He didn't know any details about armament, power plants, or electronics; the Alliance wasn't in the habit of handing out that sort of information in the middle of a war. But he knew his ore freighter could never evade them if they came after him.

And it was extremely likely that they *would* be coming after him very shortly.

It was knowing that which waked his terror, but it was the *reason* they would come after him which woke his euphoria. It was not given to many men to know, absolutely and without doubt, that they were about to die in the name of God. Bledsoe and his three-man crew had that knowledge. They had consecrated themselves to God's purpose twelve years before, when their home world was conquered, the true Faith was cast down, and the Abomination of the Desolation had come to their planet and people. The Harlot of Satan had triumphed over the children of God, but now she and her apostate Grayson puppet had come within Bledsoe's reach—within *God's* reach—at last, and if he and his comrades must die to strike down the leaders of the alliance of corruption which had perverted all which should have been good and holy, so be it. To die in God's service, bringing down the temple upon His enemies like Samson, was a priceless gift such frail and sinful vessels could receive only of His grace, for their own acts could never have earned the right to so glorious an end to their mortal existence.

In a way, it irritated Bledsoe that he and his fellows had been forced, even indirectly, to share this supreme moment with unbelievers, yet there'd never been much choice about that. The Manticoran oppressors of Masada had blathered away about their desire to bring their victims the "blessings" of more advanced technology. Their beguiling blandishments had deceived many into abandoning the stony resistance with which the true Faithful confronted their conquerors, and in his more charitable moments, Bledsoe had to admit that one could hardly blame those weaker souls for falling by the wayside. The Harlot's servants were patient, and careful to troll their lures before the most vulnerable. New medical science for the elderly and ill. The abomination of their "prolong" treatments to extend lives centuries beyond the natural span God had decreed for His children. New schools to teach the wonders of their soul-destroying technology . . . and brainwash the next generation into acceptance of their evil, secularized universe.

They swore no one would be compelled to accept any of their "gifts," but they lied. Oh, they never marched anyone in at gun point and forced them to partake, but even the best men were weak without the rod of God's discipline. The Manticorans and their Grayson puppets knew the true way to encompass the final destruction of the Faithful lay not through force of arms, which would only create martyrs and make weak men strong in God's service, but through seduction. Through slow, gradual erosion. Good men, men who should be pillars of the Faith, could be tempted by the offer of medicines to heal a sick wife . . . or the promise of centuries of life for a child. But with every step any individual took along the path of sin, *all* of God's Faithful were weakened.

Bledsoe and his fellows knew that. Had it been possible, they would have spat in the faces of the infidels and rejected all their evil enticements. Yet it *had* not been possible. Indeed, even some among the staunchest of the Faithful had been forced by circumstance and duty to God to pretend to embrace the abomination.

The occupation of Masada had never been as all-pervasive as the occupiers no doubt wished it could have been. One simply could not land sufficient troops to garrison and patrol a planet of five or six billion people, which no doubt helped explain the occupiers' strategy of seduction. The orbital bases which gleamed in Masada's night skies, bristling with kinetic weapons and stuffed with battle-armored Marines who could be inserted directly from orbit to *destroy* any who came out in open opposition, were hardly the same thing as day-to-day contact with their subjugated victims. The fallen among the Faithful who willingly collaborated with their conquerors in the systematic desecration of God's ordained way of life were another matter. There *were* enough of them, and they knew their native world well enough, to establish an effective planet-wide police force, but they had been slow to emerge . . . at first, at least. By the time enough of them had sold their souls to the Harlot, the true core of the Faithful's strength had disappeared underground, where not even traitors could find it. Many of the Council of Elders' most critical records had been destroyed before the Manticorans could secure them, and men like Shackleton, who'd served the Council's intelligence services and the Office of the Inquisition well, had simply disappeared.

Those men, like Bledsoe and his crew, were the reforged Sword of God. It was a different Sword, one which must be wielded in a more surreptitious fashion, but its edge was even keener, for the dross of the old Sword had been refined away in the holocaust of conquest. But there must be others behind the Sword, the men who supplied the sinews to make it effective, and those men had been compelled to pretend to embrace the corruption. They'd taken advantage of the new "industrial partnerships" the occupiers and their collaborationist puppet government had offered to entice the unwary. In many cases, they'd funded their own sides of the "partnerships" with tiny portions of the enormous wealth the Council of Elders had tucked away over the centuries, and none of the apostate or their foreign allies had realized their true purpose.

Bledsoe didn't know who had originated the initial strategy. He supposed it must be the present Council of Elders. Although forced underground and compelled to conceal their identities, the Elders remained the legitimate government of Masada and the guardians of the Faithful. They also controlled the secret war chest the old Council had established, and they'd diverted those funds shrewdly, establishing true sons of the Faith in critical positions in the new Masadan industrial complex. None were in position to gain access to modern weapons. The occupiers were too smart to allow any weapons production in the Endicott System. But they were able to establish other useful contacts. Like the one with Randal Donizetti.

Bledsoe had always disliked Donizetti. The man was an abrasive, loud-mouthed, irreverent infidel who didn't even pretend to respect the Faith. But he was also a citizen of the Solarian League and an established interstellar merchant (actually, Bledsoe was pretty certain, a smuggler) with outwardly legitimate trading interests on Masada and in the League. Despite his distaste, Bledsoe knew it was only Donizetti who'd made the final plan workable, for he was the one who'd managed to procure the Solarian hardware it required. In many ways, Bledsoe wished they could have used Manticoran or Havenite equipment, for there would have been something deeply satisfying about using the technology of the infidel powers whose confrontation had laid the Faithful low. The delays built into actually delivering the hardware to the Endicott System would have been shorter, as well, since Donizetti would have had to travel so much shorter a distance. Unfortunately, his suppliers were all in the League, and it was probably just as well. Slow it may have been, but the indirect, laborious delivery of the needed tools had evaded the scrutiny of any of the infidel and apostate intelligence services.

And now all was ready. The occupiers' insistence on "building bridges" between Endicott and Yeltsin's Star had been enormously helpful in bringing that about. Denied any military industry, the yards in orbit around Masada had been turning out commercial designs, including the new asteroid extraction plants and freighters for both Yeltsin's Star and the nascent deep-space industry of Endicott. Bledsoe's own command was one of those freighters, a big, slow sublight ore hauler, with none of the greyhound leanness of a warship.

But he was not unarmed.

Gavin Bledsoe let his fingertips caress the alphanumeric keypad on his command chair's arm. His ship *had* been unarmed when he arrived in Grayson space . . . in pieces. It would have taken the sublight ship years to make the trip from Endicott to Yeltsin's Star under his own power, and so his components had been shipped in aboard hyper-capable freighters and assembled on-site. It was hardly the most economical way to go about it, but the local yards were swamped with military construction, and the entire operation had been designed as a Manticoran-subsidized ploy to encourage Masadan industrial concerns to establish working relationships with Grayson ones.

But the Council had known the ship's parts would be subjected to intense examination, particularly in light of the yard which had built them, and so he'd been exactly what the specs called for, no more and no less. But his *crew* had been another matter. Hired through one of the Faithful of Grayson who, like Shackleton's partner Angus Stone, had somehow evaded the breakup of the Maccabeus network, they possessed impeccable Grayson papers. And they had been very careful to draw no attention to themselves. Bledsoe and his crew had worked hard here in Yeltsin's Star for over three T-years, until they blended perfectly into the background. They and their ship were a familiar sight, and Bledsoe himself was known by name and face to most of the GSN officers assigned to policing commercial traffic in the system.

But none of those officers knew about the repair ship Donizetti had hired for the Faithful. It hadn't been particularly difficult to find a pretext for Bledsoe's ship to take a week or two off, nor had it been difficult for Bledsoe to quietly move beyond the reaches of the outer system of Yeltsin's Star to rendezvous with the equally surreptitious repair ship. Getting it out there had cost a fortune in fees and risk bonuses, but its Solarian technicians had done their job well, and when he returned to service, no one could possibly be blamed for not realizing he now carried two shipkiller missiles in concealed launchers just inside his outer skin plating.

They weren't proper missiles. For one thing, it would have been impossible to conceal an all-up naval missile tube and its grav drivers. And it would have been equally impossible to disguise a military-grade fire control and sensor suite. But that had been allowed for, and the missiles actually had more in common with recon drones than with conventional missiles. They were relatively slow (though with vastly more acceleration than any manned vessel), but they were also very stealthy, and they carried extremely sensitive homing systems. Their drone-style drives also had far more endurance than the drives missiles used, which gave them a very wide attack envelope. Of course, despite their stealth features and homing systems, they would have been virtually useless against a reasonably alert ship of war underway. But they weren't intended to *attack* alert warships, and they should prove quite adequate for their true purpose.

The final delay while they awaited the last piece of hardware had been infuriating, and Bledsoe suspected Donizetti had intentionally drawn it out—and exaggerated the difficulties he faced—to negotiate his fees upward, but it had been delivered at last. And Donizetti's ship had suffered an "accident" as it left Masadan orbit. Bledsoe had been a bit surprised by the Council's ruthlessness in disposing of their infidel tool so speedily, but in retrospect, it made sense. It cut off their future access to Solarian technology, but if this operation worked properly, that would scarcely matter, and eliminating the infidel middle man would greatly ease their post-operation security problems.

The one thing which really concerned Bledsoe at the moment was the fact that the Harlot and her Prime Minister were on separate ships. No one had counted on that, and he wasn't certain what he should do. The beacons in the memory stones Shackleton and Stone had maneuvered the apostate steadholder into giving the targets were designed to transmit on frequencies no one used and at very low strength, which should keep anyone from noticing them until it was too late to matter. The signals they generated were not identical, however, and one missile had been programmed to home on each of them. The idea had been to assure redundancy, with one missile-beacon combination ready to back up the other if there should be a failure at any point in the system.

Study of the HD clips of the presentation ceremony told Bledsoe which beacon had been given to the Harlot and which to her Prime Minister, and he was tempted to reprogram both missiles to seek the Harlot's . . . especially since God, in His infinite wisdom, had seen fit to put both the Harlot and the apostate Mayhew aboard a single ship. No more glorious blow could be struck for the Faithful than to eliminate *both* of those targets! But until he actually sent the activation code to the beacons, he couldn't even be positive both of them were going to work, and even if they did, the geometry of the yachts' approach to Blackbird might mask one or, in a worst case, *both* of them from the missiles' seekers at the critical moment. In the end, he'd decided to leave the original programming unchanged. It was better to have at least one chance at each of the two targets than to commit himself entirely to engaging only one which might or might not be available at the moment of launch.

Now he gazed into his plot one last time, eyes fixed on the light codes of his prey, and nodded to his com officer.

"Send the activation code," he said without raising his eyes from the icons.

CHAPTER FORTY-FOUR

"That's odd."

"What?" Lieutenant Judson Hines, GSN, swiveled his command chair towards the tactical section of GNS *Intrepid*'s flight deck as the LAC loafed along, keeping precise station on *Grayson One*. The voyage out from Grayson had been a combination of boredom and intensity for Hines and his crew. Their slow pace had seemed to stretch the hours out, yet awareness of their responsibilities kept them glued to their instruments.

"I don't know 'what,'" Lieutenant (jg) Willis, his tac officer, replied reasonably. "If I knew what it was, it wouldn't be odd."

"I see." Hines gazed at Willis steadily, and, after several seconds, sighed. "Let me put this into simple, one-syllable language, Alf. What . . . did . . . you . . . see?"

"A sensor ghost, I think."

"Where?"

"Right about there." Willis threw a feed from the main plot to Hines' repeater. A small icon flickered in it, flashing alternatively amber and red to indicate a possible contact, and Hines frowned. The light code was very close to a larger green arrowhead which indicated a civilian vessel, and he punched an inquiry into the plot. An instant later, a small string of characters appeared beside the green arrowhead, identifying it as one of the Blackbird ore freighters.

"What did it look like?" he asked, his tone crisper, and Willis answered much more seriously than before.

"It's hard to say, Skipper. It wasn't much. Just a little flicker, like

517

an up tick on the ore boat's wedge strength. I wouldn't even have noticed if it hadn't happened twice."

"Twice?" Hines felt one of his eyebrows arch.

"Yes, Sir. It was like a double flash."

"Um." Hines rubbed his chin. His was the closest unit to the ore boat, and from what Willis was saying, it was unlikely anyone else had been in a position to see whatever *Intrepid's* gravitics had picked up. But still . . .

"It was probably only a ripple in her wedge," he said. "Lord knows they work those boats hard enough for the nodes to flip an occasional surge. But just in case, put us on a vector to close for a closer look. And while Alf does that, Bob," he turned to the com officer, "pass his report and a copy of his data to the screen commander."

Honor Harrington frowned. Her com was tied into the screen's net, and her earbug carried *Intrepid's* routine message to her. She approved of Lieutenant Hines' attention to detail, although it didn't sound like his sensors had actually picked up much. Yet something about the report nagged at the back of her brain. She couldn't have said why, unless, perhaps, it was that she'd picked up only the verbal report. Her runabout wasn't tied into the screen's tac net, which meant she hadn't seen Willis' actual data.

She grinned at her own compulsiveness, but the truth was that she would always be a tac officer at heart. Whenever she could get it, she wanted the raw data so she could draw her own conclusions about it. Well, why not? *Candless* was no warship, and the unarmed runabout scarcely needed fire control, but she had an excellent sensor suite. A considerably better one, in fact, than any other "civilian pleasure craft" had ever boasted, and Honor punched a command into her main console.

Candless' central computer considered the command for a sliver of a second, and then a fresh data window blossomed in Honor's HUD as her own sensors reached out towards *Intrepid's* sensor ghost. Honor noted the ore freighter and nodded. No doubt Hines was right about the ripple in the ore boat's wedge, and—

She froze, staring at the HUD as another icon blinked briefly in it. No, not *one* icon. There'd been two . . . and they were an awful lot closer than Willis' original "ghost" had been. She blinked and frowned, trying to come up with any reasonable explanation, but there wasn't one.

She entered more commands, and her frown deepened as a vector back-plot appeared. It strobed rapidly, indicating that the computer considered it tentative, but it connected the ghosts *she'd* just seen with the ones Willis had reported, and her eyes narrowed as she saw the accel value the plot had assigned. If there actually was a physical object out there, then it had to be under a high acceleration to account for that great a displacement. But the accel figure was far too low for any sort of missile. Besides, at this ridiculously low range, any missile drive would have showed up like a deep-space flare! So it couldn't possibly—

Her plot flickered again. The ghosts were no stronger than before, but they'd continued to close, and Honor Harrington sucked in a shuddering breath as the tactical intuition she'd never been able to explain to anyone else realized what she was seeing.

Her right hand shifted on the stick, her second finger stabbing the button that accessed the screen's guard channel, and her voice rapped from every bridge speaker and com officer's earbug aboard every unit of the screen and both yachts.

"Vampire! *Vampire!* Inbound missiles, bearing zero-three-zero zero-zero-two from *Grayson One!*"

Gavin Bledsoe swore softly as the nearest LAC altered course. The vector projection showed the warship's new heading bringing him within a mere forty thousand klicks of the ore carrier, yet that wasn't what had drawn Bledsoe's curse. He and his crew had accepted from the beginning that the screen would figure out where the missiles had come from after the fact, and they'd never had any hope of outrunning the apostate's retribution. But a course change this soon meant the LAC must have detected the launch, and the shipkillers' low acceleration would give the screen far too long to engage them.

Yet there was nothing he could do about it, and he closed his eyes, apologizing to God for his profanity before he offered a silent prayer of dedication . . . and for victory.

Honor's warning hit the screen and the yachts' crews like a thunderbolt. Had it come from anyone else, many of the officers involved would have discounted the absurd alarm. Even knowing who'd sounded it, disbelief held them all for precious seconds. But then trained reactions shook off the paralysis, and tac officers aboard the screening LACs swung their own sensors to the indicated bearing, searching frantically while point defense systems sprang from standby to ready status.

But they couldn't see the targets! There was nothing *there* . . . except . . .

"Well, Alf?" Lieutenant Hines snapped, and the tac officer shrugged.

"Skip, I can't *find* the bastards!" Willis said desperately. "I— Wait!" He stabbed a key, then swore savagely. "I thought I had it for a second, Skip, but it's too damned faint a signal—nothing but a frigging *ghost*! I can't get anything solid enough for a lock!"

"Shit!" Hines glared at his plot, then looked at the helmsman. "Close the son-of-a-bitch who launched them, Allen," he grated through barred teeth.

Honor swung *Candless'* nose, bringing her bow sensors to bear on the ghosts without any interfering wedge, and her strong-boned face was carved from stone as her plot refused to hold them. She'd never seen anything like it. Never *imagined* anything like it. Not in what was obviously an attack bird of some sort. The bogies were coming in very slowly, at little more than the acceleration to be expected from a long-endurance recon drone, and they obviously incorporated heavy stealth capabilities to conceal their low-powered wedges. Her sensors probably had a better look at them than any of the LACs in the screen, for she was only a few hundred klicks off the flank of *Grayson One*'s impeller wedge, and the incoming birds were obviously targeted on one or both of the yachts. But even looking straight at them, with her bow sensors against the deepest, most easily detected portion of their wedges, she *still* couldn't get a solid lock. Not the kind point defense needed.

She punched more keys, routing her sensor readouts direct to the screen command ship, and her brain raced.

They had to be some sort of specially configured drone. Nothing else was that slow and long ranged. But where had it come from? The Alliance didn't have anything like it, and neither did the Peeps, so who *had* built it? And what was it doing *here*?

She shook her head impatiently, brushing off the extraneous questions. What mattered was what they were and how to stop them, not where they'd come from.

Low as their acceleration rates were compared to missiles, they were still much too high for any manned vessel to keep away from. Worse, they were coming in silent, with no active targeting emissions. That meant they were homers and, presumably, that they'd been homing from the moment of launch, but how could they be doing that? They'd been launched from outside the screen, and their tracks had taken them within less than five hundred klicks of one of *Intrepid*'s sister ships, so why hadn't their seeking systems locked onto the LAC instead of the yachts? A LAC didn't look a lot like

Grayson One or *Queen Adrienne*, but at that close a range, its impeller signature ought to have utterly blotted out the yachts' signatures. At the very least the things should have lost lock temporarily and been forced to reacquire it, but that obviously hadn't happened.

And the fact that they were coming in silent made stopping them exponentially more difficult. They were already far stealthier than any missile ought to be, and their lack of active sensors deprived the missile defense officers of any active emissions to track. They could see the missiles only in glimpses, no more than brief flashes before those damnably efficient ECM systems blanked them out again, and that wasn't enough. Not against a target as hard to kill as a missile or drone protected by its own wedge.

Countermissiles streaked out, but that only complicated the problem. The fantastically over-powered countermissiles were even less effective than their mother ships'. Worse, *their* wedges and emissions *could* be picked up . . . and blotted out even the feeble ghost returns Honor had managed to detect.

She started to bark an order, but the screen commander had already seen what she had, and his own order beat her to it. The countermissiles vanished from her plot as the LACs which had launched them sent the self-detonation commands, and she breathed a sigh of relief as she managed to find the missiles again.

They were closer, and her mouth dried as the time to attack range counter spun downward on her HUD. Some of the LACs were firing their own point defense clusters, though the range was long for those weapons, and even their grasers at their best-guess positions on the missiles, but they had virtually no chance of hitting them. *Grayson One* and *Queen Adrienne* were also responding, turning away from the threat and rolling ship in an effort to interpose their wedges. Neither yacht carried any armament, but both were equipped with comprehensive EW fits, and their electronic defenses sprang to life. Yet there was little for those defenses to defend *against*, for the silently pursuing killers radiated no active targeting systems to be jammed, and they seemed utterly oblivious to the efforts to confuse them with decoys.

Major Francis Ney's head jerked up as Duchess Harrington's warning crackled from his earbug, and he punched a quick code into his personal com, dropping his earbug into the bridge circuits. It took him a few moments to realize what was happening. When he did, his face went pale, but he was already wheeling to throw open the stateroom hatch even as he snapped orders to his staff and the startled ministers.

Cromarty and Hodges seemed confused, but Prestwick and Earl Gold Peak were much quicker on the uptake. Fear flickered in their eyes, but they refused to panic, and the Chancellor and Foreign Secretary grabbed their colleagues and began hustling them down the passageway beyond the hatch. Ney grabbed Calvin Henke, the earl's son, by the collar and dragged him through the hatch behind them. Henke fought him for a moment, trying to break away and get the rest of the staffers out of the stateroom, but Ney was much stronger—and nastier—than Lord Henke. A three-fingered jab to the solar plexus did the job quite nicely, and he scooped the suddenly paralyzed nobleman up in a fireman's carry as he jogged down the passageway behind the ministers.

The life pod hatches sprang open as the ministers turned the final bend, and two of Ney's assistants were waiting. They threw their charges into the pods, slammed the hatches, and armed the eject sequence, and then they simply stood there, staring at Ney while their chests heaved with exertion.

He stared back, and his brain whirred. Part of him wanted to launch the pods *now*, but if those were laser heads and the people who'd launched them had anticipated such a move, the slow pods would be sitting ducks, despite their armor. Better to leave them where they were. A laser head would shred the unarmored yacht like tissue, but the small, well-armored life pods would have an excellent chance of surviving. Ney and his people, none of whom were in skinsuits, would not, but it was the best chance the men they were sworn to protect had. But if it was an old-fashioned contact nuke . . .

If it's a laser head, they've got a chance, Ney thought. *Please, God—please let it be a laser head!* he prayed, and bowed his head, waiting.

The weapons pursuing the yachts were the best Solarian hardware money could buy, but they were special-use devices, not regular weapons of war, designed for ambush scenarios. The people who'd designed them for the Solarian League Navy had waxed poetic about the capabilities they would confer upon the SLN. The SLN Weapons Division, however, had taken one look at them, yawned, and passed, for they were useful *only* as ambush weapons against an unsuspecting foe. Worse, their slow speed made them sitting ducks when their seekers were forced to go active over the last portion of their attack run.

The SLN's rejection, however, had left the firm who'd designed them with a large R&D expenditure and no legal way to recoup it. Because the weapons incorporated the very latest SLN stealth technology, their sale to anyone *but* the SLN was an act of treason, but no one really worried about that. The firms who built and equipped the SLN's warships had gotten into the habit of ignoring the technology transfer prohibition clauses in their contracts centuries ago, and no one had ever gotten more than a slap on the wrist for it. So when Oscar Saint-Just's StateSec representatives on Old Earth went shopping, an obliging salesman pointed them straight at the rejected weapons.

StateSec had been interested . . . and it hadn't shared the information with the People's Navy. It had occurred to the SS that if—or when—the final showdown with the Navy came, it would be helpful to possess a stealth weapon the regulars didn't know about. A few preemptive strikes on trouble-making Navy ships would take out the officers likely to pose problems quite nicely.

But Saint-Just had been interested in them for additional reasons, as well. Their greatest weakness was, as the manufacturer admitted, the weapon's extreme vulnerability to active defenses during its final attack run. Its passive sensors were quite capable of picking up and homing on the wedge of a target which had been pointed out to them, and it had the speed and endurance to follow evasive maneuvers far better (and longer) than any standard missile. But for the final run, it needed more precise data to achieve the proper angle of attack against a mobile, impeller wedge-protected target, which meant its seekers had to go active. And once a military target's sensors could see it, its low speed would make it an easy kill for laser clusters.

StateSec had recognized the problem, but they'd also had a solution. Homing beacons had been surreptitiously placed aboard every capital ship of the People's Navy during refits. They were carefully hidden and did absolutely nothing . . . until they received the activation command. But once activated, they would radiate a target source which the weapon could track completely passively, without ever going active. That meant it could be launched even from a ship which couldn't actually see the target . . . and would remain no more than a ghost up to the instant of detonation. And what would work against rebellious units of the People's Navy would work just as well against a *Manticoran* target if only some way could be found to get an equivalent beacon aboard the intended victim.

Nothing the PRH had could pick the new weapons up *unless* its seekers went active. Saint-Just's technical people estimated that the Manties probably *could* detect them, but not even Manticoran technology would be able to localize them well enough to generate a targeting solution as long as they stayed silent.

And so Saint-Just had reached out to Randal Donizetti. Donizetti was hardly what StateSec would call reliable, but the money Saint-Just had authorized his agents to pay him had been irresistible, especially since Donizetti would *also* be paid by the Faithful. All Saint-Just's local network had had to do was point Donizetti at the appropriate contact man for the fanatical Faithful and then stand back.

From Saint-Just's viewpoint, the arrangement was ideal. He'd controlled the Faithful by instructing Donizetti to limit the rate at which he handed over the necessary hardware, and the fact that Donizetti was a known weapons-runner had obscured the SS's involvement neatly. All that had really been necessary was to blow up the Solly's ship when he completed his task, and that had gone off as smoothly as any of the rest of Operation Hassan. Should the Manties succeed, as Saint-Just anticipated they would, in backtracking the assassins to Masada, they would find only the Faithful, who'd made their independent arrangements with a known Solarian criminal . . . and then killed him to hide the connection.

It was a tortuously complicated plan, fraught with opportunities for failure. But it had also offered at least the possibility of success without any risk of implicating the People's Republic of Haven. More to the point, it had worked, and now Oscar Saint-Just's warheads raced down upon their targets like the outriders of doom.

Honor stared at the closing icons, and sweat beaded her forehead. It was impossible to be certain, but it didn't look as if any of the LACs' defensive fire was even coming close, and even at their slow overtake speed, they were only minutes from impact. The yachts were rolling hard now and, unknown to any Manticoran or Grayson, their maneuvers had effectively cut the weapons off from their targeting beacons by interposing their wedges. But it no longer mattered. The passive sensors had a tight lock on the impeller wedges of the targets themselves now, and they arrowed onward, courses arcing and diverging slightly as they positioned themselves for pop-up attacks on the sides of their targets' wedges.

Honor gazed at the indistinct icons, lost almost completely in the futile hurricane of the LACs' fire, for a fraction of an instant longer, and made her decision.

"*Grayson One*, hold your heading and orientation," she said into the com. "Do not, I say again, *do not* alter course or roll ship further!"

"What the h—?!" Alfred Willis cut himself off in mid-curse, and his already dry mouth went even drier as he watched *Jamie Candless'* impeller strength peak.

"What's happening, Alf?" Hines snapped. "*Talk* to me, damn it!"

"It's . . . it's Lady Harrington, Skip," Willis said hoarsely. "She's going to kamikaze the bird off *Grayson One!*"

"*What?*"

"Sweet Tester," Captain Leonard Sullivan, CO of *Grayson One*, whispered as he watched his plot in horror and desperate hope. Lady Harrington's runabout was accelerating madly, at a rate not even one of the new LACs could have matched, as she raced up on *Grayson One*'s flank. The fleet little vessel rolled as it closed, turning the plane of its wedge perpendicular to *Grayson One*'s, and he knew what she meant to do.

She was turning her own vessel into the sidewall *Grayson One* lacked, deliberately positioning herself to take the missile's attack herself.

If it was a contact nuke, she would probably survive, for her impeller wedge, though much smaller than *Grayson One*'s, was just as impenetrable. But if the weapon was a laser head and detonated even slightly above or below her ship, it was virtually certain to kill her.

Yet either way, *Grayson One* would survive, and Sullivan closed his eyes to pray for the Steadholder.

"I'm in position, *Grayson One*," Honor said into the com, her soprano crisp and clear. "Alter ninety degrees to starboard, same plane, on my mark. Do you copy?"

"Aye, My Lady. We copy," a voice came back. And then, a moment later, "Tester bless, My Lady."

She made no response, watching her plot, her hand light on the stick. She felt Nimitz in the back of her brain, felt his love and courage clinging to her, supporting her, never questioning her decision. And beyond him, she could taste the terror and matching determination of Wayne Alexander at his engineer's station and Andrew LaFollet alone in the passenger compartment.

The LACs were still firing, and her mouth quirked a humorless smile. It would be bitterly ironic if one of the LACs accidentally hit and killed *Candless* before the missile ever reached her, but she didn't even consider ordering them off. Even if she'd had the authority to do so, she was in position to protect—to *try* to protect, she corrected herself grimly—only one ship. *Queen Adrienne* was on her own, for none of the screening units were close enough to attempt Honor's own insane maneuver. Which meant the only chance the Manticoran ship had was for one of the LACs to get lucky against the missiles. But the missiles were streaking straight in now, popping up higher, swinging a little ahead of their targets, and that meant they were going to go for down-the-throat shots, but they were already inside the threshold for laser head detonation, so that meant—

The oncoming missile's seekers abruptly went active, and it swerved.

"*Break,* Grayson One! *Break now!*" she snapped, and the yacht wrenched around to starboard.

Jamie Candless rode the flank of Benjamin Mayhew's ship like a limpet. There'd been no time to precalculate or rehearse the maneuver. Honor did it by hand and eye, holding her position, watching the missile roar in, seeing it vanish from her sensors at last as the belly of her wedge swung up to cut it off. It disappeared, and she held her breath, waiting for it to pop up at the last instant, and then—

A twenty-megaton warhead detonated less than fifty kilometers from her ship. For one fleeting instant, *Jamie Candless* was trapped in the very heart of a star, and Honor's canopy went black as the armorplast polarized. But even through her own visceral stab of terror, a corner of her mind exulted, for it was a standard nuke, not a laser head. And that meant there was a chance, if only—

The plasma wave came on the heels of the flash, ripping out across *Grayson One*'s course. But Honor had anticipated that. Her order to turn away had snatched the vulnerable open throat of the yacht's wedge—and her own—away from the center of detonation. The true fury of the explosion wasted itself against *Candless'* belly stress band. Only its fringes reached out past the wedge, and generators shrieked in torment as the particle and radiation shielding which protected the throat of any impeller wedge took the shock. Those generators were designed to protect the ships which mounted them against normal space particles and debris at velocities of up to eighty percent of light-speed. *Grayson One* and *Candless* were moving far slower than that, at barely nine thousand KPS, but their shielding had never been expected to face the holocaust which suddenly erupted across their base course, and the demon howl of the generators and the scream of audible warnings filled the universe. Honor yanked on the stick, jerking *Candless* away from what she hoped was still the bearing to *Grayson One*, and her darkened flight deck was a trapped, madly heaving pocket of hell as she shot the rapids of nuclear destruction.

They weren't going to make it. She knew they weren't.

And then, suddenly, the generators stopped shrieking.

Her eyes darted over her HUD, and she drew a deep, shuddery breath. One of her antiparticle generators was gone and the other was damaged—she'd be going back to Grayson at a very low velocity—but she was alive, and so was *Grayson One*! She stared at the icon of the Protector's yacht, watching as the bigger ship's wedge flickered and went down. *Grayson One* was hurt, but her com link to the yacht's flight deck was still open, and the bridge crew's harsh, staccato reports told her all she needed to know. Hurt the ship might be, but she was intact . . . and so were her passengers!

But then, on the heels of her elation, a fist of shock struck, for there was only one golden icon on her HUD.

CHAPTER FORTY-FIVE

"**S**o as soon as the last missile pods go aboard *Nicator* and *Nestor*, we'll be ready to resume operations," Captain Granston-Henley told the assembled flag officers of Eighth Fleet. "Admiral White Haven—" she nodded to where Hamish Alexander sat at the head of the conference table "—has decided to proceed on the basis of Sheridan One. As you all know, this ops plan calls for—"

She broke off in midsentence as Commander McTierney, White Haven's com officer, suddenly jerked upright in her chair. The movement was so sudden, so unexpected, it drew all eyes, but McTierney didn't notice. She only cupped one hand over the earbug she kept tuned at all times to the Flag communications center, and her startled audience could actually see the color draining from her face.

She closed her eyes for a moment, then punched a stud on her panel.

"Repeat that—in full!" she barked, and the admirals and commodores watched her shoulders slump as she listened to the earbug once more. Then she shook her head, and when she looked up at White Haven, the earl was dumbfounded to see tears in her eyes.

"What is it, Cindy?" he asked quickly, and she licked her lips.

"It's a flash priority from the Admiralty via Trevor's Star, My Lord. The courier boat just arrived and squealed it to FlagCom. It says . . . Sir, it says the Prime Minister and Foreign Secretary are dead!"

"*What?*" Despite himself, Hamish Alexander came halfway out of his chair, and McTierney nodded miserably.

"They sent the message off before they had full information, Sir. But according to what they did know, it looks like it was Masadan Faithful. Somehow they got their hands on a couple of modern weapons—some sort of stealth missile or drone; BuWeaps is still trying to figure out which—and smuggled them into attack range of *Grayson One* and *Queen Adrienne*." The Grayson officers in the compartment, already as shocked as their Allied counterparts, stiffened in unison, but McTierney went on speaking to the earl. "They were contact nukes, Sir. Somehow they managed to home on their targets, but Duchess Harrington intercepted the one headed for *Grayson One* with the wedge of her runabout." No one noticed the sudden, very personal fear which flickered in Hamish Alexander's eyes. "She stopped that one, but the other got through. There were . . . no survivors." McTierney swallowed hard and drew a deep breath.

"Chancellor Prestwick and Councilor Hodges were aboard *Queen Adrienne* with the Prime Minister and Earl Gold Peak, Sir," she said very quietly. "But the Queen and Protector Benjamin were both aboard *Grayson One*. If Duchess Harrington hadn't—"

She broke off, and White Haven nodded grimly.

"And Duchess Harrington?" he asked, trying to make his voice come out normally, knowing he'd failed, and hoping no one else would notice in their shock.

"She took it on the belly of her wedge, Sir. She survived." A rustle and stir ran through the frozen compartment as more than one officer stifled a cheer. "Her runabout took some severe damage, but the Admiralty says she's fine."

"Thank the Tester for that," Judah Yanakov breathed, and White Haven gave another, choppy nod. Elation at Honor's survival surged up in him, warring with the icy shock of the totally unexpected news, and he closed his eyes while he made himself step back and consider it with a semblance of calm.

A muted mutter of conversation sprang up all about him, but no one spoke directly to him, and he wondered if he was glad. *They're waiting*, he thought. *Waiting for me, as Eighth Fleet's commander, to tell them what it all means . . . and where we go from here. But, my God—what does it mean?*

His brain began to work with something like its accustomed speed as the initial shock receded. Of all the officers in the compartment, he was undoubtedly the best informed on the strengths and weaknesses of the Cromarty Government, since his brother was Chancellor of the Exchequer. By longstanding tradition, the person who held that post was not only the second ranking member of the Cabinet but the individual who took over as Prime Minister if something happened to the incumbent.

But that was under normal circumstances, and these were anything but normal. And if what Willie had told him about the balance in the House of Lords was as accurate as his brother's analyses usually were, then—

Hamish Alexander looked squarely into the abyss of the future, and what he saw there frightened him.

"Your Majesty, Countess New Kiev, Lady Descroix, and Baron High Ridge are here."

Elizabeth III nodded to the footman who had showed the senior leaders of the Opposition into her study as if their visit to Mount Royal Palace were completely routine. But it wasn't, and the brown eyes which met her visitors were harder than steel. There were dark circles under those eyes, etched by personal grief for a beloved uncle and cousin and a Prime Minister who had become, in many ways, a second father. But there was more than grief in those circles. There was the knowledge of the chaos Allen Summervale's death had wreaked on domestic Manticoran politics . . . and the reason her "guests" were here.

Remember that, she told herself. *Remember that what matters are the consequences, and whatever you do,* don't *lose your temper!*

She gritted her mental teeth, holding firmly to her resolve, and made herself smile as the political leaders were ushered in. She'd deliberately chosen an informal setting for this meeting, although she knew no one present could be fooled about how crucial it was, and she studied her "guests" carefully, making herself look at each of them as if they had never met.

Or trying to, anyway.

Michael Janvier, Baron High Ridge, was a tall, spindly man, with cold little eyes and a smile which always made Elizabeth think of a vulture or some other carrion eater. She knew much of her dislike for the man stemmed from her disgust at his isolationist, reactionary, power-seeking politics, and she usually tried to make herself be fairminded where he was concerned. Not today. Today she felt Ariel trembling on her shoulder, whiplashed between the grief he'd endured from his person's sense of loss and the exultation brimming within the cadaverous leader of the Conservative Association, and she wanted nothing more than to strangle him with her bare hands.

The women with him were another proposition entirely—physically, at least. Lady Elaine Descroix, who, with her cousin, the

Earl of Gray Hill, headed the Progressive Party, was a small woman, barely a meter and a half tall, with dark hair and eyes and a sweet, smiling face. On first meeting her and her cousin, people tended to assume Gray Hill was the dominant partner, but astute political observers knew who truly called the shots for the Progressives. Many of those observers also felt Descroix was even more amoral than High Ridge, and she'd become increasingly desperate as the war dragged out and the Progressives' position in the House of Commons continued its steady erosion. That had never been a problem for High Ridge, of course, since the Conservative Association *had* no representation in the Commons.

Maria Turner, Countess New Kiev, was almost as tall as High Ridge, but she was a trim and shapely woman, with long, chestnut hair in a carefully sculpted, windswept style. Her blue eyes burned just as brightly as High Ridge's, and Elizabeth hardly needed Honor Harrington's empathic ability to taste her excitement, but at least New Kiev didn't radiate the aura of indecent anticipation High Ridge and Descroix projected so strongly.

That didn't make things any better, though, for what New Kiev lacked in personal ambition, she more than made up in ideological fervor. Elizabeth could conceive of very few people with whom New Kiev had less in common than High Ridge, but the last decade had thrown the two firmly together. Much as they disliked one another, and divergent as their ultimate goals might be, they both hated Allen Summervale's Centrists even more, and all three of her visitors were painfully aware of the disasters into which their parties had wandered since the outbreak of war. Elizabeth knew the three of them had already agreed on how they would carve up the government if they ever came to power, which spheres each party's policies would be allowed to dominate. It wouldn't last, of course. They were too fundamentally opposed on too many issues for any alliance to hold together for more than a T-year or two, but that didn't matter at this moment.

"Your Majesty." High Ridge murmured the greeting and took the hand she offered him. "On behalf of the Conservative Association," he said, oozing unction, "allow me to express our profound grief at the loss you—and the entire Star Kingdom—have suffered."

"Thank you, My Lord." Elizabeth tried to sound as if she meant it and held out her hand to Descroix.

"A terrible thing, Your Majesty," Descroix said. "Just terrible."

She patted the hand she held and gave the Queen one of her patented sweet smiles, this one nicely tinged with an edge of sadness and determination to be brave, and Elizabeth nodded back, then extended her hand to New Kiev in turn.

"Your Majesty." New Kiev's soprano was cooler and graver than her allies' voices, and her eyes darkened with genuine sorrow for just a moment. "The Liberal Party also wishes me to express our grief, and especially for Earl Gold Peak. He and I disagreed over many policy points, but he was an honest and an honorable man, and I considered him a friend. I'll miss him badly."

"Thank you," Elizabeth said, and managed a small smile. But she also added, "The Star Kingdom will miss *both* my uncle and Duke Cromarty."

"I'm sure we will, Your Majesty," New Kiev agreed, but her mouth tightened and the sadness in her eyes gave way to a flicker of anger at Cromarty's name.

"I'm sure you know why I asked you to see me," Elizabeth went on after a moment, waving her visitors to chairs.

"I think so, Your Majesty," High Ridge said. Descroix nodded firmly, but Elizabeth had expected that, and it was New Kiev she watched. But the countess only glanced at the baron, then nodded in turn, and Elizabeth's heart sank. If they'd decided to let High Ridge do the talking, her frail hope of making them see reason had just become even frailer. "I would assume," the baron continued, "that you wished to discuss the formation of a new government."

"That's precisely what I want to discuss." Elizabeth regarded him for a moment, then decided to take the bull by the horns. "In particular, I want to discuss the situation in the House of Lords as it relates to the formation of a new government."

"I see." High Ridge leaned back and crossed his legs, propping his elbows on the arms of his chair to steeple his fingers under his chin so he could nod in properly grave fashion. But he also didn't rush out to meet the Queen halfway, and Elizabeth's eyes hardened a bit more as they rested on his face.

Your temper, she reminded herself. *Watch your damned temper! You don't have Allen to make sure you hang onto it anymore.*

"As I'm sure you're all aware," she went on after a moment, "the Centrists and Crown Loyalists did not enjoy an absolute majority in the Lords. The Government possessed a working majority, but that was the result of the support of two dozen of the non-aligned peers."

"Yes, it was," High Ridge agreed when she paused, and cocked his head as if to ask what her point might be.

Elizabeth bit down on a sudden spike of anger. She'd always

known High Ridge, for all his prating about the nobility of his birth, was a petty man. She'd even known he was an insensitive man, one to whom no one else was quite real or particularly mattered. But she hadn't realized he was also a stupid one . . . yet only a stupid man indeed would have deliberately antagonized the Queen of Manticore.

"Let's get directly to the point, My Lord," she told him, her voice flat. "With Allen Summervale's death, his government has lost its majority in the Lords. You know it, and I know it. The nonaligned peers' support was held together in large part by his personal relationships with them. Lord Alexander, the Prime Minister's logical successor, does not command those same alliances, and without them, he can't form a government as required under the Constitution."

"True, Your Majesty," High Ridge murmured, and Elizabeth felt a subsonic snarl ripple through the long, slender body on her shoulder as Ariel tasted his emotions.

"This is not the moment for the Star Kingdom to be paralyzed by a power struggle, My Lord," she said bluntly. "I invited you, Lady Descroix, and Countess New Kiev here, as the acknowledged leaders of the Opposition, to request your support. As your Queen, I ask you to recognize the grave challenges—and opportunities—arising from the recent turn in the course of the war. I would like you to agree to form a coalition government, with Lord Alexander as Prime Minister, for the duration of the conflict."

"Your Majesty," High Ridge began, just a bit too quickly for it to be a spontaneous reaction to her request, "I'm very sorry, but—"

"It won't be for long," Elizabeth overrode him, but her eyes were on New Kiev. "The Admiralty and my civilian analysts all agree that at the present operational tempo, and in light of the decisive technological advantage our forces currently enjoy, the war will be over within another six months, nine at the outside. All I ask is that you support the present government and its policies long enough for this Kingdom and its people to grasp the victory within its reach."

"Your Majesty," High Ridge said firmly, like a tutor reclaiming the floor from a willful student, "I'm very sorry, but that won't be possible. There have been far too many fundamental disagreements, of both policy and principle, between the Opposition and the Cromarty Government, and Lord Alexander has been too strongly associated with those disagreements. If I were to propose such an arrangement to the party caucus, half of my colleagues would flatly refuse to accept it."

"My Lord," Elizabeth showed her teeth in something only the most charitable could have called a smile, "I have great faith in your persuasiveness. I feel confident that if you truly put your mind to it, you could . . . convince the Association to support you."

High Ridge flinched ever so slightly as her pointed tone penetrated even his armor. The Conservative Association's party discipline was legendary, and everyone knew it would vote exactly as he told it to, but he seemed not to have expected the Queen to call him on his evasion, however indirectly. Yet his hesitation, if that was what it had been, was brief, and he raised his hands in a small, regretful gesture.

"I'm sorry, Your Majesty, but it would be impossible, as a matter of principle, for the Conservative Association to support a coalition cabinet under Lord Alexander."

"I see." Elizabeth's voice was chilled steel. She gazed at him for a long, silent moment, then shifted her icy eyes to Lady Descroix. "And the Progressives, Milady?"

"Oh, dear." Descroix sighed, then shook her head regretfully. "I truly wish we could oblige you, Your Majesty, but I'm afraid it's impossible. Simply impossible."

Elizabeth only nodded and switched her eyes to New Kiev. The countess winced, but her chin rose and she met the Queen's eyes squarely.

"Your Majesty, I'm afraid the Liberal Party would find it equally impossible to support Lord Alexander as Prime Minister."

Elizabeth leaned back in her chair, and the temperature in the comfortable room seemed to drop perceptibly. New Kiev fidgeted ever so slightly, but High Ridge sat motionless, as if completely calm, under his Queen's basilisk gaze, and Lady Descroix only wrung her hands in her lap and concentrated on looking small and helpless.

"I have asked you, as is my right as your monarch, to accede to my wishes in the interests of the Star Kingdom's security," Elizabeth said coldly. "I have not asked you to abandon your principles. I have not asked you to embrace or pretend to embrace any ideology offensive to you or to your party members. My only concern is the continuity of leadership necessary to win the current war and establish a lasting peace. I ask you to rise above the pettiness of party politics—of *all* parties' politics, not just your own—and prove worthy of this moment in history."

She paused, waiting, but they merely looked back at her. New Kiev's face was taut, her eyes troubled, but there was no retreat in it, and High Ridge looked no more than blandly attentive, while Descroix looked worried but bravely determined. Elizabeth felt her temper fighting the chain she'd fastened upon it and reminded herself yet again that it was her duty to get these people to agree to a compromise.

"Very well," she said. "Let's lay all the cards on the table, shall we? I fully realize that the Conservative Association, the Progressive Party, and the Liberal Party between them possess sufficient votes in the Lords, in the absence of the nonaligned peers, to form a government. I also realize that the three of you control sufficient votes to *prevent* Lord Alexander from forming a government, despite the fact that the Centrists and Crown Loyalists hold a majority of over twenty percent in the House of Commons. And I know your reasons—your *true* reasons—for refusing to form a coalition government."

She paused, daring any one of them to deny her implication that all their talk of "principles" was a tissue of lies, but none of them seemed prepared to take up that particular challenge, and her lip curled ever so slightly.

"I am fully conversant," she went on with cold precision, "with the reality of partisan politics here in the Star Kingdom. I had hoped that you would prove capable of rising above that reality, if only briefly, at this critical moment, because at this instant, I cannot *compel* you to do so, and you know it. A protracted struggle between the Crown and a majority Opposition in the Lords could have disastrous consequences upon the war, and unlike you, I do not have the option of neglecting my responsibilities to this Star Kingdom and its people in order to play petty, ambitious, short-sighted, and stupid political games."

Her contempt was withering, and New Kiev flushed darkly, but the countess showed no sign of deserting her allies.

"I submit to you," Elizabeth continued, "that however firmly united you may be at this moment, your fundamental policies and principles are too basically opposed for that unity to last. You can, if you choose, use it at this moment to ignore my wishes, but you do so at your peril, for it will come to an *end* . . . and the Crown will still be here."

There was a moment of dead silence, and even High Ridge sounded slightly shaken when he broke it.

"Is that a *threat*, Your Majesty?" he asked almost incredulously.

"It is a reminder, My Lord. A reminder that the House of Winton knows its friends . . . and also those who are *not* its friends. We Wintons have long memories, Baron. If you truly wish to have me as an enemy, it can certainly be arranged, but I urge you to think very carefully first."

"Your Majesty, you can't simply threaten and browbeat peers of the realm!" High Ridge's voice was hot as his mask slipped for the first time. "We, too, have a legitimate role and function in the government of the Star Kingdom, and our collective judgment carries at least as much weight as that of a single individual, whoever she may be. You are our Queen. As your subjects, we are duty bound to listen to you and to weigh your views, but you are *not* a dictator, and we are not slaves! We will act as we deem best, in accordance with our interpretation of the domestic and foreign situation, and any breach between us and the Crown will not be of *our* making!"

"This interview is over," Elizabeth said, and stood, shaking with fury, too angry even to notice the incredulity in her guests eyes as she violated all the solemn protocol of the occasion. "I can't keep you from forming a government. Send me your list of ministers. I want it by noon tomorrow. I will act upon it immediately. *But*—" her eyes stabbed each of them in turn "—remember this day. You're right, My Lord. I'm *not* a dictator, and I refuse to act like one simply because of your own stupidity and arrogance. But I need not be a 'dictator' to deal with the likes of you, either, and the time will come when you—when *all* of you—will rue this day!"

And with that, she turned and stormed out of the salon.

CHAPTER FORTY-SIX

"They refused, didn't they?" William Alexander said wearily as Elizabeth III stalked into the room. The glare she gave him was more eloquent than words, and he shrugged exhausted shoulders. "We knew they were going to, Your Majesty. The way they see it, they had no choice."

"Why not?"

Alexander turned to the speaker. According to the normal rules of protocol, Honor Harrington had no business in that room at that time. Duchess or no, she had never been a member of the Cromarty Government and had no official role in the formation of its successor. But Elizabeth had wanted her here, and so had Benjamin Mayhew, who was as aware of the critical importance of this moment as any Manticoran. His own situation on Grayson was much simpler, since his Constitution gave him the authority to simply select the individual of his choice as Chancellor and not even the Keys could tell him no. Elizabeth, unfortunately, did not enjoy a matching degree of authority. Her Prime Minister was required by law to control a majority vote in the House of Lords. It was part of the restrictions the original colonists had put in place to protect their own and their children's control of the Star Kingdom, and unlike many others of those restrictions, it survived intact. There had been past instances in which a Manticoran monarch had been compelled to accept a prime minister not of his or her choice, but they had not been happy ones. The Crown was too intimately involved in the day-to-day running of the Star Kingdom for a contest of wills between the monarch and the prime minister to be anything other than a potential disaster. As a rule, the Winton Dynasty had recognized that time was on its side and worked to minimize conflicts with prime ministers it didn't care for on the theory that the Crown could outlast any majority, but there had been cases when that had proven impossible and all-out warfare between Crown and Cabinet had brought the business of governing almost to a halt.

Which was the one thing no one could afford at this moment.

"Why don't they have a choice?" Honor asked. "If it's understood from the beginning that the arrangement is temporary, only an interim compromise to get us through the end of the war, surely they can give at least *some* ground!"

Elizabeth laughed, a sharp, ugly sound, and Honor looked at her.

"I'm sorry, Honor," the Queen said after a moment. "And I wasn't laughing at you. But expecting *these* idiots to give ground over a matter of principle is like . . . like expecting a treecat to refuse a celery stick!"

"I wouldn't put it quite that way myself," Alexander said, and paused to consider his words carefully. He lacked Honor's ability to feel the Queen's fury pulsing like some physical furnace, but he'd known her for years. He didn't need any special empathic ability to realize how frayed her temper's leash was, and the one thing he truly dreaded was the breaking of that leash.

"How *would* you put it, then?" the Queen demanded, and he shrugged.

"The way they see it, they have to take this opportunity, which— as far as they're concerned—is a perfectly legitimate exercise of political power, to take control away from the Centrists and Crown Loyalists. They have no choice, assuming they want to repair the damage their base of popular support has suffered."

Honor quirked an eyebrow at him, and he sighed.

"The Opposition has shot itself in the foot repeatedly. In its prewar opposition to the naval buildup and the extension of the Alliance. In its refusal to vote out a formal declaration of war after Hancock Station. In the way it treated you, Your Grace. And in the way it reacted to McQueen's offensives." He snorted a bitter laugh of his own. "I almost felt sorry for them while we were making the final preparations for Hamish's offensive, because I *knew* they were cutting their own throats by accelerating their criticism of our military policy just when we were getting ready to squeeze the trigger. But the point is that they've adopted an entire succession of positions which turned out to be wrong. Or which the voters *regarded* as wrong, at any rate; I rather doubt that people like New Kiev or High Ridge would admit they really had been wrong even now.

"What that's meant for them," he went on, "is that we Centrists have reaped the advantages of being *right* while they've been made to look like idiots. We hold a twenty percent majority in the Commons right now. If elections were held tomorrow, we could easily double that, and possibly do even better, and that's what has the Opposition—and even some of the nonaligned peers who supported Allen—scared to death."

"Excuse me?" Honor cocked her head, and he grinned crookedly.

"Think about it, Your Grace. The Centrists and the Crown Loyalists, the two parties which have always been most supportive of the Crown, have fought the entire war despite the endless obstructionism of the Opposition, all of whom predicted that any war with Haven could end only in disaster. Now, having persevered in the face of that obstructionism, we're on the brink of achieving complete military victory. . . and just as we caught the blame for 'lack of preparedness' when McQueen uncorked her offensives, we're about to get the credit for winning the 'impossible' war.

"The Opposition has been terrified ever since Hamish kicked off Buttercup that Allen would call a general election as soon as the PRH surrendered. They figured, correctly, that their representation in the Commons would be devastated at the polls. And they also figured that with a crushing majority in the Commons, plus the full-blooded support of the Crown, *plus* the prestige of having been proved a great war leader, Allen would be in a position to rout all opposition in the Lords, as well. The Liberals were afraid their demands for social reform would get plowed under, and the Progressives and Conservatives were afraid Elizabeth and Allen would manage what every Winton since Elizabeth I has hoped to accomplish: finally break the House of Lord's monopoly on the initiation of finance bills and the right of consent for Crown appointments. So even though, ultimately, they can't stand one another, the Opposition parties see no choice but to cooperate and make damned sure no Centrists or Crown Loyalists are anywhere near the peace settlement when the Peeps actually surrender. That way *they* get credit for winning the war . . . and we don't. Not only that, but it lets *them* decide when to call the next general election, and you can be certain that they'll spend a year or two repairing fences by waving domestic policy carrots under the electorate's nose before they do."

"I see." Honor's tone was leached of all expression, and Elizabeth gave her a bleak smile.

"Welcome to the reality of partisan politics, Manticoran style," the Queen said. "I'm sure from some of the things he said before I left for home that Benjamin had a shrewd notion of where our domestic politics were headed, and I don't blame him for being worried. *I* wouldn't trust the Opposition to organize a drinking party in a distillery, but there doesn't seem to be any way to prevent them from forming the next government. Which means these *cretins* will be formulating policy for the Star Kingdom, which means, effectively, for the entire Alliance, unless I publically oppose them and bring on a constitutional crisis which could be even more dangerous than letting this fumble-fingered troop of self-serving, egotistical, power-hungry incompetents run the show!"

Honor winced at the barely suppressed rage in Elizabeth's tone, but there was something else under it—a raw, driving fury, fueled by some inner agony, which had to stem from more than seeing her will thwarted or even disgust with the Opposition's partisanship.

"Excuse me, Your Majesty," she heard herself say very gently, "but there's more to it than just that. For you at least." Elizabeth's eyebrows shot up, but then her gaze flicked to where Nimitz crouched on the perch next to Ariel.

"Yes. Yes, you would know that, wouldn't you?" she murmured, and Honor nodded. She could hardly believe she'd said a word, for she had no business prying into her Queen's private affairs, but something about Elizabeth's pain left her no choice. She couldn't taste that much hurt and *not* try to do something about it.

"There is more," Elizabeth said, looking away from the two humans. She stood and reached out to Ariel, gathering the treecat in her arms, and buried her face in his fur. He purred to her loudly, caressing her cheek with one true-hand, and she drew a deep breath before she turned back to Honor and Alexander.

"Very few people know this," she told them, "and as your Queen, I must have your oaths that no one will hear of it from you— except, perhaps, Benjamin himself, in your case, Honor." Her guests looked at one another, then nodded and turned back to her, and she squared her shoulders.

"You both know my father was killed in a grav-skiing accident. What you *don't* know is that the 'accident' was nothing of the sort. He was assassinated." Honor sucked in air, feeling as if someone had just punched her in the belly. "He was, in fact, murdered by certain Manticoran politicians opposed to his military policies . . . and effectively in the pay of the People's Republic of Haven," Elizabeth went on bleakly. "They hoped to put a teenaged Heir—me—on the throne and to control my choice of regent in order to . . . redirect Manticoran policy away from preparing to resist Peep aggression. That was the long-term goal. As for the short-term one—" she smiled mirthlessly "—you will no doubt recall that it was very shortly after my father's death that the Peeps moved in on Trevor's Star. I have no doubt they counted on the confusion engendered by Dad's death to paralyze any potential attempt on our part to prevent them from securing control of one terminus of the Junction."

"My God, Elizabeth!" Alexander was so shaken he forgot the titles he was usually so careful to use in his official relationship with the Queen. "If you knew that, why didn't you *tell* someone?!"

"I couldn't," Elizabeth said, her voice bleaker than ever, harrowed and brittle with old pain. "We weren't ready for open war, and any charge that the Legislaturalists had orchestrated Dad's murder might have led to just that. Even if it hadn't, the proof that Havenite agents had actually penetrated the highest levels of our own government and assassinated the King could only have led to massive witch-hunts which would have crippled us domestically when we had to be strong and united to support the military buildup. And that sort of bitter, denunciatory mutual suspicion would only have made it even easier for *future* Havenite agents to denounce the 'traitors' more loudly than anyone else in order to get themselves into positions of power here at home."

She closed her eyes briefly, her expression haggard and haunted, and her nostrils flared.

"I wanted them dead. *God*, how I wanted them dead! But Allen and Aunt Caitrin—especially Aunt Caitrin—convinced me that I couldn't have them arrested and tried. I even wanted to challenge them to duels and kill them with my own hands if I couldn't have them tried." She smiled crookedly at the sudden understanding on Honor's face, and nodded. "Which is why I sympathized so deeply with you over that bastard North Hollow, Honor," she admitted. "But the same things which made it impossible to try them made a duel even more impossible, and so I had to let them go. I had to let the men and women who'd murdered my father out of cold, self-serving ambition live."

She turned away and stared blindly out a window onto the wondrous light show of Mount Royal Palace's night-struck landscaping, and Honor shook her head. The Peeps had assassinated King Roger in order to put a weak, easily manipulated "teenager" on the throne? If it had been possible, she would almost have felt sorry for the people who'd gotten Elizabeth III instead.

"And now this," Elizabeth said at last, so softly it was difficult to hear her. "We may never prove it, but I'm convinced—I *know*—the Peeps were behind what happened at Yeltsin's Star. The Faithful may have been the actual triggermen, but it was the Peeps who got them the weapons . . . and probably the ones who suggested to the Faithful that they ought to 'convince' Mueller to smuggle the targeting beacons on board by giving them to me and Allen."

And Mueller's paid for it, too, Honor thought grimly.

The steadholder had been impeached, tried, and condemned to death in barely one week, and sentence had been carried out immediately. There had been no question who'd handed the memory stones to Elizabeth and Cromarty, and his fate had been sealed from the moment the beacon inside Elizabeth's stone had been discovered.

She was pulled away from the brief distraction when Elizabeth turned back from the window.

"And some analysts wonder why I hate the People's Republic so bitterly," she said flatly. "The answer's simple enough, isn't it? The Legislaturalists and Internal Security murdered my father thirty-four years ago. Now the Committee of Public Safety and State Security have murdered my Prime Minister, my uncle, my cousin, and their entire staffs, plus all their security people and the entire crew of my yacht. People I've known for years. *Friends.* They attempted to murder me, my aunt, and Benjamin Mayhew, as well, and failed only because of you, Honor. Nothing changes where the Peeps are concerned. And these people—these *imbeciles*—have been prating about 'restraint' and 'measured responses' and 'peaceable resolution of conflicts' to me for *ten T-years* while Allen and I fought the war despite them, and now they even want to deny him any legacy for all he accomplished?!" She bared her teeth and shook her head, and her voice held the flat, terrible tang of iron when she spoke again. "I may not be able to stop them from forming a partisan government and excluding you from it, Willie. Not now. But I promise you this: the day will come when these people *will* remember the warning I just gave them."

CHAPTER FORTY-SEVEN

Oscar Saint-Just closed the file and leaned back in his chair. There was no one else present, and so no eyes saw what many would have sworn was impossible: a tiny tremor, quivering through the fingers of both hands before he clasped them tightly to still it.

He gazed at nothing for endless seconds, and there was a great stillness at his core. For the first time since Rob Pierre's death, he felt hope growing somewhere deep inside, and he sucked in a deep breath, held it, and then exhaled noisily.

He'd never really expected Hassan to work. He admitted that to himself now, although he hadn't been able to earlier. Not when it had been so essential that the plan *must* work. The decapitation of the Alliance had been his only hope as the military situation crumbled, and so he'd made himself believe Hassan would succeed, that he only had to hang on just a little longer.

And it truly had worked in the end. Not as fully as he'd hoped it might, true, but it *had* worked.

He'd been bitterly disappointed when the preliminary reports indicated that Benjamin Mayhew and Elizabeth III had both escaped, and he'd ground his teeth when he discovered who'd made that possible. There were very few points upon which Oscar Saint-Just and the late, unlamented Cordelia Ransom had ever been in perfect agreement, but Honor Harrington was one of them. The only difference between Saint-Just and Ransom was that Saint-Just would simply have had her quietly shot and stuffed in an unmarked grave without ever admitting he'd even seen her.

543

But as the first, fragmentary reports about the domestic Manty reaction to Hassan came in, Saint-Just had begun to realize it might actually be better this way. If he'd gotten Elizabeth and Benjamin but not Cromarty, Elizabeth's son would simply have assumed the throne with the same Government in place. At best, the result would have been only to delay the inevitable, not stop it. But by killing *Cromarty* and leaving Elizabeth alive, Saint-Just had inadvertently created a totally different situation. When the Manty Opposition's leadership announced its decision to form a government which excluded Cromarty's Centrists and the Crown Loyalists, a dazzling opportunity had landed squarely in Oscar Saint-Just's lap, and he had no intention of letting it slip away.

He pressed a button on his intercom.

"Yes, Citizen Chairman?" his secretary replied instantly.

"Get me Citizen Secretary Kersaint and Citizen Secretary Mosley," Saint-Just directed. "Tell them I need to see them immediately."

"At once, Citizen Chairman!"

Saint-Just leaned back in his chair once more, folding his hands and gazing up at the ceiling while he waited for the PRH's new foreign minister and the woman who'd replaced Leonard Boardman at Public Information. Both of their predecessors had been in the Octagon—hostages or traitors, no one really knew—when Saint-Just ordered the button pushed, and they were undeniably inexperienced in their new positions. On the other hand, both of them were terrified of Oscar Saint-Just, and he felt confident that they'd manage to do *exactly* what he wanted of them.

"All right, Allyson," White Haven said, rubbing sleep from his eyes. "I'm awake."

He looked at the bedside chrono and winced. *Benjamin the Great* ran on standard twenty-four-hour days rather than the twenty-two-plus-hour days of Manticore, and it was just after 03:00. He'd been in bed barely three hours, and he was due to attend the final admirals' briefing before kicking off against Lovat in only five more hours.

This had better be important, he told himself, and punched buttons on his com.

The terminal blinked to life with Captain Granston-Henley's face. It was a one-ended visual link—White Haven had no intention of letting anyone see him draggle-edged with sleep—but he hardly even thought about that as her expression registered.

"What is it?" His voice was rather less caustic than he'd planned, and Granston-Henley gathered her wits with a visible effort.

"We just received a dispatch boat, My Lord. From the Peeps."

"From the *Peeps*?" White Haven repeated very carefully, and she nodded.

"Yes, Sir. She came over the hyper-wall twenty-six minutes ago. We just picked up her transmission five minutes and—" she glanced at a chrono of her own "—thirty seconds ago. It was in the clear, Sir."

"And it said?" he prompted as she paused as if uncertain how to proceed.

"It's a direct message from Saint-Just to Her Majesty, My Lord," Granston-Henley said. "He wants— Sir, he says he wants to convene peace talks!"

"*No!*"

Elizabeth III came to her feet in one supple motion, and her fist slammed down on the conference-room table like a hammer. More than one person in the room flinched, but Prime Minister High Ridge and Foreign Secretary Descroix seemed totally unperturbed.

"Your Majesty, this offer must be given deep and serious consideration," High Ridge said into the ringing silence.

"No," Elizabeth repeated, her voice lower but even more intense, and her brown eyes locked on the Prime Minister like a ship of the wall's main battery. "It's a trick. A desperation move."

"Whatever it is, and whatever Citizen Chairman Saint-Just's motives," Descroix said in the tone of sweet reason Elizabeth had come to loathe passionately, "the fact remains that it offers a chance to stop the fighting. And the dying, Your Majesty. Not just on the PRH's side, but on our own, as well."

"If we let Saint-Just squirm out now, when we have the power to crush him *and* his regime, it will be a betrayal of every man and woman who died to get us to this point," Elizabeth said flatly. "And it will also be a betrayal of our partners in the Alliance, who count on our leadership and support for their very survival! There's only one way to insure peace with the People's Republic, and that is to defeat it, destroy its military capabilities, and make certain they *stay* destroyed!"

"Your Majesty, violence never settled anything," Home Secretary New Kiev said. The countess looked uncomfortable under the scornful glance the Queen turned upon her, but she shook her own head stubbornly. "My opposition to this war has always been based on the belief that peaceful resolution of conflicts is vastly preferable to a resort to violence. If the previous government had realized that and given peace a chance following the Harris Assassination, we might have ended the fighting ten years ago! I realize you don't believe that was possible, but I and many of the others in this room do. Perhaps you were right at the time and we were wrong, but we'll never know either way, because the opportunity was rejected. But this time we have a definite offer from the other side, a specific proposal to end the killing, and I feel we have an imperative moral responsibility to seriously consider *anything* which can do that."

" 'Specific proposal'?" Elizabeth repeated, and jabbed a contemptuous index finger at the memo pad before her. "All he proposes is a cease-fire in place—which neatly saves him from the loss of Lovat *and* his capital system—to provide a 'breathing space' for negotiations! And as for this sanctimonious *crap* about 'sharing your pain at the loss of your assassinated leaders' because the same thing happened to them—!"

Her lips worked as if she wanted to spit.

"The situations certainly aren't precise parallels, but both of us *have* experienced major changes in government," High Ridge pointed out with oily calm. "While everyone, of course, deeply regrets the deaths of Duke Cromarty and Earl Gold Peak, it's possible that the shift in political realities and perceptions resulting from that tragedy may actually have some beneficial results. I can hardly conceive of Pierre having sent us an offer like this one, but Saint-Just is obviously a more pragmatic man. No doubt it was the change in governments which led him to believe we might seriously entertain the notion of a negotiated settlement. And if that's true, then the final peace settlement would, in a way, become a monument to Duke Cromarty and your uncle, Your Majesty."

"If you ever mention my uncle to me again, I will personally push your face through the top of this table," Elizabeth told him in a flat, deadly tone, and the baron recoiled physically from her. He started to speak quickly, then stopped as an even more deadly hiss came from the treecat on her shoulder. High Ridge licked his lips, eyes locked on Ariel as the 'cat bared bone-white fangs, then swallowed heavily.

"I . . . beg your pardon, Your Majesty," he said at last, into the stunned silence. "I meant no disrespect to your— I mean, I was merely attempting to say that the changes on both sides of the battle line, however regrettable some may have been, may also have created a climate in which genuine negotiations and an end to the fighting have become possible. And as Countess New Kiev says, we have a moral responsibility to explore any avenue which can end the enormous loss of life and property this war has entailed."

Elizabeth looked at him contemptuously, but then she closed her eyes and made herself sit once more. Her temper. Her damnable *temper*. If she had any hope at all of stopping this insanity it was to convince at least a minority of High Ridge's colleagues to support her, and temper tantrums weren't going to do that.

"My Lord," she said finally, her voice almost back to normal, "the point is that there hasn't actually *been* a change on their side of the line. Didn't you listen to anything Amos Parnell said? Pierre and Saint-Just have been the moving force behind everything that's happened in the PRH since they murdered President Harris and his entire government. This man is a butcher—*the* butcher of the People's Republic. He doesn't care how many people die; all he cares about is winning and the power of the state. *His* state. Which means any 'peace proposal' he might extend is no more than a ploy, a trick to buy time while he tries desperately to recover from a hopeless military position. And if we agree to negotiate, we *give* him that time!"

"I considered that possibility, Your Majesty." High Ridge was still a bit green around the gills, and his forehead was damp with sweat, but he, too, made a deliberate effort to speak normally. "In fact, I discussed it with Admiral Janacek."

He nodded to the new First Lord of the Admiralty, Sir Edward Janacek, and the civilian head of the Navy straightened in his chair.

"I've considered the military position in some detail, Your Majesty," he said with the patronizing air of a professional, although he'd last held a spacegoing command over thirty years before. "It's certainly possible that Saint-Just's motive is, in part, at least, to buy a military breathing space. But it won't do him any good. Our qualitative edge is too overwhelming. Nothing they have can stand up to the new systems developed from Admiral Hemphill's work." He beamed, and Elizabeth ground her teeth together. Sonja Hemphill was Janacek's cousin . . . and the First Lord acted as if all of her ideas had come from *him* in the first place.

"Certainly they haven't been able to stand up to Earl White Haven *so far*," Elizabeth conceded, enjoying Janacek's wince at the name "White Haven." The enmity between the two admirals went back decades, and it was as bitter as it was implacable. "But who's to say what they can come up with if we give them time to catch their breath and think about it?"

"Your Majesty, this is my area of expertise," Janacek told her. "Our new systems are the product of years of intensive R&D by research people incomparably better trained and equipped than anything in the People's Republic. There's no way they could possibly be duplicated by the PRH in less than four or five T-years. Surely that should be enough time for us to either conclude a reasonable peace settlement or else prove Saint-Just has no intention of negotiating seriously! And in the meantime, I assure you, the Navy will watch them like hawks for any sign of future threats."

"You see, Your Majesty?" High Ridge cut in smoothly. "The risks from our side are minor, but the potential gain, an end to a financially ruinous and bloody war against an opponent whose worlds we have no desire to conquer, is enormous. As Countess New Kiev says, it's time we gave peace a chance."

Elizabeth looked back at him silently, then let her eyes sweep the conference table. One or two people looked away; most returned her gaze with greater or lesser degrees of confidence... or defiance.

"And if our Allies disagree with you, My Lord?" she asked finally.

"That would be regrettable, Your Majesty," High Ridge acknowledged, but then he smiled thinly. "Still, it's the Star Kingdom which has footed by far the greatest share of the bill for this war, both economically and in terms of lives lost. We have a right to explore any avenue which might end the conflict."

"Even unilaterally and without our treaty partners' approval," Elizabeth said.

"I've examined the relevant treaties carefully, Your Majesty," High Ridge assured her. "They contain no specific bar to unilateral negotiations between any of the signatories and the People's Republic."

"Perhaps because it never occurred to the negotiators who put those treaties together that any of their allies would so completely and cold-bloodedly betray them," Elizabeth suggested conversationally, and watched High Ridge flush.

"That's one way to look at it, Your Majesty," he said. "Another way is to point out that if we succeed in negotiating peace between the Star Kingdom and the People's Republic, peace between the PRH and our allies must also follow. In which case it is not a betrayal, but rather accomplishes the true goal of those treaties: peace, secure borders, and an end to the military threat of the People's Republic."

He had an answer for everything, Elizabeth realized, and she didn't need any signs from Ariel to know that virtually every member of the Cabinet agreed with him. And, she admitted with bitter honesty, her own attitude hadn't helped. She should have kept her mouth shut, controlled her temper, and bided her time;

instead, she'd come out into the open too soon. Every one of High Ridge's fellow cabinet members knew she'd become their mortal enemy, and it had produced an effect she hadn't anticipated. The threat she posed to them—the vengeance they all knew she would take as soon as the opportunity offered—had driven them closer together. The natural differences which ought to have been driving them apart had been submerged in the need to respond to the greater danger *she* represented, and there was no way any of them would break lockstep with the others to support her against High Ridge, New Kiev, and Descroix. And without a single ally within the Cabinet, not even the Queen of Manticore could reject the united policy recommendations of her Prime Minister, her Foreign Secretary, her Home Secretary, and the First Lord of the Admiralty.

"Very well, My Lord," she made herself say. "We'll try it your way. And I hope, for all our sakes, that you're right and I'm wrong."

CHAPTER FORTY-EIGHT

"**I** can't believe this," Michelle Henke, Countess Gold Peak, muttered balefully, glaring out across Jason Bay from the third-floor window of her suite in Honor's East Shore mansion. "What the *hell* is Beth thinking?"

"That she hasn't got a choice," Honor said somberly from behind her.

She had extended her stay on Manticore at Elizabeth's request, splitting her time between her mansion, Mount Royal Palace, and the Grayson embassy. Her unique status as a noblewoman of both star nations gave her an equally unique perspective, and despite the fact that virtually every member of the High Ridge Government hated her—and pretty much vice versa, she admitted—she was too valuable a conduit for anyone on either side to pass up. Benjamin knew she had Elizabeth's ear, Elizabeth knew Benjamin trusted her implicitly, and even High Ridge knew that if he wanted to hear what Benjamin truly thought about an idea, she was the best source available.

All of which meant she'd been granted a far better vantage point than she'd ever wanted from which to witness one of the most shameful episodes in the history of the Star Kingdom of Manticore.

But, then, she'd seen a lot of things she'd never wanted to see of late, she thought, and turned to Henke.

Michelle had become the Countess of Gold Peak with the deaths of her father and older brother, but her ship had been assigned to Eighth Fleet. There'd been no way *Edward Saganami* could be spared, and the trip home would have taken so long she was bound

550

to miss the funerals anyway. So she'd remained at the front, burying her grief in her naval duties, until White Haven picked her to carry Saint-Just's truce offer back to Manticore. Caitrin Winton-Henke was eminently capable of running the earldom which had just become Michelle's, and Honor knew both women had seen the press of their responsibilities as their only anodyne against sorrow.

But Michelle had been home for only a few hours. This was the first time she and Honor had been alone, aside from LaFollet and Nimitz, and Honor drew a deep breath.

"Mike, I'm sorry," she said softly, and Michelle stiffened and turned quickly from the window as she heard the pain in that soprano voice.

"Sorry?" Her eyebrows arched in surprise, and Honor nodded.

"I could only stop one missile," she said. "I had to choose, and—"

She stopped, her face tight, unable to finish the sentence, and Henke's expression softened. She stood very still for two or three breaths, eyes gleaming as she fought back the tears, but when she made herself speak, her husky contralto sounded almost normal.

"It wasn't your fault, Honor. God knows I'd've made the same decision in your place. It hurts—*God* how it hurts—to know I'll never see Dad or Cal again, but thanks to you my mother is still alive. And my cousin. And Protector Benjamin." She reached out and gripped Honor's upper arms, then shook her head vigorously. "No one could have done more than you did, Honor. *No one.* Don't ever doubt that!"

Honor gazed into her eyes for a moment, tasting the sincerity behind them, then sighed and nodded. Intellectually, she'd known Henke was right from the beginning, but she'd been terrified *Henke* wouldn't see it that way. And, she admitted, until she *knew* Henke didn't blame her for the deaths of her father and brother, she hadn't quite been able not to blame *herself* for them. But now she could let them go, and she drew a deep breath and nodded again.

"Thank you for understanding," she said quietly, and Henke clicked her tongue in exasperation.

"Honor Harrington, you are probably the only person in the universe who'd be afraid I *wouldn't* understand!" She gave her taller friend an affectionate shake, then stood back and returned her gaze to the cobalt waters of Jason Bay.

"And now that that's out of the way, just what did you mean that Beth doesn't have a choice?"

"She doesn't," Honor said, accepting the return to a less painful subject. "The entire Cabinet is united. Her only alternatives

are to accept their policy . . . or reject the united recommendations of *all* her constitutionally appointed ministers. Theoretically, she has the power to do that. As a practical matter, it
would be catastrophic. At the very least, it would produce a
prolonged constitutional crisis just when we can least afford one.
And once we get into those waters, who knows where it would
end? Creating constitutional precedents is always a scary proposition, and there's no way to positively predict whether the new
precedent would favor the Crown or the Cabinet . . . which means
the Lords."

"Jesus, Honor! I thought you didn't *like* politics!" Henke said
only half humorously, and Honor shrugged.

"I don't. But ever since Elizabeth got back to Manticore, I've
been stuck in a sort of advisory role. I'm not comfortable with
it, and I don't think I'm very good at it, but when she insisted
she needed me, I could hardly say no. Not after everything that's
happened. Besides—" her mouth quirked in a smile which held
no humor at all "—at least this way Benjamin has someone he
absolutely trusts reassuring him *Elizabeth* hasn't gone crazy, whatever the Government is up to."

"So they really are going to accept this truce? When we're only
one stop short of the Peep capital?"

Henke sounded as if she still couldn't believe it, and Honor didn't
blame her. But—

"That's exactly what they're going to do," she said quietly.

Oscar Saint-Just looked up at Citizen Secretary Jeffery Kersaint
and did something Kersaint would have flatly denied was possible.

He smiled.

The huge grin looked wildly out of place on that perpetually
emotionless face. But under the circumstances, Kersaint understood
it perfectly, for the Citizen Chairman—with Kersaint's help, of
course—had just pulled off the impossible.

"They bought it?" the PRH's dictator demanded, as if he hadn't
quite been able to believe Kersaint the first time around. "They
went for it? For *all* of it?"

"Yes, Citizen Chairman. They've agreed to a cease-fire in place,
with both sides to retain systems they currently occupy, pending
comprehensive negotiations to end the war. They request—" he
glanced at his memo pad "—that we immediately send a delega-
tion to confirm the details of the truce and begin formal talks
within two standard months."

"Good. Good! We can tie them up for months with talks. *Years* if we have to!" Saint-Just actually rubbed his hands, looking like a man who'd just received a new lease on life . . . or at least a temporary stay of execution.

"At least years, Sir. And we may even be able to negotiate an actual treaty."

"Ha! That I'll believe only when I see it," Saint-Just said skeptically. "But that's all right, Jeffery. All I really need is time to get my own house in order and figure out how to cope with these new weapons of theirs, and Citizen Admiral Theisman already has some interesting suggestions in that regard. Well done. Very well done, indeed!"

"Thank you, Sir," Kersaint said.

"Get together with Mosley and rough out a communique. I want something as optimistic as possible. And tell Mosley to set up an interview with Joan Huertes ASAP."

"Yes, Sir. I'll get on it at once," Kersaint agreed, and moved briskly out of Saint-Just's office.

The Citizen Chairman sat gazing into infinity at something only he could see, and this time he smiled faintly at whatever he found there. But then he shook himself. Time to get his house in order, he'd told Kersaint. He had that now, and he keyed his intercom.

"Yes, Citizen Chairman?"

"Get me Citizen Admiral Stephanopoulos. And requisition a StateSec courier boat for Lovat."

"Citizen Admiral, I have a com request from Citizen Admiral Heemskerk," Citizen Lieutenant Fraiser announced, and Lester Tourville looked up from the tactical exercise on Shannon Foraker's plot with a sudden chill. His raised hand interrupted his conversation with Foraker and Yuri Bogdanovich, and he turned to his com officer.

"Did the Citizen Admiral say what he wants?" he asked in a voice whose apparent calmness astonished him.

"No, Citizen Admiral," Fraiser said, then cleared his throat. "But a StateSec courier boat did enter the system about forty-five minutes ago," he offered.

"I see. Thank you." Tourville nodded to Fraiser and looked back at Bogdanovich and Foraker. "I'm afraid I'll have to take this call," he said. "We'll get back to this later."

"Of course, Citizen Admiral," Bogdanovich said quietly, and Foraker nodded. But then the tac officer inhaled sharply, and Tourville glanced back at her.

"*Alphand*'s sidewalls just came up, Citizen Admiral," she said.

"So did *DuChesnois'* and *Lavalette's*. In fact, it looks like Citizen Admiral Heemskerk's entire squadron has just cleared for action."

"I see," Tourville repeated, and managed a smile. "It would seem the Citizen Admiral's message is more urgent than I'd anticipated." He looked across the flag bridge at Everard Honeker, and saw the matching awareness in his people's commissioner's eyes, but Honeker said nothing. There was nothing, after all, that anyone *could* say.

Foraker was tapping keys at her console, no doubt refining her data, as if it were going to make any difference. Even if Tourville had been tempted to resist the order he knew Heemskerk was about to give, it would have been futile. With Heemskerk's squadron already at full battle readiness, it would have been an act of suicide to even begin bringing up his flagship's own sidewalls or weapon systems.

"I'll take it at my command chair, Harrison," he told the com officer. After all, there was no point trying to conceal the bad news from any of his staff.

"Aye, Citizen Admiral," Fraiser said quietly, and Tourville crossed to the admiral's chair. He settled himself into it, then touched the com stud on its arm. The display before him came alive with the stern, jowly face of Citizen Rear Admiral Alasdair Heemskerk, State Security Naval Forces, and Tourville made himself smile.

"Good afternoon, Citizen Admiral. What can I do for you?" he inquired.

"Citizen Admiral Tourville," Heemskerk replied in a flat, formal voice, "I must request and require you to join me aboard my flagship immediately, pursuant to the orders of Citizen Chairman Saint-Just."

"Are we going somewhere?" Tourville's heart thundered, and he discovered his palms were sweating heavily. Odd. The terror of combat had never hit him this hard.

"We will be returning to Nouveau Paris," Heemskerk told him unflinchingly, "there to consider the degree of your complicity in Citizen Secretary McQ—"

His voice and image cut off, and Tourville blinked. What the—?

"*Jesus Christ!*" someone yelped, and Tourville spun his chair in the direction of the shout, then froze, staring in disbelief at the main visual display.

Twelve glaring spheres of unendurable brightness spalled the velvety blackness of deep space. They were huge, and so hellishly brilliant it hurt to look at them even with the display's automatic filters. And even as he stared at them, he saw *another* ripple of glaring light, much further away. It was impossible to make out any details of the second eruption, but it appeared to be on the approximate bearing of Javier Giscard's flagship . . . and the StateSec battle squadron which had been assigned to ride herd on *him*.

Lester Tourville wrenched his eyes back to the fading balls of plasma which had been the ships of Citizen Rear Admiral Heemskerk's squadron. The silence on his flag bridge was total, like the silence a microphone picked up in hard vacuum, and he swallowed hard.

And then the spell was broken as Shannon Foraker looked up from the console from which she had just sent a perfectly innocent-seeming computer code over the tactical net to one of the countless ops plans she'd downloaded to the units of Twelfth Fleet over the last thirty-two T-months.

"Oops," she said.

Oscar Saint-Just finished yet another report, scribbled an electronic signature, and pressed his thumb to the scanner. It had been a productive morning, he thought, checking the time readout in the corner of his display, and not just for him.

Kersaint was doing wonders on the diplomatic front. He'd talked the Manties into holding the first round of negotiations here on Haven, and he had the fools High Ridge and Descroix had sent tied up in endless discussions over the shape of the damned conference table! The Citizen-Chairman allowed himself a rare chuckle and shook his head. At this rate, it would take six months to get anywhere close to a substantive issue, and that was fine with him. Just fine. Much of the PRH was in a state of shock at the abrupt pause in hostilities, and some people were probably going to be upset, at first, at least, over the Republic's "surrender," which was how the Manties and the interstellar news services all seemed to view what was happening. But those upset individuals were going to discover very shortly that what was *really* happening was that the Manties were no longer slicing off Republican star systems virtually at will.

And in the meantime, the People's Navy—or, rather, the unified armed services which would absorb and supplant all the regular services under SS command—was already making some progress on ways to handle the new Manty weapons. Or at least to mitigate their effectiveness. In fact, Citizen Admiral Theisman was about due for the regular Wednesday conference, and Saint-Just permitted himself a brief moment of self-congratulation. Theisman had turned out to be an inspired choice for Capital Fleet. He'd reassured the regulars, his obvious lack of political ambitions had calmed the frenzied speculation about yet another coup attempt, and he understood perfectly that he would remain in command of Capital Fleet, and alive, only so long as he kept Saint-Just happy.

Once Saint-Just got Giscard and Tourville home and tidied up those loose ends, he could turn to the general military housecleaning, and—

The universe heaved madly.

It was like nothing Saint-Just had ever experienced. One moment he was seated in his chair behind his desk; the next, he was *under* his desk, without any memory of having gotten there. And then the roar of the explosion crashed over him, battering his eardrums even in his soundproofed office, and the universe heaved again. And *again*, each time with its own deafening cacophony.

He struggled to his feet, clinging to his desk to stay there, and an entire series of lesser shocks jolted his body. They seemed to be running away into the distance, and he coughed on the haze of dust suspended in his office's air. It must have come out of the carpet, he thought, amazed his brain could function well enough to figure that out. And there was a second band of dust, higher up, which must have come from the ceiling. How fascinating. He watched the upper band drift downward, settling towards the lower one.

He didn't know how long he'd stood there before a sudden, fresh disturbance yanked him out of his semistupor. Something crashed into the side of the building, sending a fresh shock through the structure. This one was much weaker than the others, but it was repeated again and again, at least a dozen times, and then he heard the whine of pulse rifles and the lethal, hissing roar of tri-barrels, and he knew what those weaker shocks had been.

Assault shuttles. Assault shuttles blowing breaches through the tower's outer skin and then crunching into the holes to disgorge assault troops.

He spun to his desk and yanked the drawer open, snatching out the pulser he kept there for emergencies, then turned and raced for the office door. He had no idea what was happening, but he had to get out of here before—

The door vanished in a cloud of splinters a moment before he could reach it. The force of the explosion hurled him backwards, sending him sprawling, and the pulser flew out of his hand as he lost his grip on it. The weapon thudded into the wall and tumbled to the carpet beside the doorway, and Saint-Just shook his head and levered himself back up onto his hands and knees. Blood coated his face, oozing from the countless shallow cuts and scratches the disintegrating door's fragments had clawed into his skin, but there was no time for that. He began to crawl doggedly towards the pulser. His entire universe was focused on reaching the gun, then getting to his feet, and from there escaping down the corridor outside his secretary's office to the secret lift shaft to the roof hangar.

A foot slammed into the floor before him, and he froze, for the foot was in battle armor. He crouched there, staring at it, and then, against his will, his eyes traveled up a soot-black leg of synthetic alloy. His gaze reached a point twenty-five centimeters above his head, and there it stopped, focused on the muzzle of a military-issue pulse rifle.

He knelt before the foot, unable to comprehend what was happening, and more feet crunched through the wreckage of his office door. Smoke was blowing in from the outer office, and he heard distant shouts and screams, all overlaid by the unmistakable sounds of small arms and heavy weapons fire, but the sound of those feet seemed to flow straight into his brain with a perfect, crystal clarity that didn't even need his ears. There were more sets of the feet this time: three more in battle armor, and one in regulation Navy boots.

An exoskeleton whined, and a battle-armored hand twisted itself in Saint-Just's collar. It picked him up effortlessly and set him on his feet, roughly but without brutality, and he wiped blood from his face and blinked, trying to clear his vision. It took several seconds, but he managed finally, and his mouth tightened as he looked into Thomas Theisman's eyes.

The Citizen Admiral was flanked by four towering sets of the People's Marines' battle armor, and Saint-Just's eyes narrowed as he saw the pulser in Theisman's hand. It was the same weapon the Citizen Chairman had dropped, and his fingers curled, as if trying to close around the butt of the gun he no longer held.

"Citizen Chairman," Theisman said levelly, and Saint-Just bared his teeth in a gore-streaked grimace.

"Citizen Admiral," he got out in return.

"You made two mistakes," Theisman said. "Well, three actually. The first was choosing me to command Capital Fleet and not assigning a different commissioner to keep an eye on me. The second was failing to have Admiral Graveson's data base completely vacuumed. It took me a while to find the file she'd hidden there. I don't know what happened when McQueen made her move. Maybe Graveson panicked and was afraid to move when McQueen didn't get you along with Pierre in her initial sweep. But whatever happened, the file she left behind told me who to contact in Capital Fleet when I decided to pick up where McQueen left off."

He paused, and Saint-Just stared at him for a heartbeat, then tossed his head.

"You said three mistakes," he said. "What was the third?"

"Ending hostilities and ordering Giscard and Tourville home," Theisman said flatly. "I don't know what's happened at Lovat, but I know Tourville and Giscard. I imagine they're both dead by now, but I doubt very much that either of them just rolled over and played dead for your SS goons, and I imagine you've suffered a few losses of your own. But more importantly, by issuing those orders, you warned every regular officer that the purges were about to begin all over again . . . and this time, we're not standing for it, Citizen Chairman."

"So you're replacing me, are you?" Saint-Just barked a laugh. "Are you really crazy enough you actually *want* this job?"

"I don't want it, and I'll do my best to avoid it. But the important thing is that the decent men and women of the Republic can't let someone like *you* have it any longer."

"So now what?" Saint-Just demanded. "A big show trial before the execution? Proof of my 'crimes' for the Proles and the newsies?"

"No," the citizen admiral said softly. "I think we've had enough of those sorts of trials."

His hand rose with Saint-Just's pulser, and the Citizen Chairman's eyes widened as the muzzle aligned with his forehead at a meter's range.

"Good-bye, Citizen Chairman."

Author's Afterword

One of the problems with creating background for a series as long as this one is the difficulty in maintaining continuity and internal consistency. I know of a few places where I've failed in that regard (most of them, fortunately, minor), and I feel quite certain that there are those among Honor Harrington's readers who could point out several more instances to me.

In the course of writing this novel, unfortunately, I discovered yet another, all on my own.

In the background notes, which were published as part of the appendix in *More Than Honor*, page 331, it is specifically stated that the Prime Minister of Manticore must command a majority in the *House of Commons*. This is inaccurate. When I first created the Star Kingdom's political structure, I had envisioned the framers of its Constitution as kinder, gentler, more enlightened souls than they turned out to be once I got into actually *writing* them. In fact, they were much more interested in maintaining their monopoly on political power than I had initially envisioned, and I decided that they would have deliberately written the Constitutioon to give themselves and their descendants (i.e., the House of *Lords*) control of the premiership. I had changed the relevant section in my tech bible for the series by the time I write *Flag in Exile*, but somehow an earlier version of the tech bible got sent to Baen for the *More Than Honor* appendix . . . and I never noticed it when I proofed the galleys.

So those of you who thought to yourselves, "Hey! This is *wrong!*"

when Elizabeth was forced to accept a governent formed by the Opposition deserve a pat on the back for catching the inconsistency between what happened in the book and what had previously been published.

Or, as Shannon Foraker might have said:

"Oops!"